The Dead Planets' Requiem

Vol. I

Citra Tenore

Cover Art by Sue-Ellen Lamb
Cover Art Copyright © 2021 by Citra Tenore
Book Layout © 2017 BookDesignTemplates.com

The Dead Planets' Requiem Vol. I/ Citra Tenore
ISBN 978-0-9962016-3-6

To my closest friends. You know who you are.

1

Once, Quentin Frank Hanson's grandmother died.

Well, not once per se. In actuality, Agata Celia Hanson, the late mother of Quentin's father, did die twice. Yet no one else knew the true and final count. No one besides Quentin. It was a truth only he was privy to and with utmost staunchness did he withhold it from others, blood tie or no. People were aware that the woman had died, but not that it happened more than once. Only he knew of the first incident, and everyone else knew of the second. Perhaps he should have mentioned it. Perhaps the reception of his news wouldn't have been as harsh as he had thought it would be, but come the time he wondered if he should have said something, she had already been dead for five months. He knew how it would have looked; nothing short of self-promotional jibber-jabber. The only record of the first incident was purely based upon anecdotal evidence, and due to the known caveat that anecdotes tended to be dismissed or heavily doubted, a seventeen-year-old Quentin wisely swore against publicizing it. Because so much time had passed, he was left with no choice but to take the truth to the grave. He stowed it away into a mental catalog, tucked it deep in the confines of his mind. For years it would fester in there and morph from what was once a memory into a thing he couldn't help but wonder if his own mind had conjured up in brutal self-mockery of his wild imagination. Sometimes he wondered if it had even happened at all, and considering the array of peculiar events that would follow soon after his seventeenth birthday, he wasn't so unreasonable to have had his doubts.

Agata Celia was an eccentric. She was actually dementia-ridden, so there was a very high likelihood that the origins of her many eccentricities were not sound and deliberate intentions to have been eccentric in the first place, but Quentin thought her an enigma worth the time and effort of engaging. His parents, however, staunchly attempted to convince him that she was senile and needlessly occupying space on the Earth, since all she ever did since the overripe age of eighty-six was splutter disjointed phrases to herself. In fact, one night, when Quentin was ten, he silently descended the creaky stairs of his family's old colonial home to retrieve some food and squander it up to his bedroom, when he suddenly paused his careful footsteps to eavesdrop on his parents, David and Sydney Hanson, as they spoke in hushed tones in the living room, which was situated on the other side of the stairway wall. Some words were audible, but they were too few for Quentin to piece together their meaning or what exactly the couple was insinuating: *"Irreversible...Agata...Risky...Alive...Soft upstairs... Euthanasia, maybe..."* Years passed before he learned the definition of the last term, the one he had occasionally tried to apply into online search engines but inevitably misspelt badly enough to never receive an answer. It was in his junior year of high school when he learned what it meant, sitting in the middle of the classroom on a humid day in early June as his social studies teacher discussed the revived debate on the ethics of euthanasia because of its sudden legalization in the school's state of Massachusetts—a decision that had been made in the year 2036. Quentin fought back the tears that day. He never mentioned to his parents that he was belatedly upset with them for a conversation that had occurred nearly a decade before. If anything, it propelled him to visit Agata more often than he already had, because if his parents had considered killing her back then, when she was irrational but mobile, he couldn't imagine what thoughts ran through their minds so many years later, when she was altogether irrational, immobile, and sitting on an estimated four-hundred-thousand dollars, which she promised to bestow upon them in her will. He knew that, at any time, his parents were free to make the decision which only he and his younger brother, Lucas, would have been heartbroken about.

Visiting Agata was predictably discouraged, but it wasn't forbidden. There really wasn't anything Quentin's parents could've done to stop his visitations, even if they wanted to. He was aided heavily by the convenience of their brimming schedules, as his father worked long hours and his mother focused on taking care of Lucas, who had been receiving treatment for a seemingly chronic illness that he would later overcome. So, Quentin visited Agata. A lot. At first, once a week, but after discovering what euthanasia was, it became thrice weekly.

Dates, figs, and red grapes were kind on Agata's brittle teeth and shrunken stomach. Decades could pass and Quentin would still remember the tastes of the dry fruits on his tongue and the pain in his eyes from the many afternoons they spent together on the wicker rocking chairs of her front porch, how they used to squint at each other to combat the glare from the sun. Like clockwork, they spent every Monday, Wednesday, and Friday afternoon on her porch during the summer before his senior year of high school. They would sit together, bake under the natural light, and pop tiny, aged fruits into their mouths. There were times when a fig was too thick for even him to chew or when a grape contained too many seeds, so he would warn her against eating one or two of them from the plates of food until he'd inspected them, and she obligingly picked something else. When a pitted date was troubling, though, even on the days when her mind wasn't present enough to carry a conversation, she would wriggle her hand away from his and refuse to put it down. He distantly recounted the times she had cooked for him when she was younger—and saner —specifically when she used to try and replicate the wonderful food her Greek immigrant mother used to make for her and how, before every meal, a platter of dates was set on the table for pickings. When dementia had taken grasp of Agata, it became clear that she had no memory of her parents. She couldn't remember their names, and when shown framed pictures of their wedding day or them with her as a newborn, she failed to recognize their faces. But Quentin wondered if there was a fragment of her mind that knew there was some familial importance to the brown, lumpy fruit that was the date. He wondered if, in the back of that fizzling head of hers, remnants of the earlier days of her life still lived on without her even realizing it.

The clarity of her mind was fickle, perhaps, but there were moments when it fluctuated for the better and she could actually hold conversations with him, however brief they might have been. Such as one time, which just so happened to be the last time they spoke, in the summer of 2045, when she said with a newfound lucidity to her eyes, "They'll take me away from you one day. Do you know that?"

Quentin was drinking water. He put the glass down. They used to drink orange juice on those afternoons, but Agata had slowly developed an acid reflux, and because it wasn't dates that were causing the issue, she had willingly modified her food and drink choices. "No one's taking you away, Gran," he said after swallowing his water. "You're staying right here, in your house."

"If they don't take me away, you'll have to leave me," Agata said with her wrinkly, thin brows furrowed together. "You'll have to leave me, whether or not you want to. Everyone leaves eventually. You too, Quentin. You too." But then it was as if she remembered herself, her new self at least, because her eyes glazed over with a familiar, withdrawn look to them and she said, "I've realized that bees buzz for butterflies."

Quentin nodded along.

"Bees buzz for butterflies and roses rise for trees. Do you think that, My Nettle?"

My Nettle, Quentin thought with a sudden recollection of the nickname's origin, or what he knew of it through rumor. Its birth purportedly took place fifteen years earlier, when he was barely out of babyhood while she was in her mid-seventies with a mind far fresher than it would be years later. Per the allegations of his mother and grandmother, he was sitting on the ground of his family's backyard garden while the two women chatted and sipped tea on a picnic blanket nearby. At one point in their conversation, they turned to find him devouring a mouthful of common garden nettle. He was taken to the doctor immediately, as his mouth had reddened and his cheeks and throat became swollen from whichever component of the plant had irritated him, but he did survive. *"My Nettle,"* Agata had whirred to him when she stroked his face before bidding her goodbyes that evening, after she made sure he was healed. "My beautiful nettle." She probably didn't even remember the story. It was likely that she only called him the epithet out of habit.

"I guess they do," Quentin said lamely for the sake of appeasing her.

"They buzz and rise for each other?" Agata asked. "Bees buzz for butterflies?"

"Mhm."

"Good, good. Because I think so too. Did you know that?"

"Yes, Gran."

"Oh, good."

It was such a normal day, sitting in the sun and eating fruits as she spoke nonsense. It was so normal that he wouldn't have expected her to die twice over the next twelve hours.

The first time it happened, she was standing upright after he'd brought her in from the sun. They were in her kitchen and, without warning, she blinked quickly, her body swayed side to side, and Quentin lurched forward, catching her before she hit the ground. He pressed a finger to the pulse point on her left wrist and put his head to her chest to listen for a heartbeat, but no such indications of wellness were detected. He sobbed as he said his goodbyes, kissed her closed eyelids, and whispered to her of how much he would miss her. It was only after he sat on that floor for several minutes that he pulled out his cellphone and dialed for help. He cursed at himself for not dialing sooner.

When Quentin was alerted that an ambulance had been sent their way, Agata's closed eyes popped open. He watched, breathless, as she gasped. *"I heard you,"* she murmured, her head turning in his lap so she could see him better. "You have a potty mouth."

Quentin laughed, but he kept sobbing all the same.

"You shouldn't say those words, even if I'm gone."

"I promise," Quentin said. "I won't. But how did you hear me?"

"Sleepy," Agata whispered.

Quentin nodded. He slung one of her arms over his shoulders and said, "I'll bring you upstairs, Gran. Come on."

He had led her to her bedroom, moving his feet at the slowest pace possible so as to not jostle her. She blubbered nonsense again, as though she hadn't just been revived from what he swore was a bout of death. He laid her head on the cream-colored pillows of her bed and swathed her in its sheets. As he tucked her in, she ran her wrinkled thumb over his cheek and spoke of butterflies and nettles, and then of how she, too, would miss him one day.

"That day won't be for a while," Quentin said to her.

"Bees," was her response.

She had seemed so sane, as sane as she could have been, and when the emergency aid arrived, they confirmed that her vitals were normal and that there was no cause for alarm. That was why, the next morning, it drove Quentin absolutely mad when Agata's daytime caretaker, Janie, called David Hanson to alert him that his mother had passed away in her sleep.

2

The story of Quentin Frank Hanson was a simple one. At the time that elements of his life began to weave into a single, serendipitous loop, he was seventeen and stuck in that compromising age bracket in which one was no longer a child but not yet an adult. He was, in the strictest sense, an adolescent. But, really, he was only a boy. He was stubborn, lost, and continually dumbfounded by the impending threat of adulthood. His intellect was adequate at best. His sense of humor was self-deprecating. His sense of self was abysmally near-nonexistent, which was an odd fusion if one truly took the time to consider it—that someone who knew so little of himself could have harbored an abundance of deprecation for the person he didn't even know he was. And yet, while the concept of his self-loathing may have seemed pitiful for a person so young, he wasn't entirely wrong to have felt that way. He was, unfortunately, for many years, a most unremarkable individual.

Although many matters of great importance would soon revolve around Quentin, it had been the choices and decisions of the various figures surrounding him that were more sophisticated and, arguably, more critical than his own. Despite his importance, it often seemed as though he was but a leaf to their tree; a mere piece of something he hated even being a part of. For years, he fought against the path his life had taken. He felt like a shadow to the lives of others, just a thing that loomed nearby but never peeked out into the light that was reality. Yet no matter how fixedly he pushed and pulled, scurried and hid, the story of his life was indisputably *his*, and there was nothing he could have done to change that.

For the boy, Quentin, his story's inception took place in Massachusetts, in a small town by the name of Shaw, where he was born and raised. It was a humbly populated, forest-bordered stretch of terrain that housed some twenty-thousand residents, and the predominance of the population were families. The houses where they dwelt varied from opulent to shoddy, with the one consistency having been the town's center, a gaudy turf that brimmed with contemporary eateries, two separate libraries, five clothing stores, three financial management companies, and four banks. Despite how far north and west Shaw was from the state's capital and how deeply it hid in the green of New England's obstructing trees, it didn't pale against the city like most small towns tended to; it was culturally and racially diverse; modern infrastructure constituted its main roads; a small collection of notable figures had been born there. Its school buildings may have been outdated and the town severely lacking in public transportation, but its flaws were easily forgiven. It was solitary and safe, in many ways a world of its own, and had seemed quite a perfect, little place.

For all its wonderful attributes, there was, however, something terribly the matter with Shaw. The issue regarded the not-quite-adults who resided there, those being the older children. For the most part, they were healthy and happy, as young ones ought to have been, but they didn't look nearly as well as they should have. They were harried and tired, even the smaller ones in the preteens, too. The young people of Shaw didn't believe themselves unattractive. They merely thought that with a few additional hours fit into their slight sleep schedules, they too might have appeared as dashing as the adolescents in neighboring towns. But perhaps it was for the better that they were oblivious to how unhandsome, gaunt, and gray their eye-bag-dominated faces really were. "They look pretty from afar," had been the opinion of an out-of-town mother who had seen Shaw High School's varsity cheer team at a competition in 2036. Naturally, there was also the obligatory speculation of, "There must be something in the water."

The ubiquitous fatigue that conquered the lives of Shaw's children was no mystery to Quentin. He had battled it for as long as he could remember, had spent countless mornings bitterly blinking himself awake on the school bus and suffered through endless evenings of rubbing his eyes while he tried to finish his homework. The fatigue had been an inconvenience, and sometimes painful, but it was uncomfortably manageable.

Yet the worst of his brushes with exhaustion came on the 30th of October in the year 2045, which was, in all fairness to him, an objectively horrible day for everyone in the town.

On the morning of November 13th, Quentin walked his way to the public high school and, with every step he took, kicked the dirt that lined the edges of the concrete path that formed the sidewalk. He wasn't ashamed to admit to himself that the momentary unions of his sneaker-sheathed toes and the earthy clusters were unusually cathartic. It was, in his words, *Entertainingly childish*, which he thought as he scuffed his soles and raised his legs in steady beats; scuff, step, scuff, step. However ridiculous the therapy was, he needed it. *It's just…one of those days*, was his subsequent musing.

There were many times in his life when he thought all was stable and well under his control, but there were also a great many others that led him to vehemently theorize that the single, most imperative duty of the rumored God was to fuck with him without reserve or reason. Though the concept of a higher power wasn't believable to him on his best days, it was on his worst, when his anger brimmed or his prematurely astronomical stress levels pulled at the reins of his every thought that he would conveniently resort to blaming a higher, mystical entity for all his toils. When stressor upon stressor flung into his life, piled upon each other without mercy, he thought it easier to blame another. He liked to consider himself a believer in a faith he had invented, which he admittedly referred to as "Convenient Theism." It was a routine, a vice, but it certainly made him content, and so long as it wasn't narcotics he clung to for anxiety's sake, he thought the concept just fine.

The days that led up to the dreadful morning of the 13th served as models for those types of times; those days on which his theism was rediscovered. Despite the many days which had passed since the beginning of his newest troubles, he still found himself dwelling on them and thus resorted to the odd and questionable coping mechanism he had fabricated in middle school.

Quentin blamed God and continued walking, scuffed the dirt and then continued blaming God. Quentin thought of how smoothly October the 29th had opened, but also how the very opening of that day had actually been the catalyst of his revived stress. It had been so normal, so boring and perfect, just the way he preferred things. Then, in the evening, there had been conflict between himself and his parents. He tried to remember what exactly the dispute was centered on—*Grades or something,* he thought. Whatever it was, and for however long it continued, it had progressed into a screaming match so loud that he had grown exhausted of his parents' elongated bombardments, departed their pink and pleasant colonial home, and strapped himself tightly in his mother's hideous, baby-blue SUV. He drove languidly for about ten minutes until he reached the north tip of Shaw, where the best of his friends, his only friend, resided.

The friend in question went by the name of Hollis Carlyle, but for all the normalcy and blandness that the name exuded, he was drastically unlike it. What complemented the otherwise pale and plain boy was a streak of pink in his brown hair and two silver chains that hung from his neck that were accompanied by pendants forever unseen, as they were always shrouded by colorful, pastel-colored sweatshirts. He was raucous and buoyant, rebellious and rowdy. It was an oddity that Quentin was ever friends with a person of Hollis's ilk, and for years at that. But no matter how stark their differences, they were bound to each other like brothers. They had met in kindergarten, became "The best of buddies" in the first grade, but, by the second, when they had each discovered that they both had their first, innocent infatuations with the same little lass, they journeyed into their first fight; one afternoon, they were exceptionally competitive on the playground, then relentlessly tackled each other in the pickup line after school. For months, they dedicated hours of time to avoiding one another, and their mutual antipathies persisted a quarter of the way through their summer break before the third grade. It was in mid-July of 2037, at the tenth birthday party of Ewan McHugh, who was a friendly acquaintance of both, that they had at last seen each other again, and with noble maturity did they finally sever the hatred they had stretched out for so unnecessarily long. In the kitchen of the McHugh's home, they swore to never part over a girl, wielded separate butter knives, and painstakingly performed their very own blood oath, and bound by blood they remained.

As one was wont to do at seventeen, Quentin sought the company of his friend-and-blood-brother-in-one, Hollis, on that horrible evening of October 29th. They interchangeably dribbled a basketball on the Carlyles' driveway for the better part of an hour, Quentin complaining about his family affairs and Hollis listening as the sun began to set in the distance. The sky grew darker and Hollis tried desperately to remain supportive, but Quentin showed no signs of silencing his unrepressed gripings. So, the friend to whom Quentin had turned began leading him down the driveway, onto the street, past two neighborhoods, a massive pond, and then another neighborhood, until they finally made their way to a great, palatial home where there lived a fellow classmate, Amber Wood. They stood at the base of the cobblestone walkway that stretched up to her doorstep and watched as the stones shook from the reverberation of a music-player, which clearly operated in one of the front rooms of the home. Shrill screams, elated ones, were audible from where they stood, and it was mostly laughter and unintelligible yelling that busied the air of the quiet street. Somehow, Hollis succeeded in luring Quentin inside.

Quentin hated parties, but Hollis loved them. Halfway through the night, Quentin lost sight of his friend and failed to locate him in the gaggle of the sweaty under-aged. He wanted to leave. There was nothing in his midst for him to have enjoyed. He always detested beer and had recently developed a special animosity for those who partook in the lung-decimating and dully-exercised activity of indulging in electronic cigarettes. Playing beer pong and exhaling strawberry-laced haloes on a school night were not appealing to him, and besides the afflicting fact that he could neither see nor breathe in the Woods' manor because of the hazy exhalations of others around him, he was bored in the most intense sense of the word. When the clock struck eleven, he left. He left and didn't turn back, even when the scampering footsteps and slurred protestations of Hollis followed closely behind. He insisted that Quentin should stay with them. Like a needy apparition, Hollis hovered all around Quentin and refused to accept the head-shakes directed his way. He called Quentin bland and spineless, and told him he was wasting his life.

Surely if it were someone else who'd said such things to him, Quentin would have been furious. But it wasn't out of the ordinary for Hollis to lash out after imbibing three too many bottles, shots, or whatever in one night's revelry because, for all the calm and collection he radiated, he was a strangely stubborn and angry person at heart. He hated nearly everything simply because he hated conformity. He hated anything that ranged from marriage to corporate workplaces, and although Quentin could perhaps understand the idea of said conforms boring a teenage boy, to have been actively infuriated by them at so young an age and without ever having experienced them oneself wasn't something he could process.

He had heard the sermon before, and he heard it once again that night. Upon Hollis taking his frustrations out on Quentin for abandoning the party, Hollis segued the one-sided conversation into a rant that detailed how he couldn't end up like his parents, that he needed to leave Shaw, that he saw no use in investing time into his grades or attending college to feed the objective of leading a life similar to his corporate father, and so forth. Just as Hollis tolerated and supported Quentin through his rants, he similarly tolerated Hollis's ignorantly ludicrous one as well. But the problem laid in the fact that Quentin's were seldom and Hollis's were not. He partied and imbibed every week. Initially, and that initiation having been two years before, Quentin found the complaints tolerable and, on the appropriate occasions, fairly amusing despite how much he disagreed with them. There had once been a time when Quentin swallowed the strangeness of the obsession with all the calm and tact entailed for the task, but as he grew older, as college neared and his eighteenth birthday crept up on him, he began to realize how conformed a person he actually was, and that there was nothing wrong with it. He didn't have time for Hollis, for his dismissal of the realities of adulthood. The amusement had long faded by that night of October 29th, when they were seventeen. Although it was palpable to Quentin, it remained unseen by the current ranter. The annoyance clearly went unnoticed by Hollis in his latest tirade, having not realized that the more obsessive he became with verbally shredding the ways of the world to pieces, the more he was actually repelling his best friend. So, on that night, as the tolerability and humor of Hollis's complaining diminished, the situation came to a head.

Quentin snapped. He told Hollis he was a, "Whiny nuisance to society…No different from those punk-rock, suicidal, goth bitches looking for attention." He also said, "The world doesn't need any more whining hipsters."

To which Hollis retaliated with, "Oh yeah? You're an unsmart, carbon-copy of your half-assed, balding dad."

In that moment, on some street in the north end of Shaw, Quentin wondered why he had so often sustained the abuse Hollis would direct toward him during every single one of his anti-conformity rants, notwithstanding it was always he, Quentin, who would mend the severed ties after all their fights, including the ones that didn't even pertain to that matter. He supposed it was because they were each so horribly lonely, each so heavily flawed, that the only other person they could have been friends with was each other. He hated himself for the truth in the thought, for the fact that their shared desperation was the only link that kept them pieced together for all those years. But he swore not to mend the new break in their fickle link, and since then, since October 29th of 2045, he hadn't seen Hollis once.

What Quentin didn't know, however, was that he never would again.

The altercation with Hollis was cathartic, but afterward things were odd and stressful. The disagreement and disassociation were unfortunate, but undeniably ordinary experiences to have come upon in one's youth; splintered friendships were nothing short of normal. Everything was perfectly plain for a maximum of seven hours after the boys' clash, but then the true morning of toils arrived, and Quentin's world had shifted for the worse. His returned hatred for God stemmed partly from that night of the 29th, but mostly from the next morning.

No one would deny that the buses operated by Shaw's public school system were subpar in quality, but at least they functioned. Until one day, when they didn't. That day was none other than October 30th. Quentin didn't know why, and, in fact, years would pass and he still couldn't fathom the reasoning behind it, but when he woke that very morning after the exhausting night he had just suffered through with Hollis, he learned through a crackly, automated voicemail sent from Shaw Public Schools that the thirty-year-old pickup plans for the high school buses had been revoked and that no such vehicles were to arrive to any high schooler's aid on that morning and all mornings afterward. He mistook the call for a prank, chucked his phone to the foot of his bed, and rolled over to return to his slumber when, without knocking, in barged his mother.

Dressed in her favorite pair of gray pajama bottoms and an ill-fitted, floral blouse that stuck too tightly to her bosom and floated outward beneath the stomach hemline, Syndonah "Sydney" Hanson held her hands to her hips. "What are you doing here?" she asked.

Quentin rolled over to face her. "I'm in bed?"

"I know you heard the voicemail. I could hear you listening to it from the hallway. Why are you still in bed?"

"Mom, it's a prank."

"Quentin, I recognize the number," she said. "It's from Superintendent Fechner's office." Of course his mother recognized the digits. She became all too well acquainted with it the previous year, after a fight transpired between Quentin and a peer of his who had framed him for possessing illegal substances out of sheer vengeance due to Quentin reporting said peer, who actually was in possession of illegal substances on school grounds.

It was true then, the message in the voicemail. Quentin was informed by his petulant mother that his younger brother, Lucas, and all the children with whom he attended school had, as a matter of routine, already boarded buses of their own that day, and that none would arrive for those who surpassed the eighth grade. She had allegedly heard it from two mothers of children who were similarly aged to Lucas. It appeared that Shaw had made the decision to divide its youth into two groups, the young and the younger.

Fourteen days of bus-deprived mornings had since passed for the elder children of Shaw, and if they looked aged before the transportation cutoff, then they were dead people walking soon after its sudden commencement. The sleeplessness only took two days to have an effect. While the fatigue was visible before, at least their youthful blushes and glows of their skin had been detectable at first glance. Come the cutoff day plus fourteen, they were gravely different sights to behold, as the already existing circles beneath their eyes darkened and deepened, the healthy plump of their bodies dissipated from rampant, unwanted weight loss, and cystic acne induced by their stress began to color and swell their once-clear cheeks. Red speckles still danced on the tips of their noses and curved around their jaws, but it wasn't due to health and heartiness so much as it was the pinching, autumn cold through which so many had to tread every morning and afternoon. Schoolwork grew heftier, the weather colder, and their legs sorer. Many days later, the absence of follow-up announcements regarding potentially reinstating the bus lines continued. They had only each other. Those who were privileged to either drive or be driven proffered the empty seats of their vehicles to others who lacked the luxury. One morning, the aforementioned Amber Wood arrived to the front of the school during the student drop-off and, beyond the shaded windows of her father's low-riding *BMW*, Quentin saw six or seven girls piled atop each other's laps in the back row, all trying, but failing, to sit comfortably in the tight space. Quentin envied them. He couldn't be driven by his father, who left too early in the morning to make a drop-off feasible, and Quentin had no contact with his one friend after their recent altercation, who definitely would have offered to share a ride if they had still been on good terms.

The carpooling didn't last due to the inconvenience seemingly experienced by the limited number of parents willing to drive their older children to school. Few people had someone to turn to, so Quentin and most others resorted to walking. That was around the time he began blaming God again. The further his problems occupied his time, the more he did it. So, as he walked that dreadful journey to school on the morning of November 13th, he blamed the being he couldn't comprehend for the problems that polluted his life. He scuffed his feet, dragged his steps, blamed God, and poorly paced his breaths.

It was an abysmal morning, just like all the others that recently preceded it. He was cold, tired, and angry. It didn't help that he hated the weather, that there was a crispness to the air that scratched his throat every time he inhaled. He hated that he could barely see anything, that the street lamps lit his way a bit, but that the natural light of the star he desired to see showed no signs of emerging. And just when he thought the darkness of the early hours was enough of an inconvenience, a fog began to appear; it encircled him, swarmed him, and even as he progressed, it felt as though it was trapping him.

Dew formed on his shoes and the morning mist tickled his ankles through his jeans. He shivered and slumped, quit his scuffing, and became more determined with his steps. *Why drag this out?* he asked himself. *Just get it over with.*

A *"scritch"* from the sidewalk opposite Quentin's made his ears twitch. He turned to see a fellow classmate he recognized, Natalie Khan. He gave her a small, lazy wave. She glanced at the movement from the corner of her eye, but she didn't return the gesture. She plowed on with her arms folded tightly across her chest, presumably to keep warm. She frowned crossly at the fog in her way. On another week, during a simpler time, he may have faulted her for the poor etiquette. But it was seven o'clock in the morning and, having known where she resided, he estimated that she must have already walked a full hour before joining paths with him.

Quentin looked up to the dark sky. *Whatever you are... Whoever you are... We must've wronged you in some way,* he thought, and continued in the same general direction as Natalie.

3

Oscar Martinez was sniffing a glue bottle at the front of the classroom. Quentin didn't know why Oscar thought it so exhilarating, since Quentin himself had once experimented with a glue fascination of his own due to sheer boredom during an advanced-placement mathematics course, and he found it utterly revolting. He had instantly coiled backwards, as it smelled of only things he hated; plaster and an undertone synonymous to the soiled odor of the decrepit, former gymnasium which the town's board of education had the audacity to entitle an art room. And yet there Oscar sat, gaped upon by those who noticed how plentifully he took in his recurrent whiffs, and onward he went without acknowledging the halt to activity in the room.

The pupils' English teacher, a Mr. Gareth A. Halverson, sat behind his desk with his hands loosely folded together upon a notebook while his drawn eyes were vacantly set on the glue-sniffer not five feet before him. He and a great many of his students found themselves unable to detach their lines of vision from the fascinating spectacle that was Oscar's reddened nostrils flaring and sinking, and flaring once more, as he sniffed once, twice, then pulsed his breaths for a third, fourth, and fifth time. It was astounding that Oscar never noticed them, but even when Quentin fully expected their teacher to bring attention to the fact that a certain student was being watched, he instead remained, in equal measures, unimpressed, haggard, and resigned. He had nothing to say, because there truly was nothing to say. Quentin supposed Oscar could have been berated, but was it really worth the time? Surely no words could have been more apposite in conveying everyone else's disgust than the dry, emotionless expression their teacher wore.

Mr. Halverson blinked.

Quentin squirmed.

One student began to snicker.

"On to the next page," said Mr. Halverson, and the lesson resumed.

It was still early in the morning; seven-thirty, read the clock. They were all so tired, had been worn out long before their class was even in session. Most had just arrived from their laborious walks and those who didn't walk were still overtired from the daily task of fighting with their parents to search the streets for friends in need of a ride.

Quentin looked up from his textbook. He was seeing double and had to blink thrice as he examined Mr. Halverson, who was also barely keeping awake as he narrated the page for discussion. Quentin walked the thin line between consciousness and slipping into a slumber, but he was keen enough to recognize something he hadn't thought of just moments before, which was that Mr. Halverson might not have been disgusted, but, rather, jealous of one Oscar Martinez's easy route to escapism amid such a drab and otherwise unimportant day in their lives.

Quentin returned to reading the page below. He tried to, at least. As he roved the paragraphs in an effort to identify which line best matched the narration of his teacher, the low chatter of three classmates behind him began to grate on his nerves and challenge the modicum of concentration he'd managed to preserve. He squinted and tried to flush out the noise, came so close to finding the precise place, but as he reached one spot that had to have been synchronized with the sentence Mr. Halverson was reading, the talking continued. It was louder, too. Quentin finally located the line that highlighted the importance of reflective realism in political fiction with—

"Dude, yeah. I could totally see her doing that," said one of the voices behind him. "I mean, like, I don't know her or anything, but that skirt was hugging her ass. Speaks for something."

Quentin sighed.

It was Chris, the idiot. Of course it was. *Chris,* Quentin thought almost putridly, like the boy himself was some sort of odor. Quentin hated when they shared classes. Christopher Alan Laney, who much preferred the slacker diminutive of his name, which he thought made him more approachable and less priggish or stuffy, was the owner of the loudest of the voices behind Quentin, forcing him to re-read whatever dreary paragraph he thought matched their English teacher's words. Chris was the proudest of the three. He was the social one. The forthcoming one. The one who believed that the shine of his trimmed, blond hair and the dazzle of his blue eyes could have earned him anything he ever wanted. The one who, in the eighth grade, was suspended from school for two weeks due to allegedly hitting a female student's posterior and further bragging about it in an also alleged, since-deleted social media post. That was Chris.

"Nah, dude, you gotta—No, let me talk," Chris said. "Look, you gotta come off as assertive. Lay it on thick. This gentlemen's crap died off ages ago. Girls these days wanna know you want them because girls these days just wanna give it up whenever and wherever. Trust me, I know this. It gets better when they get older. I was at my cousin Ross's frat—No, I'm not lying, you know Ross is in a frat. Anyway, I was at Ross's frat party at Princeton last April and holy shit man…" The more Chris spoke, the more Quentin wanted to dunk his own head into a bowl of wet cement.

Some three minutes later, after Chris was finished detailing his premature escapades at a fraternity house, the second-loudest in the trio became firmer in his opposing views and dared to lift the tone of his whisper during their teacher's reading, which was continuing uninterrupted despite the back-of-the-class debate. "No, you're getting it wrong," said that other voice. "The less she knows about you, the more she'll want you. If a girl knows you're out there sharing your feelings with everyone, including all those mini-skirt-ass-showing randoms, there's no mystery in it. They want a guy who's approached by the randoms, yes, but he's also gotta be mysterious. Besides, chivalry always wins."

"The randoms" was probably the most unoriginal thing Quentin had ever heard in his life. He found it amusing that the other one, Terry, thought the self-coined term so fitting and inventive that it was suitable for double usage in the point he was trying to make. On the other hand, Quentin supposed that Terry was comparably better than Chris in the sense that the former thought chivalry a more appropriate form of currency whilst the latter thought the tactic of simply "laying it on thick" was the best route. But that was just about all the good Quentin could think of Terry's character.

All throughout their childhood and teen years, Terry Montgomery was perceived as the most charming of the trio of friends in question. From his mannerisms to the way he would appear and disappear from social scenes without a trace, there truly was something silken and smooth about his air. Quentin didn't see the appeal, but most others did. He always thought Terry's character was good-natured, but that his true perfection lied in his natural talents. Terry's listening skills in his classes were abysmal, but his grades were wonderful. His workout routine was questionably undemanding, but he was as fleet and slippery as a dolphin in open ocean when he moved along their school's football field. His rough-faced parents, though sweet and sociable, were plain and imperfect against the sight that was their only child, whose dark-skinned face was adorned by high cheekbones but the softest smile, which rendered him dichotomously intimidating and spirited all at once. His grades were unattainable by most, but his athleticism was artful. While others in his age range shook and panicked as they stood at the brink of adulthood, he was poised to move mountains of his own and was projected to go on to an elite university with a prestigious football program. And to complement the perfection he already displayed, his mind was equipped with a strong dose of humility that would have definitely been required for the life everyone knew he would lead. He was the perfect son, the perfect student, and the perfect athlete. Quentin was always a little envious of Terry, but never resented him. In fairness, there was not one male in the town of Shaw who didn't feel at least a slight bit inferior to that one, special boy bound for stardom and success.

Neither of them knew it, Quentin nor Terry, but it would be a great tragedy, not so far in their futures, when Terry would be stripped of all those opportunities and subsequent accolades he would have earned. There was no way for him to have seen it coming nor was there even the smallest of chances for him to avoid it; however ready and anxious he was, that dream he could have forged into an exceptional reality was never meant for him to realize. It would be years before everyone else's envy morphed into pity.

"Chivalry, huh?" Chris drawled, and Quentin could almost hear him rolling his eyes.

"Chivalry," Terry said affirmatively, like it was the simplest point. "Although I understand if it's too hard for you, considering how you're a defective in that area."

"I'm a defective?" Chris asked. He poorly masked how offended he was. "So is driving Casey home during a rainstorm after her lacrosse practice, because you forgot to pick her up, defective?"

"You–What?!" Terry whisper-yelled, to avoid drawing attention to themselves as Mr. Halverson droned on with his narration.

"Aw, man, she didn't tell you?"

"When was this?"

"Last Thursday, remember? You were busy doing…What was it again? It's lost on me, but clearly it was more important than her."

Quentin dared a glance to his right, where a teeth-grinding Terry shot back, "We said no family members, what is so hard for you to understand about that?"

"Bro, all I did was drive her," Chris defended himself. "You're the one making this sound so perverted."

"We literally agreed to no family members."

"Uh, no. We agreed to no siblings and since she's your cousin, she's fair game."

"Neither of us has any siblings, dickstick."

"Looks like someone should've corrected the fine print of the pact."

"She's sixteen."

"That's one year apart, dude."

Terry was back to whisper-yelling: *"Chris, I'm gonna fu–!"*

"Hey, hey, hey," the third voice rose up to interject after being silent for a lengthy time. "Gentlemen. Calm down."

Terry scoffed. "He literally just told us he's not a gentleman."

"Relax," said that third voice. "Cool your shit before Halv looks up and Chris gets another detention."

"He can get one for all I care."

"I know, I know. But he's just busting your balls. He's leaving out the part where Frances and I were in the car with them."

"What?"

"Yeah," said the other person. "She and Casey finished practice and their rides were late. Casey called me since I was still at school, but my car was still getting fixed. Remember? So I asked Chris to add them to the carpool. Chill out, dude."

"Thanks," Terry muttered, but to whom, Quentin didn't know.

The third voice belonged to Connor. Connor O'Neil.

No matter how many years had passed since they met, Quentin would forever squirm when he saw Connor because, too often, his face alone reminded Quentin of the uncomfortable moment they became acquainted on a first-name basis. It was either kindergarten or the first grade, Quentin didn't recall exactly, but it was the only detail of the recollection that had slipped his mind. Unfortunately for him, from the shirts they wore to the day's weather, everything else had a vivid place in his memory. It was the second day of school, that he knew confidently, and the children were assigned to pair up in teams at random. They were to close their eyes and dip a hand into a fishbowl that brimmed with cutouts of notebook paper, on which names of pupils waited to be read. On the note Quentin had blindly selected, it read, *Connor O'Neil*, and much to his surprise, what strutted up to his cubby was a spiky-haired, thin-eyed boy.

"I'm supposed to be with Connor O'Neil," Quentin had said with unabashed confusion.

"I am Connor O'Neil," replied the other boy.

To which Quentin, who was young and forgivably tactless, literally said, "But you don't look like a Connor."

Connor didn't take any offense, though. *He should have*, Quentin still thought, so many years later. Connor explained to a head-tilted, tremendously ignorant, and confounded young Quentin that Connor's mother was from South Korea and that his father was a Bostonian of Irish and Scottish descent. Connor's parents met at university, Cornell, to be exact, and it was implied that however foreign he appeared to unknowing eyes, he was American-born and completely American in terms of his cultural identity.

By the time both of them would be mere tables away from each other on an indistinctive autumn day nine or ten years later, Quentin was seventeen and Connor was nearing his eighteenth birthday. It was possible that Connor retained the memory of their first meeting, but even if he didn't, it haunted Quentin, who, just inches in front of the three friends and their debate on modern-day courtship, tried not to listen and was reddening from an embarrassment he wasn't even sure Connor remembered.

That was actually the only time Quentin and Connor had really spoken with each other. They participated in numerous group projects together and shared multiple classes, but the older Connor grew, the more conservative he became with his friendliness. There once was a time when he was willing to share smiles and laughter with someone he didn't know all too well, but, with time, he decreased his usual distributions of common courtesy in an effort to be more exclusive. But despite the fact that many deemed his exclusionary personality something of a superficial act for social suaveness, there were some improvements to his persona that went overlooked. His intellect, for one, was unmitigatedly atrocious during his younger years. In elementary and middle school, he was overwhelmingly sports-oriented and popularity-obsessed, to the extent that he barely passed each year's standardized tests, which would determine whether or not a student could proceed to the next grade. He remained popular in high school, but that was also when he became quieter and increasingly serious about the more pressing matters, like his studies and mental health. At the point where he was mediating his two friends in Gareth A. Halverson's English class on November 13th in 2045, Connor had the second highest grade point average of all the school's seniors. Quentin still thought Connor was insufferable, though. His smarts may have been a new addition to his general persona, but smart he was, and he knew it. He was attractive, and he knew it. His family was affluent, and he knew it. He said little, but his bearing said enough. Especially then, in that disgusting, moldy classroom and struck bored to tears as the English teacher read on, Connor looked like he knew he was being admired, and for good reason. Diagonal from Quentin and in a spot he couldn't see, there sat a girl batting eyelashes and hoping Connor would look over, not knowing that he was already aware of her ogling. It made sense, otherwise it would have been strange to think that the way he was sitting, then, was how he normally sat; legs parted and outwardly spreading to undoubtedly accentuate his groin; each foot extended into an aisle beside his desk to flaunt his cream-colored boat shoes; his acolytes abreast him as they mimicked his position.

Following Connor's intervention, the conversation of the three friends behind Quentin quieted down. He was able to concentrate and successfully pinpoint exactly which stanza in the textbook belonged to the author's example of a clever political poem. The lesson was boring. It was hardly a lesson and more of a recitation of one man's perception of another man's socioeconomic essay, which was ultimately unimaginative, uninspiring, and a most ineffective means to keep Quentin awake.

When the bell rang, Mr. Halverson stood and said, "If any of you have questions regarding Friday's quiz, we can discuss them in class tomorrow. Now, Group B…Where's Group B's leader?"

That was Quentin's cue. He half-raised a hand.

"Mhm," acknowledged the English teacher before he caught sight of Terry. "Oh, there you are, Mr. Montgomery. You weren't here yesterday."

"Here I am," said Terry flatly.

"You missed little due to the fire drill. You'll be just as equipped as everyone else for your group project."

"Sir," said Chris in the snidest of tones, as though the word were a preposterous form of address, "we finished the Voltaire project three weeks ago. I thought we weren't doing group ones anymore."

Mr. Halverson shook his head. "Well, as I'm sure you've heard through hallway hearsay, the annual trifecta scavenger hunt is this week."

"The what?" Terry asked, then his shoulders sank down. "Oh god, is that the stupid physics hunt Ivy told me about?"

Their teacher's mouth opened to retort, but he stopped himself and stared out the corner of his eye, back to that one particular boy whose desk was not five feet before his own. Quentin knew why. Everyone knew why. Even after Terry asked the question, he, too, immediately looked to that particular boy at that particular desk, as did all others who were listening to the exchange. Ivy was Oscar's twin sister. It spoke volumes that even the mention of her name never disrupted his glue-sniffing high.

Mr. Halverson rolled his eyes back to Terry. "You heard correctly," he said. "The trifecta is where your group, seniors, work with one of the high GPA juniors. It's tradition. Don't complain. And, Quentin, seeing as how one Ivy Martinez enjoys spoilers, you've probably heard that each group includes one or two juniors for this assignment. On each of these meant for group leaders—" He elevated a stack of freshly printed sheets of paper—"your partners' names will be listed. I'll make rounds right now." He dropped a paper onto a girl's desk, and seconds thereafter people began to converge on her in order to feast their eyes upon that group's list.

"Damn," Terry said. "Juniors? They're so annoying, bro." To which "bro" he spoke was unclear.

Chris clicked his tongue against the roof of his mouth. "Yeah, but no shit, they're the ones with the best asses."

Terry bristled and reverted back to whisper-yelling, *"Hey, cool it with the junior shit!"*

"I didn't speak specifically of Casey, did I?" Chris huffed. "Who am I kidding, though? This assignment is bull. All the junies have to offer are their bods. Hey, Halv, why do we have to work with them anyway? They're dumb as rocks, don't know crap about anything."

As the English teacher slowly made his way over to them, he pointedly remarked in that bland and vacant voice of his, "Chris, you were one too...five months ago. Also, that kind of misogynistic language isn't tolerated in this school."

"Mm. All I'm saying is, I was a cool one."

The teacher placed a paper on Quentin's desk and said to Chris, "And it's only November, so all that I'm saying is that the ratio of what you know now to what you didn't know then can't be so great that you're incapable of working with a junior today."

"You–Huh?" Chris asked.

Quentin didn't know if their teacher heard it, but under his breath, Terry said to his friend, *"Dude, you're a retard."*

Actually, Quentin presumed Terry was completely in the clear of having been overheard because, for an unspoken reason, Mr. Halverson eyed the closed, leftmost window at the other end of the classroom. To those lacking context, Quentin was simply watching a man staring out a window. To Quentin, however, he was audience to the residual effect of an incident from ten years earlier, which included a rather esteemed science teacher attempting suicide via that very fourth-floor viewport, and if one truly took the time to consider it, Quentin supposed that there always was something of Gareth A. Halverson's energy that was potentially masochistic. Suicidal, even.

"Like, for real, today's juniors are so dorky, dude," Chris said.

Mr. Halverson's obsession with the window appeared to have dissipated. He resumed his paper-passing.

Such as what the poor girl who was assigned as leader to Group A had been subjected to, the members of Quentin's group swarmed his desk. It wasn't all too overwhelming for him, seeing as how half of his group was already present and conveniently situated directly behind him.

Still, he just wanted to go home.

The friends enclosed the paper-keeper to sneak ganders at the list; Terry was on Quentin's left shoulder; Chris on Quentin's right; Connor above and exhaling warm breaths onto Quentin's fluffy mess of hair.

"So who've we got?" Terry asked. He chewed strawberry-flavored gum, which made his breaths disturbingly, and rudely, uproarious beside Quentin's ear.

"We've got us, obviously," Quentin said. "And…Derek Parker," he added regretfully.

"Are you actually kidding me right now?" Terry asked. He looked down to the paper. "You aren't."

Quentin read on, "Along with Frances Jerins, Marina Gustavsson, and Jaymes Chen."

The boys sat back down into their chairs. Quentin swiveled around to face them.

Connor rubbed a hand over his face exhaustedly. "All right. So two insane, two sane." He sighed. "We can deal."

"This isn't an Easter egg hunt," Terry said. "This is an applied physics assignment and Derek's a fucking cokehead."

"Yeah, and his loss," Connor said. "In case you haven't noticed, he hasn't shown up for English in three weeks."

"Or trig," Quentin chipped in.

Connor motioned to Quentin. "See? Thank you."

"Then what's that say?" Terry contested. "A member of our group hasn't even been seen in any important classes for three weeks."

Connor cocked his head to one side. "Do you honestly believe that Derek not being here will be anything but a positive influence on our grade?"

Terry huffed. He nodded his head, acknowledging that truth. Quentin understood Terry's frustration, how he wasn't bothered by any one specific thing regarding the mention of Derek, but was bothered and nothing else. Association with Derek was, by default, association with chaos.

Chris perked up at the realization that a certain Frances Marie Jerins was a fellow assignee, and he rambled about how staunchly he was, in his words, "Trying to score her." She was a year younger than them, a junior. Maybe that was why he was so obsessed with her. As he rambled on, it became clear that he was rather enamored by her. Not that Quentin couldn't understand it. He did, and intensely. She was his neighbor; the similarly traditional colonial her family lived in was directly across the street from his. They seldom spoke, but his eyes always managed to find her. Every day, he secretly noted the various traits that made her so distinctively herself, such as her studiousness and sweetness, her kindness and humility. There was a markedly beautiful and youthful innocence she emitted, yet young and inexperienced she did not seem. She knew loss. She knew it all too well following the death of her father when she was ten, and from that loss stemmed a uniquely observant and generously empathetic version of herself. By sixteen, she hadn't let any darkness break her, and she probably had no intention of allowing it to happen in the future. She was, simply put, quite lovely, and it bothered him to hear an individual of Chris's specimen being so wholly taken by her just as much as Quentin was.

"Fuck, are you kidding me?" Terry asked.

Quentin jumped. "Huh? What?"

Terry pointed to the paper. "You said Gustavsson?"

"I did?"

"Right there, on the paper," Chris said. "No shit, dude. Terry's right."

Quentin looked down. There, written upon the freshly printed slab of white in his hand was a name none other than Marina Gustavsson's. He had spoken correctly.

"Do we have to work with her?" Chris whined. He genuinely whined.

"Cantankerous hag," Terry bit, despite the commonly known fact that said classmate of theirs was precisely the same age as themselves. At most, she was older than them by two months.

Quentin wasn't prone to liking the raucous triad that encroached on his precious territory that day, but for the first time in all the years he knew them, he found himself welling with sympathy and a deep sense of relation. To preface his disgust for that one, special girl, it had to be known that there were many for whom he nearly felt the same way. Nearly. Disgust and dislike were sentiments vastly different and were rightly applied to different people. He reserved dislike for the intolerable social circles he had no choice but to see in his day-to-day life, such as the "goths" who harbored the most artificial and deliberate sadness in their collectively feeble attempt to appear deeper and more damaged than others. There were also the obsessive film and literary extremists who felt everyone needed insight into their every thought regarding whatever piece of entertainment the public may have been enjoying as of late. And, of course, there were those like Connor, Terry, and Chris. Those were the types of people Quentin disliked. His disgust, however, was reserved for one Marina Gustavsson. She, like himself, was a social outlier, but in the most extreme sense. He had a friend and some quasi-friends, whereas she had none. He wouldn't have minded having some more friends, whereas she probably would have minded having any. In fact, it sometimes seemed she preferred it that way; being alone. She wasn't an intriguing outcast, someone understandable. She was…She was Marina.

Marina was her own, unkind, unfeeling breed. She didn't look horrible from afar. She had thick, chest-length, ebony hair. Her hands were thin and wiry, but they were spidery and bony more than they were delicate and dainty like Frances's. Pale skin coated the bones Quentin instinctively knew were cold and stiff, soaked in a blood that was far from warm. Marina's face was roundish, which she got from her East Asian mother, whom he'd never seen. But her facial features were sharp, inherited from her Eastern European father. Her eyes were black. Black like the ones of vipers. Quentin always hated looking directly at her, directly into her eyes. Again, she wasn't an awful sight from a distance, but it was within intimate proximity, when he had to look closely, that he saw there was something wrong, something off, about her. The black, viper eyes were always keenly fixed. Her small lips were unsmiling. He didn't think he had ever heard her laugh. She was strange, yes. There was an element of her that was unsettling, definitely. But she was, undeniably, hollow. Missing. Perhaps it was presumptuous of him, but she seemed almost like a piece of a person, a fragment of the whole that she should have been.

She had a father. Provided, all people had fathers, but did they have one who was really in the picture? Because Marina's was. He was literally in pictures, and everywhere. He was in newspapers frequently. Liberal and conservative orators alike mentioned him periodically at political conventions, always in a manner that involved unbridled scorn. He traveled frequently and was scarcely sighted in Shaw. Yet, his appearance in high-profile trials made him a constant in the local news. He was a lawyer, a criminal justice lawyer, but oftentimes he seemed to embody and represent the criminal more than the justice, or even the legal. Footage on media outlets would show him representing oily-haired, small-handed, yellow-teethed men in old, chipped-wood courtrooms. Marina never mentioned him. She acted as though she had virtually no idea about his existence, but there was no pretending that she wasn't his child. One glance at her face was all it took to match her to the man in the papers and on the television screens. His black mane may have been neatly gelled while hers less tame, his hands broad while hers thin, and his face long while the shape of hers less pronounced, like her mystery mother's, but the lawyer and the student, the man and the girl, the father and the daughter, had the exact same eyes. Those dark, viper eyes. The ones Quentin hated.

"All right, chums, we got Jaymes," Connor said. "There's some hope."

"Hope?" Chris snorted. "He's a hipster."

"How is he a hipster?" Terry asked. "He runs track and wears *L.L. Bean.*"

"Only hipsters wear shades all the time, Terry. Haven't you ever been to Central Square in Cambridge?"

Terry looked aghast. "He's color blind, you moron. They're color-correcting glasses."

Chris gaped momentarily. "Oh."

"You've known him this long and didn't think to ask?" Terry questioned. "Jesus."

"Whatever. In short, it's someone sane," Chris summarized and laid to rest their bickering. "He can balance out Marina, which is all we need."

Terry reclined in his uncomfortable desk chair. "Have they even met before?"

Chris shook his head. "No. I mentioned her a couple weeks ago, venting to him about how she was pissing me off, and he said he had no idea who I was talking about. No shit, she was—"

Terry pressed a hand to Chris's shoulder. "Say 'no shit' one more time, man. I haven't heard it enough."

"Screw you, dude. Anyway, she was pissing me off so much. That bitch hated on me all afternoon in biology 'cause I didn't know what a zygote was. And when I was like 'bro, chill, just tell me,' she got all bitchy and stuff and muttered that I was mentally deficient and then legit walked away during the project. Like, legit, dude. She got up and left. I found out that she passed in her part of the assignment three periods later just to avoid me because, and I know this since she actually wrote it on the front of the portfolio, I was an 'intellectually inadequate partner.'"

Connor slowly ran a hand over his mouth. "You don't know what a zygote is?" he asked delicately.

"No. Why should I know what a zygote is?"

"Because you've been having sex since you were fourteen."

"Damn. What is it, like a UTI?"

"Oh my god," Terry said.

Connor pinched the space between his brows. "Why would they teach you about UTI's in *biology* class?"

Quentin turned his head skittishly. "It is technically biology," he supplied. It was an awkward point, but he felt it had to be made.

Connor threw an open hand in the air, which he always did when he was annoyed. "Please do not feed the beast, Hanson."

Chris groaned. "Fine. So what is it, then? Since you're all so intellectual."

"It's like that little…little thing that hangs onto the egg after insemination," Connor explained.

"Ew, Connor that's nasty!" Chris said, shrinking back. "Look, all I was saying is that Chen doesn't know who she is and he's a lucky bastard for it."

Quentin and his peers behind him stood to gather their belongings, cramming them into their bags as they readied themselves to leave.

"So where are these people?" Connor asked their teacher, who had returned to his desk.

"The cafeteria," Mr. Halverson answered. "All classes have been given this assignment. When class is dismissed, you're to make your way there, where all grades but freshmen will be present. Also, all of you, please be cautious of your language and behavior in the halls. Today especially. It's kindergarten season."

"What the hell is that?" Chris asked.

"Honestly, Mr. Laney, you know this. They're doing the annual tour for kindergarteners, and I don't want you scaring them again...*like last year*," the teacher muttered to the floor, grimacing. He looked traumatized.

Chris cursed under his breath. "This day just keeps getting better," he said. "In one hour, I'll be dealing with both Gustavsson and kindergarteners. Goddammit. Why do they keep doing these tours? Why the hell does a six-year-old even care about a friggin' high school?"

"Watch the language," said Mr. Halverson, "and I don't know why, but language like that is not what I want to hear from you when you exit this room. Now find your groups, do your work, watch your mouths, and don't trip on any children."

"Yes, sir," the boys said.

"Good," replied their teacher with definitive finality.

4

In spite of the lavish home in which Marina Gustavsson had resided all her seventeen years—a home which was excessively extensive for her small family of three, constituted only by herself and her parents —it never deluded her into thinking she was a superior being. However, whether she indeed lived in her father's ultra-dignified home of solid cherry wood, mahogany, and oak furniture, marble-girded decor, and finely woven Persian throws, or if she lived in a ragged shed held captive by weeds that ensnarled the doors and windows as the wretched thing sat upon a landscape of grassless mud, she was poised to believe that she would have always maintained her distaste for the physical state of Shaw High School, regardless of her personal dwelling. Because, whether one was penniless or grotesquely wealthy, it would have been unfeasibly ignorant to deny the decaying nature of the institution's walls, the cracks in its tiled floors, and the stale air that altogether imprisoned her and the many others who were sentenced to spend their morning within the moldy cafeteria in which she stood. It was revolting.

A pigsty, she thought. A dust morsel that originated from the leak-stained ceiling drifted down and snarled itself in the strands of her hair. She picked at the speck and wrestled it out. *What a downright pigsty*. She resisted glancing at her wristwatch for the fifth time in two minutes. Her impatience began to boil. The bell had rung ten minutes ago and yet, among the muddle of students all squeezed into that ludicrously undersized hall, the members of her project group were nowhere to be seen. She even put forth an effort to be conspicuous, as she leaned against one of the tables in the very center of the room, which she never did. Ever. She religiously evaded interactions with others, and especially there of all places. For a moment, she supposed she could enquire to one or two students as to the whereabouts of Quentin Hanson or Chris Laney, but in that same second of processing the supposition, she realized it would evidently require interacting with someone, which she ultimately wasn't inclined to do.

Marina was a far cry from what one may have considered posh or conceited, but her disposition wasn't necessarily modest either. Most determined her uncaring or, if not that, then at the very least indifferent to the qualities society tended to view as critical to being one with Shaw's social fabric. It wasn't like they were wrong. Many were accurate in their perceptions of her. She was incorrigible and unsociable, and she never denied it. She wouldn't argue that engaging her was often uncomfortable for the approaching party and that her general demeanor was innately exclusionary without her even endeavoring for it to have been that way. She did not, however, hate people. In spite of the common misconception that circulated their tiny, irrelevant school, people, to her, were not worth hating. As a matter of fact, she thought the majority of people so useless, she saw it fit to not care about any of them, because why should anyone pay heed to a thing so deeply dunked in its own futility? Her philosophy was, in some respects, similar to that of a child's mindset once they have matured beyond paying attention to the lives of their toys and, instead, opted for something more practical, like learning to bike or investing in a culinary hobby. If a person was not of value or utility to her, Marina hardly batted an eye at them.

She frightened her mother, who, at the time, didn't understand the logic and never actually would. Marina frightened her father as well, but he was able to grasp her mindset. The couple, Angela and Tom Gustavsson, hated their daughter. Angela, because Marina frightened her. Tom, because Marina was worse than him, thus she frightened him. To say Marina was the cause of the breach in her parents' relationship was harsh to outsiders' ears, but it was the truth. Angela knew there was something the matter with the girl, so the helpless mother turned to her husband to fix their daughter. Meanwhile, Tom knew there was something the matter with the girl, but he planned to utilize her in the future by setting her on a career path that was surely depraved, but lucrative—politics, perhaps. She didn't think there was something the matter with herself and wanted nothing to do with her useless mother and the opportunistic, serpentine creature that was her father, so her parents hated her all the while hating each other, and she completely disregarded them.

Such was the vicious circle of their familial life. They were an odd collection of people. They never saw each other; they never ate together or spent the weekends together. Perhaps that was why their home was so unreasonably large; they were free to disperse and live separately while technically under the same roof. Their lives rarely intertwined. Angela spent hers in long hours of solitude, home all twenty-four hours every day from an idleness she failed to address. She scarcely ate, but indulgently imbibed the finest vinos of Italy as she skimmed fashion magazine after fashion magazine or lamely gawked at the living room television. She was never awake when her daughter would return from school, typically unconscious on a chaise or an armchair. As for Tom, he passed his days at the firm, traveling, or at court, and that was really it. For recreation, he spent a few

Sundays each month playing golf with Chris Laney's father, and sometimes Chris and one of his friends would care to join them. Tom sometimes spoke with Marina during the work week, usually to guide her on which of his friends' firms would be more than willing to take her on as an apprentice after dutifully threatening them over...over something. Something she would never ask about, and something he would never detail. He liked doing that, though; bargaining to get his daughter a head start. She always had a way of refusing.

"You're a little witch, Marina," Tom said to her during the summer before her sophomore year. It was a Saturday, or so she remembered. A hot, humid Saturday, and her father had sought refuge in the dark and cool office in the left wing of their home, where he had summoned her. He was glaring. Seething. It wasn't the oppressive weather that made his eyebrows and the rest of his oft gelled-back hair frizz and poof outwardly, but, by the looks of it, he'd pulled and yanked at the hairs himself. *"Little witch,"* he grit out.

Marina stared at him. Dead, indifferent eyes met ones of pure fury.

"And dishonorable," her father said.

Marina hummed. "Dishonor, you say?"

In that moment on a sweltering summer day, Tom Gustavsson was unequivocally infuriated by Marina because, some three days before, he had informed her that she was granted early acceptance to a prestigious, all-girls university due to his ever-potent networking and the strings of influence he had pulled, only to hear that she did not, by any means, intend to go. He wanted to gift her a head start in life, but she had her reasons not to accept, one of which, she told him, was that she was not yet sixteen and her grades, whilst impeccable, were no indicator of her being fit for a higher education, even where they stood, then. That was the most negligible reason, though. While her spoken refusal pestered him, it wasn't the cause for his rage. The true origin was that, following her adamant intent to decline the offer, having stated herself that she neither worked for nor wanted the university's welcome, he discovered those few days later that she had delivered a false email under his name to said university in which "he" stated that she would not be attending and, to further ensure the irreversibility of "his" decision, she incorporated a snarky, far-from-cryptic comment pertaining to several sexual misconduct allegations hovering over the dean.

Tom Gustavsson was enraged. But he eventually let it go. He became proud, actually, but he hardly let it show. After two weeks of refusing to see her, he said one night, while they were eating their dinner together for the first time in months, "I can make a monster out of you."

A tall, flaxen-haired boy by the name of Ewan Jackson McHugh, who had eye bags grimmer than the fog that pervaded the school's grounds, waved a sheet of blue construction paper in front of Marina's face. He snapped her attention away from the gadget that was tangled around her thin wrist. She slowly looked up at him. His aquamarine eyes burst from their sockets, and in a voice far too buoyant for an hour that early, he said to her, with his single dimple in his left cheek deepening, "I decided to start a petition."

"Congrats," Marina responded.

"I'm going around and trying to get people to sign this."

Marina crossed her arms; her open blazer tightened around the sleeves of her sweater. "It's a petition for what, exactly?"

"A petition to bring this walking-to-school crap to an end. I had to walk five miles today and I heard Natalie had to do six. Plus, it's damn clear our parents aren't planning on doing diddly-shit about it."

"Squat," Marina corrected him, harrumphing. "It's 'diddly-squat.'"

"Geez, whatever, it's slang."

"Aren't you the all-star English tutor?"

Ewan shoved a flat-edged, dangerously overused pencil closer to Marina's torso and nearly tapped her collarbone, which the three topmost buttons of her sweater failed to guard in their undone state. "When I get all the signatures, I'm gonna bring this to the superintendent of schools this afternoon," he said. "I live downtown, so it'll be a quick walk to her office. You don't have to come with us. I've already got Athol and the twins to join me. But you should come, too. It might frighten that authoritarian bureaucrat to see the daughter of Tom Gustavsson in the party."

"The twins, huh?" Marina asked. "Who would've guessed that Oscar and Ivy are participating in a potentially news-covered event? I bet they're doing this for the publicity."

"So? What does their shallowness have to do with your decision? C'mon, Marina, sign it."

She said nothing, only watched him.

"Can you please sign it?" Ewan begged.

Marina glanced around the room. She hoped that, somewhere, her group members were looking for her and she could escape Ewan. "Look," she sighed out, "the superintendent will ignore it. They've probably ended the bus routes for budgetary reasons. It's cheaper for them now."

"Stop being a drip," Ewan moped at her childishly. "Please sign the sheet. It's worth a shot."

Marina's gaze shifted from uninterested to disapproving.

"Look, I'm sorry for bothering you," Ewan said, "but you don't do parties, dances, or pep rallies. The least you can do is sign this sheet of paper."

"I went to your piano recital."

"Because you had no choice but to wait for your mom to pick you up from school and you just so happened to choose the auditorium as your waiting place."

"But case in point, I attended something."

"That is not the point."

"Ewan."

"Marina," Ewan moaned. "It's for the greater good. Also, I'm using this for my social studies essay on governmental prioritization of fiscal—"

Classic Ewan, Marina thought. "Should've just said that in the first place," she said through her teeth and tore the paper out of his hand. She blotched a messy interpretation of her name in the center and smacked the sheet against his bony midsection when she was finished.

The scrawny Ewan's smile was plump with excitement. "Thanks, Marina. Hey, have you seen Roxy? She's supposed to be in my group. I can't find her."

"Don't know her. My group isn't here either. I do have someone on my list that I don't know, though. Jack Chen? Jaymes? What's his name? Anyway, he's assigned as one of my partners."

"I don't know him," Ewan said. "Sorry. See you around, though."

Before the boy disappeared in the swarm of students, Marina quietly told the air around her, "It won't work."

Ewan heard her. As he was swallowed up by the swarm of bodies around them, he stretched out his words in a pitiful coo, *"Aw... Marina..."* Then he was finally gone, deep within the cluster.

At last, she was alone. She preferred being alone, especially after a run-in like that. Ewan was brainless to think the signatures of a few, or even hundreds, of children could make a difference. That type of idealism never got anyone anywhere.

She stood against the table just as she did five minutes before, and the five minutes preceding those five minutes. Her group still wasn't in the cafeteria. She knew Chris was irresponsible and severely lacking in mindfulness of his grades, but Connor and Terry weren't so unconcerned. Frances, Marina had met twice, but she didn't know Frances well enough to assume the girl's priorities. Quentin, last Marina checked, was a bit of an under-performer; plain, talentless, and mediocre in his studies.

Behind her, someone asked, "Marina?" She turned her head over her shoulder to identify the voice's owner, but she saw that she didn't know him. He was tall, far taller than the five-foot-seven Ewan, though not nearly as unfortunately gangly as the other schoolmate of hers. His hair was jet-black and his face was pale, save for his left cheek, which was smeared with acne scars that were slightly faded. Tinted glasses barricaded his eyes, and although she was under the assumption he would eventually eject them from his head while he spoke to her, he never did. *How rude*, she mused. "It is Marina, right?" the boy asked timidly. "Sorry, we've never met. I was assigned to your science group and there was just some kid over there, I don't know him, but I heard him say your name so I kinda just came over here. Then I asked Amber and she said you were in her AP science class, so I figured you're who I should be looking for." He didn't remove his dark glasses. Marina accepted that her staring into the optical accessories was probably the closest she would come to entirely meeting his gaze.

She pushed herself away from the table and grabbed her backpack off the floor by its hangar flap. "That would be me," she confirmed. "Yes, we're in the same group." She said no more, offering no welcome in her affirmation.

"Oh, okay," he mumbled and scratched his nape. "Right. That's why you're here."

"You must be Jaymes," Marina said, and extended a hand. "I'm Marina. Marina Gustavsson."

Jaymes took her hand and awkwardly began to shake it, like he was unaccustomed to something of such rudimentary formality. It didn't surprise her. She thought he had some gall, calling someone out and refusing to remove his glasses. The handshake was brief, and very quickly did he pull himself away from her. "Sorry," he stammered out. "You're hands. They're cold. Or it might be me," he said nervously. "But everyone is." He laughed, but more at himself than at the action.

Marina didn't respond to that. Partaking in smalltalk regarding the temperature of her skin was perhaps the epitome of meaningless conversation.

Alone no longer and stuck in the company of another person of no value, she sighed. School irked her. She deemed her education imperative, but the obsession with the children's socialization was beyond her. She didn't know what to do as she threw her backpack over one of her shoulders and watched Jaymes tensely roll back and forth on the heels of his track shoes. He really was an empty individual, and yet there she stood affiliated with him in what was such an uncontested representation of useless socialization. How needless. How pathetic.

5

The flashlight that was shone into Quentin's left ear was at so high a level of illumination that he swore he felt its hot ray of light slipping into him. The school nurse lodged the pointed end of the utensil far into the depths of that little hole on the side of his head, mumbling something to herself as she pushed an eye against the magnifying glass to examine the area.

"So you do this every day?" Terry asked from the corner of the room, where he, Chris, and Connor stood beside the closed door of the exam room.

Embarrassing as it was, Quentin was obligated to attend twice-weekly checkups with the school's nurse, a Mrs. Patty Walker, for a chronic condition he suffered nearly all his life. He saw his primary care physician once a month, but the in-school nurse's office visits were more accessible, and because the issue was a far cry from complex, an actual doctor wasn't as necessary as, say, a drawer equipped with the apt instruments. The reason for Quentin's visit on that day specifically was due to his absence from the previous four visits he was supposed to have made in the prior two weeks, but as a result of his sleep deprivation and newly demanding schedule, he had inevitably forgotten about them. At the same time, they were on the doorstep to the weekend, so not only had he shirked two weeks of standard evaluations, but he also wouldn't have been able to see his doctor on Saturday or Sunday, and the doctor never took kindly to last-minute, Monday appointments.

As for the coterie of impending fraternity brothers who dawdled with undisguised boredom by the room's vitals monitor and single chair, their presence during Quentin's visit was a bit more difficult to justify. He had told them shortly after they were dismissed from their shared English class that he was overdue for a health checkup, and although he assumed they would have gone on their merry way to assemble the project's team without him, they proposed coming along to his appointment. After light questioning, he found that they each had their own reason for desiring a delay; Connor had admittedly forgotten the key elements from the previous physics lesson and wanted to review his old notes before beginning the assignment; Terry wanted to compose himself before having to potentially operate in the general midst of Derek; Chris just wanted to procrastinate. Quentin allowed them to join him. He figured their company would have perhaps made things more bearable when the nurse stuck cotton bud after cotton bud, a flashlight, and ear drops into both his ears. It wasn't relaxing, having them there. But it was less lonely than his other visits; Connor was on the chair reviewing his papers; Terry stood with his back pressed to the door, waiting for Quentin to answer his question; Chris rocked back and forth on the balls of his feet, looking unusually anxious.

"Not every day," said Quentin. "Just twice a week."

"That's a lot," Terry commented. "So when did this thing start?"

"Uh…I must've been…nine-months-old? Nine, I think. I just woke up one day and screamed, and for hours. I was checked for an ear infection but the doctors couldn't find anything. And it just kept happening; when I was a baby, when I was a toddler, when I was five, when I was fifteen, and onward. And it's like this killer thing, you know? Like, it shoots from my ear into what feels like the rest of my skull and it just stings and doesn't stop. I've been seen by some neurologists, but they haven't been able to figure it out. Tinnitus is confusing like that. If it even is tinnitus. Tinnitus is constant and not, you know, excruciating. Plus it doesn't really explain why I get it on and off."

Terry was clearly vying to appear interested as Quentin explained the nature of the auditory troubles at hand, but Terry wasn't skilled with his pretense and instead bore the face of one who regretted asking their most recent question. Quentin gaged the disinterest. He hushed himself and turned his attention to the medical professional inspecting him.

Patty Walker was a soft and chipper person. She was stout, short, and large-hearted, with wrinkles around the sides of her mouth that crinkled into half-hearts when she smiled. Quentin thought her very auntly and, since he saw her so often, she may as well have been one to him. There was, however, something shifted in the way she looked at him that day. She looked like she was pitying him.

Quentin gulped. "Find something bad?" he asked.

"No." The nurse pat his shoulder twice and gave him a solemn smile. Although sadness was an addition to the chestnut specks in her eyes, there was also a morsel of a thing he couldn't place. It verged on bittersweetness. "You're all set, Quentin," she told him. "You can leave now." She pitter-pattered her way to the main office.

The tall and lanky patient that Quentin was had no trouble jumping down from the examination table. Even as he sat, his feet were already touching the ground. He pushed off the table and flattened a wrinkle on his sweater.

"Connor, c'mon," Chris urged his friend, who remained seated on the chair and was invested in the papers on his lap. "Dude, let's get a move on. Gustavsson's gonna be a nightmare if we're late."

Terry smirked. "If I didn't know any better, I'd say you're afraid of her."

"I am not afraid of her. She's just a giant douche."

The two segments of Connor's binder loudly flopped together as he sealed it. "She's sparse with her words, man, it'll be okay," he assured. "Besides, you're the one who was just rallying for procrastination." Quentin always presumed otherwise, but Connor was quite the methodical being. He slid his navy-blue binder into the frontmost area of his backpack before realizing it wasn't placed with the other binders, but with the textbooks. He removed it just to gently place it in the back with its own kind.

After Connor warned them that the grade diversity of the project groups would only result in a scene of absolute social mayhem in the cafeteria, the four students strategically took their time departing the nurse's office. Quentin strolled while the other three strutted. They employed every plausible excuse they could just to slow their pace, like stopping to open a bag to retrieve crackers or an apple as a snack, or backtracking to get a few sips of water from one of the hallway fountains. But true to Connor's word, even after their late arrival, there still were throngs of people packed into the cafeteria.

"I hate group projects," Terry said.

Chris's shoulders slumped. "Yeah."

The three friends leaned themselves against one of the walls. Nearby, Quentin stood awkwardly. He wasn't one in their circle, but he tried to appear affiliated enough for the other group members to identify them. A long time of waiting passed, as none showed even the slightest inclination to actually penetrate the crowd and ask around.

"Do any of you have Jaymes's number?" Connor asked.

Everyone shook their heads.

Quentin looked confused. "I thought you guys were friends with him," he said.

"I mean, like, in-school friends," Chris clarified. "Not, you know…not close."

Terry knocked his hands against Connor's chest. "Hey, hey! There they are!"

By the corner of the room's centermost table, there stood a towering, bespectacled, black-haired boy. He stared down at a much smaller, brunette girl. They only accounted for two of the four that were missing, but it sufficed for the moment. Marina was mid-sentence as she spoke with Jaymes and, although both of their backs were turned to Quentin, she must have felt that familiar, chilling sensation of knowing when one was being watched without even having to look. She barely turned her head, and her eyes met his. With a most unenthused countenance, she began walking his way. From what it seemed, she didn't explain to Jaymes exactly where she was going because he looked baffled as he followed her.

"Find the others?" Terry asked Jaymes, once he and the girl began to near the group's space by the doorway.

"No, sorry," Jaymes said defeatedly.

Chris gave Marina a repulsed once-over. "Hey, Sunshine," he greeted sourly.

"Go screw," was Marina's response. She didn't look at him as she said it.

"Jaymes, great running last week," Terry cut in, probably to reduce the tension. "All that hail and rain and you just kept going, man."

Jaymes shrugged, but his grin indicated a liking for the brief flattery. "Eh, I was all right," he said, feigning shyness.

"More than all right," Terry said. "Our track teams usually suck."

"So," spoke Connor, "we've got all of us, plus you two, Marina and Jaymes. We're missing Frances and Derek, not that he matters. We're really just missing Frances."

"Actually, we do need Derek's participation," Marina countered.

"Why?" Chris asked. "What do you care about intellectually inadequate partners?"

"I don't care about them," Marina affirmed, "but in case you don't remember, our assignment got marked down because I did the second half without you."

Chris waved a hand at her. "Whatever. I am not in the mood for your...you."

"Play nice, kids, we're all tired today," Connor said exasperatedly. "Now, where do we find Derek? Have any of you seen him?" he asked, only to face a collection of head-shakes. "All right, good start."

"If push comes to shove, we could always ask Mathias," Marina proposed.

"Yeah. Great idea, Marina," Chris said derisively. "Why don't we all just walk up to that guy?"

"Trust the moron who can't even pronounce his own name right?" Terry scoffed. It was true, what Terry said. For all of Mathias Garcia's life, he delivered his name incorrectly, as though he forgot the fact that he was of Greek descent. It was like nails on a chalkboard every time Quentin heard Mathias pronounce his own name. He always said it as *"math-ee-us"* rather than the proper form of *"matt-ie-us."* It was one of the many things Quentin detested about him.

"No, I'm not joking," Marina said. "He's a loser, but it only makes sense."

Connor nodded. "They are two peas in a pod, Derek and Mathias. We could definitely ask him."

Chris folded his arms over his chest. "Well, I'm not talking to him. Just putting that out there."

"Chill, no one's asking you to," Connor said. "So, bearing all this in mind, show of hands for those who have seen them." No one lifted a hand. "Where does this leave us?" he asked.

Quentin scratched the back of his head. "This may be a bit of a reach, but you could try Athol."

"Athol?" Terry repeated. "Athol Khatri? What relationship does that kid have with Mathias?"

"Look, I know it's weird, but we were in a class the other day and he said that Mathias still comes up to him and randomly takes his lunch money or else he threatens to beat him up and stuff."

"Odd," Marina said. "Last I checked, drug-dealing was a lucrative business thanks to customers like Mr. Laney here."

"Do you ever shut up?" Chris asked. "And for your information, I went to rehab."

"That's weird," Marina said, "because I thought I saw some amphetamines fall out of your backpack yesterday."

Connor raised an eyebrow at Quentin. "So we exploit the dweeb's misfortune to find Mathias?" He shrugged nonchalantly. "Good by me, sounds like a plan."

"I saw him with his friends near the window tables," Marina informed them.

"Got it." Connor nodded again. "Let's try that."

Marina wasted no time in her journeying and swirled around on her heels, clearly intolerant to any further delay. Often when she walked, she had an especially stoic and stealth smoothness to her movements, which only fed into her elusiveness and invisibility. Her feet were usually soundless, but, on that day, she tromped through the room. She pushed and shoved her shoulders against anyone in her way. Quentin and the trio followed behind her in a botched pentagon formation. Jaymes stayed by the doorway in case Frances found her way into the cafeteria.

When the majority of the group reached the side of the room nearest the outdoor exit, where the wall was constituted solely by glass that looked upon the acres of recreation fields behind the institution, that was where they spotted a certain Athol Khatri. He was in a small dig-out of the corner with his friends, was one of many in a circle of boys seated on the slimy, tile floor that was recently mopped. Each of the boys' backpacks were piled in the middle of their perfect sphere. On their laps, open for reading, were advanced calculus volumes. Once it was recognized that an entire group of people hovered over them, every set of fingers on the hands of every one of those boys began to jostle restlessly. They didn't look at Quentin, but from the ever-unsettling Marina to the esteemed Connor and his spiffy friends abreast him, the crisscrossed myriad of students on the floor reverently stared up at the new arrivals.

Chris snorted. He leaned backwards to say in Terry's direction, "Honestly, what use will any of these dorks be?"

"Shh," Quentin said. "Give it a chance."

Connor turned to Marina. "Your idea, your bait to catch. Besides, Athol looks like he's gonna shit his pants just from seeing you."

Marina's line of sight centered on the tiniest member of the circle, a small boy dressed in a wide sweatshirt that was paired with unfit pants trimmed three inches too high above his ankles. The brown curls Quentin knew Athol inherited from his South American mother blended into the brown skin tone of his face, which he took from his South Asian father, so much so that his left eye was virtually indiscernible under his cloak of dark hair. The right eye, the one that was visible, twitched at the sight of Marina. Red, raised dots were inflamed on his collarbone, perhaps some type of rash.

"Hi—Hey, Marina," Athol stammered.

Terry looked exhausted already. "Gustavsson, get to it." He checked his leather-lined watch.

Athol's eyes widened. "Yeah, Marina, uh....Hi. How nice to see you." His knee twitched. His hands bunched together, then they came undone when he sent his fingers down to tap his knee caps. His nerves were alight.

Careless to his anxiety, Marina ambled over to him. "Have you seen Mathias?" she enquired.

Athol's knee-tapping evolved to harsh rubbing. His knuckles scraped the middle of his bony leg. For whatever reason, her question induced more jitters from him, and it was unfortunately quite amusing to Quentin, who was having an exceptionally difficult time concealing his amusement. "No," Athol said.

His friends, however, peered to him fretfully from the corners of their eyes.

Marina noticed them do it. "No?" She eyed his collarbone. "You're breaking out in hives."

"I always get hives. Pollen."

"It's November. Where is Mathias?"

Athol looked down. He shook his head.

It necessitated a lofty effort of prying, but with the assurance that she wouldn't reveal Athol's identity as the very snitch against Mathias, Marina did manage to extract the information Quentin's group needed; Mathias's whereabouts. According to Athol, Mathias was in the basement with his friend, Derek.

Friend. Derek was something like that, Quentin supposed. He thought Derek more of a narcotics partner or fellow vice indulger. To have called them friends would have been an overstatement. It was unclear just when he and Mathias first became close, but when Quentin searched his memories, it seemed to have been some time in their third grade of primary school. Derek's upbringing took place in a sorrowfully troubled home, and one could have only assumed the same applied to Mathias. Quentin seldom took the time to invest in gossip and only knew, per the local newspapers and the word of his parents, that Ethan Parker, Derek's older and only brother, was a convicted criminal released five years in advance of his full sentence due to supposedly good conduct within penitentiary walls. Although the specifics were lost on Quentin, he knew Ethan Parker had a special tendency for dealing meth amphetamines, heroin, and, naturally, what was the easiest of them all after the relaxation of Massachusetts laws surrounding it, marijuana. By Derek's teens, he began to sell for his brother and must have somehow corrupted Mathias along the way.

Athol said that Derek and Mathias were apparently bored during their earlier class and decided to hide out in the basement for a period. Had they been anyone else, that wouldn't have perturbed Quentin. But where the two of them were involved, things were not always conventional, especially if they were in the basement.

In the fifth month of their sophomore year, there had been a day when Mathias Garcia concluded his modern art class tedious, and due to that tedium, had crept into the school's basement in a forlorn hunt for some entertainment. It was rumored by the infamy-ridden Derek Parker that Mathias had read an article published by the Food and Drug Administration that was fixated on the health hazards and regulations of minors purchasing common chemical sprays that were used to lubricate creaky doors and rusted metals. The article referenced a law stating that customers had to be eighteen years or older to legally purchase cans of such substances because, following inhalation of said substances, those who breathed in trace amounts were liable to experience behavioral alterations similar to the bodily effects of common drug intoxication. The article went on to explain that just an additional sniff could result in coma or death. Stumbled upon by the sanitation workers on that dull afternoon, Mathias and Derek evidently hadn't read the article in full or simply didn't believe "coma" or "death" applied to them, as they were discovered huddled in a corner of the basement with bloodied tongues as they attempted to lick out the last remnants of a can through the serrated screwdriver holes they had poked in its metal cover. Students were restricted from entering the basement ever since.

After the news, Terry's phone dinged as they approached Jaymes, who continued his awkward hovering by the doorway and seemed relieved when they all arrived. "Casey texted me," Terry told everyone. "She and Frances were held up in engineering and are making their way out now."

Connor pointed to the hallway beyond the door frame. "Basement's right near the engineering room, let's meet her there."

They dragged their feet through the hallways and away from the cafeteria. If most of them were unenthused about the project before, they were even less thrilled after finding out Mathias's alleged location. When they made it to the other side of the building, two girls popped out of the engineering room. One had a brunette bob-cut that allowed the wisps of her waves to dance along her fair shoulders. The other had a head of immaculately knotted braids true to her Jamaican ancestry; the braids contained sleek, black hair that trailed all the way down to her hips. The girl with the short hair wore a knee-length, plaid skirt of vermilion and crimson with a collared, white top tucked into it, and the one with the braids had on a button-up blouse that floated modestly over her tight jeans. They were laughing and smiling, humored by something.

"Okay, I gotta go," the bob-haired one, Frances Jerins, said when she spotted the group.

"Actually, I need to ask Terry something," said the one with the braids, Casey Montgomery.

"Took you long enough," Terry grumpily said to his cousin.

"Well, at least she's here," Casey placated. "Anyway, have you seen Mathias? He's in my group."

Quentin opened his mouth. "He's—"

"Yeah, upstairs," Terry interrupted. "Third floor,"

"Alrighty, see you later," Casey trilled, and she went away.

Chris put his hands in the pockets of his shorts. "What the hell was that?" he asked.

"My parents told me one thing when hers died," Terry said, "and it was that I should take care of her and keep her out of trouble."

"They know this is Casey we're talking about, right?" Chris snorted. "She's a bookworm."

"I'm not bringing her down into that basement. I don't know what's going on down there."

"Actually, we know exactly what's going on down there," Connor said.

"I'm sorry, what?" Frances asked, her soft voice finally making its way into their conversation. "I thought students were banned from entering the basement."

Quentin nodded. "Yup. They are."

"Is it part of the scavenger hunt?"

"No."

"So…?"

Connor cleared his throat. "So we found out that Derek is down there with Mathias. According to Athol Khatri."

"Oh." Frances relieved an itch on the tip of her nose. The pressure left a red dot on the patch of skin she scratched. Quentin tried not to think of how adorable the upturned end of her button nose looked as the spot of red was highlighted against the darker freckles surrounding it. He wanted to collapse when she caught him staring.

"What are they doing down there?" Frances asked Connor.

"See, that's kinda the issue," Connor said. "We have a fairly educated guess. We haven't really taken kindly to the idea of proving it true, though."

"You know, since it was Marina's idea to go down there, I say we send her," Chris said.

"It was not my idea," Marina objected.

"That's unfair, it's a group project," Jaymes said.

"I don't think it's unfair," Quentin protested.

Marina didn't look insulted, just a little annoyed.

"We are all going in there," Connor decided. "Power in numbers, lest there be...Well, I don't know. But that's why we need a lot of us."

Luckily for them, the basement was one corner away, down the farthest hallway of the southern end of the school, where no one but faculty was permitted.

"*How do we get in?*" Jaymes whispered when they arrived in front of the door.

Marina lingered farthest away from the door, also farthest from the pack. In an attempt to remain hidden behind the wall while simultaneously looking beyond the corner, her neck was stretched backwards to an absurd degree, as though it was barely attached to the rest of her body. Quentin was the only one who noticed that she was acting as their lookout.

"Is this a safe idea?" Frances asked.

"*Shh,*" scolded Terry.

"Sorry, sorry. But is this really safe?"

"Probably, but Connor's being paranoid."

"With good reason," Connor argued tersely.

"Dude, whisper," Terry insisted.

"Do we need a key?" Quentin asked.

"Fine," Terry said loudly. "I get it. We're all talking now."

"We'll be okay, Marina's keeping watch," Quentin reassured. "But do we need a key?"

"Unlikely," Connor answered. "Obviously, if those two nimrods are down there, we can get there too. They probably picked the lock or something." He pushed his hands out, which successfully repelled his two acolytes and Quentin from crowding the area. Connor wrapped a hand around the doorknob and gave it a single half-twist; the door creaked open a few inches. "See, fellas?" he crooned. "What did I say? We're in business." He gave the old, rusted door a gentle punt of his foot. They watched it swing against the inner wall, creaking as it shot forward.

The first thing Quentin noticed about the path Connor opened to them was that the only source of light was a dull, flickering bulb that hung from a tattered string. They had to crane their necks to see past the doorway, and stretched before them was an unwelcoming, narrow flight of wooden stairs, most of which suffered chipped fissures that were fragile, almost too fragile, should a normal amount of pressure have been applied upon descent. Quentin didn't have to touch the stairwell to know it was unstable. It looked like one footfall could have brought down the entire flimsy thing. And that went without mentioning the utter grimness of it. Aside from its poor lighting, a musty smell arose immediately. The fusion of the darkness and the aged odor made him shiver. His nostrils began to itch.

Connor hesitantly took the first step down. Terry followed, then Jaymes, and then Frances. Quentin and Chris lagged a bit. Marina still played watchdog.

Chris swallowed some saliva, loudly. "Yo, uh, I'm thinking of opting out. Like…bro…not worth it. I dunno, man."

Marina waited for the remaining two to advance. She must have noted their resistance, though, because she said, "If we get caught, it'll be Mathias and Derek's fault."

Chris huffed and went through the doorway.

Quentin eyed the stairwell. "It looks—"

"Hanson, get on with it," Marina said.

Quentin took a step down. Marina was right behind him and made sure to silently seal the door before proceeding down with the others. One by one, from the stealthy individuals of Marina and Quentin in the back, to the raucous Connor and Terry at the front, they began their creaking journey most attentively. The farther they progressed, the more repugnant their environment became. Quentin wasn't even a quarter of the way through his trek and he was throatily gagging on the pungent, heavy odor of mold. It was grimy and thick. It felt almost like a fluid was pouring into his mouth. He even heard a dry heave at the front. On the step below his, Jaymes covered the bottom half of his face.

"Jesus, what do they have down here?" Quentin heard Connor ask, but could hardly see him. "Do they store bodies?"

"It's an old building," Frances said shakily. "I can only imagine how long the mold has been growing here." Quentin saw her trying not to mar the cascading sleeves of her white top by avoiding any potential graze of her arms against the walls that closed in on them.

Although Quentin wasn't in close enough proximity to see Terry, his complaint was at a volume sufficiently high for all to here as he mewled, "Ew! There's literal mouse shit, rat shit, or somethin' piled up on this step. What freak actually collects and piles it?"

"It does look like one of those Mesopotamian ziggurats from social studies," Connor said.

"Gross." Chris gagged. "It's perfectly shaped and everything. Shit, that's disgusting."

Jaymes started. "Are you implying someone stacked feces to look like a pyramid?"

"Hey, man, you tell me," Chris retorted, "but have you ever seen a rat shit out something the perfect shape of an ancient temple?"

Frances made a disapproving face.

"Maybe watch the language, you guys," Quentin spoke up.

"Sure, Hanson," Chris said. "Just wait till you see this. Maybe then you won't be so high and mighty."

Frances slowed her pace and waited for Quentin to descend to her step before she said, laughing, "It's all right, Quentin. I can understand, given the circumstances."

"I guess. But does he have to be so grotesque?"

Frances elbowed him. "Look around. Table manners have no place here."

"So was your morning better before this or just as bad?" Quentin joked. He attempted stabilizing himself during his small anxiety attack of disgust by loosely taking hold of the mildewed, wooden railing next to him. It was damp under his fingers. *Gooey,* he thought. "Because I used to think walking to school was bad," he said, "but now that we're—*Ow!*" He froze, and Frances squinted as she tried to understand what was happening. He realized, much too late, that his endeavor to keep steady was a faulty one. A dangerous one. He looked down to his right hand, where an enormous, twig-like extension of wood that had projected out from the old railing was notched into his palm, deep beyond the bed of its skin. Its insertion was sharp but not clean, not the way a kitchen knife would have sliced him. The splinter dug in messily with its barbed sides and unevenly pointed top. He knew it was moldy, too. He knew it was mildewy. He knew it had probably been there since the 1980s and that the bacteria woven into it was likely already contaminating him. He hated that they were down there, in that stupid basement. He really couldn't care less if his grades got marked down if he whirled around and ditched the scene.

Because of his outburst, everyone else had stopped walking. Those in the front of the line swirled their heads around to center curious eyes on him, some out of concern, others just dour from the noise he made.

Frances saw the splinter first. "Oh my god," she said. She paled, had seemed to grow sickly herself. It took her a moment to recover and not outwardly panic, but Quentin knew that she was, internally. She wasn't blind. She saw the disaster beside her. Taking in a breath, she cupped his hand in hers and turned it palm-side up for her to examine, just as her mother, whom Quentin knew was a certified nurse, had trained Frances to do. There wasn't any swelling, not yet. He made a retching sound when she touched the skin surrounding the splinter.

"Holy shit," Chris said, marveling at Quentin's hand.

Terry grimaced. He shuffled backwards and would have tripped, had Connor not foreseen a fall and balanced him with an arm. "Now that," he said, "is some splinter."

"That's really frigging gross," Chris agreed. "This is literally why I did not want to come down here, but you jackass morons commissioned otherwise. But honestly Hanson, I'm sorry for you, bro."

Be that as it may, Marina was comparatively inconsiderate to Quentin's crisis. She trudged down the step in front of her and, with an unceremonious nudge, muscled her way in between him and the doting Frances. He didn't know what Marina's intentions were or why she was so forceful to eliminate Frances from the scene, but for the first time in all his years of knowing Marina, he didn't mind her closeness because, having been encircled by the repugnant, stuffy air, a faint remnant of her floral shampoo managed to waft into his nostrils. When the momentary high of her soap scent faded, he went back to being disconcerted. She didn't look at his face, just his hand.

"What are you doing?" Quentin asked defensively. He'd never trusted her and he didn't intend on starting then.

"I'm going to take it out," Marina said matter-of-factly.

"No!" Chris screamed. "Bitch, you'll give him staph!"

Frances, to her credit, was able to compartmentalize how insulted she felt after being shoved off her step. "I don't think you know how staph works," she said to Chris. "Marina is right, though, it needs to be taken out. But we should probably bring him to the nurse or wait until—"

Marina didn't lift her head to meet Quentin's gaze and verify any show of consent on his part. Not a hint of care was on her expressionless face and there certainly wasn't any caution in her movements, because she towed his lifted hand toward herself, engulfed the jagged scrap of wood with her own spidery fingers, and yanked it out of him with a single jerk. He couldn't hold in his scream. Terry or Chris or Connor or *someone* was chastising Quentin for potentially drawing attention to the very realm they were occupying, but it hurt too greatly for him to stifle the yell. He calmed himself after the single scream, and his pain transformed to discomfort when he saw that Marina wasn't watching him apologetically, but was turning the blood-covered wood in her hands to inspect it and not him, whom she had the gall to just torment without the heart to even apologize. She rotated the object several times. It was close enough for him to smell his own blood on it, as the dark, auburn liquid of his veins was painted on the edges. His gut lurched.

After surveying the splinter, Marina's eyes finally met his. "I don't feel like suffocating," she said. "You're splinter-free, now let's find Derek and get out of here. It's like a moldy ring of Dante's *Inferno* down here, I can hardly breathe." And as though her previous display of negligence wasn't enough, she flung the wood piece aside and spared it no glance, even when it plopped onto the peak of one of the feces ziggurats Terry had forewarned was nearby. She bypassed Chris and Connor, squeezing between them, and went about her nimble trek down the stairs.

Quentin soothed his pulsating hand with a gentle massage around the extraction site and, per the advice of Frances, swaddled it with the inside of his sweater sleeve. He slinked back into the cluster that was their distracted group as they returned to descending the unstable path. They impressively, and mostly subconsciously, acclimated into a near-perfect alignment of what was a straight, single-file chain. They stalked all the way down, ever so slowly and carefully, wanting to avoid cracking a step and possibly falling through it. When they reached the ground, the tension dwindled and things returned to relative normalcy. Quentin's pulse still thrummed in his hand, but it bled no longer. Frances was relieved that pus didn't seep out.

Once a crude disruption of Chris trying to trip Terry and his new boat shoes into rodent droppings finally met its end, Quentin and the rest of the group surveyed the decaying room before them, where partly opened paint cans were strewn about on their sides, dry mop buckets were flipped upside down, and mountains of overused and outdated textbooks were piled on top of each other, their bindings ripped and their detached papers barely held to the insides. Broken school desks were stacked in a corner with a strange, yellow fluid beneath the seat legs, and Quentin could only assume what the fluid was. His assumption was, in due time, proven true the moment he saw another splotch of vermin droppings in the center of the puddle; they weren't shaped into mounds, but were spread and unsorted. A tall, thin door was camouflaged into one of the walls across the room, but the general area where it stood appeared safeguarded by a moat of that same yellow substance.

"I've got a new petition idea for Ewan," Connor said, tucking his nose into the collar of his sweater, "and it's to burn this place down before the cholera spreads upstairs."

Frances's hands covered her nose, too. "I don't think a lot of people understand just how dangerous this is," she said.

"I'm gonna be sick," Chris said.

"At least it's not as cold down here as upstairs," Terry grumbled.

"I think that's because of the humidity," Frances replied uncomfortably. "It clearly takes in water. It's the furnace and mold keeping us warm."

"I want to leave," Jaymes said.

"You and me both," Chris agreed.

For whatever reason compelled him to do so, in assessing the door on the other side of the room, Connor began advancing upon it. His feet moved clumsily as he tried to tiptoe over and sidestep various droppings and pools of urine. He, like Terry, was always wary of the pristine nature of his shoes, which maintained their suede twinkle even in the dim light.

"Connor!" Chris exclaimed. "Have you lost your mind?!"

"Come back here, man," Terry said. "This place is a pit. Let's take off."

"We can't leave empty-handed," Connor argued. His focus was unyielding. He leaped over the rancid moat of yellow in front of the closet door and contentedly, almost proudly, gestured to it.

It was a small barrier, that door. Quentin wagered that no one over the age of seven could have possibly fit through it, but perhaps someone had. Otherwise, why would Connor have fought so hard to reach it? The reception of his index finger pointing toward the entrance was mixed; Quentin took a step back; Terry and Chris groaned; Marina began a more meticulous version of Connor's journey, and she soon joined him on the other side of the basement. Eventually, everyone else finally made for the door and somehow, just somehow, Quentin found himself at the forefront of the reunited herd. He ended up closest to the door, and because it was so meager a thing, the entirety of his slim body mass excluded anyone else from coming similarly close to it.

"Well, go on," Chris said. "Open it."

"But..." Quentin licked his lips. He said in a low and sheepish voice, "I don't want to. We don't know what's gonna be in there."

"Odds are, there's nothing," Terry said. "Look at the thing, there's no way either of them could've fit in there."

"Well, Derek maybe," Connor added.

He wasn't wrong. Derek was severely underweight, so he likely could have fit past it with a small struggle. Mathias was the burly one, and Quentin was confident that he couldn't have made it inside.

"What if they're doing drugs?" Quentin asked.

Chris emphasized a sigh. "Of course they're doing drugs, Hanson, that's all they do."

"Oh, by the way," Terry said, "you each owe me ten if its coke."

"No way," Chris said. "I say weed."

"We would have smelled the weed by now," Marina said condescendingly.

"Opioids, maybe?" Frances perked up.

"Sorry, Fran," Connor said, "but if they wanted to do opioids, they could've done them upstairs without being seen."

"Shouldn't you know this already?" Marina asked Frances. "Your mother's a nurse."

"I don't know about that stuff, really," Frances said.

"You don't do drugs in a school basement unless you're doing drug, drugs," Chris educated her.

"Oh, okay," Frances said.

"Quentin, door please," Connor reminded him tartly. "We gotta get going on this project."

Quentin took in a breath. Was he scared? *No,* he thought, but then, contradicting himself, he thought, *Yeah. I'm scared.* He felt so much like a slasher film protagonist who was about to discover something spooky on the other side of the door, and the chances were that he wasn't hyperbolic to have thought that. He put his hand around the wobbly, rusty doorknob, gave it a single turn, and opened the closet. He wondered if that's what it really was, though—a closet. To have dubbed it as such was inapt, since it was more along the lines of a spacious cabinet. It was cramped with its low, sinking ceiling, squished-together walls, and an overall width of barely six feet. Cardboard boxes were stacked at each end and their margins were moistened with something blotchy, green, and most definitely a liquid; he couldn't deduce exactly what he was looking at. What hung from the collapsing ceiling, which was dipping in the middle, was another flimsy, pale string and aged light bulb that illuminated two more cardboard boxes. Unlike the others, they were positioned closely against each other and served as something of a makeshift table. On the middle of it laid an opened and colorful magazine. Quentin could only make out the page closest to him, and he really wished he hadn't, because on it was the image of a svelte young woman dancing in the most preposterous apparel of leather lingerie, knee-high utility boots, and a cabaret wig with bangs that were frayed and frizzed above her blonde eyebrows. Right-side to the choice of reading was a metal tray, on which finely cut streaks of a white, powdery substance were arranged, and squatted over them, with his lips parted in a dazed grin and his right nostril crammed into a rolled dollar bill, was a boy. He held a finger to his other nostril and sucked in a breath through the money straw as it roamed up the tray; an entire streak of the powder vanished.

That boy was Mathias Garcia. He was dressed shabbily in his torn, oversized, and muddy denim pants that dropped past his groin to expose the tops of his checkered boxers the more he hunched over the cardboard table. Four tarnished piercings adorned his unwashed form, with two in his left ear, one that dangled from his septum, and another that was gnarled into one of his thinly hairy nipples, which was accessible to the eye due to the unbuttoned condition of that particular portion of his green flannel. He was tall, had to really invest energy into his hunching just to fit his giant, muscular body into that closet. For someone who so regularly practiced intoxication, he was unusually zealous and regimented in his daily gym routine and prided himself for his strength and brawn. It was a juxtaposition Quentin failed to understand, but more so as he watched the dollar bill scoot up the tray again. Mathias inhaled another steak and then he skirted the bill over to the next line. He rubbed his nose feverishly, and before Quentin knew it, the third streak had vanished too.

Across from Mathias and atop the cardboard table was another tray, holding yet another powdery substance. Dissimilar from its sibling substance across the way, it was gathered in a colossal heap rather than organized rays, and plopped on it was a shiny teaspoon. The individual who governed the other side of the table was, in the physical sense, the drastic antithesis of Mathias Garcia, but was, in every other respect, terribly similar. His left arm was flopped down to his hollow belly, in his hand were a needle and syringe, which itself was occupied, having been lodged into a swelling vein near his elbow;

out of it bubbled a syrupy liquid coagulated with a snowy powder, which, no doubt, originated from the second tray. He gurgled a laugh. This other boy had eyes of lime-green, but his weren't like the glistening emeralds that nature had gifted to Frances. Instead, they were faded like his chalky skin. A canopy of oily, blond strands hung off his head. His figure was noticeably, distressingly gaunt; his jawline wasn't just prominent, it protruded, and his collarbone jutted out from his shoulders. The bagginess of his skin aged him by a decade. By no means did he look his young, seventeen years. As he breathed in and out, the rise and fall of his chest plate was pronounced by the fluctuation, made perceptible even through his tee-shirt. He was so ill, but he wasn't conscious of it. He was dying, but he was suffering a blissful demise. He was also supposed to be Quentin's science partner, and his name was indeed Derek Parker. There, on the floor of that basement, was the missing participant to the grade-inclusive physics project, with his back up against the rotting wall and his legs extended to keep the box-table between his slack, straddling limbs, not a foot away from his pelvis.

Quentin wanted to vomit. He felt his stomach acids burgeon up from his belly, curdling as they prepared to rebel and elevate to his mouth. But he didn't feel sick for the reason which would have seemed obvious. He felt guilty. He was extraordinarily ashamed of himself because he realized, in that moment, that he truly should have rethought his presumptions before declaring Oscar Martinez a phony, attention-starved liar two weeks before. It was a brazenly natural reaction to Oscar's normal behavior, as Oscar and his twin sister, Ivy, were more often than not serial rumor-conjurors, both in reality and on their separate social media accounts. Two weeks earlier, Oscar had been skittering about the lunch hall at noon, making rounds from table to table and boasting about how he overheard that Derek was undertaking a new, more accurate trial to determine the intensity of his brother's homemade heroin without having to inadvertently kill himself in the process. The trial, Oscar claimed, was performed by testing the drug on animals. But no one believed him. No one ever believed the Martinezes' stories. But in that basement two weeks later, Quentin realized how the claim was far from false and that he owed Oscar a sincere apology because, as Quentin stood agape, he saw that Mathias and Derek had additional company.

A yard to the right of Derek's hip and only three inches from Quentin's sneakers, there laid a stout, bushy-haired, twitching rat. Half of its whiskers were amiss, a scarred bald spot mottled the area above its shriveled tail, and punctured into its neck was a needle identical to the one that was inserted into Derek's vein. The needle in the rat even contained a similar substance. The rat twitched again, and it rolled over onto its side, on the grubby floor. It started to squawk. Mathias inhaled another powder row. Derek released a satiated moan. How they hadn't yet noticed the seven bystanders was beyond Quentin's comprehension.

Terry was the first to voice his thoughts. "You fucking wastes of life," he said into the musty air.

Frances was clinging to the closet door with one hand, and the other was smacked to her forehead as her eyesight was fixed on the rat. Chris gaped at the copious amount of cocaine Mathias persisted to take in without overdosing. Terry's arm became dotted with goosebumps. Connor was speechless, the upper and lower portions of his mouth widened and stretched apart from each other, his face like Chris's. Jaymes kept his nose covered. Marina rolled her eyes.

Quentin didn't know what to do. He did, however, know what *not* to do. He may not have been the most versatile person, in that he knew when practical limitations should have been abided for the sake of one's own personal safety. On the rarest of occasions did he think it wrong, or not worth the trouble, to enact morally correct decisions, and in that moment, he recognized that a rare occasion was at hand. As he had established earlier in the morning, it had been, as he described in his own words, "one of those days." Because Terry, it seemed, had a plan. A plan of his own. A plan which he swung by literally no one but himself. And Quentin, ever meek and conflict-dodging, simply ground his teeth and instinctively wrapped his arms around himself as Terry moved past everyone, went into that tiny closet, and with absolutely no warning whatsoever, leaned down and tore the needle of out of Derek's arm.

Chris sighed. "Well, fuck me, I guess."

"Terry, you idiot!" Connor lambasted. "You dumbass! What're you, Chris?!"

"Hey!" Chris yelled.

Terry turned around. He victoriously held the needle in the air. He looked so proud of himself, but for reasons that absolutely none of his peers understood.

Derek was everything but calm and he didn't handle the gloating well. He flew into hysteria, quaking and breaking into a cold sweat, properly venomous at Terry for disarming him only halfway through his injection. He grew pale as a sheet of paper, and he boomed out, "Give it back!" The pitch of his scream was high, but his ire was profuse. He realized that about himself just as immediately as Quentin did; how incongruous Derek's voice and emotional state were. He snarled something instead of screaming again and then, in his mounting fit of rage, crawled forward and glommed his hands all over Terry's ankles and legs in pursuit of a savage tussle to bring the drug-depriver to the ground with him. Quentin didn't think Derek worthy of being understood, but he reacted just as one should have expected of a deprived drug addict. On any ordinary day, Quentin may have sympathized with Terry. But that was no ordinary day, and on that day,

Quentin had some uncharacteristic thoughts, such as, *You know what? Fuck it. This is karma.*

No one volunteered to help Terry.

"We should've just reported them!" Frances argued.

Apparently, everything that had transpired up until that point was wholly unbeknownst to Mathias. All around him, people were shouting. In front of him, Derek was yanking at Terry, who in turn was struggling to escape the death grips on his calves. Only then did Mathias look up. He brushed away some of the white powder under his nose with a knuckle. "What the—?" he began, but no one heard him.

"All right, all right," Marina said between short breaths to everyone by the door, "we should just go upstairs and report them. Leave Terry."

Chris nodded in avid approval. "Agreed."

Connor shook his head. "But what about the proj—?"

"Hey!" Mathias broke into their discussion, eyelids red and the skin of his nostrils flaky. "How the hell did you find us?!"

Quentin backed up and nearly fell over.

Connor sucked in a mouthful of air, composing himself. "Mathias," he said, "good to see you."

"Fuck you, O'Neil."

"Ever gracing the world," Connor remarked.

Marina looked bored. "Don't bother arguing."

"Marina," Mathias said her name slowly. "This is none of your business. I recommend you fuck off, you prissy bitch."

"Shut up, trash," Connor said.

No more than two feet away, Derek wailed as he tongued Terry's left ankle and wrapped wiry arms around the nearest foot he could trap. "Give it back!" he spluttered. "I need my hit! I need my fucking hit!"

"Gah!" Terry shouted. He wiggled his leg in a desperate attempt to escape Derek's starving grip, aching as fingernails cut his skin.

Mathias punched the door; Frances, who was clutching it, tripped backwards, but she managed to balance herself before falling into the yellow puddle behind her. "Skinny prick Asshole gave us away, didn't he?!" he bellowed at Quentin, who was aware that "Asshole" had been Mathias's epithet for Athol since the sixth grade. "You wimpy little shit, you're friends with him, aren't you?!" Mathias asked Quentin.

Quentin's head turned left and right fretfully. "Uh—What?" he stuttered out. "No, no. We found you on…on our own."

"Do you think I'm fucking stupid, Hanson? I'm gonna destroy your little pussy ass and after that I'm gonna hunt down your little shit brother, too. How's that? You wanna mess with me? You wanna fuck with me?!"

Connor sauntered forward. "You know, hood, you've got a lot of nerve to act like the rest of the world owes you shit."

"Give it back!" Derek kept screeching.

"Someone help me!" Terry yelped imploringly, but no one did. Firstly, because they would've had to get past Mathias. Secondly, because they thought him deserving of the maltreatment, just as Quentin had.

Mathias, afflicted by his perilous addiction, had to actually pause the quarreling to bend over and attain another snort of the newly untidy narcotic pile on his tray. He didn't even slice it into individual lines, just sniffed what he estimated to have been close enough to the accurate measurement.

Connor chuckled. "You are such filth. Look at this guy. Can't even argue. He just needs that sniff. Don't you, Mathias?"

"Mathias, don't keep doing that!" Frances screamed. "You'll die!"

"He's a junkie this young," Chris said. "There is nothing you can do."

Derek successfully wrenched Terry off his feet. The entirety of him collapsed to the cement, which was no less damp of its mold and rodent urine. His wrist thumped against the wall and the impact fractured the glass of his luxurious watch, but most haunting of all was how the back of his head dropped onto the trembling rat, and from the fallen force of Terry's weight, the heroin needle plunged deeper into the rodent's neck, and, like a squeaking dog toy, the animal released one last gasp before succumbing to the utensil a half-second later, and right under Terry's head. He shrieked.

Connor grabbed Jaymes's arm for balance.

Frances started crying.

Marina rubbed her temples.

Quentin swallowed the vomit rising up his throat. "Did…Did you hear that?!" he yelped out.

Mathias's negligence for the recent, unavoidable devastation was astounding. He charged forward and took hold of Connor's slackened shoulders, his nostrils flaring and his forehead wrinkled as he jostled Connor side to side like he was no heavier than a rag doll. "How the hell did you find us?!" Mathias demanded.

Connor deferred from answering verbally. His knee did all the talking for him as it struck right at the core of Mathias's abdomen, which quickly granted Connor's shoulders liberation once Mathias lurched away. He stumbled, searing from the burn of his gut. He reeled and grabbed at his middle. Tripping, he unintentionally knocked his dearly beloved powder tray to the ground. What tumbled down after it was the cardboard table; Derek's tray and the pornographic magazine went crashing to the floor. A cloud of the substances billowed up into the air, up to the noses of the substance-abusers' disturbers; Quentin's face made haste behind the front of his hooded sweatshirt; Marina, Connor, and Frances covered their mouths; Chris took in plentiful sniffs of the parts of the cloud he could reach; Jaymes backed away.

The hysteria had no bearing on Derek, though, who had long since proven that his suspension of reality went beyond basic intoxication and that it was actually an innate gift. He was tireless in his loyal lust for a certain something. With a traumatized Terry laying backwards on the floor and on the deceased rat, Derek seized the opportunity to crawl up Terry's body and claw at him. "Where is it?!" Derek insisted.

Terry panted out, "You...don't...need...it! Shit! Get off me! Guys, help! Get him off me!" No one jumped to his aid and, because of it, the two of them remained sprawled on the floor. Terry's head was abutted by the slaughtered rat and he was so disturbed by it that he didn't seem as worried anymore about the persistent Derek, who was continuing to scrape and grope at everything he could reach.

"I need it!" Derek insisted. Suddenly, he looked up for the first time since he initially attacked his depriver. His eyes panned one way and then another, and they brimmed with unshed tears when he saw the state of his and Mathias's secret cave. Derek keened loudly, as if he had been stabbed. His breath grew unsteady and his bottom, chapped lip quivered against the top one as he wept; saliva dripped out of his mouth. He wept. He thoroughly wept.

Terry was stuck underneath him. The instant he saw how Connor's mess impacted Derek, Terry watched with fear in his brown-gray eyes as the scrawny creature scratching his waist readied himself like a rampant lion, and then he, Derek, pounced. He tethered his knees to Terry's shoulders and crowded all of his measly weight on top of him. Then, Derek began choking him.

Chris shook his head at the ground. He was talking to himself when he said, "Knew I should've taken those fucking pills this morning." In his next breath, he added, "Dad was right, I shoulda gone to Protestant Prep."

Connor wasn't as calm. "Ahh! That is it!" he hollered. He stalked over to his friend on the floor, had probably anticipated freeing him from the sadistic addict, but the more Connor disrupted the personal conflict by grabbing and kicking at Derek, the more firmly Derek's nails dug into Terry's neck.

Mathias ground his teeth. He snapped his body up and, without much forethought, whacked Connor's soft cheek with the back of a hand, then staggered backward. "My coke!" Mathias shouted. He motioned behind him, to nothing specifically. "That cost a fucking fortune, you preppy douchebag! And you hypocrite! You know what it's like!"

"Yeah, well, we went to rehab," Connor said as he wiped his face, where blood leaked out of a purpling stretch of his skin. "And it looks like you need it a lot more than we did." To finalize his retort, he spitefully, and passionately, punched the bottom of Mathias's jaw. Quentin couldn't see the entire act, but he flinched when he heard a grating *"crack!"* of jawbone. The result of the strike left the bottom of Mathias's face throbbing and red. He fell to the floor posterior-first, and Connor appeared satisfied with himself. "Show up to class, you prick," he said, and returned to helping Terry.

Quentin lent no effort to the Derek-versus-Terry battle, but in his defense, Terry's childhood friend, Chris, didn't either. Frances was absolutely scandalized and just held the closet door for support, and Marina and Jaymes were considerably more relaxed now that Mathias was neutralized, even if it was only for a few moments.

"How could you?!" Derek squealed. His face rolled around Terry's chest. Pathetic tears of his angst and agony dampened the *Polo* shirt his classmate donned.

Quentin's eyes shifted to the right.

Terry wasn't taking in any oxygen. The pallor of his face shifted to a graver tone. He gasped for air. They had underestimated Derek's anger, because he wasn't letting up. Connor was large and muscular, young and in exceptional shape, but he had trouble freeing his friend of the chokehold.

Mathias returned to his full height and cracked his neck on each side. He was boundlessly livid and his eyes were set to Connor, who was in a defenseless position as he tugged at Derek and started straddling him from behind.

Grow some balls, dude, Quentin scolded himself, and so he tried to. He foolishly sprang to Connor's aid by worming into the space between him and Mathias. Quentin flailed his ridiculously untoned arms out into the air to purportedly obstruct Mathias, but it didn't work. Fortunately for Quentin, Connor caught on to the incoming threat. He released Derek, briskly shot a foot into the air, and kicked Mathias in his crotch. He recovered with flying colors. Quentin should have run for his life, but he stood there, frozen in place, even when the large fist came flying toward his face. Because Marina and Chris were directly behind him, that meant that when he fell, they fell too. And hard. Marina had no warning. She only heard a single grunt before Quentin came crashing down. The back of his head slammed the front of her face, and together, their combined weight rained onto the oblivious Chris, who, for some reason, seemed entirely unprepared. A painful domino effect left the three of them piled on top of each other in a heap on the floor. Under Quentin, he made out a strangled, gurgling sound from Marina and a scathing outpour of vulgarities from Chris.

"Shit, Hanson!" Chris bellowed. "What the hell?!"

"You guys okay?!" Jaymes checked. He crouched down to probe for any dire injuries, but stopped himself before reaching them; if he wanted to come any closer, he would have had to touch the moldy, urine-soaked ground.

Quentin squirmed off his fallen classmates. He held his head and crouched on his toes, mindful of the filth that was beneath him. Guilt overcame him, even though none of what happened had been his fault. He couldn't help feeling utterly mortified as he saw Marina half on top of Chris with her hair in the yellow puddle on the floor while Chris's body was completely bathed in it. She began squirming off him, patently harried and made speechless by the impact of the fall. She cared little for the awkwardness of having to wriggle her lower body away from the front of his.

Jaymes extended a hand to her. "Hey, are you all right?"

"Get the fuck—" Marina started, but she didn't bother finishing her sentence. She made to stand, but one cursory scan of her clothing with a resigned eye stopped her. She wasn't as unfortunate as Chris, in that his whole body was basked in urine and fecal droppings, but she came terribly close. The back of her hair dripped yellow, the back of her tailored blazer was smeared with squished, brown dots, and her jeans were covered in the bed of white powders that coated the floor. She stared emptily at Quentin, which he felt was worse than being outwardly screamed at in a shrill voice—that, at least, would have indicated a change in her emotional compass. But there wasn't any of that. She was empty-eyed and detached. She criss-crossed her legs, wiped something that was either cocaine or heroin off her left eyebrow, and said nothing.

Chris still laid on the floor. He didn't make to move either, except to scoop some powder off the ground and bring it up to his nose for a sniff.

Beside them, Frances stared into the closet, where Connor was on the verge of ripping Derek away from Terry. The poor girl had been jilted the whole time, stiff and frozen. Quentin had completely forgotten she was there with them.

Derek made another screeching sound. Connor punched him in the throat.

At the same time, the pain in Quentin's head was murderous. He had to have developed a concussion from the combined sway and landing, and even though he had gaged that Marina's head was fairly small, beneath her flesh and all that hair, ultimately a skull still lurked. He crouched on the floor and balanced himself on his toes, wobbling as he peeked into the closet to spectate the ongoing hysteria. He saw that Connor had liberated Terry at last. He was balled up against the mildewed wall with his hands holding the middle of his neck and his breathing, although uneven, was thankfully present. The rotation to fend off Derek apparently landed on Connor, who vied against the pale, bony boy in another shockingly prolonged and trying wrestling match. Quentin never realized just how much needful desire had an effect on people, how it made the seemingly powerless all-powerful. Derek wasn't alone in that effect. Mathias acted similarly. In the corner of the shoebox-sized compartment, he skittered around in a fit. He jabbered to himself in his irrepressible rage as he lashed out at every item in the vicinity. He zinged a box against a wall, which unveiled the secreted skeleton of another rat with a half-used syringe stuck between two of its ribs. The light bulb on the string overhead shook as he swatted it round. His last spurt of vexation was slinging the pornographic magazine behind him, and the unfortunate Frances was introduced to another half-bare woman once the glossy bunch of papers thudded against her face and fell in front of her flat shoes, which were adorned by purple bows.

Connor smacked his elbow against Derek's nose. After so great a battle, Derek finally fell to his side. He held his bloody face; his nose was misshapen, definitely broken.

Connor moved next to Terry and pat his back to loosen up all the phlegm and whatever else had been stuck in his lungs during the strangulation. The coughs he hacked were unpleasant to listen to, but Quentin reasoned it was better to hear Terry heaving than for him to have not been breathing at all. Connor patted Terry a bit harder, and the mere help of some extra force brought out the final aftereffect of the throttle session. He cleared his throat. He coughed a few times and then produced a harsh, scraping sound. Phlegm rose to his mouth and he spit it onto the basement floor.

Mathias scoured one of the rearmost corners of the space, hungrily searching for something. At least he wasn't antagonizing the others anymore.

Quentin wondered why Derek wasn't unyieldingly vengeful once his nose was broken, or why the powder he mewled over seemed to have slipped his mind. It was puzzling, until Derek's eyes began to shimmer when they spotted the corner Mathias had exposed, back when he threw all the boxes around. In that disgusting corner, there was Derek's missing object of desire and it waited only for him. He scrambled onto all fours, retrieved the needle, and without a cautionary pause, stabbed it into the open vein of his left arm.

Frances turned pale. "I…" she struggled out. Her voice shrank and she couldn't speak.

Connor stopped patting Terry's back as soon as he saw it happen. "Ew! You fucking—Gross!"

Quentin felt like he was going to faint. Perhaps he would have, if things hadn't gotten worse. But they did.

Marina, resigned on the floor, said very tiredly, "Mathias, you can either turn yourself in now or we bring this evidence to the police and the school board."

Mathias spun around from whatever he was doing. "Did you just threaten me, whore?"

"Can you stop talking like that?" Jaymes grunted out. He rubbed his forehead with a pinched expression, his annoyance clear.

Chris sat up, wiping his shirt of the urine. It was a futile effort. "Can't believe you did this to me," he said to Mathias.

Mathias waved him away. "Shut the fuck up."

"As I was saying," Marina continued, "should you lack the responsibility to turn yourself in, we will report this. You'll probably be charged with drug possession, mainly because you're on school grounds and...Ah, that's right. This is what, your fifth drug-related offense? You can expect a nice DCS visit after school this evening. Have fun in foster care or a lockdown rehab."

Mathias scoffed. "Okay, you know what's wrong with all of you?" he asked. His head rolled in a cracking circle. "It's that you're all so self-righteous and actually think you're the shit, that you're this and that and you're god's balls. Who the fuck even are you? Hanson here, giant pussy. Marina, you're just a bitch. Chris, fuck you."

"Well, compared to you, we are this, that, and god's balls," Chris said.

Jaymes's lips parted to say something, or so it looked that way, but then he closed the tiny gap between them and began wincing at something. He rubbed his forehead again. Quentin was fairly confused because Jaymes was one of the few people left unimpaired from the basement excursion.

"Excuse me," Marina said, "but I was trying to—"

"Shut up, no one cares," Mathias stopped her.

"Will you stop being a jerk?" Frances demanded from her space beside the basement door. Her mouth was drawn into a stern line.

Mathias looked over his shoulder and laughed. The sound echoed at the base of this throat. "Well, well," he greeted her, "if it ain't Virgin Mary Frances. The fuck are you doing here, church girl?"

Frances raised her chin higher, defiant. "Is that supposed to be an insult?"

"Hey, to each his own, but you're a one-outta-ten. Wouldn't bang."

Quentin tried to stand. When he was too dizzy to do that, he attempted to reposition himself into a more stable and grounded squat, but inside his head, an ache began to pervade with an uncannily instant onset of severity. He swayed and didn't hear much of anything around him, such as the rant Chris was launching, undoubtedly a result of his lust for Frances and not quite rooted to any genuine goodness within him to defend her. But Quentin didn't care for any of it. Well, he did, just not in that particular moment. Nor could he have, because he couldn't hear a thing. A subtle pulsation was knocking on the inner walls of his skull, one he'd expected to diminish a few seconds following its sudden onset. He knew he and Marina had bumped heads, but it wasn't at an intensity level that would have produced such a reaction. Of their own accord, his eyes shut. He concentrated and tried to will the ache away.

It was no mere ache, though. Try as Quentin might to classify the searing pain as minor, he couldn't deny that it was pure, unrestricted stinging. The pulsating progressed to a more frequent drumming, so that it pained him every half-second rather than the previous pattern, which was every four. It then radiated from the back of his head to the very front, as it shot from one temple to the next and it held in his forehead every three beats. There was, of course, something else he inevitably considered a factor of the pain, but he refused to believe it was the cause on that day. Years had passed since he had been a weeping, hypersensitive child and he had long outgrown the little-known peculiarity that had plagued him for most of his upbringing. His eighteenth birthday was at the end of the month and he was used to the recent years of being joyously asymptomatic of his condition. After so lengthy a remission, he thought it impossible to relapse.

Chris was watching Quentin as his body sank lower in his squat. He almost touched the floor.

There was no further feigning serenity once the ringing started. Just as Quentin remembered, it was a soft trill, which at first sounded as though it were being played a mile away; a slight tone amid the hour's everlasting madness that already swarmed him. He wasn't going to cry, even though he knew precisely what it meant, how he knew what was coming his way. He knew the routine, however regrettably he did; the first minute was unbearable, the sixth considerably worse, the thirtieth the most tormenting, the end of the hour somewhat gentler, and the next three hours a span of sensitive recuperation. He was older and more contained, could handle a sprinkle of pain.

The headache strengthened and the sound become shriller. He didn't panic. The familiar crescendo neared, but he bottled up his discomfort. It was going to be all right. It would end, in time. He was stronger at seventeen than he was at fifteen. He could handle it.

Quentin couldn't see it because he was grappling against all odds to remain quiet, but Chris's curiosity for the squatter beside him didn't wane. Connor and Terry had made their way out of the closet and were engaging in another vitriolic exchange of insults and threats with Mathias, but Chris wasn't looking at them. He watched with enlarged pupils and lowered shoulders as Quentin gasped in his breaths, huffed them out, and was shrunken into a ball as his hands clenched the sides of his head, holding his ears. "Is this your uh... hearing thing?" Chris asked carefully.

Quentin didn't hear the question. That sound, that tone, was like a scream to him. It was miraculous how something so minuscule at its commencement had a way of developing into a torturous force a minute later. He breathed in and out. His intakes of breath were long and slow, but it was his exhales that brought him to full-form quivers every time. He hated that he couldn't lie to himself anymore, that his head hurt so much. His fingernails scraped the lobes of his ears.

Chris poked Quentin's left forearm. "Yo. You good?" he asked.

He wasn't. The crescendo arrived. It burst into his head like a punch and there was nothing he could have done to deflect the force. The screech of it was murderous. He didn't even realize it, but he was screaming too. He couldn't help it. He couldn't hear it, and maybe it would have helped him to know about it, but Jaymes was sitting just like Quentin was, knelt over with his hands prying the sides of his own head.

Someone grabbed Quentin's shoulder. "What the hell is going on here?! Why are you two screaming?!" they asked. It was definitely Connor.

"Jaymes?! Quentin?!" Frances called to them. "What's wrong?!" She tiptoed over to Jaymes and poked his arm, but he didn't respond. She did the same to Quentin, and he was identically unreceptive. They bent over, screaming with their hands over their ears.

Chris rubbed his eyelids. "Holy fuck, someone get them to shut up."

"This is blood-curdling!" Connor yelled. "Make 'em stop! Someone shut them up!"

Derek was sprawled on the floor, an arm hung over his unbothered face. He shot another dose of heroin into his arm.

It was Marina's turn to snap. "Guys, stop it!"

They didn't. As a matter of fact, they graduated from shouting and wincing to crying and screeching.

Mathias stormed out of the closet. His broad shoulders swayed back and forth as he proceeded toward the screamers. "Is this some fucking joke?!" he bellowed acidly. "What the fuck is this?! Some faggoty act to get us caught?! You think your screaming will get us caught?!"

Connor looked up at him. "God, you are such an asshole!" he screamed.

"All right, Jaymes and Quentin, enough!" Chris urged. "Guys, we're serious!"

Connor bent forward so that he was at equal level with Marina, who was still sitting on the floor. "What the fuck is going on?" he asked her.

Tears streamed down Quentin's face.

"I don't think they're faking it," Marina posited.

Mathias charged forward and kicked Quentin in the stomach. The impact sent him reeling onto his back. Everyone probably expected him to stand and express some outrage, but his hands fastened tighter around his ears. A heavier downpour of tears escaped his closed eyes.

"I hate all of you," Terry deadpanned to no one in particular, but to the air in front of him.

Chris looked back to Marina. "Get them to stop!" he begged. "Please!"

"What makes you think I can?!" she asked.

"Because you always know how to fix weird shit!"

"What?!"

"Okay, enough!" Chris blasted. "I'm serious! Jaymes and Quentin, cut it out!"

"What if it isn't an act?!" Frances questioned.

"Of course it's an act!" Mathias disputed. He bent down and punched Quentin's stomach again, but he still didn't react. Mathias just kept striking him, trying to elicit a reaction. "Cut it out, you pussy!"

"We need to figure this out!" Frances insisted. "Do you think this is some environmental reaction?!"

Since he had Quentin flat on his back, Mathias was about to stomp on Quentin's chest, but he froze to counter her. "It's an act! It's a goddamn act!" He glared to all of them individually. "You're all in on it! I'm not buying this shit!"

"Why would we be in on something this annoying?!" Chris protested.

Terry jostled Jaymes's shoulders. "Stop it, dude! Stop it!" Terry begged with a crackle in his voice. He looked around to everyone. "What do we do?!"

Derek slipped his heroin needle out of his arm and wagged it in the air. "Shoot 'em up, it'll calm 'em," he proposed.

"Should we bring them to the nurse?!" Frances suggested.

Mathias kicked the wall. "We are not taking these pussies to the nurse! They are faking it and you're in on it!"

Marina crawled over to Quentin. His shirt was raised a bit and blue bruises were blossoming on his midsection, but that's not what she focused on. She was distracted by his face, which was dampened by his incessant avalanche of tears. "He's not faking anything," she said.

"What did she say?!" Mathias asked.

"Said he's not faking!" Connor said.

"Bullshit!" Mathias punched the door that time. "Complete load of bullshit!"

Chris rubbed his temples. "I fucking can't," he muttered.

They all screamed at each other. Mathias kept abusing Quentin. Marina kept watching Quentin cry. Connor kept watching Marina in hopes that she would deliver some sort of constructive conclusion. It was so loud. There was arguing and crying and fighting, so much so that no one in their hectic bunch even noticed the school's vice principal, the janitor, and the security guard, as they made their hasty way down the rickety stairs behind them. But even when the figures of authority did arrive, which led Frances to tense up and splutter apologies and excuses while Mathias clenched his jaw and pumped his chin higher into the air, ready for a fight, neither Quentin nor Jaymes opened their eyes. They didn't look up and they didn't stop their screaming.

6

Conservatively, the aftermath of the physics project fiasco wasn't as catastrophic as the actual basement encounter. It was grueling, but nowhere near as painful. No one wanted to be near each other after their detention and questioning. They were each tired, reeked of vermin and mold, and their faces all served as reminders of the uncomely hour. In the end, they were luckier than they thought they would have been, because the school's faculty found the stench of the pupils so rancid that they cut detention short by thirty minutes. After, those who were complicit in the basement incident wanted nothing to do with the pair who had fallen victim to the oddity that was the occurrence of searing ear pain. According to Connor, his own ears had popped solely from being in close proximity to them, and Terry upheld that the outburst was indeed very annoying. And then there was Chris, who went so far as to characterize it as "Mind-fuckingly annoying." That was actually the last Quentin had heard from anyone in their group.

Later in the day, he was retrieving his belongings from his locker, all the while diligently avoiding contact between his feces-tarred sleeves and the metal door, when it struck him that he had no idea where his fellow witnesses had dispersed. He certainly knew of

Mathias's and Derek's whereabouts. Everyone in the town did by that hour; during the other students' detention session, the substance abusers were whisked away in separate police vehicles. Beyond that, Quentin knew nothing of everyone else. He assumed some either walked home or had transportation of their own, and that Frances and Jaymes were likely disallowed from participating in their extracurricular activities. Wherever they went, it wasn't any of Quentin's business. He had no interest in knowing, either. He was in an especially foul and disinterested mood, grateful to have finally been left alone, even if the cost of it was urine in his hair and ears sore from the hour-long blast—frankly, he expected the torture to have lasted longer. Everyone was depleted of their energy, and he wasn't insulted that no one wanted to partake in a chit-chat after their release. He, like the others, just wanted to go home.

One thing did manage to boost his energy, even if just by an increment. He watched from where the school buses used to stand as another mess began to unfold: Chris jumped out of the driver's seat of his car and slammed the passenger door in front of an approaching Terry. "Bro, hell no!" Chris yelled. "You are not getting into my car with that shit all over you! You didn't even take a locker room rinse!"

Terry threw his hands in the air. His belongings, which were his backpack and workout bag, fell to the ground from the dramatic rise of his arms. "C'mon, Chris, I'm freezing," he said. "It's fucking twenty-eight degrees out here."

"No way, man. No way. Ride with Connor."

"I can't ride with Connor! He left!"

"Then go with Casey!"

"She left when school ended!"

Chris crossed his arms. "This is no one's fault but yours."

"What?! How the hell is this my fault?!"

"Hey, I dunno, jackass. Why don't you tell me? Who runs up to a heroin addict and yanks the needle out of their arm? What is actually the matter with you? Now you dragged us into that crap—literally—so it's your fault. Step away from my dad's car. If there's rat piss and shit on his seats, I'm fucking dead. You saw his reaction when I barely dinged that pole last year."

Terry crowded Chris's space. "Oh, oh. I see. So never mind the two guys doing actual blow on school grounds because—"

"—Yeah, never mind that!"

Terry scowled. "Well, fuck that."

"Yeah. Get out of here."

"Fine, asshole," Terry snarled out. He grabbed his bags off the concrete of the parking lot. Quentin watched as his neighbor flounced away from the lone, silver car. Terry muttered and cursed to both himself and the sky as he hurried along in his absurdly unprepared attire of khaki shorts and boat shoes, which were paired with a button-up tee-shirt; he was nowhere near ready for the late-November chills that struck him. Things became awkward when he saw Quentin watching him, who himself was beginning his own journey by foot as he witnessed the scene take place, but Terry said nothing to Quentin, who likewise divulged no interest in communicating.

And yet, inevitably, they were moving in the same direction and, whether or not they planned for it, they were walking home together, even if they were separated by a two-way road and each confined to a sidewalk opposite the other. They were neighbors, but not friends. Yet they were aware of the glaringly uncomfortable truth that traipsing at the same pace and with the same end goal whilst separated by a stretch of fifty-or-so-feet was painstakingly awkward. So, in harmonious un-togetherness, they began to walk completely in sync, and when their single paths along the edges of the streets began to flatten into the pavement and the sidewalks long vanished in the residential corners of Shaw, they found themselves slogging the rest of their journey home side-by-side through the centers of the deserted roads. For three additional miles, they continued like that; beside each other and silent. They bore the windchill and said nothing, floundered from their fatigue and grunted as they rubbed their eyes to stay awake. But still, they said nothing. They contained their every thought to inner-monologues, which they knew the other had absolutely no interest in hearing, until Terry was the first to reach his home, and, a few minutes after, Quentin did the same.

His true misery began once he stepped over the threshold of his front door. It appeared that Sydney Hanson had heard solely that her eldest son with merely passing grades was discovered in the basement alongside Mathias Garcia and Derek Parker, and that all of them were in the general proximity of billowed cocaine and at least three, well-used heroin needles. According to her, the phone call from the school principal detailed nothing further, which left Quentin to sustain the abuse and punishment destined for one who had indeed partaken in the act of ingesting either cocaine or heroin, or both. Given the way she sentenced him to his bedroom without snacks or dinner, she likely thought that the case.

Such was his evening. He spent the later hours of the horrid day locked away and isolated in his bedroom. He showered first, and afterward he laid on his bed, constantly falling to sleep by accident. It was something of a paradox that his mother had sentenced him to his quarter of the house. On one hand, the forced seclusion was insulting and the epitome of how she often chose to ignore his explanation of whatever chaos had happened, as she always had. In her eyes, he only ever did wrong. On the other hand, he reveled in the solitude and the fact that, after so wretched a day, he finally had the opportunity to be alone and undisturbed. The last thing he wanted was to converse with his family, not when the aftereffects of his earaches still pained him, since the residual sting hadn't quite left and would probably linger well into the next morning. He had yet to complete his homework, but he put it aside and promised himself to wake during the early hours of the following morning to finish his assignments before school. He had no energy left, could barely stay awake as he laid on his bed.

He rolled over to face the window on the other side of him; from where he laid on his pillow, the stretch of his forefinger would have brought him in contact with the frosted glass. Sitting up, he undid the hook locks and pushed the lower pane up, very nearly pressing his face against the mesh screen that stood between him and the outdoors. He could see his backyard from there and took in the small expanse of green. He visually traced the terrain from where it began under their house's patio and extended all the way down to the sudden drop about a hundred feet later, where the first steps of the forest melded with the trimmed green of his father's perfectly manicured turf. Down the hill was a marsh. When Quentin was a child, a much younger child, he used to fear that ghosts from the wetland would creep up from under the edge of the drop and stare into his open window from afar while he slept. It was ironic that, at his current age, he couldn't sleep without being able to see it. Hollis would have marveled at that growth, had he been privy to it. He always said Quentin needed to outgrow his fears.

He flopped back down, and his eyes roved to the cellphone on his bedside desk.

There had been an abundance of negativity in his life that day and he didn't know how long he could live on without some positivity sprinkled into it. He couldn't believe that was how the night would end, with a mother angry at him and a head that stung from its earlier torture. The lonely, awkward walk with Terry, combined with the solitude of his mother's punishment, served as a reminder of Quentin's friendless status. Both he and Hollis had their fair share of immaturities; foibles that ought to have been long shed and pet peeves that should have faded the more they matured. But despite their many faults, it dawned on Quentin that he was lonely, that he wanted to talk to someone who actually listened to what he had to say and was empathetic to his struggles. Was he really going to throw away a link like theirs over one, overblown argument? Was he really going to spend the remainder of his youth alone?

Hollis's number was an easy one to remember, as four of the digits were the same, and Quentin knew the code by heart. He quickly typed it into the touchscreen of his cellphone. When Hollis's end rang to voicemail, Quentin dialed the number a second time. His call was answered, but not by Hollis. "Hello?" asked a voice too deep and guttural to have been that of Quentin's friend.

"Hi....um..." Quentin began. "Is Hollis there?"

"Who is this?"

"Quentin. Quentin Hanson. Wait, is this Mr. Carlyle?"

The person on the other end of the line was silent for a stretch of time that began to border on uncomfortable. "Yes," they said after a while. "It's good to hear from you, Quentin. How are things?"

"Oh, I'm fine. I was just hoping to talk to Hollis. Haven't seen him at school this week."

"Yeah, he's been pretty sick. Mono or something like that. He's scheduled to see his doctor tomorrow. He should be fine in a couple days."

"All right, well..." Quentin's nose wrinkled up. "Is there any chance I can talk to him?"

"Sorry, Quentin, but he's not feeling well. I'll tell him you called, though. He's pretty dizzy and has been throwing up all day, hasn't even watched TV."

"Okay," Quentin said resignedly. He tried not to sound disappointed. "Thanks. Hope he feels better."

"Stay fresh, Quentin," joked Hollis's father. He was the one who hung up.

Quentin powered off his phone and stretched forward to place it back on the desk when, from beyond the door of his bedroom, he heard in an eerily high and whispery voice, *"I didn't know you had friends."* He snorted and put the phone away.

"It's unlocked," he said into the air, and sure enough, his door began to creak as it pushed into the bedroom.

Lucas Michael Hanson, Quentin's brother, stood in the doorway. For his age, his stature was becoming impressive. It didn't require a prognosticator to know he would one day grow to be as tall as his older brother. He was still relatively short, but evidenced by how lanky and elongated his limbs were at eleven years of age, he would doubtlessly sprout to be of a daunting height, much like Quentin and their father. For the time being, Lucas's torso grew slower than his limbs. Quentin thought it hysterical how Lucas's arms had lengthened so much in the three weeks since he last went shopping that, by November, his shirtsleeves were barely reaching his wrists.

Lucas noiselessly sealed the door behind him and advanced to the middle of the room. Since one leg was a modicum longer than the other, his gait was uneven. It was a trait which their family practitioner assured Lucas would minimize with growth. "All in good time," the doctor had said six months ago, but it hadn't yet changed.

"Evening, scallywag," Quentin greeted with half his face stuffed into his pillow.

Lucas was unamused, his expression stony. That was a first. "Can you stop doing drugs?" he asked at once. He was entirely serious. There was no jest in his tone.

Quentin laughed. "Did she actually tell you I did drugs?"

"Apparently coke and the old her-her."

"Her-her? Is that a thing now?"

Lucas shrugged. "That's what I call it."

Quentin's eyes closed, but he had enough energy to carry on the conversation. He chuckled and recited, *"Her-her."*

Lucas raised his head higher. "I just came here to say that I hate you and I want fifty dollars because you owe me."

"Why is that?"

"Because ever since you got stoned in the basement with your friends, she's been taking her anger out on me and Dad. But we didn't even do anything. It's unfair."

"Those were not my friends. And I didn't do drugs."

Lucas raised an eyebrow challengingly. "There was cocaine on your sweatshirt. I saw it in the bathroom hamper."

"How do you know what cocaine looks like?"

"Music videos."

"Good answer," Quentin said. He narrowed his eyes. "Did you sniff my sweatshirt?" he asked suspiciously and watched in horror as a rosy flush spread across Lucas's cheeks. Quentin's upper body shot up off the bed beneath him. "Lucas Hanson!"

"No, I swear I didn't! Besides, even if I did, you're the one who just left it there for me to see!"

"That is not an answer!"

Lucas whined out, *"Can I just have fifty dollars?"*

"Believe me, Mom and Dad don't just give me money," Quentin said. "But I'm sure they'd love to give you some, so long as you just do that pouty face of yours. Now stop dodging my question."

"I didn't!"

"You swear?"

"Quentin, I swear! Really!"

"Okay."

Lucas grinned cheekily and crawled up beside Quentin onto the quilt-covered bed. "Mrs. Montgomery was over earlier," he said lowly and conspiratorially.

Quentin sat back on his elbows. "Really? Why?"

"Apparently, Terry came back to the house with rat pee and poop all over him. She said that he said that you were there with him."

"Yup, can confirm," Quentin confirmed. "That's why my clothes were in the special hamper."

Lucas blanched.

Quentin squinted again.

"Wait..." The little boy began retching. "That's not how cocaine smells, then?"

Quentin sat back up. "So you did sniff it!"

"Please don't tell!" Lucas pleaded in the smallest of voices. "Please, Quentin. I played video games as soon as I got off the bus and she gave me an earful! She'll kill me if she finds out I did this too!"

"Lucas."

"Quentin."

"Lucas, take it from my perspective. I just found out my eleven-year-old brother sniffed cocaine."

"Barely!" Lucas scooted closer to Quentin, encroaching on his territory by the head of the bed. "You won't tell, will you? I'm ruined if you do."

"Untrue," Quentin said.

"Quentin, she'd freak."

"At me, though," Quentin specified. "Everything's my fault in her mind. You'd be all right. Besides, I'm not a rat."

Lucas smiled goofily and it turned his face into a pear-like shape. "You aren't one," he agreed, "but you've certainly seen enough of them."

Quentin lightly punched Lucas's arm. "Shuddup, dweeb."

"Drug addict."

"Uneven legs."

"Oh yeah?" Lucas retorted. "Well, well...You need more friends and...and a girlfriend. Yeah, how's that?"

Quentin shrugged. "Eh. True."

"See? I win," boasted the boy.

Quentin ruffled Lucas's hair. "And you always will."

They both jumped in place at the interruption of Lucas's name being shouted on the other side of the door.

Lucas groaned. "Why does she even yell if she knows I'm in here?"

"It's for dramatic effect," Quentin said.

"Lucas?!" their mother called out. Again, she was right in front of the bedroom door and both her children knew it. There was no need for the raised voice.

Lucas chewed his lip until it swelled. "Does she ever stop yelling?"

Quentin's head shook. "Nope."

"Lucas!" their mother called for him a third time.

"I'm here!" her youngest shouted back.

The oddest thing happened afterward. The previously furious overtone of their mother's voice died off and she said, soothingly, "Come out here, honey. Come on, get out of there." Lucas was reluctant. Indeed, he was comfily compressed into the sea of blankets, comforters, and pillows Quentin had arranged for his own rest. The idea of leaving that miniature world of fluff for whatever thing she needed probably wasn't as appealing, especially if she was only taking him away for another lecture.

"Go on," Quentin told him.

"But—"

Quentin gently pushed Lucas. "Go. She won't bite."

"Not me," Lucas clucked, "but you, duh." He whispered, *"I wouldn't leave this chamber for a while if I were you."*

"Or else that dragon will set me ablaze," Quentin agreed. He frowned. "I am hungry, though."

"It's not worth it," Lucas said. "Her cooking is awful when she's angry."

Quentin smirked. "Her cooking is always awful."

"Lucas?!" their mother returned.

Quentin rolled his eyes. "You'd better go before she convinces herself that I've murdered you or something."

"Yerp," Lucas said, and off the boy went to the doorway of the bedroom.

After he left, the door remained ajar. If there was one thing Quentin hated more than being berated unreasonably, it was wanting to fall asleep but knowing the door was still partly open. He nearly swung his legs off the side of the mattress to go and close it in Lucas's wake, but halted when one and then two denim-covered legs came purposefully stalking into the room. *Mother,* he thought foully. There she was, sauntering into the room like his private space was her own turf to justly enter. Well, she was wrong. It wasn't. That bedroom was his one sanctum in their fifty-year-old home, but that didn't impede her from sashaying in as if to mark it as hers, with a *Boston Bruins* glass in one hand and her eyes refusing to meet his even as she moved through his territory. He watched the whole time as she advanced to the corner of his desk and placed the glass onto it. She turned away from him. "It's ginger tea," she announced coolly while marching back to the door. "There's lemon in there with honey and some apple cider vinegar. Drink all of it. It'll help your gut recover from that stuff you took in today."

"Mom," Quentin drawled out, "for the last time, I didn't—"

She left and slammed the door.

Alone he was, solely in the company of a hockey game souvenir with honeyed, orange liquid inside it. He took one look its way and immediately decided against touching it, regardless of how thirsty he may or may not have become later on that night. It looked repugnantly rancid, if it were even feasible for something to look its presumed rancidity—then again, it wasn't like his morning at the school hadn't already proven that true.

He once again flopped backwards and landed on the bed, embraced by a squishing swarm of his pillows and blankets. Once he settled into the warmth of the quilts and comforters, it didn't take long for him to retire to his much-anticipated slumber. He slept well that night, despite the gargantuan onslaught of stressors that hovered at the forefront of his mind. Considering how genuinely awful a day the 13th of November had been, the stretch of time during which his eyes were closed and his head was vacant proved surprisingly and pleasantly restful. For hours, the only sound that filled his bedroom came from his snores.

Pathetic as it may have been, Quentin Hanson lived for sleep. In the depths of his mind, where all responsibilities were nonexistent and where the very real, impending threat of adulthood wasn't an approaching threat, it was in there, in his head, that he was usually at peace. From another's point of view, his resentment for Hollis's desire to run away and cherish his youth might have seemed folly or hypocritical. They would have been correct to think that. Quentin didn't really hate Hollis's philosophy that conformity was damaging to one's mental health because Quentin himself adored conformity. He hated the philosophy because he believed it, and to acknowledge a truth like that would have been disheartening. It made him question what he wanted in life, which he didn't like doing. He liked possessing an unquestionable surety when it came to his future. He didn't want to be regretful of anything, and, should he have had regrets, he wanted only to tamp down on them and pretend that they never existed. But it was never lost on him that he was happiest in his sleep. There were some things he couldn't lie to himself about.

Any attempt to wake him that night would have been futile. He didn't once stir at the downstairs ruckus of his brother fighting with their mother at seven o'clock or the profanity from his father upon stubbing his toe against an upstairs wall at ten-thirty. Some dishes broke at eleven. A few birds sang at twelve. Multiple car doors were loudly slammed on the neighborhood street at twelve-thirty. Quentin heard nothing. Much to his dismay, come two in the early hours of the 14th, that was when his deprivation of proper sustenance finally had its way with him. He was mid-dream, roaming the grounds of a white, unfilled world which he would soon fail to remember, as he never recalled the contents of his dreams, when amid his life in the imagined world, there came a rupture, a cessation to the envisioning, and it was caused by a hunger pang. His eyes opened, and to the ceiling he stared. He wondered if he could put off his hunger, but he was drowsy and half-awake for all of fifteen seconds when the pangs amplified. They pinched his gut and turned into more desperate and demanding squeezes until they became so unbearable that even the heaviness of his eyes and the lasting stinging in his ears couldn't convince him to return to sleep. It felt like hours before he managed to crawl off his bed, his beautiful and warm bed. There were indents which marked precisely where each piece of him once laid, and they only fed his urge to sink back into it.

He made sure to be silent and stealth when he left to search for food. There was no reasoning with Sydney Hanson when she thought someone in her household was undeserving of any, and he would have been damned if she caught him poking about the hallways when he was supposed to be in bed, starved, and grounded with all but that hideous tea to satiate him. *To hell with that,* he thought.

It was a fantasy to have believed that the acquisition of food in the middle of night was going to be a simple task, but, nonetheless, Quentin misguided himself. At two-thirty in the morning, he stood shivering before the open door of the refrigerator in the downstairs kitchen, only to find that there wasn't any food. There were no leftovers or even evidence of his family's dinner, and nowhere in sight were there ingredients to at least formulate a decent meal. He couldn't say he was surprised. His mother, for all the hours she occupied the house every day, seldom cooked and knew next to nothing about the rudiments of the culinary arts. He didn't expect her to be a talented chef of some sort, but given the time she spent at the house and the lack of young children to care for, as both were grown and off at school, he had wrongly assumed she would, at some point, adopt cooking as a sensible hobby. He couldn't have been more wrong. But he was always wrong; either he expected too much or too little of people, never able to strike a balance between the opposites.

The tiles of the kitchen floor were freezing beneath his bare feet as he perused the refrigerator's interior. He was plagued by jitters. His sweatpants comforted him adequately, but his arms were goosebump-ridden, as they were concealed only in the spots where his tee-shirt could reach. As he suffered the jitters, he made himself jumpy in a most lousy endeavor to keep warm because he wasn't about to go hopping up the stairs to return to his room and grab a sweater. He shivered some more.

He found two brown and bruised bananas on the top shelf and a lonesome celery stick on the bottom one; the top of the stick had already been bitten off by someone else. It was a regrettable decision, but, in the end, he settled for one of the marred bananas, a full slinky-shaped package of crackers from the pantry, and two bottles of water, all of which he duly consumed standing upright at the kitchen island, where he periodically bounced on his feet to keep his blood flowing. He wiped the sleep from his eyes as he bit between banana and cracker interchangeably, drinking his water intermittently. He wasn't conscious enough to recognize how miserable a sight he made, but perhaps later that morning, when he would slip downstairs for breakfast and behold a banana peel littered with teeth marks and a forgotten cracker package torn to pieces, it wouldn't have been so unrecognizable.

When he was satisfied, he lugged himself out to the living room, took a turn, and paused at the bottom of the stairs, which he had to climb in order to return to his bedroom. He was completely spent, but for that one task, he had reserved a few morsels of energy. He had to be quiet. Per the nature of the old house, creaks were inevitable, but he couldn't make any disturbances louder than them or the typical house moans, like when the heater turned on or when the refrigerator kicked in. With his mother's infuriation peaked to a level that was inextinguishable, he couldn't have allowed himself to get caught. He refused to. His pace was glacial, his breaths were measured, and he clung to the wall as he ascended the stairs, since the spaces nearest the walls were often denser than the center section of the steps. His footfalls were light and airy, silent and unnoticeable.

He heard a creak from the second floor, on his right-hand side. It had to have been a footfall, it was too heavy to have been anything else. He hoped neither of his parents would come his way. He was grateful, suddenly, for his father's austere frugality, which did affect the lighting of their home. Where they lived was a dark, decaying place, and over the years in the house, he had succeeded in convincing his wife and children that unnecessary lighting was unreasonable. Nightlights and decorative lamps were discouraged, which Quentin once considered an unpleasant restriction to their everyday living, but as he held his breath and begged to remain unseen as the clock neared three in the morning on November 14th, he began to think the opposite.

The sound of a door opening startled him. It happened slowly, almost synonymous to the very way he himself had crept about the house at that hour. It worried him because the sound of it was too close in proximity to the staircase for it to have happened to the door of his parents' room, which was down the far side of the upstairs hall. Lucas's room was similarly far away, which meant it could have only been happening to Quentin's. And he wasn't in his room. It was his mother. It had to be. She was the skulking type, and she had such little faith in him that she was likely to poke her head in to check if he were still there, docilely sleeping through his hunger in his bedroom. That, or he wasn't as quiet as he thought he had been earlier. Either way, he had to see it for himself, and his eyes were at the point where they were well-adjusted to the dark. He restricted himself to breathing only through his mouth, since it seemed quieter that way, and he gathered all the gumption entailed for the simple act of beholding one's mother potentially walking into their bedroom and catching her in the act of sneaking around. He leaned his head forward and twisted his neck around the corner, and—

He saw a hazmat suit. Actually, he saw two.

Two, large figures in hazmat suits. They had guns looped into their belts and held flashlights in their gloved hands. They looked deliberately faceless, as they were masked, and they were creeping through the hall.

Quentin's legs wobbled. He blinked faster than normal. He retreated around the corner, to where he'd been carefully concealed on the stairs. He had to have been wrong. It was his fatigue to blame, surely that's what tampered with his mind, his eyes. It made sense. Just because he had slept deeply didn't mean he had slept adequately, and he was everything but satisfied. He took in a deep breath, reenacted his routine of slipping his head around the corner, but found that his mind hadn't deceived him. His eyes weren't mistaken. Two figures hovered outside his bedroom door, each entirely garbed in loose, but protective, attire. Their masked faces frightened him most. He wanted to know who was in his house.

The intruders walked into his room.

Quentin didn't know what he was doing and whether or not he should have even attempted to alert his parents, but when he weighed the potential tragedies of the figures finding either Lucas or their mother and father, Quentin knew in his heart that there would have been no greater pain than for him to have seen his little brother terrorized. He knew time wouldn't act kindly and that soon those unseen faces would come upon his empty bed and, for whatever reason, would be outraged by his absence.

He distantly heard muffled voices speaking in undertones, no doubt wondering where he was.

Quentin scrambled as quickly and quietly as he could. His tiptoeing accelerated and he was unfailingly silent as he slipped into the bedroom of his younger brother. He softly closed the door behind him and ran to the bed. For the moment, he forwent his caution, as he knew the quietness of his steps didn't matter once he was at the other end of the hallway and deep into another room. He produced loud thumps as he progressed to where Lucas slept, facedown and snoring. Quentin hated to wake him.

"Lucas," Quentin whispered, but Lucas didn't wake.

They couldn't waste any more time. Quentin was aware that Lucas's newfound height would impede on a relatively smooth execution of the planned action, but Quentin was supremely taller and, with some wrangling and dodging of pointy joints and limbs, he succeeded in scooping Lucas up from the mattress and carrying him.

His arms and head drooped over Quentin's shoulders and his head bobbed to the side when Quentin whispered his brother's name.

Lucas shivered awake. "Quen—?" he began.

"*Shh,*" Quentin hushed him gently. He leaned back a bit to meet Lucas's eyes, which Quentin could see with the aid of the moonlight that streamed in through the blinds of Lucas's own bedside window. "*We don't have lot of time,*" Quentin whispered. "*There's someone in the house.*"

Lucas's eyes welled with tears. "*Where's Mom and Dad?*"

"*I don't know. We'll go to a neighbor and call the police.*" Quentin held the back of Lucas's head. "*Stay quiet, okay?*"

Lucas's arms wrapped around Quentin's neck. To his credit, he didn't falter under the new strain of the pair of lanky hands around him. He determinedly paced back to where he'd entered, turned the brass doorknob with efficient silence, and poked his quivering head beyond the doorframe. He checked his right and his left, both of which seemed safe.

Until they weren't. Not one second following his assumption of momentary safety, the two figures exited his bedroom and slowly, carefully, made their way toward his parents' bedroom. Lucas saw it, too. His breath caught and he slapped a hand over his mouth, and together the brothers watched, open-mouthed and shaking, as the suited-up intruders disappeared into the other bedroom.

"*Quentin!*" Lucas cried in an undertone. He strapped his legs around Quentin's hips. Quentin recognized the cue and left the bedroom. He juggled Lucas's body and noiselessly neared the top of the stairs at the juncture in the hallway. He descended the first two steps, heard a creak from above, and hurried to reach the middlemost section.

The creaks above grew louder, more urgent.

Lucas gasped.

One of the creaks was even closer, just behind them.

Quentin froze.

"There's one more room on the other side," echoed a voice above and behind them. He knew why it did that, why it reverberated as it left the lips of its speaker; they were sheathed by the cowardice protection of their masks. The creaks moved to the other direction, ever-slow and careful; it appeared that the intruders were opposed to being discovered in kind. The duration of them moving to the other side of the house was jarring to wait for, but once the creaks became quieter and Quentin extrapolated that the upstairs pair had finally reached Lucas's bedroom, he let go of his reservations and sprinted down the remainder of stairs. He didn't look back. He held Lucas close, who in turn never loosened his hold on him.

Their second conundrum started at the base of the stairway. Part of Quentin wanted to dash out the front door, but a wiser, less naïve part of him suggested that he rethink the idea.

"Quentin, c'mon," Lucas begged. He wriggled a hand away from Quentin's neck and tried to reach for the door handle. Quentin grabbed Lucas's arm and stopped him. Lucas started to protest with another whisper, but by the time his mouth opened to say something, Quentin had ushered him to the living room.

The creaks upstairs transformed to more pronounced groans. Neither of the Hanson children were in their beds, and that had been discovered.

Quentin moved quickly. He wiggled himself and Lucas into the space between their father's armchair and the bookshelf by the television; for the first time, Quentin wondered if his parents weren't frugal but were merely averted to light, as the windows in the room were diligently barricaded by the amenities inside, which made it almost impossible to view the outdoors. In the confining space,

Quentin pulled back one of the curtains. He and Lucas peered through the glass.

The outdoors looked just as Quentin had suspected. There was a vehicle, a gray van, that lingered at the bottom of their driveway. It was the last thing he wanted to see, but not the worst. The detail that chilled him to the bone and unfurled a different type of fear throughout his belly was that there weren't one or two additional suited figures standing watchfully at the base of the driveway, but a whole pack of them. He could have missed a couple or over-counted, but he identified no fewer than thirteen. All were donned the same; black attire; masked faces; and waist belts that wielded items meant only to harm.

Lucas's fingers clenched Quentin's neck.

"Okay, okay," Quentin gasped out. "We gotta go." He closed the curtain and squeezed himself and Lucas out from between the chair and the bookshelf.

The creaks arrived to the top of the staircase.

Quentin rounded the corner of one of the living room's two exits; one would have led them back to the area by the front door, the other to the back of the house. He selected the latter, and it brought him to the kitchen.

"Quentin?" Lucas asked into the darkness.

Quentin gripped Lucas firmly and charged through the room, leaving it. He brought them to the rearmost part of the house, the sunroom. The deck was attached to the back of the house, and he was confident that they could use it to flee from the property unseen. He put his brother down. Since they were as far away from the front of the house as they could manage, he assumed running side by side couldn't hinder their stealthiness. They probably would move faster that way, when one was no longer encumbered by the weight of the other. While Quentin hastily opened the patio door, Lucas watched through the screen door between the sunroom and kitchen to see if anyone was near.

Lucas tensed. *"Quentin, Quentin!"*

Quentin jerked the boy back and scooped him up again. The motion was far from smooth, but it was effective. The fluidity of their escape mattered little, as their time had run out. Quentin hurried them out of the house. He chose against sealing the sunroom door, having known it would produce too much noise, and although they technically were outside, he didn't consider themselves clear of danger. He proceeded down the steps of the house's extension. When they were on the grass of their backyard, Lucas squirmed out of his arms. Lucas didn't part from Quentin, though, and simply held his hand instead of his entire body. Together, with their fingers knotted and their short breaths perfectly synced, they hunched their bodies forward so as to not be conspicuously tall and pronounced, even in the dead of night. They crowded themselves into the area under the deck.

"Where are we going?" Lucas demanded, frightened.

"Not to any neighbors," Quentin said. "It's too risky. Those guys might see us going there."

Lucas pointed to Quentin's sweatpants. "Do you have your phone?" he asked, scanning Quentin's person for a hint of a cellphone.

"No, bud. We're on our own."

Lucas started crying. "I...I..." He struggled to breathe. Quentin reached forward. He wiped away the tears under Lucas's eyes. "Where's Mom and Dad?" Lucas asked again. "Why didn't they take Mom and Dad?"

Quentin gulped. "We don't know that they didn't already. But we have to try and leave either way."

Footsteps from above rattled the deck, which was their only shield. The footsteps were no longer indicative of a pair of people thriving to sneakily navigate their way around. The steps were more honest, more determined. Brazenly louder. They began to descend the stairs, beneath which the brothers still hid. Quentin crouched down to engulf Lucas with all the warmth and comfort one could provide in that moment. They gasped and held onto each other. Lucas dug his nails into Quentin's shirtsleeves. Quentin burrowed his face into Lucas's clavicle and felt his breaths becoming more pronounced. Quentin covered Lucas's mouth with the palm of a hand, doing anything in his power to mute the boy.

The sound of the footsteps came closer, and then they stopped. The intruders reached the grass and stood on the opposite side of the deck stairs, a mere yard from the hidden brothers.

"All clear," said one of the two. His voice was agitated yet simultaneously shaky.

"What do we do?" the other asked.

Lucas shook uncontrollably in Quentin's arms.

There was an exhale. "We keep looking," said the one who had first spoken. "He couldn't have gone far, must have just seen us."

"I thought they were sedated."

"Must have missed it."

Fallen leaves rustled as the intruders moved about the property.

Lucas sobbed. It was pained and loud, and it hung in the air. Knowing what he'd just done, he stuck himself deeper into the curve of Quentin's body, as though hiding behind the skinny limbs of his older brother could hide him from the inevitability of the rustling leaves suddenly quieting. Quentin wanted to die. If not for the racing of his heart, it would have already felt like he had. There was nowhere to go. Behind them was the outer wall of their home's basement and abreast them were the supporting walls of the deck and sunroom. He pulled his brother closer. Although a futile action, it was for Quentin's own comfort that he tightened his hand on Lucas's mouth. They held each other and their hearts pounded unevenly, yet inordinately in unison. Stuck and in shock, they clung to one another as the leaves rustled again, faster and closer than just seconds before. Quentin didn't notice it earlier, perhaps because it only recently started, but the entire front of his shirt was drenched from the outpour of Lucas's tears. He cried and cried, heavily and hotly. Quentin just kept holding him. It was all he could do. And when beams of light flashed onto them from where the staircase ended and the lower region of the deck began, they froze. Tears stopped falling and limbs stopped shaking. Their matching breaths stopped and their bodies chilled under the new, unwanted attention.

Everything was a blur. Quentin knew there were fists, grunting, and a flurry of weak punches thrown by his ungainly hands. He knew that, at one point, Lucas was being carried away by one of the dark figures while Quentin himself was tugged by another. The brothers screamed each other's names. They scratched at the suited forms who towed them away from the refuge that the underside of their home had offered. They flailed helpless arms and tried to bite and pick at whatever stretches of flesh and bone were in their reach, but they were separated nonetheless. Quentin couldn't speak for the one who was throwing Lucas over a shoulder with ease, but the very person who restrained Quentin was not a thin thing he could just rid his body of with a few kicks and thrashes. To the one who held Quentin, he was a pliable accessory. The gloved hands that locked on his arms and yanked him back, toward the backyard, were sturdy and thick. The person was shorter, but in no way physically inferior; it was an embarrassingly simple feat for Quentin to have been pulled away.

The Hanson children were brought, lugged, to the backyard. Quentin dug the heels of his bare feet into the prickly, cold grass in an attempt to fix his body to the ground and make himself immovable.

Dangling off the shoulder of the other intruder, Lucas wailed Quentin's name, shouting and trying to break free.

"Carlson," said the one who gripped Quentin, to the other nearby. The voice was one of a male, which was a fact barely discernible due to the weight and evident thickness of the protective mask that concealed his head. He faced his partner and the little boy he carried. "The order's not for him. Put him back in the house."

"No!" Lucas screeched. "Quentin! Quentin!" He swatted his legs around and stretched his arms forward to reach for Quentin, to at least graze his soft and searching fingertips against his brother's. But, in seconds, Lucas was whisked away.

Quentin screamed after the boy. He fought against the sturdiness of his restrainer, but was met with constant failure. He couldn't move. The single hand on his shoulder and the other on his arm were both too rigid and powerful. He had never felt so impotent.

The other figure lugged Lucas up the stairs of the deck, all the while, he screeched unintelligible pleas. The only words that escaped his lips which Quentin could understand were those of his frantic, repeated question, "Where are you taking him?! Where are you taking him?!" To which, predictably, Lucas was left continually unanswered. He sobbed and screamed. Quentin heard Lucas even when he was returned to the house.

Quentin urged the one who held him, with his breath visible as he spoke, to say just where they were taking him. He demanded to know what they were going to do with him. But he, too, received nothing and he panted out exhaustedly, *"No...No..."* His words held no bearing and his movements were of no consequence. He hated himself for it. He was young and healthy, yet weak and defenseless. He hated himself for what he lacked. A stronger person would have had the physical agency to flee, but that wasn't what he was. He was weak and pliable. He was a victim.

The hand on his arm lifted, which left only the one on his shoulder. The person who had restrained him, dragged him, and then partly loosened their grip on him, stood half over Quentin's body and was reaching into their pocket, as though seemingly trusting in their own power. It was an opportunity Quentin seized. He lowered his body by a few inches and, with a brute force he didn't even know he was capable of, knocked his head back and into the space between the apex of the thighs behind him. The man bent forward. He reached for his groin and stifled an exclamation. Quentin broke free.

The thing was, had Quentin Frank Hanson been anyone else, he might have devised a better plan than the one he generated. But he was only himself, and he was stupid, silly, and inexperienced in the art of self-defense. He looked to the one place he thought he could dash into, and that was the forest beyond the hill behind him, the one that began at the end of the backyard and sloped all the way down from the peak at the backyard to the ghastly smelling wetland below, the marsh. In fairness to him, no better option presented itself on such short notice. From the front driveway to his brother's bedroom, and perhaps elsewhere in the house, all spaces were under the occupation of... Well, Quentin didn't know who. He just knew not to go there. So, he threw caution to the wind. It was so unlike him, but he did it anyway. Sensible or no, it was a plan he was set on because, *Fuck it,* he thought. *Fuck it. Anything but this shit.* And perhaps if Hollis were there, he would have been proud or even hysterically amused to see Quentin punching the already hunched-over man in the exact same spot that had previously been head-butted. Then, of course, there was the especially whimsical decision of Quentin scrambling to his feet and beginning a mad dash for the melee of dying birches and oaks behind his father's long-unused tool shed. It might have been ridiculous, but there was nothing else Quentin thought sensible. And Hollis wasn't there to advise him against it.

Quentin ran to the trees. They were thinner than the previous month, when their leaves were multicolored and large. But on that bleak November night that slowly turned into morning, the forest's canopies had already vanished and all that remained were the brittle, broken, and fallen pieces beneath his trampling feet. If his escape had been in August, the leaves would have been younger and the tree trunks not so thinly veiled. It did get a little better, though, when he progressed deeper inside the forest. Suddenly, he found it easier to conceal himself. He no longer came upon areas with just one lone pine and a few withered shrubs, but more along the lines of five pines clustered together and several shrubs tightly gathered. That was what he preferred. That was what he needed. The denser and messier the forest, the more unattainable he would be.

Yelling came from behind him. Barking, really. Someone was indignant. Perhaps it was the man whose groin was slammed by Quentin's head. Or that man's superior of some sort. Either way, it was galvanizing to hear. Then came two more voices. None of their words were decipherable, but their anger was clear. If Quentin was considering slowing his pace, the outbursts on his tail stopped him from making that decision.

For years, he had thought the hill behind his house was a small one. But not that night. On that night, he thought quite differently. It was easy to presume its volume when all he did was stare at the first few yards of it from his bedside window, but when he found himself scampering through its unforgivingly difficult path with his bare feet and the rest of him freezing from the wind gusts of a winter soon to arrive, it wasn't so small a place anymore. He had underestimated the depths of it. He felt the land tip more steeply and took note of how his body began to tilt forward.

Suddenly there seemed to be more of the trees he was hoping to see, and he went from yearning for them to wondering how he would be able to agilely twist and turn between and around them. It was difficult before, when all he had to do was battle the cold, but he faced a new challenge of trying not to get his eyes poked out by the branches as he ran. Leaves snarled in his hair. Something scraped his scalp. The seams of his sleep clothes caught against the ridged sides of bark and twigs. His pajama bottoms caught on practically everything, which slowed him. An outstretched cluster of tree limbs managed to slice the short, left sleeve of his tee-shirt into two and left both halves flapping against each other; goosebumps rose on the exposed skin of his pasty arm. He wound through a family of crooked white pines, tripped between twins of red maples, and stumbled clumsily through bushes of frayed dogfennel. Some time during his run, he was cut on the right side of his face, precisely on the pink line of his flushed cheekbone. Blood streamed down his face.

The voices behind him were clearer. They couldn't have been more than fifteen trees away. He heard someone yell, "Over there!" After which came a, "Where?!"

Quentin sped up. He tried to, that was; the deeper he ran, the forest hill proved itself unfriendlier. A spiderweb on the ground, heavily populated with strings of intermingled dead beetles, engulfed the toes of his right foot. His pants caught onto something again, that time something soggy. Another tree limb sliced the untouched side of his face, shaving off skin above his eyebrow. Tears bubbled in his eyes. He was tired, cold, and hurting. His legs felt heavier and his feet were sore and bleeding.

The yells behind him grew more distant. But, in the wake of one unclear holler, beams of bright light began to shoot through the gaps in the greenery.

Quentin made it halfway down the hill, where the bottom became visible. From above, he finally saw where the forest blended into the marsh. He continued to run and, although unwise, the whole time he snuck glances to the mysterious wetland he had never actually seen before that night. By the looks of it, the water was slightly frozen over and an obligatory murkiness plagued what might have once been a blue surface. Underneath the thin sheet of ice, everything was brown and spotty. Speckles of something gray were dotted along the top. In small sections, blobs of green hovered among the brown. Overgrowth of weeds and crooked birches were spread throughout the water. It looked revolting, even from afar, at the midway point of the hill with only the light of the moon to guide him along his way. But there was still one thing that encouraged him to progress downward and take the risk of nearing the frozen, forgotten marsh, and that thing had been land. More of it. He could see it clearly as he maneuvered his head around branches and saw that, beyond the marsh, if he were to travel through it, there was another stretch of moribund forest. He couldn't tell if it was in any way connected to the one through which he ran, but even if it was a separate land mass, he was intent on reaching it. Besides, the marsh did look small to his eyes. He could probably swim through it.

Having wasted enough time by foolishly risking glances forward, he took his eyes off the water. He knew to focus on his feet. When he did, he saw flaking and bleeding skin, where jagged grasses and crisp foliage prickled at the wounds. There was the occasional rock that cut into his soles, but he was growing immune to them; they hurt him, but he wasn't as bothered as earlier. His pace did improve, which was a small victory, as his running was far from masterful, but it was passingly acceptable. He zipped and turned through the trees. He skidded around every sharp corner. He ducked before smacking into branches and snapped his neck to the side whenever one threatened to slice his face again. His sore knees felt the strain each time he scurried lower to avoid the lights that hovered closely behind him. He thought, *I might actually escape.*

The big toe of his left foot slammed into a massive stone, about the size of a ball. It stopped him in his tracks. The nail of his big toe split, and half of it fell away. "You, motherfuc—Ah!" Quentin cried. The freezing winds kissed his red, throbbing skin. Blood was everywhere; on the spot where the piece of the nail had been; on his neighboring toes; on the leaves under him. He had no choice but to rest against the remnant trunk of a dead pine nearby.

Someone, someone close, bragged that they heard him and that they knew he wasn't far away. The beams of several flashlights bounced off the trees to his left.

Quentin shoved his wrist into his mouth, chomped at his pulse point, and suppressed an oncoming screech. The pain was brutal. He couldn't stand around, though. Not for any longer. It was too dangerous. More voices were yelling. Hisses shot out from between his teeth as he hobbled back up to his normal height. The bleeding slowed a bit, but the best he could do was a limping trek, since running seemed impossible. He balanced himself on his uninjured foot during the few occasions he paused during his zigzag down the hill. To complement his mounting troubles, the clouds above passed to the west and that crescent-shaped friend of his became shielded by the shift. He could barely make out the ground beneath him. He limped through the darkness. He felt, but couldn't see, when barbed thorns nipped at his cut shins or when an object he perceived to be one thing was something completely different, such as the presumed log that was actually the carcass of a half-eaten deer. He also didn't notice the sudden drop in front of him. He didn't see that when he lifted his leg to take one step forward, he was about to step on nothing.

It was a long tumble. Long and painful. Jagged, coarse ends of bushes tore at every bit of his exposed skin. Chains of rocks clouted at his arms. Wilted flowers curled their stems into his hair and made homes of each, individual lock. His previous wounds pulled wider every time it was their turn to scrape the ground. Then, there was his eye—his right eye. It collided with something, and he didn't know what it was, but it caused severe pain. Throughout the accidental descent, the skin around it bulged enough to partially obscure his vision. He crashed into another keen thing, one which he also couldn't observe in the fall, but whatever it was, it was substantial; the pang it gave to his shoulder was enormous and the burden of it slitting the sleeve of his shirt was just a mockery to his suffering. His tumble finished at the base of the hill, where he landed flat on his back. *At least I didn't have to run,* he thought. His momentary relief was well-founded. It would take minutes for the flock of searchers to reach that area, where he laid. They could run as fleetly as they pleased, but he had taken something of an unconventional shortcut.

He was wheezing horribly, like he hadn't breathed through the entire, lengthy descent. Maybe he hadn't. He was, however, sure of one thing, and it was that he hated nature. He was almost devoid of sight in his swollen eye, and it felt increasingly itchy. His big, left toe still oozed blood. Thorns pricked into his meatless arms and stomach. Another sting, on his left arm, captured his attention, so he raised the limb and folded up one ruffle of what remained of its sleeve, and it revealed a long, dripping cut. He tried not to think of how much he was bleeding. *At least I'm not paralyzed,* he mused, again trying to make the most of it. But he tasted salt in his mouth, and he realized that he hadn't actually stopped crying since he was separated from Lucas.

Someone up the hill loudly asked where Quentin had gone.

No rest for the weary, he thought, pushing onto his elbows. He cared little that his legs felt numb and that his feet were sensitive to the touch of the late-autumn air. He scraped his torso against the solid ground and propelled himself slightly upward and forward at the same time, so that he was on all fours, and he began a half-crawl in lieu of walking. Browned flowers were in his hair and twigs jabbed at his thighs. The air around him was putrid, just disgusting. The scents of pine sap and crisp grass barely suppressed the odor of the murky, dead water nearby. He knew he was close, so terribly close, could tell just from the smell. He stretched a hand out in front of him and, some ten seconds later, it twitched against water and ice. He felt frozen chunks knock around his swollen digits, and the unfrozen liquid swirled into the tiny cuts of his dry hand. He had finally reached the marsh. It was right there beneath, between, and all around his hand.

More rustles came from the trees. The lights shined down on some dirt a few feet away from him.

Quentin crawled forward, toward the water. His wheezes cracked into gasps as his blood-painted arms brought his body closer to the marsh, and he plunged into it. He threw in his neck, shoulders, and then his chest, but kept his head above the surface. He dropped in the rest of his body, from his core down to his hips, all the while opening his mouth for another breath, choking up the saltiness of the tears that made their way past his lips. Against his liking, he dropped his rigid legs and feet from the shore and submerged them along with the rest of himself so that he was almost entirely entrapped by the frosted water. It was the most painful relief he had ever felt. The grubbiness of that natural pool only inflamed his wounds, and he was cold. He was unbelievably cold. But, to his satisfaction, he was hidden. For that, his anxiety was mildly reduced.

He pulled away from the shore of the marsh and dog-paddled forward into the deeper parts of the water body.

A flock of the pale lights came bouncing back into sight, shooting through the trees. One beam skidded over the shore, and Quentin's sole operational eye caught sight of it. His mind functioned slower than usual as he waded in the icy water, even as he saw the light come closer. It was, once again, another uncharacteristically haphazard decision of his, but he had only one solution to keep out of sight: he sucked in a breath and dropped his head under the water. He lingered just beneath the roof of the swamp. His toes wiggled and his face contorted in a grimace. If he had to stop himself from recoiling back on land, his earlier discomfort was nothing compared to what he lived through, then, as a dagger of ice tore his sweatpants and a bushy cable of withered, but ever-strong, undergrowth ensnarled his waist. If he didn't freeze to death, he was going to be pulled down, deeper into the water. He circled his fingers around the weeds to loosen them from their lock on his middle, which was a tactic he had once learned from his father through a telling and not actual experience; it was a lesson his father thought vital, given the possibility of either, or both, of his sons finding their way down the hill when their parents were distracted.

Quentin snapped the weed in half, and he projected his head up to the surface, above the water. Either his time count was inaccurate or his lungs were proving his state of fitness poor, but he gasped in every breath. He started to wonder, perhaps a bit too confidently, about why his potential abductors were taking so long to reach him, since he was, after all, an unfit specimen.

He swam further away from the shore behind him and started to make his way to the other side, the one which touched the stretch of forest beyond the marsh. He never stopped moving. He felt weaker, but he tried to ignore the fact that his body was hanging on by a thread. He almost hadn't noticed that in front of him, originating from the destination side of the swamp, an ivory light beam came charging out to the water. It flashed right onto him, and he instantly heard the call of victory from behind the weeds, "Sarge, I found him!"

Quentin sucked in another breath, puffed his cheeks into two, chubby bags, and dipped his head back underneath the surface. Staying under the gelid water was torture, especially since the light beam held steady on the surface area. He swam to the left, but the light followed. He swam to the right, and it still tagged along after him. A bent tree branch, stuck between floras, stabbed his stomach. A frosty object gnawed at his ears while a pulpy blob, which had once been a tadpole, squished against his lips. He couldn't breathe.

A muted conversation commenced above the water.

His head started to tingle.

There were splashes nearby, and he knew they were closing in on him. He spun sloppily and turned to face the other shore, and that was when he poked his head above the water. It would have felt so good to breathe, had a figure in the water not been nearing him, their splashes were wild and wide. As for the other shore, there was no fleeing to it. Lights were everywhere, littered across the land. *What the hell?* he thought. *It's just me.* He saw boots and legs, but no upper bodies, since they vanished behind the brilliance of the glaring lights.

Someone grabbed Quentin's shoulder. He screamed. He threw his arms around like he had done earlier, in his backyard. He made blind punches, squeaked out swears. He gave the person, a man, another punch, but Quentin slipped back under the water until he was gurgling on so much of the brown liquid that he was choking and his eyes were tearing up. The man's other bulky hand squeezed Quentin's side, and he felt fingers cram down on his ribcage. With enviable effortlessness, the person dragged him back to the original shore, the one with all the torso-less figures. Lights, at least twenty of them, wagged around and settled back on the pair in the water. His single, functioning eye threatened giving out.

As he was pulled through the water, Quentin kicked his legs in a tantrum. "Need a whole fuckin' army for one boy?!" he shouted. "Get off me! Get off of me!" His head fell back into the water. He slurped in a mouthful of the swamp juice. He spit it up, hacking a cough from the wretched taste of it. As he was dragged toward the land, his carrier, a behemoth of a man, knitted his fingers through Quentin's hair and harshly snapped his head up above the surface to let him breathe. He didn't want the man's help. He didn't want anyone from that clan of thugs helping him with anything. *Who do they think they are?* he asked himself. The man yanked on Quentin's shirt, pulled him back a bit, and thrust him onto the shore.

He landed on a mattress of stones. The stones, blades of the forest ground, cut into spaces that were left untouched from his fall down the slope. More blood spilled out of him. He couldn't bring himself to move and stayed facedown on the rocks.

The one who had grabbed him, dragged him, and threw him finally came out of the water and eased himself down onto his buttocks several feet away from Quentin. The person was heaving, his crooked, but tired, face unmasked. He watched Quentin as he wept. "Jesus," the swamp-swimmer said. He tilted his head and inspected Quentin. "Oh, shit," he muttered before saying, and much louder, "Get first aid! He's bleeding in a bad way!"

That only angered Quentin. Bleeding tended to happen when one was thrown onto a bed of rocks.

A masked figure bent down, their torso visible without the light in front of them, and they handed the man on the ground a single cloth. He crawled forward. One of his gloved hands held the cloth between his fingers as he came into Quentin's space and lowered it over his forehead. In one, swift motion, the cloth was cleansing the pale boy's face of the swamp goop.

Then, in the next, the hand that held the fabric palmed his gasping mouth. Quentin's nostrils flared. His arms shot up and started swinging in every direction. The gloved hand pressed down harder, muffling his screams. He scratched at whatever he could reach, whether it was the neck or eyes, but he scraped away at the person like a feline. The hand held the cloth down firmer, tighter, until, with a gust of wind shot their way, he laid motionless.

7

July, 2046

Come the morning on which Topher Patrick Hartwell flew his long way to Dar es Salaam, Tanzania, it had been precisely three weeks and four days since the United States ambassador to Poland had died. Although, he believed calling her demise a death or a mere passing of the soul were descriptors each too gentle for something as gruesome as being shot in the chest whilst eating lunch in one's own backyard with a newborn in the wicker crib two feet away and an unsuspecting husband slicing watermelon at the opposite end of the table, their day having been halted by a shot from a neighboring house's bedroom window. It was an incredible shame. Firstly, she was young. Too young. Secondly, it was but a particle of the aggravated disunity that yet again began to plague the ever-backwards, but incongruously progressing, thing which had been known to man as geopolitics.

Geopolitics, Topher thought with a twist of his mouth. He hated the term. It wasn't politics or rising international tensions. It was the murder of a woman. Similarly, the death of the Argentine health minister during his visit to Washington, D.C. was far from a natural departure from the mortal world. Yet that, of course, had not induced an army of raised eyebrows, for he was not a citizen of the land on which he was killed, and very artfully had the genesis of his death been masked. Which begged the question, *Who are we to act sanctimonious?* Topher asked himself.

He swiped his chin with the little luxury that was the lightly-steamed towel given to him by the stewardess earlier in the hour. There was a grain—rather, if he were being more honest with himself, an entire rock—within him that craved to swipe the stress-related sweat from the top of his hairless head, but he deemed that too embarrassing to actually execute with a straight face while in the midst of so many people. He resorted to refreshing only his forehead and cheeks, and, as he did, he peered out the miniature viewport beside his seat in a desperate endeavor to distract himself from the sweat, itchiness, and general discomfort which was brought upon him from being locked within the confines of the airplane for so many hours.

He wasn't distracted. The shimmering hints of Istanbul that gleamed back at him were impressive and, quite obviously, pretty. Pretty, though not entrancing. He saw few hypnotic qualities to its landscape. As the orange daylight began to mesh with the faint, though not whole, darkness of the evening, he was left underwhelmed and undistracted, and from it, he grew restless.

Thirty minutes later, his flight came to an end. His flight, but not his journey. There was still a stretch to go.

Where Naomi Thomas-Patterson dwelt was a drab, old place in the former capitol of Tanzania, and, by virtue of being her godfather and essentially the single, last relative in her reach, Topher arched one eyebrow when she stuck her small head out from behind the door of her abode to welcome him inside, as there was no air conditioning, the furniture was decades old and tainted by its use and years, and the bends and dips of the walls and ceiling activated a most paternal, worried stupor within him.

Naomi wasn't much tinier than Topher, but in order to direct her flummoxed expression his way, she did have to crane her neck back. As she stared up at him with her legs draped in baggy sweatpants, her height seemed drastically reduced since the last time he had seen her. A product of the humidity, her once loose, brown locks were a storm of fluffy flyaways that curtained the edges of her pale and flat visage. He briefly thought that the slight bounce to her hair was a gentle softener to her appearance; it shielded the wrinkles that decorated the edges of her eyes and pulled his gaze away from the drawn patches on her cheeks.

Topher looked back to the apartment, in particular to a single board of wood that was missing from her kitchen floor.

"What?" Naomi asked.

Topher withdrew his attention from the kitchen. "Must I truly elaborate? I thought it was ragged on the outside and presumed it would get better inside."

The corners of Naomi's mouth curled up. "I'll have you know that this is *your* fault," she accused with an accompanying smirk, which was more prominent a show of amusement than her initial half-smile. "You're the one who told me to keep a low profile."

"Sweetheart, I told you to keep a low profile, not to be at a low point." Topher moved to switch his briefcase to his other hand, but was stopped when Naomi carefully grasped it into her own. "I thought I told you to stay safe, not go off-grid," he scolded her.

Naomi held the briefcase in front of her. She stood in a schoolgirl stance that minimized the appearance of her age, just for that moment. "Trust me, off-grid is always the safest," she said confidently. She leaned up on her tiptoes and graced Topher's left cheek with a press of her lips. "Besides," she said, "it's not really off the grid. I'm still in the city. I thought it would be safer to be in a most inconspicuous place."

"Last I recall, security was my speciality," Topher said. "There may not be any footage of your existence here, but I assure you, it wouldn't surprise me if one or more gangs have taken note of your presence."

Naomi's smile was still snarky, and, as pestered as Topher was by her, he had missed it beyond expression. She was a formerly timid child who grew to become an especially reserved woman, even at the best of times, so to have seen her changed, *goofy*, when he least expected her to be, was a gift he knew not to overlook. "You're only a grump because you hate flying," she said, having read him easily. "C'mon, let's get some sustenance into you."

"This does concern me, though," Topher droned on in utmost seriousness as he followed her through the living room. He eyed the peeling, cream-toned walls and the divot-littered couch and coffee table set. The floorboards were thin and barely kept together every time his brogues progressed a step forward. Perhaps, in part, the disheveled state of the apartment was made messier by the disarray of Naomi's things, like the clothing, suitcases, and binders that were strewn about uncoordinatedly. He still had his doubts. As he inspected the setting and tried to envision it wiped of her belongings, he thought it would have looked just as devastated as it did then. How she lived in there was beyond him. The kitchen and dining area was adjacent to the living room. It was there that Naomi set Topher's briefcase upon one of the wobbly chairs at her table before moving to the stovetop in order to begin truly hosting him in her home. She asked if it was coffee or tea he desired, to which he responded that refrigerated mineral water dolloped by lemon and some ice was preferred.

"Snob," Naomi commented in jest.

Just as Topher began to settle on one of the chairs, she returned with a glass of his requested beverage in one hand as well as a half-drunk, paper cup of coffee in the other.

Naomi sat herself down across from him. "You'll have to forgive the mess," she said, "but I was told you'd be here a month ago."

Topher took a sip from his glass. "Your proclivity for clutter has never bothered me," he assured. "It isn't your mess that's getting to me, Nani, it's the neighborhood. The apartment. The circle of men that hang in the hallway downstairs. What worries me is everything beyond your control. Where's the rest of the team?"

"Equally dispersed," Naomi answered. She traced the shredded rim of her takeout cup. "Some are in the airport region, others in the center. Richard is far south."

Topher cupped the glass in front of him to run his hands along the condensation. "Will he be joining us today?" he asked.

"Not sure. He came back yesterday from Columbia. But... regarding the mess," Naomi said pointedly, "there is a genuine reason for it. It would have been cleaned four weeks ago."

Topher sighed. "If that is another allusion to my whereabouts this last month, all I can say is that things didn't go as planned."

As Naomi's mood began to sober, the levity that lingered in her eyes faded. Only when it completely vanished did Topher find himself missing it. He didn't realize he'd taken her temporary lightheartedness, her revived girlishness, for granted by lecturing her upon his entry.

"I heard about Miranda," Naomi said, newly cheerless. "I mean, it was international news, but I was personally informed. Is that where you went, then? To Poland?"

"For a few days, yes. The performer of the job, it turned out, was an Irish defector acting on behalf of the UK. They must have assumed he'd be safely kept where we discovered him; he was about an hour outside of Belfast."

Naomi's eyes widened. "Bold," she said.

"You can understand my holdup."

"I haven't heard this before today."

"And you probably never will anywhere else," Topher said. "He's inaccessible because the true details of it would be too unnerving to release. But, do you remember the Belarusian operative who was sent back home last year? The one we found in northern France during that first scouting op? Not the Serbian one."

Naomi nodded.

"The intention is to blame him for it," Topher said.

Naomi nodded again. She didn't do it out of agreement, only understanding. "That should maintain some sense of normalcy," she said.

"I should hope so."

As the conversation lengthened and their voices became gentler, the initial buzz of the first few minutes of their meeting slowly began to wither away. They sipped mineral water and coffee, and then at one point, munched cookies and crackers. Throughout their time together, both godfather and goddaughter reverted back to their typical selves.

By that period of their lives, in the year 2046, they were living out a rather abnormal circumstance. Naomi's initial buoyancy and liveliness had been due to finally seeing Topher after so long, after nearly an entire year apart, when for almost all her comparably younger life, he had been a constant. Similarly, he was not usually such a shamelessly outspoken individual and, more often than not, was a more contained and considerate man who tended to restrict his opinions for the sake of diplomacy and friendliness, even when in the company of those closest to him. He was always open-minded when it came to Naomi, but given how she was recently made parentless and rendered the last of her bloodline to walk the Earth, it was that newfound solitude of hers that made him a more watchful and fastidious version of his common self.

They sat and spoke for a long while, and they continued to return to their own sense of normalcy. The goddaughter's face became increasingly neutral and her smiles started to barely reach her eyes. Meanwhile, the godfather's became warmer, softer. That was who they really were; both were cerebral, yet she was the more emotionally contained.

Topher helped Naomi tidy up the additional clutter they had made on her dining table. The paper cup was disposed into her recycling bin and the depleted glass was relocated to the kitchen sink. As they cleaned together, he told her as many of the things as he was allowed and, with deftly cryptic wording of an inside language they had created when she was a girl, he managed to slip in three stories, none of which she was supposed to know. She laughed, and it was a lovely sound. She only gleaned the complete translation in two of his tales, but since they earned him the sound that she released, he was almost as pleased as if she had intuited all three. Once the space was relatively decluttered, Naomi excused herself and left Topher alone for half an hour. He fetched his briefcase and settled himself comfortably upon the ratty, patched-up armchair beside her living room's sole window. He made sure to fully recharge his laptop after having frequently used it during his multiple flights. He considered working, even if it only would have been for thirty minutes, but the ringing pipes of Naomi's shower eliminated any possibility of him concentrating; they rang their terrible, tinny screeches to the point that it was unfeasible to focus on anything mentally taxing.

For someone who hated noise, Naomi's place was ill-suited. Topher mentioned that observation to her awhile later, when she finally emerged from the restroom in new garments and her wet hair rapidly drying on its own due to the sweltering, midmorning heat.

"I was only supposed to be here for a week," Naomi reminded him.

Topher ducked his head. "Right," he said. "My bad."

"That's all right. Two flights in one day should be enough karma to last you a whole month's delay."

"At least one of us will enjoy it," Topher murmured.

They gathered their luggage; on Naomi's end, she had two, plentifully packed rolling suitcases and a drawstring bag; Topher had his one briefcase of worn and torn leather as well as an enormous, green duffel bag. Naomi was locking up the flimsy door to her apartment when she froze the key mid-turn, giving Topher an unsubtle once-over; she wasn't judgmental as much as she was concerned. He looked down at himself, from the handmade shoes he had worn for at least five years, to the khakis on his legs, then to his long-sleeved, white shirt.

"Do you take issue with my attire?" he spluttered out in faux offense.

"Why, yes I do," Naomi said. She motioned to her cream-shaded tee-shirt, which was tucked into gray, fleece capris. "Have you forgotten the humidity of domestic flights here?"

"I can manage," Topher said confidently.

"If you insist, Toph."

He had, however, been deathly wrong when he said that; his simple assurance of managing commenced inauspiciously. Long before reaching the grounds of the regional airport, there was the horrendous two-hour period that consisted of the pair of them waiting out the congested, late-morning traffic. In the backseat of a taxi that lacked an air conditioner, their skin grew sticky and Naomi's hair further frizzed. At first, they were talkative and indulged the inquiries of their hospitable and curious driver, Jabari, with whom they laughed and exchanged jokes, along with some altered stories of their travels. But the heat became unbearable—it was August in Tanzania. The three of them lost their loquacity and soon said little, as talking had become too cumbersome when merely breathing in the hot air was an exercise of its own. Jabari apologized profusely, as if the weather was somehow his fault. Topher discreetly undid a few of his shirt's top buttons and folded up his cufflinks, but he was caught in the act; he dutifully avoided meeting Naomi's knowing eyes. As for her, she fanned herself languidly with the glossy papers of a city map she retrieved from one of her bags, but when that provided no relief, she surrendered to a few puffs of her inhaler. Topher recognized some light, Swahili cursing grunted out of Jabari's lips. Sweat pooled on the top of Topher's head, and he wiped it over with his hand.

"Oh my goodness," Naomi said at once. It was the first she had spoken in over thirty minutes. She pointed to the side of Topher's bald head. "A hair. You have a hair."

Topher was stupefied. "I do?"

"It's gray, but budding nonetheless. I suppose that makes you young again."

"Child, the days of my youth are long vanished."

Naomi shrugged. "So you may say, but the evidence is in your follicles."

At the front of the taxi, Jabari chuckled.

The driver was silent the rest of the way. They all were. The passengers sat back and watched as he took shortcuts and hidden alleys, ones he swore that no other taxi driver in all of 'Dar es' would have ever dared to stray onto for fear of losing their way. The motion sickness was an inevitability from all the extra swerving and sharp maneuvering he committed for their benefit, and though the American pair were pale and queasy upon arrival at the airport grounds, they were grateful to him. He was tipped amply, and he bid them both a very safe farewell.

In Tanzania's small city of Arusha, an olive-green United States Army truck waited outside the city's humble airport. The vehicle's roof was detached, but parked between a few thickly-leaved baobab trees, it didn't need one. Its engine murmured softly, was no louder than a whisper against the sounds of the nearby streets. Visible through the windshield and sitting in the driver's seat was a young man in camouflage attire. He was scrunching his face behind the protection of his sunglasses that seemed one size too big. Behind him sat three individuals: one a thin, brown-skinned woman in an orange tank-top, whose short, gray hair was escaping from underneath her pink bucket hat; the next a middle-aged, red-headed woman with her torso draped by an unworn windbreaker; the third a light-skinned, long-haired man, dressed in a black tee-shirt, who appeared a few decades younger than his female counterparts.

Naomi distractedly swatted flies away from her sweaty face. Topher, indifferent to the buzzing insects that fluttered around him, was the first to notice the vehicle. He waved it down by gesticulating toward himself and Naomi, and soon the truck loomed out from the parking lot's perimeter trees and began to slowly make its way toward the sidewalk in front of the main building.

"I don't know why they're hiding," Naomi said, "it's not like we've been hostilely received."

"It may not be for the reason you think," Topher pointed out. "All I know is that my phone said it was a-hundred-and-two degrees here today and judging by our late arrival, they've been waiting quite a long time."

Their ride pulled up next to them, and the woman in the pink bucket hat propped a door open immediately. She called Naomi's name and spoke of how good it was to see her after so long. Naomi reciprocated the affection; they hugged and kissed one another's cheeks. Naomi fit herself and her luggage in the rightmost seat of the back row, next to the woman, and proceeded to shake hands with the other two who were present.

Topher took the front passenger seat. "Afternoon, Mr...?" he greeted the young man in the driver's spot.

"Private Reynolds, Sir," replied the youngster.

"Oh, good day, Private. Is Colonel Brandt still up there?" Topher asked.

"Yes, Sir."

"Good, good." Topher twisted his neck around to see Naomi. "He's an old friend actually. Have I ever told you that?"

"I had no idea," Naomi said. "Now I definitely have questions."

The redheaded woman tilted her head. "Did you meet him on a past volcanic scout?"

"Oh, no, no," Topher said. "I'm not one of you. I was the security director for V2 and was only recently charged here. I met him long ago in college, before he went on to military school. I'm Topher Hartwell, by the way."

"Jane Matthews."

"Pleasure."

Naomi motioned to the other two. "Topher, do you remember them? This is Maryam Akhbul and, obviously, Richard."

The younger man smiled. "I'd hope he remembers me. That would be some godfather of yours not to."

Jane looked confused. In lowering her head to one side again, the hat she was wearing fell right above her eyes. "Why would that be?" she asked.

Richard reclined. "Well, he is Naomi's godfather," he said offhandedly. "And Naomi's my wife."

"No kidding." Jane chuckled. "I would never have suspected. She said her hellos to Maryam and me, but she barely even looked at you."

Naomi poked her head forward to see Jane. "Professionalism for in-office romance is dangerously underrated."

Topher laughed, and he turned around to face forward again. It was difficult not to; there was so much ahead for him to see.

"So, Private Reynolds," Topher said cheerily, "how goes the coexistence?"

"Good, Sir," the young man said promptly. He was incredibly young, and Topher wasn't even sure if he was above the age of eighteen. There was a softness to the private's pale face, one of pure, unhindered youth. His arm lowered and raised as he operated the steering wheel of the truck. "The People's Defense Force actually sent two more battalions last Friday. We do a lot of training together."

"That's good to hear, given the recent news."

"Sir."

Topher's sweaty hands wrapped around his kneecaps. He narrowed his eyes and took in the city, everything from the nature that had been preserved between the short buildings, and then to the sun, which said buildings failed to obstruct.

He had frequented the area many times preceding that particular visit, but the one he enjoyed the most had taken place over thirty-one years ago, when Naomi was at the tender age of five and experiencing her first time there, on that soil. While her father was busy and Topher, for the first time in months, had a day all to himself, he had chosen to spend it with her. He remembered the white, half-torn orchid that was loosely held in her left hand and the wide, unrestrained smile on her little face when she pushed her head out the rattling, half-open window of their *dala-dala*. They were being driven to a national park that was situated beyond the bounds of the cosmopolitan stretch, and all throughout their journey, her head stayed propped out that window. He remembered how the wind blew her awkwardly chopped hair, how her face soaked in the golden hues that reflected off the ground of the plains. She was enraptured, agape, and captivated by the silhouettes of towering giraffes. She bounced on her knees and reached her chubby hand to point at them, and watched their distinctive figures bob around the trees; the whole sight was west of where their bus had driven. "Mama liked giraffes," she had said, with her head still stuck out the window. Even though, thirty-one years later, Topher was being hauled through the city rather than the nearby, desolate lands from his memory, he had long retained vivid images of that one day. In truth, the mere air around him—the suffocating, humid air and its scent of flowers in bloom and oil-polluted mud—possessed a miraculous ability to bring to mind even the minutest details of a day from decades before.

His mood dampened just a little when his eyes rose higher above the windshield of the truck that was bumping its way along the dirt road. A certain mountain came into view behind clusters of buildings that were miles ahead in the distance, its body a mammoth beauty with its crown of ashen-white snow and a broad, green base. He felt his gaze darken and his stomach sink. Mount Kilimanjaro always had a way of daunting him.

——

Naomi felt Richard watching her as she made her way up the beaten driveway. He still sat in their car, a rented *Jeep* with red paint that was gradually scraping away, especially above the taillights. He waited to see if anyone was present to answer the door in front of her, at the house at the top of the driveway. She heard the rumble of the vehicle's old engine and knew he still hovered behind her. She batted the air to wave him off and, as she approached the house, she gestured overtly to the two trucks parked in front of the garage, indicating that the owners were home. One of them was, anyway. The truck on the left was Topher's, and was, in fact, the very truck she and Richard had helped Topher select from the rental agency when they first arrived to Arusha the week before. Regardless, the presence of it didn't alleviate Richard's evident anxieties. But she started to see that his concerns weren't entirely unfounded; as she progressed up the grainy path, only trees and dirt surrounded the property.

The house before her was a freshly renovated, single-level, ranch-styled outpost of misplaced, western normality. It had a quaint, small porch that traced along the front rooms and ended before the side corners began. Its faded, ivory color was remarkably untainted by the onslaught of torrential storms from earlier in the week; storms which, to the slight chagrin of Naomi and her husband, had tainted the exterior color of their own white home. Naomi ascended the steps, stood on the doormat that read WELCOME in knitted letters. She rapped at the yellow, front door.

The door flew open instantly. The space where it stood just moments before was suddenly occupied by a woman. Naomi knew that the person before her was at least in her mid-fifties, but she thought the woman actually looked younger than she did during their last encounter, and far more natural; the false blonde coloring that for so long polluted the strands of her hair had dissipated, and the locks were returned to their intrinsic, brunette shade. The stress circles that once stretched under her worn eyes had also receded to nothingness. She looked, if not happier, then healthier. It was a vision Naomi was pleased to see. "Naomi, I'm so glad you could come," the fresh-faced woman said as she pulled Naomi into a hug. They exchanged cheek kisses and marveled at the length of time that had passed since they last saw each other.

Behind them, the lingering *Jeep* departed from the end of the driveway.

"Is that Richard?" the woman asked.

Naomi nodded. "He has a conference call with Command in an hour. They want to know if he can be in Brazil next week." She tried not to let the disappointment sneak into her voice, but it did. They had already been separated for so long, she and Richard, and the last thing she wanted to do was see him leave when she had just recently arrived.

The woman smiled pityingly and beckoned Naomi into the home. Inside, it smelt of cinnamon and roses, a fusion Naomi wasn't previously aware of being partial to, but she supposed it was never too late to learn. On one side of her was the living room, on the other a small dining area, and ahead of her was a hallway that led into what she distinguished as the kitchen. A shoe rack up against the wall beside her was flurried with numerous black sneakers of similar styles but of different sizes, some clean but most dirty. The woman guiding her through the house took note of Naomi's staring and put very simply, by way of explanation, "He grows really fast. It's a new pair every month," and then continued to lead Naomi further indoors. It was a sparsely furnished home, likely due to the recency of the residents' relocation to the country. The host led Naomi down the blue-walled hallway, where, along the way, they passed locus flowers in pots upon a wobbly legged, decorative table and a silver-lined mirror that was nailed into the wall above those few items.

The kitchen was a warmer area. It was the origin of the cinnamon aroma and, without a doubt, a bright and cheery room. There were flowers everywhere; potted roses stood by the toaster oven; quartered tulips were strewn across a lone tea tray; fake geraniums were sprinkled on the keyboard of a computer on the kitchen desk, which was attached to the wall in its own dug-out space beside an open pantry. Alongside the sink and the lily-lined window above it, there were two sliding doors, one mesh and one glass, which led to a sunroom; the daylight poured inside. A tall fan stood in the corner behind Topher, who was sitting on the edge of one of the three stools by the wooden island. With his briefcase on the chair beside him, he was hunched over an open, gray laptop.

"Afternoon, Nani," Topher greeted Naomi, but he didn't look up from his computer.

In front of where he was sitting were three teacups and two mugs; one of the teacups was partially filled, but both mugs were empty. What loomed over them was a steaming kettle that smelled of lemon and ginger as well as an opaque pitcher half-filled with a thick, brown beverage that seemed to sway back and forth on its own. There were plates of cookies and biscuits too.

"Tea? Coffee?" the woman offered. "Please, Naomi, sit down. Go on, go on."

Naomi made herself comfortable on the stool beside Topher. She reached for one of the teacups; hers was adorned by delicate, metallic flowers.

The hostess was never one to sit, though. Naomi tried to recount a time when she hadn't seen the woman on her feet, but found herself incapable to do so. Even then, the woman stood half-leaned over the island with her elbows on the wooden surface and her hands clasped together. She was white-knuckled already.

"So there's a thing?" Naomi asked delicately. "I know you tried to tell me over the phone, but I'm abysmal when it comes to cryptic wording."

"A thing indeed," the woman said. She huffed at herself. "I hate that this is how we're reunited. That's life, I guess."

"It won't bore me, whatever it is."

The woman nodded. "See, I knew I would be busy back in November, so that's why I assigned McMichael to the role of tallying and confirming. Which he did, yes…but there was an open slot that had to be filled."

Naomi, holding the kettle and carefully pouring its lemon-ginger contents into her teacup, paused and set the item down. She looked over to Topher, whose chin was in his hand and his face, especially his eyes, embodied a new wave of dejection. "I take it that's no coincidence," she concluded.

Topher said nothing.

"We don't think so," said the other woman. "McMichael has been taken in for questioning. I hope, of course, it's just a product of incompetence. But I know, in the back of my mind, that's probably not the case."

"Who's the missing asset?" Naomi asked.

"The Carlyle kid. I had gone to the house and, as I should have suspected, every inch of the place was tucked up in dust. I don't even know how long they were actually gone before I discovered it."

"McMichael wasn't your hire," Topher said gently. "It isn't all your fault. Besides, you were going through a lot. I don't blame you for missing one component, not with the optimal replacement I've assigned in Hollis's place and, of course, we can't ignore all that you've had to deal with in your own life, Sydney."

"But I should have seen it," Sydney insisted. "I should have suspected something back in November, and I didn't."

"You didn't, but everything else has been set in motion," Topher said, "so it isn't all that terrible. I didn't train you to oversee absentees, that was the minutia. If anything, it's my fault for not finding a better fit to work for you; a more trustworthy fit."

"Was he vital?" Naomi asked.

"Of course he's vital," Sydney said. "One way or another, each of them is going to be of some use." She scowled at herself. "Look," she said to Topher, "I'll get to it. I'll relocate them, dig up the Carlyles' ally...or allies."

"Alleged or confirmed allies?" Topher questioned.

"Alleged. I have some reports, though. We can review them now."

"I'm really sorry to hear about this," Naomi said between two sips of tea. She pursed her lips in thought. "So, you're all here now?"

"Not David," Sydney said. "He's still in Mass. He's only visited a couple of times, actually. And...Michael is here."

"Michael," Naomi echoed questioningly.

"It's his middle name," Sydney said. "It's not too far a stretch for him to grasp. Anyway, he's here. He's miserable, predictably. Topher's tried talking to him to explain why we're here, but he doesn't want to hear it. It's also worth mentioning that he hasn't said a word since that night."

Naomi considered the news presented to her. She dragged a finger along the edge of the island, her thumb twitching as a minor show of nervousness. "You know," she began, sounding more self-possessed than she felt, "I, too, was heartbroken from it. And that was me, someone who knew everything and had been through the development. I can't imagine what's going through his mind." She froze her hand. "I could speak to him."

"You could?" Sydney asked.

"I might be able to convey what you two couldn't."

"Naomi, I don't think he's ready for that."

"I don't want to overstep," Naomi made clear, "but, with all due respect, Topher has moved him across the globe. He's away from his father. Away from his friends. He's not going to last without an explanation. A proper one, anyway."

Topher gave a permissive nod. Sydney, on the other hand, didn't. Thinking over the offer, her lips drew tight as she rubbed them against each other. All that moved on her face were those rubbing lips, but the rest of it, the rest of her body, in fact, was wholly still. She was silent for a long time, pensive throughout the quiet, and the other two were respectfully wordless as they waited for an answer, in her house. Something like five minutes passed. Topher rapidly moved his fingers along the keys of his laptop. Naomi sipped her teacup to dryness, until all the lemon-ginger was spooled in her gut and heated her from the inside.

"He's on the roof," Sydney said.

Naomi left the kitchen. As instructed, she started toward the sunroom to access the back deck, where Sydney had said that a ladder would be waiting. Naomi passed through the sunroom, which was bare of furniture and flowers, peeled apart its second pair of sliding doors, and closed them behind her when she took her first step onto the deck. Indeed, a red ladder was propped up against the rear wall of the house. The ranch, though not a colonial and nations away from the town of Shaw in the state of Massachusetts, had a first-floor layout reminiscent of the Hansons' old home, which Naomi had visited twice when she was a girl. She didn't know if that was an intentional decision on Sydney's part, if it was a weak ploy to acclimatize her child to his new and hopefully harmless reality. It certainly struck Naomi as one.

She was suddenly grateful for the single-level stature of the house. She didn't know if she would've had the sufficient gumption to climb a two-story building for the sake of reaching a child who wasn't even her own. She could scale mountains in the wintertime and active, fuming volcanoes in hot summers, but for the most ludicrous reason she couldn't place, the prospect of climbing up a ladder against a house was intimidating. She laughed at her own irony. But that ladder, she scaled. She breathed steadily and lifted her feet, all the while distracting herself from the periodic sways and creaks of the individual bars. When she reached the top, she released a breath she had held in the whole way up; it seemed that a single-level home really was a feat to her. She rolled herself onto the smoothly curved, slate roof tiles and shuffled forward on her knees for a short distance, until she finally stood half-erect.

Wind blew all around her. Another storm was scheduled to arrive in the city by the evening, and that afternoon, the sky already divulged the beginning hints of it. Behind the clouds, the perfect, blue background was slowly submitting to a gray tint that increasingly dominated. The wind gusts slowed a little, but they were stronger than before, earlier in the afternoon. Her hair flicked into her mouth, her eyes, and, most irritatingly, her ears. She was happy to have pilfered one of Richard's windbreakers when he wasn't looking—although, he never denied her of his clothing.

Naomi carefully tread upon the roof. She was fully aware that slate tiles overlaid partway upon each other, if not installed properly, could have easily ended up in a cascading mini-avalanche with one heavy step. She maneuvered cautiously, watched her every move.

That was when she saw him, the boy. He must have hidden himself earlier, when hers and Richard's *Jeep* drove up to the house, because she hadn't seen him then. But there the boy was a little later, seated on the edge of the roof at the front side of the house. His legs dangled off and his shoulders were slumped forward. His short brown hair, the hair like his mother's, was untidy from the wind.

Naomi knew he heard her. There was no way he couldn't have. She might have been stealth on stone and ice, but on curved roof slates, she couldn't help but make harsh scraping sounds. "Michael?" she called to him hesitantly. Over the years, she had learned that it wasn't the feral who were difficult to approach, but the quiet and removed.

He didn't look at her. He stared forward, over the short trees that stretched far ahead. The city was a blur from that spot on the edge of the roof. It was no more than a multicolored cluster among the green, its buildings difficult to make out if one hadn't already known they were there. From that spot, the savannas weren't decipherable in the slightest. Naomi could see the summit of the nearby mountain, though. It was clear as day, that towering beauty. There was no dissociating it from her, not since she had hiked its trails and slept on its cliffs countless times. The boy also stared at the massive body in the distance. He watched it stand fast asleep whilst the world around it was wide awake; Kilimanjaro was a dormant volcano.

Naomi bit her tongue, as the boy still hadn't turned around. She didn't intend to near him any further until she was given permission. She wanted to warn him about the slipping slate, but it would have come off as too maternal, too ridiculing. He was probably skittish, and she couldn't blame him. She wanted to ask if she could sit beside him, but she knew that wouldn't have worked to any avail. She considered saying that she was there to help, but figured that would only frighten him and make him untrusting of her.

There was, however, one word, one *name*, that she thought she might utter, but she knew it was beyond her rights to say it. And yet, as she watched his shoulders slump lower in the most helplessly lonely manner she had ever seen, she spoke it anyway: "Lucas."

He flinched. She stood behind him, hoping that he would perhaps let her near. But aside from the flinch, he was unresponsive for what felt like an eternity.

The winds grew stronger and the air more humid. The gray in the sky overpowered the blue. The mountain was less discernible, for the gathered clouds began to sweep into the south and shielded it from her view.

She decided that the time wasn't right, that there would always be another day when she could try to extend her sympathies to him. As she turned to leave, she detected movement on her right side.

Lucas was facing her.

"Oh, hi," Naomi said, surprised. "I'm Naomi." She didn't expect him to turn around, not on that day. But once she was slightly joyed that he had, she made her next bold move of motioning to a few rubbery panels that were lined up on the roof beside him. "May I?" she asked, and Lucas nodded. He watched her the whole time as she moved to sit next to him, first in a criss-crossed position and then with her legs hung off the edge, where they swung with the wind, just like his.

Lucas never took his eyes off her. His expression was blank.

"I'm not one of them," Naomi said to him. He probably knew what she meant, but, to be safe, she further explained herself. "I'm not Topher or your mom. I'm not like them. I'm a scientist, a volcanologist. I study volcanoes, so it's really none of my business to bother you. I was just coming up to say hi."

Lucas blinked.

Naomi opened her mouth to continue talking, but she closed it. Her hands stuffed into her pockets and squeezed at the tent-like material inside. She didn't know what she was doing or where she thought things would turn, but she said to him, "I know you may think no one understands you, and I know you've had many people say that they do, but…we do. Maybe not everyone. But some of us."

Lucas looked unimpressed, and Naomi felt like any sliver of hope that may have led him to liking her had slipped from her hands in a matter seconds. That last line, those last words, were not the correct things to have said to someone who was skeptical, and rightly so. She didn't want to give up, though. Not yet. She was correct earlier when she implied that there was a way to rectify his silence, and there was a reason Sydney had told her guests where her son was.

The wind blew in their faces again. It was much harsher that time around.

"It happened to me too," Naomi said to the air rather than the person beside her. "Or…someone I love. It affected me all the same. But you already know that."

Lucas looked down to his lap.

Naomi sighed. "But that's a story for another time," she said.

"Is it, though?" was the unspoken question that was suddenly displayed on the boy's newly expressive face. From the way he was looking at her, squinting and tilting his head with intrigue, he was a far cry from the blank-faced, unapproachable version of himself from mere minutes before. Naomi marked the change, and she had no intention of wasting the opportunity it presented to her. "You want me to tell it?" she asked, and as she did, she began to doubt if she was even inclined to the idea herself.

Lucas blinked again. He held his gaze on hers.

"Well…" Naomi sighed again. She removed one of her hands from its pocket and pointed to the snowy summit ahead in the distance. "It began there, on that mountain. In some sense of the word. My part of the story began there, at least. But if you really want the full picture…" She waited to provide him the time to make up his mind. And Lucas did. He faced her entirely, looking eager. "If you really want the full picture," Naomi repeated, "then we'll have to go back a long time, to when I was younger. Younger than your age, even. I must have been two, three…something like that. Anyway, there was this one day, and I didn't know what was happening, but according to my dad…"

They sat on that roof for hours, even when the rain came. It was a gentle storm in the beginning, which just so happened to arrive once she finished telling her story—what she had to tell of it, at least, because she was technically still living it. But the boy was riveted, and the woman indulging. Neither were bothered by the droplets that pelted down onto their faces, between their hairlines, and onto the other stretches of skin they had left exposed.

Did the story satisfy Lucas? Naomi didn't know. But was he grateful to finally hear it after the months of lies and deception? To that question, she very well knew the answer.

8

Quentin heard and felt most of what happened around him. The brain fog of having been asleep for what felt like ages gradually began to wane, and, with his eyes still closed, he assigned his non-visual senses to take the lead. He flinched the instant someone swung one of his wrists around, and repeatedly so. He knew the end of his arm was being battered against a solid surface, but whether it was metallic, wooden, or something else was a question too demanding for his tired mind to have actually taken into consideration. Oddly, the battering didn't hurt. He heard grunting and cursing intermittently ushered out during the expulsions of the person's breaths as they treated him like dough; they pushed and whipped his hand around to seemingly test the limits of his elasticity. He focused on the sensation of their hands, recognized how the fingers that held him loosely were lean, wiry, and cold. The voice he heard was barely detectable, but he sensed a bitterness to it.

Quentin opened his eyes. There was darkness all around him, unnatural darkness. It wasn't like the intrinsic dimness of the sky during the late night on which he ran for his safety, for his freedom. The area was artificially dark, the product of someone's choice against adequate lighting rather than the sun's nightly retire. There was a wall in front of him—that was as far as he could see—and lodged into it was a gentle, recessed light.

Nothing about him was different. He didn't know what he expected, but it certainly wasn't what he came to see when he dropped his head to give his body a glance. He saw that he was wearing his raggedy, oversized sweatpants and sleep tee-shirt, and that his bare feet were grimy with dried mud stuck to his skin; flecks of dirt were visible from under his toenails. He was unwashed and unchanged, but apparently not entirely untouched, because on the surface of the bed he was placed upon, what lingered beside his limp and long forearm was an uncannily large object that resembled a standard intravenous needle. A short, narrow machine beeped measuredly beside his wiggling toes, and, running along the side of it, was a tube that trickled from the back and snaked all the way up to his bed, connected to the tube that extended from his needle by a plastic joint. The fluid container—he assumed that's what it was—must have been hanging below the machine.

He wound his sore neck to the left to see who exactly it was that felt they had every right to absolutely abuse his arm while he was unconscious, and he ended up looking at a girl. Looking at Marina Gustavsson.

Quentin only saw her in the penitentiaries that were the various public school institutions they had attended together throughout most of their lives. For years, his only images of her were the ones she lent to the public; her in tailored blazers and jackets paired with loose khakis or dark, denim pants that resembled business-casual wear. But as he rested on that bed in the unfamiliar place and stared her way with befuddlement, she didn't look her wonted self. Her countenance was uncomely from the lack of approachability she exuded, but the rest of her, even if it was only superficially so, looked somewhat normal for once. Knelt at his bedside and fixedly hammering around his arm as she was dressed in purple pajama bottoms and an oversized, zip-up sweatshirt, she actually looked her age—normal.

He didn't know if Marina was aware of his consciousness. It would've been audacious if she were, given how demandingly she was cracking the delicate stretch of bone that connected his arm and hand. And yet, in spite of her proximity to him, she was engrossed by his wrist, which she was surveying, holding, and yet again chucking against the bed's metal support piece. He struggled to say her name. It was an absurdly difficult effort. Three syllables were all it constituted, yet he could hardly produce the first letter. What he thought would release as a question resulted in an exasperated wheeze from trying to sound out the letter M. But, to somewhat of an avail, his panting did catch her indifferent eye. She didn't stop her fiddling with his wrist, but she did meet his dumbfounded gaze.

"Didn't think you'd wake," Marina said. "You look terrible. I'm not going to ask." Quentin thought she would say more, but, after a while, it became clear that those words were all she was offering.

"Wh...?" Quentin tried to speak again, but he couldn't go any further. He tried to ask what the meaning was of their presence in that dark, gloomy, and cold place or why she was even there with him, but he literally couldn't say a thing.

Marina's focus returned to his joint. Why she was so fascinated with that segment of his body and, again, for what reason she continued to abuse it were both beyond him. She did speak once more, though. "You won't be able to talk for a while," she informed him curtly, not looking up at him when she spoke that time. "You'll be all right."

Quentin reasoned that there were worse things to wake up to. Granted, he couldn't think of what those other things were, but he knew there were other possibilities. Simply because she wasn't outwardly conniving and grating on him didn't mean she was a pleasantry for a post-abduction reunion. Her fingers were ice on his skin and her face was eerily detached. If that was God's way of blessing him with someone kind and consoling after his tiresome and torturous night, then it was wrong of Him to have assumed that Quentin would be grateful for her. All she did was make him feel small and demeaned, even when she wasn't attempting to.

"Wh...y?" Quentin croaked out when she wrestled his wrist around again. He finally looked down beyond his elbow to see what it was that occupied her and, shortly after, he started to understand her obsession; both of his wrists were anchored to the edges of the bed, pinned down by two separate steel rings. He wore shackles, essentially. He spluttered and fumed as he furiously wondered just why he was being restricted like cattle bound to be slaughtered, but, once more, he was stunted by the trouble of not being able to say anything.

Marina, for her part, was unmoved by his various expressions of impatience. He noticed after his second time glowering her way that she had, between her fingers, a mutilated bobby pin, which she knit in and out of a piece of the shackle he couldn't see, but presumed to be the one closest to her. She pushed the pin into the lock, removed the pin, and then rammed it back inside some more. At least she was helping him. He had no idea why she was there with him, but it was reassuring to know that he wasn't entirely alone. While she operated on his locks, Quentin gathered his breaths and moistened his throat with frequent swallows. It was a passing thought, but his esophageal glands felt so dry and unused, he could have sworn they had gone days without being used. It could have been the aftermath of all the screaming he'd done the prior night; he assumed that everything had happened the night before.

"You should relax," said someone behind him, "you won't be able to walk either." Their voice was just as raspy as his, but its rhythm had a slow, milky smoothness. They also were not as curt as Marina. No, in their statement, there were hints of what he recognized as concern. Quentin attempted spinning his head around to see the person, but his view was obstructed by the slanted top of his bed and the two extra pillows piled against the one under his neck.

Marina twisted her bobby pin in another direction. "I advise that you don't turn around," she told him. He sent a look of confusion her way, and she saw it. "Because, knowing you," she sighed out, "you'll cut off your own circulation and have an aneurism and die or something." Well. There she was, Marina Gustavsson. It was nice to know she regarded him so highly. Still, he couldn't complain. He yieldingly watched as she extracted the hairpin from his shackle, inserted it back inside, twirled it one way and then another, and, after minutes of toying with it, unlatched it from his wrist. Bobby pin in hand, she stood up and circled to the other side of his bed, by his still-captive right arm. Something of a routine was born. He resigned himself to lying back and calming his nerves by breathing deeply and swallowing enough saliva to smooth out the dryness in his throat. Meanwhile, she worked on his wrist with her pin that was dangerously morphed from what he assumed had been heavy use, since it gave the impression that it would snap at any moment.

When Quentin could finally speak, he asked her a question in full, "Who is behind us?"

"Frances," Marina said calmly, and she went about her work.

Quentin made a coughing sound, one which was a mixture of a second question on his tongue and the saliva he had gathered to keep soothing his throat. *"Frances?"* he repeated, completely horrified. It made him a little sick to know that. He was more outraged than he was when he woke up. When he first saw Marina, he knew that the predicament at hand was far from a simple one, but for some reason, having knowledge that his neighbor was there as well made it much worse. He was right, then, to not have scrambled over to Frances's house when he and Lucas sought refuge; the night would have ended the exact same way.

Frances appeared at once—he had spewed out her name, after all. She materialized from his left side. Above the stacked pillows, her exhausted face and form, which was outfitted in a pajama set of matching green bottoms and a long-sleeved shirt, came into sight. He couldn't help but notice that she moved towards him hesitantly, as if she didn't want to inflict any pain, and when she bent her legs to settle on the end of his bed, she stole one gander at his feet and decided against sitting. She stood nearby, but came no closer. "You're really hurt," she observed. Her eyebrows were pinched together as she stared at his scarred toes, shredded clothing, and wounded face. "They stitched you up. What happened?"

Quentin brought his free hand up to his forehead and then to his cheek, where he remembered he'd been lacerated by some branches. She was right; stitches were knitted into him. "I...uh..." he started. "Well, you know."

"No, I don't," Frances said. "I don't remember a thing. Neither does Marina." She crossed her arms. The room was really dark, and Quentin failed to see the features of her face. "It's weird that they treated you, don't you think?" she asked. "They stitched your cuts after kidnapping you. Why would they do that?"

Marina rattled Quentin's other arm around. "Kidnappings occur for two reasons only," she said as she worked. "One, for the purpose of fulfilling perverted fantasies. Two, for the purpose of having something of high value, be it for ransom or...you get the gist."

"I don't think we're of high value," Quentin argued shyly. "Maybe this has something to do with the drug bust, like we were seen as guilty or something." His eyes finally adjusted to the dark. He wasn't blind to the sidelong glance Frances sent to Marina.

"Hardly," Marina dismissed. "That wouldn't explain Ewan. Or the child."

"What?"

Marina undid the final lock and swiftly removed the pin. The restraints fell apart under his arm. "Speaking of which," she said, "I should get to them too. The girl first, though."

Quentin looked to Frances inquisitively, who nodded and came closer to him. She helped him rise up off the bed by pressing a hand to his back and balancing him when he slowly stretched his legs to the side. His feet touched the ground. To sit up and lean forward, technically unmoving, was a challenge of its own. His limbs were tingly and his toes had fallen asleep, all sore as he rested them on what was a tile surface. The monitor at the foot of his bed belatedly took note of either his waking or his absence from the mattress. He watched as the computer provided a final beep before silencing itself altogether; his vital signs were wiped from the screen.

"It's a weird machine," Frances said. "We noticed that removing the needle wakes us up, but it also seems to be tied to the heart monitor."

"But if the fluid makes us sleep, how did you guys wake up in the first place?" Quentin asked.

Frances shrugged. She appeared equally baffled. "Marina said the needle wasn't in her arm. Only next to her."

"That's weird."

"No, it isn't," said Marina from the other side of the room, where she purportedly aided a little girl. "There was a hole in my arm when I woke up. This looks like too carefully orchestrated a plan for them to have missed a needle. Or, for that matter, the pin that was in my hair."

Quentin saw Frances try to surreptitiously notice his outward panic, how he poorly masked that his head was spinning. She held out her arm for him to grab, which he did, and she helped him up from the edge of the bed. He thought it an odd interaction, with her being the chivalrous one and he the drowsy damsel in distress. But, odd as he thought it was, he found that the enormity of his stature and heavier weight didn't stop him from depending on her. Whatever was in that sedative, the fluid, its effect was merciless on his body; his lungs were tense as he breathed and his fingers were twitching uncontrollably, like a slow dose to death coursed through his veins. When his feet floundered and his legs felt like they were about to give out and crash to the floor, Frances simply assured him that it was all normal. *Some normal*, he thought. It took minutes for them to bring him to the head of his bed from where he had been sitting at the center, as his legs kept flopping and caving, and he gripped her extended arm even more tightly; he felt bad about his grip, but she showed no indication of it paining her. When they approached the top of the bed, he was no longer enraptured by his limbs. He was finally free to take in the room around him and view it as a whole, just like Marina had told him not to do. The lighting was scarce, with but a single, orange light, like the one behind him, lodged into the topmost, tile panel of each corner's walls. Four beds neighbored his, all spread around to form one widespread circle in the core of the chamber. His eyes traveled and his mind strayed as well, because between the soft, tangy color of the shielded bulbs and the unique, hexagonal shape of the room, he couldn't help but think he was imprisoned in some sort of menacing honeycomb.

Quentin saw no door. His shoulders turned toward Frances, who looked even more fatigued up close. "Is there an exit?" he asked.

"Over there," Frances said. With her index finger, she pointed to a wall diagonal from where they slow-walked.

Quentin refocused on what he first perceived as a rectangular shadow of one of the beds, but, after some intent staring, he realized that it was three-dimensional. There were indents to the lines, divots from the cracks of where it was pushed in. It was strategically imperceptible, had been less apparent from the lack of a handle.

"We tried to push it," Frances said, "but we couldn't get it to budge. We'll have to try something else."

They moved over to Marina and the bed where she operated. Frances helped Quentin scuttle along the head of the portable furniture piece to peek around it and confirm the presence of the other oddity they had previously spoken of; that a child was in their midst. And indeed, one was. Like Quentin had been when he was unconscious, she was on her back and her tiny, extremely tiny, form was hidden chest-down by the large, fluffy blanket provided to her. She couldn't have been more than six years of age—he knew that as soon as he saw her. He kneaded his eyes with his knuckles to rid them of his dotted vision and take in the child, to make out the cluster of freckles on the sides of her nose and cheeks, the brown complexion, and hair that was fanned around her face on one of the three pillows; her waves and coils were more pronounced than Frances's.

Frances helped Quentin down to one side of the girl's bed. He sat and collected his breath. He felt like he was uselessly occupying the area as Marina undid the hinges on the little girl's first shackle while Frances began to remove the needle from her arm. Marina transitioned to the other side and he witnessed that, even on this much younger subject, Marina was unforgivingly rough in her provisioning of aid. Frances, however, was incredibly gentle when withdrawing the needle, and when one neat line of blood slipped out from where the metal poker had been, she took the end of her own shirt and temporarily wrapped the area. Connected by her garment to the girl, Frances sat and waited out the absorption time until she suspected the bleeding had subsided. She unknotted her shirt from the child's arm and used it a second time to dab the area until dry.

The girl woke many minutes later, when Marina and her overused, even flimsier bobby pin were nearly finished undoing the second pair of restraints and the other two, older individuals were sitting on the edge of the bed. The tiny human shook and gasped as she glanced from Quentin, who was dumbly watching her waken, to Marina, who was doing the exact same to the girl's wrist as she had done to Quentin's. But after, the girl's hazel eyes met the emerald ones of Frances, and whether it was for that reason or another, the girl began to calm down. Frances was a calming figure. A pretty one too, Quentin recognized quite guiltily; he felt fairly immature that in his first hour awake following the madness that had swept him into there, into that dark and dreadful place, he still couldn't resist the carnal instinct of noting her attractiveness. But he must not have been alone in perceiving that truth, because the child instantly displayed an outright partiality to Frances. The little girl was mesmerized by the glowing, green pupils that shone bright and welcoming despite the otherwise palpable misery spread over Frances's face.

Frances gifted a small, sad smile. She ran tender fingers through the curls she could reach from the girl's storm of wild hair, whispering that everything was all right and that she was safe with them, the older kids. But, per the moistening of Frances's left eye, it was evident that she didn't believe a single word that was coming out of her own mouth.

Marina slipped the child's left wrist out of her final restraint.

"I'll be right back," Frances told the fourth conscious prisoner. "I promise." After her assurance, she joined Marina to take care of Ewan.

Quentin didn't feel the need to follow suit and contribute to waking Ewan. It wasn't like he could ask Ewan anything, seeing as how everyone was made mute after the removal of the sedative. Instead, Quentin sat on the edge of the girl's bed and poorly mimicked Frances's soothing statements of how things would be fine and that they were in good company. The little girl didn't believe him. It was certainly smart of her not to, and he couldn't blame her. He was a horrible liar. As she wheezed in and then coughed out, the cynicism in her eyes was nothing short of mature. She was uncomfortably far from childlike, and she made him feel ashamed of himself for thinking he could comfort her as well as his predecessor. He'd ruined the fallacy Frances tried to create for her.

"Quentin," he said a couple minutes later, when the girl's breathing was more regular and the twitching of her fingers less continual. "That's my name," he told her.

The tips of her fingers were all he could see of her hands as she hid them under the blanket, which she struggled to grasp due to her shakiness. The cynicism disappeared from her owlish eyes. "Fatima," she hoarsely said back, her voiced aged from her cracking throat. *"But my dad calls me Faith,"* she whispered afterward, like it was hers and Quentin's secret.

He felt his lips tug up a bit.

Fatima looked forlornly to her right, clearly trying to locate the friendly, green-eyed girl from before. "The one with the nice eyes, that was Frances," Quentin knowingly said to Fatima. He said it to her quickly, for fear of Frances overhearing him.

Fatima's fat cheeks dimpled as she yawned cavernously, but she never once looked away from where she knew Frances was, even though she was out of sight.

"The other's Marina," Quentin added, but Fatima gave no reaction to that fact.

Ewan's waking was par for the course; slow, cough-laden, and painful. As he recuperated, Marina's pin split from all the twisting and turning pressure she had applied when removing his first shackle. She frustratedly had to battle the second one with the salvaged halves of what had been her only utensil. The removal period for the last restraint took much longer than any other, but with dutiful fastidiousness, she did manage to extricate Ewan. He asked a lot of questions when his breathing returned to normal, and they were questions to which no one knew the answers. He asked about things that were miles beyond anyone else's knowledge and he refused to move out of his bed, even when he became relatively stable. He was selfishly tone-deaf to the fatigue of his counterparts.

"Did you have to wake him?" Marina asked Frances. The more miffed she became, the more the tip of Marina's small nose scrunched. "Carrying him comatose as dead weight would've been easier than trying to walk out of here with him conscious."

"Don't say that," Frances said disapprovingly. "You don't mean that."

Quentin thought Marina did, though.

It was Ewan's bed which they all crowded around. After that last shackle, Marina sat beside his blanketed feet and Frances made herself comfortable by his right hip. Quentin and Fatima made their way over hand-in-hand, since it was his turn, as the fully recovered one, to help the disadvantaged. The bed was large, but once Quentin placed her on top of it, she sat herself on Frances's lap as if they had known each other for years and had always sought comfort in one another. Frances was surprised, but her arms gradually wrapped around the girl's waist. Quentin settled by one of Ewan's shoulders.

Ewan asked no more questions.

Marina stared down into the abyss that was the white blanket in front of them.

Fatima fell asleep in Frances's arms.

Quentin brought one leg up and placed his chin on his knee.

He knew it didn't quite hit them earlier, when they were distracted by the frenzy of coming to and then reuniting with some of the most unexpected figures in their lives, several familiar and one not so. But as they sat among themselves in a prolonging quiet, the depths of their real-life nightmare gradually grew more apparent.

When they did speak, it became clear that no one knew much of anything, save for Quentin. But, even then, it was only in the most rudimentary sense. He was the only one who was awake that previous night. At one point during the low-toned conversation, he felt compelled to share that fact with the other captives. He told them as much information as he could salvage from memory of that last conscious night of his, from the suited figures in the hallway of his home to the unneeded presence of Lucas. Quentin was vigorously chewing his bottom lip as he tried to think back and remember the exact moment before he and Lucas were separated from each other.

"…And then, one guy told the other to put Lucas back in the house," Quentin said. "They…They said something about not having an order for him."

Ewan laid back against the pillows. "Like, a court order?"

"I don't know. They didn't say. They put Lucas back in the house, though—said that he wasn't needed or something."

Marina was contemplatively silent.

"How do we even get out of here?" Frances asked.

"None of us can kick the door down singlehandedly," Ewan said with brief disappointment before continuing, "but I'm sure we could make it work, if together we pound the thing."

"You think we could?" Quentin asked doubtfully.

"Combined, we should be okay. If we use some brute force and put our pent-up anger towards our kidnappers to good use, we should be savvy."

"But how, though?" Quentin insisted. "We can barely walk, never mind kick a door down."

"We'll rest up for a bit, then kick it down somehow," Marina said. "We already stopped shaking a while ago. We just need to recharge."

The back of Ewan's head sank deeper into the pillow behind him. "God, it feels like I died three days ago," he said.

"Who even knows how long we've been asleep," Frances said. "For all we know, it has been days."

"That…" Ewan scratched his eyebrow. "There's some truth in that."

"I just assumed it was last night," Quentin said, "because look at me. My stitches are fresh and my feet are barely healed."

Ewan looked up at Quentin's head. "There are leaves in your hair, too."

"Exactly."

"At least we can rule out a court order," Marina concluded. "No one's gassed before a trial."

"You sound kinda sure of yourself," Quentin remarked.

"I mean, her dad is an attorney," Ewan reminded him. "She would know."

"This is not how it works," Marina upheld with a dark eye toward Quentin. "Besides, you said their uniforms had no badges or logos."

"So where does that leave us?" Frances asked. "If not lawful authorities, then who?"

Ewan toyed with a loose string of his comforter. "Sex-trafficking, maybe."

Quentin recoiled and responded with a disgruntled glare.

"Thank you, Ewan," Marina said dismissively. "But where you're wrong is that traffickers love children of all ages, so that wouldn't explain not needing Lucas. And that's not likely. Look at this place. Look at the equipment. A high budget was spent on this prison…Whatever it is."

"Medical equipment is really expensive," Frances concurred. "Mom always talks about how her hospital likes to bill patients excessively just to recover the equipment costs."

"Remind me never to go there again," Ewan quipped.

"If we even can go home again," Marina said with her customary flatness.

Things were quiet again. Frances absentmindedly drew circles on Fatima's elbow. Another few minutes passed and Frances expectantly looked to Quentin and Marina, as if thinking they would say something, but they didn't. Ewan kept occupying himself with the comforter string, pulling it longer and longer. Fatima's crackly snores echoed throughout the room.

"Billionaire sex-traffickers have money," Ewan said into the silence. "And they're weird."

"Can you chill it with the sex-trafficking idea?" Quentin asked.

"I'm just saying."

"Well, don't if that's what you're gonna keep mentioning."

Ewan harrumphed into his collarbone.

"It is curious, though," Marina said. She stopped herself for a moment. "Were your parents home?" she asked Quentin.

"I don't know," Quentin answered honestly. "I know they didn't want Lucas, but for all I know they wanted my parents, too, and had already taken them into the van."

Marina reclined against the portion of the bed frame in front of Ewan's feet. "If they didn't want your parents and, as you said, they already knew the layout of your home, that may make things simpler to comprehend," she said.

"Why's that?"

"Because it could mean that your parents were complicit."

Quentin's glare instinctively made its way back across his face. "You don't know what you're talking about," he said.

"I don't," Marina affirmed. "I'm just making an inference."

"Didn't you just call out Ewan for being unrealistic?" Quentin asked. "Don't be a hypocrite."

"Don't be obtuse," Marina retorted. "They knew the layout of your home. They didn't want your brother. I don't care how deeply your parents sleep, they'd definitely hear two men walking into their bedroom. Whoever these people are, these kidnappers, they didn't invest this much time, effort, and money into us because they're some clan of child predators trying to lock teenagers in their basement. And your parents certainly wouldn't have agreed to that."

Frances worriedly bit at her bottom lip. It wasn't graceful or tantalizing like Quentin had once envisioned it to be, but toothy and painful looking. She truly was gnawing at skin to relieve some stress, and there wasn't any appeal in it like the way the films he had watched always romanticized such actions to be on female faces. When she quit tearing at her skin, she asked Marina, "Do you think it's something on, like, a government level?"

"Okay, that's crazy," Quentin said. "I'm sorry, but what would any of us have to do with the government? Plus, how do you know my parents weren't just scared and didn't want to fight? Or maybe they weren't home."

Marina's eyes bore back into his. She looked dismissive. "If your parents conveniently weren't home in the middle of a work night, which was the very night a horde of heavily-armed men showed up to your house, doesn't that just prove me right?" She folded her hands together and let them fall onto her thighs. "Besides, I never said government. She did," she said, glancing to Frances.

"But now that you mention it," Ewan said to Frances at first, and then to the rest of them, "these people sure have a lotta power."

"This is just a crazy theory we need to stop holding onto," Quentin argued. "They're just kidnappers. Why do you think our phones ping us with statewide alerts every month? This stuff just happens. You don't know that it's some bigger issue."

"Of course I do, Hanson," Marina said. "We all do. You do, too, by the way. You just like lying to yourself for some reason."

"What is that supposed to mean?"

"I just said what it means."

Quentin crossed his arms in front of his chest. "I'm not lying to myself. I'm the son of my parents and I know they wouldn't let someone kidnap me, whether they were paid off or not."

"All right." Marina nodded. Her lower neck muscle flexed just once. "Here's one inference you may be able to swallow. How about, in exchange for you, your parents were promised the continuation of their lives and your brother's?"

"You're just scraping the bottom of the barrel now," Quentin said.

"But Marina is right about one thing," Frances supported the other young woman, "and it's that our kidnappers are clearly financially powerful or backed."

Ewan nodded. "Yeah and everyone knows, like, this is basic knowledge, but the government does all kinds of cagey shit at the top when no one's looking, like, you know, war-mongering, secret investment deals, proxy killings...We've been in social studies class long enough to know this. I wouldn't be surprised if this is some stupid draft experiment or something."

"We do live in the perfect town for it," Frances mumbled into Fatima's hair. "We're surrounded by forest. No one outside of Shaw would notice a difference."

Quentin rolled his jaw. "Governments protect people," he said.

Ewan scoffed. "I mean, yes, but they still gotta test stuff in order for their plans to actually work. We're probably part of some test."

Marina's face hadn't changed from its impassive state. "If you think the government always protects people, then that's a delusion if I've ever heard one. No matter how free a country says it is, the government can always swoop a hand into the masses and pick any one of us as some lab rat. Yes, our country has done things that have made our land prosperous and free, but high ranks always have a way of secretly getting to people without being seen. I'm not an anarchist, but don't be so stupid as to think that it's clean at the top."

Ewan nodded again, and vehemently. "Look, behind closed doors everyone knows that if you don't obey, the world will wake up to a headline the next morning describing your mysteriously sudden apology in spite of how much you meant what you said. Like, this one time, this guy—"

"Stop it," Quentin said through ground teeth. "This is insane. You're both insane. We are literally going to be fine. The authorities will come, and they'll take us home. Stop theorizing about things you don't understand."

"But the thing is, I do understand," Marina said. "More than you ever would. Here's an anecdote and please, don't take it with a grain of salt. Four years ago this beloved government of yours—a specific political party, actually—came running to my father, asking for information on a loan shark who had dirt on a senator who was on their side. And do you want to know why they asked my father about said shark? It was to kill him. Apparently, that senator and a diplomat of ours had some dealings with a North Korean business executive before the senator was up for reelection, and he used that exact same corruption money for his campaign. But his party was the minority at the time and they wanted to be the majority. So, just in case the shark felt like talking any time soon, they added him to the list of possible threats against the senator's image. So, no, we are not protected."

Quentin swallowed emptily, as there wasn't even saliva in his mouth any longer. "I didn't know your dad was…I just…I'm sorry. I really didn't know."

"No one does," Marina said rather calmly. "And after I accidentally found out, my dad literally made me sign a nondisclosure agreement or else he'd legally disown me, like I was some competing law firm trying to get something on him. I only found out two years later that minors can't be bound by contracts."

"That's why people are happy," Ewan said. "That's why the economy thrives. That's why people spend their days going to work despite their unhappiness. If people knew these things, things that made them call their misery into question and made them doubt what they're serving, then the country would fail. People would gather in the streets and riot. We're supposed to go about our lives and frolic in shit like work and school and get distracted by that. Every government's seedy, it's just a matter of whether or not they can cover up their sins."

Quentin pressed his crossed arms more tightly against himself. He looked childish and he knew it, even without a mirror to show him. He knew the pout of his lips was immature and that the crossing of his arms was some form of a self-constructed cage to shield himself from Marina and Ewan. He felt even younger, almost infantile, when he muttered out, "You just want to believe that."

Marina huffed. She was exerted by him and they hadn't even been awake for a full hour. "Quentin, why would I want to believe that?" she asked. "Believe me, I'd prefer nothing more than to wake up from this dream and have breakfast with my hungover, bitch mother, but that isn't going to happen." She made a confused face, one that scrunched up her nose again and pressed her lips against each other. "You're so irrational...so emotional..."

Fatima startled awake from what must have been quite a lucid dream. Marina expressed wonder if perhaps it wasn't a strongly creative imagination that made Fatima jump from her sleep, and Marina lightly questioned her for any details of when she was last awake as well as the most recent events she could remember, clearly trying to rule out a possible PTSD recollection. But Fatima only shook her head and said it was a dream that disturbed her, not a memory of how she had gotten to be in the room with them. In murmurs, she apologized for not being able to help because she neither knew nor remembered anything. Frances pressed forgiving lips to the palm of Fatima's left hand and insisted that her ignorance was fine.

Once again, silence befell them. It was tenser that time around. Quentin avoided Marina's and Ewan's judging gazes. At least, Quentin thought they were judging him. They probably were internally, but not making it known. Marina's head was leaned against her balled-up hand. She was pensively engrossed by the exposed skin of her ankle peeking out from where her pajama bottoms were folded up. Quentin knew it wasn't her ankle she was thinking about, but simply that her eyes had to go somewhere whilst she delved into her ruminations. Ewan returned to his obsessive fascination of twirling the comforter string around his index finger, only to repeatedly unwind it. He sighed a lot, Quentin noticed; Ewan's breathing pattern predominantly comprised of lengthened inhales and absurdly stretched exhales that were somewhat of a cause for concern. Fatima's head was against Frances's chest, right under her clavicle. Frances was preening the girl like a mother orangutan, busying her hands by picking lint and dandruff out of the bed of curls that were propped under her chin. When Ewan lost sight of the string and Frances had no more impurities to fish out of Fatima's hair, the drought of speech turned the already-tense silence into a heavy-aired tedium. They all stared at each other, eyes switching from one person to the next.

Ewan exhaled gruffly. "Fine, let's get on with it," he said, and Quentin thought Ewan's voice sounded deeper than usual.

Putting forward an effort to escape was an inevitability not only for the safety and preservation of their lives, but because the childishness of the elder four inmates glaring at each other had itself become apparent. They discarded their pettiness and forced themselves off the bed. Fatima was excluded from the effort, as she had fallen back asleep. Besides, it wasn't like she could serve much of a purpose.

On the elders' side of things, an extensive bout of stretching took place. Quentin hadn't realized that none of them were particularly athletic and that they were, in fact, severely out of shape. They spent so much time stretching, he actually grew embarrassed every time he failed to reach his toes or bend his spine in a manner which Frances promised would supposedly ease their back pain. He wondered if their adjustment to mobility would have gone more smoothly if they were fitter. Their thinness and lank was due solely to the kindness of their rampant and youthful metabolisms, but none were in peak physical condition with toned legs, muscular backs, and shredded abdominal muscles. It was as if they were kidnapped for their physical vulnerability. Quentin and Ewan were tall and gangly, neither a sportsman nor a gym regular. Frances spent most of her free time studying and partaking in volunteer work, and she really only exercised her body through her triweekly, after-school sports meets. Marina was her father's daughter, which meant she probably didn't waste her time on something as trivial as bettering one's acceptable shape to be further accepted by the athletically robust. Quentin assumed she just ate the right foods and only exercised her mind, like all children of nefarious, corrupt businessmen who were obsessed with the concept of breeding their offspring to replicate themselves.

Quentin wasn't going to estimate the length of time which they were prescribed their unwilling sleep, but he assumed it had been quite a while, because once they were finished with their stretching, they cleared their path of the beds and relocated each one against the walls of the room and found that the task was properly exhausting. They left Ewan's bed in its place; far back enough that it wouldn't obstruct their run at the door, which they still fully intended to knock out.

"There's...something in that...sedative," Frances panted out, grasping at her stomach.

"Yeah...yeah..." Ewan agreed.

Moving the four beds consumed fifteen minutes of their time. By the end of it, they felt like they were dying. None of them verbally questioned how they would manage to derail the door if they could barely breathe and fight the body aches that came just from moving rolling beds, but it ran through their minds. It certainly ran through Quentin's. He tried to brush it off and convince himself that their willpower would return and that they would successfully flee, but flashes of a life he didn't want to live fluttered before his eyes; he saw only the honeycomb room in his vision. Would that actually become his life, that place with those people, his classmates, all of them forever crunched together in that orange-tinted hellhole? His stomach churned and he tried not to think of the possibility any further.

Fatima roused from her sleep and dangled her legs off the edge of Ewan's bed, wondering what she had missed. She stared wide-eyed at the rearranged beds and her hunched-over, older peers. Frances took one of Fatima's hands and said, "We're getting ready to leave the room, Fatima, all of us." Quentin didn't have the heart to tell the girl that they might fail.

Quentin, Frances, Marina, and Ewan positioned themselves as far away from the door as possible, which Quentin guessed was a distance approximately a few feet short of thirty. With all the extra space, they braced themselves, ready to pound the door full-throttle and hold nothing back. Quentin stretched his arms again. Marina dispelled her hair behind her shoulders as she did small jumps in place. Ewan lazily rolled back and forth on the balls of his feet. Frances, with a halfhearted expression, forwent the whole unenthused warmup and stood still, just staring at the door. Ewan counted to three, and they all ran forward. The charge wasn't executed as cleanly as they had anticipated. Quentin's bare feet, still scabbed from the forest scramble, caught on the ground and made him trip. The other three made it to the door, but their endeavor resulted in a series of unsynchronized, wild kicks that flailed into nothingness, each blaming the others for their lame attempt. There was so much quarreling. In the end, it took them five attempts, and not because of the presumed heft of the door, but because they were stubbornly uncompromising; the door itself was actually quite flimsy.

Later, after their skinny legs successfully knocked the barrier down, dust and plaster from the destruction billowed up and around them.

"All that for…that?" Ewan asked incredulously. "The thing's practically made of paper."

Quentin was pleased. He had expected failure. "I'm not complaining," he said.

"Just hope it's our only obstacle," Marina forewarned, dimming the bit of glow in their darkened lives.

Fatima sidled up to the doorway to stand next to them. She knotted her hand into Frances's, who welcomingly held hers back. "Yes, we're leaving," Frances said, as if reading the younger girl's enquiring eyes. "But we have to be quiet."

"I know," Fatima said. "I will be."

Past the doorway, they found themselves in a corridor. Quentin and Marina scanned the area beyond it, in case someone had heard the *"thunk"* of the door and the quiet conversation that followed. Stepping around debris from the collapsed door, he allowed the senses of his feet to determine the material of the floor outside. He felt cement. Cold, undulated cement. And the reason he had to feel rather than see was because the mere act of seeing was rather difficult, as the light panel overhead and fixed into the ceiling was similarly dull to the smaller ones in the room behind him, maybe even a few shades darker. It provided barely enough light for him to discern the corners leading to other corridors, which flanked both his left and right sides. He announced that the area looked clear, and Marina agreed.

The others exited the room and dispersed into the hallway, cautious of the door and the mess of crusted paint and unhinged screws that surrounded it. The corner on their right-hand side was silently elected as the one to approach. When they reached it, Fatima ushered herself up to the front of the gaggle despite the others' protests. She jutted her neck out and around the wall, turning back to them a few seconds later just as they came closer. She said in a whisper, *"Clear."*

Quentin held a hand up as a silent appeal for her to wait just a moment, then he ran back toward their sleeping chamber. He dreaded going back inside, but he was intent on it. He ran to the bed closest to the doorway, the one that was Frances's, and his hands roamed the fluffed comforter and pyramid of pillows, scouring the soft materials until he finally found what he was looking for.

The others stopped tilting their heads in confusion when he rejoined them in the corridor. A small blanket was wrapped around his upper body, specifically the places which his tattered shirt couldn't cover, and in his hand was Frances's used sedative needle. "For defensive purposes," he explained. "Oh, and I was cold," he added, regarding the blanket.

Ewan made the sound of a jeering, *"Shush."* He insisted that they all whisper.

For at least half an hour, they walked through what seemed to them a compound. It was a place of magnificent size, however minuscule it seemed due to the impression its narrow passages gave off. It was jarringly impossible to distinguish one corridor from another, and after leaving the one that led them to their old room, they never came upon it again. Their journey was a miserable one. Ewan was claustrophobic, and while that may have been cumbersome enough on its own, it became clear that he didn't know he had the condition to begin with. Meaning, he knew of no therapeutic methods to ease its effects. They paused a lot because of him, usually in a space between two always-locked doors that looked exactly alike, deep in a hallway that looked annoyingly similar to the one that preceded it.

In the meantime, Fatima fell asleep again. Quentin and Frances each had rotations to carry her so that neither would stress their bodies. Whenever it was his turn, Quentin would slip the used needle into the last, unripped pocket of his sweatpants for safekeeping; part of him was always afraid that it would slip and jab him in the groin, though. He was definitely feeling better, but it did hurt to hold Fatima. He still felt weak, and the cement was harsh on his bare, injured feet. A couple of his toe stitches were undone from the continuous impact of skimming the grating material of the floor.

Ewan, at one point, offered to hold her, and no one expected it, but carrying Fatima had actually pacified his recently discovered fear. The redness in his eyes lessened and his breathing became perceptibly slower.

"Mom always said that helping other people helps her ignore her own pains," Frances said. And then that same, sad smile etched onto her face again before she turned on her heel and kept walking, with Marina. Quentin knew what Frances was referring to, or to whom exactly. Steven Jerins, her father, had died of bone cancer eight years before that interaction with Ewan happened. It never slipped Quentin's mind that the day after her father's funeral, Quentin saw through his dining room window the mother and daughter of the Jerins' household packing their minivan with boxes of clothing and pots of steaming stews. Following the hiatus from school she had taken after the loss of her father, Quentin had asked Frances about it a few weeks later on the school bus. "We went to the pediatric intensive care unit, where mom works," she had told Quentin, "and then we went to an orphanage in New Hampshire. Apparently my father grew up there. I didn't know that, though. She was right. In helping others, I wasn't so distracted by Dad."

The half-hour of walking extended to a full one. They found areas which they confidently knew they hadn't encountered before. Some corridors were well-lit, their lights almost blinding, but others were completely lacking in brilliance. If Quentin was being honest, he thought the place looked abandoned, which made him doubt the notion that Marina's sedative was intentionally extracted from her arm. Due to their lack of progress, he was going to float the idea of resting, but he swore he heard something—something that wasn't quite a pitter-patter but not quite a thud. And it was close by. It wasn't the ventilation system above them, the one that ceaselessly expelled hot air from its vents into every inch of every corridor. No, it sounded uncomfortably synonymous to his own footfalls.

Quentin stopped walking, and everyone stared at him. He pressed his left index finger to his lips, until the rest of the group understood his message and they all halted near the end of a corridor, close to the next corner.

A *"scritch"* sound came from around the corner, and they all heard it.

Quentin was at the forefront of the pack, Marina at the rear. She gesticulated to the pointy utensil visible through his gray pockets. He waved her off and fumbled his hand inside to grab it, but he slipped, and he accidentally poked himself with the end of it. He brought his hand up to his mouth, licked the site of the cut.

Over Fatima's head, Ewan mouthed, "Hurry up."

Quentin nodded. He tried to dismiss his own weakness and fear so that, a moment later, he stood with his right hand up in the air, the needle held tightly in his rolled-up fingers, and his thumb lightly pressed against the plunger.

The unmistakable sound of scratching against cement came closer.

Quentin was not going to be weak. He was not going to cave in on himself. It would be customary of him to flee at the last minute, but he was the one who had the idea to bring the needle, thus it was his responsibility to act with it.

There came another scratch, and another after that one. And then again and again, right on the other side of the wall.

Quentin pounced around the corner. He didn't know why, perhaps it was so he wouldn't have to experience watching himself get struck first, but his eyes were closed. He wasn't looking and he was shaking, terrified, but he went absolutely feral. He swung his arms around, and the needle along with them. Confident that he was committing some damage, he dug up enough courage to open his eyes. Amid the swinging of his arms, the mayhem he started, the first and only thing he saw was a bicep; an exposed, burly bicep all for his picking. He jammed the tool in his hand into that one, evil bicep.

There was screaming. It didn't emanate from the person he attacked, though. It came from Frances, who had a hand over her mouth. She looked horrified. "Quentin, what did you do?!"

Ewan was gawking. Marina rolled her eyes. Fatima stayed asleep. Their reactions enraged Quentin. Who were they to judge him for his brutality? They had no idea what he'd been through in order to get into that compound. He had no regret whatsoever for lodging the needle into the mystery assailant's arm. In fact, he was warming to the idea of turning back around, pulling the needle out, and sticking it into one of his kidnapper's eyeballs. He spun on his feet to see his victim, to see whose bicep he had defiled and—

His stomach turned. Guilt had always activated that form of a reaction from him. He didn't look to his victim's face, only to the bloodied bicep area with the needle crammed in deep at an awkward angle. His eyes quickly trailed lower, drawn to a thing next to the male's arm. Quentin couldn't resist, couldn't help but notice that, on the shirt of the convulsing person, there was a wrinkled, faded print of the *Mickey Mouse* cartoon, *Steamboat Willie.*

9

Quentin's throat dried when he met the eyes that belonged to the tan face of the person crouched before him, who was clutching their arm. Their physique was burly, with large hands that felt around the injured area. They wore checkered, red-and-green pajama bottoms and, indeed, a printed *Mickey Mouse* tank-top that hung loose down their chest and under their armpits. But not even the levity of the illustration which the sailing mouse conveyed could have possibly lessened the vehement fury on the face of the shirt's owner.

"I'm...I'm so sorry," escaped from Quentin's mouth. "I didn't mean...I thought...Mathias, I'm so sorry..."

"Frances!" screeched a girl behind the foul-faced, snarling young man on the floor. It was Roxy Thompson, one of Shaw High School's junior students. She leaped around the young man crouching, ran past Quentin, and threw her comely, blushing face into Frances's left shoulder. All that was visible of Frances was a mesh of her short, brown waves interlacing with Roxy's long, chestnut locks draped over bare shoulders that were exposed from her flimsy, purple camisole.

Frances cried tears of joy. "What are you doing here?!" she asked.

"God, I dunno! I'm so glad you're here, though," Roxy said wetly, as tears of her own dropped into her mouth. "Are you guys okay?"

"Oh, Mathias," Frances said, breaking from the distraction. She pulled away from her friend to look at the person below, on the floor. "Are you all right?"

Mathias didn't say anything. Quentin didn't either. They stared at each other, the former bearing a gaze that was grimly fixated on the latter, who was batting his lids anxiously and contemplating whether or not he should scram around the corner and run for his life. Mathias kept his eyes on his quivering assailant as he rotated and yanked the needle out of his bicep. He inhaled a breath, unblinking. He clenched his jaw, then circled his hand firmly around the needle. Quentin thought he might just cry and didn't care how embarrassing it would have been if he did.

"What...the fuck?" Mathias very slowly asked through gritted teeth.

"I-I-" Quentin struggled to speak.

Mathias's hand was firm around the needle. "If you're not running in five seconds," he said tightly, restricting his rage, "I'm gonna shove this thing right up your ass, Hanson."

"You'll have to excuse his idiocy," Marina said. "He assumed you were one of our kidnappers. Evidently he was incorrect."

Mathias looked to her, and Quentin finally exhaled once Mathias's attention was directed toward someone else—someone who wasn't him. "Was he?" he asked Marina with barely concealed anger. "Was Hanson incorrect? Was this little shit incorrect, Marina? Did this fucker stick a used needle into my fucking arm when he didn't even open his eyes to see who the fuck I was? Is that the case, Marina?"

Marina's eyes were expressionless, as always. "In his defense, it made a good weapon. He had the right idea. On the bacteria front, you have nothing to worry about." She reconsidered her words. "Well," she said, "unless Frances has AIDS or something."

Quentin grimaced.

Mathias's eyebrows formed an irate line. "You know," he said, "you are one twisted shit, Gustavsson. You are fucking crazy. Has anyone every told you that? You are psychotic."

"Nice shirt by the way," Ewan said.

"Quentin?" a small voice emerged. A boy of above-average height and an incredibly, almost worryingly, lean figure came into view as he walked around Mathias, who had returned his eyes to Quentin. The boy brought himself to a standstill once he disrupted all the tension by standing between the two. Quentin almost didn't recognize him; he had a face that was identical to how it was when they last saw each other, but the same didn't apply to his stature.

"Athol?" Quentin asked.

"Yeah, it's me," Athol said smilingly.

"Dude. You're tall."

All the cheer disappeared from Athol's face and his smile dropped. "I know. I think we've been out for a while." He pointed to Quentin's face. "What happened to you?"

"Tried to run for it. Emphasis on tried."

Athol smiled a little. It was one much smaller than the last, but he was amused.

Quentin looked past Athol, where he saw a towering, spiky-haired boy tiredly leaned against the wall. His eyes were veiled by a pair of shaded glasses, ones which were rumored to have aided his struggle against color-blindness. His feet were the only pair that had shoes on them. He lifted an open-palmed hand and waved languidly to Quentin and the others behind him.

"When did you guys wake up?" Ewan asked the other hallway wanderers.

"Roughly an hour ago," Roxy said, thinking.

"We saw your mess," Athol said somewhat excitedly and motioned backwards, over his shoulder. "We must've just missed you guys. Our room was right next to yours."

"Have you been able to find your way back there?" Ewan asked. "We haven't gotten back to that area once."

"Yeah, a couple times. This place is huge."

"Excuse me," Mathias interrupted. Quentin flinched. He watched as Mathias rose to his feet; he wasn't quite as tall as Jaymes, Athol, and Quentin, but he was close to it. "I am not done here," Mathias said purposefully, like he had some sadistic plan he wanted to enact.

"You do heroin," Marina said. "You can handle some Frances blood."

Roxy looked confused. "What's this?" she asked. Quentin envied her oblivion, how she didn't have to endure the events of his last, conscious morning.

"Mathias, let it go," Frances tried to say with force, but she shook a little at the end. Her statement sounded more like a plea than an order. "This is all beside the point."

"And what is the point?" Mathias questioned.

"That we're all reunited, I guess," Jaymes sighed, not sounding convinced by his own words. He pushed himself off the wall and walked closer to the huddle.

Mathias remained outraged. "Hey, Chen, until this little asshole here stabs you with a needle, keep your mouth shut."

Jaymes was unfazed. "This is coming from the one who said he'd kill the first person he saw."

"Yeah. Saw, as in see. With my eyes. Hanson didn't even take a look, just started swinging."

"Well, you seem fine to me," Jaymes said.

"Whatever," Mathias grumbled.

"So, same story as ours?" Ewan asked.

Athol nodded. "Woke up in a room like yours. We actually looked into yours, by the way. And, ditto. All of it. Same equipment. Same beds. Same needles. I was the only one who didn't have a needle in my arm, though. But for the most part, same scenario."

"No coincidences," Ewan snarked.

"What?"

"Nothing," Quentin said.

"Yeah, so. Yeah," Athol said awkwardly. "Well, I didn't know what to do. I was facing Roxy and saw a bobby pin by her pillow and found two more in her hair. I used them to pick the wrist cuffs that were holding everyone down."

Roxy nodded affirmatively. But then she frowned. "He said he got them from me, but I don't use bobby pins."

Quentin didn't risk taking a gander at Ewan's face, which was likely to have been very proud that far into the conversation. Athol's tale was probably feeding that beast, since Quentin thought Ewan a conspiracy theorist in more ways than one.

To Quentin's surprise, Ewan didn't further enquire on the details of the other group's waking or their self-guided hallway tour.

Granted some silence and time to introduce herself, Marina ambled over to France's friend. "I'm Marina Gustavsson," she said to Roxy. Marina said it factually, unemotionally. Her name really was just a fact, and not that common courtesy was relevant in their predicament, but the absence of a smile or an extended hand made the introduction more strained than it should have been.

Roxy was confused, but she forced a smile. It wasn't an inauthentic or demeaning one, but it was likely a matter of her not expecting to be introduced to her fellow inmates so formally. Her long face softened and her lips turned up. "I'm Roxy, hi," she responded shyly. Quentin didn't know if she was deliberately speaking differently than she had a few moments earlier or if it was her delayed, natural voice, but he started to detect the distinct lift of tone and stretching of her final words at the end of her sentence as the west coast "valley girl" dialect—a dialect, which, once upon a time, was exclusive to the San Fernando Valley area near Los Angeles.

Marina's eyebrows lifted and turned jagged. "Roxy," she recited.

Roxy nodded. She pressed her pink lips together and rubbed the puffy skin line attached to her lashes; she had definitely spent a fair amount of time crying earlier. "Yes, Roxy," she reaffirmed. "Well, Roxy Thompson."

"Roxy, you say?" Marina asked. She stared, blinked, and kept staring. "Roxy's a porn star name."

Ewan's hands flew out, clearly wanting to ask about what exactly he was listening to.

Mathias huffed.

"Oh, um," Roxy stumbled over her words. "Well, I mean. No. It's normal." She fought out a laugh.

Marina leaned one shoulder farther out than the other; a minuscule show of encroachment on Roxy's space. "Is it short for anything?" Marina asked. "Roxanne? Roxanna?"

Roxy gave another contrived laugh. "I mean, it's not just Roxy. It's Roxy *Thompson*."

Marina scanned Roxy in a once-over. It was something Quentin had seen a number of girls do to one another in his time. After all, lag sessions between classes made breeding grounds of jealousy within their high school corridors. He was familiar with the judgmental squint of Marina's eyes as she inspected the flowing, chestnut hair that swooped down Roxy's back; her slim, muscly back that had a slight, inward curve near the bottom, above her shapely hips. He, too, saw the skin of her shoulders and the tops of her defined breasts showcased by sleepwear that left little to the imagination. The entirety of the moment was easy to dissect; it was just two, young females meeting for the first time, and Marina was, presumably, jealous.

"So do you think there are more groups like us?" Jaymes asked.

"Not my problem," Mathias said.

"Not mine either," Ewan agreed.

"That's pretty horrible," Frances ridiculed. "We should search for them."

Mathias flung the needle out of his hand without direction, not caring where it went. It hit Fatima, who had woken and was standing up. Luckily, he only hit her with the blunt end, where the plunger was located. She jumped back and circled her arms around one of Frances's thighs.

"Fuck," Mathias said. "I could use some blow."

"Is there ever anything else on your mind?" Marina bit.

"Oh, believe me, unrepentant bitch, there is," Mathias said. "It's the pain going up my arm from Faggot's needle. The least he coulda done was slip some morphine in there first."

"Knock it off with the slur shit, dude," Jaymes said. "Now—"

"Oh, '*The slur shit,*'" Mathias said mockingly. "Jaymes, shut the fuck up. You have no idea what I just went through."

"Look, I'm sorr—" Quentin started.

"You shouldn't be," Marina said.

"But I am," Quentin insisted.

"Well, don't be."

"Know what?" Mathias's hands went to his hips. "Fuck you all."

"Hey, excuse me," Jaymes said, "but as I was trying to say,

should we search for other groups? What if there are a lot more here somewhere? They could still be unconscious and vulnerable."

"*Or,*" Mathias said, "they could already be chopped up into little bits and buried in the ground. In which case, what's the point? Just a waste of time."

"Stop it," Frances said, stone-faced. "Stop being so cruel."

"Not funny, asshole," Ewan berated.

"We can't stick around," Athol said. "Don't get me wrong, I want to find anyone else who might be here. But, at the same time, it might be dangerous."

"Might?" Ewan repeated. "Athol, look at Quentin's face! Who's to say they're not gonna do that to us too?!"

"They didn't do this to me," Quentin said. "Not quite."

"Maybe we'd be better at saving others by finding a way out," Jaymes proposed. "We get away as far as we can and go to the authorities for help. We need to get the word out about this place."

"Except that the authorities will hand us right back to these people," Marina said.

Quentin was so tired of her. He scoffed.

"What, still don't believe me?" Marina asked.

Ewan cleared his throat. "We're under the impression that the people who took us have some sort of dominion over our parents and can skirt the authorities. Or that they just straight up own the authorities."

"I'm not under that impression," Quentin denied. "You guys are."

"It's a reasonable impression," Jaymes said, much to Quentin's disappointment. "The question is, what do we do if that is the case?"

"More like what can we do?" Ewan corrected.

"We run away," Frances said shakily again. A tear rolled out of her eye.

Mathias bent his head to look down to Frances. "Sure, Fran," he said derisively. "You got a car outside with a bunch of jacked credit cards in it? Because we don't know where the fuck we are, we don't have any money, and we gotta feed nine people."

"Maybe that's true," Jaymes considered, "but we have no choice but to start from scratch."

Marina nodded. "I think we can all agree that's the only realistic thing to do in the short term. Any future we have in the northeast is over. Sometimes my father advises clients to leave everything for a while when the dice are loaded against them." It was a rarity that she spoke so much of her father in the hours since Quentin and the others had woken. Never once had he heard her speak of him before that day.

"Where do they usually go?" Jaymes asked.

"Off-grid places. Places with no phone reception, no houses around for miles. In the worst cases, like murder or human trafficking, countries that don't have decent ties with the US work best."

Ewan rubbed a hand through his hair. "We're screwed. Royally."

"We have each other," Frances murmured. "All nine of us. That has to count for something."

"Fantastic," Mathias grumbled.

With the back of his sweater sleeve, Athol rid some runny snot from his top lip. "So where do we go?" he asked. He attempted to sound casual, but he failed miserably.

"No hotels, motels, or inns," Jaymes said, and then he shrugged. "I'm just spitballing, but I'm assuming that's how it works."

"Nah, you got your head on right," Mathias piped in.

"I went to Alabama once, as a girl," Frances said. "There are houses in open fields with miles of empty land stretched between them. That may be a good option. There's also Detroit. Whole areas of that city, really."

"No, I say we go as south as possible," Marina advised. "The north is too dangerous for us. Canada is way too obvious because it's so close, not to mention our extradition agreement with them is pretty sturdy."

"Whereas Mexico…" Mathias drifted off suggestively.

"A nation perfect for fugitives," Ewan said.

"My father has told clients to go there," Marina said.

"And food-wise?" Frances asked. "Supply-wise?"

"I guess we shoplift," concluded a reluctant Athol.

"Okay, okay," Quentin broke in. "Just hold on. How long do you guys intend on hiding in some old shack, shoplifting from *Walmart,* and living in Mexico? It's…It's not that easy…not that easy at all. And, I mean…Mexico?"

No one paid mind to him.

"In terms of finances," Marina said almost reluctantly, "maybe Mathias could always do some…*stuff* for us to earn cash."

Mathias made a bitter face. "So now you're fine with my dealing? Fuck you, you hypocrite." He sighed. "But yeah, I'm in."

"It could potentially work," Ewan said, "particularly if, and no disrespect, but if we are in Mexico."

"Are we really this desperate?" Roxy asked.

"Yeah," Mathias said. "We are."

Following the discussion, Quentin couldn't even guess just how long his group and the other roamed alongside each other throughout the never-ending array of corridors, but he knew in his heart that it was quite an extensive bout of time. Without a doubt, it was longer than the previous walk. They forwent any attempt of being quiet, probably because they had all suffered a period of going stir-crazy from the long silences and the overthinking. Frances and Roxy were inseparable, Jaymes and Mathias evidently disliked each other but kept speaking for some reason, and Ewan and Athol discovered that they found good company in one another.

About forty minutes into the trek, Fatima detached her hand from Frances's and started tugging on Quentin's blanket. "Do you want to hold my hand?" he asked, although he couldn't understand why she would want to do that. She tugged on the blanket one more time. *"Oh,"* Quentin said, understanding her request. He rid himself of the sheet and draped it over her shoulders. She looked content, and then thanked him by slotting her hand into his.

Mathias asked who Fatima was and why she was there. Frances said that, for the life of her, she had no idea.

The next forty minutes of their roaming was relatively calm, with more than half of the individuals in their lost troop drastically more collected than they were when they first ran into each other. There were no more jitters and chattering teeth from the anticipation of what may occur with every turn of a corner. Bickering, too, became identically scarce, for which Quentin was incredibly grateful; on occasion, one or two would debate over which direction to proceed, and usually Frances or Jaymes would offer their self forward to disband the spurt of conflict. The group's communication became seamless and their quietude was borne from comfort, not anger and frustration.

But, come the end of those forty minutes, the admirable patience and diplomacy began to wear thin for some and then, inevitably, for most. Quentin watched hopelessly as the people around him grew feverish, skittish, and easily pestered. A minority bore that same, imperative self-control from earlier; Marina remained the pragmatist; Frances the compassionate; Jaymes the unbothered and level-headed. But the others lost their way, and Quentin knew why that was happening. He felt the effects of the day toying with him, the fatigue and the heavy breathing and the muscle aches. He felt the dry cement of the ground scratching his skin. He breathed in that air. That heavy, suffocating air. Roxy groaned out a complaint about the recycled air, how it felt like she was never taking in enough oxygen, and that it was potentially clogging her throat; Marina snidely remarked on the impossibility of that. Athol moaned and said that his eyes hurt from the strain of not being able to see anything. Fatima pressed her free hand to her belly and whined about her hunger, how she wanted food; three others soon parroted the pain of their own famine. Jaymes admitted he had a headache.

Quentin offered some reasonably constructive advice once he suspected that they were walking in circles; he encouraged everyone to try to break down another door. They tried it many times, but disappointedly accepted that the materials of the ones that weren't already broken were thicker and firmer, made of metal rather than a flimsy wood.

"Yet another hint that everything was intentional," Ewan clucked, and Quentin wanted to punch him for it.

It didn't help when they estimated that another hour had passed, because Mathias felt it his duty to proclaim the heinously obvious. "We're going in fucking circles," he said out loud with a pause in his steps. He stood ramrod straight with his hands on his hips, scowling.

They were. They really were. Quentin had noticed the repetitive pattern of the doorways and corridors earlier, but excused it by blaming his own headache for making him delusional. He made the mistake of letting that be known.

Mathias snapped his head up. "You what?"

Quentin backed away. "No, no. I didn't know. I just had a hunch."

"Unbelievable, you fuck."

Frances ground her teeth. "Can you stop swearing? It's not just us here."

Mathias snorted. "If you're concerned about the kid, she's already been through some crazy shit. I don't think a few words'll kill her."

Fatima hid behind Quentin's leg.

"Look, can we just keep this thing moving?" Jaymes asked. "We all want to get out of here and there's no use standing around fighting."

"You want to know something else?" Mathias asked. "There's no use walking around and wasting our precious energy, especially when we haven't eaten since...I don't know, but since our last meal." He muttered out, *"Circles. Fucking circles."* His eyes flicked back up to Quentin. "And you knew about it."

"I didn't know anything!" Quentin insisted.

"Keep your voice down, goddammit!" Jaymes shouted, which only made a proper show of his hypocrisy given the volume of his own tone.

"You know, I agree with Mathias," Athol piped up, which earned him a collection of quizzical eyebrow raises. "Yes, I do. It's not the stopping that's getting us nowhere."

"We've been doing nothing but searching," Roxy said. "We're really trying."

"Thank you, Roxy, for providing the most informative insight yet," Marina sneered. "Have you any other useful facts to supply?"

Roxy was startled, but she recovered. "All I'm saying is, and I've said this before to the others, but maybe we should wait. Perhaps we should find out as much as we can."

Mathias hit the side of his head against the wall twice. "Great. This pacifist shit all over again."

Frances was uneasy. "Roxy, I really don't think we should—"

"But think about it," Roxy said. "It's an idea way better than the one we have now."

Marina nodded sardonically. "Yes, and we could just as well slit our wrists right here and surrender to our deaths before they have the chance to kill us themselves. Tell me, Roxy, does the name alone render you a ditz or is it the lingering sedative knocking around your brain cells that's making you talk like this?"

Jaymes sighed.

Roxy was aghast. "My God! Why are you so...so rude?!"

Mathias groaned and smacked his head against the wall one more time. "Never thought I'd say this, but for once I agree with Gustavsson." He motioned to Roxy. "All morning, this bitch's been tryna get us to turn ourselves in."

Roxy wiped her wet eyes.

"Can we please keep it down?" Frances pleaded in a half-whisper. *"Stop using normal voices."*

"Bro, stop whispering," Mathias dismissed. "Literally no one here is whispering anymore."

"Which isn't advisable," Marina rebuked. "Frances is right."

"Wasn't asking for an opinion."

"Hey," Jaymes said, "we're going to get ourselves caught if we keep bickering at each other. Sooner or later they will find us."

Mathias glared over to Roxy. "I wager she'd fancy that."

Roxy flared her nostrils ever so slightly.

With the revived consensus that their immaturities should be set aside, the unionized groups returned to their wonky trail of escape. Nothing in their path changed, though. Doors remained locked, sealed, and strangely sturdy—even the ones Mathias madly barreled himself against with the force of an elephant ramming a tusk into its foe. The ground was still dry, their feet were mostly still bare, and the constant adjusting to the darkness tired their eyes. It was smoother before, Quentin may have even said easier, when they weren't so high strung. But after, the energy and cooperation were strained. Their partnership became as artificial as the repugnant, recycled air around them. They walked and walked, carrying forward on a road to nowhere as their legs ached.

By what must have been afternoon, assuming they had awoken at some point in the morning, a sudden outburst from Mathias halted them again. "It's been two hours and we're still in this goddamn shithole!" he roared. He punched a wall and kicked a doorknob; a doorknob which did not rattle, much to everyone's disappointment.

"Four, actually," Athol said.

"Huh?"

"It's been four hours."

"How do you know that?"

"I've been counting."

"You've been counting? What the fuck is wrong with you, you fucking nerd?"

"Can't help it."

Jaymes scratched his head. "I find it hard to believe that it's been four hours and no one is looking for us."

"Who said they're not?" Roxy asked.

"Thought we were special or something," Ewan drawled. "Well. Screw it. I'm resting."

"Where?" Quentin asked.

"Uh, here." Ewan motioned to the floor and slid himself down to it. His head rolled back against the wall. "Feels good. You should try it."

"Yeah, guys, I'm sorry" Athol said apologetically. "I'm gone." He plonked down to the cement, his flat posterior hitting the ground. He even closed his eyes when he got there.

One by one, they sat down. Fatima and Frances rested next to each other, and Roxy joined them soon after. Mathias did, too. Marina and Jaymes didn't, as they stood in a corner talking to each other, but neither displayed any inclination to keep walking.

Quentin wasn't going to succumb to the fatigue. So they hadn't found a way out? So? There must have been something else they could have done that didn't involve lingering in an open hallway. His feet carried him away more than he premeditatedly abandoned everyone; without even realizing it, he wandered away. Despite Frances's protestations, everyone kept up the loud talking, and it proved useful, since he utilized their noise as a marker to avoid getting lost. He found himself sympathizing with Mathias, realizing that he was in his rights to have been angry earlier. Everything looked the same. Quentin would exit one corridor and wind up in another just like it, except maybe smaller or more torturous from the overheated air that streamed out from the ceiling vents.

Something miraculous did happen, though. Well, Quentin initially thought it miraculous. His afterthought was that the thing at which he was looking was actually quite disconcerting. He knew what it signified: they were not alone. They never were to begin with, but it was made a more obvious fact when he turned one more random corner and saw that, halfway down a passage, one of the doors was left open and facing his way.

Peeking around the corner with everyone later, the sight spurred on some disharmony.

"I say we go for it," Mathias said.

"No," Marina disagreed. "Too easy."

"What's too easy?" Quentin asked.

"She thinks it's a trap," Jaymes elaborated, "and rightfully so, I think."

"We may as well turn ourselves in," Marina said. "It's not worth it.

"I'm going," Mathias fought.

"Mathias," Jaymes groaned out, "do not go pulling this stuff right now. This isn't about you. This is about everyone, all of us, and we agreed to escaping."

"And if it's another group of kids or something? You saying we ditch them?"

Quentin was confused. "Weren't you literally just voting against that?"

"How do we know it's a trap?" Mathias asked. "These guys have been letting us fuck around in here all day. That's totally another group of prisoners."

"No," Marina said. "If it were prisoners like us, they'd be frantic and we'd see them running out already."

"Fine," Mathias said. "Okay. Let's say that *they* are in there. What if this is our chance to fight them?"

"Then we elude them," Marina said. "And we keep trying to get out. And am I the only one who's listening to this?"

"I'm just waiting it out," Athol said.

"I'm going," Mathias determinedly announced. He stalked away and threw himself through the open door of the room in front of them.

Frances and Fatima lingered behind everyone. "Well?" Frances asked.

Quentin made a lazy gesture to the corner behind him. "Well," he said back.

"You're not going to help him?" Frances deduced with an undertone of repulsion, only the slightest touch of it.

Quentin couldn't find it in himself to care anymore, but he knew better than to say that.

Others, however, were less diplomatic.

"If we hear a gunshot from the room, we'll take it as a warning and go the other way," Marina stated.

"Of course we'll go after him," Jaymes said. "We just…Well, we haven't heard anything so I think the coast is clear."

"Or he's already been taken out," Marina suggested.

"Can you not?" Quentin asked her.

"We should take this as a sign," Roxy said. "Maybe they're finally ready to talk to us."

"Roxy, I think they've always been ready to talk to us," Jaymes argued. "It's been a matter of whether or not we want to talk to them, which we don't. Look, we have to make sure Mathias is all right."

"I guess," Ewan said unenthusiastically.

They dithered between the options of either joining Mathias or going their own way. Shame curled into most of them, so they went onward, into the room.

"What do you think is in there?" Quentin asked Marina.

"A fish hook with worms on it," she said.

Quentin never had a chance to inspect the totality of the room upon stepping inside because, once he entered, his face was smothered by hard paper. He grunted and tripped backwards, scratched his eyes, and beheld Mathias triumphantly flourishing a yellow folder in front of him. "Here, you bony bastard," Mathias said and flung the folder to Quentin, who caught it in front of his knees.

"Thanks?" Quentin muttered, looking around.

The space was, in essence, a storage closet. The walls were tightly closed in on each other and were covered from floor to ceiling with hundreds of dark-green drawers, all of which were compressed together. A tall metal cabinet on wheels was in the center; the top of it glowed under another orange light that was fixed into the ceiling of the compartment. A rolling ladder stood by the door.

Mathias walked away from Quentin and repositioned himself on the third step of the ladder. In one hand, Mathias waved another packet of folders for them all to view. He victoriously spoke about how appalling it was that their abductors had possession of what were supposedly medical files, but then started bragging about how he acquired Chris Laney's folder, the one which was in Mathias's hand, and he spoke of how it apparently contained documentation of the recent cure to Chris's chronic case of hemorrhoids.

Jaymes recoiled, but he managed to bring himself forward and tear the files out of Mathias's hands. "That's great," Jaymes commented. "I'll put these away. I'm sure Chris would appreciate it."

"Medical records?" Quentin asked, peering down to the folder in his hands.

"Yeah," Mathias said, "med records." He jumped down from the ladder. "This is fucked up. Take a look for yourself if you don't believe me."

Quentin opened the folder to see a pile of papers clipped together in one corner. He flattened his hand against them and read the family tree that was printed in navy-blue ink across the top layer of the white sheets. He made out his grandfather's name, Arthur, and also saw Agata's. Then there were his mother's and father's. Lucas's. Quentin saw his own name, too. He saw names above those of his parents and grandparents, names of people he just assumed to precede the listed ancestors he recognized. He flipped the page and made out the words "asthma" and "tinnitus."

"Well then," Frances said by the doorway, Fatima beside her on tiptoes, peeking at the papers in Frances's hand. "This just proves our theory right, doesn't it?"

Ewan nodded.

Marina wasn't there to agree; she was the only person who wasn't in the room.

Quentin wasn't going to be sucked into the vortex of temptation any further. He shut his folder and bent down to lift the one, unripped leg of his joggers up to his calf. The bottom of his pant leg had a band inside that made the fabric tighter around his ankle than the rest of his limb, so he balanced the folder against his calf and rolled the sweatpants down, which locked the folder in place.

"We were right," Ewan said. "We've been sold out or something like that. How else would they have access to these documents?"

"We should leave," Jaymes said.

Roxy shook her head. "We can't go now," she objected. "We need to look into this, find out what else they know. We're just getting started, Jaymes. This is clearly the tip of the iceberg."

"An iceberg that I don't wanna be on," Ewan argued.

"Same," Frances agreed.

They turned on their heels, everyone leaving. Roxy sighed and trailed after them.

"We're just not safe here," Jaymes said to them.

Safe, they most certainly were not. It had been a fact that Quentin thought rather obvious, but couldn't have been made more clear when they exited the closet to find Marina standing in the center of the barely illuminated corridor, close enough to touch her counterparts but at the same time too far for them to safely reach her. Her arms hung by her sides. Her face donned its customary look of indifference. She looked like her ordinary self. Except, of course, her circumstances were perilously out of the ordinary. A tall, pale man stood behind her. He was thin with broad shoulders, long-faced but wide-lipped. One wiry hand was on her left shoulder and the other, the flexing other, was beside her right ear and pointing a gun to the side of her motionless head. The revolver shone clear as day in the soft, orange light, and there it stayed as the man met all of their gazes. He had beady, blue eyes that took their time analyzing everyone before him, and his pupils enlarged when he looked down to Mathias's hands and then to Jaymes's underarm.

"Those," the man said to them, nodding at the folders of medical records, "give them to me. Put them in front of her."

"Stay cool, just throwing mine over," Jaymes responded. He flicked his wrist forward, and a string of papers went sailing their way.

Frances kicked her finds forward, and they scraped to a halt in front of Marina's socked feet. Roxy and Athol mimicked Frances's submission and disposed theirs into the middle of the hallway. Ewan had never taken his with him, so he had nothing to return.

Quentin felt his face grow hotter. He was worried that the bulge beside his calf that had been hidden by his one, intact pant leg would be a glaring indication of his commitment of theft, but he was relieved to see that the man wasn't looking at him.

Instead, he focused on Mathias, who was peeved, to say the least. "Yours," their presumed host said to Mathias. "Hand them over."

Mathias refused compliance. He crunched the folder in on itself, crossed his arms, and started tapping his fingers against the hard paper surface.

"Fine," said Marina's holder. He pushed the barrel of his weapon closer against her skin.

"Mathias, just give it!" Frances begged. "Please!"

"I will shoot her," said the aggressor.

"No, you won't," Marina said. "You pursued us, went through so much to get us, and I'm supposed to believe you'll quickly kill one of us off like this?"

"You're not gonna hurt us," Mathias said.

There was no warning. That long-faced, haggard-looking man with white stubble on his chin extended his arm forward and towed back the trigger of the gun. A deafening ring sounded before a lightning-fast bullet ricocheted off the floor and penetrated the wall next to Athol's ankle. He jumped back, accidentally bumping into Fatima, who cried out and hid her face in her blanket, until Frances lifted her back into her arms.

Marina didn't flinch.

"Hey…Hey…" Jaymes started. He put his hands up. "C'mon, they're just messing with you. Just put the gun down. We'll go wherever you want. We'll do whatever you ask. Just…" He bowed his head subserviently. "Just hand her over. That's all we want. We'll do anything you—"

"The fuck I will," an outraged Mathias cut Jaymes off.

"Mathias, please not now," Quentin pleaded. He wasn't ready to see someone's brains get blown onto the walls around them.

"You heard me," Mathias said to the man, "we're not surrendering for shit. You can have her."

"Mathias, shut up!" Jaymes snapped. "Shut the hell up! For once today, just shut your frigging mouth!" He turned back to the man in the middle of the hallway. "Look, just let her go. Please. After that, you can do whatever you want with us."

"Please," Fatima peeped out, and it made Quentin's heart sink.

"I'm fine," Marina said.

"You have a literal gun to your head!" Ewan pointed toward her head.

"Man, just hand her over!" Jaymes pleaded.

Marina huffed out, "Jaymes—"

"We won't ask any questions," Jaymes persisted. "We'll do just as you say. We'll even—"

"Jaymes."

"Just give her back to us, that's all we want. Let her—"

"Jaymes, please stop talking."

Quentin lamely watched the entire exchange, from Jaymes emanating pained pleas to keep alive a classmate he scarcely knew whilst said classmate appeared not to care one bit.

"This is getting ridiculous," Mathias inserted himself back into the scene. He stood behind Quentin and possessed no qualms about shoving him to the side just to be more visible to the man and Marina.

"Mathias, what are you doing?" Roxy asked in a near panic. When he didn't answer, she repeated it more feverishly, in a scream.

"What none of you will," Mathias said and walked right up to the captive and her captor. His bare feet stepped all over the strewn medical records that had been thrown forward. "Ai'ght listen," he addressed their visitor. "Shoot the bitch. Or don't. Stop wasting our time. Or we fuck you up."

Quentin threw his face into the palm of his right hand. He proceeded to watch the interaction through the crevices between his fingers.

"Mathias," Marina said more calmly, "you'll only start a mess we don't need."

Mathias rolled his shoulders back.

"I swear on your useless life, do not do this," Marina said through her lips like a ventriloquist.

"There's more," said the man. He looked directly to Quentin. "Give me your files." Quentin's hand twitched, and he dropped it from his face.

"Hanson, don't you fucking dare," Mathias said threateningly. "You are not being told to do shit. Those are your records and you're keeping them."

The man pressed the gun hard to Marina's ear. She squirmed and made a small sound, but other than that she seemed oddly fine.

Mathias balled up his hands. "Okay, you know what, *GI Joe*? Shoot her if you're so damn motivated. I'd pay to see her dead."

Marina let out an exhausted sigh. "Christ," she said.

"Nice, Mathias," Jaymes said. "Why can't you just stay out of thi—?"

"No?" Mathias asked the man. "Fine. Fucking hell. Always gotta do shit myself, then." His aptitude for destructing every last crumb of order and diplomacy got the better of him. It was a reflex, an instinct; he just had to take things to the next level. Quentin's tongue shriveled up like a sun-dried grape as Mathias walked forward, yanked Marina by one of her shoulders, and chucked her behind him, face-first toward a wall; Roxy leaped forward in apt time and blocked Marina from careening into the solid surface. No one else moved. The guard, or whomever he was, didn't either. As a matter of fact, his gun was still pointed at the vacant space where Marina had been in his clutch mere seconds before. In a brief revolve-around, Mathias turned and gloatingly said to those behind him, "See bitches?" before, in a single, smooth motion, he smacked the gun out of the guard's hand. Mathias launched forward and grabbed onto the man's ears. One bash then two, three and then four, and before Quentin could take in another breath, he watched Mathias slam his fists against the man's head in a crazed, ferocious frenzy.

Roxy helped Marina to her feet, who looked up to the barbarism above them, to the unending thwacks the man was taking.

"Oh my god," Frances said.

Mathias pummeled the man from all angles. He interchanged from under the chin, to both of the temples, to square on the left eye socket, followed by a return to the side of the jaw. Mathias swung a steel arm around, to the back of his victim's long, limp, and bobbing head. Blood was spilling thickly. It splashed to the walls, to the floor, and onto Mathias, too. He wasn't being met with a fight, though. All that the man sent back were gurgles and groans. Quentin thought it would end quickly, that a short time into the unequal clash, Mathias would realize that he wasn't receiving mirrored brute force. But he didn't. He was unrestrained, incessant. If he had any intention or thought to stop himself before things grew grimmer, it had gone from his head. Quentin realized how fortunate he was that Mathias had forgiven him for the earlier stabbing, back when the two groups were united.

Fatima shrieked.

Athol's jaw dropped.

Jaymes swiped at sweat droplets on his cheeks. He ran forward, straight for Mathias. Jaymes bent his knees for stability and knotted his arms around Mathias's waist from behind, pulling back as hard as he could. But he couldn't stop him, and Mathias punted a foot backwards. His heel plunged into the space between Jaymes's legs. "Ah—Crap!" Jaymes exclaimed. He tripped back and fell against Roxy, who again caught a person just in time before another fall.

Ewan's blunt nails cut into the sides of his flushing face. He marked his skin with crescent-shaped indents. "Mathias, stop it!"

"I can't just stand here!" Jaymes lamented, in spite of cupping his groin. He was in a lot of pain, Quentin could tell. His glasses, for all their shade and width, did little to mask his blatant horror. Quentin mutely watched as he scurried forward on shaky feet, one hand still protecting his manhood. He reached Mathias a second time and just started clawing at him; pushing and kicking him. He looked like he would do anything, however ridiculous or weakly enacted it was, solely to get Mathias to stop the slaughter.

Mathias didn't stop.

"We have to do something!" Ewan urged the others. He rushed forward on uneven feet and started gripping at Mathias's midsection.

When she was sure that Marina could stand on her own, Roxy joined in. Quentin assumed she wanted to impede as overwhelmingly and messily as possible, because she leaped up onto Mathias's back, tied her ankles together in front of his bellybutton, and, with her arms crossed together around his shoulders, pulled them taut and backwards to bring his neck toward her face. She had his pulse point crammed into one of her elbows while she squeezed him. He groaned from the force of Jaymes's body, the adamancy of Ewan's tugging, and the clinging chokehold Roxy maintained while she was plastered to his spine. They dragged him down slightly, but, in total, their combined efforts didn't work. Somehow, they didn't work. Impressively, ingeniously, and disconcertingly, in impeccable order, Mathias kneed Jaymes into a wall, twisted his back and fleetingly, but thunderously, punched Ewan's face, and then shuddered Roxy off his back. Jaymes slumped against the wall, lopsided glasses cracked in some parts of the lenses. Roxy let out a high-pitched scream as she fell chin-first to the floor. Ewan gasped for air. He held his face and covered the area above his mouth, where blood from his nose poured out; Quentin knew it was broken without even having to inspect it.

Mathias spared no time for a moment's recovery. He eagerly squatted above the fallen guard, who was unmoving, and sent fist down after fist, nonstop.

Frances dropped Fatima, to whom Frances apologized for her involuntary release of the child almost immediately after she did it, seeming to not know why it happened. But Quentin knew why. The answer occurred to him all too suddenly. He knew that somewhere in Frances's mind, which was surely as frazzled but functioning as everyone else's, in a spot where only the grimmest thoughts were borne, she, too, had come to a conclusion similar to his own.

"Mathias, you're going to kill him!" Athol said.

Quentin closed his eyes.

Ewan ran forward. He helped Roxy and Jaymes to their feet, asked if they were fine, but they looked dramatically antithetical to it. Roxy's chin was indigo and mauled. Jaymes was having trouble standing.

Frances engulfed Fatima in her arms and thrusted the youngling's tiny head into the space between her neck and shoulder. "Look away!" Frances ordered. "Don't look! Don't look up!"

Perhaps the guard was in the wrong to have overstepped as menacingly as he did by holding Marina at gunpoint before everyone, but to suffer in that manner—to be struck without pause by the hands of someone as colossal as Mathias Garcia—that was a penalty Quentin had difficulty justifying, even if the guard had indeed been complicit in their mass abduction. But it was the blood, all the gushing, russet juices that sprayed all over the corridor, which made Quentin pity the filth. It was the blood that made him quake. All he could smell was iron. His nostrils were jolted by the scent. The entire corridor reeked of it. And yet the odor didn't stop Mathias, who was unfaltering.

Ewan crawled forward and wound lanky, but adamant, arms around Mathias's ankles. "Help...me!" Ewan screamed. He was latched onto Mathias, leech-like, as blood from his broken nose ran into his mouth. "Guys, hep me!"

The wobbly, but ever-supportive, Jaymes limply pawed at Mathias's arms. Jaymes had been made weaker, though. He must have hit his head at some point, because his steps were unbalanced and he was swaying. Having recognized that himself, he substituted his lost verve with yanking at Mathias's tank-top.

Quentin swallowed his slight stock of pride and hastened over. He knew there would be an inauspicious outcome, but he couldn't tolerate helplessly witnessing a potential murder. He circled his arms around Mathias's waist, imitating what Ewan was doing below at Mathias's ankles, and Quentin pulled, even as the strain in his lower back began to sting. His body was trying to tell him that it was dangerous to continue, but he went against its advice.

Ewan was grunting by Quentin's toes. "Why the…hell…is…this basehead…so heavy?!"

"Shit!" Jaymes bellowed. "Help us!"

Mathias rolled back a shoulder. The blade of it perfectly welted into Quentin's left eye, which knocked him back to the floor. Mathias then kicked Ewan, who rolled backwards and began hacking wheezy coughs, dry heaving as he clasped at his collarbone.

"Stop it!" Frances wailed. "Mathias, stop it!"

Roxy slid to the floor. She hid her face behind her knees, sobbing miserably.

Acolytes screeching, a little girl crying, and three others injured due to none other than himself, Mathias refused to pause.

Sprawled on the ground and palming one eye, Quentin's head spun. He turned on his side, and his cheek pressed on the cement when he realized that he was level with Mathias's victim. He could see welts all over the man's face—what was left of it, anyway. His sharp-featured face was morphed, twisted. His mouth was open, and glued by blood to his lower lip was one of his bottom teeth. His left cheekbone jutted out from one of his thin sideburns. The limbs of the once-lively man had gone saggy, almost weedy.

The realization of the man's death must have dawned upon Mathias, because he abruptly stopped. No one fought him anymore. No one screamed for him to stop. There was nothing for him to stop. They had fought against him, and they failed. It made Quentin recoil to wonder how long the man had truly been gone before they realized it. Was it after the second strike? The third? Did it happen when Quentin laid his eyes on him, unknowing and concerned? Was it possible that there was a moment wherein Mathias was destructing only a corpse? It was almost too much to make Quentin cry; too much for him to feel only sadness. He felt everything all at once. He was repulsed by the sight of the battered, bruised man, who was left only in pieces. He felt hatred toward himself for his weakness and inability to be someone stronger. He was sorry for everything, for the guard, for his classmates, for a child who would soon open her eyes to see a faceless man. He was sorry for himself.

"How…How could you?" Roxy asked into the iron-scented air. Her question hovered uncomfortably in the silence. Her chin smeared by wet streaks from her tears.

"We are not doing this right now," Mathias said huskily.

"Not doing what?" Roxy asked in a much smaller, quieter voice. "Discussing how you…you…You're insane."

"I'm insane?" Mathias repeated. "Right, 'cause let's see, I kidnapped us. Wait, no—" He faked confusion with a tilt of his head. "Oh, right. I didn't do that. I also didn't set up a trap and corner us. And I also didn't save one of our own, did I?" He conspicuously shot a look to the girl sitting on the floor, who in turn stared at him reprovingly. "But that ungrateful bitch has got nothing good to say about it either."

Marina had never looked so exhausted. "He wasn't going to do anything, you idiot. I was a prop to get everyone to round up and do as he said. But as opposed to us being able to keep searching for an escape, you've managed to bog us down because we now have to deal with this mess. How are we supposed to sneak around when someone is probably going to find this? And now half our group is concussed. So no, you didn't save us. You disadvantaged us with this."

The spoken "this" which Marina acrimoniously mentioned was an indistinct pile of mush that Quentin still hadn't turned away from. In the duration of his blank fixation on it, he achieved in seeing finer details. They were details he wished he could ignore. The only other dead person he had seen before was Agata, but her death was peaceful and slow, warm. The image of death on that day, in the basement of the strange compound, was not of the same ilk.

Frances didn't know it, but Fatima was looking over at the man on the floor. Youth wasn't an obstacle to the little girl's comprehension. Her subtle crying was enough of a sign for Quentin to know how aware she was of Mathias's blunder.

Seated beside Quentin on the floor, Marina studied the guard. She didn't look disturbed, merely thoughtful and ruminative.

Mathias stood, proud of himself. Quentin couldn't decipher if it was carelessness or sadism that made Mathias so prideful.

"Why would you do that?" Athol croaked. "Why couldn't you just injure him and let it go?"

"Yeah right," Mathias said. "So you all just magically cared about him, did you?"

"That's not the point!" came from Jaymes. "Look what you did!"

"Yeah, Jaymes, look what I did," Mathias retorted as he gestured to the blood that varnished the floor. "This is what I did."

"And that's why everyone's pissed at you," said Marina.

"You're lucky I saved you in the first place. You're not the kinda person people go outta their way to save. I'm out here doing you pussies a favor and this is how I'm treated? Fuck you."

"You know what, dude?" Ewan asked. "There's probably a shovel somewhere inside this building. Coulda just dug a hole and stuffed all our bodies in it, because let me tell you, that is a far more enjoyable way of burying myself in my own grave than this shit!"

"Oh, fuck you, Ewan." Mathias's eyes progressively settled on the entirety of their group. "You know, you're all the type of jackasses who run around reporting crimes instead of actually pouncing on shit yourselves."

"Oh! Oh! I'm…What, like, I'm sorry?!" Ewan stammered, still holding his broken nose. "Does that all of a sudden make me a shitty person?! Which, by the way, is rich coming from the fucking cokehead!"

"Look, the point is…" Jaymes swallowed. "You…You…You Killed a man…You killed a man, Mathias."

"He was so young," Roxy wept, sniveling.

Mathias rolled his eyes. "What the fuck is going on here?! I saved our skins!"

"On a fundamenta—" Jaymes kneaded his forehead. "No, on a moral level. You—*Ergh!* You killed a guy!"

"And now we're all cornered because of you!" Ewan added. "What do we do about him?! About this literal, dead fucking person on the floor?!"

Mathias's detachment was unwavering. "Hide the thing."

"That thing," Frances growled from her corner of the pack, "was a human being, Mathias, just as much as we are."

"Whatever, we hide him."

"Oh, like it's that easy!" Ewan exclaimed. "Look at him! Think we can just stick him into one of our folders?! Face it, you've ruined us! Now we're fucking stuck here!"

Jaymes was so frustrated that his glasses were shaking. "On top of that, don't you understand what will happen to us if we get caught? Or, given the pace of our escape, more like *when* we get caught. Can you even try to fathom what they'll say about us?"

Mathias laughed. "Jay—"

"They'll say we killed him!" Ewan yelled. "No, *murdered,* him!" He sniffed. "And we did, Mathias. We did."

"No," said Athol. "We didn't kill him. *He* did. Mathias did."

Ewan winced as he hid his mauled nose with the top of his shirt. "Fuck. This hurts."

"But they'll accuse us," Roxy said. "All of us."

Marina's drawn eyes blinked awake. "We're really going to pay for this," she said. "How do we even clean this up?"

"He's all limp and bleeding everywhere," Athol said. "And his skin is all over the place. I don't wanna touch him."

"This is the most disgusting shit I have ever seen," Ewan spat. "Nice going, Mathias."

"Guys, we gotta clean up the body," Jaymes said.

Mathias shrugged. "I say we leave him for them to find. Kinda like a dope-ass warning to not fuck with us."

"I really hate you," Ewan made known. "I think you're just pathetic."

Mathias clicked his tongue against the roof of his mouth. "Gaged and not a single fuck given."

Quentin pointed to the open storage room, the one where they retrieved their medical records. "We could...uh...put the guard in there?" he recommended in the most uncertain of deliveries.

"They're clearly watching the area," Ewan warned.

"Not really," Marina said. "He was the first guard we've seen in all the time we've been awake and now he's, of course, dead. So, no. I doubt they're watching this area. At least, not diligently."

Mathias groaned. "They kidnapped us. They drugged us. And they were going to shoot every one of us. Why are you freaking out? This is our revenge. We should be proud!"

Ewan scooted away from him. "I am actually begging you to stop glorifying this."

"If we're doing anything," Mathias said, "it's dropping this body in front of the next open door we see so that when someone else comes out, they'll get to choke on the sight of him. Like I said earlier, if I can't get out, then I'm fucking this place up."

"So we see," said Marina as sternness spread over her removed profile. "But as of this moment, you don't get a say in this."

"Oh, but you do? Ungrateful bitch. Fucking pussies."

"Not killing every person in sight doesn't make me a pussy!" Ewan vied. "It makes me a thinker! A fucking human with compassion and feelings!"

"Hear me," Mathias announced, "I'm not dying with you skinny shits."

"You just dug us our graves," Ewan said.

"Shut up. Shut up. All of you just need to shut the fuck up."

"You know what, Mathias?" Jaymes asked. "We're tired of your shit. It doesn't matter what you think. Call us what you want—slurs, pussies, whatever—it doesn't change the fact that you killed a guy. And we have a mess to deal with. Shit, what are we gonna do?"

"The closet," Marina said. "We put him in the closet and we use Fatima's blanket to clean up the…spillage."

Eight out of the nine nodded their heads.

Mathias cursed.

Later, not long in the future, although it did feel like hours had gone by, Quentin's stomach was coiling in on itself in a way it never had before. He first mistook the discomfort for a gas bubble, but then accepted it as his innate reaction to preparing for the task of holding a dead man, and, very likely, some oozing portions of him.

The ongoing scratching sounds of Ewan shuffling Fatima's—formerly Quentin's—blanket against the grating cement was an unpausing occurrence in the background.

"I just want to say thank you to Mathias for somehow making me miss my old life," Athol sliced into the quiet of their circle made up of himself, Quentin, Marina, Jaymes, and Mathias; they were gathered around the corpse on the floor.

Ewan, crouched down a few steps ahead of them, took off his sweater, because he wore a tee-shirt underneath. He threw it over to the still-sobbing Roxy, who started to help him clean the ground.

Frances kept watch of the corner by the end of the corridor. It was, in part, a ploy to stay on alert, but mainly it was to stop Fatima from turning around.

"I swear, I'm ditching you bitches as soon as we cross that Mexican border," Mathias said.

Jaymes's nail beds whitened as his fingers twitched. "Everyone ready?" he asked, bracing himself.

Quentin peered around to each of them. He saw Jaymes's chalkiness, Athol's squeamishness, and Marina's ever-unreadable face. "Let's get this over with," he resigned. Quentin and Mathias were to manage the lower regions of the guard's figure, Athol and Jaymes the shoulders and arms, and Marina the head. They bent down and picked up their allotted pieces of the man. Whenever they moved something, they heard the sounds of slop and skin. Quentin almost gagged when he first came in contact with the guard's left leg,

Mathias produced the noise of what sounded like a suppressed barf. "This goop is rancid."

"Easy for you to say," Athol said, "you and Quentin only have his legs."

It took two attempts, which was fewer than Quentin anticipated, before they had the fleshy, flaccid man unevenly juggled in all their arms. Elevating him proved difficult, with the limbs raised lower on Jaymes's and Mathias's corners and drastically higher on Athol's. Their variety of statures worked to their disadvantage, but they managed. When the five compromised and achieved a relative balance, each step they took was a slow, calculated progression. As they walked, they neglected the steady flow of blood from the man's skull and the pudding-like bounce to his limbs. Jaymes whispered a strangled bit of gratitude to Ewan, because without him cleansing the way, they would probably have slipped and fallen. Ewan didn't look up and just kept scrubbing. That journey wasn't long, but, to Quentin, it did reach an unthinkable level of dreadfulness due to the blood that squirted all over their hands, arms, clothes, and for Marina, her hair. They all strictly avoided looking at the face in her hands.

Mathias watched the blood spill over his fingers. "I'm not doing this," he said at once. Unmindfully, and rather selfishly, he released the heavy thigh of the guard.

Quentin caught it in time.

"Hey!" Athol yelled to Mathias. "Get your hands back here!"

"No way," Mathias said, "this is bull."

"You did this and now you won't help?" Jaymes asked. "This isn't our problem. It's enough that we're carrying him for you. He's dead and I don't know what you did but you messed him up badly, whether it was a giant rupture or a brain bleed or—"

"It's a skull fracture," a voice slipped in from behind, from Quentin's left. The voice was calm, pointed, and smooth. *Off-putting,* Quentin thought. Most disturbingly, he knew it belonged to not one person in the entire pack of escapees.

10

Quentin stood agape. He dithered about what he should have done; whether to drop the guard's body and sprint away, or to maintain a hold of him, speechless and still among his fellow corpse-carrying peers. In the end, what stunted his preference for the first idea was that their visitor did not appear nearly as contemptible as the last—the newly deceased one. The air of the second man, the one who appeared out of thin air, completely unannounced, was in no way even remotely similar to the lecherous demeanor of the first. Rather, their new visitor was composed and, dared Quentin think, congenial. The man's facial features were smoothly blended into each other and molded into a soft, approachable, wry, and knowing smile, as if he had suspected the panic which buzzed in the majority of their heads. He had a pair of green eyes that were dimmer than Frances's, not nearly as luminous, but were decipherable enough for Quentin to notice the almost permanent twinkle to them. Under those eyes, like the faces of the young ones before him, dark circles hung thickly. There was an ongoing war which transpired atop his head, in his hair, as an omnipresence of aged gray dominated patches of youthful chestnut. He was far shorter than Jaymes, Mathias, Athol, and Quentin, and was only a little taller than Marina. His arms were gangly and his feet were small. Copper corduroys fit loosely over his legs. His torso was hidden beneath a faded, brown flannel, which was comfortably fitted to his body. His hands were cloaked by his wrinkled pants pockets, and all that was seen at the ends of his arms were his wrists. There were faint tears and worn lines on the back of his oxfords, which were unmatched with the clothes on his body. He looked to be somewhere in the vicinity of his early sixties. To an uncanny degree, he struck Quentin as a benign figure. Fatherly, even. Or, in no more than five years' worth of time, grandfatherly. There was a wrongly benevolent air to him. The man, the gentleman, stepped forward. He was closer to Quentin, but then he swiveled back and stood behind Marina.

Fatima gasped in the background.

Athol was shaking.

Even Mathias was frozen in place, lacking his typical black-or-white conviction.

Marina was calm.

The gentleman, whom Quentin began to assume was their host more than anyone, continued to look at the presumably dead body. His hands stayed in his pockets. "Nearly dead, but alive nonetheless," he said to them. He sounded crestfallen. "I mean, I believe it's a skull fracture," he said a moment later, looking up to each of them. "I wouldn't know for sure. Medicine was never my expertise, you see. It's merely that a lot of my friends are doctors and have walked me through a thing or two about certain injuries." Hopping on his heels, he leaned his head over Marina's shoulder and analyzed the body again. "Very well, I suppose there is but one solution to this awkward quandary, isn't there?" he asked without truly asking, and switched his gaze up.

Athol blubbered out a question, "Wh-What?"

"Don't get me wrong," the new interloper said, "Mr. Garcia did a sufficient number on him and, taking into consideration his inexperience, it was an admirable job. But, with my utmost respect, of course, I am afraid it just wasn't enough to achieve complete termination."

"Complete termination?" Mathias repeated challengingly. After all his hard work, he sounded affronted by the comment.

"Who are you?" Jaymes asked coldly.

The gentleman—*The literal kidnapper,* Quentin had to remind himself—skimmed the column of his throat with his index finger. He pondered for a bit. "It seems…" he said after a beat, "that you have left me no choice but to rid you all of this burden myself." To Marina, who was obstructing his view, he sent a sideways glance followed by a dismissing nod, signaling that he wanted her to step aside. She was hesitant, but simultaneously wise enough to suppress any urges to argue with someone of whom she knew nothing. She released the broken head, which left her fingers dripping blood all over the floor, and backed away to help Athol with the left shoulder. Granted access to the guard's head, the gentleman carefully cradled it in his right hand. "Ah, thank you, dear," he said to Marina. He slinked his other hand out of his pocket. What occurred next happened so fast that it took Quentin a while to understand what he was watching, but the gentleman was pushing his free hand against the guard's neck. It looked bizarre. That was, until Quentin saw, through closer inspection, that what peeked out between the gap of the man's forefinger and thumb was the rubber butt of an object. A knife, to be precise. Blood spurted all over the place; onto the end of the man's shirt; the wall; Marina's right arm.

A small whimper was heard, and Quentin jumped. The guard really was still alive. The whimpering turned to gagging, which escaped from the guard's white and torn lips. His second assailant wrung the handheld blade to the left and to the right, and then made one long, circular motion across the middle of his neck. His jugular vein was streaming, cascading, as liquid carmine went pouring to the floor throughout the grisly process of the guard's prolonged death. The newcomer screwed the knife out of the spot where it had been firmly lodged.

Roxy was bawling. She smothered her mouth with her sleeve.

Frances covered Fatima's eyes once again.

Two minutes passed. For the duration of it, the younger individuals were silent. The older one, the de facto killer, withdrew a silken handkerchief from the breast pocket of his flannel and swabbed all of the guard's lifeblood off the knife. The others watched— somewhat reverently, but definitely confusedly—as the knife wielder silently cleaned his tool. "Patterson," he said. He dabbed at the rubber hilt. "I am Colin Harris Patterson, although you are free to call me whatever you please. It doesn't matter to me."

Dissimilar to everyone else in that corridor but Mathias, Marina was unconcerned by the dead state of the guard. "Colin," she said slowly, tasting his name on her tongue almost spitefully. "That was a placement, I take it?"

Patterson was intrigued by the question. "How so?" he asked her. He cleaned a drop of blood off the edge of the handle.

"Was he an expendable prop to make you look traitorous?" Marina asked. "Did you send him here to act crazy so it would make you look good in front of us?"

"No, child. You wouldn't have fallen for it even if I had done so to perfection."

"I don't believe you even now. This grandfatherly act of yours is really quite the charade already."

Patterson chuckled. He smiled at Marina as he finished up the preening of his knife. "I always did like you, do you know that? I have been itching to meet you for a long time, longer than you can probably imagine."

"I bet," Marina said.

Jaymes let go of his portion of the guard; without Jaymes's set of hands to help, the corpse fell to the ground. "You know her?" he asked. Patterson ignored Jaymes.

"Why are we here?" Frances came into the conversation.

"Certain things," said Patterson as he gave the knife a final pat with the handkerchief. He slid the two items back into his pockets.

"Will we like these things?" Ewan asked.

"If I'm being honest, I don't think you will," Patterson said to Ewan. "The others, perhaps. But I think it will take some time for you specifically to acclimate, never mind enjoy, the changes in your life. You've always been an immovable person, Mr. McHugh. It isn't a bad thing. Stubbornness has its perks. It just gets a bad rap."

"What?" Ewan blurted.

"What kind of an answer is that?" Frances scoffed.

"Liars and lies are whom and what you detest," said Patterson, "and in all honesty, I share the sentiment." He smiled again, and it reached his eyes. "At least on that note we have something to agree on."

"Do we?" Marina asked.

"We do."

Mathias crossed his arms over his chest. "Are you helping us or not? Because if not, you may as well leave now before I do to you what I did to this guy," he said, kicking a foot to the guard.

"Strong as you are," Patterson said, "your brawn and determination do not intimidate me. Ultimately, you failed to kill him. And anyway, I have answers. I know that despite wanting to leave, inside every one of you, the littlest one aside—although I could be boldly presumptuous—there is a craving to understand. It is in your insatiably curious natures."

"And you have an insatiably hungry appetite for us," Ewan jibed.

"That, indeed," Patterson didn't deny. He still smiled that small, gentle smile.

"Look," Marina said, "as I'm sure you've gathered through the surveillance cams in your walls, we don't really desire answers. And clearly—" She eyed Mathias—"diplomacy isn't our forte. Not to mention, since you're obviously willing to betray one of your own, why should we trust you?"

"But...I want answers," Roxy said.

"I guess me too," Athol admitted.

Mathias shot wrathful looks their way. "No one was asking for your opinions."

"Marina's right," Ewan defiantly said to Patterson. "How can we trust you?"

"Excuse me, sir," Frances started, "but is this about the drug bust?"

"But we weren't even there," Roxy said. She motioned to herself and Fatima, but forgot that Ewan and Athol also hadn't partaken in the incident.

Patterson bowed his head. "You yourself have answered Frances's question for me, Roxy. The current events do not regard the substance abuse on the school premises." He shrugged. "Although, I must say, had Mathias been my son, I can guarantee his punishment would have been something akin to the guard's ordeal here."

"You know all our names," Jaymes said. "You've been waiting to meet Marina. You know about the drug bust. You have our medical records. Access to our homes. Our parents are probably in your pocket, too. How long have you been watching us?"

Patterson slowly looked back down to the guard. "The others, I can assure you, are nothing like him. He was different. His colleagues never would have pulled guns on you, even if you attacked them in their sleep. He, however, slipped his way into here for the sole purpose of hurting you. Oh, I should have known..." he said forlornly.

"Why are you ignoring me?" Jaymes asked. "We're not worried about the guard anymore."

"And you shouldn't be," Patterson said. "You have no reason to worry about him. He will be cleaned up. As for yourselves, follow me if you like. You don't have to. You may choose to roam if you prefer to continue. I just don't recommend staying here in this drab basement. It gets awfully cold when the heating shuts off at six in these southern halls. The body will be removed, though. So, as I said, I wouldn't fret if I were you."

"We weren't," Jaymes said, his temper shorter. "You haven't answered any of my questions."

"Tea, I have learned, solves most problems," Patterson said. "If there is one thing I can agree with the English on, it is that. I could bring you upstairs, sit you down, and allow you to relax for once."

"We don't want your tea," Mathias said. "We want to get the fuck out of here."

"I want answers," Roxy spoke up again, meekly.

"Holy—" Mathias threw a hand up in the air—"will you cut it out?"

"Mr. Garcia," Patterson said, "you are free to search for an exit. By all means, go ahead. But to those who would like some tea, answers, and insight into a more reasonable method of escape, come along." He started to meander away, fully anticipating that they would all trail after him. When he heard no footsteps of followers, he turned around. "Well? Are you really not coming?"

"How do we know we can trust you?" Ewan asked.

"Because, just as you suspected, your parents do."

Everyone reluctantly trundled on behind Colin H. Patterson. As they walked, there was hushed, mild discussion of parting ways with the guard-killer, but resistance and fighting suddenly seemed all too tiring for them to continue after doing so for nearly the entire day. They had walked miles, their famine was still untended to, and they realized, all too belatedly, that their kicks and punches could only do so much damage to an institution that seemed unbreakable. Patterson exploited their fatigue, that much Quentin knew. Had they been well-rested and fed, they wouldn't have been as acquiescent as they were in that moment.

"The doors of your room," Patterson said over his shoulder, "were much thinner than all the others. I figured you would want an easy way out after so exhausting a morning."

Mathias rolled his eyes.

They reached the rooms in which the two camps had woken, and down the corridor from them was one special door Patterson unlocked with the assistance of a long, silver key. He stepped over the threshold. Everyone stayed at his heels as he made his way into another corridor beyond it. By the end of the new, even leaner strip of corridors that were identical in appearance to the ones through which they had wandered all morning and afternoon, there stood an elevator.

Ewan groaned. "So that's where it is."

"We were so close," Fatima squeaked.

Patterson pressed his pruny, right thumb against the topmost control on the elevator's button pad.

"Where are you taking us?" Jaymes asked very quietly. Everyone was squished together in that tiny corridor, so much so that surpassing the volume of an exhale mimicked the intensity of a shout.

Patterson, once again, didn't respond.

The elevator doors slid apart, and their guide traipsed inside. He was first followed by an unsure Jaymes, and then all the others when they deemed it safe to do the same. It was a struggle simply to stand in the compacted space when the doors closed, as they were pressed up against one another; Quentin's elbow stuck in somebody's armpit. As the elevator moved, the metallic walls showed reflections of their young and slim figures being widened into rounded blobs.

"Are we being punished for something?" Frances asked.

"No," Patterson said.

"Did we really not do anything wrong?"

"You really did not."

"Do you know why we're here?"

"Yes."

"Are you good?" Roxy asked. "Like, a good person?"

"I like to think so."

"Are we in any kind of trouble?" That was Athol.

"Not quite."

The upward ride and conversation ceased simultaneously, and the doors peeled apart with a hiss and blew some cold air onto them. Patterson stepped out, and the young followers cautiously proceeded after him.

"The foyer," Patterson announced pridefully, once they exited the transport. He fought through a dry cough, but he was joyously proud as he opened his palms and allowed his guests, his prisoners, to take in the drastic contrast between the new room and the previous one.

Quentin didn't consider it a room. But it also wasn't quite a foyer either. He thought it more of a hall. Walls protected by a sheen of fine, silver paint glistened against a floor that was comprised solely of unscathed and polished marble, wherein swirls of turquoise were discernible every few steps. They had to progress beyond an introductory gate of four, also marble, pillars, which were fused into the imposingly high ceiling. He beheld, with his dropped-back head, a chandelier that glimmered its pale crystals and rotated almost imperceptibly, moved by the gentle puffs that emanated from the heating vents that were clandestinely fixed into the side walls above, where a second floor began.

"Um," was all Quentin said.

"Pretty," Fatima whispered.

"Nice...chandelier," Ewan said. "Guess it pays to kidnap people."

"What the hell is this?" Mathias asked. "I don't want a tour of *The Ritz*. What are we doing here?"

Patterson smoothed out his smile. "This way, if you will," he invited with a flourish of an open hand to the side as if he were a maître d' as he said, "And thank you, Ewan, for the compliment. I selected that chandelier myself."

Ewan's eyes darted back and forth rapidly. "He knows my name."

"He knows all our names, jackass," Mathias said.

They were taken down one of the corridors adjacent to, and left of, the foyer. Multiple passages wound and bent together, extending into even longer trails, and just when Quentin assumed they would come upon a dead end, they didn't; he couldn't imagine how anyone remembered their way around the place.

There was no disputing that the foyer of their captivity compound was dignified by an undeniable regality, but the foyer, for all its architectural handsomeness, wasn't as hospitable and embracing as the corridors abreast it. The upstairs were well-kept, and soon the repugnant environs below were quickly forgotten. Before, they saw only cement and steel, but now they passed walls that were lined with decorative, mahogany writing tables that were dressed with unopened notebooks, untouched pens, and glass pots that brimmed with bunches of either trimmed roses or daffodils—sometimes both arranged together. Soaring, potted duos of kentia palms guarded each door they passed. Aromas of vanilla and berries, with touches of orange, hung in the air as they walked along the smooth and supple path of red-velvet and polyester carpeting.

"Is this a hotel?" Athol asked.

Patterson stopped at a random door, where he grabbed its chrome handle and rotated it to the right. "The dining hall," was all he said, and he entered. Quentin wasn't one to grow spoiled after the morning he just lived through, but to call the next room a dining hall was an overly formal abuse of the term. An alignment of tables was spread through the center. A serving bar attached to a wall in the back corner. Its floor was a classic linoleum that smelled of plastic. He thought it depressingly analogous to their high school lunchroom. "Do choose a table, please," Patterson requested of them.

None of them hesitated. Maybe on another day, when they weren't depleted of all their energy, they would have defied him. But they couldn't bring themselves to do it. All the walking, talking, and fighting of their presumed morning and afternoon had tired them enough. Everyone sat down on the benches at one of the gray tables.

Patterson circled the edge of the table and advanced to Ewan, who was still holding his broken nose. Something of an illusionist, Patterson extracted a small, pharmacy-brand baggie of pain-relieving patches. Ewan was looking down when he jumped, startled by the extended hand in front of his face, and he hesitantly grabbed the package. "Uh...Thank you?" Ewan asked. "Do you always walk around with these?"

Patterson grinned. "Miss Gustavsson was correct regarding the presence of hidden surveillance devices in our walls." Marina didn't look surprised by the accuracy of her extrapolation.

"You've been watching us all day and didn't bother to come down?" Ewan asked.

"On the contrary, Mr. McHugh, I only checked the monitors about forty minutes ago. I've been incredibly busy. I hope you'll forgive me. Anyway, where is Que—? Oh, there you are."

Quentin pointed to himself, his head cocked to one side.

"Yes, you," Patterson clucked back, humored. "You are not to sit with them."

"Wh-Why not?" Quentin asked.

Ewan stopped trying to open the pain-relief package. He froze mid-movement and watched the interaction with a suspecting eye.

"Why can't he sit with us?" Frances asked.

"Because he is your leader," Patterson said.

Quentin recoiled. "Their what?"

"Leader."

"Of what?"

"Of them. As of right now, you are."

"What are you talking about?"

"This is cryptic shit," Mathias butted in. "We want real answers and we want them now. Give them now or I kick your ass."

"Do shut the fuck up," Marina sighed.

"Please, you two," Patterson interjected, "you need to stop it after all these years." He looked back to Quentin. "Anyway, where was I? As captain, you are to come with me while they—"

"—No," Quentin said.

"I understand that you—"

"No!" Quentin resisted. "It's not happening. You just killed someone. I don't know you. I don't trust you. There is no way I'm going to be alone with *you*."

"I understand that you—"

"You clearly don't," Jaymes said. He stood and paced over to Patterson. "Have you any actual idea what it's like to be ripped out of your bed and thrown into some strange building in the middle the night? Quentin is leader of…whatever, but so what? He stays with us, or we come with you. You get all of us or none of us, that's how this works."

"Children, children," Patterson said softly. He fanned his hands up and down as if trying to defuse a fire. "Listen, the conversation will not benefit Quentin, nor any of you, if we do as you suggest."

"Oh, for god's sake," Ewan scowled, "can you cut the mystery-man ambiguity and just get to it? We've given you your chance, but now you're stalling."

"If Quentin could simply come with—"

"I'm not," Quentin fought. "It's not going to happen. Nothing can change that."

"Nothing?"

"Nothing," Quentin said determinedly.

Patterson shrugged. "Well then. Perhaps not just any inanimate thing will have the capacity to do the trick, but a living thing just may."

"What are you talking about?"

The door behind them swung open, the hinges soundless and the motion brisk. At a leisurely pace, a male, who was decades younger than Colin Harris Patterson, strode into the room. The group's new company had his hands tucked into the pockets of his crisp, capris shorts, with only his thumbs out in the open; his visible digits absentmindedly swiped at the seams of his belt hoops. His sweater was comfily large around his lean stomach. His light, brown hair was swept to one side of his forehead and held in place by a heavy veneer of gel. His near-white skin glimmered under the intense, bright lights above. An abundance of things had made little sense to Quentin on that day, but his mind felt like it was going to combust when his astounded, enlarged eyes watched the complacent, utterly relaxed face of Connor O'Neil show a subtle smile. He stopped walking. He swept his hair farther back with one hand as if he hadn't been groomed enough already, then defensively pushed that same hand forward. "Chill," he said. "Don't freak. I sure did. I can explain."

"What's going on here?" Roxy asked. "I don't get it."

"Neither did I," Connor said, "but it just takes a bit of explaining. Patterson can help, so long as you do as he says."

"Friendship through compliance?" Ewan asked. "No way."

Mathias rose off the bench at the table. His hands were flexing. "O'Neil, why are you helping this guy?"

"Connor, you can be honest with us," Frances said. "Don't bend out of pressure. If he's forcing you do to this, tell us."

Connor lowered his hand. "Guys, you can sit down. It's okay. I'm fine. It's just complicated. It's not gonna be easy at all, but you just gotta do as he says. I'll stay here with everyone, meanwhile, you," he said to Quentin, "go with Patterson for a few. Only a few. You'll be back with us in no time."

"No," Frances said. "Quentin can stay here."

"I'm sorry, Fran, but he can't." Connor turned back to Quentin. "Really, Hanson, you'll be fine. Just go. We'll meet up after. I promise."

Quentin stood up, but he made no move forward. He didn't know what to do, as Mathias looked like he wanted to kill Patterson, and Jaymes looked like he was readying himself to lunge forward and punch Connor. The last thing Quentin intended to do was insert himself into a potentially messy confrontation between the four of them. He looked, rather helplessly, to Marina, who was already fixed on him. He wondered if his face reflected his inner helplessness and unabated confusion or if she simply suspected what he was thinking, because she gave him a small, permissive nod as if having sensed that he was desperate for even the smallest piece of advice. It was a barely noticeable gesture, to others an inconsequential, downward nudge of her chin.

"Where will you take me?" Quentin asked Patterson.

"On a walk," Patterson said chirpily. "A short stroll, really. Although, I am more than inclined to the idea of a brief tour of the finer attractions here, should you request one."

"Uh…No…I don't think so."

Radically unsubtle compared to Marina's display of support was Connor's repeated nodding. "Go on, Quentin," he all but shooed the other boy away. "You'll be fine."

Quentin stepped forward. He tried to put it out of his mind that Patterson had just stuck a blade into a person's jugular vein.

"It'll be fine, man," Connor assured. "Everyone else, I'll take care of them. We'll all be fine. And go easy on Patterson, all right? I know what you're thinking, but trust me, you don't know the half of it." Quentin tried to not have any imaginings of what that meant.

He followed after Patterson, who was already leaving the dining hall, and walked behind him along the fabric-lined floor. Quentin was mindlessly transfixed by the rises and falls of his toes. He stared at each one as they flattened and then fattened with every step. He put forth a concerted effort to set his attention on anything other than the hammering of his heart and the sweat that slid down the sides of his face and leaked profusely from his armpits. He was doing everything in his power to distract himself from having a panic attack. When they reached the end of an intoxicating, flower-petal-scented corridor, they rounded the corner and were greeted on the other side by a fiddle-leaf fig tree and a moist bucket that accommodated a small, corn cob cactus. They continued walking.

When he was confident that he wouldn't cry, Quentin ventured into the foreign art of initiating an actual discussion with his kidnapper. "You've been watching all of us," he said shyly. "But why?

What's the use? I have nothing for you. I'm not like, you know, special or anything."

"No, you are not," Patterson affirmed neither maliciously nor disparagingly, and onward he went with a new pep in his step, a bounce to his heels. The response was gratingly direct. Quentin didn't know whether to feel offended or thankful. It was a good thing, a reassuring one, but it also had a way of squashing his confidence. He thought it would be ironic if his own lack of exceptionalism would be the very thing that ended up saving his life. Maybe he didn't matter to this Patterson man all that much. Hollis would have thought the notion pathetic, would have said something along the lines of, "If you do something long enough, you'll be right one day, I guess." But Hollis wasn't there, so Quentin held onto the small hope that he was blissfully unimportant.

Patterson wasn't finished, apparently. "It is your generic, decidedly bland existence that has made you a target," he said.

Fuck, Quentin thought. His heart sank.

With his arms behind his back, Patterson laced his fingers together. "It's not a flattering statement," he acknowledged. "And it isn't my intention to offend you either. But it is the truth. You being a typical, run-of-the-mill youth is vital. Still, you have what I see as some unique quirks. That is true, is it not?"

"I'm no...I have nothing unique to offer, sir. I'm actually quite boring. Usual. Ordinary."

"That, you are. But on the subject of your ears...Now, they are something."

"Yeah." Quentin flinched. "Wait, what?"

On that note, with the boy on edge and his query unanswered, all Patterson did was mumble something unintelligible before going on to spend the subsequent length of their walk in silence. They exited the last corridor of their route and wound up in the foyer again, and together they walked upon the shimmering marble, Patterson ahead of Quentin. Patterson didn't seem to mind the lagging. At one point, when Quentin wasn't looking, the host glanced around and chortled at the nervous wreck that was his prisoner and guest, at how he just kept watching his toes. Eventually, Quentin walked into something that looked like a glass box. He finally lifted his head to see that Patterson was already ascending the twelfth step on one of the massive flights of stairs—that being the left-hand set from where they had all stood during their initial entry. Ascending the artificial incline, he laughed when he saw Quentin's squirming face reflected along the silver railing, which turned him into a stretched and plumped interpretation of himself, much like the doors of the elevator had.

"Come along, my boy," Patterson bid rather buoyantly. "It isn't half as daunting as you think."

Quentin climbed up. "Why glass?" he asked nervously, inspecting the transparent steps under him.

Patterson was at the top step, which flowed into the second floor; there were two more levels above. He patiently waited for his guest. "Frankly put, it is an old, unoriginal, architectural illusion. Glass and mirrors deceive the eyes into thinking something is far larger than it actually is. The vitality of such a magic trick should become evident to you over time."

"Over time?" Quentin asked. "How much time? How long are you keeping me here?"

Patterson turned away. Quentin chased up after him, and when he made his way to the top, to the second floor, he wisely stopped himself from making the mistake of peeking down to the foyer below. He kept his eyes trained forward.

Welcoming them on their left was a seating area, where three, circular, black tables stood unattended, each accompanied by a pair of thin, metal chairs. It was a common area, almost like a balcony, for one could oversee the sweeping staircase if they were to lounge on one of the available chairs. On Quentin's and Patterson's right, the insides of a nearby room were both visible and yet not so due to the intentional, frosted coat of its glass outer walling. Quentin could only make out a long, boat-shaped conference table and a clean-slated whiteboard beside it—*Probably where they brainstorm their crimes,* he thought, annoyed. Across from the conference room, there was another area that was closed off and had a small, rectangular screen with the eye of a closed-circuit camera on the wall beside it; their two figures were displayed on the screen as they walked past. Patterson saw Quentin looking its way and said, "The infirmary."

As they strolled down the first corridor, Quentin noticed that the second level was almost entirely identical to the one below it. He plodded after Patterson. "So what're all these doors?" Quentin asked. "What do they lead to?" The question was innocent-sounding, but it was his political way of asking if they were storage facilities for more children. He didn't know if it was a reach, if Patterson couldn't glean the implication.

Still, Patterson didn't reply. Instead, he advanced to a door constructed of a hefty cherrywood. Affixed to it was a large, bronze doorknob. He turned the knob and pulled it toward himself, slowly swinging the heavy door back only halfway to the wall, as that was all the width needed for the two of them to enter. "Please, Quentin," he said, "see yourself in." Quentin looked to the doorknob. After, he looked back to his wriggling toes as they scrunched bits of the carpeting between them. He didn't want to have his back to Patterson, but entered anyway.

Quentin's nostrils tickled when whiffs of aged wood and traces of incense engulfed him once he stepped inside. His roughed and scraped feet were softly received by a widespread rug, but the new one was not red-velvet, but instead flaxen-and-brown-toned and embellished by a floral design. The air was pleasant, and the temperature comfortable, as it carefully walked the line between warm and hot. But the new room was by no means humble. A lamp, frilly and beaded, stood beside him and the open door. A cabriole sofa positioned against the rearmost wall was neighbored by a fireplace that blazed authentic flames within a small dig-out. Above the waving fire, atop the mantelpiece, a gathering of golden, electronic candelabras flickered dim, pearly lights, and above them, fixed to the wall, was a painting of what he assumed was Uranus; in school, astronomy wasn't his strongest subject. Opposite the cabriole sofa, and on the other side of the fireplace beside it, a chaise lounge of a deep, dark red color was dappled with puffy pillows; two swan feathers poked out from the zipper of one of the covers. A thick-legged coffee table stood alone, in a corner, and on it was a white mug with brown finger stains. All around him, from one end of the floor to the other, multitudes of towering, pitch-pine bookshelves, which were keenly stained to match the brown rug on the floor, flaunted piles of books. Atop each shelf laid open-lidded bottles of quills, and their podiums were shared alongside mounts of old volumes that were filled with bristly parchment; the pages danced under the impact of what he saw was yet another heating vent.

Of their own accord, his feet brought him deeper into the room. He looked up to the high walls, where arrays of threaded tapestries hung on either side of him. One was a green spread of a legion of Arthurian swordsmen galloping through the misty Dinas Emrys of Wales; another bore an impression of a sleek, black stallion standing pristinely among a bed of lumped sand with classical Persian wording haloed around the horse's erect ears.

He hated, absolutely hated, the incontestable appeal of the room. The comfortable space warmed him and let loose some of the tension in his muscles, and he felt like a traitor for feeling so enraptured by it.

"What is this place?" Quentin asked.

Patterson smirked amusedly. "Quentin, I know you have the capacity to recognize a library when you see one."

"No, not the library. This place. This entire building, I mean. Like, who are you people? That tapestry alone—" He pointed to the one with the Welsh art—"it's gotta be thousands of dollars."

"Tens of thousands," Patterson corrected nonchalantly. "My decision was scorned upon, but I thought it a good investment. I'm glad you noticed it. That shall be put in the pipes of my colleagues and they may smoke it when they meet you. Come," he said as he moved away from the closed door behind them, his disregard unrelenting. He ambled to the end of the room's first level, and it seemed that the area where he and Quentin lingered was only a fraction of the library's entirety. Another swirling staircase rose at the end of the room. It was made of a wood synonymous in color to that of a pistachio nut and stretched long, like the lowering clouds of a foreboding tornado. It had been recently polished, and its luminosity caught every ripple from the fireplace as well as every sway of the pendant lights that hung above it. Patterson mounted the first step. Quentin followed obediently. By the time he was a few paces up, Patterson disappeared around the twirling corner. But, as usual, the man was patiently waiting at the top when Quentin further ascended to join him. "The library loft," Patterson said when Quentin reached the pinnacle, sending an arm out and bidding Quentin to take in the sight.

The loft was an extension of the downstairs, though not nearly as great in size. Although the previous region was rich in its design detail, the new segment was humbler. *Homier,* he thought. It was simultaneously fashionable and soothing. There was a chandelier, yes, but it was a melding of mahogany and oak, as opposed to glass and crystal. The walls were closed in more tightly, and significantly smaller bookshelves lined them. In the center of the room was a vast sea of massive throw pillows and blankets, each as long as Quentin was tall, while a shore of fuzzy, neon rugs and a clutter of open books and fashion magazines were sprawled around the space. Beside the oval of spilled blankets and plushy spreads, two suede sofas stood opposite one another. The softer color schemes, combined with the disarray of items in the center, made Quentin realize that the building was an often occupied and busy place, and it was simply that he was there at the quietest of times.

Patterson eased himself onto one of the sofas, so Quentin hurried over to the one in front of Patterson's and stiffly settled there. They took in one another, Patterson an embodiment of calm whilst Quentin frozen and still somewhat covered in the dried blood of the dead guard.

"Now," Patterson said, "in order to get your answers, you must promise me one thing. One thing is all I ask of you Quentin."

"Oh…Okay."

"You must promise to bear with me, that you will listen all throughout my ramble. That way, you will not think I am crazy or lying. I will drift at times, but you must promise me that you will always keep an open mind. Do you think you can do that for me?"

"Yes," Quentin lied. "I'll keep an open mind."

11

"I'm not going to pretend this is easy for me," Patterson said. "You see, I have a daughter, whom I care for more than anyone else. Whom I love more than the world itself. I took you for her. And before you scream with outrage, I know you feel similarly for your dear brother, that you would do anything to keep him safe. But, Quentin, I took you for him too. I took you and your friends, your classmates, for every person and animal alive right now, and even the ones that will come to be in the future."

"What?" Quentin asked, embarrassed by his uncreative and undemanding response, but he reasoned that it wasn't the worst thing he could have said.

"I did a terrible thing, Quentin," Patterson said, downcast, "and there's no use in my denying it. But it was, without a doubt, for the greater good."

Quentin kept his mouth shut.

Patterson sighed. "One thing I must make clear to you is that, despite a couple helpful character traits and a hearing disorder, you are not incredibly…Well…You are not incredible. In any manner, really. This is not intended to be a disparaging remark, Quentin, it is more like a…Oh, how do I say this? Yes, a backdrop to set the stage for what I have to tell you. Do you understand?"

Quentin nodded, but he had no sense of where the conversation was headed.

"But, as I noted earlier," Patterson went on, "you do possess some helpful qualities. They are partially the reason why you are here. The other part is somewhat pure luck of the draw and being born into the wrong place at the wrong time, and to the wrong people. Or, depending on how you may end up looking at it after further enlightenment, the right place at the right time—born to the right parents. Now, you may be asking yourself, 'Why am I here?' In truth, you are a bit of a vitality. A bit. But, as with many things of consequence, you are here because you were born with a connection to what I have to tell you.

"I know you don't want to hear this, but I have known your parents far longer than you have. Your mother, anyway. I only met your father shortly after you were born, but I've known your mother a very long time. If it weren't for her, believe me when I say that you wouldn't be here, in this place. With me. Anyway, putting that aside, I will have to return to that point later. And I promise I will. Everything will tie together. All I need from you is more of the show of patience you are displaying right now." Patterson cleared his throat. "My own daughter, her name is Naomi, was supposed to be in your position. She was supposed to be here, in this room, on that couch where you sit at this very moment. It should have been ten years earlier, not ten years too late. And yes, yes, I see you looking at me like that and I know, as a parent, that what I say sounds heartless and, well, simply that. Heartless. But I can vow to you that I had, and still have, good intentions. Or else my dearest Naomi never would have agreed to it. She has known my line of work for nearly all her life. More importantly, she knew of the sacrifices which I and my colleagues oftentimes have to make. And she, like you, was born with that same condition, the one that you have. Being touted as a malady, said condition is always mistaken for the auditory health condition known to man as tinnitus. Yes, I see your confused face, Quentin. Don't worry. I will get around to what I mean.

"See, years ago, when my Naomi was two years of age, I was horrified by her pain, and as I'm sure you recall, a seething pain, which she had in her ears one night. She shrieked all throughout the late hours of some random Wednesday. I didn't know what to do. But something I've learned is that the experiences which you, Naomi, Jaymes, and little Fatima have had were just magnified perceptions of what millions of us feel and hear on occasion."

"Fatima has tinnitus too?" Quentin asked.

"What appears to be tinnitus," Patterson said.

"So if it appears to be tinnitus and is actually another thing, then what are we hearing?"

"Sound waves from space," Patterson said.

Quentin laughed. He couldn't help it. "Sir, I'm...I'm sorry?"

"Oh, you heard me correctly, Quentin. Millions, dare I say billions, of people can actually feel and hear sound waves because the shape of their inner ear enables them to register tones in the range above five kilohertz. Ever wonder why we sometimes twitch or shiver at random? It is because our bodies are simply reacting, are naturally sensitive to the disturbances in the environment, even from afar— from places not on Earth. The four of you can simply hear them more intensely than other people because, essentially, and I can't put this any other way, you have what we in this field of study call 'Electromagnetic ReverboHeads.' Acoustically, that is. For short, we interchange between 'ReverboHeads' or simply just 'Listeners.'"

Oh my fucking god, Quentin thought.

Patterson put his hands up for a moment. "Now I know, I know, that they are not the most professional of nomenclatures, but they are certainly apropos, are they not? You see, the shapes of the inner parts of your heads, and in particular the cochlea of your inner ear, make you more attuned to high-pitch sound waves. Of the millions with the condition, roughly three percent are like you, Naomi, Jaymes and Fatima. The reason you three are here instead of them is due to just one factor, that being the parents to whom you were born. In your case, that would be your mother."

"Mhm," Quentin heard himself utter. "Um…uh…" he began to speak, "but what about the tinnitus thing? Are you saying that everything from my doctor's diagnosis has been total nonsense? Because I've seen good doctors. I've been the patient of some really reputable people who are in the top of their field."

"And I mean no disrespect to them," Patterson said. "As a matter of fact, I am well-acquainted with those doctors of yours. They have offered, or surrendered to me, information from virtually every one of your visits over the years. But what they have wrong is that your perceived, tinnitus-type affliction is, in fact, curable."

"So if you knew what was happening to me for all these years, why didn't you say something?" Quentin responded tersely. He sat up a bit. "Wait. Am I being kidnapped for some type of clinical trial? Are you, like, a drug company CEO or something? Is this a—What's the word? Am I in a conglomerate building or whatever?"

Patterson let slip a quick burst of laughter, but rapidly strove to contain himself. Still, his chest heaved several times as he fought back the humor needles. "Ah, she was wrong, Quentin," he said, wiping a tear from his right eye. "She was so very wrong. You are quite keen when you want to be. I wonder why she said otherwise."

Quentin didn't bother asking who "she" was. "So I'm right?" he asked.

"No," Patterson said, sobering. "Although I have to admit, of all the guesses I have heard, that one is by far the most realistic, and isn't there always some truth in the best comedy? In contrast, Mr. O'Neil's was comically farcical. That surprised me, seeing as how he is usually a most rational young man, but I suppose we all have our off days. At any rate, no. No, no, no. This is nothing of the sort. Where I *work*," he said, like the word scarcely sufficed for the weight of his job, "is a place that is no stranger to you. That said, you know only of its public image and not of its inner makeup or its true mission for the past decades. You know of the tall tales, the discoveries—some real, some boldly unreal. And while it will be hard to believe, I swear on my sweet Naomi's life that I am being one-hundred-percent forthright with you. The place at which I've worked nearly the entirety of my adult life is where I met your mother, your father, where I met Jaymes Chen's father, and where I met nearly all your friends' parents."

"Well, my mother's a housewife."

"No, Quentin."

"And my father's an engineer for a defense contractor company. They specialize in, like, making weapons for the military and stuff like that."

"Yes."

"So do you work at one of those engineering companies?"

"No."

"Oh."

"Well..." Patterson bit the inside of his cheek. "I sometimes collaborate with the one at which your father is employed."

"Oh, which spot?" Quentin asked. "Cambridge? Burlington? Out of state?" Having known all the locations of his father's various offices in Massachusetts as well as a few in other states, Quentin tried to test the veracity of Patterson's statement.

"All of them," Patterson said.

"Really?" Quentin challenged. "What...Well...What...How many years in Cambridge?"

Patterson gave a deep chuckle. It reverberated in his chest. "A solid, spontaneous reaction, Quentin. It only confirms I made the right choice of leader—captain, actually. Our years in Cambridge were 2014 and 2015. But what you must understand is that I don't focus on that specific company. Where your father works is, shall we say, a branch of government. You know this, Quentin. I know you do."

Quentin nodded.

Patterson opened his hand outward. "Therefore it shouldn't be too difficult for you to imagine that a powerful, invisible hand from a more significant tier of government may swoop in to...to...shall I say...Ah, *ask* things of their employees. But, Quentin, your father's involvement in this whole effort really is minuscule at most. We should be segueing to other things."

"Oh."

"It's just that, because that company is, as I have reminded you, something which our government turns to quite often, it is safe to assume that most of their vetted employees possess certain loyalties to our nation; they must all go through an arduous security clearance process."

"Okay."

"Thus I was quite supportive when your mother said she wanted to marry your father."

"My mother, the housewife?"

"No, your mother the sleeper agent."

"The what?"

"I'm sorry, I'm sorry," Patterson apologized. "I should clarify that. She was, for a time, a sleeper agent. She was only reactivated about...Hm...I want to say...When you were about fourteen? Yes, that seems about right. Fourteen, I think. Maybe fifteen. She didn't always work for the CIA, you know. She was quite an army major bound to become a colonel one day. She graduated from West Point with highest honors."

Quentin's knees hit each other as they shook.

"Anyway," Patterson said, "she was a major before she switched over to intelligence. She's actually quite new to the CIA, I should have you know. She was intending to stay in the military but then you were born and…Well, let's just say the phone call from NASA made her redefine her loyalties. It wasn't a drastic shift in her prerogative, of course, since it all ties down to one nation in the end. But her career change and her perception of the concept of a family certainly shifted."

"NASA?" Quentin asked.

"NASA."

"And my mother is a…double agent?"

"No! Lord no, if there even is a lord. No, Quentin. Your mother is incredibly loyal to us. She was a *sleeper* agent, and then a deep cover agent, and I believe she is now going through additional grooming. But never, ever a double agent. She has always been a dyed-in-the-wool supporter of our cause."

"Okay, but my mother is literally a housewife," Quentin said. "Like, I…I don't even think you realize how, um, you know, far-fetched your lie is because, like…um…She doesn't do anything. Like, she's…you know…a housewife. But not like…not in the homemaking kinda way. She really doesn't do anything. She can't cook to save her life and—Okay, how about this? She can't even do basic math. Like, she's not…not all there."

"You know, I always thought that was funny on her part," Patterson said. "She told me that she'd play up the ditzy act for you children. All these years, and I still can't get enough of it. She always was something of a comedian, however unintentionally."

"You're lying," Quentin snapped. "You said you would be— what was it, forthright? And now you're just...What is this?"

"This is the truth, Quentin. I am giving to you the truth."

"But she's, like, really dumb!" Quentin forced in a breath. "I love my mom, and I feel bad saying it, but she's not capable of that. Like, she could never be an agent and in the military. Never mind a major."

"Quentin, what do you know of your mother. Really? What do you know about her?"

"I know enough. I know that she can't cook. Doesn't clean. Doesn't read. Doesn't do anything. She and my dad have gotten in fights about it. And I doubt someone who was militarily disciplined would put up with the absolute mess that our house can be sometimes."

"But she is home a lot?"

"Yeah. She's a housewife."

"Do you know what she does when she's home during the day while you and your brother are at school and your father is at work?"

"Well...No. It's why she and my dad fight all the time. Because he always says he goes out and provides while she does nothing."

"I see. And do these fights always happen in front of you?"

"Um, yes."

"They don't ever contain their anger, not even in front of their children?"

"No?"

"So, if I am correct, your parents deliberately display the frustration of that very issue in front of their sons?"

"What about it?"

"Does it not seem as though someone is trying to convince you of that idea instead of it actually being a problem?"

"Um…"

"What I am saying, Quentin, is that being a housewife is the perfect cover for an espionage operative. It gives one the opportunity to be home alone in a most unsuspecting sense and little to no one questions it and—"

"But—"

"*And*, especially when one's entire town is completely in on the operation," Patterson breezily said.

"Wait, what?"

"Quentin, your hometown is everything but what you think it is. Technically, it is a town. But that's not its purpose. The innocence of its existence is simply a veneer. It is a full region of housing designed and secluded for one division of this mission's personnel. What this mission is, I will come to in a minute. But, in any case, the town of Shaw is a housing institution at which intelligence agents spend round-the-clock time working. Your town is a lab. Nearly every day of your lives, yours and those of your classmates here today, have been under our close scrutiny. Everyone's close scrutiny. Your school teachers, your principal, your police force, your parents…they work under me, Quentin."

"How can I believe you? Because you're sitting here? Because you're distracting me with this big place and your big words and—"

"You must take my word for it," Patterson said, almost with regret. "I know it's hard to believe. I wouldn't either if I were in your position."

Quentin wiped the sweat from his forehead with his sleeve. He wanted answers and didn't want himself getting in the way of receiving them, nor did he want to vex the man whom he just witnessed commit blatant homicide.

"I will continue whenever you're ready," Patterson offered sympathetically. "With you, I knew this would happen."

Quentin sniffled. "Why do you do that? Why do you say things like that? As if you know me." It was rhetorical, that question. But he felt so impotent, so exposed, and he found it unsettling that Patterson managed to make him feel that way in the short amount of time they were acquainted.

"Because, Quentin, you have been under my watch for nearly your whole life."

"Why are you studying me? What do you want from me that you can't get from others?"

"But you see, I can," Patterson said. "I can indeed receive your same capabilities from other people. It's simply that those mystical others don't have parents who are already employed in the same way. Your mother was in the military, so she was easily accessible. She is also trustworthy. Who else could we turn to and trust to hand us their child other than a decorated major who herself was married to a vetted employee of ours? Her undying loyalty to our nation is incomparable. So when we, NASA, approached her, she said yes. She willingly switched over to intelligence, which allowed for her to be both a full-time mother and a loyal operative to raise and ready you. And to study you, too."

"But why have you been studying me?" Quentin repeated. "What does NASA care about...about...ListenerHeads?"

"Electromagnetic Reverboheads," Patterson corrected him casually and straight-faced, like it wasn't the most ridiculous thing Quentin had heard in his entire life.

"Right," Quentin said, just accepting the nonsense as fact.

"We studied you because you hear things, Quentin. We are discussing things which most others cannot hear. Many can feel them, maybe get a cold tingle down the back of their neck or get a slight ringing in their ears on occasion, but to hear them, to be affected by them so strongly, that is a rare form of reception, even rarer when you whittle it down to just the offspring of the people who have the right knowledge and security clearances to investigate them appropriately."

"But how do you know I'm hearing things from space? How am I supposed to believe that?"

"You know, I've only just realized how much I digressed, but we've covered a lot of ground, so I suppose it all came full circle. Anyway, my daughter. May I return to that?"

"Naomi," Quentin supplied. "Go ahead."

"Much appreciated. Now, when Naomi was a toddler, she underwent one of your notorious earaches. Two years beforehand, I had just been reassigned from my prior position to become the director of one of our main radar installations, one that captures and interprets, or at least attempts to interpret, electromagnetic waves. Quentin, before I go on, I must ask, are you familiar with the varieties of content which our radars are able to recognize? I know some of our findings have been made public, so perhaps through those reports, you know of them. Some have headlined in mainstream media sources over the years."

As quickly as he could, Quentin gathered memories of the nights on which he studied for his science homework, and after a minute of straining his brain, he recalled something that could suffice as an answer to Patterson's question. "I read a thing," Quentin mumbled, "a couple years ago, in a news article. It said that those huge NASA radar dishes can capture all kinds of stuff like images, outer space sound waves, gamma rays, and—"

"So you are aware that we can detect many things from deep space, all kinds of things resulting from electrically charged particles undergoing acceleration from almost unimaginable distances beyond Earth? Far beyond Earth in deep space and beyond our solar system?"

"Uh, yes, I am...I know one of the tele—I mean, radars—captured a tiny blip of a star collapsing or...exploding. Something like that."

"The former," Patterson said.

"Okay."

From the corner of his eye, Quentin glimpsed an errant teddy bear, fluffy and small with a green, silk bow draped about its pudgy neck, lodged beneath one of the legs of Patterson's sofa. After some consideration, Quentin thought himself rather similar to the fake bear, from a most figurative perspective. He was the young, lost, out-of-place object being toyed with by the higher powers of that institution. He thought of himself as the stuffed animal, and God the leg of the couch, thus God was painfully stepping on him and refusing to withdraw. Just like that, he found himself blaming God all over again.

"Quentin?" Patterson asked. "Are you still with me?"

"Yeah," Quentin confirmed quietly. "So these radars or, um... electromagnetic waves, what do they have to do with me?"

Patterson clapped his hands together and sat back, as if their conversation reached a pinnacle. "I promise to come around to that," he said. "Okay?"

"Um, uh, okay," Quentin said. *Then why did you mention it?!* he thought, wanting to wring Patterson's neck.

"Circuitously," Patterson said, "but just as I warned you, I am going to drift off on a tangent for a few minutes and then return, if that is all right."

"Mhm."

"And, Quentin, you can stop me whenever you please for questions."

Quentin scratched his forearm nervously.

"So," Patterson continued, "After many years of analyzing electromagnetic waves...And allow me to call them EM waves for short. Got that? Okay. So, after years of analyzing EM waves detected by the dishes and overlaying those results onto what our visual observations found, my team became extremely conversant in matching the waves—which your schooling has likely taught you, can travel at the speed of light—with what was causing them. Common causes, you can imagine, were the likes of star collapses, asteroid collisions, etcetera. For example, when we would pick up a certain click pattern, we knew that we had an asteroid collision and that a different type of click pattern was indicative of something else, like a star collapse. When we would hear an asteroid-related click pattern, all we had to do was query our asteroid-tracking visual observation system and match them up with which asteroids had disappeared from view to know which had collided. Of course, that was within our own solar system, since we mostly cannot see into others beyond it. Similarly, sets of clicks that indicated a star collapse would lead us to our mapping system of the galaxy and allow us to make strong assumptions that a red giant, for example, had had its day. We also had a visual observation system for some exoplanets and the moons of exoplanets. You were taught what an exoplanet is, correct?"

Quentin nodded. "A planet in…in…another star system?"

"Good, good. You remember. With that knowledge, you can understand. So, we were also receiving distinct click patterns from our radar that indicated the destruction of an exoplanet or an exoplanet's moon. We knew exactly which click patterns were related to asteroid collisions, which indicated red giant implosions, and which told of the destruction of exoplanets and their moons."

"But I thought you could only map, not actually visualize exoplanets because they are outside our solar system," Quentin said.

"We could. At the time, it was technology vastly advanced. We kept it under wraps because of the implications of what types of advantages a country might have via that technology, and I'll come back to that. I promise. Anyway, each time a click pattern indicated the destruction of an exoplanet or an exoplanet's moon, something else would be heard just before the distinctive click pattern. Let's call them 'tones' for short. But, better yet, these specific tones were being received in an exact time range of thirteen to thirty hours before an exoplanet would disappear."

"Or its moon?"

"Yes, or an exoplanet's moon. You're cooperating. Good. And you're correcting me." Patterson chuckled. "I was worried the sedative may have been too strong. Anyway, anyway. As I was saying, not only that, the tones were specific to the destruction of an exoplanet or its moon…but nothing else. Not asteroids, not red giants…nothing else. They have never indicated any other type of event. But what's really amazing is this: years after the first tones were heard, my team had a major analytical breakthrough." He beamed. "Not only could we pinpoint a pattern in these tones, but for the first time ever we could foresee when we would receive the next tone and the soon-to-follow click pattern of an exoplanet or moon destruction." He paused to let that fact sink in.

"So…?" Quentin asked.

"So," Patterson chirped, "things happen out there, cataclysmic things that radars sense only as tiny, tiny clicks and, more importantly, only when they happen. But these tones…they tell us when something cataclysmic is *about to happen* to an exoplanet."

"But exoplanets are light years away. If it takes lightyears for these tones to reach your radars, they're still not predicting the future. These tones give just—Oh. Half a day or like thirty hours' notice before an object will become extinct? But isn't that just notice of something that already happened years ago?"

"Excellent! Excellent observation, Quentin! Yes! You got it."

Quentin reddened. He didn't know what was going on.

"What did I get?"

"Well, you are one-hundred-percent correct that a cataclysmic event occurring many light years away from Earth will take that same number of years to reach Earth. Where you were wrong was in your assumption that our radar had picked up those. They never did. They only picked up click patterns thirteen to thirty hours later. The tones were not picked up by radars at all. They were picked up by people. Certain people. *Certain* people with Electromagnetic ReverboHeads, to be more precise. This is where Naomi comes into the picture, which means your relevance to this is coming quick.

"My Naomi had her first ear-shredding experience in 2011, when she was two years of age. The very next morning, approximately fifteen hours after her screaming fit of agony ended, I was driving home from the hospital to get some much-needed sleep when I received a phone call from a colleague of mine, Drew Flanchard. Drew excitedly informed me that our radar had picked up the distinct click pattern for the destruction of an exoplanet or moon. It turned out to be a moon very close to an exoplanet. Then, just four months later, Naomi had another ear-piercing experience, and wouldn't you know it, I got a call from Drew some fifteen hours after that one, too, again informing me of the same click pattern. This time, the exoplanet that had just lost its moon was now gone, too."

Quentin swallowed and his pupils shrank. His eyes darted side to side.

Patterson's eerily kind eyes enlarged at him. "Oh no. I've lost you."

"No, I'm—So, are you insinuating that your daughter and I are...are...are you saying that I am hearing something beyond Earth? More specifically, these...tones?"

"It isn't an insinuation," Patterson contended. "It has been proven as fact. Keep in mind that EM waves are made up of many things we didn't know actually interacted. If you hadn't been kidnapped, you would have reached lessons on the impact of ionizing radiation. These can cause chemical reactions in living cells. Combinations of elements within EM waves do that to people, and the outcome for some are unbearable, high-pitched tones. And, to ensure at the time that my suspicion of the tones was correct, I instructed a team of twenty—let's call them agents, for brevity's sake—to scour local medical records filed on the same two days of Naomi's hospital visits. The agents reviewed the medical records of those individuals who had visited doctors and hospitals for reasons of severe ear pain, earache, or ear infection."

"Isn't that overreach? Oh wait, governments can..." Quentin stopped talking. He remembered Marina and Ewan, and their claims that governments didn't always function with the purest of ethics. He wiped some more sweat off his face. "So what did the agents find?"

A sparkle of impressed satisfaction snuck into Patterson's eyes before he continued his explanation. "They came upon three similar medical cases to Naomi's, and they were cases that also saw people suffering immensely from what the visited medical professionals described as ear-piercing tones that started and ended at the exact same time as Naomi's. With those results in mind, I subjected my daughter to close observation for years. She was a key to this mystery, my team and I concluded."

Quentin bit his lip. "Kind of a strange coincidence that you were in charge of these radar system telescopes and stuff and it's your daughter who was suffering from the tones."

"Well, I may have worded it in a way that sounds completely coincidental. But actually, the knowledge that some people working around such radar can pick up sound waves from space dates to the 1940's, and...Well...My late wife and her father were such people."

"Is the condition genetic? Like, hereditary?"

"Yes and—"

"Did you marry her before or after you took your radar station job?" Quentin blurted.

Patterson gave another bemused look.

Quentin recoiled in shame. *What the hell am I ashamed of?!* he scolded himself.

Patterson rambled on, as he warned he would. "So, Naomi was a key to something significant, something which we desperately needed to comprehend."

"Which means I am also significant to this?"

Patterson nodded affirmatively.

"These *tones*," Quentin said, "why are they so important to you and your…people? What does it matter that me, your daughter, and the others can hear them?"

Patterson laughed. "Because, and this is where I begin to sound the most absurd, but we scientists are humans, too. And trust me when I say that I think humans are not the most intelligent beings to exist."

"Me too, sir," Quentin whispered.

"Please, it is merely Patterson."

Quentin nodded.

"There are many things that have remained secret, hidden from the public," Patterson said. He lifted himself off the sofa. He fluttered across the carpet, his mood still cheery, and approached one of the bookshelves behind where he had been sitting. He pat the bindings of a collection of paperback and hardcover volumes, his search for his desired choice delayed as his rummaging took longer than he must have anticipated. Quentin was still seated when Patterson returned to join him on the sofa across from his. He had a pasty, gray textbook loosely held in his hands and, as he sat, he casually flipped a third of the way through the partially torn, but still glossy, pages. "Here," he said a minute later.

Quentin took the weighty volume into his hands. He cradled it carefully, since he didn't know if it was a belonging of import. He realized, once he looked down, that what he was meant to be paying attention to wasn't the textbook at all but, rather, a folded sheet of paper that had been stuffed into it, as if leveraging the fat hardback as a protective folder. "Do you want me to open it?" he asked, wary of his every move.

"Yes, go on. Please."

Quentin unfolded the sheet onto his lap. It was a map, a planetary one. *A star system*, he thought after considering the images and scanning them for a longer period of time. Ten, circular dollops were spread on the paper, one of which was half the size of its counterparts, with shadows that served as illusionary pedestals beneath each orb so as to reflect their three-dimensional reality on the paper. Centermost was the irrefutable graphic of a star, its pearliness not lost in the darkness of the map. The other little, shadowed orbs bore underlined, bold titles; John-P; Ted7; NEX; PROBER24; CrX; N-BULA; 23KCJ-0H; GPh; JALV. Underneath, the neighboring star read, Inverness2.

"It's a solar system," Patterson said. "It is a region situated far away from our own, far out in the depths of our galaxy. The system's star goes by the closely kept name Inverness2, after it was discovered not so many years ago by a Scottish professor, who once taught me, by the way."

Quentin raised the map closer to his face, inspecting it. "I've never heard of Inverness2, and we had to memorize a lot of the named stars of the Milky Way in science class last semester during our junior year. It was the second most important assignment for our GPA of the year."

Patterson glanced at the map in Quentin's hands with another conspiratorial glance. "The fault for your lack of knowledge regarding it isn't your own. It wasn't allowed any time in the lime light." His visage was faintly dejected when he said that. "Sharing knowledge has always been something I rather enjoy. I love to teach, love to see others learn. But any public mentioning or study of it was prevented, and information regarding it was kept classified."

Quentin let the slippery sheet flutter down to his lap. "This is classified?"

Patterson gave another sigh. The faint dejection Quentin swore he saw was palpable, then. It was boldly written all over Patterson's face. "The strange thing," he said, "is that on one hand, I am here telling you that this star system exists. Meanwhile, on the other, I am also here to tell you that it doesn't. Rather, it barely exists." Quentin took another look at the graphics of spherical, hued planets and the single star with its pictured light rays that girded its body like a necklace. "Those beauties you see in there, they all are gone," Patterson mourned. "The only things remaining are the star and the two gaseous planets in the top left. No, not those, child. The top left. Correct."

"All of these are gone already?" Quentin asked as he ran his fingers over the string of pictures.

Patterson's saddened expression turned grim. "Yes, and gone are the days of coincidences. We lost every solid planet on that map. Not instantly. It was a long process, quite gradual." He righted his recline and sat up to continue the exposition. "In 1984, the moon farthest from us, one of Prober24's moons, was reported missing after we heard the telltale click pattern. That was the first ever record of an exoplanet body's disappearance, and it would be another twenty-seven years before we discovered the exoplanet click pattern and put two-and-two together. Then, in '89, we lost the actual Prober24. In '96, one of CrX's three moons. Six months later, a second CrX moon. In 2003, its third moon and CrX itself. Then, in 2011, NEX and its four moons were wiped from space. No, don't worry, the moons aren't shown on the map. There's no need to look down. Anyway, 2011. That was the year of the story I just told you about; Naomi's experiences, our breakthrough discovery of the tones' relevance to exoplanets as well as the realization that the click pattern was reliable.

"Having realized the relevancy of the tone-to-planet and tone-to-moon pattern due to my own daughter's incidents, we began another search. We issued a team of agents to sweep the nation's hospital and physician records. They were commissioned to sift through medical records that ranged anywhere from 1984 to the year of our discovery, 2011. Naturally, however, the search process was delayed to early 2012 since we needed to obtain permission to even begin it in the first place. Anyway, permission was granted. We wanted a spacious range of data to really confirm our thesis. And, sure enough, we found several patients in those aforementioned years who had suffered through ear pain approximately the exact same time during which our radar detected the clicks. Obviously, not as many were listed as we would have liked. I'm sure many chalked up the pain to a temporary condition, because it was so rare an incident that there was no need to call a doctor. And as you know, once it has passed, there's nothing else to dread. Very few people actually called into their physician's office to complain about the key words 'ear pain.' But all we needed were a few.

"The first piece of evidence we found of an incident we matched up was in 1989. One patient was a middle-aged male in California, the other a nine-year-old girl in South Carolina. Both had on record the mention of undergoing severe ear pain that was reportedly so excruciating that it sent them to the emergency room. As you probably recall my saying, 1989 was the year of the Prober24 planet's loss." He pointed to the map, to the orb on the top left. "That one there. The find was enough to push the researchers to keep looking. They identified that, in '96, there was a spurt of seething ear pain reported by three persons—one was a man well into his late sixties, the other a teenage girl, and the third a mid-twenties male. That mid-twenties male, you ought to know, is now the father of Jaymes Chen, which is further evidence that your conundrum has been caused by hereditary ties.

"But, anyway, back to 2011. I'm sorry for constantly going adrift, by the way," Patterson excused himself. "So, back in 2011, before the team reached the most satisfying conclusion, they wondered if perhaps all those disappearances, or even those tones, were the strange results of the theorized black hole nearest Inverness2's star system. And, yes, there was a theorized black hole, near Inverness2. Your gawking is most humorous. Oh relax, child. It isn't scarcely relevant, as we came to realize that the very black hole I speak of would have devoured every one of our satellites in the vicinity as well. So, at the end of the day, the black hole, as raucous and daunting as we assumed it may have been, proved itself irrelevant to the situation."

Quentin was trying to follow, truly. But he had to stop the momentum of the conversation. "I'm sorry, black hole? I thought those were just theoretical."

"Exactly so, Quentin. Exactly so. But an estimated guess is an estimated one, nonetheless."

"And a guess is a guess nonetheless," Quentin mumbled.

"I like the keen thoughts," Patterson goaded. "They fit you, don't try to repel them as you always do. Now—*Ahem*—where was I? Ah." He pushed his palms off his thighs and stood. "All that being said, allow me to veer to the crescendo of this discussion, if you will. In 2045, which, to you, surely feels no more than yesterday, something very significant was taken from us. It was one of Pluto's moons."

Quentin stared up at the man.

Patterson chuckled.

Why does he always laugh at me? Quentin wondered.

"You heard correctly," Patterson said. "Indeed, my boy. A moon of Pluto."

Quentin's mind shifted gears. To that point, all conversation centered on the mystical exoplanets had seemed like a dull, theoretical science lecture. He could tolerate going along with it to simply get along, scraping on the edges of diplomacy and obedience for the mere sake of not getting his own throat stabbed. But he had trouble faking it, then. Patterson was crazy. Quentin looked around and bit down on his tongue so hard that he tasted blood. He gulped and harvested all the mandatory courage to express his doubt. "No offense, sir—I mean, Patterson. But, um, that sounds pretty, um…far-fetched. Kinda hard to believe, I mean. How can I believe that?"

"How can you believe that?" Patterson recited. His hand was on his belly and he clucked his tongue in amusement. When he finished chuckling, he asked, "Your medical files, did the guard take them?" Quentin flinched at the mention of the guard. But in response to the question, he shook his head and brought his right leg up and onto the couch. With his knee in front of his nose, he reached his hand into the tightly scrunched bottom of his sweatpants. He removed his rolled-up files, which, after being confined into a tubular shape, resembled the form of a baguette. Patterson waited, always patient. When offered the paper baguette, he took it into his hands and opened it. "While you sit in your firm state of disbelief," he said in another amused, but in no way derisive, manner, "allow me to say that, before I read this, Naomi was born in 2009. Do you remember the age at which she had her first severe ear pain?"

"Two?" Quentin cooperated. "She was two, I think."

"Good." Patterson smiled. "You listen well, Quentin. You make my job so much easier."

Only because I'm scared to shit, Quentin thought to himself.

"Alrighty," Patterson began, reading from the pages below him. "In 2034, your school nurse reported that you experienced searing ear pain during the day along with one of your fellow classmates, Jaymes Chen. The incident occurred at nine o'clock in the morning eastern time." He looked over the edge of the files' paper binding. "One of John-P's moons was discovered missing at ten-thirty PM that same day." He looked back down and switched between the medical records and the planetary files. "In 2043, you experienced bad ear pain again. This time, it was in the middle of the night. Twelve hours later, Houston called me while I was in D.C. and alerted me to the disappearance of John-P. Previously, in 2039, you had yet another earache. That was when we lost the smallest of John-P's moons. In 2037, you had another episode, which also happened to be just when we lost the largest of John-P's moons. In December of 2031…indeed, another earache. N-BULA vanished off the radar. And indeed, the loss of N-BULA's single moon coincided with your massive earache of 2030. Ah yes, 2029…your ears pained you excessively on the same day that 23KCJ-OH was gone. And then of course, your first ever episode took place earlier that year when you had just turned one, and that signaled the impending doom of JALV." He glanced down. "Might I add that the mother of a particular four-year-old girl by the name of Fatima Jennet sent in an ear pain complaint to her doctor during the year 2043. Then, most recently, alongside your friend Jaymes and little Fatima, you were all *ear witnesses* to the disappearance of one of Pluto's many moons, Nyx." He seated himself and shut the folder. He handed it back to Quentin, who flinchingly took it back. "Oh, and one more thing I deem important to add is that all the planets and moons which disappeared were constructed of solid surfaces. This I must emphasize. All that remained were the star and those two gaseous planets. I think that strange, do you not? As I said before, Quentin, gone are the days of coincidences." Quentin must have looked pale and sickly because Patterson said, "Quentin, I am no threat to you."

"No, I know," Quentin lied. He scratched the back of his neck. "I mean, this is some pretty heavy information. I think my friends would benefit from knowing it too. Can I see them?"

"I know, Quentin. But now is not the time."

"Right. The...the time. Right. Of course. Um...What else do you want to tell me?"

"Quentin, I am not going to hurt you."

"Okay."

"Really, Quentin."

Quentin shook all over. "May I ask you something?"

"You may ask anything you like."

"I guess what I'm trying to ask," Quentin said, "is...how do I know any of this is true?"

"That is not for me to decide. True belief is only summoned from within yourself. There is, however, more to help you decide. Much more. More to this explanation, perhaps more easily ingested with a walk and a change of scenery. So, would you like to take another walk, look around, or do something else for a couple minutes? Perhaps even get some food? That is, with the exception that you cannot see your friends just yet."

Quentin shook his head. He looked to the carpeted ground, where his toes were clenching and unclenching. He felt really sick, nauseous and dizzy. He also felt demeaned.

"Do you want to stay here?" Patterson asked.

Quentin nodded.

"But are you ready for me to go on?"

Quentin shook his head.

"All right," Patterson relented. "We shall slow it down. It is a lot to take in. I've had the privilege of processing this since my daughter was two. You are doing great, considering your ripeness."

Quentin stayed stiff. "*Why* am I here?" he pressed.

"As I have said, you have been recruited to help me, to help your brother, and to help everyone and everything on Earth."

"But recruitment implies consent," Quentin said. "Okay, just...What am I helping you with?"

"Those two gaseous planets of the Inverness2 star system are still untouched," Patterson said. He scratched at the thin layer of five o'clock shadow around his chin.

"Okay." Quentin sighed. "I'm sorry. I really am. No....I'm not...not *sorry*. Just, no more of this. I get it, I hear the impending doom of long-lost planets. Why couldn't you have just told me this during lunch break in the cafeteria at school? Why drag me out to some underground, windowless, industrial building?"

"Not only will that be explained to you and your friends in just ten minutes, but you will all have the freedom to go wherever you please before the hour is out."

"Okay...Ten more minutes..."

"You have my word."

"All right. Then I'm listening again. Sorry, just ah..."

Patterson waved him off. "Please, Quentin, do not apologize for your confusion and honesty, as they are necessary and demonstrate your level of seriousness."

Quentin played along to stay on Patterson's good side. "So what's wrong with the two planets?"

"Not one little thing," Patterson objected and gave a short-lived smile. "Nothing at all. That's what's so wonderful. But at the same time, not. One of the most important things you need to understand about their persisting existence is that, without their specific compositions, that being their inherent physical makeup, they would not still exist."

"Their compositions?"

"The remaining two planets have one thing in common. They are either gaseous or have an atmosphere of gaseous nature. The one highest and furthest left on the map is an entire body of gas whilst that other one, down below it, is cloaked by a gas or gases. Are you catching on to what I am telling you, Quentin?"

Quentin shook his head.

"All right. Hm…Okay. Allow me to elaborate. They are both either gas or cloaked by gas, are they not?"

Quentin nodded.

"And all the other planets and moons in that system were not, correct?" Patterson asked.

"I guess so. You never mentioned the composition of all the moons."

"Oh, excuse the omission. Yes, they were all solid objects. So, to my point. They were all solid objects therefore…therefore what, Quentin?"

Quentin half-shrugged his shoulders. "Therefore only the planets with gas are still in existence?"

"Exactly!" Patterson verified in relief. "And not only that, but whatever it is that had demolished the star system seems to have moved on from that very one, Inverness2, to ours. Almost like *they*… *it*…whatever…doesn't care about gaseous or gas-covered planets. So you may be asking why this is happening…"

Quentin wasn't asking.

"And please," Patterson said, "bear in mind that planets consisting entirely of, or concealed by, gas, are in no way life-sustaining or inhabitable." Then, he sat down, closed the palms of his hands together decisively, and offered a satisfied look to Quentin, as if they had together just solved some great mystery. Quentin, by contrast, regarded Patterson with a disturbed, inquisitive expression. "You don't get it," Patterson said in a flat, matter-of-fact tone.

"No, sorry."

"Think about it. *Really* think about it. The pattern of extinguished planets, the composition of them, and the unharmed nature of the uninhabitable planets all point to one summary inference. Whatever destroyed those planets only did so because they were solid, and whatever it is continues to do so on a path that now includes our solar system, and inevitably, Earth."

Quentin cowered into the backrest of his sofa.

"Quentin?"

"Uh...that's a leap," Quentin said bashfully. "You know, to piece that together from the tiny dots of a few exoplanets not showing on a telescope? I mean, planets come and go in the night sky all the time. I can't see Venus all the time. That doesn't mean it's...y'know... gone. Not like, gone-gone. Just gone. It doesn't make Venus dead. And even if it were, why would I assume *something* destroyed it intentionally? Why are we even discussing this? I just want to know why we've been kidnapped, and to pull this on me...Just give me a straight answer...Please, sir. I don't care about your space stories. Are we under arrest, or what? Did we do something? Like...Really, what?"

"None of those things. Just calm down. Just indulge me another minute. Literally, one more minute, and it will all be clear."

"Fine," said Quentin. "Fine. I'll play along. Okay, so here's where I'm supposed to ask, 'So, how can you be certain something is purposely destroying solid planets?' Happy?"

"We are not one-hundred-percent certain, but it is a supremely educated guess based on deep probability testing. In fact, we were able to predict the sequential blinking out of the last three bodies, the nearest exoplanet, that planet's moon, and the expired Pluto moon, Nyx. The odds against getting those predictions right were so high that Vegas casinos never would have taken the bet, because they could never have afforded the payout. Odds of billions to one, and yet we were spot on. Our theory is both stronger and more provable than The Theory of Evolution."

"Theory being the operative word," Quentin grumbled.

"Let's, for a moment, say that you are a remarkably advanced being somewhere out there, living in another corner of our galaxy."

"Okay..."

"And say that you want to prevent the prospect of allowing a whole different species of intelligent beings from ever threatening the existence of yourself and the entirety of your own kind. What, with all of your advanced faculties, would you logically do?"

"I don't...I don't know. I guess...I just never really thought about it."

"Think, lad. You are responsible for preserving your entire species. You have no choice in that position. You would go on the offensive, wouldn't you? I mean, if you had the advanced technology, weaponry, and wherewithal to do so," Patterson suggested.

"I suppose, maybe, but—"

"You would, Quentin. Eventually, any leader would, in order to preserve their own planet and kind," Patterson added convincingly. "If you had the capability to destroy the totality of a potentially threatening planet, you would invest your power into that mission if you were a being predisposed to self-preservation and strategic thinking. Right?"

"But—"

"So what do we, as humans, do? What do we do when this is what we believe something, or some *being*, inside our galaxy is doing to all these poor bodies?"

"Something? Nothing? I don't know," Quentin said. "Not kidnap a bunch of high schoolers and some kid."

Patterson chuckled. He didn't seem to mind the insult and pushed through his agenda. "If you were under the suspicion that something or someone were on its gradual way to killing you and every living thing around you, what, realistically, would you do?"

"Fight back?"

"Ah! Yes! But, to do that, you must first locate whomever or whatever it is which is bound to antagonize and kill you. Correct?"

Quentin swallowed. "Mr. Patterson," he cracked, "what does this have to do with me?"

"You are here to help us find them before they find Earth," the man said.

"But how?"

"Each consecutive time you experience 'tinnitus,'" Patterson said while making quotation signs with his fingers, "the volume increases, and the tones become more painful. Over time, we observed, in all four of you, that the more intense or strikingly loud they became, the more pain you felt, and the closer this danger was to us. But here's the clincher. In the last instance, the one with a Pluto moon, you had the pains a full thirty hours before the moon blinked out. Don't you see? You, Jaymes, and the child Fatima are both an early warning system as well as a set of tracking devices. As the distance closes, your sensing of the tones, combined with our knowledge of the bodies within our solar system, means we can track down and anticipate where our doomsday attacker is and likely will be…and *when*."

"Where are we?" Quentin begged.

Patterson, that time, chose to neglect his guest's distressed plea. "We were going to persist with our Earth-based sound search, truly we were. If anyone is to blame for your presence here today, the groups at fault are actually our adversaries back home."

"Adversaries back home? What do you mean?"

Patterson sighed. "You know, politics and war are never delightful things to engage in. It's why I chose to pursue the sciences, but life has a way of making us face the things we dread most." He shrugged. "You had a good education growing up. Surely you must be aware of certain geopolitical tensions our country suffers with others, correct? If we are not enemies with some other place, we do have governmental stress. Take Russia, for example. Touchy, I am aware. But consider it. It is a nation, its innocent people aside, that has famously failed to see eye-to-eye with us on most issues. Or, our government has failed to. Either way, both governments are rarely aligned where it counts."

"Yes," Quentin said.

"We would only align with them if we had no other option or if they, for once, proposed something which our politicos were inclined to agree with. Isn't that so?"

"I guess."

"And yet, we disagreed with them on this very matter. We presented to them what we thought to be a logical solution, but they disregarded it."

"I mean..." Quentin coughed. "I never kinda thought the Soviets or Russia were exactly illogical...just...different from us and our means of...of normal approach..."

"'Different' is a diplomatic term, I shall hand that to you," Patterson acknowledged admiringly. "Oddly enough, for an art that sounds so easy, diplomacy is actually rather difficult. Kudos to you. I have chosen well."

Patterson's false belief that his obsessive, science-fiction fantasy was at last translating into real life made Quentin squirm, but so did the observation of his supposedly deft wielding of a difficult art. "With all due respect, sir," he said, "I think you're mistaking diplomacy for me trying to phrase something delicately without sounding too...American."

Patterson burst out laughing. But then, in a matter of seconds, it was as if the middle-aged gentleman with his double chin forming from his lowered head had lost his focus on Quentin. For a short, but seemingly long-feeling while, his heavy eyes didn't blink, and he was wholly distracted by a thought. His hands remained pressed against each other and he stared off into a landscape of pillows. Quentin wondered if he was witnessing a mental breakdown.

Some moments later, Patterson's sad, lime pupils rested on Quentin when he seemed to regain traction of his thoughts. "Are you familiar with the Krakatoa explosions of 1883?" he asked.

Quentin suppressed a groan. *Goddamn. Not another tangent.* "Um, yeah. We learned about it briefly in school last year."

"What did you learn?"

"Well, they were a series of volcanic explosions near India. No wait—Indonesia. I think. What was it? Mr. Jenkins, my science teacher, he didn't discuss the actual eruptions as much as he did the aftermath. So, I can't say much about them. Sorry."

Patterson's elbow sagged off the armrest of his sofa. Quentin's admittance of unknowing seemed comforting to Patterson. "Quentin, it was no mistake that Mr. Jenkins centered his lessons on the aftermath of the volcanic explosions as opposed to the explosions themselves." Happily, he bowed his head sideways with a small show of his teeth in a smile. "Jenkins was instructed by my team to only teach you of the aftermath."

"Huh?"

"Because," said Patterson, "the aftermath of that volcano and all like it are gravely tied to this mission of yours."

"I really think you have the wrong kid."

"The details of our planetary findings were shared among several countries we believed could aid us," Patterson said. "We quickly came to accept that the threats soon to occur warranted a multinational approach and that, if we wanted to ensure our Mother Earth's safety, we would need to involve other nations. We could not succeed in the overall safety of our home on our own. Not to mention, it would be rather thick-skinned of us to withhold intel such as this from our allies and nations whom we have, in the past, scorned for keeping things from us. Thus we allowed Canada, England, France, Germany, Japan and—" Patterson huffed, wrinkling his nose with repulsion—"China and Russia in on our findings."

Quentin frowned. "Sir, I don't understand your disdain for Russia. I might not read the news a lot but my social studies teacher was talking about how they've had, for the first time, a fair election and a genuinely elected president."

"You're referring to the 2043 election, aren't you?"

"Mhm."

"You listen well then. But, Quentin, I'm afraid that even the fairest of elections can end unfairly."

"But President Karev seems like a cool guy. I mean, I don't know a lot, but he seems better than the last guy."

"That's because he is," Patterson said. "And in a perfect world, Karev would win reelection for a second term, which, believe me, I want more than anything. My issue with Russia is not the pro-democracy, free-and-fair-Russia of Karev, though. My issue with Russia is the very real threat of the fascist minority party and its opposition leader, Rustev."

"But you said he's in the minority party. Why should you be worried about him?"

"Because, my boy, no one remains in the shadow of another so long as they have powerful figures to back them and push them into the light. But I promise you, we will come back to this. Just hold that thought."

"Okay."

"Now, the great meeting. So, in the company of the globe's arguably most powerful nations, we delved into the gravity of the situation—pun unintended—and discussed the missing planets and tones. However, none of us from our home nation or other seven delegations could have fathomed how the discussions would turn. Much gratitude to the Russians, but a dispute emerged because they put forth a most ridiculous proposal for how to diffuse our ever-nearing threat and others disappointingly backed their play. In a matter of hours we were divided, revolving tensely around two drastically antithetical proposals...ours and theirs. The two proposals were essentially A, dispatch a troupe of the necessitated scientists, a subdivision of NASA-issued paramilitary, and genuine military for protection and warfare—the former's job would be to determine the location of our mystery enemies whilst the latter two would be intended to eradicate as much as humanly feasible. Or B, which was to disguise Earth in a way that made it appear gaseous and uninhabitable in the hopes of eluding an attack."

"Both options sound unrealistic," Quentin mumbled. "Like, we went to the moon once and we can't even get there a second time or reach Mars with people."

"I must oppose that notion, Quentin," Patterson debated. "NASA possesses such an abundance of advanced spacecraft and weaponry from the Department of Defense, but the extreme secrecy surrounding them meant that the information had never been revealed.

Needless to say, we were met with rebukes from those who were none too pleased to be told of this news. I'll explain more about that after. Now, what do you think about plan B?"

"What? Oh, disguising Earth? That sounds impossible. Besides, what do you mean 'disguise?'"

"Quentin, do tell me what happened after the four major Krakatoa explosions occurred."

"I don't see how this is—"

"No, do tell," Patterson pushed, and sternness was suddenly drawn all over him.

"Okay...The ash, debris, and stuff formed dust clouds that were really thick...really dense. It covered the Earth, and from Asia to Europe. Some people reported they couldn't see the sun. There was this, like, massive layer of ash and smoke left all over the world for years. Oh, and it cooled it down. The Earth cooled down."

"Did you ever get to see what the Earth looked like at the time?"

Quentin nodded. "There was old, black-and-white footage of the ash-filled atmosphere. Everything was smoky, and Earth's temperature dropped for a while, and it looked like a—Wait. Do you mean to say that they're...?" He paused. "No."

Patterson smirked. "You're quicker on the uptake than O'Neil," he teased. "Yes, that is precisely what certain parties were proposing, Quentin, and included in the band of support were the UK and China. They thought it a sensible idea to detonate massive amounts of explosives within and below some of the world's largest, most menacing volcanic bodies in order to deliberately create a gaseous atmosphere."

"To disguise us as a gas planet?" Quentin gurgled. "Actually, that doesn't sound like a horrible idea. Sounds a lot easier than tracking down some super alien force and winning a war in space. B doesn't sound like too bad an option, if I had to pick one."

"No, it does not," Patterson concurred. "However, all in the proposal is swell until you begin to think through the details."

"Like?"

"Well, it is simple. Isn't it? Imagine an entire race of humans with asthma-like symptoms. That's not to mention the one billion asthmatics who'd die immediately. And the decrease in temperature. The lack of sun exposure. The sure destruction of at least the nations that harbor the volcanoes in question."

"Oh…right," Quentin murmured.

"'Oh, right' indeed," repeated Patterson. "Now take the Krakatoa explosions, multiply them by some factor of ten to twenty, and you're somewhere in the range of an unbreathable, unlivable atmosphere for years and years, perhaps even extending for more than three generations. What then? Not even then, but before then? Would there even be a 'then?'"

"We all die in the short term," Quentin realized. He was so overtired that for an unnerving spurt of time, he was disturbed by the prospect of his family dying from the possibility of a volcanic eruption, until he remembered, *This guy's cracked.*

"It is blatant suicide," Patterson said. "Not even a roll of the dice. Even if you downplay the air quality, as the UK did with wildly woolly science, you still end up with a decimated food chain, and farm yields would shrink so much that billions would die. How many billions? No one could even project a decent estimate. You can genetically engineer and modify food for only so long. Which is why, of course, we could not proceed with that proposed operation.

"Thankfully, an agreement was reached that said if either of the plans ever commenced, all parties would come together under that plan and support it with whatever means possible to make it succeed.

The only issue is that some people tend to go against their word. Five years after our first meeting, Chinese troops moved into some African nations with volcanic activity. Thus, two protection leagues were formed, one the Global Defense Op, the other, the Global Offense Op.

"What you must understand about the original formation of the Global Defense Op is that the meeting in question that brought our opposing nations together took place over twenty years ago. And at that time, it was awfully unfortunate to have the volcanic proposition ever be voiced, more than today. Russia, then, was not a democratic nation. The UK and China were letting slip the first splinters in their bureaucratic relations with us." He put his hands up a bit. "Now, there was some splintering among themselves too, don't get me wrong. The UK proposed an all-out bombing blitz on Krakatoa since it had previously proven its worth when it came to destroying the planet. Somehow, despite all its natural riches and three hundred million inhabitants, they deemed Indonesia a land worth sacrificing and that the world would survive it being be blown off the map, so why not utilize its one defense tool. Heartless perception, no?"

Quentin nodded.

"Yes," Patterson said. "Very, very heartless. The only reason China objected to the Krakatoa proposal was that it would obviously negatively affect Chinese soil and economics. So Krakatoa was temporarily off the table. Besides, the UK realized soon enough that a lot of their manufactured goods are made in Indonesia, not to mention the vast forestry and plants that feed the biopharma industry. Moreover, Germany and the others on our side made it clear that we would sanction the hell out of the UK if they attacked Indonesia in such a manner. Follow the money, Quentin. Just follow the money. So where did that leave them? Well, those three nations, The UK, China, and Russia, were more than cozy to the concept of forcefully inducing volcanic eruptions as long as they didn't risk greatly impacting their own land and power. They decided, in the end, to instead erupt multiple smaller, but still massive, volcanoes that were both far enough away to leave said countries somewhat unharmed while causing great harm to virtually all others. Do you see why this may not be the best option?"

Quentin nodded appeasingly.

"Just as I thought. So their pact had changed and they had a new plan. International operatives of ours unveiled that, altogether, they were intending to target volcanoes within—How may I put this? —nations which they deemed to be of lesser value than others. And you may be thinking, why would any of the nations who were seen as lesser ever agree to this? Well, Quentin…They didn't. As I said before, a fair election does not mean a fair result. Shortly after the 2035 election in the Congo, the United Kingdom intervened and overthrew the democratically elected president with someone they deemed more…*suitable* to the people. Which, in other words, meant someone who was glad to take a payoff and flee the country to permit British troops to do as they pleased with Mount Nyiragongo. Similarly, the Chinese government did the same in the Ecuadorian election of 2042 in order to stake claim to the nation's twenty-seven dormant volcanoes. Then, there was the invasion of more African nations, that time by China, and it was an especially strategic move on their part. Not only would they be detonating land which would not hurt themselves, it would also leave the world more dependent on Asian manufacturing. Horrible, horrible. But, yes, it is true. So do you know what dormant volcanoes are, Quentin? Oh, you do. Good. Again, you make my job very easy.

"In terms of Russia, they themselves had laid claim on a volcano of their own, and it is in Columbia—Mount Ruiz. But then 2043 happened and Karev was fairly elected. He kept Russian troops on the mountain but not for the same reason as his predecessor.

Karev's reason for military occupation on the volcano was, and to this day is, to guard the body from anyone who wishes to set it off. Not to detonate it at any given time like his predecessors would have liked to have seen."

"So Russia is on our side?" Quentin asked.

"In some respects, yes."

"It sounds like they're completely on our side."

"The majority is. The minority isn't. Karev may have the people's love, but Rustev is deep in the pockets of the United Kingdom and China. It wouldn't surprise me if Karev's reelection results will either be rigged or end with him assassinated. Or both. The opposition leader is slowly rising, but often overlooked. We've sent some of our own troops to Mount Ruiz to aid the Russians, but as Rustev receives more and more funding by the day, it's hard to tell how permanent a fixture democracy will be there."

"Oh."

"Don't lose hope, Quentin. In terms of the Global Offense Op, we similarly have territories of our own. We've suffered some losses, though, I won't deny it. Unfortunately, the previous president to the Congo was a dear ally of ours. But then the election happened and we lost our grip on them. We have Brazil and Tanzania, though. We aid their governments with our troops and promise them to keep their land whole and safe, and they in turn allow us the opportunity to stand en garde of their dormant volcanoes. Although, Brazil has a strong enough force that doesn't need much support. But Tanzania needs it."

Quentin perked up. "Mount Kilimanjaro is in Tanzania, right?"

"That, indeed. Our troops are there right now as we speak."

"I haven't heard it on the news," Quentin countered skeptically.

"Because things like this do not make it to the news, Quentin. It would worry people, hence its secrecy. It was hard enough to let their government in on it."

"So we're there to keep it safe?"

"We guard the mountain day in and day out alongside the more prominent occupation of the Tanzanian People's Defense Force. It's a good placement for us. After all, it puts us quite close to the Congo. For safety, we've also sent troops and air defense systems to Indonesia, because even though China was initially against the prospect of erupting any of Indonesia's volcanoes, one never knows how things may swing. Plans change rapidly when it comes to the selfishness of saving one's own skin.

Patterson sighed. "And there you have it. The two teams. Both mean well, but have different ways of executing their perceived wellness. China, the UK, and technically parts of Russia make up the Global Defense Operation whilst ourselves, Russia's current ruling party, Canada, Japan, Germany, and France make up the Global Offense Operation."

"I—" Quentin stopped himself. "France?"

"Yes, Quentin, France."

"Okay," Quentin said. "So, uh, is that the end of it, then?"

"The end of what? The summary?"

"Yeah."

"Not quite."

So, there was still more. Quentin wanted to scream. "So you've...what? You've sent forces into space to go find and battle the...whatever?" he asked doubtfully. "Well, at least the volcanoes won't hurt them."

"Indeed, a search league. And no, the volcanoes will never hurt them here...*us* here."

A long pause filled the space between the two of them.

"Here?" Quentin asked. "What do you mean 'here?'"

"Well, Quentin," Patterson said calmly, "considering how neither you nor any of your contemporaries came upon a conventional exit the entire time you wandered around, that can truly only be indicative of one thing."

"What?"

"You, my boy, have in fact already been recruited into said top-secret project. But, circumstances did not allow for the project to work from Earth. You are part of the search league. And by search league, yes, I do indeed mean the one which has already been deployed into deep space. We hear their cries, their little screams for help. They are sounds that almost seem to mourn their deaths. A mass, so to speak. We must take those tones as a cautionary tale...to not have one ourselves or else the funeral of our planet will be soon." Patterson's head spun around on his shoulders as he scoured the room for something. "Always so funny. Enjoy as I might these all-telling discussions and my guests' reactions, they leave me so dreadfully parched. Do you see any errant water bottles lying on the ground? Given the state of things, germs are seldom a worry of mine. I wouldn't be afraid to drink from one. Ah! Ignore me! Here's one! Ooh, I could do with some ice. Would you like to go get some proper refreshments, Quentin? Quentin?"

Quentin sat very still. By that period in his life, tirades of pure inanity were things he had grown accustomed to, courtesy of Agata Celia Hanson's senile state and Hollis Carlyle's rants. But Patterson's mind suffered a different ilk of mental instability. He had a mind which Quentin had the capacity to understand, and it was because of that very fact that he was properly petrified. *He's absolutely delusional,* is what he thought. The twists and turns of Patterson's flowery-phrased speech and the genuine belief in his tender eyes that his fantasy had come true were most disconcerting. Agata was an outpouring river of wonderment and curiosity, unfulfilled but hoping that one day she could have seen what others could not as she dragged through endless days of a mental haze. Hollis was something of an unrealistic dreamer. But Patterson wasn't like them. Patterson was different. He was unhinged.

While Patterson chugged his—or someone else's—water, Quentin, although still in his sheepish slouch, said as brazenly as he could manage through his trembling lips, "You drugged him."

"Quentin?" Patterson asked with an inquisitive frown.

"Connor," Quentin said. "You did something to him. You're one of those psycho rich guys, aren't you? The type that knows billionaires. I know your kind. I see it in the news. You weirdos love that escapism stuff and want us all to be a part of this whacked-out fantasy of yours so you can pretend you're in some movie or something. Maybe you are a billionaire, I don't know. But you're the type that can pay off law enforcement and our families. The type that traffic kids just to make them live out your creepy fantasies."

"Quentin, I desperately wish that the situation we are living through were a fantasy but, unfortunately, it is not."

"What did you do to him?" Quentin asked. "You drugged Connor, right?"

Patterson bobbed his head in a half-serious, half-bemused surrender. "Why, of course I drugged him. I drugged all of you. Actually, your mother was supposed to, but she ultimately failed at that. But yes, you were drugged. Was I supposed to bring you here conscious? You never would have agreed to it, evidenced by your reaction now. I can see how horrible a night you had. But that was not my doing."

Quentin's teeth ground together behind his lips. "That's not what I mean," he said. The bushy eyebrows of his meek face interlaced in his glare. His appearance wasn't wholly infuriated, given the held-back tears that polished each of his eyes, but his fury glazed on him enough for Patterson to minimize the somewhat lighthearted, upward curl of his lips; after all, if everything he had stated was true, then he, more than anyone, was perfectly able to read Quentin's swift broadcast of anger. He asked one more time, "You drugged him, didn't you?"

In a pacifying tone with his open hands raising in the air, Patterson said, "Quentin, please, I would never do that here. I promise you."

Quentin shot up off the couch, livid. The maps and medical records sprang off his lap. The items fell across the carpeted floor and smacked against Patterson's oxfords, but Quentin didn't care. He wasn't going to hide his frustration any longer. Why should he have to continue to sit there and obediently take that farce as truth? While he put up with the charade that was likely a distraction, his classmates were probably undergoing the presumed torture Connor had gone through. "How can I believe that?!" Quentin asked. "I've known Connor since elementary school! Since we were kids! He's smarter than this, he never would've given in unless you forced him to!"

"Quentin, I truly never—"

"And that can only mean one thing, right? That means…That means you'll drug me, too. And…and…and persuade me to say swell things about our situation to the next bunch of victims. Right, Patterson?"

"Quentin, I sincerely mean it when I say that I did not drug Connor in order for him to believe me, nor have I ever used such tactics on you. I never even instructed him to intervene on my behalf earlier. That was purely his own initiative. The boy must have been eavesdropping and decided to make things easier for me. It was kind of him, really. I thought he'd been sleeping."

"The others, my classmates, are they still in that cafeteria?"

"That would depend on whether or not they wished to stay there. There is lots to see, after all," Patterson answered elusively, softly. He creased his forehead in concern, observing Quentin. "You've lost a lot of your color," Patterson commented worriedly. "I understand that you're perplexed, or more precisely, feeling as if you shouldn't or don't want to believe me, but deep down, you do, and you have to see that it all pieces together in only one possible way. It all makes sense. But it's all right. It is all right if you're not ready to accept what I've said on face value just yet. You do have months, years, to warm up to it. It will take some time to absorb, and I can help you through it. I can be—"

Quentin's hands slinked up his cheeks. His uneven nails tore at his white skin while he panned reddened eyes to the wooden chandelier. He started to cry. His head was drumming, ramming the insides of his skull and rattling it against the flesh of his brain. He dragged his skin farther down, then massaged his temples under his bed of straggly hair.

"Oh, dear Quentin," Patterson rustled out compassionately. He scanned every corner of the nook. "I think Amber left a box of tissues hanging about, seeing how naggingly ill she was the other day."

Quentin dry heaved. *"Amber?"* he croaked. With vivid recollection, he thought back to the freckly, honey-haired girl, the captain of Shaw High School's cheerleading squad. "What is she doing here?" he asked.

"Oh, I wonder where she put them," Patterson mused aloud as he stretched his neck to acquire a better look of the area. He stayed intent upon the mystery of the missing tissue box. "Oh well. You'll be washed up soon. I'm assuming you—"

Quentin cursed.

"Pardon?" Patterson asked. "I can show you your quarters if you like."

"You are..." Quentin started, but the rest was too quiet to hear.

"Sorry?"

Quentin slid his face into his palms. He whimpered and uttered out, "You are crazy."

Patterson sighed a breath of understanding. He clamped his hands into a knot on his knees, and said touchingly, "Oh, Quentin. I know you've been taken advantage of somewhat, like you've only been handed unfortunate curveballs, but I assure you, I can—"

"No!" Quentin screamed. He tore his hands away from his face and opened his eyes. "You are crazy! You are fucking crazy!"

"Quentin, I am here for the sole purpose of helping you."

Quentin staggered back, toward the staircase.

"Quentin, where are you going? Don't be so frightened. Things will be better, I swear. You have your friends, you have this ship, and you have people depending on you for their safety. You will adjust to it. We have it under control. If you let me, I can—"

Quentin walked backwards. He neared the top of the stairs. "Lemme guess, help me? You are textbook insane."

"Which, my boy, were essentially the very words of Connor, Terry, Amber, Derek, Natalie, and everyone else here when they first arrived. Yet, here they all are, healthy, well, and dedicated to the cause, one they never could have imagined they would follow and devote themselves to."

Quentin was flustered. "There's more?"

"And every single one of them trusts me with their life," Patterson said with the grace of a man who had dealt with that specific dilemma time and time again. "They believe in the cause and are willing to fight for it, gain fulfillment from the sacrifice. They aren't alone, having one another, and very happily will they have you by their sides."

A blazing migraine began to ignite in the front of Quentin's head. "What did you do to them?" he asked. His arm extended behind him, his hand feeling for the railing of the staircase. He walked back a few steps, until he finally felt his foot drop and knew he was on the stairs. He didn't take his eyes off Patterson.

"Everything they feel, think, and do is a product of their own, deliberate, independent thoughts," Patterson said. "Whether or not they are content with being here holds no relevance to me. I never forced Connor or anyone else to grow into this ship, they chose to."

"You changed him," Quentin said. "Someone like Connor wouldn't have...wouldn't have just seen sense in literally anything you've said to me. He's not stupid, and...Oh, god..." His hands flew to his stomach. He was going to throw up. "I'm leaving."

"Quentin..."

"You will regret this," Quentin threatened. "When the real authorities come and find you, you will regret this."

Patterson poorly masked his disappointment as Quentin staggered backwards, distancing himself from the loft by descending the steps of the swooping stairway. For as long as he stayed in close proximity to the upper level, he never peeled his attention away from Patterson, who sat in place with slumped shoulders and pitying eyes. Quentin defiantly descended another couple of steps, to which Patterson arose and slid his hands into the pockets of his pants. As Quentin left, the man sighed. He sat back down on the sofa, unperturbed. Like he had seen it all before.

12

Quentin squeezed through the library door and all but flung himself out into the corridor. He had trouble breathing from the constant intake of the fragranced, recycled air. The perfumed wafts made him dizzy, like the story he'd just sat through in the library. Despite his sight having been set upon his feet earlier, when Patterson moseyed the two of them through the first two floors, Quentin had secretly taken note of each and every corner and different floor pattern. To his luck, his memory retained everything, and his bare feet were fleet as he traced his way along the mental map he had created for himself. He scrambled past unnamed, gold-inlayed doors he had seen before, on the few occasions he had looked up to see beyond his feet. As he ran, he began to realize just how far they had walked earlier. He cut seemingly endless amounts of corners before he finally passed the infirmary and the small conference room.

He went to the staircase, squinting the whole way down to block his eyes from the luminance of the crystals high above that were latched into the chandelier. The steepness made him squeamish, especially when he glimpsed through the transparent glass and down to the marble. He hated heights, but he wasn't about to bolt down the staircase with his eyes closed. He'd hurt himself enough in his swamp escapade.

Right before he touched the marble of the foyer floor, he screamed Frances's name. Then Jaymes's. Marina's. Athol's. Even Mathias's. *The goddamn irony,* Quentin thought. Once downstairs, he went in the direction of the cafeteria. When he found its door, he entered quickly.

There wasn't anyone inside. No brainwashed Connor O'Neil. No little girl. None of the other captives. Quentin's bloodshot eyes saw only dirtied, plastic bowls and crinkly paper cups on the formerly empty table where he and his fellow inmates once sat together. "Are you kidding me?!" he fumed. "Jaymes?! Ewan?!" He didn't get a response. "Goddammit!" He decided not to loiter. He would have to find them eventually, but with Patterson nearby and Quentin alone and vulnerable, he couldn't stand around, couldn't spare any time. He ran out of the room. Door after door and hall after hall on that first-floor level, he hollered all the names of the people he knew were indoors with him. He called out for every single one of them, but a shout of his own name was never reciprocated. He moved like a gnat, as he zigged and zagged through the channels of the place.

There was a silver, oval mirror nailed over a patch of one of the hallway's walls. When he passed it, he caught a glimpse of his skinny limbs, shaggy hair, and feverish face. He looked just as pathetic and pitiful as he felt.

A little later, he passed by an open door, through which purple lights gleamed onto him from inside, but kept on with his scampering. He tried to ignore the interior.

But he couldn't. He stopped running. He propped his chin onto his right shoulder and peered behind himself. He saw the purple lights again. There were also yellow and green, each shaped like laser beams. He detested himself for being pulled in because he knew there was no logical justification for tiptoeing back to indulge in the curiosity of peeping past the agape entrance. Faint as it was, there was a sound. Music. That was what he heard. It was a waltz harmony, and euphoric notes of an aggravatingly cheery symphony hopped through the air. He put his head through the doorway and, in that spinning mind of his, concocted expectations of a laser torture chamber purposed solely for fulfilling the barbaric fantasies of one Colin H. Patterson. Maybe he liked playing music while he tortured people. Quentin didn't put it past him. But the chamber Quentin confidently anticipated seeing, the one he just assumed would be replete with clubs and needles of unthinkable sizes and uses, or teeth-welding laser guns with machete extensions flacking their shafts, wasn't what he saw. The walling, whether painted or lined by paper, was black and overruled the brightness the room could have achieved, had those walls been lighter. Lined against them was a five-foot-tall *Pac Man* arcade game and an unnamed virtual reality, spaceship-flying game set with goggles and controls that were discarded upon the console. Humming in the middle of the room, with side speakers that suddenly emanated the voice of a computer-generated referee shouting despite the lack of occupation, was a weighty air hockey table; a metallic puck had found balance in one of the table's corners, and it hovered a few millimeters above the surface. To the right of it was a dessert parlor guarded by a lime-green countertop. Taking up space on the counter were two, plump goblets, each with melted pink liquids congealed in their bottoms, both stood forgotten on the edge of the bar. Five turquoise barstools were turned backward, not facing the bar.

Quentin brought himself back into the hallway. He tried to forget the oddity that was the arcade, and he resumed his haphazard flight in search of an exit.

Later, following two, subsequent harried runs through numerous vacated corridors which he was sure to have entered before, he came face to face with the elevator doors in the foyer. *What?!* he thought, furious. *What the hell?! I didn't retrace! Think, dumbass.*

Think. He led us up here. There's nothing here on the first floor. It's got to be down...in the basement. It wasn't an unreasonable estimation. When he put his mind to it, Patterson had been suspiciously intent on escorting everyone upstairs rather than letting them linger below. Quentin tapped his foot and nibbled the edge of his mouth, debating what he should do. He pressed the button, the only button on the elevator control panel wired into the wall. When it didn't open promptly, he unrelentingly slammed his finger against it, and the doors hissed apart. During the ride down, which felt painfully longer than the earlier ascent, he watched his reflection. He saw slimy skin with beads of sweat rolling into each other, and they made puddle-like splotches on his forehead. His face was ridden with deeply embedded stress wrinkles. His fluffy hair was limp, sagging down to his nose.

The elevator dinged and the doors slid apart again. When he exited, Quentin darted his way through the secret passage Patterson had unthreateningly introduced to everyone after previously ending the happened-upon guard's existence. At the final steps of it, once Quentin opened the door, he launched himself into his scouting venture. It was an unconventional and unforeseen quirk for him to find solace in the underbelly of the complex, especially since they were the very walls he had ardently despised before. But he was comforted by them. He couldn't explain why. Perhaps it was because, in there, he was hit with recollections of where his tedious day had begun alongside those whom he, mostly, trusted. And he began to think that he much preferred the honesty of the basement, in that it wasn't one giant guise of prestige like the place upstairs, where falsely pleasant flower scents and velvety floors tried to convince him that his situation was better than it seemed. The palatial upper levels were just a distraction, and he didn't appreciate it. The basement, on the other hand, was a hellhole. It was all cement and low-lighting, rough and unwelcoming, just the way things should have been to constantly remind him of how disastrous his life had become.

He tried to remember every fine detail that soared over his head from when he and the group were hurrying around those corridors earlier. He tried to pinpoint even a moment of possibility for an exit, but all that came to mind were Jaymes and Mathias unsuccessfully attempting to throw themselves against immovable barriers. Quentin swore he ran for ages. He had no idea how long he floundered around the basement, but he was tired of doing it.

Eventually, he did see an open door in front of him. It wasn't either of the barriers that had been taken down by the previous group of escapees after they woke in their separate rooms, nor was it the one to the file room, where the dead guard was still laid outside; despite Patterson's insistence that the guard would be removed, he was still on the ground where they had left him, only paler and more odorous. *Don't fall for it this time,* Quentin chastised himself as he looked at the open entrance. *Not this time, idiot. Not this time. It's not inadvertent, you've learned the stupid lesson. Don't.* But he had no other choice, and he was unmonitored and alone. He had no one to tell him not to do it. The other inmates were elsewhere and Patterson was upstairs, probably rambling to that teddy bear under the sofa leg about exoplanets' destructions.

Quentin stepped inside. The space was a bit larger than the file room from earlier. It was darker too, but everything in the basement was. He saw, arrayed by the door, hooks that were nailed into the walls on both sides of him, and from each hung long, durably crafted, dark-blue jumpsuits with multiple breast pockets and holster straps that were loosely strung around the upper halves of the left legs. He had seen them before and not a long time ago; they were identical to the attire his abductors wore on the night of his kidnapping. On the floor, beneath the dangling garments, translucent plastic boxes that contained metal-bottomed boots. At the end of the compartment, there were two, swinging doors. He extended his hands forward and pushed his palms against the doors. They were heavier than their appearance let on, but an extra shove managed to open them. Behind him, when he stepped out, the doors soundlessly swung back into place.

The new space was slighter. Its contents were different, in the sense that it was completely vacant. The faint lighting, however, was similar to the previous compartment, as one flat, fluorescent light winked dully at his sickly face. He was overcast with disappointment once he saw that an identical set of swinging doors was but five feet ahead of him. *"To hell with it,"* he muttered. He pushed the doors in front of him, saw rather than heard their soundless impact, and stood in yet another room, which he hesitated to even consider a room in the first place. *Closet,* he thought. *It's a closet.* The space was even smaller than the others. It was equivalently empty, but matchlessly uncomfortable. His shoulders brushed both walls as he moved, that was how small it was. The other difference he identified was that there was a chilliness to the air that he hadn't felt when he was in the last compartment. But the temperature aside, it was all the same. He rolled his eyes when he came upon a third pair of swinging doors. "Yeah, real funny, Patterson," Quentin said into the space, hands on his hips. Quentin pushed the next set of doors, and he wound up in another compartment. "Motherfucker!" he thundered.

The door ahead of him wasn't a double, swinging one. He was grateful that it wasn't, since the repetition started to wear on him. That door was, on the other hand, quite unforgivingly set in its place. There were no handles nor any plates of metal to indicate where one should place their hands to push it open. It was just a door, like the torn-down one from the room in which he had woken; if he hadn't been staring intently, he also would have mistaken it for undulated wall. Lodged into the cramped space with its oddly frosted metal walls and flooring, he was freezing cold, colder than he had been in the last closet. He recalled that his kidnapping had taken place in November and that the weather was already suffering the winter bite, and assuming he had been sedated for a while, long enough for Athol to have rapidly grown another foot, it wasn't so unreasonable to presume that it was at least midwinter already. Quentin wrapped his arms around himself and set his eyes on the barely visible door ahead. Beside the door's seam, on the wall left of him, a metal plate protruded from the surface, and a spring-loaded cover made from carbon fiber in the shape of a half-dome was on top of it. He saw the edge of a button, within which he assumed was the unlocking mechanism for the door. With the tips of his index and middle finger of his right hand, he casually attempted to flip up the gadget's cover.

It didn't move. The cover was spring-loaded to such a high degree of tension that it must have served, he again assumed, as an additional mechanism to require deliberate opening and ensure that the purpose of entry had been thoroughly considered. Well, his purpose had certainly been. He wanted to escape and one button wasn't going to be the impediment on his endeavor. He made a second attempt, outstretching his hand and placing considerable pressure on the cover and raising it, but the lid pinched down hard on three of his fingers as soon as he gained a small amount of movement. The half-dome didn't release his fingers. "Ow!" he yelped. The tightness of the compartment, which he formerly loathed, suddenly worked to his benefit as he reacted fast and braced his right foot on the opposite wall for leverage as he tried to pry his hand from the mechanism. He freed himself with a single jerk. *"Shiiiit! Shit! Shit!"* he whisper-yelled. He dropped his foot from the wall, cowered over, and jammed his hand against his stomach. There was blood, that awful smell again, but there wasn't enough to stop him. Nothing would stop him. He looked up to survey the wretched protection scheme that had just eaten his fingers. As the pain in his hand subsided, he thought to himself, *Oh, this bitch has got to be it.* He propped his sore fingers into his lips, slathered warm saliva onto them, and then released them from his mouth; it was so cold that the saliva solidified almost the exact instant he popped the fingers out of his mouth. Attempting once more, he squatted below the plate. He hoisted his thumb up and under the edges of the semicircle. He grunted as he began to elevate the lid off the base. But where he met with minor success, his jittering from the numbing cold slipped his grip, causing the lid to snap back down, back onto his fingers.

"You bitch!" Quentin boomed, spit globs shooting at the wall and freezing into tiny pellets. "Fuck you! Think you're tougher than me, Fucker?!" He was never one to assign personality to inanimate objects that refused yielding to human desire, but he thought himself quite a changed person since the abduction. In an all-out struggle, he again resorted to squatting beneath the four-inch-wide device and applying full force above him with the palm of each hand, as he had seen done by the power lifters in the *Olympics*. "Think you're tough, huh?!" he burst out. "*Not* tougher than me, Fucker. Wanna play that way? You wanna? I'm better than you…better and tougher…and smarter, you little bitch…" His new tactic finally achieved the intended movement of the cover to reveal its tightly guarded interior; a single, red button on the center of the plate. Any pride he accumulated from the victory waned as he began to feel the downward force fighting to once again lock the device closed. "No you don't!" Quentin yelled at Fucker. He couldn't risk moving a hand from the cover in order to press the button. With it mere inches from his nose, he quickly settled on using that extremity to push it inward. With a steady movement, he applied pressure with the tip of his nose. But, even then, the button didn't give in. Neither did he. He propped one foot against the wall behind him, positioned his forehead directly in front of the button, and locked his tongue behind his clenched teeth as he made his fifth attempt. Hands shaking from the strain, he thrust his wrists under the chomping cover, pushed off the wall with all the power he could muster, and smacked his forehead onto the red object. The cover bit down. He let out an echoing scream.

At last, the wall-and-door-in-one opened.

Quentin wobbled back. A frigid blast of air kissed his skin once the hard-won opening awaited his entry. The cold, he noticed, was significantly worsening the pain in his fingers and forehead. But what really irked him, what really ground on every single nerve in his thin, pathetic body, was that, in front of him, obstructing his way, stood an exact replica of the wall-door he just defeated. *"You gotta b-be fucking-ing kidding me-me,"* he said through his shivers. He wasn't going to risk freezing to death in the new compartment, and he set on repeating the button-unlocking regimen immediately. Unhinging the second lid should have been easier since he had a proven method of attack, but the steadily decreasing temperature took a toll on him. His fingers couldn't stop quaking. He was freezing, genuinely freezing. His thighs were stock still. His lips were drying. His almost iced-over nipples were uncomfortably hard under his shredded, half-intact shirt. It felt as if multiple, blunt knives were slowly shaving off his skin. His face stung too. He couldn't even feel his ears, like they had chipped off the side of his pulsing head. There was no feasible way to shirk the room's excessive chilliness, so he settled on employing his deep freeze to his benefit. He punched the button cover with the front of his freeze-dried forehead.

The single door, that one portion of the wall in front of him, cracked away from the surfaces around it ever so slowly, as if reluctant to open him to what he just knew would be yet another closet-tight space, and the fifth one at that. When the inching barricade finally revealed the other side, he was proven correct. It was another cramped, freezing chamber. Quentin pulled down the bottoms of his ripped sweatpants to cover his feet as best as he could to form a protective layer against the crisp floor. He wrapped meatless arms around his torso. He wasn't wheezing due to fear or trepidation anymore, but because he was cold. His pinching eyes clashed against what he was certain was subzero air.

Opposite him, there stood a door and not one, but two, button plates were affixed to the wall beside it, both of which, to his profound infuriation, were also shielded by the same painful, half-dome protective covers. The two metal plates weren't the only distinctions between that puzzle piece and the previous one. The new one, now closed off from its sibling behind him, had an inconsistency in one of its walls. There was a window. It had slight, white grids checkered all over. He was overjoyed to have found it, caring not one iota that it was tiny, as he was just grateful to finally find one. He hardly had to walk forward to reach it and the wall plates; a few shuffles of his feet were all that was necessitated. He squinted to gain sight beyond the glass's thick, single layer, his frosted lashes clinked against it. He saw another compartment the same size as the one he was in, but unlike the current, it was more similar to the first closet he had entered; the one with the clothing articles and boots. To his elated surprise, it contained additional arrays of outerwear, which dangled from hooks. He was freezing, so he planned to continue forward, to grab some of those clothes for himself, get outside, and run as far away as he could.

He bitterly recognized that in order to progress, he had to resume with the ever-tedious exit regimen. He settled his shaky hands around the bottom of the half-dome shield closest to him, lowered his knees to the ground and repeated the excruciating routine all over again, forcibly unveiling the first button. With his body convulsing in shivers and the tops of his two fingernails chipping off as blood oozed into sight, he pressed down on the switch. He noticed, as he made physical contact with the button, that it wasn't the same color as the other ones. A blue glow was on its miniature plate, caused by a ring of tiny blue bulbs surrounding it. He wondered why that was, but only for a split second, and then pushed down on it. The door in front of him didn't give way. Not even a crack. He angrily smashed his fist against the wall. Then, amid the loud teeth-chattering that pounded through his head, he heard something. Something beyond that compartment. The sound didn't originate from behind or along either of his shoulders. Instead, it came from a short distance in front of him, past the lonely, little window and within the new room with the clothing he so desperately needed. His unfeeling thumb lingered above the round, blue-hued switch that was next to his lower abdomen. He peered through the frosted glass; up against the hazy window, he saw his breaths. It appeared that he hadn't unlocked the exit to his chamber, but, by some inadvertence, the exit of the next one. The sound he heard grew louder, was relative to a forced, rusty scowl and it came from the opposite side of the wall-door-window-thing in front of him. From his side of the glass, he made out the exit doorway of the chamber ahead as it began to open. Then, the sound stopped, even though the entrance was still in motion. Halfway through its rigid, iced-over phase of unfastening, the clothing undid from the hooks and flew out the doors, into the shadows of what Quentin initially thought were the dark grounds of nighttime New England.

But it wasn't Massachusetts. It was nothing like his home. It was beautiful, yet dauntingly revolting. It was something which, for years, he had dreamed to see from a similar vantage point, but not one that close. Not so close that he could see the danger in the beauty, how the darkness consumed everything beyond the open doorway. Only a few, subdued twinkles shone in the distance while two dusty clusters danced before him. Everything else was a deep black—not only the backdrop, but the outdoors's entirety. The clothes were somewhere out there, somewhere in the great darkness, in the beautiful, unimaginable darkness, which meant that if he had been on the other side of that window, he would have similarly been pulled out.

Quentin looked away and fell to the ground. He started vomiting.

The figure of a person loomed out from a back corner of his compartment. Smooth on their feet, they ambled forward and crouched down next to him, draping a wool blanket onto his shoulders. Quentin didn't have to turn around to know who it was that stooped beside him. "Why did…Why didn't you tell me?" he pleaded, vomit frozen on his lips.

"I tried to," Patterson said.

Quentin closed his eyes. "H-How long?" he asked. When he didn't receive an answer, he asked again, "How l-long, P-Patterson?"

There was a sigh. "A year. We've reached late-November of 2046. Your nineteenth birthday was last week."

13

February, 2047

Quentin leaned his head against the post of his bed. It was a platform bed, a metal one which was fixed into the floor, with a lighted frame that glowed softly behind his pillows. He had laid awake all night before sitting up to examine the men's sleeping quarter.

Connor once told Quentin, and that was back in December of 2046, that occupants of the ship preferred unconventional sleeping locations to match the lack of convention in their lives. Most residents preferred either an empty living room couch or unclaimed library chaise to the tradition of dozing upon actual mattresses. Quentin was of a dissimilar opinion; he preferred the traditional means. True to Connor's word, the sleeping quarter was completely empty. There were over sixty beds, but except for Quentin's, every single one of them was unoccupied. Patterson had promised that once everyone was comfortable with their new living situation, they would each be given a key to their individual bedrooms on the topmost floor, the fourth. But, for the time being, he was adamant that there was a distinctive importance for communal support during the phase of adjusting to their dramatic circumstances. Quentin thought that rationale was stupid and that Patterson should have handed over the keys, then.

As he stared out at the empty beds, Quentin realized something glaringly obvious about himself, something which he hadn't previously recognized: he wasn't just fine with conformity, he craved it. Even though he technically wasn't born into it, it seemed he was gifted with the uncommon aptitude of not only performing menial and mundane tasks without complaint, but he favored such things over the thought of going about his life in a unique and non-conformist way. He wasn't his adaptive mother or his flamboyant best friend, Hollis. Quentin was Quentin. He liked having hours of homework. He liked the idea of owning a house in Massachusetts, living out his days in the state he was born into. He genuinely liked being just a son, a brother, and a student. His new life, despite having been prescribed to him, was not, it turned out, for him. Thrust into an ecosystem of raucous plans and eclectic notions, the world Patterson had molded for Quentin was the last thing he wanted. He wasn't creative. He wasn't versatile. He couldn't adjust to something he previously knew nothing about.

He thought back to December, on a certain afternoon when his new home bustled with activity, as there were still loud catchups between friends who hadn't seen each other since November of 2045. Besides Connor and the few others Patterson had offhandedly mentioned when he first met Quentin, there were more present as well: Chris Laney, Casey Montgomery, and Oscar and Ivy Martinez. The noise was bothersome, and, with their lunches in hand, Quentin and Connor sought refuge from it and retreated to a downstairs conference hall.

"Relax, you'll have help," Connor had told Quentin that day.

"Help?" Quentin asked as he blew over the steaming pea soup, which had been made by Natalie with the assistance of Fatima.

"Look, you don't need to worry," Connor said. "There's a chance that you being captain doesn't even happen. If things go to plan, that is." He swirled his own bowl of soup around with his spoon. He didn't look very attracted to it. "At the top of our ranks is, obviously, Patterson. He was the architect of this operation, so everything goes by what he says. Although, it's not, like, you know, an autocracy. Sleeping right now in some cryogenic tubes in the basement are about a hundred additional personnel."

"What are they supposed to do?"

"Half of them are military, handpicked individuals with the best skills and training. The other half are scientists; physicists; astronomers; geologists for when we get to our final destination; I believe we also have some neuroscientists. We also have, from the medical world, some neurologists, psychologists—"

"Hold on. Hold on. Our final destination?" Quentin asked.

Connor sat back. "Patterson didn't tell you? What *did* he tell you? Because I told everyone else everything."

"Um." Quentin put down his spoon. "Only that stuff about the tones. And a search league of some sort."

"Are you kidding me?"

"Well, it's not really Patterson's fault. I kinda ran away and then, like, slept the last few days. I vomited a lot too. Like, a lot. Patterson had to give me this weird smoothie thing with electrolytes every hour."

Connor sucked in a breath. "All right, how's this? I walk you through the purpose of all the personnel and then move into what our final destination is. Cool?"

Quentin nodded.

"So," Connor said, "the fate of the world thankfully doesn't lie in our hands. There's no need to panic. We have Patterson, our architect and director and the Global Offense Op, the various military figures who aren't needed right now as much as they are just backup in case stuff, you know, goes down. And then there's us."

"Us," Quentin echoed, his tone doubtful.

"Us," Connor repeated. "You, Jaymes, and Fatima are going to be the subjects of multiple studies because there's clearly some correlation between your health issues and everything that's going on beyond our solar system. Well, now in our system. You know what I mean, though. So we have some of the best neuroscientists on board with us here and a fantastic group of astronomers and astrophysicists, and the objective is that they pursue this collaborative study into, not only the origins of why you guys are going through this, but what we, as humans, can do to utilize it for the better."

"So the goal is for my ears to become a tool?" Quentin asked.

"Yeah."

"Why couldn't we do this back home?"

"Because," Connor said, "it's not safe there anymore. Our ambassadors and allies were getting killed overseas. Our top scientists, who were covertly cooperating with us from all over the world, were getting gunned down in their own homes. And even though Shaw was heavily protected by people outside and inside the town, you know how it is. There are operatives everywhere. It's even harder to tell who's who and how to hide from adversaries now that old allies are against us. So, the logic was to dispatch the most valuable figures up to a place where their safety could be guaranteed." He shrugged. "Besides, if the Global Defense Op could get their head start with the volcanoes, who's to say we couldn't get ours up in space? But, do you remember that bit I just said, how the other nations got their head starts by taking over volcanic territories?"

"Mhm."

"We got our head start too."

"How so?"

"Twenty years ago—I think that was the time, I could be wrong—after the Congo's territories were overtaken and barraged by a couple of our adversaries, we launched a different league into space, which consisted of the world's then-best scientists on this subject."

Quentin slurped some of his soup. "Are they still up here? Are they near us?"

Connor shook his head; a single, overly gelled strand of hair fell down to his face. "The first league? They are far out. They probably arrived to Titania years ago. They should be well into establishing a colony there with their families. We sent military up there too, obviously. Actually, what you have up here on our ship is minuscule compared to what we sent up before. Apparently, we dispatched a ton of people. Thousands. Patterson wasn't specific, but he made it clear that it was a lot. I know you're probably thinking that for something called The Global Offense Op, it seems pretty US-based, but that's not true. Where it's really global is when it comes to the people waiting for us on Titania. Establishing a base there was a collaborative effort. It's home to a population of people who originate from all corners of our world. It has Japanese natives, some French, some Russian, and many others. *And* it even has some defectors from countries that are now our adversaries."

"Titania is a moon of Jupiter, right?" Quentin asked.

"No." Connor's expression was flat. "Uranus."

"Right. Did you get a lot of comments?"

"About Uranus?" Connor's laugh was short, clipped. "Yeah. Anyway, where was I? Titania. Yeah so…We're essentially just the add-ons to an already undertaken mission."

"Why aren't the scientists and military members on our ship awake now?"

"Why?" Connor repeated, surprised by the enquiry, like the answer was the most obvious thing known to man. "Let's see, those in the military were young and in-shape when they were awake. Why would we age them unnecessarily? We need to preserve their youth as

long as possible in case things do go badly. And the scientists and doctors? Those people are well into their fifties and sixties. Patterson even said some of them were retirees in their seventies but came back to join the cause. Again, you and I are just a fraction of the team. So relax. We're minuscule at most."

Quentin was even more baffled, though. "So, then, what's all this stuff about me being a captain? It doesn't sound like I'm in charge of anything. Not that I'm complaining."

"All right, so…" Connor laughed, but Quentin didn't know if it was from genuine amusement or outward sarcasm. "How do I phrase this elegantly?" Connor licked his lips and considered his words for a moment. "Young military personnel included, you and I are way younger than most of the people who were in on this operation years ago. That's undeniable. And the thing is, because you, Jaymes, and Fatima are arguably some of the most important people here, we need to keep you alive. So if you add up all the very real possibilities of the smarter elders dying and, say, you and I still being alive in thirty to forty years, we couldn't just be roaming around Titania without any direction. As a whole, we are one research league. As I said, at the top is Patterson, second in command are the fellow scientists and medical professionals, then military, and then us. We're lowest on the subordinate chain. The idea was that if we are somehow separated from the wiser, older people or if they just straight up die, we would have to defer to our own organized system. The secondary system—which again, is our backup system—would be one league comprised of two divisions, each in control of various military personnel of choice. Each division will have one captain, one advisor to the captain, one doctor or nurse, two pilots, and the rest with proper experience in a miscellany of expertise." Connor pointed to himself. "I'm in Division One. My captain is Casey Montgomery. Patterson thought it would be a good idea for her to be captain because, not only does she thrive academically and have a very fair outlook on the world, she's obviously surrounded by a group of young men who have known her almost her entire life and would definitely take up the idea of protecting her if push came to shove; she has Terry, her cousin; Chris and I, Terry's lifelong friends. Captains need to be surrounded by people who they know would want only the best for them. I'm Casey's advisor, which means that pretty much any decision she makes or wants to make must first be vetted by me. Natalie Khan is our paramedic-in-training right now, but once the medical professionals are awake, they will train her to be a doctor. Derek will train to be our chemist—"

"Chemist?" Quentin stopped him.

"Yeah, he spends hours at a time in one of our labs playing around with gases and whatnot. Patterson's cited his and Mathias's experimentation with the rats from back home as proof of their, I guess you could say, caution and willingness to follow the scientific method when it comes to harsh chemicals; they both know to act only on evidence-based things rather than just jumping all in at the risk of their own health. And honestly, I can bash him all I want, but Derek's become something of an alchemist, really."

"Sure."

Connor smiled stiffly. "As of late, Chris, Oscar, and Ivy don't have assigned jobs, but what Patterson told me was that when people have generally healthy bodies but don't fit a specific, academic role, they just go on to become military-trained personnel."

"I can see that," Quentin said.

"Yeah. And then on your end, Division Two, things are a little different..."

"Different?"

"Look, I'm not trying to be rude or anything," Connor excused himself preemptively, "but there are a couple things about you specifically that Patterson thought might change for the better due to the benefits of being a captain. But, I'll say this, there are also things about you that should prove to be merits. For starters, and no disrespect to Casey, but you don't share that type-A personality she has, which a captain normally needs. But one could also argue that, because you are a very quiet and reserved guy, people won't really think much of you and therefore won't resent or want to kill you or anything. They'd be more willing to help you because you just seem like a nice guy."

"Thanks," Quentin said drily. He wasn't flattered.

"No offense," Connor said, "but we were all really surprised when Patterson told us you were captain. But he said that people can change and that you might grow into the role. Who knows? Besides, there is a clear safety benefit to it; a security reason for you being captain. You're a Listener, which is incredibly rare and imperative to the whole Global Offense Op's ability to tracking what's out there, so we can't just have you dying on the job or something. And anyway, captains can't just go missing. And they can't just run away or abandon a mission for the hell of it. Their advisors have to be in on everything, not only to guide the captains, but to ensure the safety of them too. So it's killing two birds with one stone, really. You being captain ensures your safety as a Listener and you're a pretty likable guy that everyone should want to keep safe." He allowed himself a laugh. "So, my condolences, but Marina is your advisor."

Quentin stopped ingesting his soup. "What?"

"I know, man." Connor grinned. "Patterson thought she'd be a good fit. He likes her no-nonsense ways. He just likes her. He said the same thing about me."

"That's different," Quentin grumbled.

"I am flattered. But it won't be bad. This is all just in case, Quentin. No one knows if this operation will even be needed in twenty years, and what are the odds that everything goes careening out of control after the decades of planning? Besides, you've got others with you. Frances, in terms of her occupation, will be in a similar boat as Natalie. Your pilots will probably be Ewan and Athol since they're both super smart and technologically-oriented...Although, Patterson did seem warm to the idea of training Athol to be a neuroscientist. Mathias looks like he's going down the same road as Derek, where they'll be rehabilitated until they get on the chem or engineering track, or both. Roxy seems like she's definitely got the physical discipline to be paramilitary. But for now, you, Jaymes, and Fatima should be most at ease."

"Why are all the Listeners in one division?"

"It's only temporary," Connor said. "Patterson's thinking of switching Fatima into my group when she's a little older and maybe less attached to Frances. He'd probably swap her with Oscar to even out the imbalance between the potential military folk in my group and yours. But that's it, man. I'm just surprised you had to hear this from me."

Quentin looked down sheepishly. "I haven't really been into listening to anything lately."

"Brace for it. You've got a lot to listen to."

Quentin glanced over to the clock on his bedside table, which had metal legs that were fixed into the identically metal floor; the time was two-thirty-five in the morning. He slipped out of the bed, and his socked feet touched the ground. Without purpose, he left behind the sleeping quarter and adjacent shower area to walk through the brighter hallway just outside. He tentatively descended one of the foyer staircases. The lights of the chandelier weren't as piercing as they were during the ship's scheduled daytime. Throughout the sleeping hours, when everyone was supposed to be tucked in their beds but wandered elsewhere, the lights dimmed to a degree that wasn't quite as dankly dark as the bulbs of the basement, but with the reduction of one or two more notches in the settings, they would have been the same.

When he passed the second floor's entrance on the staircase, he saw, through the smoked-glass walls of the miniature conference room, that three figures were huddled around its table. Papers were everywhere and the whiteboard was made messy by unreadable handwriting. He knew who was inside without even having to gaze at the fogged view for more than a few seconds. He could easily make out the bodies of the other captain and the two advisors. He didn't know how they did it. Every night, or so it appeared to him, the three would gather about a table in any one of the many conference areas, sometimes the miniature, smoked-glass one, sometimes the larger one on the first floor, and there were even times when he spotted them entering the auditorium, which was also downstairs. They seemed inseparable, their own little triad. They would hop around from location to location, with notebooks and pens and pencils in hand. They never ate at the same times as everyone else and they rarely socialized with anyone who wasn't them. He never knew what they were doing, and he had no interest in finding out. He had no interest in anything, really.

Unlike him, the majority of their humble population was motived by their changed circumstances. But not Quentin. He watched not all, but many, as they moved on without him. They attached themselves to new hobbies and habits, established routines for that new phase of their new lives while he loitered, hid, and loitered again, looking on from the shadows. That wasn't to say that the others lacked their own spurts of depression. They did, but they didn't suffer the way he did, because, beyond their dejection, they were equipped with something he didn't possess: direction. Schedules formed and abnormal became the new normal. Fatima took up culinary lessons from Natalie. Terry taught Ewan how to weight-lift. Athol helped Chris improve his mathematics skills. Frances dove nose-deep into the textbooks that introduced her to a variety of medical studies. Roxy, Oscar, and Amber ran laps through the hallways together for exercise. And then there were Casey, Connor, and Marina who were doing something which Quentin probably should have participated in, but chose not to. It was frustrating for him. He didn't understand any of them. How could they have moved on so quickly? They would look out the windows, the windows he so often veiled with curtains and refused to acknowledge, and they would not only be entranced by the darkness and glistening specs of the outdoors, but they wouldn't vomit every time they saw the view. Whereas he did, and every time. He hated their new outdoors. He hated the windows. He hated everything. He didn't want that view. He wanted to go home. Why didn't they want the same?

As he neared the bottom of the foyer stairs, he was still disturbed by the sight of the captain and the advisors all congregated around a wooden table and babbling about things they likely didn't even know existed back in 2045. He was bitter, he admitted it. He was jealous too, there was no point in denying that. They were more mature than him and the alignment of their priorities did make sense, but it didn't mean he had to be happy about it—happy for them.

He found Frances sitting in the middle of the second-to-last step of the staircase he was descending. She must have heard his clothed feet sliding along the surface, because she turned her head over her shoulder. She had an open book on her lap, and she quickly plonked it closed. "You look better," she commented. She wasn't lying. In the last week or so, his face had healed significantly from the impact of his night in the marsh.

Quentin sat down beside her. His long legs stretched out and his toes touched the marble base in front of them. "I couldn't sleep," he said.

"Neither could I," Frances sympathized, but it went without saying; she was alone at the bottom of a staircase in the middle of the night. She thumbed the binding of the book on her thighs. It was a large volume. He couldn't see the front cover.

"Still reading that introduction to phlebotomy?" Quentin asked.

Frances smiled. "No. I finished that pamphlet yesterday. This is just a…Well, a bible."

"You don't have to be weird about it," Quentin told her.

"I know," Frances said. Her head tilted. "Are you religious?"

Quentin snorted. "You trying to convert me?"

"Yes, Quentin," Frances said, sardonicism in her voice. "I am so trying to convert you at three AM as we approach Mars. Name me a better time." The few hard lines around her eyes softened. "No, really. Out of curiosity, are you an agnostic or something?"

Quentin thought of his convenient theism. He had certainly resorted to it more frequently ever since he met Patterson. "I've got something."

"So you do believe?"

"Er—Not quite. It helps me sleep, though. That's about it. My faith is pretty flawed."

"What's the flaw if it puts you to sleep?"

Quentin shook his head. "It's not really a peace-inducing thing. It just helps me ignore stuff."

"I can tell," Frances said, much to his surprise. "I don't know what you're doing, but I see what it does to you. You don't talk to anyone. You don't join those captain-advisor meetings. You haven't even spoken to Marina once since you found out about this place. I'm not trying to be mean. Patterson said we all take time to adjust and that it varies."

"Did he?" Quentin asked coldly.

"He's not the enemy, Quentin. Or else your mother wouldn't have trusted him."

"My mother," Quentin said slowly. "It sounds like she's the type of person to do anything she's told."

"No one's telling you to do anything," Frances said. "But no one's telling you to continue doing nothing either." She yawned and covered her mouth with her hand. It was a deep yawn, so deep that her belly pulled backwards from the long breath. "I should get to bed. I have to watch this training video tomorrow on how to set broken extremities. You?"

"Soon," Quentin said. "See you tomorrow."

Frances plodded up the stairs.

Quentin stayed on those steps for a while.

14

Unlike the bright, open spaces that constituted the rest of Quentin's new home, Patterson's office was a dark and chilly place, but Quentin supposed it was in something of a welcoming way. The coffered ceiling was black. The walls and their beams were black. The porcelain tiles, which amplified the sound of Quentin's sneakers as he walked inside, were also black. Patterson's desk, however, was not. It was a rich oak, faultlessly smooth and free of any ridges. It was an enjoyable escape from the twinkling chandeliers and blooming flowers. The heating was refreshingly milder; hints of the artificial warmth were tangible, but not so overly noticeable that he felt like he was suffocating.

Patterson was seated behind his desk, a laptop open in front of him. He wasn't alone. Aside from Quentin, who had only just entered the office, there were three others present. Their expressions weren't as clement as Patterson's when he looked up to see Quentin making his way over to them. One was Marina, who was markedly irritated by Quentin's tardiness. Beside her was Casey, whose face was taut with disapproval. The other was Connor, who looked more tired than irked, but his annoyance subtly manifested itself with a frown.

Quentin stood next to Marina. "You're late," she said. What she didn't add was, "to our first meeting."

He didn't respond, just looked at his peers, in particular to their countenances, which reverted to strict and unshaken expressions. He noticed that the stances of their bodies were different from his, that their shoulders were elevated, their hands were knotted behind their backs, and their chins were held high. He gracelessly mimicked them.

Patterson reclined in his swivel chair. "Well, look at this," he marveled. "A team." He was smiling, but then it reduced to a less stretched grin. "Nevertheless, greatly as I appreciate your order, I would prefer you all to be far more at ease. We are human, and we never would have made it this far with our sanity intact had we acted so formally these last few months, now would we?" Casey's shoulders slackened their upright bearing and her hands slid into the pockets of her jeans. She dropped the stoic expression and embraced the naturally rounded shape of her face; Quentin thought her cheeks looked fuller compared to when he last saw her, when she was seventeen. Connor crossed his arms, but not out of defiance, just loosely. Marina let her hands tie together in front of her waist. At the change, Patterson hummed approvingly. "Much better," he said. "Now, on this twentieth day in the month of February of 2047, I welcome you all to our very first meeting. I know how exciting this is indeed. We have a few things to go over together. It's an informal briefing is all." He scooted forward, his body hitting the edge of his desk. "We are in a new year, and with new years, there are always things worth looking forward to. Now, I had intended to hold this meeting back in January, but things at the time seemed a little too tense for me to do that. But don't you worry, the one-month lag didn't put a crimp in our plans at all. Today we are going to discuss the objectives for this year as well as everything bound to come next year, in 2048. It will be a special year, 2048, and hopefully things by then will have calmed down emotionally, to the extent that you and all your friends can focus on your new work."

"Work?" Quentin asked.

"Something like that," Patterson said. "This year, which you should all take pleasure in knowing, is the year of you."

"Of us?" Casey asked. "As in our new jobs?"

"No. This year, under the Rebirth Plan, is a time of hiatus. It is entirely about clearing your heads and granting yourselves the time to rest and process everything that has happened. From here on out to December 31st, you have no duties."

Marina looked aghast. "That's ridiculous."

"In what way?"

"Well, with all due respect, we've already wasted a full year sleeping and it's not like we're getting any younger. We should act now on whatever you have planned."

"I can't, Marina. You are an extremely adaptive person when reason calls for your adaptability, but others, I am afraid, are not. Don't pretend like you don't see the depression that hovers around some of the members in this ship, and in your own division, might I add. In order to begin job preparations for future professions, I have to examine the versatility of everyone for me to even assign the proper jobs to the proper people. Right now, it's too early for me to finalize my determinations. Sure, there have been some exceptions, such as with our future paramedics and suchlike, but beyond that, only time will tell."

"So real stuff happens January of next year?" Connor asked.

"Officially, for some people, yes," Patterson confirmed. "Although, I am very impressed with the efforts of you three—" He looked at Casey, Connor, and Marina—"for your unofficial leadership in striving to understand the mysterious threat at hand." He turned to Quentin. "You are more than welcome to join their brainstorming sessions any time, but I won't think less of you if you still need time to settle into things."

Marina muttered something.

"Thank you, Patterson," Quentin said shyly. He tried to ignore the carping girl beside him.

"For comfort's sake," Patterson said, "and to preserve as much of their youth as possible, the older adults on board are to remain in cryogenic hibernation until February of next year, at which point your subordinates will all be assigned jobs and the proper preparations for said jobs. The intention is for you to study under my peers' tutelage for five years, and afterwards, everyone, young and old alike, will undergo a ten-year, cryogenic sleep period as the ship further embarks on its way to Titania. Okay?"

"I thought the journey from Earth to Uranus was nine years," Casey said. "I read it in a book once."

Patterson smiled. "You know, some of your friends are not entirely wrong to have doubts regarding the legitimacy of my agency's various publicized claims. Most are true, some are stretched truths. Publicity, if you will. In all honesty, modern science hasn't quite accelerated to the point of being able to travel that quickly for long periods of time and *safely*. For a satellite, it is entirely possible. For a craft with humans, not quite so. Do you understand? When dealing with people's lives, the process of great achievements takes much longer. But," he said, "that doesn't mean some fun cannot be had before February of 2048. Beginning in January of next year, once per week for the next five years, before our ten-year sleep, you will have to complete the mandatory environmental preparations to brace yourselves for the grounds of Titania. EV Prep is to consist of tiring, but very beneficial, one-to-two-hour sessions of grueling exercises designed to ready your minds and bodies for the harsh environs of that specific moon. This doesn't entail advanced supervision, so I am qualified to be the sole supervisor. Besides—" He let out his signature, under-the-breath chuckle—"to my benefit, I would like to boast to my peers of how great a job I did with all of you while they were sleeping."

"When does EV Prep start?" Connor asked.

"January 2048. But if you desire the date, that would be the 1st."

Connor looked pleased to hear that. "Straight into the new year," he said.

"Straight into the new year," Patterson repeated. He drummed his hands against the desktop for a second. "For now, though, I advise that you be gentle with yourselves and be kind to those around you. Recognize that you have been gifted an opportunity that many can only dream of having." He chuckled again, and Quentin wanted to lunge forward and strangle him. "So many of you have proven surprisingly and admirably sane considering how you weren't even asked to participate in this," Patterson said. "Now, you have yourselves a good day. Treat one another well. I hope to see you all at dinner." He flourished his left arm, waved them off with another smile, and, as if they weren't all standing before him, fixed his eyes on the computer screen in front of him and started typing.

Quentin followed the others outside. The office was deep into the second floor, which made it a long journey back to the foyer's staircase. He walked with Casey, Connor, and Marina, but none of them really seemed to have any destination in mind.

"That was interesting," Casey said.

"It was stupid," Marina voiced.

"What was?" Case queried.

"Having to wait. Imagine the faces of our adversaries if they knew how much Patterson were coddling us. They'd be doing cartwheels."

Casey shook her head. "It's not that bad. We've already colonized a moon."

They rounded a corner.

"Either way, I think the full year's a mistake," Marina professed.

"I know you do," Casey said, "but the rest aren't like us." She stopped and turned, was eye-level with Quentin and looked right at him. He didn't remember her being so tall. "We're going to the conference room downstairs. We've set up camp there for our meetings. Want to join? You could get some insight into what we're trying to figure out."

"No, I don't think so," Quentin said. "Maybe I'll read a book or find something to do." That was a lie. He was depressed and unmotivated, and he knew it.

"You sure?" Connor asked. "Every opinion's needed."

"Don't overwhelm him, Connor, he's *adjusting,*" Marina said.

Connor shrugged, and he and Casey went their own way.

Before Marina joined them, Quentin gathered up the gumption to say, "You don't always have to be so patronizing."

"How am I being patronizing?" Marina asked.

"You know how."

"Are you or are you not still adjusting?"

"Um…yes?"

"Then why do you have a problem with me excusing it?"

"I don't have a problem with you excusing it, but you and I both know that you were just deriding me."

"How so?"

"By your tone of voice."

"Ah, by my tone," Marina said, and she walked away, like they weren't even having a discussion.

When he was alone, Quentin remembered how much he hated having so many hours on hand, how every minute slowly passed, and he felt the futility of his existence nibbling away at him like a cancer. He went to the dining hall and ate some food, then walked a lap around the first floor to help with his digestion. Later, not knowing what to do with himself, he went to the third-floor living room, which he considered a decent retreat. Worst case scenario, he would fall asleep on one of the couches and sleep the day away. He had done it before and didn't mind the possibility of doing it again. But when he made his way to the room he had in mind, it was far from empty and was boisterously occupied. *SpongeBob SquarePants* was showing on the flatscreen television, which was affixed to the pink wall. Fatima was on the carpeted floor with Frances, who was verbalizing her interpretation of *A Christmas Carol's* meaning and advising Fatima on how to better read novels to understand their every metaphorical and literal facets. Mathias sat on one of the couches, his arms spread over the top of it, claiming the piece as his own, whilst he soberly watched the cartoon show. Under the television and across from him was the room's second and only other couch, which was taken up partly by Ewan, who spoke to an inattentive Mathias. Athol, reading a book, was next to Ewan.

"Quentin!" Ewan exclaimed. "Come over here, help a guy out."

"Nah, help her," Mathias said, motioning to Fatima.

Quentin shut the door behind him. "What's up?"

It seemed a weighty battle for Mathias to pull his eyes away from the television, but he managed. He kept sneaking glances back to it as he spoke. "Fran's got the kid doing ELA," he said.

Frances exaggerated an exhale. "Education is important, guys. I don't care that we have a year off or that Patterson thinks she's fine without school, she's getting her studies done somehow. And all we're doing is discussion, we're not even reading right now."

Quentin frowned. "The news reached you guys too, about the year-off thing?"

"Casey popped in and told us earlier," Athol said, not glancing up from his book as he spoke.

"I've gotta meet Natalie in the infirmary and do some studying myself," Frances told her student. "Remember this lesson, all right?"

Fatima nodded. "I will. I'll retain it in my brain."

Frances smiled. "Good vocab." She and Quentin passed each other as they swapped positions on her way out. Once she left, he joined Fatima on the floor, who was already engrossed by the television.

Ewan snapped a finger at him. "Excuse me."

"Huh?" Quentin asked dumbly.

"I need your help on something," Ewan said. "I've been tryna convince these two—" He signaled to the very disinterested Mathias and Athol—"that NASA's a bunch of bull."

"What?"

"They're bullshit," Ewan said earnestly. "For example, I was reading this news article once that was talking about how, for over a decade, they lost track of this satellite, right? You got that? A satellite, which they casually just lost like a sock in a washing machine. But okay, fine. Whatever. They lost all intel on it, couldn't receive even the smallest hint on its location, and you know who finds it? You know who friggin' finds the thing?"

Quentin sighed. "No, Ewan."

Athol turned a page of his book. "Nor do we care," he added.

"An amateur!" Ewan shouted. "An amateur astronomer. Literally, this is regarding a high-tech satellite from, supposedly, the top space agency in the world…and yeah, what do ya know? An amateur discovers it. An amateur."

"Okay?" Quentin acknowledged dismissively. "Look, Ewan, everyone's entitled to their own opinions, but we really—"

"And they're indolent. For a supposed space agency, if that's even what they are."

Quentin's head started to hurt. "You don't think they're a space agency?"

"Doesn't this whole operation, the Global Offense Op, prove it? These people aren't astronomers, they don't study the universe. It's an enormous cover-up, a genius one, too. When you think about it, who's possibly gonna question what seems to be an innocent clan of scientists? I sure as hell wouldn't. But…I am not like everyone." Ewan smirked, boasting. "I'm not. And here's the thing, how the hell else would they be able to take billions of dollars in taxes from us every single year in a way that would make us feel good about it? The only way would be to feed into the fantasy that everyone eventually has, which is exploring outer space."

Quentin blinked thrice in one second. "Wow," he said. "That is certainly quite the leap."

"You done?" Mathias asked Ewan.

"Don't believe me yet?" Ewan asked. "Okay, how about this? They maintain that the moon landing wasn't a publicity stunt of a fake event, but if we've already gone, how come they keep talking about going back or talking about going to Mars? If they already had gone to the moon, wouldn't it be easy just to, I dunno, go back? And what is with their social media back home? Every goddamn day was a post about Mars. Didn't anyone else notice this shit? We supposedly sent bots and all kinds of stuff there ages ago, so why is it a new discovery every single day? It's all they post about."

Athol put his book down. "Because we're passing Mars right now, you dolt," he said. "How else do they distract other governments from thinking they're up to something as top-secret and controversial as this mission? Are you forgetting the fact that half the world doesn't agree with this? That half the world has had nukes aimed at our town since the news of the Listeners' births? Knock it off. This isn't just about you and your hatred for NASA, all right? Take your conspiracy theories somewhere else."

"I'm just saying I don't believe them," Ewan said. "They're obviously an intelligence agency that just so happens to have some astronomers in the ranks."

Athol inched away from Ewan. "Fine, but will you stop being so hyper? It's way too early in the morning for this." He turned to Quentin. "Anything else new from the meeting that we should know about?"

"Not really," Quentin lied. He didn't feel like detailing anything Patterson told him.

"Liar," Athol called him out. "I'll ask Casey later."

"What do they do, anyway?" Quentin asked. "She and the advisors, they're always running around holding meetings about stuff."

"They're trying to understand what the thing is that keeps destroying planets and their moons. Apparently, there hasn't been a lead on what it is, so it's an unsolved mystery."

"Oh."

"I never see you with them, though."

Quentin couldn't look Athol in the eyes, so he turned to the screen, to the cartoon he used to religiously watch in a life he once hated but had come to ardently miss. He didn't feel comfortable in the room anymore. "I'm gonna go," he said, but Athol, who was reading his book again, didn't seem to care. When Quentin hurried out the door and wound up back in the hallway, he let the tears fall.

15

Since September of 2046, Lucas had been a homeschool student. His work was predominantly taught online rather than in-person with a parent, but considering how he was home-ridden, it was, in the most technical sense of the word, homeschool. His mother sometimes helped him with his studies, but she was often too busy or too preoccupied to aid him in learning about things like the Pythagorean theorem.

Since Quentin's disappearance, their mother traveled a lot. One week she was in the United Arab Emirates to negotiate a protection deal for the country's lead volcanologist, whom Lucas knew was a woman named Maryam Akhbul, the bubbliest member of the Kilimanjaro-based volcanology team. He almost never saw his father, who remained in Massachusetts, but his mother had allegedly come upon him in Pennsylvania, where his company had sent attendees to a conference that was being held the week of her own visit. The last, and the only, two visits from Lucas's father were identically long and uncomfortable, and the same applied to his mother. The demeanors of both his parents were stiff when they spoke with one another. At first, he was taken aback by the rigidity of their interactions after all that had happened in their once tight-knit family.

But if their marriage wasn't the most enjoyable of ties before, why would it have been, then, after the vanishing of one son and the relocation of another? Such was his life. He lost the brother he dearly loved, had a father he scarcely saw, and lived with a mother who obsessed over her work.

Naomi once told him something that wilted his dwindling happiness more than it comforted him. After finishing the story of her life on the day of their first meeting, she had said, "The emptiness does pass. The loneliness will bother you, but in time things will be all right." He wondered if she actually meant those last few words. He didn't think she did. He presumed it was her way of coping with her own, internal vacancies.

If Lucas were being honest, Naomi was the only constant in his new life. Time-wise, she had a predictable schedule. She and the others on her expedition team would spend two weeks on the heights of the volcano that loomed over the city of Arusha, and then, for the next two, would be limited to the flatlands, where they aggregated their research and analyzed their findings before repeating the cycle again the next month. He saw her more than his own mother, who, despite officially residing with him, was either in her poorly painted office day and night or traveling and meeting with people she undoubtedly deemed more important than him; when Sydney was out of the country, Topher stayed with him. Lucas definitely saw Naomi more than his father, who, by that point in Lucas's life, became something of a memory, a relic of the life he used to live, back in a town called Shaw, in a faraway state called Massachusetts, which felt strangely faraway in the past. He tried not to mull over the many losses he had suffered, all of which were caused by those early hours of one November night, back in 2045. He still never spoke, hadn't said one word, but Naomi didn't take any issue with it. She had told him her story, which naturally intertwined with his, and for that reason, his words were unneeded. She knew what he was going through. She probably knew more about him than he did, and she definitely understood him more than anyone else. She wasn't lying when she had promised him that.

There was a stretch of time when he was panicked that she might have forgotten about him. After he first met her in mid-July, he neither saw nor heard from her for another four months. Something inside him warned that she was another adult to have slipped into his life who would later evaporate into thin air just when he needed her, like nearly all the others. But one day, the thin-haired, round-faced volcanologist did slip her way back into his life. Her husband did, anyway. In late November of 2046, Lucas spotted that dented, scraped, dirt-ridden *Jeep* he had once seen creep up to the end of his mother's driveway back in July, the one that dropped off Naomi. Behind the wheel was a man, one who could not be categorized as young but, by the same token, was too young to have been considered old, and with his window pulled down, he yelled up to the boy, who was doing his schoolwork on the roof of the house, "We pinged your mom! We just got back! They're at the tavern now! Naomi was asking if you wanted some food!" Lucas's breath caught. He sealed the notebook in front of him, the notebook which contained all his history notes. Down the ladder he went. He tossed his belongings into the sunroom and, not one minute later, was seated in the passenger side of the *Jeep.*

The tavern bustled with conversation, ones started by the mysterious researchers who would appear and reappear in the city, some young-but-not-young whilst others in the same age range as his parents. They spoke in technical jargon he didn't understand and referred to risks and frights he wished he could have experienced with them. Naomi spoke to him all throughout the dinner. When the others began to discuss the more serious matters, detailing their finds, Naomi dissected and explained each element of every statement to Lucas. She guided him through geological terminology, particularly the terms that related to volcanoes, and took apart each mentioned intricacy in their discoveries, just so he could understand. Over the meal of grilled meats and spiced porridges that were split among everyone, she told him tales of a father she missed and a mother she knew a lot about, but had ultimately never met. He still never said a word, and Naomi still didn't care. He sat back later in the night, when the cold brews were settling in the adults' bellies and the volume of their intercourse had returned to normal levels, as he had begun to finally see, not quite for the first time, that for those who had suffered losses like his own, there were ways to find joy again.

When December came, Lucas hadn't noticed any drastic changes in his life. Not even in the weather. He realized that the kind-faced woman who operated his favorite fruit stand in the city hadn't been lying when she told him that rain was the only threat to the Arusha heat. The singular exception he could discern was the one on the mountain, where snow had fallen a mile lower than usual and covered a large swathe of the natural wonder, rather than just its peak; its middle was basked in a shimmering coat of white.

"It's beautiful, isn't it?" Naomi asked him in the next year, 2047, on the 23rd of February. She had a *Polaroid* in one hand, which depicted the snowy glacier wall of the mountain. February 23rd was the researchers' second-to-last day on the flatlands until they were to return from the mountain in March. She and Lucas were sitting at the dining room table, drinking orange juice together after eating a dinner hosted by his mother, who was in the kitchen cleaning up the dishes and chatting with Richard and Topher.

Lucas looked down at the photo. The glaciers mesmerized him in a frightening way. Naomi must have read the fear on his face.

"Scary, right?" she asked. "They're a lot smaller than they were ten years ago. Climate change tends to do that."

Lucas offered up an understanding frown.

"The picture doesn't capture it all that well," Naomi said. "Honestly, a video probably would have been better." Her face lit up and she poked his shoulder. "Hey, your mother tells me you have a knack for filmmaking, said that you used to film mountains with a drone."

Back home, in Massachusetts, Lucas was quite skilled with a camera, and he especially loved drones. In the summers, when the weather in the northeast of the United States was warm but not oppressive, he and his family used to vacation in New Hampshire, Vermont, and Maine. They would swim in the beaches and lakes, and hike in the mountains. When they did hike, Lucas was always ten steps behind his parents and Quentin, fussing over the remote control for the drone camera. He was relatively amateur with it, and the videos were typically a few shakes beyond professionally acceptable, but his editing techniques often compensated for his filming blunders.

"You know…" Naomi stopped herself for a moment and ran her thumb over each of her fingers, pondering. "Kilimanjaro is a unique mountain," she said. "It's something of a five-layer cake, as I like to say, because there are five climate zones. The first is a rainforest. The second is the heath, and it's like a dry forest. The third is the moorland. The fourth is the alpine desert, and the fifth, up by the summit, is like the arctic. A lot of people think it's a ton of steep climbing, but it's actually quite gradual, often flat. It's the altitude and oxygen deprivation that get to everyone. But with the right precautions and the right crew, it is quite an enjoyable hike. The minimum age to be on the trails is ten years old. So…" She couldn't contain her suggestive smile. "We have a mini-scout this week. It's only a short way up, about four or five days' worth of climbing. The full height of the mountain is about nineteen-thousand-four-hundred feet, but we would only be going up the first nine or ten thousand. And then the way down will be another three days, give or take. Anyway, that's still a lot shorter than our recent trips, which were two weeks at a time up there. How would you like to film those glaciers up close? Richard has a drone. It doesn't connect to internet, so it's entirely harmless and we shouldn't be hacked. Would you like to use it? He hasn't touched it in ages. And it won't be an awful hike, we'd only be going to the desert."

Lucas didn't know how many nods he gave but it must have been a lot, because one second Naomi was sitting there smiling and the next she was holding his shoulders, telling him to calm down before he gave himself a concussion. His mother and Topher weren't as permissive of the idea when Naomi and Richard broached the topic later that evening, right after all the used pots, pans, and silverware from their meal were loaded into the dishwasher.

"What?" Sydney asked. She lowered the coffee mug she had to her lips. She switched her bewildered gaze between the young couple and the boy who was excitedly rocking back and forth on his heels beside them.

"Sweetheart," Topher said to Naomi, parsing his words, "these expeditions are not meant for touristic purposes. You know the government halted tourism once the military came into the picture."

"No?" Naomi questioned with a wry smile on her lips.

Topher sighed. "No, Nani. The visits from your childhood don't count. Those were not recreational."

"Is that so?" Naomi was smiling ear to ear. "So what were they, then?"

Topher opened his mouth, then snapped it shut. He shook his head, but ended up nodding. He shook it again, grabbed his mug of coffee and chugged the liquid, even though it was omitting billows of steam. Lucas's throat hurt as he watched.

"Just bring him back in one piece," was all his mother said.

Little did any of them know that, not only would Lucas return in one piece seven days later, but he would be brought back with his speech in tow.

Richard had explained that where there was either the great success or survival of a climber, there was, in their shadow, a talented troupe of guides. Lucas had no past knowledge of it, but the men and women who climbed the great Mount Everest each owed their lasting breaths to the aiding hands of Tibet's Sherpa people, who worked for hire to bear the large brunt of juggling their clients', the tourists, belongings; tents; clothing; food; oxygen tanks. Guides and porters were also medically trained to run health checks on their guests, to check their blood pressures and measure their oxygen levels. Similarly, Tanzania had their own valiant locals who offered themselves as helpers. Richard said the volcanology team used to hire three or four at a time, but due to the increased frequency of the team's visits as well as the ballooning Tanzanian and United States military occupation on the mountain, that most critical part of their company was reduced to one or two.

The expert porter on Lucas's trip was a man named Abul Ibrahimu. His face was a light-black tone, but the rest of him was immensely darker. He had a sandpaper smile, with teeth as yellow as naked husks of corn, while the upper row was jagged in some spots but soft in others, much like the mountain's peak. His height was astonishing. Lucas had never met a man as tall as him, and he was the son of David Hanson. Abul was from Arusha, but his grandparents were from the Chagga tribe, who lived near the base of the mountain.

His sons, one eighteen and the other twenty-three, were infantryman in the Tanzanian People's Defense Force, and they just so happened to be stationed at the volcano summit the very week of Lucas's climb. He really liked Abul, who, similar to Naomi and Richard, took no issue with his lack of speech and spoke to him just as one would with any other person. But it bothered Lucas to see Abul's days spent hunched forward all throughout the climb, as Lucas's things—two, fully filled backpacks—were propped on Abul's back in addition to his own belongings. In fact, the first question Lucas ever asked of him, but still without the use of his tongue, was whether the hauling of all those objects hurt. With a worried pinch to his face, Lucas pointed to the load on Abul's shoulders as a gesture of enquiry.

"Your things?" Abul asked, laughing. Lucas nodded. "Have you seen how small a boy you are? You are my easiest client yet." Lucas was reassured a little. He supposed that, when compared to Abul, he really was a small person.

Lucas was forewarned that the first day would be the easiest. Indeed, it felt like he was climbing any ordinary New England mountain, like Monadnock in New Hampshire or Cadillac in Maine, merely that they were in rainforest and not surrounded by dry pine. Come the afternoon, his legs were fairly sore but he gradually adjusted to the demands of the path. It wasn't difficult for him to keep up with the others.

It seemed that the presence of a child was a refreshing addition to the research team. The two other women present were childless themselves, like Naomi and Richard. There was another scientist with them, one who wasn't a part of the dinner congregation back in November. He was a man named Jack Rowling. He had straggled, blond hair and a face that betrayed his youth; he was said to be forty-two, but he looked about sixty. Lucas, apparently, reminded Jack of his eldest son, whom he rarely saw due to his unconventional work life. So, Jack and Lucas raced themselves to spots they would point out at the last minute. His first day was fun.

His night, however, was not. That first night on the mountain was so hot that he couldn't sleep. He rid himself of layers of clothing and hoped no one in their flimsy tent would roll over and see him indecent while he changed. It was just so hot. It was a sweltering heat that was nothing like the soft warmth of New England. When he slipped back onto, rather than inside, his sleeping bag after shedding his three shirts and opting for only one, light tee-shirt, he rolled onto his right side and looked over to Naomi and Richard.

He didn't know how they didn't die from heat exhaustion. Not only did they sleep fully clothed, but she was curled into his side, her head on his chest, and both of her legs were tangled around whichever one of his was closest to her.

On their second day, Naomi and the other researchers began their actual work. Lucas tried to eavesdrop on everything they were saying and glean the purpose of the strange equipment in their hands, but he failed to understand the meaning behind any of their conversations. It appeared that Naomi had only introduced him to the basics of geologic terminology. During the daytime, when the researchers worked among themselves and Lucas sank into irrelevance, Abul demonstrated how to set up a tent in a manner robust enough to defy the frozen winds, which they would be sure to face over the next few days. He told Lucas of the beautiful summers up in the alpine desert ahead, the way the sun would gleam off the stones of the path and how the rays would shine back down to the plains below. While they were still in the rainforest, he brought Lucas to cliffs and corners where the flatlands were still visible.

Eventually, the drone came into use. From the bag that was strapped to Abul's back, Lucas withdrew Richard's unused device and a telescope Lucas had possessed all throughout his childhood, but for some reason left equally untouched. He would scan, with the latter utensil, to find wildlife and, with the former, subsequently film his finds. His film work was worse than he had performed in New England, likely because he hadn't touched a camera in so long. But like his editing skills to his shakiness, where the camera failed, the scenery compensated. His faraway shots of red-billed oxpecker birds still captured every turn of their heads and twist of their ears, and the zoom-ins on insects sneaking up trees were immaculately detailed.

But, without a doubt, his favorite shot from the trip was of himself and Abul. Lucas took it on the third day, when they were higher up the mountain and the temperature around them shifted from the warmth of the tropics below to an ongoing cold from the winter weather above. He had the drone camera focused up close on the two of them, himself and Abul, so that it was shooting right at their noses, which were scrunched up from their cackling. Then, Lucas let it zoom out. He sent it back, so it showed their entire faces. He sent it even further back, so it showed their bodies on the edge of the large, barren cliff. He sent it back one last time, so that they looked like minuscule, ant-sized figures on the side of the mountain, while behind, but closely above them, the winds blew the clouds to the right and the sun seemed mere inches over their heads. The research team's director, Jane, laughed out loud when she saw the clip for the first time. She suffered an even bigger fit of laughter when she asked to see it again. She simply couldn't get over the beginning, how the video had started so close that she could see the nose hairs of the boy and the guide. She was also in magnificent awe of the beauty in the final capture at the end, where the two figures who once seemed so large and dominant became tiny dots on the cliff that protruded outward and into the sky.

The cold of the higher points may have been gentle in the late afternoon of their third day, but the soreness in Lucas's legs was not.

Richard sidled up to him. Or, back to him, as Lucas lagged at the rear of their group, dragging his feet. "Tomorrow's our last day of ascent," Richard assured. His triple-gloved hand patted Lucas's arm. "We reach the end of the heath and go into the alpine desert. After that, it's down. Down is always easier."

Lucas's expression was forlorn and doubting.

"I really hate to do this," Richard said regretfully, "but Jane just reminded me that your camera can't be out tomorrow. There are at least two battalions training up there. That's where their temporary base is, actually." Lucas nodded. He was too spent to dispute it. Not that he would have, anyway. He hadn't met anyone as kind and accommodating to his unique circumstances as Naomi and Richard were, even though they scarcely knew him. When he handed over the devices, Richard ruffled Lucas's hair. "Are you having fun, buddy?" he asked, as if suspecting the heavy thoughts that ran through the boy's mind.

Lucas was happier than he ever thought he could be, notwithstanding the ripping soreness in his calves and quads, of course. His head bobbed up and down. He was tired, but he was truthful. He smiled through the spittle that escaped his mouth, and he snorted when he wiped it away with the back of his hand.

"I know, I know." Richard laughed. "It always hurts the first few times. You're good at this, though. You're doing great. Seriously, I don't know if I'd had the guts to do this at thirteen."

Lucas grinned widely.

Their final destination was the makeshift military base Richard mentioned, which was situated in the general vicinity of the ten-thousand-feet mark. Lucas was a little disappointed that he didn't get to see the glaciers Naomi had spoken of, since they were located by the summit, but come the evening of that third day, the air had grown too cold for him to crave anything colder. He no longer moved with ease, as he was shrouded in an absurd amount of layered clothing and jackets. The number of sleeping bags and blankets they scattered within their giant tent exceeded the amount of people who slept inside. Hot chocolate and herbal teas became staples in his diet, and his vacuum flask was more prized than his plastic water bottle, although he did drink more water than he ever had in his entire life.

Abul checked all their vital signs. Everyone's came back normal. "We have to do this the colder it gets," he explained. "Not to mention the risk of high-altitude sickness, which happens the higher up we go. Tell me if you have any headaches or nausea, okay?"

Lucas nodded.

"And I'll get you another windbreaker," Abul said. "By evening, the winds will be crazier."

Lucas never admitted it, but those winds frightened him. From the early evening to dawn, he swore the gusts became wilder than they were when the sun was in view. Abul must have sensed Lucas's fear because, the next morning, which was their fourth day, Abul said during their breakfast of peanuts and fruit seeds, "Never has a tent blown away on my watch." Perhaps a tent hadn't yet, but Lucas thought his body may have been susceptible to being taken by the wind. It had grown far stronger overnight, and he was having trouble climbing against the forceful waves of air.

In the afternoon of their fourth day, the winds roared through the plains of the first few miles of the alpine desert as Abul held Lucas's hand. They abutted themselves to each other in an effort to keep the boy stable when they reached the climbing portion. There was a moment in their climb when Lucas peered up and hurt his belly from giggling at the way the wind drew Abul's cheeks back and shaped them into air-filled bubbles. They prevailed together. Lucas clung to Abul throughout the whole day, for fear of potentially being swept off a cliff and permanently becoming one with the mountainside.

Kilimanjaro was a strange body. In some parts it was so steep that Lucas dreaded turning his head to look back. In others, it was flat, which was why, much later in the day, just before dusk, the volcanology unit and their single guest saw the first scatter of green tents from the temporary military base. The land up north turned out to be flatter than it was in the introductory heights of the mountain. A helicopter pad was set up on a perilous cliffside, which they had to pass in order to proceed. Lucas and Naomi shared a bottle of marshmallow-covered cocoa as they walked, when they heard the marches of incessant, measured footfalls. As they neared, the "hut-hut!" sound came from a drill sergeant. Lucas was so tired, he didn't even bother trying to match the voice to a face. He knew there were soldiers all around, and he felt shy when he sensed some of them rubbernecking his way. It belatedly occurred to him that he was probably the only child they had seen in months.

He and Abul were left behind by the researchers, who said they needed to report to a certain colonel. "Colonel Brandt, that's the name," Jack told them. "We'll be back in a few. See that large tent over there?" He pointed to the one of distinctive length and width, which stood in the middle of the base. It was larger than all the others. "We'll be in and out in a jiffy."

As the sky darkened, small camp fires flickered into being. The night hadn't yet arrived, but it was approaching apace. Men and women in uniform, some from Lucas's home country, but most from the native land of the mountain, bundled themselves in jackets and snowsuits. With the extra time on their hands, Lucas joined Abul as he asked a few young People's Defense Force soldiers, who were dawdling by the medical tent, if they were familiar with the names Jamil and Baraka Ibrahimu, whom Lucas gathered were Abul's two sons. One of the soldiers said that Jamil and his unit were lucky to be alive following a recent ambush. The interviews of those random infantrymen made Lucas wonder if he would one day have to do as Abul did, should something happen to Quentin. Would Lucas be informed of Quentin being hurt, or would Lucas, too, have to desperately question strangers on the whereabouts and safety of his older brother, like Abul had to with his children?

"Michael!" a female voice called. "Over here!" It took Lucas a moment to recognize that he was being singled out with his new name. He hurried over to where he heard it being yelled.

It came from Naomi. She stood outside the large tent, the one in which she had gone with the other scientists. It was closed behind her, sealed up neatly, and it looked impenetrable despite the high winds. Beside her stood a man of remarkable height whose thickset physique was visible even underneath his snowsuit. His face was shadowed by his peaked service hat, but Lucas very well discerned a scowl fixed onto the man's face, making his features appear locked in a grimace.

Naomi was smiling, though. "Colonel Brandt, this is Michael Hanson."

The colonel bent down, even though there wasn't much of a need to, as Lucas had sprouted considerably since turning thirteen. A tight smile splayed onto the colonel's lips, and Lucas couldn't tell if it was genuine. "Michael Hanson," the colonel said.

Lucas tensed. He thought there was something intimidating about the man's partially covered visage.

"You know, I'll say this," Colonel Brandt said gruffly, "only a son of Sydney Hanson would come climbing up here for fun at your age."

Lucas relaxed.

The Colonel's chin lifted as he looked down at Lucas, surveying him. "Your mother and I go way back, Michael. We served together for a long time, even graduated together." He grunted and raised his eyebrows for a second. "But then she decided to marry an engineer, and she moved into intelligence. I would say it all worked out, though, didn't it?" He shot his arm forward and patted Lucas's shoulder. He even gripped it. "She's an exceptional servant to our country. You do right by her. Am I understood?"

Lucas nodded.

The colonel snapped back up to full height. He turned to the glowingly prideful scientist. "Thank you for introducing him to me, Naomi. Thank you. What a kid, coming up here with you."

Naomi shrugged. "What can I say? He's Sydney's son."

Sydney's son, Lucas remembered as he tried falling asleep that night. Was that supposed to be a compliment? He couldn't tell if he really was his mother's offspring. How could he be, if all he had previously known of her up until November of 2045 had been one, giant lie? Should he be proud that others thought him parallel to her? She gladly gave up one child, mentally destroyed the other to the extent that he hadn't uttered a word since he was eleven, and was everything but devoted to the man who was not only her husband, but also the father of the children whose lives she entirely wrecked on one cold, November night.

He rolled onto his side, away from the wall of the tent, and looked over to Naomi and Richard. Lucas watched them with the aid of the electronic lantern that stood on the fabric floor; he was very much aware of the way its metal handle rocked and squeaked under the influence of the high winds. The couple slept in the exact same position as before, with Naomi's head on Richard's chest and both of her legs entwined around one of his, the only difference being that one of his hands was draped over one of hers. Richard's hand twitched in his sleep. Naomi snored very softly. Lucas thought back to the emptiness Naomi had spoken of in the prior year, the one he wasn't sure pertained to her or to him. Or perhaps it was meant to refer to both of them. He wondered if it eased her pain and potential emptiness to have someone like Richard in her life. Did it quell that hollowness she had spoken of, to have someone who loved her subtly when in the company of others, but adoringly when he thought no one else was looking? Suddenly, Lucas began to understand his fascination with them, which was that the connection they shared was not one to which he had ever bore witness. It was nothing like the one his parents supposedly had with each other.

He plopped himself onto his back and closed his eyes. He tried to sleep, he really did, but then there was a ruckus of some American soldiers outside as they messily sang a rendition of an old, Irish sea shanty. He swore he heard a cowbell, too. It sounded like it was deliberately dinged every time the soldiers reached the chorus.

His eyes popped open. There was no sleeping that night.

Richard wasn't being deceptive when he had said that the fifth day would be easier than the others. Their trajectory finally changed, in that north was the past and south became the future, and the trail became far less demanding. The hike was all the more enjoyable for it. They still had to brace the gelid winds and Lucas spent most of the day clenching Abul's hand to cement himself to the ground, but at least he wasn't so distracted by the soreness in his legs and a constant throbbing in his calves that he couldn't take in the beauty of the sky around him. They were engulfed by the clouds and, for the first time since the day he filmed his favorite drone shot with Abul, Lucas finally took everything in and enjoyed it.

When Richard sidled up to Lucas on that day, Richard had to genuinely hurry his pace to advance to the boy. "Hey, do you want the drone back?" he offered. He began reaching his hand over his shoulder, to his backpack.

Lucas shook his head.

"Oh. Okay." Richard was evidently surprised and perhaps even a bit disappointed.

Lucas stared ahead. The ground he treaded upon was relatively flat. It was a stretch of earth he recognized, and his astute eye knew from memory that it would be the last bit of flat terrain they would approach for a while, that it would become uneven very soon. Richard was asking Lucas something, something he ignored because he was fixed on the sight of a boulder. He tapped Richard's stomach and started running toward the rock.

"Hey!" Richard shouted after him. "You gave yourself a head start!"

Lucas just kept running.

Despite having begun their descent, the wrath of a lingering winter was still quite a rather violent force to reckon with. Come the first night of their downward hike, it didn't quite matter where one was on the mountain, because, so long as they surpassed the warmth of the rainforest far below, the cold was bound to attack. Remaining near the sky, they were likely to spend their night half-frozen. The chill of the winter winds evolved from sporadic and burdensome, to constant and cruel. Lucas wore three pairs of pants, two shirts, one jacket, and one pair of wool gloves. Everyone slept deeply, including him. Their collective slumber was bumpy in the beginning from all the shivering, but their physical and mental fatigue overwhelmed them so powerfully that the cool of the night and the movements of their bodies went peacefully unnoticed.

Lucas didn't know why he woke. It was possible he heard movement or simply sensed a shift that disturbed the stillness inside the tent, which would have been ironic given the vicious beating their shelter was taking from the wind gusts. In any case, he woke in the middle of the night. His eyes opened, and, without moving his head, he saw Naomi uncurling herself from around Richard, who shifted in his sleep as though he, too, sensed she was no longer knotted into him. She crept forward, grabbed the lantern off the floor, and slipped outside through a small crack in the tent's zippered opening. She didn't make a single sound. Lucas looked over at the tiny fissure in the tent wall. If Naomi could fit through it, so could he.

Emerging outside, he spotted Naomi a few paces to the right of the entrance, sitting on the rough, patchy ground. He wasn't as quiet in his movements as she had been, and she heard him immediately. "What are you doing out here?" she asked, her voice made quieter from the winds. He wondered if she could even see out the furry sides of her red parka's hood. As he approached, she must have seen his raised eyebrows with the help of the clear moonlight, because she looked down briefly. "Excuse my hypocrisy," she said good-humoredly, "but you're shaking."

Lucas was, in fact, shaking. He was freezing.

Naomi unzipped her topmost jacket, the parka—she had another one layered underneath, above her snowsuit—and beckoned him over with a wave of her hand. Lucas didn't hesitate, not for one second. Like a joey would slip into the pouch of its kangaroo mother without heed or debate, he lowered himself to the bit of ground in front of her, crawled over, rested his back against the front of her interior jacket, and let his head fall against her unexposed neck. She zipped up her parka over them.

"I like to come out here at night sometimes," Naomi said to him. "Not just here, though. Any mountain, really. So long as I know that I'm near the peak, I feel like I'm a part of the sky. Which we are, kind of." She exhaled. Lucas felt her chest deflate behind him. "I feel like I'm closer to him when I'm up here, closer to my father. Sometimes I wonder if any of those stars above are him, if they're his ship. Things aren't all that bad if I think of it that way."

"I miss Quentin," Lucas said in a small voice. Those were the first words he spoke since November of 2045.

He felt a pressure applied to the top of his head, but it was gentle. It was a touch of Naomi's lips to the hood of his jacket. "I know," he heard her say. "I know, Lucas. I know."

———

Topher grinned out the driver's seat of the *dala-dala.* "My, aren't we bright-eyed and bushy-tailed today?" he asked.

Dragging three, overstuffed backpacks, Richard tapped the roof of the vehicle. "You drive these now?"

"I figured I'd try it out. I come here so often, why not ingratiate myself with the ways of the country? So, I rented one on a whim. I thought it would be a fun way to pick you all up instead of letting you get onto some humid bus."

"Excellent forethought on your part."

"Well, to have good forethought is my job," Topher asserted.

He leaned his head to the side in order to look past Richard, who was obstructing the view of the sloping, dirt path that was a short distance away from the truck. The porter, Abul, whom Topher had screened and hired himself, was racing Sydney's son, presumably to their ride. One of the other geologists, Jack, who was a few steps ahead of them, suddenly dropped his bags and crouched down to brace himself. Without even being told what to do, Michael Hanson jumped onto Jack. With the boy strapped to him like a bag, Jack shot forward and went racing against Abul by proxy for the child, who was laughing. At the back of the pack, with Jane and Maryam, Naomi lifted a handheld camera and snapped photos of everyone.

"You know what? I support this friendship," Richard said. "Michael and Naomi."

Topher's face grew wrinkly in his smile. "Oh, is that so?"

"Very much so. It should stave off her maternal cravings for a while."

"Hmm." Topher tilted his head. "And you are…not inclined to it?"

Richard turned to him. "No, of course I'm inclined. I'd love to have kids. But you of all people know that things haven't been particularly safe lately."

There was a new, more uproarious bustle on the path. Michael, who had fallen off Jack and accepted that he wasn't going to win the race through sprinting, leaped to his feet and tried tackling Abul to the ground. They were covered in dirt, and Abul started tickling the boy. Naomi, laughing, came up closer to snap some more photos.

"Richard," Topher said, "between you and me, our lovely Naomi was an accident. Really. Emily used to say the exact same thing, that it was too dangerous and that times were too unpredictable. But one has to lead their own life at some point. You two have already lent so much of yourselves to this operation."

"I suppose," Richard said, "but bear with me, while we have a kid in the picture who has a tenuous relationship with his parents and is currently satiating Naomi's desires of motherliness—" He chortled mid-sentence—"I don't see the need to produce some offspring of our own. At least, not for now."

"To each his own, Rich," Topher said respectfully.

There was a *"thunk!"* and then some laughter at the back of the vehicle.

Topher huffed. "May we bid the week's peace a fond farewell. It seems you've turned him back into the little boy he's supposed to be."

Richard patted the driver's door.

"To the tavern again?" Topher asked.

"You, my good sir, know the drill."

16

March came and Quentin was depressed. He didn't know the dates of the days or the hours at which he tended to wake. His skin was crinkly from its dryness, his eyes were always heavy, and his legs were stiff from the many miles he spent in meaningless, directionless ambling through the corridors.

Others had it better. When they weren't warbling on in their meet-ups about things he didn't care for, Casey, Connor, and Marina were, if not productive, then more grounded in their handling of the situation. Casey liked to read, but not fiction. She was a science aficionado at heart—he had always heard of her prodigious mind— and when she wasn't playing basketball with her cousin and his friends in the gymnasium or spending time with Frances and Roxy, she was in the loft of the library with her long braids drooping into the pages of a quantum physics volume. Connor became a more extroverted version of himself. He remained selective in his choices of socialization, but he was more open to spending time with those who were starkly antithetical to Chris and Terry, and he would occasionally be found in the billiards hall with Athol or in the second-floor chemistry lab with Derek and Mathias. Quentin rarely saw Marina. Frances and Natalie were overwhelmed by the basics of their medical training. What was added to Frances's load, however, was the unneeded, but nonetheless executed, endeavor of hers to teach Fatima basic math, science, and history. He used to believe Frances embraced the uncalled-for undertaking due to a sort of unaddressed, maternal instinct. Yet, as he watched her labor through her workload and additionally take on Fatima as a pupil, he saw that it was for a different reason. It was all a distraction, a coping mechanism so as to never feel sorrowful, useless, and lacking—like Quentin. He imagined it was easier to have a heap of things to achieve in every waking moment than to have no purpose at all. But he recognized that having purpose was not the only path to happiness. There were ways to feel happy in an otherwise meaningless life. Such had become the case with Mathias, who seemed calmer, content; he had a new world in which he could start over, plus a quasi-legalized narcotics gig to keep him sane.

There were, however, others like Quentin. They were similarly antisocial and undyingly dejected. They, too, felt vacant and purposeless. Terry was morphing into one of them. Where his little cousin thrived, he jealously slipped into the abyss of living through the nothingness of a directionless life. He became the quiet one, and Casey the bubblier, more popular figure. She always was that way, but more so, then. Quentin felt bad for Terry. Quentin was ashamed and pitied the fact that, for so many years, he was envious of the spotlight that was bound to shine upon one Terry Montgomery, the athletic firebrand who was supposed to have emerged from the strange and unheard-of town that was Shaw, Massachusetts. But he was robbed of that dream. Quentin saw the efforts Casey made to make her cousin happy, to remind him that a life without stardom and accolades was a life still worth living, but her tactics—her blind encouragements— never worked. Quentin saw the way Terry skulked, how his tall, dark figure roamed the corridors like Quentin's.

The twins, Oscar and Ivy, fell victim to that same syndrome, too. The formerly flamboyant, almost socialite-esque, figures of Shaw High School became quiet and invisible. Oscar was shedding weight at a worryingly rapid pace; Quentin scarcely saw him at mealtimes. Ivy, on the other end of the spectrum, grew heavier; eating became her sole comfort. Between the Montgomery cousins and the Martinez twins, the utter sadness that polluted their once happy and innocent relationships transformed their dynamics into toxic twists of envy and respective eating disorders. There didn't seem to be any way for them to win their separate, internalized wars. And Quentin, for his part, didn't know how he would fare with his either.

With Marina set to be the advisor and Quentin the reluctantly advised, it surprised the unwilling captain that he seldom saw his second-in-command, and it pleased him. Even by the third week of April, she seemed unmotivated regarding the concept of engaging him just as he was revolted by the concept of being engaged by her. But he wasn't so sure if she was avoiding him or if her reduced presence was simply a product of the mayhem that arose within the trenches during the middle weeks of that specific month.

He didn't know what happened exactly or how it came to pass, but things went further askew. Three weeks into April, he realized that he no longer saw much of anyone. The change in the ship's atmosphere had slipped past him in the earlier weeks of the month due to the ceaseless stream of depression which had gradually overtaken every aspect of his life. But later, when he was a little sharper, he realized that he could count on one hand the number of times he actually crossed paths with someone. He knew something had gone awry, but before he could comprehend the origin of whatever it was, said mayhem contaminated their new home.

Hints of a growing social turmoil began to materialize in the last week of April. The air felt thicker. The ship was quieter, and it somehow seemed smaller. An unrelenting gloom swept through the halls and, save for a few, everyone replicated the rare disassociation which was previously exclusive to Quentin and some select individuals. He saw less and less of people, like each person was a fog that thinned out the moment the sun swept into its place in the sky. Patterson, too, became sneakily unattainable and randomly vanished without notice.

By the 30th of April, the place that was once manageable for all became unbearable for most. The few peers Quentin saw became oversensitive and brusque, like live wires ready to spark upon contact. He watched from afar as intermingled friend groups between unlikely individuals splintered, with some snapping back to the sophomoric, exclusionary mindsets they had once harbored in their school days, back home on Earth. Decency and kindheartedness melted away. The daily routines of arcade games and group cooking sessions in the dining hall no longer took place. What joy they had created for themselves wilted at every turn. Happiness seemed an impossible sentiment to reclaim.

The culprit, Quentin came to believe, was that the two divisions had vied so restlessly to acclimate to their new setting that they had forgotten the tragedy of why they were even there in the first place. All that their forced happiness had done was string them along for a contrived, soulless approach to an operation they hadn't even fully taken into consideration. It made him realize that he wasn't alone or uniquely depressive, that he wasn't a singularly directionless waste. Others were simply faking their adjustment and had brimmed with artificial cheer. He had no reason to feel guilty for his despondency. None of them were ready to be adults, much less carry the weight of something which their parents had dedicated their entire adult lives to.

April was only an oddity, but May was much worse. The invigoration of the operation faded. The recycled air became bothersome. The home-cooked meals were no longer being made, and the ration bars which substituted for their genuine plates of engineered meats and unfrozen vegetables weren't sitting well in their stomachs. People became ill at the mere sight of the same faces they saw each and every similarly passing day. The realization that everyone was bound to be together for decades to come was ghastly for them to even imagine. Social circles switched daily. They switched and switched, and then fighting would commence, and more switching would betide until, some two weeks into the new month, no one was friends with anyone. Those like Chris were struggling to fathom how they ever tried to bond with someone as skinny, studious, and unpopular as Ewan. Casey and Connor no longer sat next to each other at breakfast, lunch, or dinner. Marina's appreances were rare. Mathias and Derek split up their narcotics operations and each claimed separate chemistry labs as their own; Quentin never saw them, but he heard through rumor that Derek was experimenting with gases while Mathias pushed his limits with oxygen, as he had tried to see if there was any way to give himself a rush from it. Meanwhile, Fatima asked around to try and lure someone into helping her bake chocolate-chip cookies to sweeten the recycled air, but the older counterparts were either too tired, too disinterested, or too short-tempered to fulfill her request. At the same time, no one knew where Patterson was.

By the arrival of June, not only was everyone lacking in friends, but they were childishly churlish and easily agitated. Nearly all were bitter and bratty, and they became animalistic; decorum was lost and kindness vanished. There were moments when Quentin was startled by how gratingly rude and foul-mouthed he became, considering how he spent so much of his life surrendering to the comfort and ease of being compliant and invisible. But the repetition of the days nibbled at his sanity, which was the very sanity Patterson, wherever he was, had once praised. Quentin even began to wonder if Patterson hadn't disappeared at random or if he had foreseen the emotional unhinging that happened and had wisely hibernated for a time to avoid it. It wouldn't have been so unthinkable; due to his seniority, he was in possession of access keys and codes to the restricted, cryogenic chambers in the basement. Quentin would have done the same if he could—napped the days away.

Quentin became something of a voyeur. His mental state was in shambles, but bearing witness to the calamity of other people's lives tended to make him feel better about himself. It probably wasn't the healthiest of practices, but just like his convenient theism, at least he wasn't endangering anyone. He felt superiorly civilized when he heard that Terry had a fit while exercising in the weight room and, for no reason other than superficial perturbation at life in general, he allegedly flung one of his thirty-pound dumbbells toward a mirror and mindlessly gawked on as the glass collapsed to the floor. No one offered to clean it. Then, on a separate morning, when Amber and Casey stumbled into each other in the dining hall after bickering about something minuscule, they commenced a vicious fight. The beasts were released when Amber thwacked Casey's stomach with a serving tray and Casey kicked her rival into the booth. No one attempted to separate them, until Jaymes entered the room and pried them apart. Fist fights broke out like wildfires. The combatants would leave in their wake coffee-stained carpets, scraped walls, and flower petals strewn across broken tables. Natalie complained that they were prematurely running out of their monthly supplies of painkillers because of the endless stream of punch-drunk patients who spilled into the infirmary on an almost nightly basis. She and Frances tried to find Patterson to request more bottles, but he was still nowhere to be found. All the while, food rations disappeared from the shelves, partially because of hunger, but mainly due to gluttony. It was a mess. Philosophically, yes. But in a literal sense, it was just as unnerving. They, Quentin included, were odorous and unclean. The idea of washing and preening was beyond so many of them, as they felt there was no use in attempting to impress. Showers went unused and for a long time no one spoke, for when they did, the stench was a storm from their teeth and gums which they idly, or in some cases, refused, to brush. Razors lacked rust, as everyone rejected the labor of removing their extra hairs.

The Dark Era, Quentin thought. *That's what I'll name this shit.* And name it, he did. He said it once to Athol, when they were both scavenging the kitchen cabinetry for food one night. The name spread a few hours later, perhaps from the lips of Athol or those of an eavesdropper, and soon the bout of misery, grime, and irritability was coined that title by everyone.

As for Quentin's civility, it was put to an end in mid-June, when he once again hunted for food late at night and came upon an equally hungry Chris. One thing led to another and the two partook in a brutal feud after Chris said that he would "bag and rag" Frances and that Quentin would never in his life be able to because he "sits on the sidelines like a lil' bitch." The ship was quiet and the bodies of their peers didn't stir in their sleep, even when a pile of frying pans flew and the clamor echoed through the air vents all the way up to the residential fourth floor, where at least some of them were sleeping. When Quentin saw Frances a few days later in the computer room, he intended on telling her that Chris Laney was a predatory swine whom she ought to be wary of, but she just looked so tired. She wasn't listening to a single word Quentin said, which, he learned, was due to a prolonged expedition of hers to locate a missing Fatima. Frances had scoured the ship all day just to find the child burrowed deep in a pillow fort beneath the ice hockey table, encircled by days' worth of empty cereal boxes. There had been frantic questioning and afterward indignant scolding, since Fatima had apparently used some adopted terminology from Mathias's lexicon in her explanation for her absence.

And then there was one day, somewhere in the middle of that mess, when Quentin contemplated intervening on something which he might have once thought reprehensible, had they not been living through The Dark Era. It was a Tuesday morning, and he was passing a hysterically crying Ivy, who was sitting on the floor under one of the windows in a hallway of the fourth floor, when he saw Ewan around the corner, with a bottle of spray paint in hand, as he vandalized a silver-edged NASA panel on one of the walls.

Just below the big, bold N and proceeding in a downward vertical from it, Ewan sprayed new lowercase letters, O and T.

He then moved to the first bold A, hesitated, and left the area below it blank.

Beneath the bold S, he sprayed P, A, C, and E.

And underneath the second bold letter A, he guided the stream from the can to form the letters G, E, N, C, and Y.

Late in the night on the 16th of July, Quentin was watching a movie on his laptop in the library loft. The ship was quiet, as it normally was in that era. He uncurled himself from the warmth of the sofa, which he managed to hog for himself, and went out into the hallway to make his way downstairs to fetch some water. During his three-AM journey, he took note of the peculiarity that was a crack of the door to Mathias's chemistry lab. That door was never left open. Quentin hadn't even seen Mathias since April and knew only of his alleged oxygen experimentations. A curious Quentin pushed the door back and poked his head inside, which allowed him to see Mathias on the ground, his legs covered by a fallen lab stool, and his head atop a bed of broken glass shards. Glass pieces were scattered everywhere, some basked in the experimenter's blood while others shimmered spotlessly. With the words "glass" and "overdose" rushing from his lips, Quentin ran through the halls and, like Paul Revere on his midnight ride to alert the sleeping Minutemen in 1775, Quentin screamed for help, waking everyone.

Patterson appeared.

There was terror all throughout the night. The ubiquity of the panic was inescapable. Tears leaked out from the eyes of those who weren't even fond of Mathias. However many people tried to soothe Fatima, the child was inconsolable. Her breaths issued erratically and her face was red from her overwhelmed state. Jaymes was stressed. Ewan was angry, but at what, Quentin didn't know—NASA, maybe. Ivy, Amber, and Casey strung their hands together and stayed that way the whole night. Even Marina presented herself. She squatted beside Ewan on the floor outside the infirmary, her eyes in a steady squint and her face drawn tight, looking lost in thought, like she knew there were no words that could suffice in expressing how she felt in that moment. Everyone laid themselves outside the infirmary. Blankets, quilts, beds, and throw pillows were ejected from their sleeping spaces and relocated to the corridor, where the residents waited impatiently, eagerly, for even the slightest news pertaining to their ne'er-do-well peer. They planned to sleep until the clock struck six, resting on the ground in their ring of disheveled comforters and additional, strewn coverings. Some of them occasionally woke to see if the door to the infirmary had opened, but it never did—it was locked shut. The hands of Ivy, Amber, and Casey all remained interwoven in their sleep. Jaymes and Roxy held Fatima as she continued to weep into their shirts. Minding the sleeping bodies near them, Ewan and Marina spoke in undertones for hours, neither letting the conversation go, just as Oscar and Terry did the same in their own corner. Connor slept restlessly, and the same applied to Chris and Derek, who struck up a strategically distracting conversation in which they theorized Patterson's recent whereabouts. At some point in the night, Derek departed their ring, the cause of his leave unclear.

Quentin once thought he hated Mathias. But all throughout that night, Quentin, like so many others, accepted that he didn't. He disliked Mathias, but for all his flaws, he was one of them; one in their humble home. Despite the complete dysfunction of their new world and the few people in it, at least they had each other. Patterson's vision came true, after all. He wanted them to grow attached to each other, and they did.

"He doesn't mean half the shit he says," Athol said later, in the early hours of the morning, to Quentin and Ewan. The three of them were huddled under one blanket in their own corner of the hallway. "Mathias, he's a jerk," Athol continued, "I know that. But he's insecure. All the slurs…the bullying…the violence…all that shit…"

"It's a cover-up," Ewan said, as if knowing where Athol was going. "A way to mask how much of a loser he is."

"It's sad, really," Athol said. "I feel bad for him. But I get why he's intimidated by other people being comfortable with who they are when he has nothing to like about himself. But that doesn't mean I wanted it to come to this."

"If this is what it takes to get him sober, so be it," Ewan said.

Quentin felt himself nodding.

When the arrow of the hallway clock struck six, everyone decided to wake, and they sat there in silence, stunned that no one had come out to inform them of any news. So few believed it possible that Mathias could have overdosed on a supply of oxygen, since that was what he told everyone he'd been toying with during his excessive bouts of free time. But later, much later, after Natalie, Frances, and the enigmatic Patterson spent their whole night in the restricted ward with their patient, the reason for Mathias's critical state was finally revealed. What had been kept from everyone's knowledge for so long was that Derek and Mathias were infusing microscopic doses of nitrous oxide into their separately manufactured amalgamations of homemade narcotics. They infused the doses solely for amplified effect. According to Derek, nothing "normal" had been able to invigorate him and Mathias any longer, thus sprang forth the rationalization that something potentially lethal could suffice, which, evidently, it did.

"Coke…weed…they're nothing compared to that shit," Derek confessed to the enquiring captains after they were ordered by Patterson to search the different levels of the ship and find him. Mathias wasn't yet conscious, so their sole conduit of information was the only other known substance abuser in the community.

The creatively engineered amalgamation indeed worked, fortunately not for killing but for coming damn close to it, because visitations to Mathias were finally permitted at ten in the morning, soon after he woke. He looked horrible. Both his septum and lip piercings had been extracted during the resuscitation procedure, so the holes in his skin were gaping and wide for all to see. The oxygen mask had imprinted purple divots along his cheeks and chin. His speech was slurred. His eyes were baggy. But he was alive. It was clear how little he knew of his surroundings or what was even happening, but his peers didn't care. They cautiously crowded around him. Some sat at the foot of his bed and others stood or squatted in a simple effort to see his face. Fatima, little and lithe, climbed onto the cot and ensnarled his right knee into her arms, her chin on the peak of it.

Frances and Natalie exhaled exhaustedly, like they hadn't breathed in hours.

Thirty minutes into the visit, Natalie insisted that everyone let the patient rest. Scattered members of the two divisions filed out the doorway. Quentin wrapped a loose arm around Fatima's shoulders. He attempted enticing her to leave with him and the rest of their group, but she refused to budge. She clung to Mathias's leg.

Quentin smiled. "C'mon, you gotta let him go."

Fatima unwound her delicate, polka-dot-sleeved arms from around Mathias's thigh. Quentin expected her to follow after him, but she shuffled up the cot and deftly wriggled her way under every wire and tube extending from Mathias's form. She molded her body into an accommodating shape that would suit both patient and visitor for an extended period of time, with her small head tucked into the curve of Mathias's open armpit and her legs brought up to lean against his stomach. Once she was settled, the baby fat around her bloodshot eyes puffed as they fell shut. Quentin studied the scene. Frances did, too. She seemed amused. Quentin couldn't decide if the friendship between Mathias and Fatima was a good thing, a healthy one. But he had to wonder, what worse harm could Mathias possibly inflict on Fatima compared to what her parents had already done to her? Mathias was disrespectful and daring, vulgar and impulsive, while the place they had called home was discreet and diplomatic, but exploitative and manipulative. When Quentin tried to look at their predicament from her perspective, it hit him that she must have credited Mathias as the only protector in their group, because for all the vitriol the older kids had hurled at him the day he had tried to kill that guard, he was still the only one who outwardly displayed a desire to fight for them, which must have comforted her young, impressionable mind. As Mathias's and the little girl's breaths synchronized into a steady, relaxed pace, Quentin uneasily accepted the strange reality that unfolded.

That day, the 16th of July, marked the end of The Dark Era.

———

Patterson had thoroughly confused Marina. She didn't know how to process the fact that her superior officer believed it was for the greater good of his subordinates' mental health to have them spend an entire year without performing any mandatory preparations. In her eyes, the sniveling of her peers was shallow water against the deep sea that was the imminent, imposing threat at hand. He knew she thought lesser of him for the choice he had made, but he didn't seem to care. Sometimes she scoffed at the irony of his behavior, at the pretense that he was devotedly mindful of everyone's mental health. But if he were so mindful, he would have abandoned the Rebirth Plan for its potential to drive rational people absolutely mad.

The advisor to Division Two's unconcerned captain wasn't a jealous person, but in early December, when the majority of the ship's community had idly sniveled, wept, and shut down emotionally, she wished she could have robbed Natalie and Frances of what they had and she didn't—jobs. Marina had nothing to do, nowhere to go, and, although she was in the continual company of so many, she had no one to talk to. The demise of everyone's energy and the wildness of their crying prickled every nerve inside her until she couldn't stand the sight of their flushed, weeping faces every day. They thought her jagged and immovable, and she thought them pathetic. She concluded it would be best for everyone if she withheld involving herself in their community until the universal misery and self-pity waned.

In January, she had mistakenly thought most of her peers had begun to compose themselves. She admitted she was fooled, but in her defense, things had taken a promising turn. Different cohorts of hers woke earlier than needed and habitually participated in group activities every single day—rituals which, to her disapproval, although never to her surprise, were only temporary. Why did she ever believe Athol would remain consistent with learning to weight-lift under Connor's tutelage, or that Amber opening a book club centered on Albert Einstein's *The World as I See It* would go beyond five days? The act was insufferable. The three words "We gotta grow" was a slogan which, per the sources of rumors, was crafted by none other than Oscar Martinez. Those three words were spoken in what Marina thought was the most pretentious, inorganic effort to prove one's false strength. With rising popularity, it made its rounds. She heard it everywhere and all the time, ironically only regurgitated by those whose misery was glaringly detectable, like Ivy, Terry, and Roxy. Every breakfast included the recurring antic of her peers plastering smiles onto their faces, smiles that never reached their swollen eyes, in an unabashedly ridiculous endeavor to bury evidence of the previous night's crying. They were so unsuccessful and they looked so stupid, and they didn't stop. From the final half of January and deep into February, they applauded themselves for the speedy development of their own maturity. But it was all strained and unnatural.

"To our bravery," Ivy toasted one dinner with a cup of oat milk. That statement was the last straw for Marina, who was already full from her meal; she stood up from the table's bench and walked away.

In time, the faux cheer predictably disappeared and the gloom of the past snuck its way back into their new home. Marina was there for it. She was there for all of it, from the beginning of April to the middle of July. But she made sure to never be seen, since no one was worthy of engagement, except for Casey and Connor, whom Marina misunderstood for being mature and innovative back in January, only for them to spiral into a spurt of sadness themselves. From afar, she watched the turbulent moods of her peers shift dramatically every week, watched them revert back to the childish persons they'd once been. She witnessed the gloom shift into anger, the anger shift into aggression.

She reveled in their self-proclaimed Dark Era. As everyone fought and screamed and cried, every day and night, she moseyed about the floors of the ship with a book in one hand and a water bottle in the other. She walked over every inch of their new home and interchangeably sat in every nook and cranny she could find, but to keenly remain active in preparation for the inevitable tasks of the year to come, she often chose to pace rather than sit. For miles each day, she read and turned pages of paperbacks that she never would have read back in her real home, but, for boredom's sake, she read them there, on that ever-moving ship. She hardly saw anyone, but when she did, and those occasions were very rare, she made her inclination for solitude evident. She wished only for The Dark Era's continuation.

It didn't continue, though. She should have known.

One day, in May, Marina was basking in the calm of her serene day and reading a novel, which was a lauded literary classic, when out of nowhere, Jaymes Chen started walking beside her. Except, he wasn't quite beside her. He was actually walking backwards and facing her. He still had those dark glasses on his face, "And what are we reading today?" he asked, as though it was any of his business to intrude on her private relaxation period as she read and roamed in her pajama bottoms and over-sized, NASA-issued sweatshirt.

Marina didn't answer. She didn't have to. She could do as she very well pleased without being interrogated. By then, The Dark Era had been in existence for over a month, so did he not have anyone else to pester?

To satiate him, she decided to throw him a bone by saying in a clipped tone of voice, "*Anna Karenina.*"

Jaymes raised his head. "Is it good?"

Marina didn't answer him.

"Do you ever get lonely?" Jaymes asked.

Marina slammed the book shut. "What are you doing?" she asked.

Jaymes kept walking backwards even as they rounded a corner. "I'm on suicide vigil," he said.

"You're what?"

"Patterson's assigned me to keep track of everyone's mental health," Jaymes said. "I go around and investigate, report back to Frances and Natalie in the infirmary, then I do it again the next day."

"Do you genuinely think it's a productive idea to go around asking people about their mental health?" Marina asked.

"Who said I ask around? I said, I investigate."

"You're asking me right now."

A corner of Jaymes's lip curled up. "Only because I know you'll see right through me if I don't." He pointed to the book. "So, is it good?"

Marina sighed. "No. It makes no sense. After everything Tolstoy puts the reader through, he has her pitch herself in front of a moving train in the end."

"Interesting." Jaymes continued walking backward as Marina progressed forward. He looked smug. "You aren't using that book as inspiration for dealing with your own mental health problems, are you?"

Marina scowled. She whirled around and left him alone in that random, third-floor hallway.

July arrived and Marina swore she would never forgive Mathias for singlehandedly dismantling The Dark Era. While everyone around her wept on the carpeted ground near the second-floor infirmary, she sat narrow-eyed and still, speechless and in deep thought as she tried to comprehend how that fucking idiot ever managed to overdose on oxygen. She only looked up once during her contemplation and saw that, for some reason, Quentin Hanson was staring at her.

17

Quentin put the keys to his bedroom in the front pocket of his duffel bag. The meeting metals gave a jingle. He had a spacious bedroom, which he appreciated. After suffering through months of sleeplessly rolling side to side in the open area that was the male sleeping quarter, he knew it would be more comfortable to finally have a space that was his own. This, his personal bedroom on the ship, was practical and similar in size to that of his back home, in the pink colonial on a hill in Shaw. A metal desk was fixed into the wall beside the door to the fourth-floor hallway. Above, but slightly beside it, were two glass panes, and dark-blue curtains that could cover them were slid back on either side. There were also windows right by the bedside of his single-level bunk but, to his great relief, that glass was shrouded by its own pair of fabric veils. He snooped into his closet and pulled open all the drawers and little doors. It seemed that, in addition to the articles of clothing he had been wearing since his arrival in the previous year, other pieces were waiting to be used, some of which he recognized. There was the occasional, standard-issue pair of sweatpants or folded pile of tee-shirts and NASA-branded sweatshirts, but there were also the running sneakers he wore to school every day throughout his senior year of High School. There was even the blue, collared shirt he wore on the last day of school of his junior year, and the black one he wore to his grandmother's funeral in the summer of 2045. There were corduroys that were three sizes too small for him, but also khakis that had once been oversized when he was fifteen but, at nineteen, could fit him perfectly. One sweater still smelled of pine. A green tee-shirt was marred by a single, stubborn toothpaste stain; the pink-and-yellow striped one which Lucas had always insisted on buying.

Quentin walked out of the closet, shoes squeaking against the paneled floor as he advanced to the bed, where he sat down, slouching. The clock on his bedside table read one o'clock in the morning, but he wasn't tired. How could he have been? He hadn't done anything all day. There remained a hectic commotion that permeated throughout the ship due to Mathias's release from the infirmary after his two-week stay, but besides the celebratory dinner, staying up to watch a movie with some others, and Patterson distributing everyone's bedroom keys, none of the day's events made Quentin exert himself in any way that would justify sleeping.

He would think of something to do with himself. But for the time being, he laid down and kicked off his shoes, settling onto the bed with his lower body hanging off the edge of it. When his head pushed back against the pillow, he felt something solid extending out and hitting the back of his neck. He sat up and peeled the pillow off the bed to unearth the mystery item.

It was a diary. He slid his hands over the frayed, leather covers and the rusted metal ends of its binding. Knitted into the bottom-right corner, in satin-red string, were the initials ACH, which led him to wonder with rightful curiosity if it had once been the possession of a certain Agata Celia. When he opened it, he flipped through the whole thing. Nearly all the pages of it were empty—all but one. The first sheet had some writing on it. Inscribed in the middle of its creamy, pink paper was a passage that read:

Do bees buzz for butterflies....my nettle must know…
Nettle knows that bees buzz for butterflies

Quentin shut the diary and tied his shoes back on. He ran out of the room, and he went hurrying through all the floors of the ship. He looked everywhere for Patterson, but, once again, couldn't find him. His office was empty. The library had only Frances and Fatima. Derek worked alone in his lab, and Mathias's was vacant. Ivy was eating in the kitchen all by her lonesome. Jaymes, Chris, and Oscar were working out in the fitness room, laughing among themselves but then shaking their heads when Quentin asked if any of them had seen Patterson since dinner. When it struck Quentin that the older man must have retired for the night to wherever it was he normally hid, Quentin succumbed to the unlikelihood of successfully completing his search and plopped himself onto the lowest step of one of the foyer staircases, just like Frances before him, when he had found her in the middle of the night, back in February.

Diary in hand, he flipped through it. Page after page, all the lines but those centermost two on the first one were empty. That written question was the one clear, but dichotomously ludicrous, thought Agata had had in her last years of mental fragility, so much so that she felt inclined to write it down in permanent form. She must have written it just before she died, some time when he wasn't looking. But that would indicate that she had given the question forethought before he went to visit her on the day of her death. It also indicated that the passing thought wasn't passing at all, but was, in fact, something genuinely on her mind, which, were that the case, would have been unusual. For the last ten years of her life, she seldom harbored thoughts that stayed in her mind for more than a minute, so what would have made it different, then? And how could she have written it? He couldn't even recall a time when she had written anything by hand. His father always handled her paperwork and likewise her nurse, Janie, sorted and read Agata's mail deliveries for her. She couldn't even hold a pen, as her knobby, bruised fingers were afflicted by an acute case of arthritis. It was Quentin who pitted their fruits during his visits. It was Quentin who poured her drinks and held open the doors. Sometimes he even fed her by hand when she was too weak to hold her cup or a fork. It didn't make sense. None of it. Not the thought, not the adamance of that very thought, and especially not the potential, physical act of her writing it down, and neatly too. Why was that question so important to her?

Quentin started roaming without direction. He walked up the stairs, through the second and third floors, and then found his way back to the foyer again. He just needed some time to think.

When he returned to the first floor about an hour later, Casey spotted him. He wanted to turn around, but it was too late. Her round face with its pinked cheeks smiled as she made her way to him, pushing her dreadlocks to one shoulder. "Hey, Quentin!" she called to him. "You're awake!"

Quentin faked a smile. He hoped it wasn't too tightly pulled. "What're you doing?" he asked, but he didn't need to. He saw that, over her low-cut cardigan, a brown strap cut across her chest and trailed down to her left hip, locked into a sand-colored messenger bag. He saw the papers and pens peeking out the poorly fastened top. Casey pointed to the door behind him, and Quentin glanced over. *Damnit,* he thought, when he saw that he had been roaming outside the large auditorium. "You should come in," Casey suggested, "we'd be more than happy to have you join."

"Oh, I don't—"

"Come on, Quentin. You're a Listener. If there's anyone we need at the table, it's you, if not just for the sake of having one at our meetings. And, as captain, it is kind of your unofficial, civic duty to attend."

"But—Well—I was getting tired and—"

Casey laughed. "No, you weren't. Don't lie." She bumped her elbow into his and started lightly pulling at his sweatshirt. "Come along, you big baby."

"No, seriously. Whatever you guys are doing, I can't help."

"All help is welcome," Casey optimistically dismissed him. He was infuriated with himself for obliging as he followed her through the heavy door of the room. If she noticed his unending reluctance, she refrained from berating him for it.

Never once had he stepped into the auditorium, and the depth of it was a wonder to the uninitiated, like him. He wouldn't have suspected that a door as narrow and normal as all others would lead him to a place as grand and gaping as the room they entered, but, he supposed, he shouldn't have been taken-aback; soon there would be a great many people in their company, enough to fill the many of seats around him. Casey led him down the aisles of seating, and he watched as his shadow covered her body. Low, orange, recessed lights in the corners glowed gently, but an askew spotlight suddenly shined directly into his eyes the farther they went in. While shielding his face with an open hand, he heard, but didn't exactly see, Connor, Marina, and Athol speaking at the bottom.

"…unlikely to prove it works…" That was Marina.

"A thermal sensor is always the best bet," replied Connor.

Then came the customary Athol, "Yes, but, Connor, you're excluding the very real possibility that it isn't something thermal in the first place. It could be cold-blooded. In fact, the data indicates that it probably doesn't even have blood."

"It has blood," Connor said.

"You don't know that," Marina said.

Connor's tone was much curter when he rebuked, "Well, how the hell can it be something bloodless, Marina? Can you explain that?"

"I'm not trying to explain something I don't understand. I'm referencing the data."

"Fine." Connor used to be so quiet that his recent loquacity frightened Quentin, as it was indicative of the very uncomfortable fact that there were some people who indeed thrived in their new living conditions. Quentin thought Connor never seemed more in his element than he was in 2047. Perhaps all his years of acting closed off were not due to a problematic complex of social superiority but, rather, a lack of desire to enter into matters which he considered of minuscule consequence; parties; sports; Shaw High School's social scene. Perhaps he wasn't as stuck-up and shallow as Quentin had assumed.

Quentin's and Casey's sloped walking ended below the final row of seating, where, through the cracks of his fingers, he finally saw Connor and Marina. Each were seated on one side of the head of an enormous, boat-shaped, wooden table in the center of the bottom level; Quentin counted thirty chairs encircling it. A rolling whiteboard stood behind the head seat, but it was untouched by the blue and red markers that waited in their holders on the edge of it. Connor, in a white, buttoned-up tee-shirt, was flipping through a hefty volume of paper-clipped pages, his free hand white-knuckled in a clenched fist. Marina seemed undisturbed. She was comfily garbed in a flannel, and one of her sweatpants-covered legs was pulled up on the chair, so that her arm rested on her knee as she read from an open journal. She tapped a pencil against the table. Athol was similarly cloaked in draping pajama clothes that were much too large for his form; he curled and uncurled his hands around the ends of his overly large sleeves. He sat beside Connor, reading through the same, paper-clipped pages.

"Look what the cat dragged in," Marina said without looking up.

Quentin dropped his hand from in front of his face and saw Connor looking at him. "No kidding," he reveled at the newcomer. His mood visibly improved, evidenced by the smile that etched onto his once tightly wound face. "It's about time."

Casey spun around. "See, Quentin? They don't bite." Quentin just nodded and mimicked her in joining the others at the table. She took the seat at the head, and he took the one on Athol's left.

"I decided to join the fun," Athol explained.

"Fun," Quentin commented. "So what do you guys do in here all the time?"

Connor put down his paper pile and reached a mug that was on the table. He sipped from it and asked, "Have you been briefed on the information we have about the beings who led us on this wild goose chase?"

Quentin shook his head.

As she jotted in her journal, Marina raised an eyebrow.

"That's okay," Casey said. She retrieved a notebook of her own, with stickers and pen marks peppered across its front cover.

Quentin was suddenly reminded that a diary sat on his own lap. He hoped that he wouldn't be compelled to use it, not after just finding the only known and preserved relic of his favorite person was hidden inside. The last thing he wanted to do was taint it with transcribed notes of their little project.

"Quick briefing..." Casey said. "Basically, the conundrum scientists have been facing is that there are no physical signs of the beings that have destroyed the exoplanets and, thus far, one of our solar system's moons. Literally no one has any clue what they look like or what they're made of. Satellites have been sent to detect traces of their existence in those areas, but nothing's come back with a positive read. Over the decades, we've dispatched…I think it was somewhere in the area of two thousand sensors. Anyway, some thermal sensors and motion detectors, but nothing came back and *still* nothing comes back. Ever. Granted, the machines haven't had the time to reach the part of deep space where the exoplanets were located, but that's still concerning."

Connor sighed. "And nothing's come back from Titania, even after the destruction of Pluto's moon, which is equally distressing because, when you think about it, the distance between Uranus and Pluto isn't so astounding that you can't detect action if you're located on or near either one. So you can see how this is worrying. We even enabled all kinds of detector mechanisms on the satellites. But they yielded nothing."

Casey's chair swiveled left to right, right to left as she rocked in thought. "We think it could be some type of advanced, invisible shield that's guarding them from our detection, or perhaps something like the stealth technology, like the type used in stealth aircraft."

"That wouldn't explain the lack of physical detection, though," Athol said. "Or the fact that there hasn't been a readable shift in space. There are discernible ripples when an asteroid moves or when a planet orbits. There haven't even been registrations of gravitational pulls or anything."

Perhaps it was because her book was on his lap, but Quentin thought of Agata. He thought of all the nonsensical things she used to warble about every day for as long as he could remember. "Maybe it's not a physical being," Quentin heard himself say.

Marina's response was a disbelieving and disapproving frown. "Quentin, what are you talking about?"

"Nothing," Quentin said quickly.

"No, go on," Casey encouraged him.

"It's dumb, Casey," Quentin said. "I shouldn't."

Casey's face was firm, completely serious. "Yes, you should."

"I just…" Quentin licked his bottom lip. "Look, maybe you're thinking about this from the wrong point of view, our point of view. The view from Earth. You're asking how you can uncover a disguised creature but maybe…maybe it isn't disguised."

"It has to be disguised," Connor said.

"But that's what I mean," Quentin said quietly, hesitantly. "You're only saying that it has to be disguised because that's all you know about things that show up on a radar or other sensing devices. Because that's what it's like on Earth. Back home, if things aren't seen on a scan, then they either aren't there or they're well hidden. But maybe they are there, but not hidden." His insides squirmed when his words hung in the air and no one said a thing. Against his better judgement, he added, "It's…You…We're perceiving it from our perspective."

"That's what perceiving means," Marina retorted.

"What're you insinuating?" Athol asked.

"I'm not insinuating anything," Quentin said defensively. "I'm just theorizing."

"You clearly have some thought," Marina said.

Quentin sighed. "I guess what I'm getting at is that they could be invisible by nature. I mean, think of chameleons, how they can blend into their environments without even trying."

"So you're saying they're chameleonic?" Casey asked. "That they can change color or even blend into the dark matter around them?"

"Maybe?"

"That wouldn't explain why our physical sensors can't pick up anything, though," Athol said, returning to that point. "You can still read a color-changing animal's movements via the displacement of air and dust particles or shifts in light. And there's plenty of light in that exoplanet solar system. Not to mention, in ours too."

Casey pulled her legs up on her chair and crowded them in front of her chest. "Maybe these beings are more advanced than we've thought. It's possible they're equipped with enough knowledge about us and our technology to deflect our sensors or even manipulate the data streams before we receive them."

"Can they be that advanced?" Connor asked.

"I mean, they are advanced enough to make solid bodies disappear without a trace," Casey said. "So I'm betting yes."

"Are they actually gone, those planets?" Quentin asked.

"Before you go there," Athol said, "yes they are. We had the same thought a few months ago, wondering if maybe the planets and moons were masked like the being potentially is. But our satellites have scanned the very areas and orbital paths where those bodies had been before, which is the telltale sign that they are, in fact, gone."

"Okay," Quentin murmured. "But why do you keep assuming that the beings, or being, are, like, physical or something?" He wanted to shut up, but he couldn't get himself to stop talking. He didn't know why he was losing himself in the conversation. Maybe it was all his months of boredom finally wearing on him that made him invested. Part of him wanted to punch his own throat for cooperating.

"Are you assuming that they aren't physical?" Athol asked.

"Physical indicators of their existence have come back, Quentin," Connor said. "Remember, sound is a physical indicator."

"I know *that*," Quentin said. "I also now know that the planets and their moons are physically gone for good too. But that's not what I'm trying to say. Look, we know that these beings can make detectable impacts, tangible ones, but that doesn't have to mean that they're tangible too, right?"

Connor crossed his arms. "But how can something non-physical impact something physically?"

Quentin squirmed under all the attention. He never should have followed Casey into that room. "I...I don't know," he spluttered.

Casey started fiddling with an errant string on her pajama bottoms. "I suppose we always considered things only from the limited realm of human knowledge, which is ridiculous when you think about it. I suppose it's insular-minded to approach new things in a limited, earthly context."

"I dunno," Connor said, exhaling. "It's not feasible."

Athol shrugged. "Well, to each his own, but I think you're proving Quentin right."

"Why's that?"

"Because, like Casey pointed out, you're only willing to consider things from the Earth-based realm of knowledge," Athol said. "You also aren't willing to actually think of something beyond our comprehension."

Marina dropped her leg from the chair and sat upright, resting her elbows on the tabletop.

"Our Earthly mindset is inappropriate," Casey expanded. "We're not supposed to be thinking in an Earth manner because we're tackling something that originates beyond our solar system and maybe even beyond our galaxy. Who are we to set limitations on something we don't even know the slightest thing about?" She puffed out a laugh, almost sardonically. "You know, my dad was an astrophysicist and I always thought he was just a hyperbolic daydreamer. I kind of... I don't talk about this, but I didn't have a lot of respect for his field. I always wanted to be a physicist, never an astrophysicist, though. I thought they imagined too much. I thought their conclusions were excessively theoretical rather than literal. But it was only recently that I realized how he actually wasn't wasting his time by thinking of stupid—or seemingly stupid—ideas because, when you think about it, we really only know a tiny, tiny fraction about our own solar system. Even after all that we've uncovered over the years, he was sure we had missed at least a billion other things. Why should we apply that limited knowledge to areas that might be vastly larger, more complex, and far more ancient than our own?" She smiled at Quentin. "Thank you. To be honest, I hadn't seen just how limiting I was being this whole time."

Quentin felt even more uncomfortable.

"So how do you recommend we detect an undetectable body?" Connor asked impatiently.

"Why are you jumping to the conclusion that it's a body?" Marina asked. "If it's not a tangible being, there's no body to find. It's just a life."

"A life?" Connor's disbelief morphed into frustration. "How are we supposed to find a life? Life's not physical. Nor is it something that pops up on a screen."

"There are manifestations of life," Athol said. "Hints of it. Then again, I'm just referencing the impacts of a life as opposed to the actual life itself. And what even is a life, or a soul, if not just an energy? A machine can't quite pick that up either."

Casey perked up a bit. Her shoulders raised in her bettering of the long-lasting slouch. "I don't think that's so true."

"To be fair to Connor," Marina excused the other advisor, "there hasn't been any scientific evidence of a life—or as Athol said, a soul—being readable. Findable."

"I mean, this topic has been a hotbed for debate since the beginning of time," Connor said. "Especially in recent decades because, well, political and ethical arguments have always correlated this type of discussion with abortion rights. And the argument from those who support a woman's right to choose has always been that there is no way to know when a life begins, therefore on what actual basis does the government have the right to infringe on their ability to terminate a pregnancy? We can't resort to the formless life idea. So many already have."

"Hold on, hold on." Athol drummed his fingers against his armrest. "Eighth…? No, sorry, ninth grade biology class. You guys remember when Mrs. Landon said a heartbeat can be detected at around five to six weeks after insemination?"

Casey nodded. "Plus the bit in our textbook said that some can be found at three or four."

"This is not helping at all," Connor injected. "A life is a life, but a heart is a physical thing."

"Does every creature need a heart to live?" Quentin asked meekly.

"No," Casey said. "Jellyfish don't have hearts."

"Neither do plants," Athol added. "Bacteria. Fungi. Parasites. All are living organisms. No hearts there, though."

"Or souls," Casey said.

"I think," Marina said slowly, "for simplification's sake, we should focus only on sentient and brain-functioning beings. Let's try and steer clear of the plant discussion. We are, after all, pursuing a creature that can develop premeditated thoughts and exercise select destructions. It—*they* aren't—thoughtless. And they definitely aren't inanimate objects either."

Casey took in a deep breath. "*Life*," She said at once, mulling over the word. "So life is a concept we believe we understand. Without physical manifestation of it being inside someone, we probably wouldn't even think it existed and we probably wouldn't even exist to see it. Correct?"

"I don't think that's really true," Quentin spoke up.

Everyone turned back to him.

"Two years ago," Quentin said, "in the summer before we were kidnapped, my grandmother died. Once in the day, and once again that night, in her sleep. I was spending some time at her house. We had lunch, talked a bit and just kind of hung out until the evening. I was helping her into the house—so keep in mind, I was holding her —when her eyes glazed over and she fell down. I checked her pulse. Nothing came back. And guys, I checked every reasonable pulse point. Also, she wasn't breathing. By the time I had gotten up to call an ambulance, a lot of time had passed. *A lot.* I was pissed at myself, and I swore up and down for reacting too slowly. But when I hung up the phone, she was wide awake. She was on the floor, staring at me, laughing and telling me that I had a potty mouth. She told me that her being gone was no excuse to use the words I'd said. I asked her how she could hear me, but she couldn't explain it. She said everything went black, but that she heard me the whole time. She said she heard *everything*, from my breaths to my swearing…to the dialing of the phone.

"When the ambulance arrived, she didn't remember anything from when it was just the two of us or even the short amount of time when she was talking to me after coming back. It shouldn't have surprised me, since she had really bad dementia. So when the paramedics came in, they chalked it up to me being overdramatic and told her to increase her fluid intake so she wouldn't get another fainting spell. I didn't bother telling them what had happened and that she had no pulse and wasn't breathing. I knew I would've sounded crazy. I tucked her into bed right after they left, and I went home. When her nurse went to the house the next morning, she said that my grandmother had died in her sleep. And that was the last of her, I guess. Her burial was a week later." Quentin's breath caught. "I've uh…I've never told anyone that."

Marina glanced down to her journal. "Now that..." She drifted off and wrote something down. "That's really interesting because it indicates that life is autonomous."

"Was it, like, a cardiac arrest episode or something?" Athol asked. "My mom's a surgeon, so I know a bit about that stuff."

"I don't know," Quentin said. "I didn't tell the paramedics anything else, only that she fell and hit her head earlier."

"It could have been a coma," Athol said. "Your grandmother's ear canals may have been in optimal condition throughout it. Plus, it doesn't sound like she really died, only that she was in a prolonged unconscious phase."

"That wouldn't explain the cessation of breathing," Marina said. "Or her lack of a pulse."

"Wow," Casey gusted out. "Sounds like she died twice."

"I think so," Quentin mumbled.

Casey's eyes widened. "That would mean that her body had given out, but not her. As in...*her. She* heard you, while the physical her didn't. And despite what Athol said about the ear canals possibly being fully intact, I contest that it's possible a life can be fully aware of things even without its body. A lot of living beings attach their lives to a body. It's more of a default setting in our nature, but that might not be the case for something else. Someone, I should say. It's possible that life, for other creatures, is an autonomous entity. Maybe they aren't dependent on their bodies like we are. Maybe they can switch into and out of a body."

Marina glanced down to her notes. "So we're actually veering into more of a metaphysical discussion?'

"Oh, metaphysics," Casey said, sighing, "how I detest thee."

Connor's arms tightened against each other in their fold over his chest. "So we need some system that can detect, basically, what Quentin's grandmother was doing when she died the first time."

"That's near impossible," Athol said.

"Brain waves?" Casey asked.

"Can you even detect brain waves?" Connor wondered suspiciously.

The Division One captain scoffed at herself and extracted a handheld device from one her pockets. "I'm such an idiot," she said self-deprecatingly. "I forgot I had this."

Quentin tried to see the object in her hand. "What is that?"

"It's essentially a phone, but not a phone. Just a browser, really. It's a log of all the information from major search engines back home, so it's technically off-line internet. It has data as recent as when we left home; 2045." Casey slid her thumb against the touch screen and began rapid-typing on it. "All right, let's see…"

"We've picked up brain waves before," Athol said in the meantime. "I swear we have."

"I wouldn't know," Connor said.

Casey rejoined the lagged conversation a minute later, with a web page open under her chin. "So," she began, "according to this one source, brain waves occur around week twenty-eight of a baby's life and are, in fact, detectable."

"Wait, wait," Connor interjected. "I'm really sorry, I hate to interrupt, but brain waves are unrelated to everything. Again, a brain is physical. A physical piece of a body. We're now trying to understand the situation of a non-physical being, Casey."

Casey tartly flicked the cover back onto the web surfer. "Right. Right. Crap. So what do we do now?"

"This is impossible," Marina said.

"It can't be," Quentin said. "If my grandmother had the capacity to hear every single one of my words, doesn't that mean we could have the capacity to know she was there?"

"It's not scientifically possible, however reasonable it may sound," Athol said. "I know it would make sense. I know the intermix, the…the concision makes sense logically, but we can't do it. We don't have the scientific maturity to even go there."

"But we do have scientists on board to help us with any theory we have," Marina said.

"Hey, aren't there people who claim to see spirits?" Quentin asked. "Or, life forces. Call them what you will. We know there are people who are said to sense spirits and paranormal activities."

"But it's all anecdotal," Marina said.

"Like, mediums?" Casey asked somewhat condescendingly. "Sure. The problem is that we're not talking about spirits and paranormal activity, though. Ghosts are a whole different…" She paused when she saw Quentin's face change. "No. Don't."

"But are they really any different from what we're discussing?" Quentin challenged her. "A ghost—the thing we label as a ghost—is just a formless life, right? You said it yourself that my story about my grandmother indicated that a life doesn't always need a body, and so if the body dies, that doesn't necessarily mean the life dies. What we're basically agreeing on is that the life can use a body as a host but that life itself isn't necessarily physical. A ghost doesn't have to be seen as a ghost, we could see it as a formless life."

"Nevertheless," Marina said, "regardless of what a life is, we still need something that transcends modern science to even register a thing like that."

"Maybe it's not a machine that would register it," Quentin proposed.

"Pardon?"

"Touching on the medium thing again," Quentin said, "we could—"

Connor groaned. "But those people are more often than not delusional. Besides, where the hell in deep space are we gonna kidnap a medium? And they're crazy, man. All of them."

"Now, wait," Casey came around. "I did say earlier that life can be autonomous. Mediums—sensors of ghosts or spirits or life, if you will—are not always traveling circus members, attention-seekers, or liars. There's no denying that certain types of individuals are proven to have a sixth sense."

"And who, Casey, would that be?" Connor drawled.

"Infants."

"Infants?"

"Infants," Casey said. "You and I can't find a life on a whim, Connor. And scientists can't find one either. Doctors have tried for decades, and failingly so. But children can. Young children. Babies, for example. Human babies have always been able to see things that we can't. *Once*," she said, "I was at a baby shower for my cousin. One of the guests brought her eight-month-old, and I kid you not, I walked into the room where he was supposed to be napping, but instead of seeing a sleeping baby, do you know what I found? I found him sitting upright, laughing. Laughing at the wall. Literally at a wall. There was nothing on that wall, Connor. No paintings. No bugs. Nothing. It wasn't even colorful. It was a plain, white wall. I went further into the room and stood in front of him, but he wouldn't look at me. He was looking at a space beside me, almost…almost through me. And he was laughing. He just kept gurgling that creepy, baby laugh."

"Casey," Connor said carefully, "that's just something all babies do."

"Exactly!" Casey exclaimed.

Marina wrote a few words into her journal.

"That is what I mean!" Casey all but screamed. "Why, at random, do babies laugh at things we aren't aware of? Things we can't see? And why are we accepting of that? They can clearly make out something which we can't."

A decades-old memory dawned upon Quentin as Casey and Connor bickered. In it was a two-and-a-half-year-old Lucas sprawled on their parents' bed, giggling ceaselessly at the ceiling. Nothing that could have registered as humorous had been in place on that ceiling. It was just chipped plaster.

"I've never seen a baby do that," Marina said. "Laughing at nothing? Never."

"I have," Quentin said. "My brother would do it sometimes. He used to freak out my mom."

"And in your mother's defense," Casey said, "she was rightfully freaked."

Athol nodded to himself, the butt of his chin hitting his chest as he did. "We need some type of mechanism that enables us to mimic that extra, observational sense infants possess in hopes that we can sense what they can."

"Well, not just infants," Marina said, "but dogs, too. Dogs have a sixth sense, a sharp one."

Connor unfolded his arms and looped his hands into each other on his lap. "All right. That seems more logical than before. If that's our final decision, I'm sold."

Athol reclined. "Actually, you know how we were talking about embryos and how people don't know if a life is there before or after an embryo is created? Okay, here's this. When I was about ten, my golden retriever, who'd lived with us for over five years by that point, started acting irrationally protective of my mom. He would bark whenever she'd leave the house or if my dad and I even dared go near her. He'd never been protective of any of us, even when she had an asthma attack or when Derek and Mathias would egg my house on the weekends. But five weeks later, after that behavior change, do you know what happened? She took a test and found out that she was pregnant with my little sister."

"That's a little…a little different," Connor said. "How do you know he knew that? Your mother was pregnant. Women carrying are constantly hungry, always eating. They experience tangible, probably sniffable, hormone changes. It could've just been that he was following her around all day because he wanted more treats and goodies and she was constantly eating, so why not?"

"But why would he bark every time she tried to leave the house?" Quentin asked. "And that wouldn't explain why he'd get angry every time Mr. Khatri and Athol would go near her."

"Where does this even leave us?" Casey mumbled.

Athol filled his cheeks with air and then blew it all out. "We mimic the brains of a baby and a dog."

Connor shot him a puzzled look.

"It'll take years just to design this technology," Athol said. "We would have to make synthetic brains with accelerated sensory systems. We'd assemble a team to design two different models, electronic ones. One prototype would be of an infant, preferably less than nine-months old. Another would be an adult German Shepherd, since they're one of the most observant breeds in the world. And before any of you say that it's impossible, we have with us some of the smartest people here, in our home, downstairs in the basement. Why not at least mention this to them? Maybe they'll laugh. But they're scientists, maybe they won't. They shouldn't. I bet they'll give us a chance."

"Assume they don't," Marina said.

"Assume they will," Casey countered.

"We would first need Patterson's clearance," Marina said. "A theory as aspirational and, possibly unprovable as this would consume so many resources and supplies, I don't even know if he'd approve it.

And even then, if he did, we'd have to fly it by the research league when they wake up this coming February."

"Or," Connor cut in, "we propose to Patterson that we're allowed to at least build the basics of the machines. That way, when the senior officers wake up, they can use that as our educational training through the years that we're awake until our second cryogenic phase. Besides, they don't even know what they're up against. Last they were awake, they were just as lost as we were thirty minutes ago. And they're more likely to say yes to something we've already started, rather than just shooting in the dark with them. Simple politics say that we act like we have everything together on our own, even if we don't, and that we're letting them in on the operation. We don't know the science, but if we've already started the project—however bad we are at it—they'll have no choice but to join."

"That's true, that's true," Casey whispered.

Marina looked down to her journal and then up again. "We should request a minor curriculum change in Natalie's and Frances's studies. The neurology specialists aboard—I checked their records— two are in their sixties, the other in his early seventies. They're not going to be around forever. We should have them educate our trainee doctors while we have the chance."

"Damn, Marina," Quentin said to her, insulted.

"I'm just being honest. Natalie and Frances need to have some neurology expertise if we're going to engineer this. And let's face it, a project like this is going to take us a long time. For one, we don't even have a baby or a dog up here."

"I'm all for this," Connor said supportively. "Besides, they hauled us into this place. The least they can do is grant us permission to help them with a project they haven't even excelled in themselves. Maybe it's a far-fetched theory, but it's better than their complete lack of one. Besides, its pursuit could lead us down some tangential, unforeseen paths that end up solving the problem."

Casey scratched the tip of her nose. "I'm gonna need to amp up my bioinformatics learning if we're going to do this. But I'm in. We should get this over to Patterson tomorrow morning. In the meantime, Connor and Marina, plan to write our request overnight." She turned to Quentin and Athol. "And thank you both for coming. You've helped us immensely."

"No problem, Casey," Athol said.

Quentin just ducked his head. He didn't have anything more to say.

Dew from the steaming mug of roasted coffee was sticking to the shallow stubble under Patterson's lower lip as he scanned the sub-operation request, which the two advisors had dutifully dedicated their overnight hours to writing, as evidenced by their sagging eye bags and sallowed skin. Patterson absorbed the pages, sipping his coffee sporadically. He ignored the four people in front of him.

Quentin was swaying despite trying to stand firm. He'd also barely slept through the night, could barely keep his balance.

Patterson hummed when he finished reading the pages, and he slid them back into their rightful place in the orange portfolio provided with them. "My, my," he trilled. He took another sip of coffee. "It seems that there was, in fact, a great merit to all those months of idleness, wasn't there?"

"Sir?" Connor queried.

Patterson grinned. He fully, shamelessly grinned. "Between flight calculations and ship management, I scarcely have time to wonder about any of this—" He gestured to the closed portfolio— "although I am beyond pleased to see you all doing a much better job than I ever could have hoped. And if the other superior officers were awake to see this, they would be just as pleased. Relieved too, probably. You've spared their elder brains the mental exhaustion you clearly withstood to come up with this. You see the universe in a manner that is entirely new. You are untrained in it, thus you are more imaginative. A backhanded insult, it may seem, but trust me, by applying scientific reasoning to that which objective analysis has yet to be applied, you have very possibly breached an area of science that neither I nor my peers ever would have."

"So is that a go-ahead?" Casey asked with visible pleasure, but also suppressed impatience.

"It most certainly is, Miss Montgomery. I see no issue with at least formulating the rudiments of an experiment and testing the theory, if you so desire."

"We desire," Casey said immediately.

"Then by all means," Patterson said smilingly, "you have my permission."

18

The sub-operation, which was then entitled The BDP, short for The Brain Development Pursuit, was all that people spoke of after the news of its approval first broke. Some were impressed, some felt antithetically. Others were ecstatic. Natalie and Frances, for example, were reinvigorated in their approach to their medical studies and increasingly elusive ever since Patterson had agreed to a few tweaks in their curriculum. They were irretrievable, as they spent all hours in the library. As for the disgruntled, Ewan represented that category.

Under the harsh lighting of Derek's chemistry laboratory, to which Ewan had been summoned during the week after The BDP's conceptualizing discussion, he stood stiffly erect next to the low-shouldered and bored-looking Derek. "You really want me to work with….with *him*?" Ewan asked. His finger projected out to the young man beside him. "Have you no consideration for my feelings?"

Quentin hated being captain with a furious passion. "Look, Ewan, I know it's not ideal," he said, "but Connor and Marina agreed to—"

"—Quentin, I am not working with this crackhead."

"I have never, ever done crack," Derek said. "Heroin… weed…shrooms…speed…ahh…downers. Coke a bunch, but not crack though. That shit's whack."

Ewan, flustered, rotated his head to face his assigned partner. "Do you honestly think I give a crap about the technicalities of your personal pleasures? I am fucking paraphrasing."

"Ewan," Quentin said as he rubbed the back of his neck, "this isn't about you. This wasn't even my idea. I'm sorry, but the sub-op needs perfect designs. I know you can make one, and Connor is confident that Derek can too. This is a collaborative effort between our two divisions to keep things balanced. Will you help us?"

Ewan didn't answer. He muttered under his breath.

"I know I can," Derek said. He jammed his thumb against his left nostril to alleviate a tingle.

"You reckon so?" Quentin asked.

"Yeah, I can. A sturdy exterior that'll hold all the electronic elements and satisfy the other requirements?" Derek nodded. "It's a simple collagen, dude."

"Good to know." Quentin eyed Ewan. "And you?"

"Fine," Ewan surrendered. "I'll do it."

Unbeknownst to Quentin, the project's inception occurred sooner than he had anticipated. Athol and Casey hastened themselves to a collaboration regarding the potential interior engineering of the two synthetic models. Night after night, like the fledgling medical students in the library, Athol and Casey would hover in the dining hall with hoards of food, scribbling and sketching and conferring. Quentin was obligated to join various portions of their meetings—yet another cumbersome virtue of being captain. He would always half-listen to the things they said to each other, whereas Marina and Connor avidly took notes in order to document every concept and plan, lest someone grow forgetful after all their hours of work. Quentin would hear things like, "Can my programming coincide with yours?" coming from Athol, and then an overly enthusiastic Casey responding with, "I think you should start by making one unit, one synthetic brain, which would initially be preprogrammed by you before I do anything." Quentin would overhear many such snippets, but he was typically too wrapped up in his own thoughts to actively pay attention.

He was conflicted. On one hand, he was hopeful that there was some prospect of him being able to understand the mysteries that were his grandmother's multiple demises, but on the other, he wondered if his participation was a direct betrayal of all his beliefs. He still didn't want to be useful, to lend what slight wits and intelligence he had to Patterson's operation. That resistance grated on Marina, Quentin could see it, but he was so tired of being away from home and frustrated that he had fed the starving beast that was their mission by mindlessly helping to formulate a subsidiary one. *I am such an idiot,* he scolded himself.

"No, Connor, I was not saying that," Casey interrupted Quentin's thoughts. "I'm saying that his and my work can only be compounded once I can take in the layout of his design. If I'm going to be making a converter, I need to know what I'm working with and how to make my device compliant with his programming. Then I can test their interactivity. For now, I'll just be shadowing him."

"The functionality of Casey's device depends on the structure of mine as well as what it detects," Athol explained. "But in order for any of this to be possible, I need a descriptive outline of Frances's and Natalie's research so I can know what to look for, and possibly mimic. We need those brain examples. So, Quentin...Quentin?"

The begrudged captain lifted his head. "Hm?"

"Will you go to them?" Athol asked.

"To who?"

"To Natalie and Frances. Tell them I need an ETA on their research."

"Right. Got it. I will."

Unusually, because it had become something of their de facto home as of late, Quentin didn't find Frances and Natalie in the library loft, but in the computer room that afternoon. Natalie was seated before one of the desktops while Frances stood behind her, interchangeably looking to the screen in front of them and writing into the notebook in her arms.

"...and the brain of an average dog is three times smaller than that of the average human's," Natalie was saying. Her greasy, brown hair was knotted into a messy bun at the top her head, a few curls trickling down to her neck as she shifted a bit. "Did you get that?"

"Yup," Frances said.

Neither noticed Quentin proceeding toward them.

Natalie gave the screen a weird look. "So why do you think they're sub-perceptive, then?"

"Probably because they're instinctual, not intellectual," Frances guessed. She squeezed herself between Natalie's chair and the one beside her, so she could point to the screen. She circled something with the tip of her pen. "Our cerebral cortexes are enormous compared to theirs. Maybe that's why."

"Yeah, the pooches' cortexes are small."

"Very."

Quentin produced a deliberate squeak by skidding the edge of his sneaker against the linoleum floor. "Hey," he said.

Natalie glanced at him, but she quickly returned her gaze to the computer.

"What's up?" Frances asked.

"It's Athol. He's asking for a time estimate on the research."

Frances momentarily faced the computer. She studied the graphs and x-rays on the screen before facing him. "I think another two months or so. Is that okay?"

"Well, he didn't really say. He probably wants you to take as long as you think is necessary. We don't want to rush this."

"I know. I can get the canine data to you in three to four weeks, the human's in nine or ten."

"Okay." Quentin stood in front of her lamely. "All right, I'm gonna…"

"Go back to being useful?" Frances asked. He swore her eyes were smiling.

"What?"

"Just something Marina said." Frances laughed. "We were at lunch the other day and she said you were, and I quote 'of surprisingly decent utility.' Or something like that."

"Nice," Quentin responded.

"Hey, coming from her, that's like a gold medal. I do think it's great, though, that you're helping out. It's a good change. I hope this works." Quentin had never seen Frances so excited before. "I'm actually really looking forward to this. A scientific advancement like this poses great promise for the medical community. Maybe for once there won't be any more conflict between religion and medicine."

"Maybe."

"See you around?"

"I guess," Quentin said. He smiled for her, but dropped it as soon as he left the room.

The rest of July passed quickly. Perhaps it was the revived bustle of their small community or that the darkness that had plagued them for the first six months of 2047 had finally made its departure without leaving behind any crumbs of its existence, but the days felt shorter. Despite his hesitance to take a liking to the new project, Quentin couldn't entirely disregard the fact that providing some contributions of import gave him a refreshing sensation.

The ship's fragrances of faux rose, tulip, and cherry were minimized due to the overpowering predominance of molten glues and singed metals and plastics. Derek's chemistry lab was open for everyone all day, every day. Ewan may have been a griper, but in spite of their stark contrasts, they operated well in one another's company. That once spoken-of, but never-approached, room on the second floor became not only the centermost hub of The BDP, but, in some sense, the new social heart of the ship. Those who had become permanent fixtures in the sub-operation spent most of their days working in there. Those who were exceedingly curious would watch them perform their every activity. Those who were bored would simply pay a visit.

And so, Quentin was put to use, however minuscule it was compared to the deed of having helped conceptualize the operation in the first place. Because he detested meetings, he aided the unofficial engineers by fetching their supplies, acting on their orders to pin their sketches to the walls for future reference, and, when they trusted him to work diligently, he would follow their illustrations in a most detail-oriented manner to craft scale models for them. He became their personal lackey. It was busywork, but just as he had realized back in February, keeping his hands occupied was what he did best, and he didn't think that there was anything wrong with that.

"Oh, and get us Fatima tomorrow," Derek said, on the 6th of August.

Quentin was halfway through the first scale model. He wiped the cardboard particles from his hands. "Why?"

The scrawny blond pulled a sealed measuring tape container from an open drawer beside him. "Gonna need a real-life brain if you wanna see me do it right," he said. "And until one of our bitches gets knocked up, she's the closest thing we got to a baby brain."

"It's fine, Quentin," Ewan said. "We'll minimize the size once Frances and Natalie get back to us with the proper measurements."

Quentin nodded. "Okay."

"Oh, by the way," Derek said.

"Yeah?"

"Try not to do the next model as shittily as this one."

"Yes…Derek," Quentin responded. He suspended from his mind the very irony of taking orders from Derek Parker, of all people.

The 7th of August was the most boisterous day of the year. The laboratory felt significantly smaller, for it seemed as though everyone complicit in the operation had decided to spend their entire day in that very room. Derek and Ewan were sketching at one table while also occupying another as they attempted to formulate a collagen-rubber amalgamation that could maintain a perfect hold for electronic insides. Natalie and Frances, binders in hand and looking as though they hadn't slept in weeks, were communicating with Casey and Athol about the most relevant and imperative of their findings. Connor and Marina were outlining the month's schedule and intermittently editing the captains' shared, introductory presentation that they intended to give to the senior officials once they woke in February.

Come mid-afternoon, Fatima pranced inside. Her glassy eyes panned from one corner to the next. She waved to Frances, but she was too busy to return the gesture. Fatima subsequently saw Quentin performing his manual tasks, and her squishy cheeks flattened in a becoming, little grin. "Hi, Quentin," she greeted.

Quentin winked her way. "Hey, bud."

"Jaymes said you needed—*Ow!*" Fatima kicked her arms around, but Derek was heaving her into the air with his hands under her armpits. "Let me go!"

"Yeah, yeah," Derek said. He carried her to one of the empty tables and placed her on the edge of it; her legs dangled where the stool had been. "So remind me again why we can't just use her brain?" he questioned in a sober tone.

"Excuse me?" Quentin asked.

Derek pointed to one of the printed X-ray's, which Natalie had taped to a whiteboard. "I dunno, man, that baby head looks just like hers."

"You're a freak," Quentin said.

In one hand, Derek started unwinding his measuring tape. He none-too-gently flung Fatima's hair behind her shoulders and began looping the tape, starting from the crown of her head. He wrapped it all the way around to the back.

"You're mean to me," Fatima said matter-of-factly, her small nose scrunching up in her frown. "Mathias isn't mean to me."

"He sold his soul a while ago," Derek said.

"He doesn't sell things."

Derek rolled his eyes.

"If my daddy were here, he would say that you're a bully," Fatima said. "He wouldn't like you very much."

Despite not finishing the measurements, Derek put the tape down and looked the child dead in the eyes. "Oh yeah?" he asked. "Well, get this. Your daddy probably didn't like you very much either, otherwise you wouldn't be here with me now, would ya?"

Quentin put his pencil and mini saw down. "What the hell, Derek?"

"You're really mean," Fatima said. "That's shit."

"What—?"

"Fatima!" Frances lambasted at once.

"Sorry..." Fatima murmured. "I meant that it's stupid."

Days turned to weeks, and the weeks rolled into the end of August. By then, Quentin was fairly at peace. He scarcely saw his advisor, he often saw his manual labor, and he sometimes saw those whom he liked, such as Frances, Connor, and Athol. Quentin worked throughout all the hours of his days, both when he was and wasn't told to do so. The engineers, medical students, and advisors were doing identically well, if not better. As September approached, Quentin produced two of the four models, which won everyone's approval, so much that they felt inclined to relocate the project to a more practical location.

"Long-term," Casey said at dinner one night, "we need to utilize the synthetics to detect things outdoors. We need a place that lends itself to that."

"What's wrong with the cargo hold?" Connor asked.

"For one, we're not allowed in there," Marina mentioned.

"Oh. right."

"How about the observatory?" Ewan suggested. "The glass is sturdy and, let's face it, that's gotta be the easiest and safest way to situate everything as close to the outdoors as possible."

"I vote observatory," Athol said.

Everyone else agreed.

The relocation was a group effort. Groups of theretofore irrelevant division members swarmed the laboratory to haul tables, stools, computers, and Quentin's scale models. Everyone dragged furniture and all the articles of import during the late hours of a Saturday afternoon, scratching the transparent ground.

Without a doubt, the observatory was the room Quentin hated the most. It was a glass dome, and essentially nothing else. There were no curtains, no proper walling. There was nothing that could distract him from the utter horror of being in what was, essentially, unprotected space with all but a clear shield to protect him from the cold, dark realm outside.

Patterson walked in on the relocation effort with undisguised stupefaction. "What in heaven do you think you're doing to my observatory?" he enquired of Casey and Quentin, who were both simultaneously taken aback, and they looked down to the scratch marks and papers that were littered along the translucent ground.

A dumbfounded, "Uh," was all Casey said.

Athol put down the stool he was carrying. "It was easy to develop the synthetic in the lab during the embryonic phase," he said, "but now we need to really put it where it belongs, that way, when it's complete, it can actually sense things outside. We'll set up camp on only one side of the room. That'll leave you some space."

"A fair compromise," Patterson accepted. "No harm, no foul."

Quentin loitered near Patterson. "It doesn't freak you out, being in here?"

Patterson smiled coyly. "Though wildly unfathomable to some, I myself find unusual peace in coming face to face with what bothers me most."

"Oh. You get bothered by outer space too?"

"Quite."

"Which is why you hang out in here?"

"Precisely."

"Oh," Quentin repeated. Not knowing what to do with that information, he shuffled away to help Ivy and Mathias with one of the lab tables.

Chris and Amber were loading the main portion of a portable welding station. They were encroaching on a vacant corner when

Chris asked, "So I guess we men shouldn't feel so guilty about pushing for abortions now, huh?"

Amber expelled her shining, red hair from her face as she fought to keep up with him. The metal edge verged on slipping from her grasp. "How...so?" she panted, both in annoyance and pain.

Chris pivoted them around, so that he could walk backwards to the destination. "Cuz the life doesn't need a body, obviously," he said. "So the procedure's harmless. Yeah, you're killing a baby. But it's just the baby body. Nothing to feel guilty about."

With an enraged uptick in her energy, Amber rammed the station piece into Chris's chest. He stumbled backwards, fell, and quickly rolled to the side; the station very nearly squished him. "Hey!" he shouted. "What gives?!"

"Position it yourself, asshole," Amber snapped, and she stormed away.

"I must say, I am certainly impressed," Patterson said on the 21st of August, when the observatory was entirely overhauled to become the new laboratory. Gathered around him were the captains, their advisors, and the medical students as well as Athol, Ewan, and Derek. "I'm glad to see your faces looking weary and drawn. It means you've been working hard."

"Weird compliment, I will say," Ewan replied. "But thank you, Patterson. We couldn't have done this without you kidnapping us."

"Now that is a truth, Mr. McHugh. But for now, I order that you pace yourselves and rest. That is my first ever direct order as your superior officer. I want you all taking at least a week off. Am I understood?"

"Yep," Frances said cheerily.

"Can do," Athol said.

"Very well." Patterson sighed contentedly. "You make my job so easy. Sleep well tonight, my pioneers. You deserve it."

19

For Lucas's thirteenth birthday, which took place on the 25th of August, Naomi sent him dental wax. She told him it worked miracles, miracles that few orthodontists in Dar es Salaam were in possession of because the inaccessibility of the product made it such a rarity. He wondered how she knew to purchase it for him, but when he put his mind to it and tried to recount the details of the weeks prior to his birthday, he recalled having mentioned the bothersome state of his inner mouth to her. Once or twice, Lucas had offhandedly complained that the metallic hooks and brackets of his braces would shred the skin of his inner lips and cheeks without even having to talk or chew for it to happen. Sometimes the stinging was so intolerable that he could hardly concentrate on his studies—or so he told his mother, but she knew better than to play into the feeble fib. Still, while one would have been right to think that the pain wasn't so egregiously enormous that it would induce nights of undone homework, that didn't mean it was negligible. Which was why, on the 27th of August, when he peeled apart the red ribbon wrapped around the blue, tin box from Naomi, he was all the more touched to realize that she had actually listened and acted upon the things he said as opposed to purchasing him a gift of slight substance. There was a note inside the tin, layered above the clear, cold wrapping that protected the wax from melting.

L,

I hope you're doing well. R and I are in D.C. this week and guess who had a dentist appointment on their second day back. Three cavities and a root canal later, I'm starting to sympathize with you. May this miracle-working wax ease at least one of our mouths.

N (...and R but he thought this gift was lame)

Lucas folded the note with a cautious gentleness and slipped it into the breast pocket of his tee-shirt. When he looked up to the person sitting across from him at their table of the cafe, where they were waiting for their food, he said, "Wax. For my teeth. They hurt a lot."

Abul nodded, his cheeks dimpling. "Very thoughtful," he replied. "Will you use them to eat?"

"Uh-uh."

Where they waited to dine was a humble establishment by the name of Kawaha na Ng'ombe, or "Coffee and Cow," as Abul had translated. It was located in Arusha's eastern block and was a token of the city's older, less refurbished days. Its owners made a concerted effort to dodge the growing pressure of modernization. Said owners were a pair whom Lucas was most privileged to know, those being Abul and his wife, Bahati. Beside the dirt road of the city block, Lucas sat at one of the tables on the outdoor terrace, his body strategically hidden behind a faux pink-ivory support beam to avoid the sunlight that threatened to burn the left side of his face. The decorative, similarly inauthentic leaves above him provided some protection as well. While the outdoor extension of the couple's cafe withstood the onslaught of midday rays, the indoor section was more uncomfortable, as the single air conditioner weakly thrummed behind the cashier's booth and emanated only the faintest hints of cool air. And yet, Lucas loved the place, partly because the aromas of cumin, bananas, and teas that made his growing belly grumble, but also because Abul and his lovely wife owned it.

Abul gazed through the curtain of tangled vines that dangled in front of a window diagonal from them. He was looking at a gathering of fifteen camouflage-clad young men and women, some in People's Defense Force uniforms, others in the attire of the United States Marine Corps, all cackling and crooning as they raucously devoured their plates of various rices with beef and chicken. They drank from clay mugs with iced teas and chilled coffees. "I don't know where we would be without them," Abul said. "After the ban on tourism was announced, we were so worried. We didn't know what we would do. I love my tribe and my people, but my parents left that area for me to find something different. I thank God that these soldiers eat like lions, that they train near us. They keep our business alive. I'm very grateful for them. For many other, more important reasons, yes. But also for this."

Lucas nodded. "I get it," he said. "You should be able to keep living normally even after everything that's happened."

Abul turned back to him. "The food will be done soon, I think. I will go to see."

Lucas purposely waited for Abul to be far out of sight and in the back of the kitchen before reaching into the tin to separate the wax with sweaty fingers. Even though he couldn't have the wax inserted while eating, he was much too curious to wait. He had seen Quentin fix it to his own teeth, back when he had braces when he was twelve. He used to part the hardened substance into tiny bits, let it soften on the pads of his fingers, and then awkwardly pull his cheeks back to stick the wax tight against his lower teeth. His fingers were always drenched in his own saliva by the end of the unflattering undertaking. While no one was watching, Lucas enacted the weirdness of placing a wax piece into his own mouth. At least, he thought no one was watching. Unfortunately, mid-plastering of the wax stick to his top-right teeth, with his cheek yanked back by his pinky and his left hand entirely jammed in his mouth, he made eye contact with a hard-jawed, blond, American solider who was drinking out of his mug and squinting confusedly in Lucas's direction. Flushed in the face, Lucas looked away, returned the wax to the tin, and wiped his hands.

Abul returned. He held three yellow plates with plain meats and spiced rice in each hand. Behind him, the much smaller Bahati waddled along and was responding to something he had said over his shoulder to her. Two bowls with soups, one green and the other reddish, filled the palms of her hands. Atop each of the bowls was an empty plate, and she was patently apprehensive about them tilting and falling every time she took a step. Lucas stood and helped to ease her hands of the cumbersome weight. As she gave him one of the bowl-and-plate sets, strands of her graying, black hair escaped the left side of her loose headscarf, so much that Lucas could see a dolloped, pea-sized birthmark on the column of her throat.

"Thank you, Bahati," Lucas said.

Her wrinkled, thin hand, the unoccupied one, squeezed his shoulder. "Happy birthday, Michael. May it taste good again." After she placed the rest of the food onto the wooden table, she went waddling off and disappeared inside the cafe.

Once again seated across from Lucas, Abul pointed to the plates between them. "That's *mishkaki* and *wa nazi,* do you remember?"

"Yup. Naomi actually made some before she and Richard left."

Abul rolled his sleeves up to his elbows. With a giant ladle that was laying on one of the napkins, he began scooping the coconut-dunked rice and some pieces of brown meat onto his empty plate. Lucas followed suit.

"And where is Naomi now?" Abul asked.

"Washington, D.C. I think. That's what she told me, anyway. You can never really know, right?"

"Very true," Abul said. He dipped his right hand down to his plate and gathered the meat and rice between his fingers.

Lucas was about to grab the only fork on the table, the one provided for the westerner, but he stopped himself. Smirking, he imitated his host and began eating with his hand too. Abul didn't conceal his surprise. "It's weird," Lucas said, laughing with his hand in his mouth. "*Gah.* That's really weird." *But,* he thought, *no weirder than sticking the wax into my mouth...and tastier.*

"That's why I gave you a fork," Abul said.

"But I wanted to try it."

"You are very adventurous, Michael. You remind me of my sons. They always like to try new things, too. Did I tell you Jamil has been promoted to Sergeant Major?"

"Reawy?" Lucas asked through a mouthful of his food.

"Last month, yes. I didn't mention it, did I?"

"No." Lucas gulped his chewed food and grinned. "But now we have two things to celebrate."

They were eating and talking, but Abul really spoke the most. Because Lucas was predominantly surrounded by those who were decades older than himself, he comfortably accepted his new position as an audience member rather than a speaker. He wasn't among schoolchildren any longer, but was entirely in the company of adults, and he felt intellectually diminutive. So, like all his other days with his mother, Topher, Naomi and Richard, plus all their volcanology colleagues, Lucas quietly sat back and absorbed, rather than provided, opinions on what Abul had to say. By listening rather than speaking, Lucas learned throughout his belated birthday lunch that the current international conflict was extremely personal to Abul, who, along with his family, had actually endured several attempted invasions by two completely separate forces.

"I'm sorry," Lucas said sympathetically.

"They would come with tanks and missiles and these odd, toxic chemicals, just trying to open the mountain," Abul grimly recounted. "But she is strong. She doesn't yield so easily. And my boys…they were very young. They remember all of it, though, before the multinational intervention. You know, I didn't want them to join the military for good. I wanted them to do something like this." He gestured to the terrace around them, and to where they were sitting. "I wanted them to build something for themselves because they have that opportunity. But I never really considered…never really thought of what it was like to live through that while so young. That's all they've ever known. I realized they were not being…hm…*idealistic*. Do you know what it means to be idealistic, Michael?"

Lucas shook his head.

"It is like being a dreamer, being a bit unrealistic."

Idealistic, Lucas cataloged for later use. He thought it would be a good word to use when he grew up.

"So there was nothing I could do," Abul said. "I was an adult when we lived through those events—to me, those years were shorter compared to the ones I had already lived. But for my sons, that was their childhood. And who am I to tell them that they should think of something better when that was their reality? And that is when I realized that I was the one who was being idealistic."

Lucas started wiping remnants of the food from his hands with a napkin and some water from his cup. "Can I ask…Why are you still a porter if you have this restaurant?"

Abul smiled pitifully. "I only go a few times a year, that way I don't deprive the tribespeople who actually need the work. But for me, it's a good way to check on my sons. It's the only way I can be with them these days, even if it's only through hearing about them rather than seeing them."

Lucas realized how fortunate he was to have lived a large portion of his upbringing in Shaw, Massachusetts, which was a relatively untouched slice of land. He only recently become aware of how shattered much of the world was whilst he and his brother resided in a comfortable home and a safe nation that hadn't been compromised. He was still very young—inevitably, some elements of the geopolitical warfare were too bloated with complexities for him to fully understand—but he wasn't blind to his privilege. He recognized that when Abul's sons were ten and thirteen, spending sleepless nights under rains of bombings and detonations, Lucas and Quentin were themselves five and twelve, being educated in well-funded public schools during the early and late months of the year and then happily venturing across New England in their summers. It made him a little nauseous to think of the juxtaposition, of how wrong the world was.

When he and Abul began their dessert of fruit puddings topped with sugared nuts, Lucas's mother poked into the cafe. She shook Abul's hand and tried to give him the estimated amount of cash dollars that would compensate for the two meals, but he closed his large palms over hers and vehemently shook his head. "No, Mrs. Hanson," he said, "Michael is a friend."

"If you insist," she resigned. She walked around the table and pulled her sitting son into her arms for a tight hug. With his head stuffed into her underarm, he felt sick from the waft of potent perfume that was stuck to her clothes. "I'll be back soon," she said. "Topher will pick you up after he drops me off at the airport, okay?"

Lucas nodded.

His mother released him. "Thank you, Abul," she said to the cafe owner one last time, "you've been very kind."

"Mrs. Hanson, your Michael is deserving of all the kindness."

Topher wasn't the worst nanny. He was boring and responsible, but he was always very considerate. Despite managing the security of a most imperative piece of land, Topher was quiet and kept his head bowed. He was a sad man, and Lucas had no idea why that was. Yet, Topher's sadness never dampened his days enough to halt his determination, and onwards life went—and he with it. In spending so much time with him, Lucas began to understand Naomi more than he ever thought he did. Stories were one thing, but bearing witness to exactly how one was raised was another. She had told him that she was raised by two widowers, one of whom Lucas had come to know while the other he heard of through retellings of a life she had once spent with him, that person having been her father. Lucas then saw the irony of how he and Quentin were being simultaneously bred by either of the two men who themselves had bred Naomi.

Topher was meticulous and preferred neatness to clutter, but he didn't nag about things that clearly displeased him, such as the cups and silverware Lucas left on the tabletops after his meals or the music that was volumes too loud and resultantly distracted Topher as he attempted to concentrate on his work; in the end, he always resorted to bearing the brunt of working while Quentin's old CD of his favorite songs would blare from the littler brother's bedroom. Topher and Lucas would joke and play boardgames, and sometimes Topher helped

Lucas with his schoolwork, when he was periodically stumped by a question.

After Lucas's mother left, he and Topher shared the meatloaf and potatoes she had made for them earlier in the day. As they ate, Topher helped Lucas with his algebra and social studies, and after they were well fed, they put the schoolwork aside to clean the dishes together. Lucas couldn't remember a time when he so much as filled a used cup with water before he arrived to Tanzania, but something about watching Topher clean their mess all alone didn't sit well with him, so Lucas adopted the habit of cleaning up after dinner, just like all the adults did.

With each of them holding abrasive, steal wool pads that stung his fingers, they took turns scrubbing the glass pan in which the meatloaf had been baked. Mid-scraping, Lucas asked, "Where do you think Hollis is?"

"Hollis Carlyle?" Topher asked. He rolled his sleeve farther up his wrist before reaching the underside of the pan. "There are many possibilities. That's the unfortunate thing about his case."

"I feel bad for him."

"You do?"

"He's all alone. He can't be alone."

"You knew him well, Lucas?"

"Yeah." Lucas scrubbed harder at a stubborn stain. "He was best friends with Quentin. When Mom and Dad would let us bring our friends on family trips, Quentin always brought him. I always brought my friend Ron."

"Do you miss Ron?" Topher asked.

"Sometimes," Lucas answered, as honestly as possible. "But I don't think Ron would understand me anymore. Plus he's not allowed to. Right?"

Topher softened his expression. "I'm sorry," he said.

"It's okay. It's just true."

Topher paused the conversation to turn away and wet his pad under the faucet. When he circled back, looking a little transfigured in the face, in a way Lucas couldn't place, Topher took a breath and said, "I think…Well, I try not to think the worst. The best thing we can do is hope that Hollis is safe."

The meatloaf pan was stainless. They transferred it to the drying rack.

"I wish Hollis were with Quentin," Lucas said as he began to clean one of their dinner plates.

"Why is that?"

"Because Quentin can't be alone either. They pretended like they didn't need each other, but they were both bad at it. Even though they fought a lot, they were best friends."

"Where Quentin is, he's safe. He's in good hands, and with good people. But where Hollis is, we don't know. I wouldn't worry too much about your brother."

"Okay," Lucas said resignedly. "Do you think Mom will find him, though?"

"Find Hollis?" Topher ducked his head to inspect a stain on the pan he was cleaning. "Your mother can find anything she puts her mind to. I'll bet you a hundred dollars she finds him by this time next year."

"If you say so."

When they finished cleaning, Lucas brushed his teeth and Topher caught up on his unread emails, and when they both had finished, they played chess while sipping ginger tea. Afterwards, they made their beds, said their goodnights, and went to sleep. Over the next couple of days, they would do the very same things in the very same order, until Syndonah Hanson's planned date of return.

Lucas's mother was supposed to return to Tanzania on August 30th. Supposed to. She didn't. Two more days passed after the 30th, which swept them into the month of September, yet she still hadn't returned like she said she would. He knew not to worry, though. It wasn't the first time she was either sidetracked by an overlapping case or had to entirely reroute her trajectory and travel to some other place he similarly wasn't allowed to know anything about.

Naomi and Richard, on the other hand, returned to the country at the exact time they had intended to. On the 2nd of September, they came by the house and gave long hellos. Richard ruffled Lucas's hair, and Naomi took him into her arms to hug him. She gave the warmest embraces. The couple, Lucas, and Topher all reunited with a quick lunch in the kitchen, eating sandwiches and drinking juices while they caught up on each other's news. Lucas was happy to have an excuse to be away from his schoolwork, even if it was only for an hour. He asked about the United States and if they enjoyed their stay, but Richard declared that it was as bland as ever.

Something managed to disturb Lucas that day, and it had no relation to the continued, unaddressed absence of his mother, but pertained to Naomi and Richard's relationship. Lucas didn't notice it earlier, when she was squeezing him to breathlessness with her hugging arms, but later, as he watched the two interact, he saw that something was wrong. Not with Richard, it seemed, but with Naomi. Her smiles fell flatter than they used to. Her laughs were quieter, slower. A heavy darkness appeared under her eyes, like the shadows Quentin used to have when he would wake for school every morning. And Richard, for his part, was more expressive. They were usually so reserved a couple, even in the privacy of the Hansons' home, but not on that day. If he were passing his wife while she sat at the table, he would give her shoulder a squeeze. If he had to reach for something behind her, he would reach a hand forward and rub her hip lightly, but far from secretly. His eyes hovered on her longer than usual, and in a manner that verged on concern, sensitive, as though she were something delicate that required his monitoring, which she wasn't. She was strong, willful, and very independent. Lucas didn't know what it was exactly, but through the unreciprocated affections and the decreased expressiveness from Naomi, he suspected that something bad had happened. He assured himself that if time passed and the secret still hadn't been reveled, then it probably wasn't anything to worry about. He tried to remind himself that he was only a child, that he knew nothing about marriage.

Time did pass, and quite a bit of it. Yet no signs of Lucas's mother were unearthed. Two weeks after the day on which she intended to return, Topher made phone calls to people he knew and trusted, people he swore would look high and low for her. He told Lucas not to worry and that she was probably held up with certain people; once again, people who were never described nor specified.

He didn't really know what to make of the news, or lack thereof, so he dedicated himself to his schoolwork, since it was so confounding that it was guaranteed to distract him for hours at a time. By then, Naomi and the geology team weren't scheduled to return to Kilimanjaro for at least another eight days, so when he wasn't investing his time in schoolwork, he spent his spurts of freedom with her. She became his interim chess opponent and, when he wasn't looking, would clandestinely slip notes with answers to his math equations into his binder. He enjoyed his time with her, but it wasn't enough of a distraction to pull him away from the very obvious tension that took place on Topher's end.

And then, of course, there was the mysterious thing that was evidently bothering Naomi. Lucas continually noted the undisguised slope to her smiles and the ceaselessness of Richard's affections, how he pecked her cheek whenever he came into the same room and rubbed her hip when he passed through a slim space behind her. It wasn't a horrible change, but Lucas recognized that it was radically unlike them. But, still, he watched silently and asked nothing about it. Only time could tell with something like that.

The night preceding the volcanology team's dispatch, Topher decided to leave. To where, exactly, Lucas had no idea. He never had one, not since Quentin had been kidnapped. But Topher insisted that he must, that he was the only one who could successfully situate the missing Sydney Hanson. Tensions rose in Lucas's house. Naomi and Richard argued that Lucas couldn't be left home alone in a country he hardly knew, with both of his parents far out of reach, one of whom was declared missing in action the day before; Lucas didn't know if it was a grave status, but it didn't sound pleasant.

"Take him with you," Naomi urged. "Wherever you go, take him. You're just searching anyway."

"He's safer here," Topher argued. "That's why he was moved here. No one would dare come here. It's leaving that's dangerous, Nani."

"But he can't be here alone," Richard said.

As Topher and the couple spoke among themselves in the living room, Lucas just sat on the couch and listened to them argue over him. The room was in a complete state of disarray. Topher had turned the space into his office during the time Lucas's mother hadn't returned. There were papers everywhere and a laptop open on each table. Lucas knew that for Topher to be messy, it meant that something must have gone drastically awry.

"We can stay here and miss a week," Richard floated the idea to Naomi.

"But Jane…"

"Honey, she'll understand. This is Sydney's son after all."

"No, I have a plan," Topher said. "I'll contact the colonel. We're old friends, remember? He can send a couple men to watch Lucas for the next week."

Lucas sank into the cushions of his couch. He reached for his mother's purple afghan and curled it around himself. It was going to be a long night.

"You sure?" Richard asked. "Really, we can talk to Jane."

"You two have work to get done," Topher objected. "It will be fine. In the meantime, I've contacted David. We'll figure out when it's best for him to come."

Lucas's stomach dropped. He couldn't explain it, couldn't understand it, but the prospect of seeing his father for the third time since November of 2045 wasn't one he looked forward to. He didn't know if he imagined it, but he thought Naomi didn't look happy about it either.

A Private John Reynolds and Corporal Danny Matthews were sent to the house the following morning, at dawn on the 15th of September. They weren't dressed the way Lucas thought they would be; in military attire. The pale-faced, younger one, whom he learned was John, wore faded jeans and a crisp, blue tee-shirt that had one wrinkle on the left shoulder. The tan-skinned other, Danny, wore creamy cargo shorts and an oversized *Yankees* sweater.

They were waiting for him at the kitchen table with Topher. "Michael," Topher began apprehensively, like he himself didn't know how his plan would unfold, "these fine, young men will be watching over you for a while. I should be back in six to seven days. All right?"

But Lucas didn't nod. He wasn't going to accept that Topher had intentions of returning. Lucas wanted Topher to prove that he would come back, unlike his mother.

To his surprise, coexisting with the military men was an untroubled phase of his life. They respected his privacy—and he, theirs. Save for their hour-long morning runs, the private and the corporal spent nearly all their time in the living room. At night, each man was fixed to a couch, and there they slept the darker hours away. During the day, when Lucas's online school was in session, they would watch television on the flatscreen that was bolted to the wall, beside his mother's bookshelf. He seldom conversed with them for the first few days, for the purpose of squashing any opportunity of awkwardness in the household. But after the first three passed, his own boredom began to not only irritate him, but keep him awake and hyper at night. So, he succumbed to the daunting temptation of starting a conversation with the two, temporary guests.

On the evening of the 19th of September, when his day's schoolwork was finally completed and he had the later hours to himself, Lucas hesitantly crept his way into the living room. The men were sprawled on their separate couches and yawning as they watched *Top Gun*. Quentin used to love that movie, and Lucas wondered if he still did.

"Hey," Lucas said quietly, meekly.

Danny Matthews turned his head over the armrest to see the boy behind him. "Hey," he said, sitting up. "Wanna watch with us?"

"No," Lucas said quickly.

John Reynolds swung his legs off the couch and reached for the remote on the coffee table. "You want to pick the movie?"

Lucas eyed the chessboard.

"Oh, I'm down," Danny said when he caught on to Lucas's request.

John reclined on the couch. "I'll watch and learn."

But the chessboard ended up untouched. *Twister*, they decided, was a far more interactive game.

When Topher returned to the house after seven days, on the 22nd of September, just like he intended, his face was morose and his skin was drawn and pasty. "Nothing," he said to Lucas. "Absolutely nothing. I couldn't find anything. I'm so sorry. I'll keep looking. She's out there. She's out there somewhere. I know she is."

September turned to October, and October slowly bled into November. Such a magnitude of time had passed that, come the anniversary of Quentin's kidnapping, Topher still didn't know where Lucas's mother was. By then, the man had left the country multiple times, most trips persisting for a week. Sometimes he was gone for shorter durations, depending on the distance between Tanzania and his target location, which, even then, Lucas never knew anything about except that Topher was there and Lucas wasn't.

It wasn't until early November that Naomi and Richard stayed and watched over Lucas themselves, since Naomi was so paranoid that Jane, the director of their unit, wouldn't take kindly to the concept of two, absentee employees. It turned out that Naomi never even mentioned the missing state of Lucas's mother to Jane, but once the volcanology unit's director found out that Sydney Hanson's son was in the hands of two, low-ranking military men in their early twenties, she relegated the couple to more ground-level-appropriate work; work they could surely perform from Lucas's home. On paper, Naomi and Richard lived in a quaint, contemporary house in the heart of Arusha. Unofficially, when Topher was away, they lived in the Hansons' small, single-level, white ranch south of the tiny city. They stayed there with Lucas all throughout the weeks whenever Topher vanished without a trace, off to new lands to once again find that one, missing woman.

Again, the couple became Lucas's only constant. He preferred them to his own parents, in fact. Naomi and Richard were functional and communicative. Healthy. He couldn't speak for why they took pleasure in watching over him as if he were their own child, but he had his suspicions. He imagined that Naomi liked being in his life because she saw shreds of her younger self in him. He wondered just how alone and empty she had been at his age, when she was motherless and probably sensed, in the back of her mind, that the last of her two parents was bound to leave her at some point in the future. He saw, then, that it was possible for the children of abandoning parents to be more alike. He recognized that he and Naomi were similar in many respects. Her childhood couldn't have been very different from his own, he figured. She had made it clear that she wasn't a stranger to the discomfort of severe alienation throughout her youth. As for Richard, Lucas didn't know what had drawn him to stay at the house except that he was married to Naomi. Only, they weren't just married. Not like Lucas's parents were. Richard could read his wife. He knew her every thought. It was an obvious fact that he knew everything about her, which, perhaps by extension, meant he knew a thing or two about Lucas, and maybe that was why Richard lingered even when he didn't need to.

The three of them living together worked, and wonderfully. They ate breakfast together. Lucas did his schoolwork in his bedroom, and the couple occupied the sunroom during their working hours. The house brimmed with energy. When lunch hour would come around, they paused their duties, ate together, and then resumed their earlier activities, going their separate ways. And then, when the sun would begin to set and the neighboring mountain would slip behind a shroud of clouds, Lucas would help Naomi cook dinner while Richard cleaned up the day's mess. They all stayed up late, usually until the eleventh hour, clinking teacups and battling each other in board games or watching television shows. Naomi and Richard spent so much of their lives at the house that, every two weeks, when the volcanologists made their return, the business lunches of the scientists were often held at the Hanson home. Jane, Maryam, and Jack would come barging in with their equipment and folders of never-ending papers, bidding Lucas brief greetings before he continued on with his schoolwork. The routine became everyone's new normal.

In November, during the familial visitation period for the volcanology unit, it was at the Hansons' that the non-professional brunch was held. On that summer-like Saturday, Naomi and Richard barbecued in the backyard, sautéing steaks and vegetables on the grill beside the perimeter of baobab trees. Lucas played in the yard with Jack's two sons, one five and the other eight, while Maryam's college-aged daughter, Sofia, blushed furiously as Jane introduced her to the towering, burly sons of "our favorite guide, Abul." Jack's wife, Michelle, was on the deck with Bahati, and the two talked among themselves as they sipped pomegranate juice. Lucas invited John and Danny that day, too, and they clinked their beer bottles as they placed their bets on which of Jack's children would win the wrestling match against Lucas.

Existing in the orbit of Naomi and Richard was a life Lucas could get used to. They were distractions, but they were also so much more than that. They were his family. He knew that because, in even the quiet times, when there were no social brunches or barbecues and boardgames being played, he still loved being in their company.

He was doodling over the assignment instructions for his essay on women's rights in the Gilded Age—*Whatever that meant*, he thought —when he caught Naomi staring at him. He looked up at her quizzically. "You do that a lot," he said," stare at me."

"There are a lot of people who care about you, Lucas," Naomi said. "I hope you never know what it's like to be alone."

Lucas stopped doodling. "You don't feel alone now, do you?"

"It's been a long time since I last did. But it's hard to forget what it felt like." Naomi cleared her throat and stood up. "I'm going to the store. You want anything?"

Lucas put his pencil down. "Can I come with you? I saw you try to carry that rice bag into the house last week."

"Now there you have me."

It never slipped Lucas's mind that every time Topher came back, he looked even more tired than when he left. He looked harried. Older, even. He always greeted Lucas with downcast head-shakes. "Not yet," he would say, hedging his bets. "Not yet."

Yet, Lucas thought. He doubted the word. Would she really come back? Or had she, like his father and Quentin and all of Lucas's friends, just become a thing of the past? Sometimes the thought made his throat swell and he couldn't take in air; once, he asked Richard to take him to the hospital because of it. Other times, he felt nothing.

Once, when Lucas was shopping with Naomi in early December, she warmed his heart.

"Should we just get the pre-made frosting?" Lucas asked her.

"No, we'll keep looking for all the ingredients, even if it means going to two more stores."

"But why?" Lucas asked. "It's quicker. And you're always tired after work. Maybe we should take a night off cooking."

Naomi shrugged. "Yeah, but I like cooking with you." She bumped his shoulder. "Come on, plantains and confectioner's sugar are this way."

On December 13th, Topher came back one last time. There was no leaving anymore. Lucas knew that just by looking at the man, at the lines around his small mouth and the dryness that plagued his bald head, how skin began to flake off the edges of his ears. There was a look of finality on his face, something like a surrender.

K.I.A. That was the verdict. Lucas knew what it meant. He had heard it in a movie once, in one of the blockbusters Quentin and Hollis used to rent on the weekends, when they let Lucas join them in watching whatever violent, vulgar thriller they had chosen to entertain themselves.

So, that was it. Everyone related to Lucas by blood was either absent by indifference, involuntary leave, or death. That left him with what, then? His father? Would he even return after the news or would his disinterest surpass all emotional permutations imaginable? And would Quentin even be able to know about the news or would he live on blissfully ignorant while Lucas, by contrast, was subjected to bearing all the troubles alone again?

Lucas had nothing to say, so he stayed quiet. It took him by surprise when it was Topher who was the first to shed a tear.

In December, not only was the question of his mother's absence answered, but so was the question about the unusually open intimacy of Naomi and Richard's marriage.

It was during the week after Topher's final return. Lucas and Richard were quiet, sitting on a couple of lawn chairs they had scraped up the deck stairs after the clouds of an ending storm had cleared and the humid rains faded away. They were just sitting there, saying nothing. Naomi was fast asleep indoors, in the guest room that had become the couple's.

"She always wanted kids," Richard said into the sticky air; it frizzed his hair and made him sweat, even though all they were doing was sitting.

"Why'd you never have any?" Lucas asked.

"She can't. We only found out in August. That's why we were in the US, we were seeing her doctor there. She always wanted some of her own. Topher wanted that for her, too. She didn't have a normal childhood, not one with two parents and a household of siblings and siblings' friends. Topher always said that when we wanted to start a family, we should get out of the business, maybe move into education. She liked that idea. I did too. I know it kills her to see that she can't have that. Can't really anyway."

"Can't really?" Lucas repeated.

"Then you came along," Richard said. He smiled slightly.

Suddenly, it all made sense to Lucas. All the comforting, unreciprocated kisses and hugs. The morose, downward pull of her face. But, at the same time, her happiness in staying at the house and working with Lucas under her care. It made sense why she was more than happy to make his bed and cook with him, to settle into the domesticity of being his temporary guardian.

Lucas couldn't stop the next words from escaping his mouth: "I wish I could always stay here with you guys."

He heard, deep in the darkness of the night, the words he desperately wanted to hear, "Me too."

The tears burst of out of Lucas's tired eyes. He hadn't cried in ages, not since he was carried away from Quentin. Lucas felt arms wrap around his shoulders from behind him. He curled forward, sobbing. He sobbed about the death of his old life. The change of his name. The loss of his brother. The loss of his mother. The scarcity of his parents' involvement in his changed path. The loneliness had been tearing him apart, as had the lack of blood relatives and friends his age. All he wanted were friends and a family. Could he not be given that?

Richard tightened his arms around Lucas.

Maybe that would be enough.

———

Children were not the solution to marital strife. David had known that, but Sydney hadn't. He would never forget the summer of 2033, when his wife told him with rosy cheeks and showing teeth that a second child was growing in her womb. She told him of how long it had lived within her, of how she felt; how she was sure that it would resurrect whatever vanquished happiness they had lost from their lives. David wondered if she really thought him that obtuse or if she was faltering from a disruption in her own sanity. Did she honestly believe, in the depths of her uncontestedly keen mind, that he didn't know what she had done? The addition of a second child would never distract him from the inevitability of Quentin being taken away from him, no matter how adamantly she fought to make it seem that way. It wasn't lost on David that she had signed away their son's life. Nor was it lost on him that on Quentin's fifth birthday, he was effectively disowned by his parents and put into the hands of that pompous professor, Doctor Colin H. Patterson.

There were other options. They were less elegant than David would have preferred, but they were feasible. Defection was the most obvious, most achievable one. But Sydney never agreed. It was her country over her children and never the other way around. And it was all his fault, David's. He was aware of it. He didn't have to fall for the enigma that was the brunette beauty, the woman who was like no other when they met and continuously proved to be that way all throughout their legal union. She was loyal, which he had once thought endearing, but by the time he realized that her loyalty was one of her biggest faults, it had been too late to do anything about it. Their son wasn't theirs anymore, but the property of some governmental branch David hadn't even known existed until she received the ominous phone call one afternoon, after Quentin's sixth doctor's appointment in a single week, back when he was four.

Lately, David wondered how different his life would have been if Sydney never broke off her engagement with that stiff, unsmiling, unlovable Second Lieutenant Brandt and if David himself had chosen a nice woman, one who wouldn't have driven his own mother mad with the suspicion of her son being in a relationship riddled with one-sided affections. But it was only when David's rental car was bumping along the dirt roads south of Arusha that he realized it was the very things he and Sydney loved most about each other that had eventually led to their marriage's downfall. He loved her for her overachievements, for the fact that she was a walking medallion of perfection and intelligence. She loved him for his outward displays of emotion and his prioritization of family values. But admiration wasn't love, and neither of them had understood that. The point hadn't hit home until one of them was dead and both their children were out of their reach.

———

The visit from his father shouldn't have shocked Lucas, but it did. He didn't know why his father flew such a long way to see him, if that was even why he arrived. It had been three years since Quentin was taken. Three years since Lucas was eleven years of age. Three years since they were a family, with a mother and a father and two beautiful, healthy, happy sons. It had been three years, and his father hardly batted an eye in his direction. Lucas had never seen a countenance as drooped, yet austere, as his father's was on that day, in late December. Not once did the man meet his son's eyes as he entered the house, looking embittered, as if he had been coerced into journeying to see his own child. That may have been the case. Lucas would have believed it.

He had never seen Naomi angry—no, incandescent. But she was. She was white and fuming. "What are you doing here?" she questioned his father.

"I'm here to get my son," David answered defiantly, which Lucas heard as he hovered in the hallway entrance to the kitchen, where the adults were.

"Your son?" Naomi asked. "Where were you, then? Were you there when he didn't say a word for more than a year? Were you there for that?" She pointed with a finger to the printed picture on the fridge, on which Lucas, Abul, and Jack were shown racing to the end of the Kilimanjaro trail, a snapshot from February. Lucas's father didn't even look to where she was pointing, so Naomi dropped her hand.

Richard didn't say anything. His eyes were closed as he forced himself to level his breathing, to keep it even. His hands were balled up on the kitchen island, clenching and unclenching. For the first time ever, Lucas saw a gray hair on the man's head.

"Do you know that Lucas wants to be a documentary filmmaker?" Naomi quizzed the other man. "Do you know that he likes to cook in his downtime? Do you know that he's learning Swahili? Do you know any of these things?"

Lucas had to leave the house. He made himself do it. He couldn't listen to the highly charged argument. He ran out the front door, stomped down the steps, and brought himself to his favorite tree in the front yard. He fell to the ground, his knees hurting from the thick roots that were tangled in the earth and protruding up from the dirt. He stared out at the muddy driveway, where Naomi and Richard's *Jeep*, Topher's truck, and Lucas's father's rental car were all parked alongside each other in an uneven row. Lucas stared at them for no particular reason, wiping newly formed tears from his face.

He didn't want to leave. He couldn't leave. There was nothing for him back in the United States. What family members he once had were either vanished or dead. What friends he once had wouldn't understand him.

He was blind to Topher approaching him. He hadn't seen the older, soft-faced man leaving the house. Topher crouched down in front of Lucas, holding up the parts of his khakis above his knees to avoid wrinkling them. "You have to leave, Michael," he said carefully. "I know you've enjoyed your time here, but your real home is back in the States. You can't stay here anymore."

Lucas's eyes kept watering. "Why can't I be called Lucas anymore?" he asked.

Topher forwent the care for his pants. He sat down next to the boy, right on the dirt. "Because it's no longer your name," he said.

"But that is my name. That's who I am."

"No, that is not who you are. What is a name, if not just a title assigned to you? Everyone here, on this soil, has had many names. Take your mother, for example. Your grandparents called her Mary. Your father, Honey. You, Mom. And the rest of us called her Sydney. Your mother had many names, but she was still herself, no matter what she was called. A person can name their self whatever they like, but that doesn't change who they are. In the end, it changes nothing about what is inside. Names change for all kinds of reasons. In the case of you and your mother, it was for your safety."

There was yelling from within the house. They could hear it from the driveway.

"I wish I could send her back with you," Topher said. "I would love for her to have a fresh start, like you will. I'm always trying to get my Nani to leave. She refuses."

"I've had my fresh start," Lucas contested. "Going back would also mean going backwards to who I was before Tanzania."

"I am sorry. I am. But this is the only way now."

Lucas heard his father bellow, *"He is my son, goddammit!"*

Richard's response came fast, *"Then where were you?!"*

Soon after that exchange, the front door swung out, almost detaching from the wall of the house. First came Lucas's father, plowing down the steps and making his way to his car. Then came the younger couple by the door, eyes welling with tears as they watched the man mark the dirt ground with his heavy footsteps.

Lucas shot up to his feet.

Topher rose very slowly.

David Hanson stood beside his car, staring at his son, who fully expected his father to grab him and forcefully drag him back to America, which was, according to Topher, where Lucas belonged. But instead, they stood for a very long time, looking into the each other's eyes. There was an unmistakable grief in David Hanson's stare, and in its shadow were hints of submission. "What do *you* want?" he asked.

Lucas said nothing. He didn't move either. He didn't know what to say. Part of him wanted to scream at his father, but another part felt him unworthy of hearing Lucas's voice when those who were truly deserving had been with him all throughout his lowest and loneliest points in life.

His father barely took Lucas's silence into consideration and just stood there, as if there was nothing he could say to persuade him.

"Lucas," Naomi said imploringly.

The humidity was intolerable and the sun beat down on all of them. A bug moved across the back of Lucas's neck. Everyone's eyes were on him, awaiting his answer. From the heat of the air to the gazes of the men and the woman, he felt the pressure of the moment amplifying.

But what could he have said to encapsulate everything he felt as a simple answer to the question his father had asked? What did Lucas want? He knew he wanted his brother beside him on the soil of Earth, or even the return of a mother whom he hardly knew anything about, but cared for him nonetheless. He wanted to live in the house upon a certain, steep hill in the town of Shaw, Massachusetts, where, in the cold autumns, he and Quentin used to rake the fallen leaves into piles and then wrestle each other for what seemed like hours. Lucas wanted to scale Kilimanjaro all over again, but completely next time, and with Naomi, Richard, the volcanology team, and Abul. He wanted New England's warm summers and frosty winters, but, at the same time, Arusha's sweltering heat and Kilimanjaro's frozen winds. He wanted whatever could ease the pain of having to remain true to himself despite his life's many changes.

Lucas didn't break his gaze with his father.

Naomi hitched a breath.

The face of his father became unreadable. He stared solemnly at the last of his sons. After an elongated blink, he turned away. He opened the driver's door to his car and seated himself inside. Following a brisk close of the door, he backed out of the driveway. No one moved, even when the rumble of the departed car's engine was but a whisper against the songbirds in the nearby trees.

Several minutes later, Lucas walked past Topher and ascended the three steps to the house's front door.

Richard embodied his relief. Lucas didn't recognize just how wrought and tense the man was before, but the creases in his forehead suddenly flattened and the unnatural rise and push of his shoulders swiftly went back to normal. Naomi's cheeks were puffy from the freshly dried tears. She took one of Lucas's hands into both of hers and pulled him against her. She wrapped herself all around him, and Richard led the three of them back into their home.

20

A *"thud!"* jolted Quentin awake. Were it allowed, he would have slept another ten hours, would have laid prone on his uncomfortably firm, twin bunk if it meant he could melt into the sheets and shirk his existence that day. Despite January only being a day away, he still hadn't identified if it was genuine fatigue or debilitating depression that made him dread the arriving month—it was probably both.

Someone of unique slightness set their weight onto the corner of his bunk, and it forced the rigid mattress to a disproportionate dip.

"Up," Quentin heard Ewan say in a tart voice. "Quentin, get up." He had food of a crumbly variety between his pearly teeth on one side of his mouth, making his right cheek larger than the left. Quentin cringed at the way the stuffing mutated Ewan's words into unclear syllables, but Ewan didn't care. He acted oblivious to the granola torrent that fell from his mouth with every open chew.

Quentin slapped some of the sugary crumbs away from his blanket. "Really?"

"Really," replied the boy on the corner of his bed. "And you really left that captain-issued alarm clock in the communal bathroom, which means it went off for thirty minutes, nonstop."

Quentin flopped an arm over his face. "Patterson..." He yawned and slurred his words, as if not all synapses were firing yet. "Can't miss...meeting..."

"You should've been awake an hour ago. Captain my ass."

"How'd you even get in here?"

"You fell asleep with the door open. Why are you still in bed, anyway?"

"Okay, Ewan, we don't all go to bed at geriatric hours."

Crumbles plummeted onto the portion of blanket beside Quentin's left thigh. He brushed them away. "Dude, no food in my bedroom. Besides, Patterson wants this place all pristine and stuff."

Ewan widened his granola-filled mouth and chewed a bit louder. "Yeah, well kidnapping is illegal and morally reprehensible," he snarked. "But he doesn't seem to mind that much, does he?"

"What?"

Ewan gulped the final clogging of granola. "Same as every other day. Get up, you sloth."

Quentin rose from the bunk. He washed his face in the restroom and slowly dressed himself in his bedroom, indeed at a pace like that of the famously slow-moving mammal. He made the decision to forgo breakfast once the clock struck nine and he forced himself to briskly make his way downstairs to Patterson's office.

After arriving, Quentin was startled to see only one other person in the room besides his superior. It was Casey. She looked tired but calm, calmer than in their last meeting, when she was fizzy with excitement at the launch of the BDP.

"Ah, Quentin," greeted Patterson, who sat at his usual spot behind his desk. "Good to see you. Do join us please, and we'll get started."

"No advisors today?" Quentin asked.

"I'm afraid not," Patterson said. "This meeting only pertains to scheduling. I figured they could sleep in a little." He examined the sleepy captains in front of him. "Oh, how I've missed this, seeing you two on duty."

Comments like that one made Quentin hate him.

"Now, proceeding to the news of the day...I've made the calculations and adjusted some engine controls. It would appear we are a week's worth of Earth time away from our irreversible approach to the asteroid belt. This may seem like something we should act upon instantly, but despite its close proximity, we won't begin even the slowest penetration until each division's pilots are properly and optimally trained. As you know, it's not a dangerous area to pass through. It's only hazardous if one were to travel at full speed. But I am obligated to ask, how have they been doing?"

By December 31st, the appointed pilots were Amber and Oscar from Division One and Athol and Ewan from Division Two.

Casey shrugged. "I don't know anything about flight training, but they're acing their simulation tests. Amber and Oscar seem to get along well too, which is a benefit. They've become good friends."

"Same," Quentin said.

Patterson nodded. "I just needed to check in is all. Don't you worry, it'll be years before either set is needed."

"All right," Casey said, but she sounded a little flustered.

"On a more serious note," Patterson said, "good luck tomorrow. EV Prep is not as easy, keep that in mind."

"If you say so, sir," Casey responded.

"Casey, your division will be going first tomorrow morning. Quentin, your session will take place some time around noon. And when your groups do wake for the day, please advise them to eat and drink plentifully preceding the exercise."

Quentin thought back to Ewan and his one granola bar. "Okay," he said.

"Good. This is wonderful, actually. Dismissed. Oh, and by the way…" Patterson didn't finish his sentence. He pulled out one of the drawers beside him, on the far side of his desk, and lifted into view two silver wristwatches. "For tomorrow," he said, and he held them out for the two captains.

"But you already gave us those last month," Casey said.

"I can assure you, these are quite different."

Quentin took one into his hands. "What are they for?" he asked.

"Soon, you will see," came Patterson's unsatisfactory answer. "Tomorrow morning, you will see."

When the following morning arrived, Quentin mourned the end of 2047, when responsibilities were unassigned and moping was societally acceptable. He hated the arrival of the 1st, had stayed up all night thinking of how it was closing in on him, almost taunting him. A part of him pitied himself, and another part felt justified. Before, he was sure of his stance, was remorseless when it came to his purposeful indolence. For the first time ever, he was conflicted.

Although the 1st of January made him feel differently, the actual morning of it differed little from the ordinary. Breakfast wasn't a single degree removed from normal. As usual, Mathias dozed off at the table with his chin propped on his elbows, the skin there forming rumples under the weight of his skull. Frances listened attentively as Fatima read the first chapter of *Charlotte's Web* for her weekly English assignment. Quentin attempted striking up a diplomatic chat with Marina, since they were bound to continue seeing so much of one another in the coming months, but the instant he delivered his first few words of small talk, she yawned over her mushy oatmeal and then snapped her jaw shut, looking at anything but him.

He was about to leave the table, maybe catch another nap before the unavoidable noon requirements, when a shrill, screech-like sound erupted from the new watch on his wrist.

Mathias jumped awake. "What the hell is that?!"

"Shut that ear-rape off, dude!" Derek vociferated.

"Derek!" Frances yelled reproachfully.

"Sorry! I—*Oops*—Sorry!" Quentin stammered. He scrambled to disable the blaring device as he experimentally twisted and pressed some of the buttons that lined its platinum-silver edges.

Roxy choked down a chunky glob of softened cereal. She squirmed, her shoulders making their way up to her ears. "Why did he give you that thing?!" she asked. "There are clocks all over this place!"

"He was worried we'd forget about today," Marina said in a normal voice. They could barely hear her.

Roxy's arms shook at the shrieking of the gadget, as if further presentation of her discomfort would somehow convince the device to stop. "Seriously?!" she asked over the noise. "Why, as head of our division, would he forget our first preparation day?!"

"Not him, you vapid minx," Marina said. "Patterson. In case he slept in."

Quentin situated the correct control, clicked and turned it, and at last his device stopped its audible torture. "Ah, got it!" he happily announced as he sealed the glass cover over the watch. He sighed out in relief, but noticed that no one else felt the same.

He saw that most were frowning, while Roxy was gaping.

"Actually, no," Ewan inserted himself into a conversation Quentin knew nothing about. "The watch was meant for Quentin, not Patterson. Roxy was right."

Marina's gaze relocated to Ewan. "I don't recall asking for your input."

Roxy laid her hands on the table and shot a glare at Marina. "Friendly much?" she asked.

"Yes, I try," said Marina. She pitched her legs over the bench of their table and snatched her food tray into her hands. She made for the door, tossed her mainly untouched meal into the garbage bin, and seated herself on an empty space of the bench at Connor and Athol's table.

Roxy gulped, blinking fast. "I was just making conversation."

Quentin made a dismissive waving motion toward Marina. "No one should ever feel insulted by her," he said.

Derek pulled his fork out of his mouth, which was filled with food—turkey sausage and the yolk of an egg, it seemed. *"Prolly dat time uff da month,"* he poorly enunciate before swallowing. "Tried to get her loosened up the other day, but she walked away from me. Bleeding, I guess."

"Ew," Jaymes responded.

Frances was clearly about to say something scornful, but she changed her mind and turned to Fatima. "Why don't you go get changed? I laid your clothes out for you on your bed."

The girl frowned. "Why can't I wear my polka leggings?"

"Because Patterson probably won't want you to wear them for EV Prep. Go on, I'll check on you if you haven't come back."

Fatima was still tiny enough to jump off the bench of their table. When her feet met the floor, she hurried away.

Frances swiveled her head back in Derek's direction. "You really don't know how to control yourself, do you? You don't belong near children."

"Aren't you the one that brought her here?" Derek asked.

"Cool it," Jaymes said. "Can we just eat our food in peace?"

Conversation became infrequent. They ate purposefully, never lifting their heads from their plates and trays to make eye contact with each other, except by accident, like when someone would stand to get a refill of their breakfast beverage. After their intake of food, the second division still had a couple hours to themselves. They dispersed. Some went to the gym to warm up whereas others retreated to their beds for a quick wink. Quentin chose to nap for an hour and then walk once he was rested, as he'd heard Marina and some others had planned to do. He knew that the assessments during their approaching undertaking were going to be strenuous, so he thought it wise to ease his stiff legs into the day with a low-maintenance stroll.

When the hour was up, Quentin dressed himself in the attire Patterson had provided them all the night before. Quentin slid his head through a long, black turtleneck and shoved his legs into a pair of heavy and baggy, fleece cargo pants. He picked at the top, hating how tight it was, and when he descended one of the staircases of the foyer after leaving his bedroom, he had to constantly pull his pants up to stop them from cascading down to his feet.

In the corridor that lead to the gymnasium, he saw Ivy sprinting in his direction. She was overjoyed, verged on twinkling, and waving as she brought herself within a foot of him. Her rouged lips limned a broadening smile, and her long mane flapped behind her head as she reached him and started jogging in place; the section of hair that wasn't restrained by her high ponytail's elastic band swung back and forth behind her head, threatening to whip him even from where he stood. Sweat stains were dotted all over her. She must have thought herself subtle as she simperingly glanced to the wet blotches that highlighted the curvatures of her breasts, shoulders, and waist, but he knew what she was doing. After the total disaster of the first half of 2047, she had been quick to regain her confidence and improve her mental health. She started eating well, taking care of herself, and now, it seemed, she was quite in tune with her body's every desire.

"How was EV Prep?" Quentin asked. He thought that a safe question.

Ivy swung her arms back and forth. She verged on swiping his jaw with her elbow. "Woah! Whoops! Sorry, Quentin! Super scary! Super, super scary at first but holy shit, it was so cool!" In a secretive tone, she whisper-yelled, *"Quentin, Quentin! You. Will. Love. It."* Her voice returned to normal. "Or you'll hate it. Whatever, it's so cool! And Connor…Oh my god, Connor almost pissed his pants and I mean, who can blame him? But it was so fun!"

"Connor? But he seemed fine at breakfast."

Ivy kicked her legs higher and shook her head madly. "Oh, no, no, no," she told him in short breaths. Her rubbery neck moved in all directions, and her ponytail finally thwacked his face.

Quentin stumbled back, astounded by the sharpness of her hair. "You don't say," he replied as he rubbed the space where she had struck him.

Ivy laughed animatedly. "He was losing it! Gotta go, Quentin. This whole prep thing's released some kinda crazy endorphins I never thought I had. I'm gonna run through the ship and—Oh my God! I just got a thought! You should join me some time!"

Quentin scratched his head. "Oh, I'll see if I—"

"See you!" Ivy exclaimed, and she ran off. A breeze from her swinging ponytail was the only lingering indicator that she had been in the hallway with him. She disappeared as quickly as she had appeared. In a matter of seconds, Quentin was alone.

When he did arrive to the gymnasium, he had no idea what Ivy was talking about. Standing shoulder to shoulder with his equivalently baffled peers, Quentin watched as Patterson flourished his arm and gestured to a multicolored, rock-climbing wall that was sturdily bolted to the interior of the gymnasium's four walls. Quentin surveyed the apparatus, an article which fell victim to great athletic scrutiny. The vertical obstacle course was sectioned into four parts; the first was hot-pink; the second, sky-blue; the third, green; the fourth, yellow. It wasn't twenty-feet-tall, had an evident mash of forged rubber foundations, and incorporated child handles beneath every sixth, faux stone that protruded from its surface. *What did I expect?* Quentin thought. *Another pathological lie from a Martinez, and I believed her.*

"Patterson, what am I looking at?" Mathias asked.

"A rock-climbing wall, Mr. Garcia."

Roxy laughed. "Ooo, how scandalous, Patterson, you didn't put safety pads on the floor."

Straight-faced, Ewan said, "It's okay, Roxy. Thankfully we have the kiddie handles."

The curl of Patterson's lips flattened. "I promise that your endurance, both mental and physical, will be challenged." He leaned forward and extended a hand, reaching out to the puny child who stood between Frances and Mathias. Fatima shuffled forward. She didn't like lifting her feet when she walked, so she slid them along the laminate flooring with squeaks and skids that were so annoying that Quentin plugged one of his ears with a thumb, feigning an itch. When she reached Patterson, she took his hand and refused to let him go. "Fatima will eschew from today's preparatory screenings," Patterson informed them. "She will be with me, watching you and studying to prep herself for the day, a day many years from now, when she, too, will have to do the same, but perhaps under your tutelage rather than mine."

"Dude," Mathias said, "she'd be just as good as any of us. That wall's gotta be fifteen-feet high, tops."

"Fourteen," Ewan said.

"Twenty," said a nonplussed Patterson. "It may provide an initially underwhelming impression, I am aware of that, but traveling around all sides of the gymnasium is more difficult than you may believe. I advise that you avoid underestimating the dimensions of this room."

Mathias clicked his tongue against the roof of his mouth. "I used to lift four days a week."

"As I was saying," Patterson lilted on, "whether or not one has pumped iron for ages, you are going to feel your muscles contracting and burning. *'Scorching,'* if I may quote some of your friends from the previous session."

"When do we start?" Ewan drawled.

"Now," Patterson said. "You start now."

He ordered that everyone warm up, but they didn't recognize the value in it. The admittedly egoistic division refused to abide the request, but he made it clear that they wouldn't begin their assignment until they obliged him. Some jogged. Some walked laps around the room. Roxy disappeared for a total of nine minutes to allegedly change out of her uncomfortable clothes, but never actually did because the attire was mandated by Patterson. When the warmup was deemed sufficient, everyone formed a line at one end of the rock wall. Quentin, the reluctant captain, stood at the front, followed by Marina, Jaymes, Ewan, Athol, and so forth, with Roxy bringing up the rear.

Patterson and his little partner hovered in the core of the room, where the others had recently congregated. "Do you see those ropes hanging from the top, Quentin? Once you start, yours will be the first you come across. Marina, you start your climbing when he approaches yours, then you take that second one as your own. Jaymes will follow Marina, then Ewan, Frances, and all the way through until it is Roxy's turn. You should get the picture. Are you ready, Quentin?"

"Shouldn't it be the other way around?" Roxy disputed. "Shouldn't Quentin go to the rope farthest from him, then Marina takes the second to last one?"

Patterson unveiled an uncharacteristically goofy grin. "Last I recall, you were so unconcerned by the exercise that you spent the entirety of the warmup in the lavatory."

Roxy's shoulders dipped. She dropped the complaint.

Patterson pointed to the ropes again. "Quentin, if you will," he said.

Quentin stepped forward. He came face to face with the first rock closest to him. He lifted his hand up to touch it, feeling the inauthentic coarseness of its surface.

"This is so stupid," Mathias said.

Ewan looked back to Patterson. "You're still here? To watch *this*?"

"I for one find the first moments quite fascinating," Patterson said.

"Most fascinating," Fatima complemented, her hand still in his.

"Why exactly can't she join?" Frances asked. "It'd be good for her to exercise."

"Please, Quentin," Patterson requested lightly, "we need to get on with our day. We mustn't waste any more time."

"Fine, fine," Quentin said. He buried the tiny, but nonetheless present, morsel of pride that lived inside him just so he could elevate his right leg and set his boot-covered foot onto the bumpy rocks nearest to the floor. He tried not to think of how ridiculous he felt doing it, and that somewhere at home there were scientists and politicians who had fought for him to be on that ship, had risked and lost their lives, all for him to be climbing *that*. He brought the rest of himself up and began his sideways climb, progressing about two yards.

By the end of the short distance, he noticed how heavily he was breathing. It was a windedness that didn't lessen. He stopped and concentrated, but he somehow felt worse. His limbs felt heavier, but his fingers thinner. When he reached the blue rope, he strung it around his waist, but just like his pants, it hung loose on him, more like a lasso than a belt. Even tying it was exhausting. As he approached the second rope, he felt spent. Everything was sore. His fingers burned. Sweat gathered under his clothes, moistening his skin. He leaned an arm against the pebbly, hot-pink wall and drooped his head against his forearm as he tried to regain his energy. He balanced himself with each foot on the edges of their separate rocks, one hand clinging to the rope. His blocked ears barely made out the sound of the others' jeering laughter. He tried to move again, but he felt something, something he couldn't see, yanking him down.

"What the hell is going on?" Ewan asked.

Quentin peeked over his forearm to see the line of people near him. "I…I…I don't…" He gasped for air. *"Ergh!"*

Mathias and Ewan shared a snicker.

A special someone who still stood in the center of the gymnasium then said, "Enhanced gravity."

"What?!" Quentin yelped. He didn't even bother turning around to see Patterson.

"No way," Jaymes said, sounding invigorated.

Ewan opened his palms resignedly. "Now that…Okay. You have me, Patterson."

And Patterson, whose buoyancy returned, said through his staying smile, "I promised I wouldn't disappoint."

Quentin bent his body rightward and leftward, downward and sideways. At every turn, he felt the constant pull of the invisible force.

He heard Athol cheering him on, but it wasn't motivating at all. Moving took longer than any of them thought it would. One step and then two, and two eventually swept into six. In seven, Quentin was victoriously lingering beside Marina's rope. Sweat dribbles splayed across his forehead, his breathing was ragged, but he was there. Behind him, Fatima was clapping, and the smacking of her hands echoed throughout the enormous room. Mathias's claps were slow and mocking. *Oh, like he could do any better,* thought the drained climber.

"I guess you're going mobile," Jaymes said to Marina, and she advanced upon the wall.

"Go slow," Quentin recommended.

Marina nodded in acknowledgment. She, like him, started with her right leg.

Thirty minutes later, all of Quentin's contemporaries were suffering the same physically challenging battle. They groused at the pain and tenderness of their muscles. No longer were any of them embarrassed about the hassle of the exercise, as they all wallowed shamelessly. Even Quentin couldn't deny that it was a little exciting.

At the forty-minute mark, Ewan discovered bags of chalk nuzzled into the occasional crevice, several of which Quentin had already passed and overlooked. Many were grateful to ease their hands of their slipping. For Quentin, the white pieces offered some solace, but following reapplication, they did next to nothing.

Patterson was probably looking on with another knowing grin. When Quentin turned to verify it, he saw that the man wasn't with them anymore. Nor was the child. Quentin called attention to their missing superior, but no one else was concerned about it.

"He must've gotten bored," Ewan said.

Jaymes pushed his glasses up his nose. "Wow…This gravity is kinda…kinda pulling my glasses."

"*Definitely* enhanced," Quentin whined.

"As if anyone was having doubts," Athol remarked.

"Legal suffocation," Roxy muttered to herself.

Ewan slipped. He nearly hit Jaymes, who swung to the side with the assistance of his rope. "Sorry, man." Ewan apologized.

"No, I get it," Jaymes said. "It's fine."

"Is it just me...just me or...?" Frances hacked a cough. "Or is it...stronger now?"

"That's probably where he went, then," Marina said. "It's likely he just pumped up the gravity."

"Keep moving, guys," Jaymes said. "Let's try to end this. C'mon."

But it was so hard. Had it not been for the rope he had strapped like tape around his midsection, Quentin didn't know if he would still be climbing. He stopped more often, paused every couple of minutes. He wasn't alone. Others were slowing, too.

"Feels...like it's...pres...preshu...pressurize...ing," Ewan griped, diagonal from Quentin and slightly above him.

"How do you...figure?" Quentin asked, even though he wholeheartedly believed it.

"Cuz no way...no way I'm weak as *you*..." Mathias spat.

As much as Quentin wanted to disagree, he couldn't. He stopped once again. Catching his breath, the only movement he made was to shift enough for Marina to work her way up and around him, letting her advance. After a struggle of her own, she was at superior footing, alongside Jaymes and Ewan, who still hovered over Quentin.

Ewan readjusted his rope around his stomach, twining it into a tighter knot. "If I had to guess," he said, "I'll bet Patterson just made the change."

"Should we stop and conserve our energy for a while?" Quentin asked.

Roxy looked doubtful. "Because that's helped you how much?" She gestured to herself, Jaymes, and Ewan. "We've been moving nonstop and the rest of you have been conserving your energy, but we're all here right now. None of us can move. This isn't going to work."

"Please lower it!" Ewan shouted into the air.

"Guys…" Jaymes was about to prolong the debate, but he blew out a strained breath, deciding against it. "Damnit. Just keep going. Save your air. We'll talk later."

Quentin silently went along, as did everyone else.

———

There once was a time when Colin Harris Patterson had a daughter. He technically still did, come the year 2048, but the odds were against him ever seeing her again. He was older, and yet he felt his new life was only just beginning; everything else, everything before 2045, had been a preclusion to what now unfolded. He knew Naomi understood that. He knew that after she had grown, after she completed her education and started working in his world, that she finally understood her formative years of deep solitude and loneliness, that she finally understood why her godfather frequented her home more often than her own father, and why her father, when he was home, often slept during his few hours of respite. She understood it all, and she forgave him. But her understanding wasn't the catharsis he thought it would have been. In the end, he realized that he never wanted there to be a reason for her to forgive him for anything. He thought it wrong for a child to have to forgive their parent.

But forgive him, she did. When she had reached the point of understanding, they, for the first time, became close—something he had always wanted, but for many years considered an impossibility. She graduated from high school with honors and then, under the tutelage of the very people who had once schooled him, completed her university studies. He waited with open arms, hoped she would choose to further mold herself into his realm of expertise, which she did. Partly. He thought geology and its many branches quite boring, but he wasn't one to complain about her choice, because it still brought her into his sphere.

But then they were separated again. There were no pop-ins in the middle of the week, nor were there apologetic phone calls like the past ones that detailed his misery for having missed her volleyball games or how he was sorry that he wasn't at the house to wish her and her date a safe drive to her senior prom. This was different. He didn't know what she was doing on the 1st of January, in 2048. There was no phone he could pick up to contact her, just to hear her voice. There was no car he could drive to sneak away from his work and watch her from afar, like the many days when she would hop off the school bus and run into their home, where Topher was sure to be waiting. There was no way Colin could steal glimpses of anything anymore. He could only guess and hope.

Was how he felt, then, in 2048, just how she felt all throughout her childhood? She wasn't allowed to know much of who her father was or what he did. Was it karma that after all her years of solitude and suffering whilst he worked on clandestine matters, that he, down the line, was the one to suffer the same? He thought it was. God, he assumed, was not an entity based upon science, but Colin had to admit that after all his years of observation, there was one thing that had become clear to him: the universe had its ways of getting back at people, even the good ones.

So, while his daughter was likely living in normality back home, probably rocking a child in her arms—one who had Richard's thick, brown eyebrows and her bright eyes—Colin made due with the few resources in his midst that could potentially ease his loneliness.

For instance, Fatima.

He admittedly knew little of dealing with small children, since he was hardly in Naomi's life when she was a sprouting, miniature figure of her mother, who, had she lived long enough to see their daughter, would have been speechless at the chilling likeness. But he reasoned that dealing with small children must not be too trying a duty, because if Mathias Garcia could tame Fatima all by himself, well…How could Colin H. Patterson, father of one and former vice administrator at NASA, possibly fall short?

With Fatima beside him, Colin stroked his chin as they stared toward the narrow window together. He was fixed on it, but her eyes drifted. The table before them, too tall for her to see beyond, was the thing at which she rubbernecked in awe. It had neon buttons, voltage meters, and a plethora of gauges and touchscreens strewn all across its surface. She didn't seem to care about the window a few feet beyond it, but was hypnotized by the bouncing lights and twinkling, electronic color schemes.

He crouched down. Balanced on his toes and stooped to her diminutive height, an aroma of her coconut shampoo whisked into his nose. "Do you know what room this is, Fatima?" he asked.

Fatima bit her upper lip.

"It's okay if you don't. But do you have any idea of what it may be?"

She shook her head.

"Well," Colin said, "do you see them?" With his forefinger, he pointed to the long, rectangular sliver of glass which constituted the window at the front of their room. Beyond the transparent barrier was a view of young, striving bodies of various statures, each grappling against unseen impediments as they scrambled sideways along a rock wall. "We can see them, but, but, but…" he said, with exaggeration for a flair of suspense, "they cannot see us. Now, they don't look like they're having much fun, do they? They look a bit…"

"Tired," the girl said.

"Tired indeed. Not only would it be entertaining for ourselves, but it would be a wonderful gesture of charity on our part to allow them some fun. Don't you think?"

Evidently, Fatima didn't have a clue as to what any of the flowery terms from the older companion's lexicon meant, but she grasped the general idea fairly well. A mousy smile drew onto her chubby face as she nodded, and her long brown hair bounced against her cheeks.

"Would you like to make it funner for them?" Colin offered.

She nodded and eagerly gave consent for him to scoop her up to a height more conducive to touching all those buttons on the console. His neck was in her hands as he rose to full height, her frame in his arms. She was patient, but excited, as she awaited his command. Her gaze followed his every move as he activated a control on his right, a green button that protruded from its metal pedestal on the table. He stepped closer to the console desk, which brought her closer, too. He pointed to a glowing, pink button beside the green one.

"That button," he whispered, *"will make things funner."*

"The pink?"

"The pink one, yes. But see, the problem is that I cannot touch it. Only you have the power to. It is a special button. What do you say? Do you still want to help?"

Being young, Fatima was innocently gullible despite the lack of artfulness in Patterson's persuasion. "I'm ready," she squeaked.

Patterson leaned his body forward, and she giggled at the way the inclination made her tip backwards. "Very well then," he said, "the floor is yours, cadet."

Fatima reached forward and dropped her thumb to the pink button. A beep elicited from the edge of the desk. When nothing happened, she eyed him skeptically.

"Hold on," Colin said. "All in good time. See this table? It can do anything you want. You just have to be patient."

———

The veins in Quentin's legs pounded as he moved and sporadically held still. He could almost feel the green lines in his legs bulging and then decompressing. He didn't know what Patterson was thinking when he deemed enhanced gravity sequences as appropriate training, other than it being a mechanism to make them all feel guilty for their year-long sedentary natures.

"There is athleticism, and then there is gravity," Athol said above Quentin.

Quentin gasped. "Yeah."

Athol laughed. "Took me five minutes to get to the nearest person just so I could say that."

Quentin gave a thumbs-up. "I...*mm*...honored."

Marina, Jaymes, and Ewan were far away, all the way near the end of the first wall. Roxy and Mathias had lagged a bit, but they were still closer to the other three than they were to Quentin, Frances, and Athol, who were farthest back. Ewan was unique, though. His energy fluctuated in the luckiest of ways, where sometimes he could climb fleetly for five minutes and then rest only for two.

A while later, as his eyes watered and his calves burned, Quentin felt the invisible force pushing down on them begin to thin. He took in a breath, and it felt like his lungs bloomed wider and were able to take in more air. For the third time in the hour, he rested his head against his forearm, panting. *"Thank you,"* he whispered. The enhancement remained prominent, but not so powerful that it was oppressive. His movements improved greatly, enabling him to reach the halfway point of the first wall. Frances and Athol flanked him, and Jaymes, Marina, and Mathias were no longer far away; as others thrived, the three of them began to plateau. A few minutes later, Quentin progressed so well that he eventually hovered underneath Ewan and Jaymes.

The high did come to an end, though. Five minutes later, Quentin was stopping for air again.

Frances climbed up beside him, closer than she already was. Her face glowed happily, like her bob-cut hair wasn't flying over a majority of it and sticking to the sweat. "You know he only increased the gravity, right?" she asked. "And it is decreasing."

"Well," Quentin managed to say through his lips as he puffed his cheeks, "the…gravity pushes…down…on the…the lungs…Makes them…shrink…"

"I'm pretty sure that's mind over matter, Quentin. If your lungs were being squished by gravity, then I guess those flat-Earthers really are correct."

Quentin flushed and gathered his breath. "I just aligned myself with the dumbest fringe of society, didn't I?"

Frances's smile was nauseating.

"Wanna race to Jaymes?" Quentin offered.

"If you want. But you're looking rather inadequate."

"Wow. Okay. Rude."

"As a trainee medical official, I must prepare for being the bearer of bad news to my future patients." Frances dropped her smile. "But in all seriousness, this race starts now."

Quentin felt like a child on a jungle-gym. He snorted as he bumped himself against her, deliberately batting her body away as he tried to advance beyond her reach. She deftly lowered herself so that she was a few inches under his feet and began her climb around him. Jaymes, their target, was resting and talking with a well-advanced Athol. Frances yelled for Jaymes to stay where he was, which confused him for a moment, more so when both Quentin and Frances were closing in on him. Athol started climbing away, not looking keen to the idea of being crowded at random, but just as he made to move, the gymnasium shook violently. He grabbed onto Jaymes. Quentin dug his feet into the wall, hugging his rope. Frances tightened her grip on the rocks by her face.

The walls fluttered, and it seemed as though the floor wobbled too. Quentin couldn't see much of anything. With the shaking, everything was hazy and out of focus. Someone screamed. Athol looked down to Frances, who was lowest in the entire group and closest to the floor. He asked her if she was okay, but she didn't answer. The room kept shaking. Quentin fastened his rope tighter around himself.

Jaymes began to slide down. He had to be twenty-feet high. Marina, who had begun to lag, was under him and she registered his instability, so she scooted to the side in case he lost control—which he did. Athol, right next to where Marina had been lingering before she moved, was still preoccupied with Quentin and Frances, so when Jaymes went falling down, Athol, at the last minute, threw himself to the side. He tried to help the falling figure, reaching forward and grabbing Jaymes's rope, but all it did was birth subsequent trouble. With Jaymes's cord ensnared in Athol's hand, the momentum sent them both hurtling toward the floor. Their ropes grew longer, and swung right next to Quentin. He grabbed them both and bunched them together in his hands, which burned, as the rough material scraped his palms. He almost let go. Luckily, Jaymes and Athol each caught onto clusters of rocks and held them. When they could support themselves, Quentin released their ropes.

The walls didn't stop shaking, and the rocks were loosening.

"You guys all right?!" Quentin hollered down.

Athol and Jaymes shouted that they were fine.

The room stilled.

Everything went silent.

"What the hell was that?!" Mathias asked.

Athol stayed near the bottom, but Jaymes climbed back up. He approached Quentin. "Thanks for grabbing on," Jaymes said. He wiped the perspiration off his left cheek. "I wouldn't normally consider a twenty-foot drop fatal, but…" He pushed his glasses up. "Man…this gravity's insane. Listen. Let's all stay as close together as possible from here on out."

"Yes," Quentin concurred.

Jaymes raised an eyebrow. "Look, I don't have any idea what Patterson thinks he's doing, but I don't see how this is going to help us prepare for—"

Quentin heard a click. He thought he did, anyway. Jaymes must have heard it too, because his mouth was open, but words weren't coming out of it.

"Did any of you hear that?" Athol asked up to them.

Quentin hitched a breath. "Yeah," he said.

Frances began to shake.

"I wouldn't worry too much," Quentin said to her lowly, comfortingly.

"Quentin, I'm all right," Frances said.

"You're shaking. I just figured—"

"I'm not shaking."

"Yeah, you are."

"No, Quentin. I am not shaking. Everyone and everything is. You included."

Quentin glanced to his free hand. He watched how it shook uncontrollably. The stone beside him did the same, the one he gripped with his busy hand.

Jaymes hugged his rope. Athol produced a squeal below. Above and relatively far away from Quentin, Mathias's and Ewan's feet bounced against the stones they were balanced upon. Roxy was talking to herself with her eyes closed, looking skittish and green. Marina let go of a rock by accident, but she returned her hand to it instantly.

As for the floor, it, too, released a couple grips of its own. It split into two, right down the middle, leaving a small gap between the symmetrical halves.

Cold air rushed up to the wall-walkers.

The shaking stopped, but the movement of the ground did not. Backwards and away from each other, the halves began to recede as the room's temperature dropped precipitously. They slowly peeled back, each retreating underneath a base on opposite ends of the room. The crack between them wasn't gaping...not yet. It was, however, wide enough to make the bile start rising in Quentin's throat. Through the crack, he saw something that looked like a dusty, multicolored laser beam. He didn't know what he was looking at, but then the two segments of what had previously been one solid floor pulled farther back, until they were nowhere in sight, and only then did he understand what that colorful line was and why it was speckled, clouded and not truly clear. A non-solid body shone under him, where the floor was, and surrounding it was the onyx-like outdoors.

Roxy screamed.

"Patterson, put it back!" Mathias roared.

Ewan was hyperventilating. Frances climbed closer to him, telling him to, *"Breathe, breathe,"* which she whispered measuredly, as if she weren't stricken with fear herself. Quentin thought it ironic that the claustrophobe couldn't handle the opened state of their room.

"What do we do?!" Athol asked hopelessly.

Marina had one hand on a rock and lowered the other, guiding it to the latch of the cord connector mechanism on her rope. Gradually and purposefully, she felt around and abruptly disassembled it. Off came the rope and its cords. She extended her arm and held the assistance mechanisms above the black void below.

"Chill! Chill!" Quentin called to her.

Everyone looked over to them, trying to understand the frenzied interaction.

"What are you doing?!" Athol sputtered at her.

Marina outspread her fingers and released the rope. It shot down and plunged to the horrifyingly groundless gymnasium. But it wasn't groundless, only seemingly so. Her rope and connector mechanism hit a transparent surface, and the sound from the collision reverberated through the room.

Around them, the walls recommenced an erratic shake and a *"crack!"* from high above, from the ceiling, drew everyone's attention upward.

"What was that?" Athol asked.

Frances turned to Quentin. "You don't think Patterson means to—?"

"I think he does," Quentin said.

The shaking intensified, and plaster rained from each of the ceiling's four corners. Soon, the shaking and quaking morphed into infrastructural twitching, and Quentin jammed his elbows into a newly formed fissure in front of him. Akin to the parting of the floor, the domed ceiling split open with one final *"crack!"* It parted its inner layering, but unlike the two split pieces from earlier, the ceiling disassembled into four, and its dome separated. It wilted apart like the petals of a flower. Shards of a creamy color landed in the dip of Quentin's left shoulder.

No matter how much he wanted to, it was hard to look away from the top of the room. That familiar sea of blackness greeted him not only from below, but from above as well. He swallowed vomit.

"Why?!" Athol bawled."Why is this necessary?!"

"We're in space, we get it!" Ewan cried.

A new rush of freezing air smacked into them.

"H...Hey!" Jaymes shouted to Marina, who was hugging the wall like a koala to a eucalyptus branch. "My rope! You want mine?!"

"I'm fine!"

"You sure?! I can—"

The vibrations worsened, were stronger. Quentin felt ill, like he wanted to puke again—not from repulsion that time, but because he was being jostled. A puffing, sigh-like sound emerged. The puffs sounded something like air brakes on a train, not quite as strong as the distinct *"fwishhh"* that Quentin and the others knew so well, but familiar enough that they couldn't turn away from the mystery. He moved his head side to side to see from where, or from what, the sound originated. A shorter puff released. It came from behind him.

On the other end of the room, where thankfully no one occupied the space, the wall shot up so much higher than theirs that they had to look up at it. Quentin couldn't tell how far the wall rose, but when he gazed up at it after the movement finished, he felt like a miniature being. He rather naively thought that his side of the gymnasium would remain unaffected by the shift, but when another short puff emerged and the vibrations again intensified, he looked down and recognized that they were pulling farther away from the fallen ropes and cords that rested on the glass below. Marina's tools looked smaller. Saturn seemed farther away. Their own wall started rising, as did the two perpendicular to it, until all three were transformed from their mousy height of twenty feet to a towering alternative, a number Quentin didn't even want to imagine as he dangled from his rope and held the stones in front of him.

The violent redesign, paired with the preexisting shakiness, slammed his face forward against one of the rocks. He grunted at the pain from the shot to his cheek.

So much screaming echoed around him that he felt like his eardrums might burst.

He didn't look down. He had the restraint not to. He did look up, though, to the stretch of rocks and jagged walling that had extended beyond the original twenty feet; there was a fairly extensive space between the sea of darkness and where he was situated.

"What…Whadda we do now?!" Jaymes asked. "I'm serious! What are we supposed to do with this adjustment?!"

"I'm gonna pee," Athol said, and Quentin instantly thought back to how Ivy proclaimed that Connor nearly soiled his own pants during their early morning session. Quentin shed his disbelief. She wasn't lying.

Frances climbed toward Marina. "Are you sure you're okay? Can you go without your rope?" Quentin didn't listen for her answer. He could only imagine what that rise had been like without the safety of his rope to comfort him.

"Door's still there," Mathias observed. He gestured to the bottom of the wall opposite them.

"Basketball hoop, too," Roxy said half-amusedly.

"So do we just…climb to nowhere?!" Ewan asked.

Quentin heard a buzz. He felt two, brief squeezes around his wrist. Supporting himself with one hand splayed across a few stones, he drew back the sleeve of his left arm to expose the wristwatch

Patterson had given him the day before. Quentin flicked the cap of the gadget away from its rim, where the watch ended and where his scrawny arm began. The screen didn't display the time, only a message in light-blue text.

Grav. Level: 2%
Total Height: 130 ft
Hanson, Q: 40 ft, 3 inches
Equipment: 130ft
Exposure: 30 mins, 15 secs.

"Hey, hey!" Quentin exclaimed. "My watch! There are instructions on my watch!"

"What does it say?" Athol asked.

"So…Okay. The total height of the room is a-hundred-and-thirty feet. Our gravity has been enhanced by two percent…" Quentin sucked in a breath. "It has a read on my location. It says I'm at the forty-feet mark, which should apply to most of us right now. Our equipment is located at the full, one-hundred-and-thirty-feet mark and…and…Oh. Oh shit."

"What?" Marina pressed. "Quentin, what is it?"

"We have thirty minutes until…until exposure?"

"Exposure?!" Ewan panicked. "What does that mean?!"

"I think we all have a very clear idea of what the fuck it means," Mathias said. "I'm not wasting another precious second. Let's get to that equipment. And fast."

The truly mad scramble began. Breaths were huffed and limbs were strained. No one complained anymore. They couldn't waste their energy on something as futile as talking. Communicating wasn't a luxury they could afford.

Frances advised Quentin against checking his watch every time he halted to gather air, but he couldn't help it. He was dissatisfied when he read that it took him three minutes to climb ten feet, or another five minutes to climb an additional fifteen. The reads only ever discouraged him, but they were addicting. The only solace came from looking down to the faraway state of Marina's stranded ropes.

A little later, when pausing again, he checked his watch. The update didn't comfort him one bit.

Grav. Level: 1%
Total Height: 130 ft
Hanson, Q: 85 ft, 1 inches
Equipment: 130ft
Exposure: 16 mins, 15 secs.

"Anything good?" Athol asked, when he caught up to Quentin after falling back for a while.

"Decrease in gravity by one percent," Quentin said. "We have sixteen minutes."

"And where are we?"

"Eighty-five."

"We need to keep this pace or faster."

"Yeah."

By the time there were fourteen minutes remaining on the watch, Division Two was well spread out. Quentin and Frances were the lowest, Athol and Ewan were diagonal and above them by a few feet. Jaymes, Roxy, and Mathias were directly above the latter three. In case her grip failed, Marina made sure to always be positioned somewhere between the two groups.

When there were eleven minutes left on the clock, the watch read that Quentin was at the ninety-nine-feet mark. He was decently encouraged.

"How much time do we have left?" Ewan asked a bit later, against Quentin's wishes.

"I'm not checking anymore," Quentin said.

"We have to know! It's better we know than—!"

Just then, eye to eye with one another, the two jerked away from where they were climbing to dodge a rock that dropped toward their faces. Jaymes was slipping above them, as the rock had been under his foot before it went catapulting out of the wall. But it wasn't just there that the anomaly took place. It happened all around them. On each wall, every fifth rock popped out from the surface at an alarming speed. One hit within an inch of Marina's head, which she guarded with her forearm. Frances gave a scream when a projectile hit her square in her stomach, but she maintained her position and didn't falter. A rock supporting Mathias suddenly went whizzing away. He slipped and dangled by his fingertips before recovering with a barbarous stream of profanities. Each rock's brief flight ended with a sharp crash to the glassy floor, leaving scrapes and divots in the clear layer. At first, Quentin didn't understand the utility of the torture, but when he focused on the scrapes and cracks, he watched as the slits in the glass broke into fissures. He thought he understood the purpose of all those tiny fractures.

He looked back down to his watch. "We have nine!" he announced.

"Move! Move!" someone was pushing them all, and Quentin did as they said.

He climbed, and he didn't stop once. His lungs were crackling and he was heaving in breaths, but the growing awareness of the slowly shattering glass and the ever-ticking gadget on his arm did him the favor of galvanizing him to keep moving.

At the eight-minute mark, Mathias was the first of their entire cluster to reach the pinnacle. A ray of light from a star ages away shined upon his sweaty face as he threw his hands onto the top of the wall. He removed a foot from one of the little boulders and propelled himself up to the peak by pushing his foot off Jaymes's shoulder, treating him as a springboard of sorts.

"You prick," Jaymes said, slapping Mathias's foot away.

Mathias threw the upper half of his body over the top and stretched across the narrow platform. He stood up, smug, with defiance etched across his face; the healing hole where his septum piercing had once been was more defined under the light of the stars.

"Start looking for that equipment, asshole!" Ewan barked up to him.

Mathias unbuckled his rope cords from around his waist. "On it!" he complied. He looked around for a second. "Hey, where am I supposed to find them?!"

"Use…your…eyes, dumbass!" Athol told him.

"This thing's two-feet wide max!"

"Just look!" Jaymes yelled.

"Easy for you to say!"

"Mathias, go!" Athol screamed.

"I'm trying!"

"Look harder!"

Mathias carefully began to walk in the direction to the right of where everyone was climbing.

At the seven-minute mark, Roxy was the second to conquer the wall. After she untangled her rope, she was more generous with the advantage than Mathias was and utilized her spare time to hoist her teammates' ropes up, saving them valuable climbing time.

Ten seconds later, Jaymes and Marina made it to the top. They chose against walking and instead opted for the more cautious manner of travel: crawling.

Roxy and Mathias were over at the east wall, where they were scrounging at the floor, trying to locate gaps or nooks wherein the safety equipment may have been hidden.

Quentin felt like he was going to die. After nearly freezing to death from the blasts of cold air, he was overheated. His lungs felt tight, like he couldn't take in any air.

When there were six minutes and forty seconds left on the clock, Athol made it to the top and started crawling to meet the others, who were on the corner where the east wall ended and the southern one began.

"C'mon, guys!" Ewan urged Quentin and Frances, who climbed beside him. "We can do this!"

"Try…ing!" Quentin responded.

They were close. They were so very close. Quentin could see the edge of the ceiling, could practically touch it. Ewan already was. He gripped the edge and heaved himself up to the top. After some squirming, he reached it. He put out his hand, proffering it for the closest person, and Frances grabbed it wantonly. There was a lot of awkwardness in how he helped pull her up—several times his hands had nothing to grab except for the lower parts of her body, and twice her face went into his chest. But it worked. They were both at the top, and when they were, five minutes and thirty-five seconds remained. They quickly looped their hands around Quentin's rope and tugged at it together, sparing him further agony. At last, he flopped onto the peak. He felt smooth tile under him.

"Jesus, Mary, Joseph, and the Greek fucking gods, we're okay," Ewan huffed out.

Quentin laid on his back, a hand over his face. He laughed tears of exhaustion as one leg hung off the edge and the rest of his body was supported by the glass dome beside him.

"Hey!" Frances screamed, but to whom he didn't know. "Anything yet?!"

"Nothing!" Athol replied. "Absolutely nothing!"

"Get up and help us!" Marina shouted from the other side of the room.

"Shoot. Okay." Ewan jumped up carefully, so as to not go toppling over the edge. He unhooked the locks of the rope around his waist; Frances started doing the same, and Quentin shortly thereafter. Unencumbered by his support system, Ewan crawled in the direction toward the others.

"C'mon," Quentin muttered as he tried undoing the buckles around him.

"Quentin, what time do we have?!" someone yelled.

He looked to his watch. "Four minutes and fifty seconds!"

"Fuck!"

Frances rid herself of her rope and let it fall down the wall with everyone else's. She pointed to their right, where Ewan was. "Everyone went there, but we should head the other way," she said to Quentin. "There's no luck down there. They haven't found anything."

Quentin detached the rope from himself and followed after her. On all fours, they made it to the first corner of the west wall. He was crawling carefully, until Frances stopped short. "Is there something wrong?" he asked. He hated stopping. He strictly avoided looking over the edge of the thin platform while also trying not to look forward at her posterior.

He heard laughing. Then yelling. "Guys, I found something!" Frances was chuckling. "This bit is hollow here!" To Quentin, she spoke with a normal tone as she turned around to face him. "The equipment…it's here."

"Woah, careful," Quentin warned her, and she stopped moving. "What's hollow?"

Frances smacked down hard on a space of their makeshift floor. He saw that it wasn't of the same texture and smoothness as the rest of the ceiling, but was a more raised and pronounced pane that was aesthetically out of place on the faultless plain of rubber and tile. It was also a light-blue color, whereas the surface surrounding it was darker, more earth-toned. She punched into it with her elbow, and he joined her in the endeavor to break it. As they crumbled it, he looked around and saw that the others were barely at the corner of the south and east walls. They were running out of time. At once, Frances leaped to her feet and started kicking into the pane. It fractured even more. Quentin did the same as her, watching victoriously as it cracked.

The room shook. Rocks began shooting from the walls all over again. Quentin, in turn, teetered.

He fell.

"No!" Frances screeched. She knelt and grabbed his left hand before he could slip down, wrapping both of her sweaty palms around his.

Quentin's eyes wandered to his watch, and he saw that there were just three minutes and nine seconds left.

Frances's blistering, chalky fingers loosened. She dug her heels into the edge of the ceiling, where the glass of the dome was. "I…can't!"

Quentin made the mistake of looking down to the glass floor, to Saturn and the dark.

Frances sobbed. Her face was basked in starlight and her freckles drowned in a red flush. Spittle escaped her mouth and a surge of tears leaked out of her eyes.

"Pull, Frances!" Quentin begged, his face swelling. "Just pull!"

"I'm trying! I'm trying, Quentin, I'm trying!" And she was, she really was, but her arm was so bony and she was wincing and straining. She couldn't bring him up.

And then, out of nowhere, when there were two minutes and fifteen seconds left on the watch and Frances herself was nearly tipping off the edge no matter how deeply she squatted to stay in place, two spidery, pale hands crept around her sides and gripped Quentin's left hand. He didn't have to see the face of the helper to know who it was. He saw two, ebony strands of hair poking around Frances's hip and knew, instantly, that the person was Marina. She mimicked Frances's position, but then she rose to hunch over the other young woman. He didn't know how she had gotten there so fast, how she made it to them when she had just been searching with the others. But there she was, having mysteriously popped into the picture right when he and Frances desperately needed an extra hand. Marina gasped for air, all but growling. She lowered her hands and wrapped them around his elbow, gritting her teeth; he thought he could hear the two rows of bone scraping against each other. Frances yelled something over her shoulder. Marina didn't respond. Quentin's arm began to slip out of their hands. Until that moment, he'd never realized that Marina was as thin as Frances. It took hanging off the edge of what had once been the ceiling of a room for him to realize that he was dependent on two, tiny pairs of arms.

Through the wetness that poured down her face, Frances asked Marina, "Yank on three?!"

"One!" Marina grunted out by way of answering. "Two!"

" Three!" Marina and Frances counted together.

They pulled.

Something popped in Quentin's left arm.

He reeled from the agony of it, but he wasn't so distracted that he didn't notice the multiple pairs of hands all over him. Some belonged to Frances and Marina, another pair was from Ewan. He thought Athol was grabbing him to check on him, but it was only to read his watch; they had one minute and forty-five seconds left.

Jaymes and Mathias kicked the pane in on itself, until it gave out and the flimsy material went crashing down. The gap in the ground—the ceiling, that was—must not have been any more than a yard wide. "You're the skinny one," Mathias said, but, for the first time ever, his commentary on another's physique wasn't intended as an insult. Jaymes understood the implication, and he plunged himself into the gap.

Before Quentin crawled closer to the others, Frances lowered herself in front of him to see his mutilated arm. She gently took it into her hands. "Oh my god. We didn't do this to you, did we?"

"It's fine," Quentin said.

"Maybe not. We may need to climb again, Quentin." Frances took in a breath. There were no more tears in her eyes, but she seemed regretful. He didn't understand. "Okay…Okay…Here it goes. Just try not to freak out."

"Why?" Quentin asked.

Frances lifted his arm, held his forearm with her left hand and his elbow with her right. He mutely obeyed as she ran her soft fingers over his skin, but then she shed her gentleness and snapped his limb back into place. He mewled, bent over, and shed tears. "That's it," she said to him. "It's done. I promise, it's over."

"Jaymes! Anything?!" Marina asked.

Jaymes didn't directly respond to her, but he technically gave an answer to everyone. He was deep within the crevice Frances had discovered, and all that they saw of him was one of his hands and a glass-fronted helmet, from which there hung a string and a baggie, one which was synonymous to the shape and size of a teabag.

"What is that?!" Quentin asked, pointing to it with his healthier arm.

"There are suits in here too!" Jaymes alerted them.

"Well, hurry up!" Roxy berated him. "We're almost out of time!"

Mathias took the helmet out of Jaymes's grasp, and the unseen person's hand went slipping back into the crevice. Mathias plucked the bag away from the helmet, which tore the string in the process. From inside it, he retrieved a paper note that he held up for all to see.

"What's it say?!" Athol asked.

"Uh...'*To apply Grains...place firmly against walls between cavity and nano...nasopharynx.* '" Mathias looked up from the packet. "Whatever the fuck that is! What the fuck is this?!"

Frances left Quentin stooped on the ground. She squeezed her way between Marina and Ewan to see Mathias. "He means the nasal cavity!"

"He wants me to stick this shit up my nose?!"

An assembly line was initiated, with Jaymes tossing up helmets and suits, and Marina and Ewan catching them before distributing them to everyone else.

"Just do it!" Frances ordered. "What's even inside?!"

Mathias shook the baggie labeled GRAINS over his open palm. Two tiny, pea-sized, metallic beads fell into his hand. "What the fuck is this?!"

Frances looked encouraged by the sight. "It's probably an oxygen supplier! Go ahead! Put them inside your nose!"

The vibration of the walls returned. Everyone held the edges of the ceiling to keep still as they gingerly passed around the helmets and suits.

Roxy held the ground tight. "Quentin, how much time do we have?!"

"Thirty seconds!"

"Okay! Fuck! I'll do it!" Mathias gave in. With the pads of his fingers, he slid them up his nostrils. "They won't stick!"

The glass below started to crack. Marina's fallen equipment started to shake.

"It said the nasal cavity!" Frances instructed. "It needs to go as far back as your fingers can reach!"

"Okay!"

"Just one big push, Mathias!"

Mathias inhaled, and with the Grains on the tops of his index and middle fingers, he rammed them up his nose. His fingers flew out as quickly as they went in. "Ah! Shit! Fuck!"

"Does it hurt?!" Ewan asked.

"Like a bitch! Jaymes, gimme my suit!"

"I was right...I was right..." Frances said disbelievingly, having almost doubted herself. "Everyone, do the exact same!"

The rounds were made quickly. The Grains were put in place before anything else, just as Frances ordered. Mathias was right, they did hurt. It took Quentin three attempts before he successfully shoved the electronic specks up his nose, but after they were correctly lodged inside him, he was slightly comforted by the cool air that pumped into his system from those two pieces alone. Some others weren't as fortunate in their placement attempts, like Marina and Jaymes, who were donned in their suits but not their helmets, both still struggling to get the Grains to stick to their fingers in order to apply them.

"Ten seconds!" Quentin announced.

Ewan crammed himself into one of the pant legs of his suit. He threw his helmet on at the same time.

Mathias, fully wiggled into his uniform and protected by his fastened helmet, was already retying his rope and cords around his waist. "Later, pussies," he said. "I'm dipping." What no one knew until it was too late was that when he said he was "dipping," he meant it literally. He spread his arms out, and, in the nonchalant manner of a man who placed his unreserved trust in the ropes strung to him, he pitched himself backwards and went flying off the edge of the ceiling.

"Bitch. Bitch. Bitch," Quentin muttered as the zipper on the chest part of his suit stuck to his turtleneck.

Roxy put her helmet on and reached for her rope.

Jaymes whisked around. "Hey!" he called to Roxy. "Can you help me and Marina?! We can't get our Grains in!"

"Oh…Sorry, Jaymes! I'm just…I can't!" Roxy strapped the rope and cords around herself, and she went rappelling down after Mathias.

"She ditched us!" Jaymes exclaimed to Marina, who merely nodded in agreement.

They had five seconds.

Ewan and Athol left next.

"Marina! Apply it with the pads of your fingers!" Frances guided her. "There's a sticky side! Use that for application!"

Marina tried that. "Got it!" She lowered her helmet over her head.

One second was left.

Those who were less fortunate and remained at the top—Quentin, Frances, Jaymes, and Marina—were, by that point, fully clothed in their gear. Marina was the first of them to leave, seeing as how she was lacking the extra safety of a rope. Almost immediately after she started her descent, the other three strapped on their ropes, because the room shook again, and when it did, it made them so unstable that the thought of dawdling at that peak and delaying their climb any longer seemed foolish.

Quentin climbed slightly above Marina, since she had a head start. He was asking her about the Grains, about whether Patterson had ever mentioned them before. She didn't answer. She seemed distracted by the helmeted head of a peer below her—Roxy. One second Marina was climbing and listening to him. The next, she sent her booted foot down, kicking Roxy square on the head.

Quentin didn't know what to do. Girls had fought all the time throughout elementary, middle, and high school. But not like that. Not like the young woman who punted another's head, eliciting a horrific scream of fear as she fell, perhaps to her death, had Jaymes not reached out and grabbed her rope; Roxy clung to him for a few moments, catching her breath, until she was comfortable enough to detach from him and compose herself, solo on the wall.

It seemed that a single, genuine threat to a person's life was all it took to return the sadistic chamber to its previous state. In a few seconds, from the dome to the cracking floor, the unsettling, inescapable sea of blackness disappeared and was replaced by the same bland gymnasium and the children's rock wall at the unassuming height of twenty feet.

Quentin scrambled to the slippery floor, as did his teammates. Once they touched that real floor—no glass or puffing plaster in sight —Mathias fell onto his back and closed his eyes. Jaymes leaned against the once-formidable rock wall, heaving in air. Frances, Athol, Ewan, and Marina began extracting their Grains. Roxy was sitting on the ground, stock-still and her head plopped on her knees.

The door to the revived room swung upon. Patterson stormed in, and zooming behind him at his heels was a fretting Fatima. "You fell," Patterson worriedly said to the petrified girl on the floor. "Roxy, are you all right?"

She lifted her head. She looked terrible; her unkempt hair like a jumble of weeds; her face sticky and sappy from the wealth of sweat.

"Why did you fall?" Patterson questioned her.

Roxy glanced to Marina.

Frances followed the look. "You pushed her?" she asked.

Quentin knew the truth. He bit his tongue, though.

"That is ridiculous," Marina said. "I pushed no one. She was far too absorbed with herself to notice my foot hovering over her forehead."

"It didn't *hover*," Roxy snarled. "It plummeted into my skull."

"Well, it's no wonder you fell," Marina said. "You didn't even rappel correctly. You're not supposed to gently put your foot on the rocks, you're supposed to dig into them. No kidding you ended up the way you did."

"I didn't gently put my foot on anything!" Roxy insisted. "And unlike you, I know when people around me might need some help."

"Yes, you evidently do. You just don't do anything about it."

Patterson silently watched the exchange.

Quentin just stood there with the truth on his tongue, but his silence prolonged.

It was decided that the second division's environmental preparations were finished for the day.

21

Quentin shifted on his feet. He tried to compose himself as he stood before Patterson's desk, beside Marina. Patterson had asked Quentin if he was all right, and rather offhandedly, but the question nagged at him. He wasn't fine. After being saved by Frances and Marina, he felt emasculated. After watching Marina kick Roxy, he felt confounded.

As with all of their meetings, Patterson sat at his desk with his folded hands upon the surface of it as he looked up. On that occasion, he was in the midst of Quentin and Marina. Their appearances were starkly dissimilar to the last time they were gathered in Patterson's office, and in a most uncomely manner. Quentin's normally pale face was heated and red, and his hair of straggled waves had devolved into clumps of limp, sweat-sodden strings that hung in his eyes, making them itch. Marina was just as grim a sight. One side of her forehead was bruised from one of the projectile rocks, and the other side glowed—not attractively, but because of the sheen of sticky sweat that coated her. Her sunken face was thinned from the fatigue that dragged her skin down.

Patterson and Marina were staring at Quentin expectantly. He blinked himself back into the moment. "What?"

"Don't you agree?" Patterson asked.

"To what?"

"That it went more smoothly than one could have imagined?"

"What did?"

"EV Prep, Quentin."

"Yeah."

"Are you all right?" Patterson asked once more.

"Yeah. No, I'm good. Just tired."

"I see. That was to be expected. And yet, in spite of your immense fatigue, you and your teammates were astounding in your efforts today and should all be very proud of yourselves." Patterson moved his lower row of teeth to one side as if making to chew his upper lip, but he readjusted his mouth. "Regarding your efficiencies in teamwork..." He opened his palms. "I'm not going to say it was bad. It was, as I said, smoother than I could have imagined. Marina, I have to applaud you for your miraculously fast-paced approach to saving Quentin despite being all the way on the other side of the room."

"He's a vital component," Marina said.

"And you would do it again," Patterson finished the sentence for her. "I'm glad I can trust you on that. To be an advisor is to guide your captain. His safety is in your hands. Good job today."

Strategic basis or not, she did save my life, Quentin mused.

Patterson coughed. "Now, look, I must ask, Marina...And not because I don't trust you...On the contrary, I find you very trustworthy. I want to establish that fact. But you see, the thing is...I wouldn't be much of a commanding officer if I didn't ask whether or not you had any idea about how Roxy maneuvered so horribly wrong at the end."

"I can only assume it was from her own inattentiveness," Marina said levelly. "It was a stressful scene. Odds were that one of us would lose balance."

"Except for you? The one who was cordless?"

"I felt optimal."

Patterson nodded. He rose off his chair. "I'm not making any presumptions, nor am I placing any blame on you," he disclaimed, "but, Marina, I want us to be honest with one another. Please don't take any offense when I ask, did you kick Roxy?"

Marina blinked. Quentin saw only placidity on her face. "I did not kick Roxy."

"Neither intentionally nor accidentally?"

"Neither intentionally nor accidentally."

Before he could restrain himself, Quentin said, "I was there, next to her."

"Yes, I am aware," Patterson said.

"I would've seen her kick Roxy. I was right next to Marina the whole time."

"Yes, Quentin."

"Right, right. You were watching us the whole time."

"That, indeed."

Quentin bit his lip.

"Quentin, teamwork is one thing," Patterson said, "but loyalty is another. Marina saving your life should have no impact on this discussion."

"I—It doesn't."

"So you saw nothing of a kick? Or, say, the thrust of a foot?"

Quentin shook his head.

Patterson turned back to Marina. "And you, similarly, committed no action that would provoke rightful suspicion?" When he was met with a subsequent nod, he sighed. "Very well then. Sleep well, both of you. Rest up."

When he and Marina left the office, Quentin closed the door behind them and nearly gagged out a breath.

"Are you ever not having a panic attack?" Marina asked.

"How about you be a little grateful, okay?" Quentin shot back. "I just saved you."

"You didn't have to," Marina said as they started down the corridor, side by side.

Annoyed, Quentin scratched his forehead with his knuckles. "Look, you and I aren't exactly what one would call ideal partners, okay? So you saving me kinda hit me as some type of grand gesture and I just...I freaked out back there."

"It wasn't a grand gesture. I was doing my job. If anything, you made us look really suspicious."

"I do not need your commentary right now." Quentin stopped walking, and she did too. "What I need is an answer."

Marina's small, probing eyes darted side to side. "To what?"

"Gee, I dunno. Maybe the fact that you kicked our teammate off an enormous rock wall in plain sight. Right next to me. And with Patterson watching. Which made me, just now, look like either a complete dumbass or a total liar for saying that I saw nothing of you kicking Roxy."

"No one told you to do that."

Quentin's hands held his hips. "Why'd you do it?"

"My foot barely grazed her."

"You pushed it down."

"It was an accident."

"Bullshit."

"Look at you," Marina said with fake reverence, "caring about your teammates all of a sudden."

"Like you care."

"Exactly," Marina said. "I don't. And you were absent from anything mission-related for over eight months before Casey coerced you into a meeting, so get off your high horse and stop pretending like you genuinely care that I kicked Roxy off a wall."

"Hey, me not liking the mission has nothing to do with the fact that Roxy is a sweet and innocent girl who didn't deserve that. You are so petty. You've been nothing but mean to her since you met her. Why? Is it because she's, like, a really attractive girl and you feel intimidated? Is that what this is?"

"Do you genuinely believe that was my reason, Quentin? If that were the case, since every guy on this ship has had a thing for Frances at some point in his life, why didn't I kick her off instead? If we're really going to talk pettiness, let's take the gloves off and actually do this."

"Well…" Quentin struggled to find the words to counter her. "You…"

Marina huffed. She looked even more tired than she did in Patterson's office. "Wow. Go ahead. Finalize your monologue on rationalizing my jealousy for Roxy. Do your thing. I'm going to take a shower." Quentin mutely watched as she took several strides forward and left him alone in the corridor.

When he went to the men's lavatory to wash up, he spent over an hour under the steaming water, internally scolding himself for his behavior in Patterson's office. If anything, it served to solidify Quentin's hatred for Marina. Why did she always have to make things so difficult? Why did they have to be paired together? His shower was stressful; unlike everyone else's, it didn't relax him.

It was three o'clock in the afternoon when he finished washing. He went to find food and hopefully speak with someone who wasn't Marina or Patterson, but he was met with complete silence. Their home was quiet, like it was the dead of night; even the nighttime lighting had been activated.

"One went to sleep an hour ago," Fatima informed him. There was only her, in the foyer by herself, drawing on sheets of paper, which she had girding her body as she sat on the floor. True to her word, many of the older occupants were nowhere to be seen. "Frances went to sleep. I think everyone from Two did. Casey set the ship to night mode, but it's the middle of the day. Don't you think that's weird?"

"We're all very tired," Quentin told her.

"Are you going to sleep too?"

"Probably. I think I'll go watch a movie or something first, though. Care to join?"

Fatima shook her head. "No, thank you. I'm good here."

Quentin waved, and proceeded to the third-floor living room. He hoped there wouldn't be anyone else inside. He could use some solitude after the hectic morning, but when he lingered at the doorway, he heard voices on the other side of the barrier.

"…it's not like we didn't just find something you're good at…" He recognized Casey's voice.

"What's that supposed to mean?" the other person asked. It was Terry.

"No…I didn't…Terry, I didn't mean it like that. But you can't pretend like you didn't just tune out all of last year."

"I did not tune out."

"It's okay that you did. I understand. After everything—"

"So you pity me? Is that what's going on here? You're glad that I can finally fit into the mold of being the physical, dumb grunt? I'm not an idiot, you know. I was a straight-A student back home. I don't deserve this."

"That's not what I'm saying. I know you're smart, I just hated to see you struggling last year. Why can't you be happy that we found something perfectly fit for you? Something you can put your superior athleticism toward, now that football is out of the picture."

Quentin felt dirty standing outside that room, beside the door. Yet he couldn't stop himself from infringing on their privacy.

Terry released a humorless laugh. "I'm nothing without football, huh? Look, I'm sorry we're not all perfect scientists-in-the-making who can just blend into Patterson's little world of astrophysics and stuff. I mean, you're essentially just lumping me into the group of people like Hanson."

Quentin's mouth dried. A breath caught in his throat.

"I did not say you're like Quentin," Casey said fiercely. "I'm glad that you got over your depression is all."

"I wasn't depressed. I was angry. I still am. Fuck this place. And Patterson too, for that matter. I'm glad you're settled in here. I'm happy for you, but it's not for me. Or Chris."

"Is this Oscar's influence again?"

Terry emitted another dry laugh. "Nice to know you don't even believe that I can think for myself anymore. You know what? Speaking of influence, I think Patterson's getting to you."

"Terry…"

Quentin stepped back into the middle of the hallway. He quickly fled the scene, wary that either of the cousins might angrily tromp out of the room once their arguing came to a peak. As usual, he tried walking off his problems, to avoid taking it personally that Terry thought so little of him. But Casey…Quentin thought that if they weren't friends, then they were at least trusting in one another's capabilities. He wasn't insulted, but he was discouraged. Is that how everyone thought of him when they assumed he wasn't listening? Was he really pathetic in their eyes? He listened to some music and walked all the upper floors, until an hour later, he made his way back to that same living room, which was finally empty. He didn't even bother turning on the television to distract himself from the disheartening musings that played in his head like an endless loop. Utterly exhausted and a little lonely, he shut off the lights, threw himself down onto a couch, and dozed off.

He slept for ten, undisturbed hours. His lethargy that day was more toiling than any of his sleep-deprived school mornings back home had ever been. The physical demands, combined with the mental hits, sedated him deeply. There was no rolling over. He never woke for water or to relieve himself. He didn't even snore. For the first time in a year, his sleep was long and restful.

At two o'clock in the morning, his languishing came to an end when a visitor to the room sat not on his couch, but directly on him. He flinched awake. He was sore, so sore, from the hours of EV Prep, and the applied pressure of that person's body weight shot pains through his torso. He swung his arms out and shot upright.

The interlocutor, whose face was indistinguishable in the dark room, squalled and bounced off him. "Who the—?!" they burst out. "Whoa!" They fell to the ground.

The lights turned on.

Quentin, gasping, turned to see that the person on the floor was Connor. "Oh, shit. I'm sorry, Quentin," a stunned Connor apologized without delay. "It's just me. Sorry, dude."

Quentin rubbed his forehead. "It's okay…Damn."

He detected movement by the doorway. Jaymes was there with a hand on the light switch and a smug pull to his lips.

Connor stood up. "Couldn't have turned that on before we came in here?"

"Not all of us are so specially unaware," Jaymes replied as he entered the room. He gave his head a backwards bounce, letting his glasses go higher up his nose. "My bad for assuming that you weren't."

Quentin grunted as he rubbed the sleep from his eyes, his fingertips doing circles over his closed lids. "What time is it?" he asked, his voice cracking.

"Two," Connor said. "In the morning." He sprawled himself on the couch adjacent to Quentin's. "A bunch of us got up to grab some food. Look's like we're on a night schedule now."

Jaymes harrumphed. "Says you, but Casey just set it back to normal." He went to the only other unoccupied couch and plopped himself upon it lengthwise; his long legs dangled over an armrest.

"Did she really?" Connor asked. "How are we supposed to adjust now?"

"Oh, hey, I think the remote's under one of my cushions," Quentin said to them.

"We weren't coming here to watch anything," Jaymes said. "We just wanted a place to hide out from people."

"People," Quentin said. His reason for being in that room was the same as theirs, it seemed.

"Library's full," Jaymes said with chagrin, "arcade's busy, and the bedrooms…We spent all day there, it would be weird to go back now."

"I get that."

Connor hummed. "It's nice to avoid the drama, what with the rumor mill going off in your group. What happened, anyway?"

Quentin yawned. "Marina…" He yawned again. "Roxy claims Marina kicked her off the wall during EV Prep."

"Everyone's convinced of it," Jaymes said. "I'm not. Marina's strange, but she's not emotional or violent, more like perpetually impatient or something. She likes her space. I can't see her actively seeking out fighting someone."

"Can't see it either," Connor agreed.

"And I saw nothing," Quentin told them untruthfully.

"Hang on there." Connor tilted his head off the side of his couch to see Jaymes. "You turned twenty-one this week, didn't you?"

"That, I did," Jaymes confirmed.

"No shit."

"None."

"2048, man" Connor said half disbelievingly, half frightened. "Where do you think we'd all be, if we were back home?"

"If we were this age and back home?" Jaymes asked. "That's too surreal to think about."

The thought made Quentin shiver.

"Let's see," Jaymes said, "I was already eighteen when I was kidnapped. I hadn't yet decided on which college, but...Jesus. I'd be graduating next year. From college."

"What were you thinking of being?" Quentin asked.

"Social worker."

Connor turned his head to Jaymes's direction again. "Really? You?"

"Yeah. I wanted to teach sign language or art therapy. Or both. What about you?"

"I was thinking something in finance," Connor answered.

Jaymes snorted. "You didn't need to tell us that."

"Hey—"

Jaymes held up a hand. "You were *such* a prick back home."

"What are you saying, that people who work in finance are pricks?"

"No," Jaymes said, "just the people like you who work in finance." He leaned his head back. "What about you Quentin? What were you thinking?"

"Computer sciences, software engineering track. That area."

"I'll bet you guys a hundred dollars," Connor said, "that if we were to turn this ship around right now, Chris would still go on to work in sales."

Jaymes laughed. "Oh, no question. Now, I think in the case of Ewan—"

A blaring sound rang throughout the room. It was one loud, foul screech followed by another, then another. It came from the red-bulbed emergency alarm which was blinking repeatedly, in the back, by the doorway. Quentin covered his ears. They were always so sensitive, and although it had been years since his last episode of what he once thought was tinnitus, the piercing volume of the interrupting sound still stung; he wondered if there would ever be a time when they weren't tender. Lifting his hand from his right ear, he heard Connor telling them to make for the foyer.

Due to the dimness of the nighttime setting for the hallway lighting, running downstairs was heavily burdened by staggers into tables and corner walls. A mishap that was more embarrassing than it was painful involved Quentin running face-first into a tall plant. He and Connor floundered into various objects. Jaymes was more adroit than them, seamless in his running.

The foyer was crowded. As the three of them shuffled their way down one of the wide staircases, Quentin looked through the glass under his feet, and the first thing he saw was Ewan crouched down in front of Fatima, covering her ears with his hands as she cringed at the sound of the alarm. Except for Patterson, Frances, and Natalie, Quentin tallied that everyone else was present.

At the bottom of the staircase, Chris greeted the three. "Morning," he said in a half-asleep state. He brushed a crumble of eye wax off his face.

Connor tried getting Casey's attention, but she couldn't hear him over the incessant alarm. *"Damnit,"* he muttered. "Chris, where's Patterson?"

"Not here," someone else—Oscar—said.

"Neither is Frances," Quentin said without thinking.

Connor slowly turned his head back, an eyebrow arched high up his forehead.

"And Natalie," Quentin rushed out.

The alarm stopped screeching, and Quentin heard footfalls coming from his right-hand side, from one of the nearby corridors. He tapped Connor's arm and motioned to that particular wing, which they looked upon with anticipation. Heads collectively turned to see a colorless Patterson emerging. Until that night, Quentin had never seen Patterson move so fast. The way he strode out with pronounced steps made the loose material of his corduroy pants flare and flap as he walked. His fluffy, green sweater was soaked with sweat. His face was red. Frances and Natalie followed behind him, the former holding two binders and the latter cleaning her hands with an antiseptic wipe. They struggled to keep up with him.

Connor slid his hands into his pockets. "Patterson? Is everything all right?"

Patterson halted when he reached the middle of the foyer. His expression was so strained, it was almost as though he had to convince himself to stop moving. He briefly turned and shot a look to the young women behind him, who must have been well-versed in the translation of what his eyes were trying to convey, because they immediately parted ways; Frances weaved around everyone to climb upstairs; Natalie pressed the button of the elevator door and hurried inside as soon as it opened.

Patterson addressed all the others. "I'm…" he said, and then he stopped.

"Patterson?" Casey asked, stepping closer. "Can you speak up?"

Patterson swept several fingers through his hair. "Come," he said to everyone, motioning for them to close in one him. "Come here, all of you." Feet scraped forward. Ears honed in on his every word. "We're on our own," he said. "We…" His breath caught. "We're on… on our own. I went to wake them, to bring them back to us…

They're…" He paled. "They're gone. They're all gone." His eyes frantically focused from one person to the next, from Derek to Fatima, from Fatima to Ivy, from Ivy to Roxy. "They're gone. Dead."

Casey stepped into Patterson's space. She put a hand on the underside of his elbow. "Who? Who is gone?"

Patterson withdrew from the crowd and drifted to the bottom of a staircase, where he sat on one of the lowest steps. He scratched the space between his eyebrows. "I must be frank with you," he said to all of them. His hands were wound together with the lower half of his face hidden behind them. "It's one of the many things I owe you: honesty." He closed his eyes and opened them after several beats, gathering more composure in order to speak.

"What's going on?" Connor pressed. He advanced to the staircase and stood beside the railing. "Why did you call us here in the middle of the night?"

"Because they're gone, Connor."

"Who is? Who's gone?"

Patterson's eyes were glazed with tears that never fell. "My friends," he said, and then again, "my friends. My colleagues. Some from work. Some from school. Some from happenstance. Some from the draft. The ones who were meant to train you, to teach you. They're all gone."

"How do you mean?" Connor asked.

Quentin's left pinky twitched against his thigh.

"I went downstairs to check on them," Patterson said, his eyes hollow and his voice crisp. "I had Natalie and Frances with me. We were going to bring them back from their sleep. Their vitals were normal, or so it said so on the monitors. But they…they weren't normal. Not when we opened the chambers. They're gone," he repeated himself.

Connor ground his teeth. "How are they *gone*, Patterson?"

Patterson shook his head. "By God, if I don't figure it out myself...I have to know..."

Terry rolled his jaw. "An entire group of people doesn't just die, Patterson. That was our one hope."

Patterson swiped his hands over his face. He rubbed his chin, his forehead, his cheeks—anything he could feel to center himself. "We've wasted too much time," he said. "Earlier, when I was planning...and when they were alive...I thought...But no...Now, we can't waste any more time. You're all adults now. You're not children anymore. And we're alone. For the first time, we are truly alone. You have to be the adults."

"Be the adults?" Casey recited. "How can you expect us to go forward with this when you don't even know why the real adults are dead?!"

Patterson closed his eyes again. "There is no one else. Only us."

A formerly bleary, inattentive Derek became sharpened by the conversation. He slapped his hands against each other. "Great. So what do we do?"

Patterson didn't respond.

"What is your plan, Patterson?" Casey asked.

The man blinked. He massaged his forehead. "There's only one option."

Quentin's fingers continued to twitch.

Patterson stood up. He paced from the bottom of the staircase to the middle of the foyer. "If we really are alone and my colleagues are gone, then there is only one thing we can do." He covered his mouth with his palm before letting it slide back down to his side. "We have to reach our destination faster...and go very soon."

"Titania?" Athol asked in a tiny, shaky voice. "But that's... Patterson, that's impossible. We'd have to pass through the belt at full speed to—"

The expression on Patterson's face was grave, downcast.

"No," Amber said from the front of the circle. "No, no...not soon."

"Patterson, we've just started training!" Athol screamed.

"You can't...We can't..." Amber started. She was already fully in tears. "We're not experts! I'm not a pilot! I am not ready!"

Patterson walked right up to her. He planted gentle hands on her shoulders and lowered his head to look straight into her rapidly blinking eyes. "And time will do little to change that, Amber," he said. "All it will do is age us—me, especially. But we must go forward. You must learn fast while you can, while I'm still sound enough to guide you." He reached for Athol's forearm, and though he couldn't reach Oscar as well, Patterson made sure to lock eyes with him during that moment. "My pilots, we can do this."

"We can't," Athol said. "Patterson, we're new to everything. We're not ready."

"You weren't ready for your environmental screenings either, but both of your groups did exceptionally."

Casey shook her head. "That was different, it was a *screening!*"

Oscar turned on his heel. He was out of the foyer before Quentin could even register the fact that he was walking away.

"Oscar, get back here," Connor said. He tried appealing to Casey to help him in pulling back their departing peer, but she was speechless, gazing at the floor and looking like she was about to punch the shiny marble.

"Patterson," Athol continued, "we can't."

Amber was dry-heaving, and Ivy scampered to Amber and brought her into her arms. *"Sh...Shhh..."*

"We are not prepared for this," Connor insisted.

"I never said we would be perfectly prepared," Patterson acknowledged. "But we have to do it. Against greater odds..." He sighed. "There's no other option. Either we fly at our current pace and safely arrive to Titania years from now, when you are older and the mystery beings have picked off more of our neighbors, or we go now...now, while you are all young. The sooner our flight, the faster our arrival."

"How long?" Ewan asked.

Patterson blinked fast.

"How long do we have?" Casey questioned him.

Patterson swallowed, and Quentin heard the saliva slipping down his throat. "I'm giving you until February 2nd," he said.

22

The rest of January was bound to be horrendous. It was a shame that after their full year of emotional healing, it all came undone with a single night's discovery. Life had been going a little too well—a cataclysm of some sort was bound to happen. Quentin thought he finally understood that peace was a fragile thing.

It had been made clear to him during the early hours of the 2nd that Patterson placed immense hope and trust in his colleagues, but that he never once asked himself if he could live without them. *Why?* Quentin thought. *Why did he never ask that question?* But, then again, could one have even expected the conundrum that was theirs? Quentin didn't think he could have. He was a cynic, but even he hadn't imagined a reality in which his last vessels of expertise and insight would somehow slip from his reach.

Later in the day, on the 2nd, Patterson did little to abate the fresh anxieties. For the first time since Quentin met the man, he bore neither pity nor sensitivity for his pupils. Perhaps it was the sudden demise of his lifelong friends or the utter horror of having to prolong his role as the sole guide without anyone wiser to turn to, but he was finally, unabashedly, authoritative. He was adamant that the de facto pilots train from five in the morning to five in the afternoon every day, for six of the seven days per week. He told the captains that they, as well as anyone else who wasn't a pilot, were to immediately declutter the ship, locating all loose items, be they books, linens, or culinary supplies, and store them in the foyer until they were allowed disposal into the cargo hold in the basement.

"That's it for now," Patterson said during his meeting with Quentin and Casey.

"Don't you think five to five is too much for our pilots?" Casey questioned. "They're so new to it. Even if it's just simula—"

"It's not just simulations," Patterson said, his mouth rigidly set. "It's pod dispatches, pod returns, and temporary pod flights in lieu of the actual shuttles. Simulations are not the only thing. But they have no choice. We have no choice. If we want to make it through that belt next month, we have to advance."

"But—"

"Dismissed."

Casey was taken aback, insulted by Patterson's terse delivery. She nodded her head and departed his office with Quentin, who was staving off a jarring migraine.

"I don't know what to do," Casey lamented to Quentin. "How are we supposed to do this? *How?* A month? Quentin, we aren't ready for this. He's overshooting his expectations. If we force them to do this, we'll…we'll…"

Quentin wanted to tell her to relax, to calm down and stop freaking him out on top of his preexisting stress, but he couldn't get a word out. As he listened to her, his headache became murderous.

"I just…" Casey sobbed, but no tears escaped her. "I need to be alone."

"What about our pilots?"

Casey looked like she was going to break down. He thought she looked younger, like she was sixteen all over again. "Can you give them the news?" she asked him. "Quentin, I...I need to sleep. I need to go get some sleep."

"Okay," Quentin said. "Go ahead. I'll tell them."

Casey left him.

Quentin rubbed his pounding head.

A week passed, which brought the calendar to the 10th of January, and the migraines became a regular condition. They were grating in the day, especially when Quentin would perch himself upon a library stool and load books into cardboard boxes for hours on end, but they were nearly unbearable during the nights. Sleep was difficult. When he could sleep, he suffered nightmares and woke with cold sweats, panting into the blackness of his bedroom, pretending not to notice the outdoor darkness beyond his bedside window. When he couldn't fall asleep again, the migraines intensified. It was a vicious circle.

On the 10th, he asked Frances if there was anything she could do to remedy his situation. Her hair was longer by 2048, and it hung over her face as she glared toward him. "Quentin, look around," she said. "There isn't a single person getting a good night's sleep right now." She glanced to the array of medicine selections lined along the walls of the infirmary. "I'm not going to prescribe you something you don't need." It was the last thing he wanted to hear, but he accepted her honest response and chose not to pursue the matter further.

Through the labors of his days, he took nonprescription painkillers and drank plenty of water. Sometimes he felt like he was going to faint. He asked Jaymes and Fatima if they were experiencing anything similar, in case the severity of the pain had anything to do with the special condition of being one of the selected subjects, but they both denied experiencing any headaches. *So,* Quentin thought, *it's just me.*

He nearly pitied himself. Nearly. But there were things he witnessed that tore his heart apart and made him rethink his sympathy for himself. When he couldn't sleep and attempted strolling his troubles away during the nighttime hours, that was when he often saw Amber. Whether she ever noticed him was a mystery he didn't feel the need to unravel, because the important thing was that he saw her. She would pace alone, in her sleep shorts and humungous tee-shirts. She sat in rooms by herself, the lights turned off, and she would stare into the nothingness of the walls as those red locks of hers drooped in front of her face. There were nights when he spotted her in the kitchen, binge-eating the way Ivy had once done, in 2047. Seeing Amber humbled him. It reminded him that his misfortunes were nothing like hers. He couldn't imagine how she was feeling, as the weight of everyone's lives was placed upon her shoulders, and with time now working against them—against her.

Quentin rubbed his temples. The darkness outdoors, made visible by the transparent walls of the observatory, loomed ominously on all sides of him. Looking at it was unavoidable. He wanted to run out of the room.

Casey and Athol were inspecting their barely developed BDP models. To Quentin's surprise, Derek was in the room with them.

And then Derek said, unexpectedly, "We should turn this ship around."

Casey slowly lifted her head.

"If we turn it around," Derek said, "that's two, maybe three, years until we're back home. There are plenty of scientists there who could finish this project for us. Are we really going to risk a ten-year wait to meet a group of people we know nothing about?"

"They're the best and brightest," Casey said. "Many were volunteers. Yes, there are great scientists back home, but the best chose to leave. And that's where we're headed. To them."

Derek picked an eraser off the work table and started turning it between his fingers. "You would risk years of ours and our home's safety for one group of people?"

"Patterson thinks it's best."

"And look where we are now because of one man's singular vision. Couldn't even keep his own friends alive. I say we turn this thing around at full speed and get home as fast as we can. Maybe we can even get there a year earlier."

Athol scoffed. "Became a strategist overnight, did you? What do you want?"

"I already said it. I'm being frank with a pilot and our captains. Do not do this."

"It's not like we have a choice," Casey said, regretful.

"Of course we do," Derek insisted.

Athol sighed. "No, we don't. We're going to be on autopilot, and that program only allows us enough manual control to steer thousands of miles off course to avoid obstacles while in motion. It doesn't allow for any degree of backward movement. Besides, your plan of running home at full speed wouldn't work, because full speed has a time throttle. The ship is programmed to only allow two weeks at full speed every six months. Clearly, they planned well to avoid rogue moves like the one you're suggesting. It's designed to protect us from ourselves. It wouldn't work."

Derek tossed the eraser into the air before letting it fall back into his palm. He did it a second time. "Yes, it would," he said. "Oscar agrees with me. Apparently, there's some way to bypass—"

"Derek, shut up!" Athol snapped.

Quentin and Casey tensed up.

Derek ran the nail of his thumb over the eraser. "I'm just saying."

By the 13th of January, the foyer was overloaded with boxed goods and errant furniture, but there remained plethoras of untouched items on the upper floors. On one rare occasion when Patterson emerged during the daytime hours, Quentin and Marina cornered him about the overgrowth of items and how it was impossible to maneuver around the horde.

"Shouldn't we load this into the cargo hold now?" Quentin asked.

"Not yet," Patterson said.

"But this area's getting full. Are we really just going to put it all downstairs at the last minute?"

"Yes," Patterson maintained. He didn't look at Quentin when he spoke. Patterson examined one end of the foyer to the next, peeking over piled tables and pyramids of cardboard and metal boxes that overflowed with miscellanies of contents, like baskets of pillows, coffee tables, and an arcade game with a backup supply of men's shampoo piled atop it. Quentin followed Patterson's eyes, which appeared to be scanning for someone, as if to ensure that the three of them were alone. "I don't want anyone in the cargo hold except for you two, and Casey and Connor," he said. "No one else."

"You mean for us to bring all of this downstairs on our own?" Marina asked.

"You are not alone. There's four of you."

"There's eighteen of everyone," Marina pointed out.

"Only myself, captains, and their advisors are currently permitted into that cargo hold, Miss Gustavsson. No one else. Do not question this. Not for now, at least. Not until I've figured out how and why my colleagues are dead."

Marina looked like she unequivocally understood him.

Quentin, on the other hand, did not. When Patterson left, Quentin gave Marina a quizzical look.

But, "Don't be a moron," was all she said.

The nightmares were always about Lucas, and the cold sweats that followed were sticky and uncomfortable. When Quentin was asleep, it was never for long—he was too haunted. When he was awake, the migraines were heightened, since his insomnia very clearly fed the ailment. Sometimes he wondered if his sleeplessness stemmed from his anxieties about their hastened flight or if they were borne from another bout of depression that was developed by his renewed futility and irrelevance. Once again, he didn't know the answer. He also didn't want to know it. But whatever it was, it took a toll on him.

Every night, he roamed the hallways. He knew them by heart, even with his eyes closed. Sometimes in his aimless journeys, his throat felt tighter, like he couldn't take in any air. There were a few times when he swore he couldn't breathe.

Natalie, like Frances, was initially unfazed by his complaints of insomnia. It was only when he mentioned choking on air that she submitted and prescribed him a bottle of pills. "To help you sleep," she said. "If this happens again, come back immediately. Just like tonight."

It was the 18th of January, precisely fifteen days away from their extended flight, when Ewan and Oscar engaged in their very own altercation. Ewan was chasing after Oscar, who was stomping out of the foyer elevator. At that moment, Quentin, Casey, and Connor were speaking among themselves after dropping off some cabinetry and table decor into the ever-growing pile. They stopped short at the disturbance.

"What the hell was that?!" Ewan thundered. He grabbed Oscar's shoulder and spun the shorter, trainee pilot around. "You left me mid-tilt!"

"And if Athol passes out or something?" Oscar responded. "You'd have to do it on your own, anyway."

"You purposely tilted us. You were not trying to help me for training purposes."

"I didn't purposely do anything."

"Load of shit, asshole. We both know for a fact that you've been deliberately flunking your tests since the announcement was made."

"Fuck it. Report me, then."

"You can flunk all you want, but that doesn't change the fact that the trajectory is set and we launch at the end of the month!"

Oscar brushed Ewan's hand off his shoulder and stomped away a second time. The heaviness of his boots pounded into the marble and released a clamor that maintained its distinctive volume even after he abandoned the area. Ewan didn't chase him down a second time. He just scowled while the blue of his eyes shrank against the abrupt enlargement of his black pupils.

"I'll go talk to him," Connor said, referring to Oscar. "He needs to get his shit together. We need a plan."

"Oh, he has a plan all right," Ewan said.

"Do you think—?" Quentin began to ask.

"Yes, Quentin, I do," Ewan said. "I very well do."

Quentin never took his pills. For so long, he yearned for them, but once he received them, he couldn't bring himself to swallow a single one. He wanted to, but it would have felt like a misdeed, as he considered himself the last person deserving of the treatment.

The pilots had it so much worse. Athol's loquacity vanished. Ewan's blitheness was replaced by a seething undercurrent that threatened to burst into outright rage at the slightest annoyance. Oscar became a bitter, vengeful version of the happy, energized person he once was. Amber, like Quentin, transformed into a raging and restless insomniac. But unlike Quentin, Amber didn't seem to be receiving any aid. It made him wonder, *Why am I deserving? Why did Natalie give me something, but not Amber?* More than a few times, he thought of approaching her and gifting the bottle of untouched pills, but then he remembered that the bottle's label listed brain fog as a common side effect. He rationalized that he couldn't share it with her for the sake of her mental clarity during her training. He didn't want to be the cause of her missing anything vital to flight safety.

"I want him kept away from the pilots," Casey said to Terry one day. She was talking about Derek. "Quentin, you agree with me, don't you?"

Quentin awkwardly played with his bowl of cereal, twirling his spoon around and watching as the flaky food became squishy in the pool of milk. "Well, I don't have much of an opinion," he said.

"Why do you want Derek kept away from them?" Terry asked his cousin. He traced the top of his glass cup with his index finger.

"Because of the crap he spews," Casey said. "Don't pretend like you haven't heard it."

Terry pushed the glass aside. "I'll be honest, Case, I have to agree with him."

Casey looked scandalized. "What?"

"It's not too late to turn around. We can do it if we get the other pilots to agree."

Quentin didn't say anything.

"Do you think that's what your mom and dad would have wanted?" Casey asked. "After everything they sacrificed for us?"

"For us?" Terry asked, incredulous. "Not for us. For *him*. For Patterson and all the delusional folk like him. He's exploiting your trust right now, making you feel like your little project will come to life one day with the help of those Titan people."

"Titania," Casey corrected him.

"Titania, Titan…I don't care. That guy just wants to hog your intelligence for his own cause and has never once looked in the mirror and wondered if you'd be better off somewhere else." Terry's left hand balled up into a fist. "And the same goes for Mom and Dad."

"You think they exploited me?"

"I do. Fuck them."

Quentin squirmed. He was no longer the spectator of a mission-related conversation, but a family affair.

At three-thirty in the morning, on the grim day of January 20th, Quentin heard retching coming from the second-floor women's lavatory. He rapped on the door with his knuckles. "Hello?" he called. "Is everything okay?"

"I'm…m'kay. I'm fine," someone struggled back.

Before he could stop himself, Quentin said, "I'm…I'm coming in." He didn't know why he said it. Was he that lonely? He wanted to act like he didn't just say what he did, but it was too late. If he left at that point, it would have made him look negligent and two-faced, and maybe even selfish.

He wasn't met with any objection, so he flattened his hand against the door and pushed it forward, into the dark room, where only a slight bit of light from the hallway peeked in. The nearest stall was open, and a girl was sitting on the floor beside the toilet, one arm upon its open seat; the unsanitary nature of it made him recoil.

"Amber?" Quentin asked. He had to squint to make out her face in the dark.

Amber sniffled. "I've been doing this a lot lately, vomiting" she said, "Don't worry."

Quentin squatted down beside her.

"Sorry," Amber murmured when she saw that he was sitting on scraps of toilet paper.

Quentin pointed to her midsection. "You're not, like, pregnant are you? I won't tell…or judge."

"No, no." Amber allowed herself a laugh at his guess. "I ate too much, that's it."

"Again," Quentin blurted.

Amber went still. Quentin was about to shamefully admit that he had been silently watching her misery all month, but then, behind her shroud of hair, her face grew sad as she watched him look down; next to her limp legs, he spotted a prescription pill bottle.

"Insomnia drugs?" Quentin asked. "Natalie gave me some too."

"No." Amber sniffled again. "They're…" She couldn't stop sniffing. Her arm dropped listlessly from the toilet seat. "They're amphetamines."

Quentin stayed quiet. It was what he did best.

"I…" Amber wiped her nose with the back of her sleeve. "I don't have an attention deficit disorder or anything. It's only that I…I…need to be….I need to be perfect. I want to be aware of everything when we're out there, during training. We've been dislodging pods from the ship, flying them for hours. I…" She wiped a tear from under her right eye. "Just explaining this makes me feel pathetic, Quentin. I just…We need to be perfect, right? Because if we're not perfect, we'll…we'll kill us all. And Oscar's not stepping up to the plate, so…" She cried harder, letting out tiny teardrops that slid down her freckly cheeks. "I don't want to kill anyone."

"You're not going to," Quentin said confidently. He didn't know where his newfound conviction came from or why he never used it with himself, but he miraculously found his voice for it in that moment. "I've seen how hard you work," he said. "You know this stuff. Your results are fantastic, Patterson says so. But it's also true that you're overworking yourself."

"Quentin, if I mess up—"

"It's on autopilot. It's already doing half the work for you." Quentin frowned. "How often are you taking these?" he asked, pointing to the bottle on the floor.

"Twice a day. Ivy said she used them to get through finals back home. She would buy them through Derek."

So that's the origin of her boundless energy, Quentin thought.

Amber wiped her eyes.

"I think you should stop taking these," Quentin said.

"But if—"

"I know you haven't been sleeping lately. I know they've wired you up enough that you're overeating but not gaining any weight. And, not to be that person, but you just told me some incriminating stuff that could land you in some serious trouble with Patterson."

Amber sniffed.

Here goes nothing, Quentin thought. "But," he said more softly, "I won't leave you stranded without something to help." He withdrew his own prescription bottle from a pocket of his sweatpants.

"These are some pretty weak sedatives, but they'll work well enough. I'm supposed to take them a couple nights a week, but I figured that I'm the last person who needs them, since I'm not training like all of you." He dropped the bottle from his wiry, left hand and placed it in one of her palms. She didn't close her fingers around it. "I want you to promise me that you'll take them," he said. "There's nothing better for your head than a good night's sleep."

Amber closed her fingers around the bottle.

"You should know that one of the side effects is brain fog, though," Quentin warned. "Try to only use them on the bad nights. But I wouldn't be too wary. It's better than…"

"Being a speed addict?" Amber simplified for him, saying what he was afraid to utter.

"Put it that way, yes."

Amber gave him a smile, and it stayed on her face a little longer than the other one. "Thank you, Quentin," she said.

Athol had his share of problems, just like everyone else did. The only difference Quentin noticed between Athol and the other pilots was that he was better at concealing his. He resisted the urge of divulging sentiments that may have presented themselves similarly to Oscar's outward aggression, Amber's sadness, or Ewan's frustration. Athol didn't lose sleep, overeat, fight to hold down food, or transform into something of a meth abuser. He looked composed, but his composure was a pretense. He subtly overworked himself. Despite his constant work, he spent his evenings in the observatory with Casey to further the development of the BDP. He would sit in a lab chair, his dinner in a paper bowl on his lap, and review all of her findings. He must have assumed that, because he was both a pilot and one of the architects behind the project, that he was the best positioned to save the group from a potential lag. But he, like Amber, forced himself to exhaustion. He could act as collected as he wanted, but his eye bags spoke for his tamped-down misery.

The month neared its end, and the state of the pilots was worse than ever. With Oscar angrier, Amber sadder, Ewan more distant, and Athol pretending like he wasn't an emotionally repressed version of the person he once was, Quentin felt useless. He wanted to offer whatever help he could, but he had neither advice nor pills to provide to anyone. He had only loneliness, a ruinous case of insomnia, stinging migraines, and poorly veiled uncertainty about whether any of them would even be alive the following week.

23

It was on the 1st of February that Quentin, Marina, Connor, and Casey were at last allowed access to the restricted section of the basement, that being the cargo hold. Early in the morning, while everyone else was asleep, Patterson escorted them through a labyrinth of hallways in the lowest level's eastern wing, through which they walked until they finally came upon a pair of swinging doors and entered the mysterious, great space. It was, in many respects, a glorified industrial garage; monstrous storage units were inflexibly fixed into the cement ground; several forklifts awaited duty. Quentin didn't understand why Patterson was so firm in his stance of not allowing anyone else inside, but then they made their way deeper, into the heart of the hold, where a towering escalator ran up to the highest point of one of the walls. Where the steps ended, a platformed walkway began, which led to the ship's main control room.

"Main control room?" Casey asked.

"*The* control room," Patterson said. "It's where I spend nearly all my time. A home such as ours requires constant attention."

"Is it the most powerful room?" Quentin asked.

"I would hesitate to put it in those terms," Patterson said. "Although, it is the most important. For now, you still aren't allowed entry. But one day, maybe a year from now, you and your pilots will be permitted. As of this moment, your main concern is loading everything down here, but do be discreet." He turned to walk away, but stopped. "Casey and Quentin, don't forget the other meeting we spoke about."

"Four o'clock?" Casey asked.

"Yes, that is correct," Patterson said, and then he made his way to the elevator, leaving the four of them to their devices.

For hours, Quentin, Marina, Connor, and Casey hauled the goods from the foyer down to the cargo hold. By the afternoon, Quentin's back was so sore that he could barely walk. He felt bad that Marina and Connor were left with the rest of the work by four, at which point Quentin and Casey were needed in their own engagement, but as he watched the other two attempting to fit three mattresses into the elevator at the same time, he was guiltlessly relieved that he had the chance to be excluded from that—it wouldn't have done his back any favors.

Walking away from the labor, Casey asked him, "What do we do if something goes wrong tomorrow?"

"I try not to think about that," Quentin said.

"But if something did go wrong," Casey persisted, "if our systems malfunction or if a pilot hyperventilates...passes out..."

"Please," Quentin said, "don't think about it." He wasn't going to tell her to shut up, but he wanted her to.

"Which room did Patterson say, exactly?" Casey asked.

"He was kind of vague, said eighty-five or eighty-six and that it didn't matter. Also that we should wait outside."

"So I'm not spiraling?"

"Nope," Quentin comforted her while he picked at the sore spot in his lower back. "What's this meeting about anyway?"

"He didn't say. He's been so elusive. I don't even bother asking him questions anymore."

When they arrived to the eighty-five-to-eighty-six range of room numbers, they dawdled in the hallway. The pilots joined them; Oscar and Amber were first to arrive, and Ewan and Athol came after. With them huddled together and confused by their unclear directions, Quentin thought it reminiscent of his first day in that basement, in 2046.

"Did we get the wrong hallway?" Casey asked Quentin when such an abundance of time had passed that the overexerted pilots were blinking themselves awake.

Many minutes later, Patterson showed up and excused his tardiness. His hair was disorganized and puffed, like he had spent hours stressfully pulling the untended strands. Having gone without seeing him for so long, Quentin didn't realize how much the last month had aged Patterson. "My apologies," he said to Casey and Quentin. "I briefed the advisors yesterday, but I figured your catchup would be better if held with the pilots. Please, Ewan," he said to the blond, who stood beside the eighty-fifth door, "if you would be so kind as to open it for us. Yes, that room there. Thank you."

Ewan pulled the door back, but there wasn't a room on the other side of the threshold. The space was similarly sized to one of the closets that would have served as a portal to Quentin's near-demise into eternal blackness, over a year ago; he wasn't oblivious to the way Ewan started to teeter at the sight of the setting's slightness. Quentin made out a long, aluminum ladder that trickled up to the ceiling, but he couldn't see where it ended above.

"What is this?" Oscar asked.

"The entry to our second division's control center," Patterson answered. "There is a passengers' quarter inside as well. It's where they will be staying for the week, during the flight."

"It looks like the entrance to a bunker," Ewan said.

"It is, in essence, that very thing, Mr. McHugh. You will have to climb up a distance, but you've managed more trying heights."

"In open spaces," Ewan muttered, and yet he was the first to step inside. He visibly readied himself before he climbed up the ladder with the feigned collection of a first-time performer trying not to panic before an entire gathering of spectators.

Quentin was the third to enter, after Ewan and Amber. Quentin's tall body squeezed between the confining walls as he clumsily balanced himself on the ladder. About halfway up, he saw a large, circular cut above, in the ceiling, through which light escaped. From the edge of the cutout, Amber's red hair swished over her face as she looked down at him. A similarly circular, lid-like object protruded off the ceiling, which was hers and Ewan's floor, and was open beside her head. Quentin thought Ewan's comment over. *A bunker indeed.*

Reaching the higher room, Quentin asked Ewan and Amber, "How many rotations did it take you to remove the lid?"

"Twice clockwise," Ewan said, glancing to the handles in the center. "It's heavy, though. Steel or something."

Quentin put his hands on the edges of the circular gap in the floor and hoisted himself up by his elbows. He climbed over the rounded edge of the opening and crawled away to make room for those behind him.

The new room—his home for the coming week—was gray and cold, expressionless. He wasn't conscious of just how pampered he had become from the time spent in the extravagant upper floors, having passed all his time in a home of tapestry-laden walls, tables of fine woods, subtly artful and glorious chandeliers, and couches replete with goose-feather-stuffed throw pillows. He was unenthused when he saw the two aisles of seating in the middle of the room, each stiff and scarcely cushioned, likely incapable of reclining or revolving; protective harnesses that connected to the ceiling were propped above each seat, just waiting to be pulled down, as though they were all about to embark on a discombobulating roller coaster ride. Behind him, there were three, closed doors, and almost jutting into one of them was a table that was attached to the closest wall. On the other side of the room, which he assumed was the front, where the pilots would be, there was a single door, dead center where the alley between the two aisles of seating ended.

Quentin puckered his lips. "Well, it's certainly…"

"Practical," Casey said, climbing up after him.

"Drab," Oscar grumbled when he came up a few seconds later.

Patterson was the last one to climb through the little entry basin. He brushed off his wrinkled corduroys and stood against the table as Quentin and the others wandered around. "This is the passengers' quarter. You will find a bathroom, a small closet, and a storage room. Inside, there's food, medical supplies, inflatable mattresses and such." He gestured to the side of the room that had only one door. "That there is the control room. Only pilots should ever be inside, but if additional help is needed, only captains and advisors can be additionally included. Is that clear?"

Everyone nodded.

"Good," Patterson said. "So, you may be wondering why the shuttle's main control areas are situated in the middle of the basement and why we had to climb up into it, but the fact is that the ship is not quite a ship."

"I have no idea what you just said," Oscar responded derisively.

"The ship is divided into three shuttles, all of which are mergeable, regardless of the layout in which we are living now. For example, you could swap the first floor with the second, and the foyer stairs would still adaptably align. The ship isn't one, whole body. To have a single craft, we thought, was too unsafe; too susceptible to complete destruction if some type of problem were to arise. And, not to mention the unlikely, but nevertheless viable, possibility of us having to travel at full speed. We figured it would be simpler, easier, to fly and maneuver individual shuttles rather than one, gargantuan ship. Of course, when they are combined, they form one body. But that is why your training consisted of individual pods rather than practicing on the total body that is this ship. Flight-wise, each division will be in charge of a shuttle. I will man the third one, which consists of the fourth floor. Casey, your pilots will be in charge of floors two and three. Quentin, yours will bear the brunt of the first floor as well as the basement."

Ewan cocked his head a bit. "Any piece can connect with another?"

"Correct. That way, again, should something unfortunate happen, the livability of your home remains intact."

"And is this room the standard layout for all our shuttles or is ours different?" Amber asked.

"They are all the same," Patterson said. "Yours is identical to this one. Are you familiar with the always-locked door on the second floor, the one beside the computer room?"

"Yes."

"That one is yours." Patterson lowered himself to the floor and sat down with his legs crisscrossed. It was evident through his new way of sitting that their visit was far from over, so the others mimicked his seating style and joined him on the metallic surface. He continued speaking. "It technically isn't required, but when you are in here, I do recommend you wear the gravity-enhancing boots that will be provided."

"You can't enhance it in here like you did with the rest of the ship?" Casey asked.

"It's not that I can't, but only that, because you will be in full flight, you will want a backup mechanism for gravity, especially if it gets somewhat...bumpy," Patterson floated the word delicately. "It's a personal choice. As for oxygen, I would apply the same rationale. There's already a healthy flow of it passing through here, but you should definitely be using your Grains while the shuttles are in motion, in case anything does go wrong. And in case there are any delays, should our flight take longer than anticipated, remember that Grains only contain a one-week supply. You must remember this. Be sure to change them if we pass their limit." He glanced to the control room. "I cannot stress it enough that you are not to allow anyone who isn't a pilot, a captain, or an advisor into that room. Given certain sentiments buzzing around upstairs, I feel the need to emphasize the point." He stroked his jaw. "I feel like I'm forgetting something."

"I actually do have a question," Casey said.

"Yes?"

"Should all the Listeners be in one shuttle?"

"I don't see much of a problem with that," Patterson said. "The risk of something tremendously horrible happening is quite low. You're on autopilot. The shuttle's sensors are astute to say the least, and your pilots have proven themselves adaptive." He folded his hands together. "Right. I remember what I wanted to say. What I did want to mention to you, Casey, is that I have temporarily assigned Roxy to your group."

"Not that I have a problem with her," Casey said, "but why?"

"Casey, I'm sure the hearsay has reached you. Quentin vows that he didn't live through a dangerous moment of contention between Roxy Thompson and his advisor, but the fact that there was even an accusation is worrisome to me. I don't want any form of conflict, emotional or physical, during your flights. I want you all surrounded by people you trust, and I don't want certain persons feeling bullied or uncomfortable, especially if they're going to be in extremely tight quarters with each other for the entire week. Isolation and fear can lure people into doing things they wouldn't normally do. It helps having a support network around us."

Quentin caught the hints of an oncoming glower from Oscar, but it never came to full bloom. Quentin didn't think Patterson saw it.

"I have faith in all of you," Patterson said to Oscar, Amber, Athol and Ewan. "I trust that you will work together with your respective teammates, that you will do the right things. Remember, you can request a pause in the flight if you want to rest. Always bear in mind the fact that you can, and should, take care of yourselves as much as everyone else around you." He took in a long breath. "There is one more thing you should all know. I said it before, but I didn't elaborate at the time, but we are…we are effectively on our own from here on out. We always were, but more so now. Not all of you are aware of this, but from where we are, on this side of the belt, contact with our home has been possible. As of right now, it can take anywhere from two to six months for both parties to send and receive messages. Once we cross the belt, however, our ship-to-base communication time is unknown. It could take two months, it could take two years. Things get complicated the farther we travel." He wiped a hand over his face. "But you know…so long as you take care of each other, we can get through it. Something struck me today, something I had overlooked. It was that, even though we lost my colleagues last month, you never really needed them last year. Neither they nor I took care of you when you experienced the worst phase of your lives. It was you who saved each other." He cleared his throat. "The launch time is scheduled for six o'clock tomorrow evening, but I will see you around four."

Their meeting drew to a close. As the pupils climbed their way down the ladder, Patterson stayed behind, saying that there was a whole chain of system startups he needed to run in preparation for the following day.

As everyone walked through the basement and tried to situate the elevator, Amber tapped on Quentin's elbow. She signaled for him to lag a few steps behind the others, poorly masking her caution for being overheard. A twist of the lips signified a sheepishness in her, but the glow in her eyes alluded to some semblance of happiness. "Those pills," she said quietly, "they really helped me a lot. I've been sleeping better. I can't remember the last time I slept seven hours straight before them."

"I'm glad," Quentin said sincerely.

"I guess I didn't realize just how much the other ones were messing with me." Amber folded her arms and covered herself almost protectively. "I can't believe I spent all those nights staying up like that. I can't thank you enough. If there's ever anything you need, feel free to ask. You saved me at my lowest, at my most embarrassing. I'm not proud of it. I owe you."

"You're about to pilot an entire shuttle," Quentin said, "I would say it's the rest of us who owe you."

Amber ignored the flattery. "Where are you off to now? Does anything else need loading? I can help if you need it."

"We're not allowed to have anyone else in the cargo hold," Quentin said. "But thank you."

In the foyer, the pilots split up, which left Quentin and Casey together. She told him that she had to leave, that she promised to help Connor in securely relocating the BDP's models. "Marina won't be there to help him because Patterson told her to meet with Frances over something," Casey said.

"I'll come with you," Quentin proffered.

Casey waved for him to follow her up one of the glass staircases. "I would hope so. The project wouldn't really exist if not for you."

Quentin squinted up at the chandelier above them. "Hey, shouldn't that come down?"

"Oh, I already asked Patterson about that," Casey said. "Apparently, through the control room of my group's shuttle, I can retract it into the wall, where it'll be safely locked away. There are all these protective barriers that rise into place—they're hidden in the floors and the walls—and they block off the shuttle floors from each other, for the whole autonomous-shuttles thing, I guess. Patterson told me he wants us to barricade all the hallway entrances before we take flight."

"Why?"

"Something about the ship fumes being toxic. He doesn't want them reaching our shuttle's control rooms."

"Got it," Quentin said.

In the observatory, Connor was delicately handling the BDP models. The room was already quite bare, as the tables and chairs had been removed a week earlier and the whiteboards had been rolled into the cargo hold that morning. All that remained were the physical sketches and the five, delicate, first-draft sculptures that rested upon their wooden pedestals. They carefully slid the pieces into their hands.

After they tucked away the physical adaptations of the BDP into their own, secure corner of the cargo hold, Quentin finally felt the relief of having finished the job of clearing the upstairs. He, Casey, and Connor surveyed the spacious area, their eyes roving over some of the furniture and repositioned fineries; the single chaise from the library; the bunk beds from the separate male and female sleeping quarters; curved-back chairs; pots filled with parched flowers; the spinning stools that once stood half-turned in front of the arcade's ice cream bar.

"So this is it, then," Casey said later, when they were back upstairs, wiping their hands at the accomplished cleanliness of the ship. "We've done it. It's all cleared." She smiled a bit dejectedly. "It's weird...I never realized how much those stupid, contrived comfort items actually helped me adjust. Now it just feels like we're living in some shell."

"It's temporary," Connor reminded her.

The three of them perambulated around the foyer, not so sure where they were to proceed next. They did get hungry, so they decided to find themselves a meal.

The elevator dinged behind them, and Athol lazily ambled out.

"I thought you were taking a nap," Connor said to Athol, who was coming their way.

Athol shook his head. "Someone had to lock the training pods. The others are all out cold."

"We were all just about to eat, actually," Casey said. "You should have a splurging dinner before tomorrow. You'll need the sustenance."

"Yeah, I'll join in on that." Athol was about to say something else, something that darkened the friendliness of his face, when he caught sight of Marina exiting one of the hallways adjacent to the foyer, a backpack slung over one shoulder and a box of electrical wires in her hands. "Hey, do you have a minute?" he asked her. "Patterson was asking for you. He's in our shuttle control room."

"I'll be down in a second," Marina said. She moved past them and disappeared around the other side of the nearest staircase.

"So," Athol said lowly to the others, "I was working with Oscar and Amber today, before your meeting. He's such a...I don't know how else to say it, but he's horrible. He's vile and patronizing… just a piece of crap. He treats her like complete garbage. I don't wanna call it sexism because he's been a jerk to everyone lately, but he's cruel to her."

Connor didn't seem surprised. "He was a prick all of January, it would be naive to expect him to change overnight."

"I just think maybe one of you should stay in the control room with them tomorrow," Athol said. "It is allowed, right? Captains and advisors in the control room?"

"Patterson said it was fine," Casey affirmed.

"We can take turns, switch it up every once in a while," Connor proposed. "Anything for them to work together."

"It's him who's being toxic," Athol said. "She gives it her everything. He doesn't. Anyway, I'm starving. Let's go grab a bite."

———

It was nearly impossible to see anything in the freezing tunnel that was the entrance to Division Two's shuttle, but Marina managed to feel her way up the ladder, despite her clammy fingers slipping off the metal every few steps. As she climbed up and onto the floor of the passenger area, she was struck by how poorly lit the room was. It was even darker than when she and Connor were given their private exhibition. Patterson seemed to hate luminance.

The man had been awaiting her arrival. He was in the passenger seat closest to the table on her right side, the one that was attached to one of the walls.

Marina rose up from the floor. "You asked for me," she said. Although it wasn't a question, there were traces of confusion in her statement.

"I did," Patterson said. He curtly gestured with his left hand to the bench affixed to the table. "Take a seat." Marina slowly proceeded toward him, aware of his tells of unease, from the way he restlessly rubbed the tips of his thumbs against his index fingers, to the tension shown in his pupils and clenching jaw as he watched her approach him. At the bench, she saw that there was an orange folder on his lap. "For you," Patterson said. He extended his hand to her with the folder between his fingers.

Marina gingerly took it from him.

"Read it cover to cover," Patterson instructed her. And then, as if he wasn't in her company at all, he rested his hands on his stomach and closed his eyes. Whether or not he legitimately dozed didn't concern her, and she dutifully peeled the folder open to begin reading.

Marina read and reread for what must have been at least an hour; never once did she look to the clock by the control room door or to the watch on Patterson's wrist. When she finished, she closed the folder and slid it to the edge of the table, right in front of him.

"I read it all," Marina said a long while later. "Cover to cover. Twice."

"So I heard," Patterson said, opening his eyes. He never did fall asleep. "I couldn't present it in bits and pieces." He leaned forward, hunched over. His elbows rested on his knees while his hands, still clasped together, hung in the space between his legs. "It had to be delivered in its entirety or else my conclusion and my final decision, which you have no doubt inferred by now, would have probably seemed...There's no other way to phrase it, but inflated."

"I take it you want me to execute this inflated decision of yours," Marina said.

"In a word, yes."

"And should I keep it to myself?"

"Preferably."

"Preferably, but not necessarily?"

Patterson laid a hand on the closed folder. "At least until we've finished this week's flight. After that, I fully intend to come clean. Hopefully, by then, I'll have a way to elucidate it without making everyone read all thirty-six pages. But, yes, until we pass this obstacle, I want this clandestine."

Marina narrowed her eyes. "So, to be clear, you want me to take care of a prospective problem?"

"Is it prospective?" Patterson questioned, almost indignant. "My colleagues are dead. That guard who held you at gunpoint somehow managed his way up here. Those are not possibilities... prospective things. Those are realities. The fact is that you and your contemporaries could have very well been killed last year and there was nothing I could have done to stop it. Kudos to Mathias. And did you never wonder, in 2046, why some of you had grown physically despite having spent a year in a cryogenic phase? If not, I should tell you that our systems faced unusual and uncanny pauses in the scheduled deep-freezes. But were they unusual? No, I don't think so. One might even consider those disruptions interceptions, deliberate attempts to prematurely age you all." He pursed his lips. "The real question, of course, is whether or not you can do what I'm asking of you."

"I think I can."

"You think? I can fold in Connor if you need the help."

"No, don't do that," Marina objected. "He isn't like that. Not yet." She hesitated before saying, "I think Quentin should know. I know you believe freedom is the best way for adjustment, but that's not how it works with him. He needs to be personally compelled, personally attacked, to do anything. Literally, anything. Other than that, he doesn't...I don't want to say *care*, but he's not invested." She motioned to the folder. "Maybe this sets him off. And, should things go messily on my end, at least he'll know where I'm coming from and won't ask a thousand questions in front of the others."

"Very well," Patterson accepted.

Marina stood to leave.

"Marina," Patterson said quickly, just when she was about to exit. "How did you know?" he asked.

Marina blinked. "I didn't."

"Really?"

"Really."

"How unlike you. So it was only a hunch?"

"It was only a hunch."

Patterson smiled to himself, amused. "Well, now you must tell Athol. When the time is right, of course."

"Why is that?"

"Because it is proof that the mind is more powerful than we give it credit for." Patterson sighed out, serene that time rather than tense. "When they are ready, as you said, *one day*, he will find that knowledge fascinating. Worth studying, one might say."

"I see," Marina said. "So you really do believe in the BDP?"

"That, I do. Even more so now."

"Have a good night, sir," Marina said.

———

Dinner was far from relaxing. They were presented with platters of baked potatoes, peas, and chicken breast, but save for Athol, Chris, and Derek, people scarcely touched their food. Most stayed quiet throughout the mealtime hour, eyes fixed on their plates, but never making a move to indulge in it.

Quentin sat with Casey and Connor. Marina never appeared for that final meal.

"You two aren't touching your food," Connor said to them.

Casey pointedly stared at Connor's plate, where there was a squished potato overrun with fork marks and two slices of chicken that were halved but not eaten. "Says you," she retorted.

Connor swiped his hand over his mouth. "Fine. I'm nervous. It feels like my insides are burning. Happy?"

"I don't like that you're nervous," Casey said. "You never are."

Connor's eyes found Oscar, who was at one of the tables in the middle of the room. He was joined by Derek and Terry.

"It's not like we can do anything to change the unlikely friendship," Casey said gently, knowing what was bothering Connor. "We'll be okay."

Because he wasn't eating, Quentin saw no use in staying at the table when he could be catching up on sleep. His back demanded it more than his eyes. Excusing himself from the table, he brought with him one slice of chicken to munch on during the walk to his bedroom.

"Call time's four PM tomorrow," Casey said to him.

"Can't miss it anyway," Quentin assured her, raising his arm to remind her of their watches.

"Good night."

"Night."

When he was in his bedroom, Quentin took in its empty state. There were no late-night protein bars piled on the desk nor the usual unread book flopped on the floor beside his hamper. Except for a clean desk, a bed with exactly one flat pillow and a comforter, and his backpack on the floor, the room was vacant. Where there used to be sweaters hanging on the hook on his door, there was only his rugged outerwear for the approaching launch.

As he climbed onto the stiff mattress, something from the corner of his eye grabbed his attention: from under his backpack, which had been haphazardly tossed to the floor, an orange object peeked out. He didn't own anything orange. He slid the heavily stocked backpack aside.

He found an orange folder.

He wanted to sleep, but curiosity got the better of him. Settling into bed with his pillow propped up against the headboard and his comforter swarming him, he pulled his legs up to abut the folder. It only took him about forty minutes to read the files, but it was the exercise of processing their content that kept him locked in place and numbly staring at the papers for a total of two hours.

His back hated him for it, but in the middle of the night, while others slept and he desperately needed to do the same, he tiptoed out of his bedroom with the folder in tow. He stealthily crept downstairs, to the library. Once inside, he closed the large doors behind him. He poked his head around the bookshelves and walked up to the loft, checking to see if he was alone. When he verified that he was, he went back to the library's first level and stood before the fireplace.

Sighing, he focused on the slight weight of the folder under his arm. "What do you say, Gran?" he asked into the quiet blaze. He closed his eyes, but he could still see the flames jumping up and down in front of him. He felt their heat, felt them waving and whirring. He saw their red tints, their orange hues, and their hints of yellow, all drifting one way and another. "Would you be mad at me if I did it?" he asked, opening his eyes.

The folder under his arm felt heavier.

The fireplace didn't have a cage.

"Not that it matters," he said, louder than before. "Because you're not here anymore, are you?"

The flames waved. The hearth was warm under his bare feet.

Agata wasn't there to tell him otherwise.

He threw the folder with its contents into the flames and watched as the contents burned up with it. Some pieces disintegrated and others lived on as ashy sprinkles that dappled along the black plinth, and he was hypnotized by them. As he smelled the decayed fragments of the papers and saw the flames engulf what was left of them, he swore he had never been so at peace.

Quentin's peace on the night of February 1st was ephemeral. Not only was he upset that the 2nd arrived, but he found out, not long after his breakfast, that he, Marina, Casey, and Connor, had missed a spot in their effort of clearing the ship of its upstairs belongings. Somehow, they had forgotten about the kitchen.

The fridge was emptied, but the same didn't apply to the rest of the room. Pots still hung above the ovens and stacks of unused pans occupied the pantries. One of the walls was caged off—in order for one to access it, the hinges would need undoing—revealing rows of stainless steel utensils as well as shelves that housed collections of can openers, blenders, mixers, and a variety of other electrical and manual kitchen tools.

"Damn," Connor said. "Good thing we woke up early."

Casey rolled up the sleeves of her jumpsuit to free her hands of the extra fabric. She kicked open one of the ground-level cabinets. "You know the drill, bring down as much as you can."

Quentin, for good measure, slid open one of the drawers. He groaned. "Guys, we forgot the silverware too."

They gathered caissons, canisters, and cylinders constructed of plastic, glass, and ceramics. They stuffed as much as they could into those vessels, mixing together everything, from forks and spatulas, to toothpicks and napkins. Casey and Connor gamified the task of hauling the huge volume of pans down to the basement, as they sprinted back and forth to the cargo hold like relay racers. In the meantime, Quentin and Marina filled whatever containers they could find with all the forgotten objects.

About fifteen minutes into the routine, Casey decided to accompany Connor to the cargo hold so that she could stabilize the two massive boxes of pots that wobbled precariously on his two-wheeled dolly. Left alone with Marina, Quentin was squatted on the floor with her, the two of them sorting through silverware.

"There's no need to get those," Marina said, glancing up to the alignment of sharper knives that were on the wall beside one of the ovens.

Quentin bunched some forks together. It was a delayed response, but after he placed the utensils inside a plastic container, his fingers twitched in the open air.

Marina didn't notice him staring at her until a full minute passed. She uncurled her hand from around some spoons and dropped them into the same plastic container. "They're fine where they are," she said, not looking at him but definitely feeling the weight of his immovable gaze.

Had Ivy not knocked on the kitchen's open door at that precise moment, Quentin probably would have vomited. He needed to gain control of his gut. His retching reactions were getting out of hand.

"Hi," Ivy said to them. Her brown hair was tied up into a bun, and the dimples of her round face were more prominent in her greeting smile than they typically were on other days, when her hair was down and flowing. She had in her hand a rectangular, touchscreen pad.

Quentin pretended to focus on the forks in front of him. He did everything in his power to avoid Marina's eyes, which were already directed up to Ivy. Marina calmly enquired on the matter that brought Ivy there.

"Patterson was asking for your fingerprint IDs to add to the protection software for the main control room in the cargo hold, just in case of…" Ivy bit her lip. "Of…you know, something going wrong and the ship winding up in your hands. You can make your copies here."

"Sure," Marina said.

Quentin was green and glaring when Ivy came to collect his biometrics, but he was grateful that all she did was show her deep dimples and smile without adding a comment regarding his twisted face. After she left, he swiftly and shakily went about his silverware packing. Marina exuded her usual calm. She wasn't taking her precious time, but she wasn't as overzealously speedy with her movements as he was.

With the exception of the knives beside the oven, the captains and advisors cleared the entire kitchen by three o'clock. They were sure it was their last removal job of the day, because after their earlier discovery of the overlooked objects, each captain ordered a division-wide sweep of the whole ship; by four o'clock in the afternoon, two separate teams confirmed that the job had been completed.

In the foyer, at four-thirty, everyone congregated one last time before the flight. Stood upon the marble and gated in by the perimeter pillars, they were appropriately garbed and fresh-faced from recent showers. For once, Patterson was dressed identically to them. He seemed more poised than the last time they all met there, on that sad January day, torn from their beds by the dramatic change to the course of their once fairly predictable year.

Just as the arrow on Quentin's wristwatch struck four-thirty-one, Patterson greeted them with a simple, "Welcome back."

Quentin gulped.

"The last time we were here," Patterson said, "I gave you all quite the scare. I know I induced some anger along the way and that you were very frightened, and while your anger and fright might not have abated over the last month, your determination and resilience have grown. On countless occasions, I have, admittedly, pulled the rug out from under you, and you have, without fail, consistently stomped down on it and taken back control of your lives. I trust that you will continue to do that throughout this week. What you are soon going to do, what you are going to accomplish, is more than anything which I, my superiors, and your parents could have ever expected from you so soon." He smiled. It wasn't his old one, the one that would crinkle the corners of his eyes and lift his cheeks, but it was a slight upturn, a virtually imperceptible curl.

"Now, my pilots," he said, "you are who I am most proud of. I won't be with our two divisions to help them, guide them, and comfort them. It will be you. The lives of your friends are in your hands, and you have proven worthy of that weighty responsibility. For years, I saw the way Athol and Ewan pored over their schoolwork, trying to ace their tests and earn the best grades in order to prepare for the eventualities of their futures. In Amber and Oscar, I saw two quietly considerate people who only ever wanted the best for their friends, and, in his case, his sister as well. Additionally, I trust our advisors to supportively, although never in blinding loyalty, hold firm at the sides of their captains, whom they are to assist if anything goes awry. But let's hope nothing does, so that several days from now, you will find yourselves back together as one ship, here in this foyer. But, for now, it is with utmost pride and trust in individual and collective agencies that I say, expectantly not for the last time, you are dismissed. Call time is five; twenty-five minutes from now. Do not arrive any later than five-thirty. After that, the ship initiates its separation processes. Stay safe. You will all be back here again soon."

24

As soon as Quentin sat down, his thighs sank into the light cushioning of his seat. It seemed he had been mistaken when he previously assumed that he would be uncomfortably perched for the entire week.

"Plush," Fatima commented. She was the only one who had her harness pulled over her body. On one side of her was Mathias, and beside him was an unattended, but reserved, spot, which was made clear by the presence of Marina's duffel bag left on top of it. On the other side of the small gap between the aisles of seating were Quentin's seat, Frances's, and Jaymes's, and in that order.

Frances stuffed her backpack into the storage compartment under her seat. "I won't lie," she said, standing erect, "plush is not the word that came to mind when I first saw these."

"It makes a good ass-warmer," Mathias said.

Frances rolled her eyes. "Thank you," she said, and plopped herself between Quentin and Jaymes.

"Why was our call time so early?" Jaymes asked, adjusting his glasses.

"The ship exhaust," Quentin said. "It runs through the entire place, except where we all are now, apparently. That's why we had to empty out everything."

"Oh, I thought Patterson was being paranoid," Jaymes said. "I thought he was acting the way airports do when you have an international flight, how they want you to arrive a few hours in advance."

Frances snuck a peek down to Quentin's watch. "It's ten-past-five, why isn't she here?" she asked, raising an eyebrow toward Marina's empty seat.

"Athol and Ewan had a few questions for her," Quentin said, "She's probably up front with them. Don't worry, it wouldn't be like her to be late."

"She was probably the first to get kidnapped," Mathias said.

The remark elicited a chuckle from Jaymes. "Just, like, threw herself onto the ship. Didn't even have to steal her."

"I miss airports," Fatima said at once.

Frances shivered dramatically. "I used to hate them. They gave me awful anxiety. The thought of planes…flying…creepy."

At five-twenty, Ewan came barging out of the control room. The automatic doors shut behind him as he advanced down the narrow path between the aisles of seating. He furiously fixed on Quentin.

"Mind offering me some context?" Quentin asked.

"Yeah, how's this? Your little advisor said she'd review some stuff with us but never showed." Ewan glanced to the closed restroom door. "Tell her to finish whatever she's doing and get up there."

"No one's in the bathroom, Ewan," Frances said. "I was in there thirty minutes ago. Why isn't Marina with you?" She spun her head to Quentin. "Where is she?"

"We thought she was with you," Jaymes said to Ewan.

"And I thought she was with *you*," Ewan retorted.

"I'm sure she'll be here soon," Quentin tried to assure everyone in a feeble feign of nonchalance. "She's always punctual."

"Exactly," Jaymes said. "Thus a cause for concern. Call time was ages ago. She's advisor, and she isn't in the cockpit, the bathroom, or, apparently, the control room."

Mathias elbowed the bag on the empty seat next to him. "Her stuff's here, though."

"Find her," Ewan said.

"But she'll come, I'm sure," Quentin said.

"Find her before it's too late and the shuttles start spewing toxins everywhere."

Frances jumped out of her seat. "We can do a quick search. Quentin, what's the time?"

"Five-twenty-one."

"Is it okay for us to be running around the halls right now?" Jaymes asked Ewan, also standing up.

"No," Ewan said. "But Marina isn't here. It's not like we have much of a choice."

"Okay, okay…" Frances nervously rubbed her hands on the pants section of her suit. "How about we split up and go looking for her?"

"Not me, I'm busy with the flight initiation," Ewan said. "Just make sure to be back by five-fifty at the latest. And remember, whether or not you're back, the shuttle will leave."

"You can't control it?" Jaymes asked.

"Not the actual push. Patterson scheduled it and there's no stopping it."

"All right, c'mon," Jaymes urged, making his way over to the closed lid on the floor.

Ewan disappeared into the control room.

Quentin stayed still.

"Quentin, let's go!" Frances yelled to him. She was already on the floor with Jaymes, the two of them groaning as they turned the hefty, steel lid counterclockwise and opened it.

"Well, I…" Quentin stammered.

Jaymes dipped himself over the edge of the opening. Starting his climb, he said, "It shouldn't be too hard to find her. The other shuttles have to be walled off by now. Come on."

Frances began her descent above Jaymes. "Mathias, you too. Let's go."

"Nuh-uh," Mathias refused. "Someone's gotta close that thing in case you don't return."

"Unbelievable," Frances muttered. Quentin could hear her from the other side of the room, but her second snide comment to follow went unheard once she traveled lower, beyond the edge of the gap in the floor.

Fine, Quentin thought. *Fucking fine.* He undid his seatbelt and raced toward the circular exit. He thought of only one thing when he began climbing down the ladder, and it was the orange folder he had found in his bedroom.

When he exited through the eighty-fifth door, Frances and Jaymes weren't in the hallway outside. Quentin stayed in place for a moment, listening as the other two called for Marina but were never answered. He could tell solely by the distance between himself and their voices that they were roaming into the southern end of the basement. He discerned the racket of them busting open random doors and slamming them shut. He told himself that he needed to find Marina before either of them had the chance to.

His watch read five-thirty-five.

As Quentin charged in the other direction, to the northern end, Frances's and Jaymes's shouts were fainter-sounding. Thin billows of a filmy, black fume started to gather in the corridors. Quentin coughed a bit, and his eyes began to sting. The soft lights of the hallway were reduced in visibility because of the smoky substance. He had to navigate his way from memory and periodically put his face against a door number to ensure he was still on track to reach the elevator.

Frances was yelling behind him. She was far away, and he wanted to keep it that way.

With a squint, he saw through the haze of the sooty exhaust and identified a door that was labeled with the number TWENTY. *Nearly there,* he encouraged himself and sped past it. He allowed himself a glance to his watch, which radiated a gentle, white hue along its glass perimeter as an automated response to the darkness; it struck five-forty.

He heard something like a sigh come from the walls, like the ship itself was discharging a long-held breath as it readied for the powerful departure. Seconds after that sound, the expulsion of exhaust grew more constant. The air felt thicker, heavier. Quentin started choking. *What did Ewan say?* He tried to remember. *Be back by five-forty or fifty?* He couldn't recall. All he knew was that he hadn't reached the elevator and that Jaymes's voice sounded closer.

A ray of fizzling gray ejected from beside the doorway of the room Quentin was passing. He breathed it in accidentally, coughing as it streamed down his throat. Whatever was in the fumes that swirled around and into him, it hurt. He tasted it on his tongue, metallic, chalky, and burnt, even somewhat ashy. His body responded to the foul intake with brimming eyes and a tightening chest.

When he reached the elevator, he punched the button on the panel. The interior of the compartment was bereft of the fumes, and he reveled in the clean-aired sanctuary during his trip.

He was relieved that the smoke hadn't permeated the upstairs as thickly as it did in the basement. He could still make out the foyer's bright corner lights, which had been enabled while the chandelier was withdrawn. It was the brightest he had ever seen the area, but it wasn't lost on him that the amplified fluorescence would slowly lose the battle against the exhaust fumes that trickled in. On the ground level, he couldn't see much of anything. He could, however, see above the first twenty steps of the two staircases. The second, third, and fourth floors were walled-off by their once secret, movable barriers, which made searching them impossible. Smoke began shooting out by the high ceiling.

Quentin weighed the idea of calling out for Marina, just as Frances and Jaymes were doing downstairs. But then an ashen, steely taste made its way onto his tongue and he felt himself inhaling it. He wheezed and felt heavier. Breathing in the fume made him dizzy, and he stumbled into one of the marble pillars, where he rested a moment as he tried to inhale. He heaved in a breath and slid his hands along the cool marble of the pillar. He pushed off it, balanced himself, and swiveled on a heel to face the elevator, intending to leave. But it was then that he smelled something putrid, at five-forty-eight. It was that disgusting smell of iron. Even as the exhaust poured into his nose, he knew the smell. With watery vision, he squinted and walked around the other side of the pillar. The scent was stronger.

He found Marina. She was crouched down on the marble and had made herself so small that he nearly stepped on her. Her expression was dazed and she was gasping for air. Blood was everywhere; in a puddle on the floor; on the soft edges of the pillar beside her. She had a hand pressed to her left hip, and although he couldn't see what it was she gripped, he saw the pooling blood and knew it wasn't anything kinder on her body than the rest of the littered messes all over her. He saw a slit in her cheek, just like the one he had years ago, from his nighttime escape in the moribund forest behind his home in Shaw. There were pink scrapes on her forehead, chin, and collarbone, under which there was a tear in her jumpsuit. Through the opening in her clothing, he saw another slice in the skin. More peculiarly, her neck was cut too. By some miracle, she was still on that floor breathing. He thought, *She should be dead. How is she not dead?*

The elevator dinged behind him. Frances and Jaymes were calling for him, asking where he was and if he had found Marina.

Quentin, obviously, had. The issue at hand was whether or not he wanted to make that fact known.

"Quen...tin?!" Frances probed for him.

Quentin peeked around the pillar. The other two were in the middle of the foyer, hobbling and hacking coughs as they wandered through the exhaust, their backs turned to him.

Marina was panting faster. The hand on her left hip held it firmer.

"We should go back!" Jaymes told Frances.

"But—!"

"Let's go!"

Quentin chomped on his lower lip. *"Ah, fuck it,"* he muttered. He left Marina, ran around the pillar, and shouted over to the others, who were retreating, "She's here!"

The billows of exhaust were bombarding them, clogging up the hall, but through the gaps in the fumes, he saw Jaymes and Frances chase after his voice. Quentin ran back around to the other side of the column, where he got down to his knees and threw one of Marina's arms over his shoulders. Beside her, the foul odor was stronger. Her blood smeared his clothes as he held her.

"Oh...Oh...my god," said a gasping Frances when she arrived. "Your blood..."

Marina winced as Quentin stood up and elevated her.

"Jaymes, help him," Frances said. "You two are about the same height."

In guiding them out, Frances stayed barely ahead of Quentin and Jaymes as they carefully lugged Marina through the foyer. Frances hit the elevator button, and when the doors peeled apart, the young men discarded their caution and crammed Marina inside before any exhaust could enter with them.

The elevator closed.

Jaymes retched. His grip on the hand Marina had dangling off his shoulder never loosened, but his stability wavered.

"Did…did none of us put Grains…in?" Quentin asked, but he didn't get an answer.

Frances leaned a hand against one of the walls behind her to propel herself forward. When she was closer, Quentin saw that she was crying. "Do not close your eyes," she said to Marina. "Stay awake. Am I clear?"

Marina wheezed.

In the basement corridors, the smoke felt fuller, almost solid. Except for the glow of his watch, Quentin couldn't see a thing. He and Jaymes held their respective sides of Marina's waist a little sturdier as Frances blindly zigzagged them through the hallways. Every few seconds, they paused to breathe in the remnants of oxygen around them. Advancing slowly, Frances looked like she was going to topple to the floor at any moment. Jaymes's feet stuttered. He went crashing to the floor, and Marina slipped from his grasp. Quentin caught Marina before she fell. She didn't make an effort to hold onto him. For all he knew, she had already passed out. Or passed away. He couldn't see enough of her to tell the difference. Meanwhile, Jaymes was hunched over the cement floor and prying at it for purchase. Frances clung to a random doorknob, crying as she swallowed more of the exhaust. Quentin opened his mouth to motivate them, to get them to stand up, but exhaust shot between his lips and down his throat. His legs shook. His lungs felt overheated. He pushed an arm out and slapped it against the wall beside him to avoid crashing down like Jaymes had. Frances was wobbly. She rested a hand on the only part of Jaymes's body that Quentin could see, which was Jaymes's left shoulder. She tugged him to try and bring him to his feet, but all she accomplished was using him to break her fall as she similarly crumbled down, coughing uncontrollably as she did.

Quentin's eyes burned. They stung so much. He thought, *We should leave her,* as he examined the limp body he was propping upright. His grip on Marina began to loosen.

As Quentin began shucking Marina's arm off his shoulder and pulled his hand away from her waist, a figure came into view before them, a burly body cloaked in one of the jumpsuits. Their head was hidden by a helmet, which was fogged up. Through the few, clear spaces in the opaque glass, Quentin saw Mathias's face. He leaned down and grabbed one of Frances's and Jaymes's shoulders each and yanked them up, almost a bit too aggressively. Then, having brought the two of them back up to their feet, he plowed past the gagging pair of hobblers and shouted to Quentin, with his voice muffled from the helmet, "Here, give her to me!" Quentin obliged. He unhooked Marina's arm from around himself, which sent her tipping forward. Mathias bent down right before she hit the cement, and he threw her entire body over one of his broad shoulders. He turned and trudged away.

Quentin knew he had to follow after Mathias or else they'd never find their way back. He tried to be a semblance of the stronger man that Mathias was, so he weakly tripped along and pulled at Frances's and Jaymes's hands. He led them forward. The three of them clumsily bumped into each other and fought the desire to stop and dry heave. With their hands intertwined and their elbows locked together, they persevered and returned to the basement's eighty-fifth door. Jaymes slammed it behind them. Mathias and Marina were nowhere to be seen, but the entry lid in the ceiling was wide open, so they must have already ascended. Quentin's climb was a toil. He was coughing badly all throughout it.

Back in the passengers' quarter, he sprawled himself on the floor. Frances and Jaymes did the same.

"What…What happened?" Frances struggled to ask Marina, who was blinking herself awake, haphazardly plopped down beside them, which was definitely Mathias's doing.

Mathias was already out of his suit and helmet. He kicked down the lid, squatted, and turned the handle to seal it shut.

Quentin's watch read five-fifty-five. "We're five minutes to launch," he warned everyone.

"*What* happened to her?" Frances asked him.

Mathias put his hands in the air. "I've learned not to ask when it comes to this bitch."

"Thank you…for getting us," Jaymes said.

"First…First aid…" Frances said. "For Marina."

Quentin sat up. "Later. We're too close to separation."

Frances pointed to Marina's neck. "It is impossible for her to be alive."

"Clearly it isn't," Jaymes said. He helped Frances up, cradling her elbow and holding one of her hands. "Better sit down before this place starts rolling."

Frances wrenched her hand free and stayed on the floor. "I'll use my gravity boots if I have to, but I *am* closing that wound before she dies." She crawled to the storage space under her seat and retrieved her extra footwear. "I need that medical kit. It should be in the storage room. Someone find it for me before we separate, please. We don't have time to waste."

"Fine," Mathias said, entering the storage closet.

"Is there anything you need us to do?" Jaymes asked Frances.

"Help me ready her," Frances said.

Quentin and Jaymes rolled Marina onto her back and placed her head on Frances's thighs. Just by touching her, they were covered in her blood.

Frances wiped her eyes with open hands, so that only the bottom of her face was visible. "Lord, I am not prepared for this," she wept.

"Frances, listen to me," Jaymes said. "You can do this. You can fix her."

Quentin's watch read five-fifty-nine. "We're a minute away," he announced.

Jaymes roughly clutched his knees, and his knuckles lost their color.

Quentin's eyes found Marina's neck again. Blood ran out of it and down to her chest, where it pooled under her layers of clothing.

Frances noted him staring. She lowered her hand to that spot on Marina's body, trying to suppress the outpour. "I have to stop it from flowing out. I need that kit, Quentin."

"But we're going to—" Quentin said.

"I have my gravity boots and I'll hold her down. We'll be fine."

Jaymes patted Quentin's shoulder. "Let's sit down, at least during the separation. Frances, we'll be back to help you as soon as we're stable again."

Five-fifty-nine remained the time on Quentin's watch as he returned to his seat and maneuvered the harness over his body. He sat down just as a low rumble began to sound off, underneath the floor. The room quaked. He expected an intercom message from their pilots to perhaps alert everyone to stay seated at that time, but no such order was given. Following two massive rumbles and a side-to-side shake, the shuttle lurched forward. Somewhere in the storage room, there was a clatter of objects falling and then Mathias swearing. The shuttle moved slowly at first, but it shed its gradual push and accelerated.

Their environment never achieved full stability, but when the worst bouts of thirty shakes per minute subsided to ten or fifteen, Quentin and Jaymes unbound their harnesses, grabbed their own boots, and returned to the floor with Frances. A hunched-over Mathias rejoined them. He was grunting as he plodded into the room with a steel trunk that was approximately the same size as his torso. The right side of his face was indented with red marks.

"You okay?" Quentin asked.

"No," Mathias said. He dropped the trunk, and it thudded into the puddle of Marina's blood.

"Are you sure those are medical supplies?" Frances asked.

"Yeah," Mathias said. He carefully shuffled over to his seat and acquired his boots. "That ain't no kit, by the way. That's a whole infirmary."

Frances pressed her hand harder against Marina's neck. "The more the better," Frances said, using her free hand to unhinge the lid of the trunk. She had trouble reaching inside and sifting through to examine the products.

Mathias sighed and crawled back over, taking up the task himself. "What do you need?"

"There should be some type of suturing kit. Get me that. And some scissors, rubbing alcohol, gauzes...and antibiotic ointment." To Quentin and Jaymes, she said, "Please check her for more wounds."

"Are you kidding?" Quentin asked. "She's injured all over."

The shuttle swerved.

Mathias jammed the trunk between his legs to rein it in.

Quentin planted his hands on the floor to sturdy himself.

Jaymes fell back onto his heels.

"I'm aware of that, thank you very much," Frances curtly replied as she unzipped the front of Marina's suit. "But I need to know if any of them are nearly as bad as this one." She motioned to Marina's neck. "I'll get the neck first, obviously. And then her cheek. Is anywhere else as bad?"

Frances pulled wider the many split portions of Marina's suit. When that didn't aid her in performing a closer inspection, Frances unzipped the top half and carefully folded it down below Marina's hips, which wasn't uncomfortable for any of the involved parties, since she was wearing a pair of sweatpants underneath. The view of her body was, for the most part, bared. Almost every inch of her was cut. Some incisions were superficial and drying, most deep and dripping. Her legs were relatively unscathed, marred only by rips in the fabric of her suit. Her back was fine.

From the trunk, Mathias pulled a transparent, glass canister, inside which were five needles, a single pair of scissors, toothed forceps, and a ball of what looked to be white thread. Those were, doubtless, the stitching materials.

Frances must have noticed something with Marina's left hip, because she lifted the folded-down pieces of the suit to expose the skin there. Marina flinched and sent her hand down over the spot. "Remove your hand, please," Frances said, and Marina did as told. "Will you two hold her down?" Frances asked Quentin and Jaymes, who similarly did as requested of them. But even with Marina tethered to the floor, Frances still couldn't see the hip, as she was too preoccupied restricting the blood flow from Marina's neck and didn't want to move away from it.

Quentin took charge of the examination. He husked Marina's leg of the tattered suit material that surrounded it. Something was inside her. She wasn't bleeding out, but it was almost like her flesh and blood were corked in by a circular, black object that had a circumference similar to that of a squash ball. "What is *that*?" he asked.

Marina lifted her head to see it.

Frances pressed Marina down again. "Stop that! Stop moving!"

"Should we get that thing?" Quentin asked, referring to the hip.

"Neck…more important," Frances distractedly said, shivering at the hot blood all over her hands.

"How do you need us to help?" Jaymes asked.

Frances's hands didn't stop shaking. "I need you to…um… stitch up her other wounds?"

"Is that a question?" Jaymes asked. "Are you asking if that's what we should do or if you need us to stitch her up with you?"

"The second one."

Mathias placed a plastic bottle onto the floor. It was labeled ISOPROPYL ALCOHOL, 32 FL.

Frances weakly tried to compose herself. "We…We'll need to dilute that."

Mathias was appalled. "Dilute it? Fran, look at her. She's gonna fucking die on your lap."

"True, true. Okay. Um—"

The shuttle swerved.

The bottle rolled away and the suturing kit tipped over.

Frances's fingers verged on penetrating the cut as she pinned her hands down even harder on Marina's neck. "Here's what we'll do," Frances said. "I'll get her neck, then her face. In the meantime, all of you tackle whatever you can. Watch me stitch the neck, and you'll see how it's done. Quentin, that cut on her arm looks pretty bad, so you'll take care of that one. Mathias, you get the one on her chest.

Jaymes, you clean the wounds and sterilize our equipment. Mathias, are there gauzes? Please get gauzes."

Mathias dunked his head back into the trunk.

Quentin picked up the glass suturing kit. As he unscrewed its top, he was unpleasantly aware of the fact that the blood on his hands was staining the sheer borders of the canister.

"And that antibiotic ointment," Frances said to Mathias once he found the gauze pads and wraps. "Also, a hair tie please."

"But what do we do about *that*?" Quentin asked her, pointing back to the thing in Marina's hip.

"We'll save it for last. My biggest concern right now is her neck. God, Marina, you should not be alive right now."

"You really want us to stitch her up?" Jaymes asked disbelievingly.

Frances wiped her eyes. "What else can I do?" she asked shakily. "I only have so many hands."

Mathias fetched all of the utensils and laid them out on the floor for Frances's selection. She guided everyone through their usages. Quentin learned quite a few things, such as the needles available were of the cutting variety, which were meant to heal tissue and skin, whereas tapered needles were for more invasive procedures. He and Mathias paid close attention to everything their panic-struck guide had to say. As they listened, Jayme dabbed the open pieces of Marina's skin with a cloth he repeatedly dipped into a plastic cup of purified water and the rubbing alcohol; without fail, a strained groan escaped her every time the cloth made contact with her.

"Knotting it at the end should be the hard part," Frances said. She wound a line of dissolvable string through the looped end of a needle, her gloved fingers deftly tying the two into one. "Just leave the ends to me. The most important thing is closing up the openings. Did you see how I did that, by the way? How I set up the string? If you think you can do it, try and do the same."

Her apprentices gloved their hands, reached for their own sets of string and needles, and began to imitate her work.

Jaymes ran to the restroom to wring out his dabbing cloth. When he rid it of most of Marina's blood, he returned, and Frances lifted her hands off Marina's neck. Jaymes poured some alcohol onto the cloth and touched it to the gash. Marina squawked out something of a shriek.

"Shh!" Quentin berated her.

Marina's eyebrows came together and her lips tightened in a snarl, like she was trying to communicate to him that he didn't have even the slightest idea of what she was living through.

"We can't distract our pilots," Quentin said to everyone.

Frances's hair fell in front of her face again. She threw her head back in a quick movement to fling all the layered waves behind her shoulders, but the strands had reached the compromising length at which they were neither long nor short, but completely unmanageable. When it was out of her face, she said, "The pilots needing quiet has no bearing on this." And then her hands were nearing Marina's throat, one end of the open area slowly pierced the tip of her needle.

Marina sort of squealed. Her teeth ground and she moaned loudly. She wriggled at the lasting stings from the alcohol and made discomforted noises from the sensation of Frances's stitching. As Quentin watched her writhe and produce squealing sounds, he realized that, in that moment, she had never seemed so ordinary to him. He had never seen her in agony. He wondered if she only knew physical pains, not emotional ones.

Frances pulled the needle up, and the string followed closely behind, until the knotted end of it met the tiny hole that she had created in the skin. She brought the tip of the needle back down to the opposite end of the cut and continued her sewing. Marina adjusted to the odd feeling of the procedure and calmed down.

"So what do you want me to do?" Mathias asked.

"I already told you," Frances said. "Find a—"

The shuttle lurched to the side.

The movement sent Mathias and the open container of supplies zinging into the nearest wall.

Frances was unfazed, except to mutter at the hair that flew into her face again. "Did you find me a scrunchy?" she asked Mathias.

Crawling back to them, Mathias picked up his needle along the way. "No, Frances, I did not find you a scrunchy. As you can see, I don't even have time to put my boots on."

Frances wove her needle back to the first side to penetrate a new hole and form a perfect pattern—or as perfect a pattern as her steadfastness could bring her in the tumultuous environment. She was remarkable, though. Quentin didn't know how she did it. He was constantly overpowered by the instability of their shuttle and found it difficult just to clean the wound he intended to seal, which was the one on Marina's left arm.

"So just…stitch her?" Quentin asked.

"Yes, just stitch her," Frances said.

"Is this, like, safe for us to do even though we're not nurses?"

"No," Frances said.

Mathias turned over the flappy bits of fabric around the object in Marina's hip and lowered his needle, verging on puncturing the skin that bordered the foreign object.

Frances intervened when she saw what Mathias was about to do. "No! Not the hip!"

"Chill! Why not?!"

"You'll trap that inside and it'll get infected! I need to remove it first!"

Mathias innocently put his hands in the air. "Okay, okay. Fuck."

Quentin pricked Marina's arm with the needle. She flinched. He twice looked over to Frances to try and mirror her neat alignment of string and flesh.

"The one on her chest, right here, you'll take care of this," Frances said to Mathias. She butted her elbow downward, gesturing to a cut that was below Marina's collarbone, on her right side. They didn't have to undo the buttons of her shirt to access it; the fabric had been ruggedly torn apart for them to see it. With Frances instructing him on how to begin, Mathias shuffled over on his knees and took in the information. Jaymes cleaned the area. Frances loudly talked over Marina, who was groaning. Quentin thought she sounded uncannily reminiscent of the doves from his old neighborhood in Shaw, back when they used to belt unflattering pleadings to mate with each other in the springtime.

Mathias poked Marina's skin with his needle. He pulled the string, laced the two pierced sections closely together, and began a second set of holes. The skin on her chest was thinner, so it must have hurt her more.

"We should knock her out," Quentin said. "Ewan and Athol will hear this."

"We are not knocking her out," Frances argued. She ducked her head down and resumed stabbing, sowing, and once again stabbing Marina in the neck. "With this type of blood loss, that'll do nothing but kill her." She switched her hands to ease the tension in them as she stitched. "How is she alive...someone tell me how she's alive...Maybe if I—"

With his sterilized cloth, Jaymes patted Marina's left hip, the one with the weird thing. She screeched through her teeth.

"*Maybe,*" Frances said, trying to get her sentence out, "if I use some lidocaine that I thought I saw, I might be able to quiet her. What I'm not sure about is—"

"Lidocaine?" Jaymes asked. "What's lidocaine?"

"A numbing agent. Like novocaine. I could try it later when we have to surgically rem—"

The shuttle swerved down in one, sharp bounce. Quentin and Jaymes flopped sideways. Mathias's needle slipped out of his hand. The motion moved Frances. Her right fist shot up, and the needle in it stabbed the underside of Marina's chin.

"*Aaagh!*" Marina gurgled.

"I'm sorry! Oh my god, I'm so sorry! " Frances slobbered out. She sheepishly resumed her stitching. Her eyes grew teary as she tried to ignore the choking sounds Marina made. Quentin didn't know if Frances saw the new puncture in Marina's body, which had been made by none other than Frances herself.

"What were you saying?" Jaymes asked Frances. "About lidocaine?"

Frances's tongue wagged out the side of her mouth as she poked another stitching hole. "That it's a numbing agent. We'll use it later on her hip...to—*Shit,*" she cursed, perhaps for the first time in all the years Quentin knew her. Marina's blood made Frances's gloved hands slippery, so much so that gripping the utensil became a challenge on its own. "The lidocaine...We'll use it when we want to remove that foreign object."

"Can you use lidocaine on a hip?"

The question made Frances burst into tears. "I don't know, I'm pre-med!" She nearly poked her right eye out with the needle in her hand as she wiped her face again, sobbing. In touching her cheeks, Marina's blood painted her face.

There was a shout up front, from the control room. The message was indistinct, but the sentiment wasn't. The person was enraged.

"Okay, you need to calm the fuck down," Mathias said to Frances, who nodded and continued looping the needle into Marina's neck. But for all the calm Mathias appeared to exude, his beginner's luck faded. His first few stitches were uniformly even, optimal in terms of closing the wound. But after those initial few, the strings were sewn lopsidedly from his rushed frenzy to get the task over with. He didn't know what he was doing. His work was disastrous. The farther he traveled down the wound, the more it looked like he was deliberately knitting a crooked smily face pattern into Marina's chest.

The shuttle bounced again.

The string in Frances's needle snapped in half from the jolt. *"Shit,"* she whispered. She reached for the suturing kit to retrieve a new string, and she knotted it into the one that was already inside Marina. But, once again, to Frances's misfortune, the shuttle bounced while she was applying the new string to the circular back of her needle. It made her hand jump and, just as she had inadvertently done to Marina, Frances stabbed the pad of her own left index finger. She winced. Blood trickled down her digit. She grabbed a gauze and some tape to wrap it, but with another unexpected veer of the shuttle, her hair dropped in front of her face. She couldn't see anything in front of her. "Goddammit!" she exclaimed. She set the needle and the string down in the column between Marina's clavicle, grabbed the scissors, and, in ten seconds at most, boorishly chopped the length of her hair in half. Quentin and Mathias gawked her way, watching as clumps of it fell into Marina's open mouth; she spat up the strands. Frances had definitely seen better days. She looked terrible. Her hair was jaggedly uneven, cut right below her chin, and her naturally wavy texture only added to the hectic appearance. Nevertheless, the transformation did work to her benefit. Granted the gift of uninterrupted sight, she returned to her work and even finished it, knotting the strings at the end of the row of neck stitches.

Thirty minutes later, she closed up the cut in Marina's cheek and then took over for Quentin and Mathias when they completed their own stitchings. Jaymes asked if they should address the smaller lacerations, but Frances said that they weren't emergent. They had more dire problems at hand. Now, the most worrisome of them all involved the object in Marina's left hip.

"I am so lost," Mathias said at the end of the hour, when they were all taking a break.

He and Quentin were in the cockpit's restroom, the door left open for them to remain in contact with Jaymes and Frances outside. Mathias and Quentin nearly drained the soap container in their effort to rid themselves of Marina's blood. Their clothes were doused in it. Their fingers and everything they touched, from their faces to the doorknobs and their boots, were equally streaked in that sickening, rich, iron-scented liquid.

Frances was sterilizing a pair of suture scissors at the table outside the restroom. "A wise man once said he learned not to ask questions when it came to her," she said.

When the four of them were cleaned—as much as they could be—they split among themselves a single canteen of water Mathias had pilfered from Quentin's backpack. They sat on the floor, gripping the sturdy legs of the table for support so as to not go zooming across the room every time there was a flinch of the shuttle. They faced Marina, rubbernecking at her. Frances downed the refreshment from the bottle until there was but one swig left inside its walls. Never once in her chugging did she stop looking at Marina, who was laying on the floor.

Propped up on her elbows, Marina suddenly felt their eyes on her and looked their way, frowning. "What?" she asked.

"Venture a guess," Quentin said.

"Did the cut miss her voice box?" Jaymes asked Frances.

"Maybe?" was Frances's unknowing response. "I don't know."

"Clearly," Mathias said.

Frances huffed. She crawled forward, stopped herself above Marina's head, and helped her take in the last few drops of water from the canteen. Frances tipped back Marina's chin, holding her there, and let the water fall into her mouth.

"So now what?" Quentin asked.

Frances wiped Marina's mouth of the water droplets that didn't make it inside her. "Her stitches are holding up well," Frances observed. "We should get to that thing in her hip. Do we have any surgical pliers or other tools?"

"They're in the bathroom, already sterilized," Jaymes said.

When the tweezers, pliers, a new cloth, and the bottle of isopropyl alcohol were set up around Marina, the others encircled her like participants in a seance.

"You're wearing pants underneath, right?" Frances asked Marina, who nodded. Frances lifted the upper half of the suit that was draped over Marina's hips, exposing her sweatpants. "Right. I forgot. Okay, so…we're just going to remove your suit so I can get a clear image of…" She analyzed the thing in Marina's hip. "Of whatever that is."

They stripped Marina of the suit, which left her donned only in her sweatpants and long-sleeved undershirt. Frances's dainty fingers moved gently as they pressed around the inflamed skin that bordered the circular object. It was made of a hard plastic material—at least, the exposed part was.

"Can't we just rip it out?" Quentin asked.

"Not quite," Frances said. She flattened herself against the ground to be at eye level with Marina's midsection. "There's a pretty imperative vein that runs through the hips, I believe. But I'm not so sure. I think it's almost like the wrists and the jugular. I can only assume it results in serious damage if we disturb it too much."

Quentin didn't think it was even possible, but Marina looked worse. She looked like she had been dead for a while. The bags under her eyes were black, no longer gray, and the laceration that was stitched on her face had swollen at the edges; privy to the unnatural enlargement of the skin on Marina's face, Frances had given Marina an antibiotic pill during the cleaning break.

"All right," Frances said, inhaling. She was knelt on the floor, her face at Marina's hip, studying the mystery object up close.

"Can you tell what it is?" Jaymes asked.

Mathias, who was by Marina's calves, lowered himself down beside Frances. Had it been any other day and had he not been in the sourest of moods, Quentin may have snorted at the odd sight of Frances and Mathias, an unlikely pair, hovering their heads just above the apex of Marina's thighs to obtain decent views of the plastic, circular thing embedded into her. But it wasn't any other day, and Quentin was infuriated with Marina as he was with himself, so he didn't laugh. He just sat there, on his knees like Jaymes, and awaited their commentary.

"What the hell?" Mathias murmured in wonder.

Frances was gaping. "God, Marina, what did you do?"

"What?" Jaymes asked. "What is it?"

Frances dropped even lower to the floor. "Are those...? They look like twisted *teeth,*" she said, horrified.

"Yeah, like metal teeth," Mathias agreed.

Quentin, by Marina's head, also lowered himself to see the object. Because he couldn't see it too well from his side of Marina, he delicately tore back some of the surrounding sweatpants fabric. She flinched, and he paid her a bland, unemotional apology. When Frances and Mathias made no indication of moving aside for him to see the mysterious injection, Quentin turned on the miniature flashlight in his wristwatch and brought it close to Marina's hip.

"Oh, good idea," Frances applauded. "Bring it up again, Quentin."

Both Quentin and his wrist inched closer to Marina's left hip. He saw out the corner of his eye that she was straining her neck to see the thing as well, but he blocked her view when he tilted his head down to fully take it in. Frances was right, the best way to describe the oddity was a collection of twisted, metal teeth. Fangs, almost. They extended from the underside of the circular portion. The metal pieces were wide at the top and thinned near the bottom, hence its ability to clamp into her. It was chomped into her hip, sunken into bone and flesh and veins.

Quentin swallowed. "That is disgusting." What he thought was more repugnant, however, was the new puffiness of the surrounding skin. "Hey, is that an infection festering or—?"

"Could be," Frances said. "I don't know exactly."

"So what do you know, by the way?" Mathias asked.

Frances drew back, aghast. "Must I remind you that the people who were supposed to educate me are all dead? Natalie and I have only had books and prerecorded med classes to learn from, okay? I'm doing my best here."

Still leaned back on her elbows, Marina edged up a bit to obtain a gander of the object.

"Oh, no, no, no," Frances scolded. She pushed her hand against Marina, forcing her to back to the floor. "I need you to stay dow—"

The shuttle sprang to the right. Frances fell onto Marina. Quentin hit the floor. Jaymes and Mathias collected the nearby medical gadgetry before the various items could go scattering about the room again.

When they had regained their previous placements, Frances fixedly said to Marina, "That is exactly why I need you to stay down. It's enough that we're dealing with turbulence. Lay back. We can't have you moving. Jaymes, hold her down."

"Yup," Jaymes said. At Frances's behest, he placed his palms on Marina's shoulders, pushing her against the floor.

"But what…what is it?" Marina insisted, fighting to speak. "That object, what is it?"

Frances picked up the tweezers and looked to Jaymes. "You sanitized this part of her earlier, right?"

Jaymes nodded. "And I sterilized the tweezers."

"What, you're just gonna pull it out?" Quentin asked.

"No…" Frances bit her lip. "Well…I mean…Yes. I'm going to try that. Carefully, of course."

"Isn't that kinda dangerous?" Jaymes called into question.

Frances nodded quickly. "Mhm. Yes. Yes, that's why I'll need to stitch her as soon as it's removed or else she might bleed out." She glanced down to the floor, to the puddled blood. "Again," she added.

"Is that post-extraction protocol?" Jaymes asked.

"I think so."

"You think?" Marina repeated.

"Look, you've made it this far, Marina," Frances said. "I just stitched together your neck. You should've been dead an hour ago, so stop doubting my abilities all of a sudden." Quentin wanted to remind

Frances that the only one who had outwardly doubted her prowess was, from the beginning of their flight, herself. Everyone else was simply asking questions.

Frances's first attempt to extract the object from Marina's hip was pure mayhem that ensued for five, full minutes. She slid the flat-head tips of the scanty tweezers between two of the prong-like blades that bit into Marina's skin. With the tweezers, Frances tried to push the blades up, but it didn't work. They stayed firmly in place. Marina was huffing and puffing, her teeth grinding against each other in pain. Loud moans resounded throughout the shuttle, and always three or four seconds after her production of guttural sounds, the shuttle would veer and bounce, which made it unnervingly clear that their pilots were very much aware of the ruckus behind them, but were simply too preoccupied to interfere. Frances's frustration mounted to a boiling fury. Seeing her like that—heatedly angry—was shocking to Quentin. She was always the level-headed one, the placating constant who tended to center others.

Ten minutes later, Frances's efforts only proved to have worked against her. Her tweezers were lodged between three of the object's blades, and it showed no signs of loosening from under them. Frances requested the scalpel.

"What?" Marina seethed.

"I'm really not in the mood for your enquiries right now," Frances said to Marina, who was trying to appeal to the others with secretive, sidelong glances that she be saved from their blatantly confused medical head.

"Is a scalpel really a good idea for this?" Jaymes asked.

"Just get it for me," Frances demanded.

Jaymes acquiesced. They may have all doubted her, but they also had to admit that they probably couldn't have handled the situation any better than she. With the scalpel in hand, Frances slid its thin blade between two of the prongs that had entrapped the tweezers. She craned the utensil upward. For the first time all evening, the thing began to lift at one corner.

Frances exhaled with relief. "Thank God…Oh, thank God."

"Whatever you're doing, keep doing it," Jaymes said.

Mathias, whose head was still beside Frances, snidely said, "Such words of wisdom. Great advice, Chen."

Sweat streamed down Frances's forehead and dewed her eyelashes. "I'm going to give it a push up," she said. She bent her wrist, trying to compel the object higher.

It didn't budge.

"You could always try—" Quentin began.

"Ripping it out?" Frances proposed.

"What?! No," Quentin said. "Don't you have something a little more practical? More complex?"

"I take it you've never watched a c-section birth tape, but I have," Frances said. "It's horrifyingly primitive when a baby's head is stuck behind a rib or wound inside its own umbilical cord, so excuse me for not being complex enough."

"What do they do in that scenario?" Quentin asked.

"Rip the child out. Or so I saw…once."

"That's not a baby," said a small voice behind them, Fatima's voice. She had been so quiet all night that Quentin forgot she was even there with them. But, near the front of the passengers' quarter, her tiny head was looking over the harness of her seat and she had a hand pointed out, calling attention to the thing.

"See? Thank you," Mathias said, an arm extended toward Fatima. "Look, Fran, you gotta be carefu—"

"You think I don't know that?!" Frances rolled back the baggy sleeves of her suit, all the way up to her elbows. "Fine. No scalpel. I'm just going to try something else, then. Marina…on three. Okay?"

"Uh, " Marina started, her head shaking. "No, I—"

Frances counted to three and yanked at the top of the thing. Marina's body jerked. She mewled as loudly as her stitched neck allowed.

The shuttle jostled to one side.

Frances didn't stop pulling.

Marina didn't stop making noise.

"This hardly seems right!" Jaymes shouted.

"Quiet down!" Quentin scolded them.

Frances paused her pulling. "Sorry," she said to the wincing Marina. "One more try. One more."

Unable to shake her head, Marina blinked hard twice. She took in a breath. Frances didn't bother with a forewarning countdown to the second pull. She dropped her body lower to the floor, kept her right hand latched to the plastic top, and gave one, snapping yank. For what felt like the hundredth time that night, Marina screamed through her teeth. Her outcry reverberated around the metal walls of the cabin. Quentin shot a hand down over her mouth, muting her. Frances tugged. Marina kept screaming. Mathias squirmed in discomfort at the whole ordeal and even went so far as to push the thing up with the tweezers while Frances pulled. The screams Marina released were deeper, hoarser. Eventually, from the sweat and blood that were smeared on her fingers, Frances's hand slipped off the object.

Following the failure, Mathias tried to wriggle it, but it didn't budge. "Damnit!" He punched the floor. "It just ate our tweezer!"

"All right, one more time," Frances said.

"Yeah, okay."

"No," Marina managed to voice. "S-s-top. What're you—?"

"Trying to save your life, bitch," said an increasingly agitated Mathias. He grabbed the bottom end of the tweezers again and waited for Frances's mark; when she pulled up, he pushed the utensil's ends against the blades.

Marina made another gurgling sound.

"Okay, stop!" Jaymes interjected. "Stop it! C'mon, guys, that's enough! I'm sure we can pull them out another way!"

They didn't, though. The further they pursued their seemingly hopeless endeavor, the more Quentin felt Marina's tongue coiling against his palm as he muffled her.

But they were approached, all of them. Quentin heard it first, the breeze-like whoosh of the control room door sliding open behind them. Just as he had expected it to happen, they were caught in the midst of their compromising operation. He wondered how riotous a spectacle they made, with Frances squatting and tugging at the thing, Mathias laying on the floor with his face right above Marina's pelvis and his burly hands wrapped around the tweezers, and the other two restraining her shoulders and mouth. Quentin pressed his hand down harder onto Marina's mouth. Ewan was properly startled and perplexed.

"Out!" Quentin ordered. "Get out!"

Frances tugged.

Marina groaned again.

Quentin didn't know how it worked, but Ewan took two steps backwards, flinchingly walked himself into the control room, and vanished once the automatic door slid back to where he had been standing and watching them from afar.

By some similar stroke of luck, Frances and Mathias won back the tweezer. It was bloodier once extracted, wetting Frances's hands as she juggled it.

"I can't believe this," Frances said. "I stitched up her neck, yet I can't remove a...a...*thing*."

"It is a thing with fangs," Mathias said.

"What the hell is it?" Jaymes asked.

Mathias transitioned to a squat. He stared at the circular object, silent.

Quentin pulled his hand off Marina's mouth, ignoring the glare she sent him for having been smothered for over five minutes. He rubbed her saliva from his hand. "Why don't we take a break?" he asked. "We've been at this long enough. Let's rest and tackle it later."

Frances swiped at a teardrop that ran down her cheek. "You're right. It's too much stress on her body after so much blood loss."

Marina dropped her head to the ground in relief.

"I'm so sorry, Marina," Frances said. "Would you like anything? Some water maybe?"

Marina closed her eyes. "I want you to stop touching me," she said with miraculous smoothness, like she hadn't been cut in her neck.

Frances bit her lip again. She and Mathias glanced down to the object in their patient's hip.

"What?" Quentin asked them. "What's wrong?"

"I…" Frances sniffed. "I think we're worse off than before. After what we did, it looks a little deeper on one side."

Yeah, no shit, Quentin thought. "Do you have a medical manual or something?" he asked. "Something you can turn to when you need help?"

Frances's bottom lip didn't stop shaking. "No. I mean, yes. But it's…There's the database in the computer room, but that's on the third floor."

"So Division One's shuttle," Jaymes sighed. "Great."

"There must be something I can do," Frances said mournfully.

"No," came from Marina. "Don't do—"

"Marina, stop moving your mouth," Frances told her.

"You know…" Marina began, gathering in air, "for someone who—"

"You're moving your neck and cheek too much," Frances said. "You'll undo the stitches."

Marina closed her mouth.

Mathias bounced on his toes as he stayed squatting. He was biting at a fingernail when he stopped mid-chomp and stared at the mystery object once more. "Wait a minute," he said, but didn't finish his sentence.

The left side of Marina's face touched the floor as she laid limp, but she moved her head enough to see him.

"That...that thing," Mathias said.

"Yes?" Frances asked.

"I know how to get it out."

"How?"

Mathias came down from his squat, transitioned onto all fours, and closed in on Marina. She attempted squirming backwards, away from him, but he wrapped a hand around her right ankle and tugged her back into place. "Jaymes, hold her down," he said.

"Yeah, no way," Jaymes objected. "She's been through enough already."

"Hanson," Mathias said. He wasn't asking.

Quentin weighed his options. On one hand, he didn't care about Marina. On the other, he would have really liked to be up in his chair, watching a movie or reading a book to pass the time of their flight, not just spending the rest of his first night in a pile of blood—her blood—and playing assistant nurse. He said nothing, though.

"Get off her!" Frances interfered with Mathias's plan. "We've exacerbated it enough already!"

"No," Mathias said. "I know what I'm doing."

"No, you don't!"

"And you do?!" Mathias broke his stare at Marina's hip to focus on Frances. "You've been playing tug-of-war with that thing for ten minutes now! We're on the same education level here, Frances. Your teachers are dead, and you've never handled anything like this. Like or not, we're even."

Frances shoved a hand against his arm. "That is not true! I know far more than you do!"

Mathias shrugged, his right hand encircling Marina's knee and dragging her closer to him. "Whatever, I'll save our second-in-command if you won't."

"No!" Marina whisper-yelled.

Jaymes wrestled with Mathias, trying to get his hands off Marina. "C'mon, that's enough! She doesn't want your help! We can't dick around like this, Mathias, she's Quentin's advisor!"

Mathias elbowed Jaymes in the gut, and he cowered over, moaning.

"Jaymes!" Frances screamed, moving to him.

"Which is my fucking point," Mathias stressed in response. "It is important that we do this now. If you won't make that choice, I will."

"My…choice!" Marina growled up at him.

"Uh, wrong, Gustavsson," Mathias said. "You're advisor, so this is all our lives in your hands. Not just yours." He moved his hand to her hip, to the object.

It fell to Quentin, then, to do something. He thought of intervening, of saving…of saving whom? Marina? The very person he wanted to abandon in the foyer? He didn't know what to do, so he watched. He watched as Mathias's bulky fingers tightened around the circular, plastic thing with the blades, watched Marina feebly swat a hand at him, and watched as Mathias twisted it. And then Quentin's eyes followed that same, bulky hand as it lifted into the air. In Mathias's palm was the disk, and protruding up from it was the halo of small blades, each caked in Marina's flesh and blood.

Marina stopped wiggling.

Frances held her chest, breathing hard.

Quentin said nothing.

Mathias was smiling. No, beaming. He was giddy. Goofy and boyish, in fact. He had never looked so young, even then, when he had just reached his twenties and had aged as quickly as the rest of them. His beam turned into a grin, a grin of pride and smugness, sticking to his face as he said the two words, "Blender blade."

25

After Mathias had extracted the blender blade from Marina's hip, he and Jaymes carried Quentin's overtired advisor into the storage closet, where they laid her down onto an inflated air mattress; Quentin was the one who had spent twenty minutes blowing it up. Marina instantly slipped into a deep sleep, and Frances seized the opportunity of having an unflinching patient to finish the minor stitches, which was a task she completed by midnight.

No one slept the way Marina did. She was deadweight and snoring once the clock struck eleven. The others wished they could have lost consciousness as thoroughly as she had, but the fact was that everyone else remained conscious for that entire first night aboard their individual shuttle. The jostles and jerks of their environment worked against the closing of eyes, and the mystery of what Athol and Ewan were viewing in their advancement of the shuttle was most unsettling; Quentin was thankful for the absence of windows in the passengers' quarter. In an effort to distract themselves from the unnerving experience, Mathias put on his headphones and listened to some music, Jaymes eased himself with breathing exercises, and Frances asked Quentin about what he thought might have been the cause for Marina's tardiness and injuries. He said he didn't know, but he very well did.

Their flight came to a stop at six o'clock in the morning on the 3rd of February. Neither of the pilots emerged from the control room to say so, but the group that was confined to the rear end of the transport gleaned it on their own when the shuttle came to a complete standstill that lasted for over fifteen minutes. They finally closed their eyes. Their bodies unwittingly decided that the days would become their nights, since that was the schedule of their pilots; as long as they were in motion, there wouldn't be any sleeping.

During the daytime hours of the 3rd, Quentin fully expected a flummoxed Ewan to make an appearance with a myriad of snippy questions that needed answering. But he never did. Some time in the evening hours, everyone felt a rumble and knew, per the renewed shaking of the walls, that their forward flight had resumed. However curious Ewan may have once been regarding the torn-up state of the captain's advisor, he must have deemed it negligible when compared to the gravity of his job.

That night of the 3rd as well as the earliest hours of the 4th were blurry and bouncy. Had he not been so petrified by the prospect of crashing at any given moment, Quentin may have considered the time boring. Because of the whimsical jerks and jumps of the shuttle, board games couldn't be played, books couldn't be read, and Mathias discovered that not even the highest volume of a music player could mute the screeches of metal rubbing against metal every time they reeled a certain way. Quentin never had the opportunity to consider the journey in such a bland light, though. He spent his every breath whispering to the god in whom he fickly believed, pleading to live to see the later hours of that same morning. He would slam his eyes closed for an hour at a time, but wouldn't ever sleep. In the darkness his lids provided, he recalled visions from the drastically different days of a simpler life he had once lived; sitting with Hollis atop the roof of their middle school on a warm weekend night, nibbling on potato chips and sipping cheap beers; flinging snowballs at Lucas on a winter afternoon, cackling as their ever-petulant mother bemoaned the frosty, white orbs that careened against the living room windows as she attempted to watch the television inside their house. To his disappointment, Quentin found that the memories were dwindling in their vividness. They were hazier, the details harder to remember. Immersing himself in the fantasy of living his old life became a challenge. He was stuck with reality and he had to accept it. He dealt with the fact that he wasn't sitting on a school roof with Hollis, but was in the shuttle, eating tasteless, chalky protein rations. He wasn't flinging snowballs with his brother, but was, instead, something of a hurled snowball himself as the shuttle zoomed up, down, and side to side, occasionally half-turning and threatening to collide into outdoor objects. His mother wasn't even griping at him, and he grimly reminded himself that she would never have the opportunity to do so again.

His sleep during the daytime hours of the 4th was terrible. The shuttle was unmoving, everyone around him was snoring, and he assumed the same applied to the pilots, whom he hadn't seen in two days. Quentin, however, continued on in restlessness unabated. He chose to remedy his conundrum and went, rather begrudgingly, into the storage closet at the back of the passengers' quarter. It was for the best—at least, logistically. It wasn't like he could go there in the night, when their pilots were awake and the small act of walking across the room put one at risk of careening into a wall.

Once he was inside, Quentin soundlessly sealed the door behind him.

A soft, orange light dimly shone in the top-left corner of the space, letting him see a wide-awake Marina sitting up on the mattress and slathering one of the stitched and healing wounds on her arms with a cooling gel. The wound she slathered was the one Quentin had stitched; rather unexpectedly, it looked the gnarliest of all the repair jobs, to the extent that Mathias's sloppily executed one was healing faster. The hairs on Quentin's arms raised as he took in Marina. She was still in her old clothes, her sweatpants and long-sleeved shirt, which were stained with blood blotches. Crooked lines of absorbable strings were crocheted into almost every expanse of her skin; he could probably count on one hand the parts of her that weren't surgically modified.

Quentin leaned back against the door. He felt the front of his hands dig into the small of his back as his knuckles pushed against his spine. He asked, "Do I even want to know?"

"You have a pretty strong imagination," Marina said. Her voice sounded better. She laid the tube of healing gel beside the mattress. "Wager a guess," she challenged him.

Quentin's voice was neutral as he asked, "What is actually the matter with you? How do you blindly follow orders like that?"

"I don't blindly follow anything."

"But you do. You did. There was no evidence to—"

"It was perfectly evidence-based. Your mother—"

"I don't care about my mother," Quentin said. His own voice sounded foreign to him. "That was her choice. All of it. She calculated the risks. She dealt with the consequences. That doesn't apply to me. I didn't choose this life. Whatever she got herself into, whatever she had to do for this…I don't care, because I'm not going down that path, too. I'm more than just Sydney's son." His hands found their way into the pockets of his suit. "What are your values anyway?"

Marina quirked a brow. "What do you mean?"

Just as well. Quentin didn't expect her to understand the question. She was heartless in that way. "It's a simple question," he said. "What are your values? Do you value life? Do you believe that there's dignity to existing? No, you know what? Fuck it. Why'd I even bother?" He bid her no goodbye and exited the closet, quietly closing the door behind himself.

As he entered the main room, Frances came from the adjacent restroom. "Oh, you went to see her," she said, sounding pleasantly surprised. "Did she tell you anything?"

"Nothing," Quentin lied, and his chest felt heavy as he said it. "She's asleep."

Frances stepped closer. With the small distance between them, he noted just how uneven and unkempt her new haircut looked; straight and wavy wisps curled around each other in the occasional tangle, some dangling down to her collarbone and others knotted up, just below her ears. "She's been out since we placed her there," she said. "I woke her last night, but she was so tired that she could barely tell me what hurt and what didn't. I've had to force her to take her antibiotics." She scratched her chin. "Maybe we should wake her now. More forcefully, I mean. Whatever it is she went through…we have to know. *You* have to."

"She needs to rest," Quentin said.

"But—"

"Frances, whatever she got herself into will come out eventually. There's no need wearing her out when we can interrogate her later, when she has energy. She'll be fine."

"I know she'll be fine but—"

"And I'm saying that she stays in there," Quentin insisted. "She'll wake up when she's well rested and then we'll get our answers."

Frances bit the inside of her cheek. "If that's what you want, I guess," she yielded.

"It is."

Despite having gone without sleeping, their conscious hours during the 4th improved his mood. Athol and Ewan seemed to have learned and followed a decently predictable rhythm to their flying. The ride was far from perfect, but it was better. For the first time since they went independent, Mathias and Fatima took advantage of the relative stability to indulge in a few rounds of chess, aided plentifully by the magnetic bottoms of the pieces, which made them stick to the metal board, no matter how many bumps and bounces threatened to thwart the fun of their matches. Jaymes closed his eyes to an audiobook and then a full playlist of music. Frances attentively flipped through the pages of a textbook on childbirth; "You never know, with everyone on the ship being so young and fertile," she explained awkwardly. Quentin passed the time watching a few pre-downloaded episodes of a domestic comedy from 2035.

Even on the 4th, no one saw the pilots. They were undoubtedly alive and functioning, but they never made an effort to interact with the others. It thoroughly took Quentin aback that Ewan and Athol never called for him to enter their area and provide an explanation for the events that had happened on the 2nd. Quentin wasn't complaining, though. The explanation wasn't one that could have been easily delivered, being looped into coinciding elements of a greater story he didn't want to tell. It was better, easier, that way.

"You would choose to side with the people who killed your own mother?" Marina asked Quentin during the day of 5th, when all the others were asleep and the two of them were locked away and speaking openly in the privacy of the storage closet, bound to go unheard.

Quentin didn't know why he went to Marina. His disdain for her had only intensified over the course of the week. He questioned his decision throughout the entire time he sat across from her, especially during the lags in their conversation, when they would pause to nibble at their ration bars. But he felt, rather pathetically, that because secrets were so aggravating to keep, it was greatly relieving to be able to discuss the matter with someone, even if that someone was Marina.

"You never struck me as the type to prioritize blood over sensibility," Quentin said.

"I'm not," Marina affirmed. "But you're a different story."

She zipped up the vest that he had brought to her along with the food and water. She wasn't as awful a spectacle, then. Newly capable of performing small movements, she had changed into a fresh pair of sweatpants and a new sweater, which she topped with the article Quentin had brought to her.

A few minutes later, after she finished her humble meal and drank some water from the canister that stood beside her mattress, she asked him, "Did you tell the others?"

"No," Quentin said.

"When will you tell them?"

"I don't want to."

Marina sighed into the spout. "You can be so exhausting to talk to sometimes."

Quentin folded the wrapper of his protein bar, having finished eating too. "Why can't you do it?" he asked.

"I've done my part. I'm not a captain. It's your story to tell. Make sure you do it before the end of the week."

Just as he had done before, Quentin abruptly stood and exited the closet with no forewarning or farewell. He returned to his seat with a loud *"thunk!"*

In the night, when everyone was awake, he told Frances that he had paid Marina a visit, spurring her to hopefully ask, "Anything?"

"Nothing," Quentin replied for what felt like the hundredth time that week, even though he had only visited Marina twice. He supposed he hadn't appreciated the weight of the guilt that was birthed by his lie, and the longer he perpetuated it, he swore it was heavier and applying pressure to his chest. "I fed her some food and she gave me the silent treatment," he said. "Maybe next time."

The 6th's hours in motion were seamless and verged on effortless, the stablest the shuttle had ever been. In spite of the occasional jolt, when considering everything they had endured the prior four days, Quentin found it most peaceful. Frances cuddled up and read on her chair with her harness undone, a fluffy blanket spread over her legs and a long pillow on her lap, wholly undisturbed, her pages neither flapping nor flicking from any sudden movements. Jaymes was stretching beside the table and listening to music, humming along with the tunes that directly streamed into his ears from his headphones. Mathias and Fatima were finally out of their seats and gathered on the floor with the chess board between them. They vied against one another for two hours straight, until Fatima grew bored of her same opponent and requested that the unoccupied Quentin swap in for Mathias. Later, when she tired of playing with Quentin, who won every game despite trying not to, she begged for the young men to square off against each other for her entertainment.

At five o'clock in the morning—figuratively the evening for them—a recurring beeping sound rang loudly from the front of the shuttle. They ignored it at first, but when it didn't stop, they grew worried.

"Do we ever get a break?" Mathias asked some two minutes later, when the beeping hadn't died off as expected.

Quentin put down the black pawn he was preparing to move.

Frances closed her book, too distracted to continue reading. She squinted and studied their environment. "We're not flying," she said. "Have you noticed that?"

Quentin looked up to the harnesses that were stiffly in place above the unattended seats. He glanced to the restroom door, which was ajar, but not rattling like it always did mid-flight.

"You think I should go see if they're okay?" Quentin asked.

"Might be best," Jaymes said. "You'll kill two birds with one stone by updating us on how they're doing while you're at it."

Quentin stood up and shook out his legs, which tingled after having spent an abundance of time in the same position. When he approached the door to the control room, he scanned his thumb on the keypad beside it. Walking past the threshold and hearing the door slide shut behind him, he realized that he had never been in that quarter of the shuttle before. There wasn't any need for him to have explored that section, unless there were an emergency of some sort, which he doubted was the case—he hoped, at least. He thought he would find himself inside the control room, but he was proven wrong when he had to hunch lower to continue forward. The walls were crammed more tightly together, and the ceiling was low enough to form a tunnel-like chute. A dark-blue radiance emanated from the ceiling's recessed lights.

To avoid startling the preoccupied pilots, he walked with pronounced footfalls, making himself louder as he saw four seats ahead. An enormous gap split the seating in half, and through it Quentin could see a desk that glowed a collection of colors and controls. A window made up the entirety of the front wall. He stopped short, suppressing the urge to faint as he stared at the massive darkness directly in front of him and the intimacy of being in such disconcerting nearness to flying boulders of all shapes and sizes, the kind he had only ever seen as illustrations on the walls of his science classes back home.

"...But the link couldn't break," Ewan was saying, and then he leaped up, stood in the space between the rows of seating, and leaned over to press a button on the desk. To Quentin's relief, Ewan's form partially obscured the window. As Ewan began to turn around, Quentin materialized from the tunnel. "Christ!" Ewan flinched, a hand over his heart. "I didn't see you there."

The beeping sound was even louder up front.

"Sorry," Quentin said. "We were just wondering if everything was all right."

Athol rose from his seat. With his suit half open, the only thing that concealed his torso was a zipped-up sweatshirt. "We picked up a signal indicating that One and Three are on the move," he disclosed, "but the problem is that we can't...can't...move."

Quentin's gaze followed Ewan as he walked over to one of the two doors bordering the tunnel on each side. One, Quentin assumed, hid the control room's lavatory. Ewan opened the other, revealing an electrical closet. Quentin turned away and indulged in a moment of tourism, surveying the bunk beds stuffed against the far-left wall of the control room and the mess of extra clothes and jumpsuits that were strewn across the bit of floor outside the other door, which was the presumed restroom.

"Define 'can't,'" Quentin belatedly responded.

"We *can't* move," Athol said with a touch of force. "We've tried almost everything, even ran a scan on the engine for any malfunctions. Nothing's working, Quentin We don't know what to do." Tears gathered in his bloodshot eyes, and Quentin wondered if the pilots had been sleeping as much as everyone else or if they had been suffering like him.

"How long have you known this?" Quentin asked.

"A little over three hours. We received a warning earlier, around two in the morning. But we put it off, and now we're stuck. The system wasn't lying to us. That's why the shuttle's powering down now. We've officially stopped."

Quentin hated the sound of the alarm. It reminded him of a slightly less deafening version of his lifelong earaches. His right hand worked its way up to the side of his head, where he fumbled with his earlobe and rubbed the area to reduce the ear strain, even if only momentarily.

There was a knock on the control room door. It was audible above the beeping, but barely so, as it had intensified over the last few seconds. "Hello?!" someone—Jaymes, it seemed—called to them. "Is everything all right in there?!"

No one in the control room bothered answering a question of such insignificance. They couldn't answer it even if they wanted to.

"Is there anything you need me to do?" Quentin offered.

"Dude, I don't even know what *we're* supposed to do," Ewan said over his shoulder as he rummaged through the closet.

The door at the end of the tunnel whirred and opened. There was only one other person capable of entering besides those who were already inside—indeed, it was her. Marina had one arm thrown over Frances's shoulder as she hobbled through the tunnel. The door automatically slid to a close behind them.

Ewan still had his head stuck into the closet, but Athol's eyes were available to take in the state of Marina. He didn't seem to care about how she looked, though—that, or he was supremely skilled in concealing his confusion. "There's an issue with the shuttle's mobility," he said to her. "In that it refuses to move."

As Frances brought her closer to them, Marina asked, "Is there any way we can contact Patterson?"

"We're in close enough range where we might be able to try an emergency call sign," Athol said.

Quentin frowned. "But I thought that we couldn't—"

"We're only about ten miles away from him, not hundreds," Athol said, "We might be able to."

A low murmur of the engine sounded from beneath them. Quentin looked down to the floor. He watched his feet tremble with the sound.

"Ewan, what did you just do?" Athol asked. "Whatever you did, keep going. It's working."

Ewan turned around. "I didn't," he said. "I'm looking for my inhaler."

"But we just heard…Did we?" Athol asked, made unsure by Ewan's dismissal.

"Yes, we did," Frances said.

Athol grabbed the armchair of his empty seat. He cleared his forehead of the sweat beads above his brows.

All of a sudden, there was a leftward bounce of the shuttle followed by a higher-pitched beeping sound. The magnitude of the jolt wasn't enough to throw them off their feet, but they braced themselves to avoid falling over. Quentin and Athol grabbed the back of the same pilot seat, Athol's, while Ewan hugged the open door to the closet, and Frances and Marina sturdied themselves against the edges of the tunnel walls.

Frances gasped. "What's happening?"

"Is it running again?" Quentin asked.

"I don't trust it," Athol voiced. He rolled back his shoulders and picked at the corners of his eyes, which further reddened from the strain of staring at a screen on the desk for one straight minute.

The beeping sounded again.

Athol returned to his seat, but he didn't pull down the harness, as if he wasn't ready to settle in yet. "I'll try and send a message," he said. "Ewan, run another scan on the engine."

Ewan acquiesced. He plopped himself back down in his seat and began to type into one of the touchscreens on the left side of the desk.

The beeping stopped.

"Did you do that?" Athol asked his partner.

"No, I was just pulling up the messaging screen on the computer. What do you want me to say?"

Quentin's fingers tightened around the rubber edges of Athol's armrest.

Facing Marina, Athol noticeably ignored Quentin. "What suits this situation?"

"What you just told me, that'll do," Marina said. "Put in that thing about our loss of mobility."

"Okay," Ewan said. His fingers hovered over the glowing screen under his hand. He lowered his pointer digit to the letter P, which was all that Quentin could see from the other side of the room.

The lights flickered.

Ewan stopped typing.

"What are you doing?!" Athol asked. "Keep going!"

The lights flickered four more times before blacking out. Quentin heard another gasp from behind him, probably from Frances again, and they all stood perfectly still. The only brilliance they relied on were the glowing controls on the desk, as the shimmers beyond the window were too gentle and remote for their radiance to be useful.

Ewan resumed typing.

A strong knock came from the other side of the door at the end of the tunnel. "What are you doing in there?!" Mathias hollered. "What the hell's that sound?!"

"There's clearly some problem here," Quentin said.

Ewan scoffed. "Thank you, Quentin," He continued typing out his message. "Great. Everyone's scheduled to meet at the end of the belt tomorrow, meanwhile we're doomed to fall behind with this crap."

The lights flickered back on.

"Oh, good. Any ideas while we can see?" Quentin asked.

"None," Athol said. His hands were out and his palms were open, as though he were appealing to the shuttle to provide an answer.

Answer him, it did. The shuttle jerked forward. One second, Quentin was gripping Athol's armrest, the next he was flying backwards toward the young women behind him. He slammed into Frances and Marina, crashing all three of them to the floor. They groaned and winced under his weight. There were a couple shrieks from behind them, in the passengers' area. One sounded like it came from Fatima, and a surprisingly higher-pitched one from someone else followed—it could only have come from Mathias or Jaymes.

"You guys all right?!" Ewan shouted over the back of his seat.

Quentin and Frances rolled off each other and massaged the backs of their heads, each crawling up onto all fours. Once he was up, Quentin felt around for blood. He was relieved to discover none on his hands. Marina laid on her side, holding her left hip, where the freshly removed blender blade had been lodged into her. He realized that he must have struck her there. He didn't apologize.

Athol pulled his harness down and only removed his hands from it once he heard the mechanism click into place. "Did any of us do that?" he asked Ewan.

"I'm typing out a message over here, man," Ewan replied.

"This is impossible! You must've done something!"

"I'm telling you, I didn't! I can't even type out a message!"

Banging came from the end of the tunnel. "What the fuck?!" Mathias roared. "No warning?!"

"You know what?" Athol turned around. "Let them in. Maybe they accidentally hit something back there."

When she saw that Quentin had replaced her in aiding Marina to her feet, Frances volunteered to open the locked door behind them. Mathias furiously stormed in, but Jaymes lingered in the doorway to keep it from closing. Past them, Quentin saw Fatima sitting in her seat, her harness protecting her body.

"Did you two touch *anything* back there?" Athol quizzed them as soon as they came into view. "Did you touch anything you weren't supposed to or something unfamiliar, something you didn't recognize? Maybe in the closet or the electrical box? It could've been accidental."

Jaymes and Mathias both shook their heads.

Frances took Marina back from Quentin.

"Ewan, how's that message coming along?" Marina asked.

"I can't type anything," Ewan admitted, dread on his tongue.

"Elaborate," Marina said.

"I can't do *anything*. It's frozen, Marina." Ewan smacked the edge of the desk. "Fuck."

"Where's Patterson?" Quentin asked.

"Our monitor says he's still about ten miles away," Athol answered. "But who knows if that's true. We don't even know when's the last time our monitor was accurate. For all we know, it's been frozen since last night."

Ewan pulled a leg up to his seat and wrapped his arms around it. "We should try and find him, though. Maybe we can reattach, transfer, and go the rest of the way paired with his shuttle."

To everyone's surprise, Marina said, "Absolutely not."

"Why?" Ewan asked.

"If ours is this unstable on its own, I don't want it paired with his, not if his is perfectly fine. For all we know, this is some type of preprogrammed hack that'll make it impossible for him to decouple from us later. We're not taking that risk with his shuttle."

Ewan put an elbow on his knee. "Who could've sabotaged the layers of security installed in here?"

Marina sighed. "For one, that guard who held us at gunpoint sure had hours of free time on his own, didn't he?"

Quentin swallowed dryly.

Athol pinched the bridge of his nose, standing up. "Look, let's just try a reboot. Or restart, whatever you want to call it. We'll have to leave the cockpit and go into the basement."

Ewan joined Athol in the aisle between their seats. "Engine room is which one?"

"Eighty-seven, I think."

"Is it safe for you to go down there?" Frances asked skeptically. "The fumes will get to you, won't they?"

"We'll wear our helmets and Grains," Ewan assured. "And it's not like we haven't been shut down for some time now, so we can go to—"

The shuttle shot forward.

Everyone was instantly propelled backward, through the open entryway and into the passenger area. Athol and Marina flew down the aisle and were hurled against the closed door of the restroom, all the way at the back. Jaymes, Frances, and Mathias slammed into Quentin's seat. Ewan and Quentin ended up across from each other, gripping the baseboards of the walls just outside the closed control room door. Fatima screamed, but had the presence of mind to lock herself into her harness. The shuttle never stopped shifting directions. It shot upward, then forward. It tilted back and shot up again.

"Do something!" Jaymes urged.

"How can I?!" Athol countered. Deep into the other side of the room, he clutched Marina's wrist to guide her over to the bolted-in table in the corner. Lest the unpredictable ride toss them again, they latched themselves onto its legs.

Mathias and Frances clung to the back of Quentin's seat. She wrapped trembling arms around its harness.

"Ewan!" Athol shouted. "Get in there! Now!"

Ewan released a hand from the baseboard and moved it up to grip a seam in the wall. As the shuttle tilted back even further, he swung his legs forward and positioned his feet just above Quentin's head, which was opposite him. "Shit!" Ewan exclaimed.

"C'mon, you can do it!" Mathias encouraged. Grunting, he curled an arm around Frances's back to push her closer against Quentin's seat, helping to keep her in place.

There was no way Ewan could continue moving vertically. He flipped himself over, so that he faced the floor. With his feet safely pressed against the wall behind him and his hands pressed against the wall in front, he shuffled down to the keypad and scanned his right thumb, keeping his other four digits affixed to the wall. The door slid open. He shuffled sideways, pulling in his stomach and leveling his breaths like they had done in EV Prep. He held his position, a plank of some sort, and kept moving.

Quentin couldn't keep hanging off the edge of the wall. He feared a backwards fall that would send him shooting against the restroom door like the impact Marina and Athol had braved—the landing could have paralyzed them. Wanting a different fate, Quentin decided to mimic that same, supported plank position Ewan made, but Quentin went facing up instead of down.

He made the mistake of glancing into the control room as he traveled. Through the window, he saw that their shuttle had covered a great distance in the short amount of time they all spent rolling, hanging, and recovering. He was open-mouthed and drooling as he saw where they were headed: at full speed, they were hurtling toward a gargantuan rock. They were catapulting toward an asteroid.

Athol shrieked.

"Quentin, keep the door open!" Ewan commanded.

Quentin ground his teeth and rejoined Ewan in the sideways shuffle. Quentin approached the doorway, which was just beginning to close as Ewan persisted his scrambling down the tunnel, making his way beyond the entrance. There, Quentin carefully turned his body over and sat as comfortably as the small space allowed. The beginning of the tunnel was narrower than the adjacent walls of the passengers' quarter, so he put his feet up against the tunnel wall and crunched up his legs, bringing his knees to his chest. He spread his arms out, kept them stuck to the wall behind him, and stiffly held the position. That was all Ewan required of him; Quentin just needed to stay in place. *This is how I die,* he thought. *This is how I actually die.*

Ewan, still facing down, came within a yard of the tunnel's end.

In the passengers' quarter, Marina and Athol crawled up the table and latched their hands onto the edges of the top surface, their bodies spread all over it.

Fatima was crying.

Quentin thought the asteroid looked closer.

Ewan reached the start of the tunnel. "Okay....How do I do this?" he asked himself.

"Hurry up!" Athol shouted.

Ewan threw a leg down. The other followed. He pushed his hands off the wall, took advantage of the forceful motion, and disappeared into the room. The others lost sight of him, could only trust that he would find his way to the desk at the front.

"You've got this!" Athol yelled.

Quentin's eyes trained on the window, where scrapes and scratch marks peppered the glass. His stomach flipped. The shuttle was being peppered by debris, the debris of minerals that had split off and lingered in the orbit of the asteroid. He swore he felt the shuttle's unanticipated flight accelerate; his opinion was seconded by Fatima's screeching. All that he saw through the glass ahead was a brown surface. He didn't know how much longer they had, but he knew it couldn't have been more than another minute.

"Ewan!" Mathias groaned out.

The pilot finally became visible. Hanging off the back of Athol's seat, Ewan's fingers dug into the harness. He rolled over the seat top and fell into it. He didn't bother with the harness. Instead, he opted to push his left arm forward against the invisible force around them to reach for a control on the desk.

So much debris was clashing with the window that the dominant object ahead of them was overshadowed by the gray of all the scrapes on the glass.

"Fuck!" Mathias exclaimed. "All right, listen up!"

What the fuck? Quentin thought.

"You're my fucking mates!" Mathias professed. He was crying and his nose was scrunched up, like the statement actually caused him some form of physical pain. "Didn't wanna say it before….never would have...But you're my mates!" He reached a hand down to the front of the seat he was holding, which was Fatima's, and held the small hand that had risen to meet his.

Frances sobbed. Her legs tightened around Quentin's seat.

Jaymes shook his head vehemently. "I am not dying...I am not...not today…"

They were so close that Quentin could see divots in the asteroid's surface.

There was a grunt ahead, from Ewan. "I'm sorry!" he told them. "I can't!"

Quentin closed his eyes. He recalled the discomfort of sitting upon the rickety wicker chairs on Agata's front porch, could taste the dates and figs she had so dearly feasted upon along with the tangy stings of her fresh, organic orange juice. He thought back to what must have been her last question before passing: "Do bees buzz for butterflies?" He thought of his brother, too. Of course he did. But his imagining of the boy's face was blurrier. Through his effort of remembering Lucas, Quentin knew that one day, should he live a full life, there would come a time when every freckle and uniquely shaped frown of Lucas's face would slip from memory. With a defeatist touch to his senses, Quentin reasoned that perhaps it wouldn't have been so pitiful a thing to leave his life behind at that moment. Did he want to live long enough to experience the nightmare of being unable to remember Lucas's face. While most of the others' became erratic, Quentin's breathing slowed. He heard the screams of his counterparts, felt the instability of the ship around him, but he remained serene. He dared to think that he was at peace. Agata and Lucas were all that Quentin came to see and hear. He saw his brother's smile and heard his grandmother's inane question.

This is how I die, Quentin thought, but, that time, with the acceptance of a man who was satisfied with the life he had lived. He was ready to leave it, ready to move on and reunite with Agata.

Ewan pulled the shuttle up.

Unlike all the other days, they didn't spend the 6th sleeping. They huddled in the control room in a circle on the floor. The door to the passengers' quarter was locked behind them. Fatima was bundled up in a blanket, and Frances's legs were curled around her. Athol, Marina, and Mathias sat under Ewan's seat, and Ewan remained upon Athol's, with Jaymes and Quentin slightly in front of him on the floor. No one spoke. They didn't have to. The silence did it for them.

With the exception of the heating and oxygen supplier systems, Ewan had shut down the ship to reduce the risk of any more whimsical malfunctions occurring suddenly. Quentin's wristwatch and the few backup controls on the desk were the only illuminations permitted, and since no one wanted to spend the aftermath of the catastrophic morning in the pitch-black passenger area, everyone gathered up front, in the control room.

"It was Roxy," Quentin said.

He thought his advisor would display perhaps a minute hint of surprise, but she looked like she wasn't listening to him.

"What about her?" Athol asked.

"It was Roxy all along," Quentin said, bringing his legs up to his chest and hugging himself. He felt small, childlike. "Patterson told Marina to take care of her before the dispatch." He motioned to Marina with his elbow. "That's why she looks like that."

Frances lifted her head up from Fatima's hair. "What?"

"Hollis," Quentin said, looking at nothing specifically. "Hollis Carlyle was supposed to be here. Roxy's in his place. Patterson knew I was close with him, so he wanted me to have a friend up here. He thought it would be good for me. But Hollis wasn't home to be kidnapped that night, so Roxy got the slot."

"But how does that make any of this her fault?" Frances asked.

Quentin ignored her. "I remember wondering why…why his strict parents would let him skip school for so long…would let him stay home, claiming a sickness, all those days. But he wasn't sick. He didn't have the flu or mono or anything. They were hiding him." He spoke more to himself than to the people around him. "I knew his father was acting weird that day, when I called the house." He blinked and remembered where he was. He needed to speak more clearly, for his sentences to be more cohesive. "Apparently, my mom worked in intelligence. I didn't know that. I thought she was just a housewife. But not the homemaking kind, just a trophy wife. Just a dumb, useless housewife, who wouldn't cook, clean, or do basic math. Come to find out, that wasn't the case. Not exactly, anyway. She couldn't cook or clean, but she could sure as hell memorize a phone number by heart. I remember that."

Everyone was staring at him.

"So when she was assigned to go looking for him, for Hollis," Quentin clarified, "whoever the Carlyle's cut a deal with to keep him safe must have gotten to her, probably as promised." He added, with the driest tone and the droopiest eyes, "So, she's dead. She's been dead. And Hollis is nowhere to be seen. But Roxy is in his place. Roxy, who cried the most when we all thought Mathias killed that guard. Roxy, who Marina never trusted. So, there's that."

Frances was crying into the back of Fatima's head. "Your mother's dead?" she asked whisperingly. It was no surprise to him that she was upset, as she had known the Hansons for almost her entire life. After all, she had been their neighbor.

"When did you find out about this?" Jaymes asked.

"The day before the flight."

"The day *before* the flight and you didn't think to tell us?" Athol asked angrily.

Mathias clenched his teeth. His jaw popped out. "That's why Roxy wanted us to stay back, during that first day in the basement," he said. He sounded both amazed and insulted. "That's why she told us not to go looking for an exit. Because she already knew where we were and knew we'd die if we found one. She always did know."

"Before any of us," Ewan said.

Frances was glaring Quentin's way. "I saw your face, you know. In the foyer, earlier in the week, when we were looking for Marina. I remember wondering, '*why* is he so angry looking?' But now I know the answer to that. You never wanted Marina to make it out alive, did you?"

"I thought I was doing what I had to do to get back home," Quentin said.

Jaymes's mouth hung open. "Quentin, Roxy's people killed your mother."

"And that's a mess my mother got herself into," Quentin said without shame. "I didn't choose that for myself."

"How can you think like that?" Ewan asked. His disgust was evident in the way he vocalized every word, how he slowly said every one, like a foul taste was on his tongue.

Quentin felt no shame. His lowered head rose up for all to see an unabashed show of contempt and anger. "I did something for once," he said. "Just like everyone wanted me to do. I haven't heard the end of it these last twelve months. Every day, someone's calling me depressed or lazy or unmotivated…and no shit. What did you think would happen? But now I've finally lived up to what you all wanted me to do, right? I did something. I took matters into my own hands for the sake of my future."

"*Your* future, yes," Athol pointed out. "But at the cost of millions—no, billions—of others. That is not what any of us meant when we said we wanted you to grow up and accept your role."

"My role?" Quentin repeated. "And what role is that? Lending my ears to a bunch of people my parents knew? That's not a future of freedom and choice. That's slavery. Glorified slavery."

"Everyone in this room knows that is not the case," Jaymes disputed.

"Oh, it isn't? Kept captive, forced to live out the rest of our lives for—"

"You know," Frances said, cutting him off, "I've had it with you. With your selfishness. I thought maybe you would change, but you never did. You're still seventeen all these years later."

Quentin laughed at her. "Okay, fine. I'm sorry that not all of us are perfect students like Casey and Athol and Ewan; people who are prominent in these types of environments. Maybe you revel in playing the hero but—"

Frances unwound her limbs from around Fatima, who knew to crawl away. "Revel in?" Frances asked, revolted by the implication. "Do you think I have fun knowing that, at any minute, one of our fertile women on board can get pregnant and I wouldn't know a thing about how to help them? Do you think I enjoyed what happened the other day, trying to keep your advisor alive? Who, I just found out, you tried to let die? Do you really think I enjoyed any of that? That I wouldn't rather be back home in a good school, getting actual medical training, and at the same time being able to live like a normal nineteen-year-old? Why would I want that, right? Why would I want that when I can be up here, barely getting by in saving people and losing out in saving our second-in-command to a person who used to be the biggest drug addict from our high school? Yeah, why would I want anything else, Quentin?" She closed her eyes and inhaled. "I'm sorry, Mathias. I didn't mean it like that."

"It's fine," Mathias said, understanding.

Slowly, Frances worked her gaze back up to Quentin. "To suffer, to deal with things that aren't easy…That's part of being an adult. But more importantly, that's part of what it means to put yourself second for the greater good. Not all morally good things call for happiness. Unfortunately for you, the pains for an end goal like this are worth suffering through. You just need to grow up."

"I need to grow up?" Quentin asked. "I need to, when the rest of you are being unrealistic? You really think we can actually save the world from complete ruin?"

"Maybe the odds are against us," Ewan said, "but it's always better to try than to downright ignore something we could possibly fix on our own, even if we have a slim chance at best."

"Then that's the fundamental difference between me and all of you. I am pragmatic, you're idealistic."

Marina rolled her eyes. "A true pragmatist recognizes that, where there is an opportunity to end a threat against one's life, it is always best to seize the one chance of eliminating that threat rather than pretending it doesn't exist."

"So you're pragmatic, then?" Quentin asked. "Marina, look at you. You can't even move your left cheek without it bleeding. That's how far your pragmatism has gotten you."

Worn out by the conversation, Athol said, "Sacrifices always have to be made. Just how many times do we have to tell you that? Whether it be our education, our youth, our happiness...It's all irrelevant. When the world might not even exist in thirty years, what does that brief happiness guarantee? Nothing. Only more death and more destruction, you selfish prick."

Quentin shook his head. "I am not selling my soul for this cause."

"Who do you think you are?" Frances asked. "What gives you the right to hide at home while the rest of us choose to stay and fight the uphill battle? I'll say this, and it's that nobody else came to me asking for insomnia pills last month. Not our overworked pilots...Not Natalie, who could have very well snuck some since she worked in the infirmary and knew I'd never tell. But, for some reason, you felt deserving of the special treatment."

"Wanting to be happy is not special treatment. It's human."

"Bullshit," Mathias said.

"Rich coming from you," Quentin said. "Wasn't it you who we all crowded around because you overdosed? So much for your usefulness. So much for ignoring indulgences."

"Well, that's the other thing about this, isn't it?" Mathias asked. "You never care to ask how others are doing. Maybe a couple people, but you assume things. You don't know that, after I overdosed, Patterson assigned me to be the main engineer responsible for constantly increasing our supply of Grains. You don't know that I spend countless hours with Frances and Natalie so they can guide me in my job, because you never asked. Because you never wondered. So we never told you. Fact is, you shut down, Quentin, and the rest of us moved on."

"You have the chance to right this wrong," Ewan said. "None of us are perfect, Quentin, we know that. But unfortunately, up here, you're as good as dead if you don't accept that life isn't fair."

The frustration in the room subsided, but it didn't evaporate. It was partly from mercy, but overwhelmingly from lethargy. By the end of their contentious discussion, Quentin's wristwatch struck eight in the morning; most days, they'd have been sleeping already.

Despite being in close proximity to the others, he never felt so alone. A new wave of guilt festered inside him. As a result, his head throbbed and his throat started to swell up.

"So now what?" Jaymes asked. "Where does this leave us?"

"I sent a distress call to Patterson," Ewan said. "I kept the communication system on, so we'll hear a ping if he sends anything back to us."

"I meant with One," Jaymes said. "You think they know about this? The rest of them?"

"If they do, then that's dangerous for us," Marina said. "Their behavior all of last month was atrocious."

"And that was before they had a way out," Athol added.

Ewan sighed. "It wouldn't surprise me if Roxy talked to them about her ulterior motives. And I'd bet anything they welcomed them with open arms."

"You don't know that," Frances disagreed. "There's stress and then there's wanting to abort the whole mission."

"You think Oscar wouldn't be all for it?" Athol asked her. "Ewan and I have been working with him and Amber all month. We know he's against going forward. Given the opportunity, he'd pounce on it, if he knew he could get away with it."

"Not even," Ewan disagreed.

"It's true."

"Our main concern should be Casey and Connor," Marina said.

"Why Connor?" Jaymes asked.

"He can be tough to read. For all I know, those times when he was lecturing his teammates could have been shows for Patterson."

"Casey is smart," Frances attested, "she has a lot of common sense and enjoys being a part of the operation…but there's Terry. We all know his opinion on things, and she loves spending time with him."

"She's grown up now, though," Athol said. "She can think for herself."

"I don't think anyone doubts that," Frances said, "but where he's concerned, she'll always have an irrational soft spot. Mr. and Mrs. Montgomery took her in after her parents died in that car crash when we were in kindergarten, remember? They gave her everything, and really, she spent all her free time with Terry and his friends. It was only in recent years that she started socializing with people outside of her family, probably due to the trauma and wanting to have a normal life again. But you have to understand that she'll always do what's in the best interest of her cousin. She lost her parents and was raised by her aunt and uncle. Back home, Terry was an older brother figure. But here, he's probably something more like a substitute father. It's one of her few flaws, even if it is trauma-born."

Mathias held in a yawn. "Quentin, what's the time?"

"Eight-thirty," Quentin said.

"When did you send the distress call?" Athol asked their other pilot.

"Forty-five minutes ago, around there," Ewan answered. "The message got wiped in the process, so it's only the call for help."

They hadn't expected to wait hours for a return ping, but that was precisely what happened. They brought their pillows and blankets into the control room and fell in and out of sleep from eight-forty to twelve, shifting positions on that cool, metal floor in a constantly failing pursuit of slumber. But, having narrowly dodged their deaths, most of them couldn't sleep. They simply laid back and pondered.

The ping came at two o'clock.

"So much for a rapid emergency response," Ewan grumbled from his chair. He pushed aside the pillow on his left armrest, where his head had just been, and reached over to the computer. "Now that he's acknowledged us, what should I write?" he asked. Everyone knew he wanted Marina to answer; Quentin felt informally relegated to a unranked member.

When it was discovered that Marina was one of the few people in the room who had actually fallen asleep, Athol spoke for her. "Just tell him what happened and let him call the shots," he said.

"Besides, maybe it's not something as grim as Marina thinks it is. Maybe it's an engine glitch."

"I'm no pilot, but a glitch doesn't do that," Mathias said.

Athol's face darkened defeatedly. "Maybe you're right."

Much to their surprise, Patterson's second response was received only three minutes following Ewan's message of explanation. After an interaction which probably should have taken up about ten minutes of their time but, instead, lasted twenty-nine minutes, the pilots were instructed to stay in place and pause the flying indefinitely.

"He'll come to us," Ewan said to everyone, his attention on Marina as Frances shook her awake. "I don't know if he's considering docking. He only said that we should stay put and not turn anything on."

Athol rubbed his eyes. "Easy enough. Where is he?"

"He's within the fifteen-mile radius. He shouldn't be long." As Ewan returned to his seat on the other side of the control room, his face reverted back to its earlier display of astonishment. "So do you really think that Roxy had something to do with this?"

Athol made his way up to his seat, stretching his legs out in front of him once he was down. "Are you kidding?"

"I mean, I'm aware that she's not quite one of us, but this specifically?"

Frances was teary. Quentin only just remembered that she had considered Roxy a friend, and a close one, at that.

"What if it's something else?" Ewan asked.

Athol made himself comfortable on his seat. "Something like what?"

"Like…more than one operative. She had to have been let on by someone equally guilty of treason. Or, maybe not treason if they're not American. But someone guilty of interference."

"Anything's possible in this situation," Marina said. "But there's something else too. Something I didn't get to tell Quentin." She turned to him. "I wasn't planning on using one of the kitchen knives and the…well, the other blade. Patterson told me to go down to the armory in the basement, not that I even knew we had one."

"Neither did I," Quentin said.

"So I went there, but it was mostly empty. I found a couple things, but I didn't think they were useful. That's why I used the knife as backup. But that would imply that whoever robbed us of our weapons is intending to perform a complete onslaught sooner or later. You didn't load any guns or anything like that into the cargo hold, did you? Maybe one of those days when I was busy clearing a different floor?"

"I think I would remember that," Quentin deadpanned.

"So Roxy's got her own agenda," Mathias concluded.

"But if that's the case," Jaymes said to Marina, "why didn't she just shoot you that day?"

"I honestly don't think she was expecting me to jump her. I guess she set them aside for something else. I don't know what's going on in her head either."

"One thing I know is that it's nothing I want to be a part of," Athol quipped. "I guess our only hope right now is that the guilty parties are just the ones who work in the vetting system; the people who approved of every one of us. I'd hate to think the infiltration runs any deeper."

As Quentin considered the point, he detected movement from the right-hand corner of the window, just behind a cluster of rock bodies he adamantly tried to avoid staring at for the duration of time he was inside the control room. It looked like a tiny thing, a dot among the darkness, as it slowly soared forward past the obstacles that hovered between itself and their shuttle. From afar, the silver-colored object slowly advanced its slight body through the pitch black. He realized that he had never actually seen the exterior of their ship, but he finally did in that moment, even if it was only one segment of it.

"Quite serendipitous if you think about it," Ewan said. "Shit hits the fan as we near the end of the belt flight."

"I would hesitate to call that serendipitous," Athol contended. "It sounds more like a measured intention."

"How much longer do we have, anyway?" Frances asked, standing up with Fatima fast asleep in her arms.

"We were supposed to exit the belt around ten tonight," Athol said, "but who knows how things will go today. And we haven't gotten any sleep."

"That should impede on things," Jaymes added.

As the third shuttle flew at a slow pace, only Athol and Marina continued to track its every move. Patterson was still about two miles away.

"So if One is armed to the teeth—" Mathias said, but was cut off.

"Roxy," Frances said, leaning back against the wall beside the restroom. "Roxy only. She doesn't speak for everyone in Division One."

"You keep telling yourself that," Mathias said. "But my question is, what do we do? She already tried killing our second-in-command, so who's to say she won't do the same to us or Patterson?"

"I'm sure he has a plan," Quentin said. "I hope he does, anyway."

A ping rang from the desk.

"Is that him?" Frances asked.

"Yup," Ewan said. "We're just supposed to wait now, remember?"

Their attention returned to the approaching shuttle, which, up close, seemed of much greater size. They watched it float closer. It was a lengthy distance away, but the fact that it was bound to encroach on their space kept them enthralled. When it grew massive-looking and was, according to Athol's calculations, no more than half a mile away, it started to turn to the right, so that it wasn't facing them head-on.

"What's he doing?" Ewan asked.

That question made Jaymes trepidatious. "You don't know what he's doing?"

"Well, I thought he was coming directly toward us, but he's not."

"Should we page him?" Athol proposed.

"No, give him some time to do his thing," Ewan said. "I don't want him to be distracted if he's planning to couple."

Once the third shuttle was entirely turned away from them and all they could see of it was one side of the chassis, it moved no further.

"Give the guy a minute," Ewan comforted them. "You saw how long it took for him to send a message."

"And that never once struck you as unusual considering how it was an SOS?" Marina asked.

Ewan was pointedly unresponsive.

Several more minutes went by, but Patterson's position didn't change. The circumstance was the exact same. The only trait that made the faraway shuttle stand out from the solid rock bodies that surrounded it in unsettling nearness was the reflective shine from the metal edges of the craft. Quentin's eyes had to stay trained on it in order to retain that it was, in fact, a shuttle and not a meteor of significant glow.

Without a ping to notify them, the third shuttle began tilting back and facing up. Quentin couldn't help but think that the movement of the shuttle before them was troublingly synonymous to what their own shuttle had experienced earlier that same day. Unspeaking, he witnessed with a wary gaze as it started moving, not at a gradual pace, but a disturbingly brisk one. The shuttle streaked up, so high that Quentin and those who weren't in the pilots' seats had to scramble up to the front of the control room to see where it was going; in the back of his mind, Quentin had a suspicion that he hoped wasn't true, and he even further hoped that he wouldn't have to see it.

Technically, he didn't see anything. By the time he made his way around the desk, he witnessed only the aftermath, as scraps of metal, glass, and hard plastics were adrift in the darkness, spread out in front of one of the closer rock bodies.

26

In the silence of the continually worsening afternoon, Quentin realized that there probably was a part of Colin H. Patterson that always knew he was going to die. Why else, during his address to everyone before their week-long flights, did he speak of their future, but never of his own? The signs were all there, laid out for Quentin to read with ease, but he simply never took the time to see them. It was easy to have wanted Patterson dead, but it was mortifying to actually see it realized. The guilt sank in, because Quentin thought of his mother, of how easy it was to both accept and neglect her death when he never once took the time to visualize what she might have looked like, lifeless and forever gone from the world which he, too, had lived in, not long ago. Death, he remembered, was terrible. He just needed to see it again. He just needed to call to mind the uncomfortable truth that not everyone was as privileged to leave a lifetime as pleasantly as Agata had.

All too late, he conceded that Roxy should have died on the 2nd of February. It should have been her whom he left to rot in that smoky foyer. He had just been too blind to see it, was too engrossed in his aching for his home, for Lucas and Shaw—but that was an unattainable future, anyway. Marina had been right, even if she hadn't predicted it, but to justify the death of Colin H. Patterson would have equated to justifying the murder of Quentin's own mother. *What have I done?* he thought. *Am I any different from Roxy Thompson? I could be her. Slap a different name over mine and put me in her place... We're the same person.*

Athol was crying in his seat, poorly hiding his misery as he attempted covering his face with one of his hands. Open-mouthed, Ewan stared at the touchscreen beside him, like he was anticipating a message, perhaps a few words that would disprove what they all knew they saw. Frances and Fatima hugged each other as they walked to the back of the room. The veins of Mathias's neck protruded as he sat on the edge of the desk, unaware of all the buttons and controls he crushed with the weight of his body. A downcast Jaymes and slow-blinking Marina were on the floor, under one of the blankets, but where his gloom was tangible, her calm was indubitable, as she breathed normally, regularly; she seemed unsurprised. Quentin stood stoically, but he had to hold onto one side of Athol's seat to avoid collapsing. Quentin hid that his legs were trembling.

"We're alone," Mathias said, dropping to the floor to sit next to Marina. "We're actually alone now."

Frances wept into Fatima's hair, who herself had her face down dejectedly. It seemed unattainable, but they hugged each other closer.

Quentin slid down the back of Athol's chair, joining those who were on the floor.

"What do we even do now?" Ewan asked.

"Don't couple with One," Marina said. "However tempting it is, do not do it."

"We can't really be alone," Athol said, cleaning his snotty nose with the back of his sleeve. "I don't know how we can be alone. We don't know much of anything."

The new unknown was anguishing. Quentin wanted someone to say something that would pacify them, something that would wane the tension. Aware that no such thing would be told, he felt like he couldn't breathe, as his throat wouldn't stop swelling. He didn't draw attention to it, though.

"We aren't alone," Marina said. "There's an entire colony of people waiting for us."

Ewan sniffed, accidentally pulling the water of his teardrops into his nose when he did. "That's *years* from now," he said, sounding stuffy. "We don't have that kind of time. We're on our own now, Marina. And we have to merge with One. They're all we have left."

"We have the most powerful piece of the ship, Ewan. We have the strongest control room, the main one, here in our basement. We go on without them."

Frances was repulsed, and she showed it on her face. "Is that your answer to death and destruction? Abandoning our friends?"

"Your friends," Marina said evenly, "are in the company of the girl, the woman, whose people killed Quentin's mother. They're the people responsible for everything that has happened today. I don't know how they did it, but they did. The time is four. Right, Quentin?"

Quentin didn't answer.

"Quentin?" Marina pressed.

"What?"

"What's the time on your watch?"

"Four-fifteen."

"Ewan," Marina said, "you need to listen to me. Any moment now, One is going to request that we merge with them. You said we're almost at the end of the belt, correct?"

Ewan nodded. "Yes..." he answered, not really listening to her.

"Deny their request. We keep going on our own."

"But why?" Frances asked. "Why do you have to be so heartless about it?"

"That shuttle is packed with people who want this mission to fail and have railed against everything Patterson has said and done," Marina told her. "There's a select few who are in favor, but that isn't worth the risk. You tell me what's the smarter choice."

Frances hiccuped. Despite choking as she cried, she did respond, "I'm talking of the ethical choice here, Marina. Roxy and... and many of them are opposed to this mission, I know that. But there are a few, maybe many, good people there."

"Do you think we're going to risk it all for a few good people?" Mathias asked. "I agree that it's unfortunate for those who aren't like Oscar and Terry and everyone like them, but they have the guns. We don't."

"We can't afford to risk our lives over unneeded kindness," Marina upheld.

"But we've known those people since kindergarten," Jaymes said.

"Which is exactly why I'm not taking the risk," Mathias said. "We've known them almost our whole lives. We've seen how Derek acts when he wants something. We've seen how Terry gets in his cousin's head. We've seen the way Connor is loyal to his friends even when they're fucking crazy."

Athol removed his hand from his face. He sniveled. "Frances, if you want to talk about the ethical choice, leaving them is the one. How are we helping people back home by risking our lives to save a few people when there are billions who are dependent on this?" He swiped his cheek with a tissue from his pocket. "Mathias is right. The tension was clear all month, and that was when Patterson's colleagues were found dead. Now that Patterson himself is gone, how do you expect to win them over this time? They'll try and take over this shuttle. *Our* shuttle. The one Patterson left to us. I don't think it's any mistake we were given the first floor and the basement even though we're in the second division."

"I still say we meet them," Frances said. "We give them a chance, rule out the traitors, and then move on."

"And I say we all take a vote," was Jaymes's contribution to the disagreement. "Who thinks we should move on without them?"

Marina raised an index finger, and Mathias and Athol a hand each.

"Anyone else?" Frances asked, impatient.

Quentin thought of the empty second row of seating in the passengers' quarter, how Roxy was supposed to be in one of those throughout the week. The thought caused him a brief panic, but it wasn't enough to compel him to leave behind a whole ship of innocents. Regardless of her complicity, he remembered Amber, who appreciated him. Natalie, who was kind to him. Casey, who always encouraged him. And Connor, who had become something of a friend to him.

No one else raised a hand.

"That carries it," Frances said defiantly, verging on boastful.

"Ewan," Marina called the pilot's attention, "wasn't it you who Oscar ditched during training?"

"He's an idiot," Ewan said, "but he doesn't deserve to die, stranded out in the middle of nowhere. They'll starve and freeze to death once they're out of supplies and can't function on their own. They don't deserve that."

Mathias huffed. "Your funeral."

"No one's dying," Quentin said with all the conviction he could gather. "We join with One."

They stayed in the control room only for another hour, until the ping of the first division's merge request finally reached them. The pilots, drawn and sallow from their sleep deprivation, informed the others that the speed of their flight was to be at the fastest setting yet.

"We should reach the end of the belt by nine at the earliest," Athol said.

Again, they waited. It felt like the thousandth time that week that they sat in the back room, fiddling with their fingers, blind to everything outdoors. Quentin thought it rather fitting that Mathias and Marina were the only two adults on the other side of the passengers' quarter, Fatima in between them, while those who opposed their agreement to leave lifelong friends behind were sectioned on the other side of the aisle.

With the free time on hand, Quentin should have caught up on sleep. Instead, he spent the hours toiling through breathing exercises, trying to banish from his mind the memory of all that metal and glass strewn across the dark sky. Frances read from her bible, which she had apparently packed with the rest of her carry-on luggage. Jaymes did nothing.

At nine-twenty, there was a steady rocking and backwards burst of their shuttle. Quentin recognized the sensation; they were docking.

Did he regret his choice? No, he didn't. He was terrified and sweating, but he couldn't reject morality. Not anymore. He did it once. He couldn't bring himself to do it again.

The pilots, for the first planned time all week, exited the control room. They were noticeably avoidant of one another's gazes. Ewan appeared nervous. Athol was smoldering, like he was going to snap at the first person who said a word to him.

That time around, Mathias was the one to help Marina to her feet. Frances never made a move to help her, which Quentin initially thought was a result of prolonged disgust from the earlier dissent, but she left for the storage room instead of staying still for the sake of holding a grudge. When she returned, she slid forward the enormous medical supply trunk they had retrieved on the first day of their flight. She removed the slide and began rummaging through the supplies, extracting from the pile an unused scalpel. "If we are to meet with some contention," she said, "we should have some things on us that may lend to keeping us safe." She looked over to Marina. "You would know best of everyone here that household appliances can be fairly lethal."

"Fairly," Marina said, slinging an arm over Mathias's shoulder.

Frances kept the scalpel and gave another, the only other, to Quentin. Mathias handed Marina over to Athol and went into the storage closet on his own, returning with a screwdriver in one hand and a wrench in the other, giving the latter to Jaymes. Quentin found a scalpel for himself. Frances stood to give Ewan one of the lidocaine syringes, an unfilled one, but Mathias interrupted the interaction.

"Uh, no," Mathias said matter-of-factly. "Hanson takes one of the needles."

Ewan raised an eyebrow. "Wielded it well, did he?" The hint of a smile was on his lips, even as he winced while removing his Grains from his nose and disposed them onto the table behind him; Mathias did the same.

"Let's just hope we don't have to use any of these," Athol said.

Hope, Quentin thought. *Can we still do that?*

The foyer was empty. It was sooty and sordid, but empty. Quentin didn't like the ship, still hated it with every fiber of his being, but even he was disheartened to witness the marble and glass of the once-resplendent hall tainted by the exhaust that had permeated throughout it for days. The lights in the corners shone dimly, as the covers to their bulbs were masked with the moist darkness. The staircases were no longer translucent; where before one could look at one side and instantly see the other, he couldn't make out the opposite end of the hall.

Everyone stood outside the elevator, all eight in his group, with their backs to the door. Having decided to remain as close to the exit as possible, they didn't move any further. Their makeshift weapons were concealed, stuffed into pockets and slid into sleeves just above the spot where one's arm ended and the wrist began. They weren't loitering a long time when a commotion from the second floor, on the left side of the foyer, drew their attention upward. With their heads tilted back, they listened and watched as someone yelled. Then, there came a grunt. There was the scream of an expletive, and it came from a female voice.

Fatima was standing between Quentin and Mathias. When her breath hitched, Quentin felt the rapid air flow wrinkle the back of his jumpsuit's pants.

Quentin stuck his thumb back, toward the elevator. "Should we...?" he driftingly asked Marina, who was behind him.

Marina pressed the button herself.

Nothing happened.

Marina pressed it again and again.

"Why isn't it working?" Ewan asked.

Marina pulled her hand away from the pad. "We're locked up here," she said.

"Should've voted against this," Mathias muttered under his breath.

Quentin heard Connor's voice coming from the second floor, where the protective barrier had recently slipped back into its place in the wall. But Connor wasn't the first to come into view. It was Terry. His suit was shed, which left him garbed only in a pair of unwrinkled jeans and a blue tee-shirt. He had a cut on his left arm; small but perceptible, even from downstairs. He was staggering back, his body hitting the railing of the balcony. When he turned his face to notice the second division watching him, in spite of the darkened state of their surroundings, the purpled bruise of his left eye was unmistakable. Soon, Connor emerged with an apoplectic scowl on his face. Blood seeped out the corners of his mouth, and his shoulders were tautly pulled back. Terry didn't look afraid—he was rarely afraid of anything —but he did back up again, toward the stairs. He stepped down each one carefully, facing Connor the entire time, who also began a descent.

"I can't believe you!" Connor shouted.

"Stop it!" a frazzled Casey cried out, beside her Oscar and Chris. One of her dreadlocks was messily unknotted, which unleashed a puffy line of curls that dangled by one side of her face. Her half-undone jumpsuit flapped against her abdomen as she joined the young men beside her in pursuing Connor and Terry.

"What in the hell?" Mathias asked.

Terry reached the first floor.

"Who do you think you are?!" Connor fumed, following after him.

Chris attempted mediating the apparent fight. "Hey, man, stop it!" He ran down to Connor and took hold of his right bicep, but the action infuriated the seething advisor, who turned around and shoved Chris into the one of the railings.

"Don't you fucking touch me," Connor said, his face only inches away from Chris's.

Oscar yanked them away from each other. "All right, knock it off. Connor, get off him."

Connor whirled around to Oscar. "Get off him?! Real hypocritical, don't you think?!"

Marina pushed the elevator button again, but it didn't open.

Casey bypassed her three peers and skipped the last steps with a single jump. She ran up to Terry, inspected his face, and asked if he was all right, but he shooed off her unease with a lazy wave, assuring his cousin that nothing was the matter.

"He's just overreacting," Terry said to her.

"Oh, I'm overreacting?" Connor asked as he made his way down again, that time finally reaching the first floor.

As Oscar and Chris reached the bottom, Natalie and Amber were the next pair to come out and storm down the steps.

Connor brushed past Terry and walked forward, toward the group that silently hovered by the unavailable elevator. Quentin felt his face overheat as the bloody-mouthed Connor and his fixed scowl kept coming closer. His steps faltered a few times, like he had somehow injured his leg. When he came up to Quentin, who gulped twice, Connor looked over the captain's shoulder, to Marina. He grimaced as he examined the state of her. To Quentin and his teammates, she appeared impressively healthy, but he understood that, in the eyes of others, she was an alarmingly grotesque version of the person she had once looked like, and only a week ago. "I know everything," Connor said to her, licking away some blood on the corners of his mouth. "I know enough, at least. About Roxy. About you. Patterson."

"What happened during all that time you were away?" Frances asked.

Connor sighed. He half-turned to his group, still catching his breath as he said, "We're a day in. A day in, got that? One minute, we're doing fine; Oscar and Amber are flying; the rest of us are behaving ourselves in the passenger area. The next thing I know, our flight stops at midnight and I'm being shoved into the storage closet, all alone."

Natalie and Amber reached the first floor.

Roxy was at the balcony of the second floor, slowly coming down.

"And *she*," Connor spitefully said, pointing up to the newcomer, "is going into the control room with the permission of one Captain Casey. I got my answer this morning. You can imagine how that went."

Terry took one step forward. His hands out, his palms faced Connor's way. "So this is how it ends, then?" he asked, straightening out his shirt.

"We're not ending anything," Connor said. "We're sorting this shit out."

"Please, enough of the fighting," Amber pleaded. Her face was flushed and drawn. She nervously pulled at the ends of her suit's sleeves. "We don't have to do this, guys," she said to her group, to Casey in particular.

Casey stood in the middle of the foyer, patently displeased. There was a glint of annoyance in her glare. "You think I don't know what you were up to last month?" she asked Amber. "Do you think I was completely unaware of the fact that you were a drug addict for the sake of pleasing Patterson? Who do you think gave the go-ahead for you to take literal meth? Who do you think told Natalie to ignore all the bottles that went missing every week? *Me.*" She pointed to herself. "I did, and it destroyed me every day. I don't want to keep ruining my friends' lives for this stupid operation. I'm sick of it."

Shame curled onto Amber's face. Hives began to bloom on her neck.

Derek loomed out from the second level, right behind Roxy. He followed behind her, and eventually their walking evened out until they were beside each other on the journey down.

"Fantastic," Mathias bitterly said. "Decided to join the show, have you?"

"Shut your fucking mouth, " Derek replied when they reached the bottom.

"Nice," Athol sneered.

Connor was still focused on Casey. "You're blowing this whole thing out of proportion," he said. "We both know last month was an exception."

"Last month was no exception, Connor!" Terry objected. "Patterson made it damn clear that even he didn't know what the point of all this shit is. It wasn't him who came up with the BDP. But hell, even that's just a theory, right? He couldn't even keep his friends alive, never mind us."

"And anyway, he kidnapped us," Casey said.

"Since when were you mad about that?" Connor asked. "Last I checked, you were more than happy to cooperate, unless you mean to tell me that your toxic, manipulating cousin is getting into your head again."

Casey stepped back. "How dare you?! Do you really think I am so lacking in…in…basic agency that I can't think for myself? I was younger than all of you when I was kidnapped. I was sixteen, too young to realize at the time that it was Patterson who was toxic and manipulative, that it was him who tried distracting us with this fancy home, coddling and flattering us every time we did the bare minimum of cooperation. I didn't recognize just how much I'd fallen into his trap, so pardon me for being a little naive. You saw the way he was with us, treating us like we were special and all that crap. Frankly, I'm surprised that you never realized it too."

"You know what I think?" Connor asked.

"What do you think?"

"I think you don't believe a single word you just said."

"Excuse you—"

"*I think*," Connor said, enunciating his words, "that you knew that reason sounded like the better argument. You're using it to cover up that you just want to leave. That's it. You just want to go home, regardless of how much you're needed up here. And whatever Terry has told you, whether it be that you can go home and get into a good school and become a trailblazing scientist or something, let me just tell you, it's not true. This is our home. This is our life."

"You say that like it's a thing to be ashamed of," Oscar said, bringing himself forward, to the center of the foyer. "You act like we should feel guilty for wanting to have control of our lives, to live normally again."

"You couldn't get that life back even if you tried," Ewan said. "Let's say we do turn the ship around and we're back home, on Earth. We can't live the way we used to, we'd be hunted. Being up here is unavoidable now."

"That's surrendering, not satisfaction," Casey said.

"I'm willing to surrender my happiness if it means serving the greater good," Ewan voiced.

"You could go home," Roxy spoke up, her voice even. "You'd be offered protection. My superiors would take you in. So long as you're outside the US, you can safely live in a normal way again."

"Your superiors, huh?" Athol asked.

Connor put his hands on his hips, his shoulders slouched forward. "If you're under the impression that I'm about to go committing treason to live with—"

"Oh, don't get me fucking started on treason," Terry said, laughing to himself in the stiffest manner Quentin had every heard. "It was our families who were the treasonous ones. Those fucks sold off their own kids to Patterson, so don't go spewing out a lecture on deceit and betrayal when they're the guilty parties here."

"Then what's your genius plan?" Mathias asked. "You wanna take over this ship? Wanna kill every one of us, like the way that spy bitch outright murdered Patterson?"

"You do make it sound so easy," Derek said rather lecherously.

"You are sick," Frances said.

"Are we?" Oscar asked. "Weren't you the one reading some intro-to-psychology book a few months ago? I'd think you, of all people, would know what Stockholm syndrome looks like."

Frances glowered at him, but she let it slip from her face. She separated from her division, went right up to Casey, and took Casey's hands into her own. "Don't do this," Frances pleaded. "This isn't you. I know you. We all saw the way you worked and…You're meant to be here. You're incredible and smart and meant to do something as wonderful and…and monumental as saving so many lives."

Casey ripped her hands away from Frances's. She walked herself backwards, to Chris and Natalie.

"Come on…Natalie," Frances whispered.

Natalie shook her head, looking down.

Frances turned to Amber, but she similarly shied away from sharing gazes and directed her vision elsewhere. That left Frances alone, frozen in place, misery polluting her soft countenance. She rubbed at her eyes.

"We're friends," Connor said to Terry. "What are you doing?"

"Friends don't ignore each other when one of their lives has gone to complete shit," Terry said. "You haven't looked at any of us once since we got here. You became Patterson's lapdog. You spent all your time with Gustavsson, who you once hated, might I add. You never once made any effort to talk to your actual friends. Forgive us for moving on."

"Is that so?" Connor asked. "Explain all that time I spent with Casey, your cousin."

"For what she brought to the mission, yes. Not because you genuinely care about her. Not because she's your friend. You only spent all that time with her because you thought you had to, right? You don't care about any of us. Matter of fact, you didn't see any of us volunteering to play enabler for Patterson when Hanson's group woke up, did you? But you were first in line that night, jumping on board and willing to rationalize all of that guy's sick and twisted shit. Admit it, you love the power. You've always loved being in charge."

"I enjoy leading something that can help people, yes," Connor said.

"Don't do that," Terry said. "Don't pretend you're doing this because you care about others and not just so you can be at the top of something."

"I do care," Connor said. "Why the hell else would I invest my time into this? I love my family and I love my friends, and their families too. I'm doing this because I want to help people. Get a clue."

"This isn't—"

Connor reached the end of his patience. "Look, life goes on, Terry! What do you want me to say? That I'm sorry for moving on, unlike you? Not all of us are stuck in the past, all right? Not all of us spend every waking minute mourning the fact that they never got that professional football career. You are fucking pathetic."

Terry stalked up to him, pulling an arm back. "You pious bastard!"

"No!" Amber screamed. She ushered forward and tugged at Terry's shoulder, but he shoved her away. She went stumbling back a few steps.

Oscar walked up to her and grabbed her by her shoulders, forcing her to look at him. "You want to be a washed-up crackwhore by age thirty? Go on and ask Mathias what it's like by seventeen, I'm sure he'd love to enlighten you."

"But—" Amber said.

"Because *that's* where you're headed with this prick in charge," Oscar said, gesturing with a flick of his hand toward Connor. Oscar let go of Amber.

"Stop the fear mongering," Athol said. "Amber, this last month's been crazy. We're pilots too, we know that. But it was a unique situation and you have to remember that."

"For the last time, it wasn't," Chris said. "Weird shit keeps happening up here. Patterson is dead, even."

"Yeah, because Roxy killed him!" Athol vied.

"Here's what's going to happen," Oscar said, coming even closer. "You're going to calm down, get out of our way, and let us get into that shuttle."

"Into the *basement*?" Ewan asked. "No! No way!"

"Like hell," Mathias said.

"Ah, you," Oscar said to Mathias. "I know why you want to stay up here. Why all of you do. A useless fringe to society like you, a loser, could never live past twenty-one back home. A dork like Athol could never be relevant the way he is up here." His eyes roved to the back. "And a psychopath like Marina could never get away with her shit without a megalomaniac like Patterson being there to justify her actions." He glanced to Frances. "Then there's you. I know how you religious freaks always like to run around playing hero."

Frances took in a long breath. Her teeth started grinding. "I swear, if one more person—"

"You are a depraved sleaze," Ewan said to Oscar. "How can you side with someone as evil as Roxy? After everything? Her people murdered one of our agents, Quentin's mom!"

Quentin's stomach hollowed. He wished Ewan hadn't said that.

"Roxy's here to help us," Oscar said, ignoring the comment.

A movement from the second floor caught Quentin's attention again. He saw Ivy sitting down on the step connected to the balcony, a resigned expression on her tired face. She made no move to join the rest of them downstairs.

"To help us, is that it?" Connor asked. "By what, killing us? What are you going to do if we refuse?"

"I'd rather not think about that right now," Oscar said.

"And what's that supposed to mean?" Frances asked, her voice shaking.

"All right, we need to set things straight," Connor said. "You're not telling anyone what's about to happen. This is out of control."

"The only thing out of control is this entire operation," Casey fought back.

"No, no. You're the one openly admitting to—"

"To what? Prioritizing my happiness? Is that really such a bad thing Connor? I've tried to talk to you about this for months."

"No, you haven't! This is entirely revisionist history! We were both..."

The voices went unclear in Quentin's ears. Everything they were all saying became a blur when he felt a light, but insistent, tug on his right pinky. He looked to his hand and saw Fatima by his hip. She gave another tug to his finger as well as one to Mathias's, but he was distracted, watching as Terry hovered closer to the scene of bellows and crying. But Quentin was aware of Fatima's plea to be noticed, moreover the way she wasn't looking toward any of the people to whom she was appealing. She was staring ahead, at Derek.

Derek was lingering at the edge of his group, beside the staircase on Quentin's left. He was wary of how half of Derek's right hand was in the front pocket of his sweatshirt, how he had himself angled toward Oscar, almost fully concealed by the pilot, who engaged in an argument with Athol. Quentin was fully capable of taking in the entirety of the blond; the disdainful twist of his face, the way his wrathful expression grew nastier the more Connor spoke; the handle of the thing in the half-hidden hand, which Quentin couldn't see, but thought appeared suspiciously akin to something Marina said she had once gone looking for. Fatima never once looked away from Derek, entranced by his silent intention, which, admittedly, all the adults in the room had somehow overlooked; leave it to the child to perceive the seemingly imperceptible.

The shouts grew louder. Terry and Connor were fighting again. Ewan was trying to convince Amber that things would be better in time, that patience was all she needed to live a better life; she refused and shook her head. Casey rejected everything Frances tried telling her, about how Terry shouldn't be the sole domain of her every decision in life; she was once again affronted and started screaming back insistences that she was more than capable of independent thoughts. Marina was warning Athol to not provoke Oscar, as they were the ones who were disadvantaged by the lack of escape route.

When Terry threw a punch at Connor, it was Mathias who stepped in. Then, Chris inserted himself into the mess, seizing the opportunity to finally strike one of the members of the other division.

Quentin knew he had to do something, something responsible yet realistic. What he chose to do may have seemed cowardice to some, but, to him, it was the safest and most sensible choice: he crouched down, scooped the frozen Fatima into his arms, and hurried them away. He hid them behind the nearest marble column. He must have just fled the mayhem in time, because an influx of screaming and shouting ensued immediately thereafter.

Frances begged for Derek not to do something.

Mathias was swearing profusely as he grunted, and why he was grunting, Quentin tried not to imagine.

Fatima quivered in Quentin's arms. He brought an index finger up to his lips, and she diligently covered her nose and mouth with both of her hands. He spun on his heels, looking for the closest way out, which he saw was one of the hallways adjacent to the foyer. Such as he once did with his brother, he ran himself and the girl away.

27

Derek wagged the gun in front of Marina's face. All she could see of it was its barrel. "Up the stairs," he said gruffly. "And put your hands up where I can see them."

Composed, Marina relented and put her hands in the air. There was no use in arguing. She was exhausted and, deep down, knew to have expected a confrontation like this. What she couldn't believe was that her peers had been so naive as to think that there was utility in reasoning with those people, with the first division. What she couldn't believe was that she was involved in such a debacle.

"I fucking told you, you fucking morons," Mathias berated their group, stepping backwards beside Marina, which made them the first to follow Derek's order of ascending the staircase on the left; the one which the first division members previously traveled down.

Athol, Ewan, and Connor, who had hung back in the center of the foyer nearest the people with whom they argued, were the next group that Derek approached. "You too," he said to them, and they trailed after Mathias and Marina without a fight.

Jaymes and Frances were the last to be shooed into place.

As Derek dangerously encroached on Jaymes's space, the latter's nose almost tapped the front of the weapon. "You know, you almost had me there," he said. "I almost wanted to go with you. I would have loved to go home."

"You gonna have him shoot us all?" Connor asked Casey, looking down at her from above, on the stairs. "Admirable heroics there."

"We're not shooting anyone who doesn't wish harm on us," Terry said. "Now up the stairs, *all* of you," he specifically said to Frances.

Due to being singled out, she refused to leave.

"Just do as they say, *please*," Amber implored.

"You are pathetic," Athol said to her.

"Up. The. Stairs." Derek was commanding Frances, who still hadn't moved.

"Roxy didn't even have to manipulate you," Frances said. "All she had to do was exploit your selfishness."

"Get moving."

"Casey, please," Frances appealed once more. "Casey!" she cried, trying to win over her attention.

Derek rolled his eyes. "Jerins, get your ass on that staircase."

"Wonderful," sneered Connor, from halfway up. "Real nice. Is this who you're really siding with? This white trash cokehead?"

"Who, believe it or not, has more sense than you right now," Chris said. He had to bend his neck back to look up at Connor on the stairs. "People change. You certainly did."

Derek, who was in possession of the most power, and Terry, who was something of a middleman, led the reluctant group up the stairs, all the way to the second floor balcony, where a doleful Ivy moved aside and made room for them to pass. Where they were being escorted, Marina didn't have a single hunch, but they were directed to keep going backwards, deeper into the second floor.

"Hey!" Oscar yelled from below. "Where are Quentin and Fatima?!"

The coerced group stopped walking. Beneath them, the hard ground of the balcony began to mesh with the softness of the second floor's first corridor.

Marina turned her head over her shoulder. Oscar was right. Quentin and Fatima were nowhere to be seen. *Hanson finally used his brain,* Marina thought.

Derek turned to Marina irritatedly. "Where'd you send him? Where'd you tell him to go?"

"I didn't," Marina said calmly.

"You lying, little bitch, you tell me where they are right now."

"What does it matter to you?" Marina asked, her eyebrows quirking on her expressionless face. "Do you really think that incompetent moron and a child will dismantle your plan?"

"I told you we needed the Listeners," Roxy was saying to Oscar, Terry, and Casey, down on the first floor. "Find them now, and fast." Through the gaps of soot plastered on the staircase, Marina saw the three disperse. They left the foyer quickly, as Roxy had instructed them to. Each discharged down different hallways.

"She your captain now?" Connor asked Derek.

"Down the hall," was all Derek said with Terry still behind him, like he was itching to pounce at any moment.

"I-I don't understand," Frances said. "Why do you need the Listeners?"

"Oscar, we're on the second floor!" Terry announced.

"Coming!" Oscar shouted. He climbed up the glass path and reached them.

The majority of the second division were led into the library, herded through the enormous, cherry wood doors like cattle. As they begrudgingly stood by the doorway of the unlit room, Oscar hurried past Derek and Terry, told them that he would be quick with whatever it was he needed to do, and then he disappeared. Marina couldn't imagine what any of that meant, and it wasn't until Terry shut the door and she heard a click that she realized Oscar must have locked the room from inside the first division's shuttle control room.

Frances flicked the light switch up, which illuminated the fake candelabras that were installed into the mantelpiece above the fireplace, but the engine pollutants had glommed onto the room's every surface and dimmed the lights' effect.

Mathias launched himself at the doors. They didn't give under his weight.

Connor smacked one of the bookshelves.

Ewan kicked a wall and then dropped to the floor, squatting in a corner with his head in his hands.

"What the hell do we do now?" Connor asked Marina as he paced back and forth, a hand in his hair, brushing his fingers through it twice, until he was grabbing it, like he wanted to yank every strand out of his head. The bits that fell in his face and prickled his eyes suffered the strongest pulls.

Marina didn't know what to do. She hadn't planned that far, and certainly not for that form of a predicament. Had the night's events played out her way, they would have already been thirty more miles out, in the safety of the seemingly endless obsidian realm, and on their own. But they weren't isolated, and they weren't in the sole company of their own division. She groaned at the fact that she was confined to the dusky, first level of the library with a head that throbbed and a body that was barely healed, trying to ignore how she felt herself stiffen every time she made even the smallest move. She leaned against one of the bookshelves, the one Connor had abused, and started palming her forehead. She held one of her frigid hands up to the warmer skin in the hope that the cold of her fingers would chill the warmth of her face.

Mathias never stopped trying to break the door down.

"There's no use barreling yourself into it," Marina said. "Conserve your energy."

"Why are they so adamant about finding Quentin and Fatima?" Jaymes asked. "You're right, Marina, they can't be that threatening."

"I have no idea what runs through the minds of our adversaries back home," Marina said. "I don't know who they think are or aren't threats."

Mathias stopped attacking the doors. He turned around, his back up against them, and he dug his hands into his hips. "I just want to say thank you to all the fucking idiots who got us into this shitshow. I swear to fuck, when I say you don't reason with those people—"

"How were we supposed to know?!" Ewan defended his decision in unbridled horror. "They were our friends once! A *week* ago."

"They were never our friends," Marina said. "They were always just acquaintances. Growing up with people doesn't make them your friends."

Connor started biting the nail of his left thumb. Without realizing it, he ended up digging lower; blood leaked out, but he didn't seem to notice. "I've been with Terry through everything. I've been his best friend since we were four. Since pre-school. And Casey... Chris and I treated her like a sister when her parents died. We've all been there for each other from day one. How do you just throw all those years away?"

"Because they're selfish motherfuckers and you never once tried to see it," Mathias said. "I've known this shit for years. You were friends with assholes, O'Neil. You always were."

Ewan shook his head. "There's assholery and then there's—"

"We warned you!" Athol reminded them. He walked back and forth by the fireplace. "And you of all people should've known, Ewan! I mean, fucking hell, dude! We spent a month working with Oscar! You knew more than anyone that he'd pull this crap!" The fury splayed over his dark face wasn't visible from the candelabras as much as it was from the stars that glowed on the other side of the exposed window beside him; the draping curtains had been stripped from the wall and placed into the cargo hold before the flight. "Look where you got us, dumbass."

"Excuse us for having hearts," Jaymes bit.

"Hearts have no places in war," Connor said.

"Stop being so dramatic," Ewan dismissed him.

"I'm not being dramatic," Connor said. "It is a war, invisible as it is. But that's how geopolitical ones always are."

Marina gritted her teeth. "We don't have time for this."

"For what?" Mathias asked.

"For *this*." Marina motioned to the general area around them. "Wasting our energy arguing."

"How long do you think they'll keep us in here?" Jaymes promptly changed the subject.

"I can't say," Connor admitted defeatedly. "I don't know anything. God knows how long they've been concocting this reality in their heads where we're the evil ones and they're the...Well, not the heroes. But a reality where they think that they're the ones in the right." He chewed into his cut bottom lip, drawing more blood. "I just don't know why you didn't tell me," he said to Marina, displeased, his voice tinged with hurt from having been mistrusted by her. "Patterson gave the order the day before the flight. That was more than enough time for you to talk to me. Why didn't you? I thought you trusted me."

"Connor," Marina said his name curtly, "for the last month, your group has been acting fucking neurotic. I wasn't going to take the chance telling you, not when I had no idea what was going on inside your head. For all I knew, you would've done the same to me as Roxy had. By the way, do you even know how long Casey has sided with her?"

"I don't," Connor admitted. "It could have started last week… three weeks ago. God, maybe even a year ago. I literally don't know. But I suspect it wasn't long after Patterson gave us permission to enter the cargo hold, or some time before that. I don't know when she decided to derail our mission. I don't know shit."

Despite his rage, Athol yawned.

"We have to find Fatima," Frances said. "And Quentin," she added, but everyone knew he was an afterthought to her.

"When did your flights take place?" Marina asked Connor. "Day or night?"

"Night," Connor said. "Like yours, right?"

The pilots nodded.

Connor frowned. "Why do you ask?"

"We haven't slept in a little over twenty-four hours," Marina said, "so we're in no condition to go flouncing downstairs and attempting to stop whatever they're doing. If there's any benefit to this night, it's that, should Quentin stay hidden, the others will waste their time looking for him and maybe tire themselves even further. After the long day we've had, our best hope is that he stays hidden."

"And if he doesn't?" Frances asked.

"It's Quentin we're talking about," Mathias said. "All that pussy knows how to do is hide away and pout."

"Exactly," Marina said. "In terms of the ship turning around, they would still need all the captains' and advisors' biometrics. Granted, at any moment they could force Connor and I into cooperating, but so long as they can't find Quentin, we should be fine."

"Or the bare minimum of 'fine,'" Athol said.

"We can work with the bare minimum." Marina's eyebrows pinched together in thought. "They turn it around via the main control room, correct?"

Athol nodded. "Yeah. The basement, which they've no doubt hijacked."

"Is there any way we can break out of here?" Connor asked. "Some kind of vent or something?"

"You've seen them, they're too small for us to fit into," Mathias said disappointedly.

"The visible ones are," Ewan said.

"There are invisible ones?" Connor asked.

"No, just well concealed," Athol said. "When Ewan and I went over the ship's blueprints after we learned that the ship is made of multiple shuttles, Patterson showed us that there are larger vent systems that run throughout the ship. They're not exclusive to one shuttle. They were designed to be large enough for a person to fit themselves into so we could, you know, four times a year clean up the oxygen tanks or drain and clean the water dispensers. Stuff like that. Patterson usually did the maintenance on his own and was planning to start assigning people later, once we exited the belt, but he didn't trust us with that information. Not yet."

"But they do connect to each other?" Connor asked. "I mean, shuttle to shuttle?"

"Yeah," Ewan said. "You could travel from the third shuttle down to the first." He licked his lips awkwardly. "Of course, we don't have a third one anymore."

"But we could, if we wanted to, go downstairs from here?" Marina asked.

"I think so?" Athol replied unsurely. "I don't see any reason why not. That's what I remember, anyway. There's an entrance to them in every room, just well hidden so that no one decides to go stirring trouble or hiding from everyone. Like, there was one in the arcade. It was hidden behind the pool table. You can probably find it way easier now, though, since we've removed everything from all the rooms."

"Do my division's pilots know about this?" Connor asked suspiciously.

"I wouldn't know."

"That settles it," Marina said with an emphasized exhale. "We escape through the vent system. File out. Go look for the vent."

She was the only one who didn't participate in the search. While everyone else slid their hands against the walls and floor, feeling around for the tiniest of gaps or surveying the surfaces with the small bits of light from the mantelpiece and the window, Marina perched beside the fireplace and turned on the switch abreast its cage. Fifteen minutes later, Ewan was the one who located the vent. He found it in the loft upstairs, where it was strategically placed between two bookshelves; before their flight through the belt, a cascading, Armenian tapestry once hung over it.

"We go when we're rested," Marina said.

"Surely now," Frances debated, but she clamped her lips shut to stop herself from releasing a massive yawn.

"We're spent," Marina said. "We won't sleep the entire night, just enough so that we can function. We can't take the risk confronting them in this shape. They have the guns. All we have are a few medical supplies we might be able to weaponize and our bodies, plus something I found but wouldn't use unless absolutely necessary. By the way, Mathias, do you still have that screwdriver? We need a way to get into the vent."

Mathias pulled the tool from a pocket of his suit. "Right here."

After their inspection of the escape, they returned to the library's first floor, by the fireplace. It was there that the pilots apprised Connor of the mayhem they had all withstood in the belt, when the ship reeled out of control and their communication with Patterson had lagged. Connor didn't know about any of it.

"Hey, Marina," Connor said to her somewhat questioningly, "you said you had something, a thing you wouldn't use unless absolutely necessary."

Marina dipped a hand into the breast pocket of her vest. Behind the fabric, her fingers wrapped around a small object; a little, mechanical orb with an indented, honeycomb-patterned surface that made it easy for her to maintain a tight grip, even with a loose hand. She held it up for all to see.

"What is that?" Mathias asked. He looked repulsed by it.

"It's a Nox Bomb," Marina said.

Athol raised an eyebrow. "A what?'

"'Nox', as in N, O, and X, like the ones in chemistry?" Ewan asked.

"That's what I thought," Marina said, but she shook her head. "I found it in the weaponry, in the basement. It was all that was left over after Roxy raided the place. There was a guide under its display. Apparently it consists of three gases. The 'Nox' is for 'noxious.'" She spun it around. "If you open it, there are three buttons; blue, red, and black. Like a grenade, it detonates after three seconds. Each button is reserved for a different gas. Blue releases nitrous oxide, which can knock a person out. Red releases sarin, which can obviously kill a person. And black—" She turned it over one more time, before putting it back in her pocket—"is for the rare occasion when you need to use both at once."

"How inhumane," Ewan commented.

"Is it?" Mathias asked. "Look at the situation we're in."

Once the reveal of the weapon ended and the conversations around it waned to low-toned murmurs, everyone rested. Mathias sprawled on the floor and passed out, as if the Nox Bomb had granted him instant solace. Connor sat back, reclined against the newel of the stairway that led up to the loft. Jaymes laid down on the floor, his eyes closed under his glasses, but Marina knew he wasn't asleep; he sighed intermittently, and his fingers twitched every so often, usually once every couple of minutes. Frances wasn't likely to sleep at all that night, not when she and the little girl, who was far from her reach, were separated. Marina attempted lulling herself into a slumber, but it proved quite the trial. She wasn't distressed or frenzied, but she was cold. Her discomfort was probably due to the sore, stiff state of her body. She wasn't sure when her eyes closed, as she had no way to tell time, since the clocks that had been attached to the walls were removed before the flight, but when she did slip into sleep, with her arms curled around herself and her tongue repeatedly laving her lips to keep them warm, she was the last of them to finally surrender to unconsciousness.

———

Connor didn't sleep long. He doubted anyone else actually did, except for Marina. She was different. She could cast aside even the most upsetting stressors to will herself into a night's rest, but the others weren't like that; sometimes, her lack of empathy grated on him.

He must have had his eyes closed for only thirty minutes before he woke to find himself in the same position as when he was wide awake. His head spun and he couldn't get it to stop.

Ewan similarly wasn't asleep. He was sitting upright, scooting closer to the fireplace. He didn't seem aware that another person was conscious, because he drew up his legs and started kneading the back of his hands against his eyes. Tears rolled down his cheeks.

"Can't sleep?" Connor asked him quietly.

"No," Ewan mumbled. His Adam's apple bobbed in his throat when he swallowed. "It's my fault, partly. But it's still my fault. We took a vote, whether to leave you all behind or to keep going. We never would have wound up in this mess if I'd just voted against going back."

Connor managed a smile. "Maybe you got yourself into this mess," he said, "but you gave us a chance. I can't tell you how much it means to me that you all came back, especially after what my frien—" He caught himself. "After what the others did."

"I guess," Ewan said, unconvinced. "But I'm one of the reasons we're outnumbered by those assholes. I'm one of the reasons Quentin and Fatima are missing."

"You think they're assholes?" a woken Jaymes asked.

Connor snorted. "Is anyone here asleep?"

Jaymes laid on his back, but he sat up on his elbows. "I asked if you think they're assholes."

"I think any country that's willing to sacrifice innocent lives is in the wrong," Connor said. "The excuse of doing something for the greater good doesn't legitimize small evils. Evil is evil." He tilted his head. "Did you really mean it back there, when you were talking to Derek? How you said that they almost had you?"

Jaymes nodded, far from shameful. "I always viewed it a little differently. If I try and place myself in the shoes of a pacifist, and resultantly try and think authoritatively about the safest route forward, I'd choose the hiding method. It may come with unfortunate costs, environmental health costs, but I think it's the ideal one."

"So, if you were president," a stirring Mathias said, "you would choose the Defense Op?"

"Now, I didn't say that," Jaymes denied. "There's a difference between sympathizing and acting in a similar fashion. I feel that's an important differentiation."

"That doesn't answer my question," Mathias retorted.

"Fine, yes," Jaymes said. "I'd choose the Defense Op."

"Seriously?"

"Seriously. It's the one method that lacks risk. See, if our little ship had been caught within the first year by these evidently advanced beings, I'm sure they'd have figured out our place of origin, which obviously grants mankind and Earth a survival rate way lower than if we'd stayed back. Through research, we know they move slowly, despite their acceleration in travel lately, and mankind would have at least another forty years before they approached Earth. Now, if I'm a leader who wants a risk-free guarantee that I can stretch out Earth's survival for at least another few decades, I'd choose hiding."

"And the Patterson part?" Ewan asked.

"That's one of the only reasons I opposed it. Personal drivers make our decisions for us, not logic. I understand both sides is all. I'm fine with both, in fact. If I didn't know about Quentin's mother or, say, Roxy killing Patterson's colleagues and Patterson himself, I'd be fine with the ship turning around. But I'm not unfamiliar with those people. And, again, that's only due to personal drivers. Under different circumstances, where Roxy doesn't kill people, I would go with her."

"That's a logic loop if I ever heard one," Ewan said. "Doesn't that just mean that, so long as you didn't know him, you would think killing Patterson is justifiable?"

"In essence," Jaymes admitted. "But I'm imperfect that way."

"At least you're honest," Ewan said.

Frances rolled over, facing them. "What's going on?" she asked sleepily.

"A discussion on the fickle ways of man," Jaymes said.

Frances yawned, covering her mouth with a loose fist. "I don't consider myself fickle."

"Jaymes was just saying that, under different circumstances, he would have sided with her," Connor said. They all knew who the "her" was.

Frances clambered forward to the other advisor, who was asleep next to Ewan. Concern drew onto Frances's face as she took note of the irregular breaths from Marina, the way her chest rose, fell, shook twice, and then fell again. "It is cold in here, isn't it?" Frances asked, rubbing her hands together.

"Yeah," Connor agreed.

"You guys just need some meat on your bones," Mathias said.

Ewan pointed to Marina. "You sure it's not just her injuries? They're looking gnarly."

"I hope not." Frances sat back. "Then again, I left her antibiotics in our shuttle. She still had three more rounds to take."

"We really need to get our floors back," Mathias said resolutely.

"But we should sleep," Connor said. "Marina's right, no matter how hard it is, we have to. Oddly enough, I do think our futures depend on these next six hours, assuming we rest up."

Ewan laid back down on the floor, shivering. Frances did the same, her hands back under her head, pillowing it from below. Connor further reclined against the bottom of the staircase, and he closed his burning eyes.

———

Marina was freezing. She didn't know how long she had slept, but she couldn't continue. Her lips quivered. Her fingers pulled at the ends of her sleeves, but they never elongated enough to bring her warmth. Her toes curled in on themselves inside her sneakers. None of those remedies worked. She sat up and rubbed her legs, and it wasn't lost on her that, as she exhaled, a visible cloud danced before her face and fizzled away after a few seconds.

She wasn't the only one who had been yanked from the solace of her slumber. Multiple pairs of eyes skittishly set on her as she tried to warm herself. Others shivered just as she did; Athol, Jaymes, and Frances were crunched together, their arms around each others' waists and shoulders; Connor, Ewan, and Mathias held their hands up to the fireplace, sometimes shifting to bring them up to blow hot air onto them from their mouths. Marina scooted closer to the flames by moving up to the hearth.

"Wh-What's happening?" Marina stuttered out.

Athol shook his head a few more times than normal. "Dunno. Maybe they shut off the heat."

Frances inched closer into Jaymes's side, and he gladly welcomed her closeness; his ears were blue. "Why would they shut off the heating?" she asked, having to lean past his chest to see Athol, who was identically closely clung to Jaymes. The three of them hugged each other.

"We are in *their* shuttle," Mathias said brusquely. "On their turf, basically."

It was so cold that the soot on the floor wasn't staining their clothes anymore, but had instead become a hardened varnish.

The others' suits were zipped up, but Marina wasn't in possession of one. Her sweater, vest, and checkered sleep bottoms would only last her so long. After noticing that detail, Connor moved over to make more space for her by the hearth, so that she was close enough that her hair was perilously near the flames. The left side of her face dried from the heat of the fire, but she had to stay there. The stitched wound on that side of her, on her cheek, desperately needed heating because the cold had made it tighter and more painful. In addition to those troubles, she hadn't taken a painkiller in over twelve hours.

"How long has it been this bad?" Marina asked.

"A while now," Connor said. "It started off as a chill earlier, when you were asleep. Some of us were up and awake. Maybe an hour ago it got a little worse. Then about thirty minutes ago it was like this, and it's been this way since."

"But it hasn't changed in the last thirty minutes?"

"No."

"We should leave," Mathias said.

"No, not yet," Ewan disagreed. "It might be the second shuttle cooling down or something."

"How do you mean?" Athol asked.

"I don't know, man. Maybe it has to wind down after all those hours in use."

"Bullshit." Athol rubbed his hands together. "I don't trust this. I checked the thermostat five minutes ago and couldn't control anything. The screen's black."

"It's too early for us to leave," Marina said.

Jaymes's glasses bounced on his face from his ceaseless jitters. "But we'll freeze up here," he said.

"If we leave now, then we're stuck in the vents," Marina said. "They're clearly awake. What chance do we have? Where do we go from here? We haven't even devised a plan."

"Then let's do that," Connor said, mainly to her. "We do that right now. What's the plan?"

"We don't even have an idea of where any of them are," Marina reminded him. "We can't just travel through the vent, exit through some random room, and hope we don't run into one of them. That's how we get killed. And before anyone says that they wouldn't dare kill us, just think back to that fiasco in the shuttle, which, apparently, they knew about."

"For sure, we know someone's in the control room of your shuttle," Ewan said to Connor. "That's how they shut the heat off." Ewan took in a breath. It sounded like a wheeze.

"You all right?" Frances asked.

"Yeah, just..." Ewan coughed, wheezing again. "It's cold."

Marina hugged her legs. She felt the fire warming the back of her head, through her hair.

Connor bunched a hand into the fabric of his suit, right over his chest. His face wore a strained expression. "I'm..." He squirmed. "I don't feel so good."

"Why?" Jaymes asked. "What do you mean?"

"Just...not *good*."

"Yeah, none of us do," Athol said.

Connor was having difficulty speaking. "No...like...like..."

"Relax," Frances said. "Just calm down. It could be anxiety."

"I don't..." Connor's face formed a pinched expression. "I do *not* have anxiety."

"We all do in some way," Frances said very gently, considerate in warming him to the prospect of having the common mental affliction.

"Well, I don't."

On one side of Marina, Mathias began wheezing. He fixed his large hands onto the edge of the metal hearth. His fingers tightened whenever he inhaled, and they relaxed, just slightly, with every exhale. It took her a minute, but she eventually pieced together the fact that the two men flanking her, he and Connor, were suffering from breathing difficulties.

Ewan, on the other side of Mathias, fell forward. Ewan saved himself from toppling face-first by pressing his hands down to the wooden floor. He sounded like he was choking.

"Ewan!" Frances called to him. She and Athol clambered forward on their hands and knees. They rubbed his back and arms, trying to goad a response out of him.

"What's going on?" Athol asked, slapping the side of Ewan's face. "Tell me!"

The candelabras flickered off.

The flames of the fireplace died out.

Marina pushed herself away from the hearth. She was about to approach Ewan as well, but then Mathias and Connor were themselves producing strangled noises. Connor's eyes closed and he grabbed at his throat. Mathias fell to the floor, coughing.

Ewan couldn't prevent himself from collapsing anymore. His chest rose and fell unevenly, and he plummeted down to the wooden surface.

"What's going on?!" Jaymes asked. He dug his hands into Athol's shoulders and jostled him. "Athol, tell us!"

"I….I don't…" Athol said.

"Athol!" Frances screamed.

Athol started crying. "It might be the oxygen! They may have shut off the oxygen!"

"C-can't…bre…breathe…" Mathias struggled out.

"That's impossible," Marina said to Athol. She kept her voice even. "They can't shut it off without all the captains' and advisors' biometrics. Even in their own shuttle, they can't without all of us."

"There can't be any other explanation!" Athol said, his hands fisted in the collar of Ewan's shirt as he and Frances turned the collapsed pilot onto his back so she could inspect him.

Marina thought back to the moments before her division left their shuttle, how Ewan and Mathias had removed their Grains from their noses. Connor must have done the same.

Frances seemed to pinpoint that same recollection. "We have to give them some of our Grains!" she told Marina, Athol, and Jaymes.

"How will we survive?!" Jaymes asked.

"A person can manage on one! Hurry!"

Athol winced as he tore one out of his left nostril. He gave it over to Frances, who applied it to her index finger and shoved it up one of Ewan's nostrils. Jaymes did the same for Mathias, and Marina for Connor. The latter two's conditions bettered instantly, their troubled breathing abated and returned to paces that, although far from normal, were significantly improved. The red of Mathias's face and the blue of Connor's were beginning to fade to their lighter skin tones. The same couldn't be said for Ewan. The guttural sounds he produced only became deeper, louder. Frances forced his mouth open and pressed her lips to his. She willed hot, gasping breaths to shoot into his body, but when she was unsuccessful in performing the lifesaving method, Mathias volunteered to replace her. Burly hands pounded against Ewan's chest, and then Mathias's chapped lips slammed against Ewan's. But nothing was working. He just kept convulsing.

"He has asthma…" Athol said, wiping his face of tears, the same way he had done following Patterson's death, like he was ashamed of his sorrow. "His inhaler…His inhaler…Must have left it…" He was slobbering his words, shedding uncontrolled tears as he clenched Frances's hands, holding her like his life depended on it, like he would fall forward, too. "He left it in the shuttle...He....He left his inhaler in the shuttle..."

Mathias kept striking Ewan's chest.

Jaymes fell back, a hand over the lower half of his face. Sobs ran free from his mouth.

Marina pulled back from the scene. She watched as Athol and Frances released each other to take Ewan's hands into their own.

"Please," Athol whispered. *"Please, Ewan...Please. I'm sorry. I'm so sorry. Ewan...Don't leave...Don't leave me..."*

Ewan stopped convulsing.

Mathias was knelt over, his elbows on the floor in front of him and his head bent into the space between his arms, gasping not from any abrupt deprivation of air, but because of his horror, from his inability to accept what was happening. Jaymes and Connor grabbed at each other's arms, not quite embracing each other, but supporting one another so as to not tip over from their tremors. Marina, however, sat against the cooled walls beside the fireplace, her lips slightly parted and her pupils shrunken to beads, not a tear slipping from her dry eyes. She knew what had happened, that there was no rectifying it. Athol kept begging Ewan to stay with them, and Frances was kissing Ewan's soft, blue knuckles, whispering that he couldn't leave them, that they couldn't go on without him. But the fact was that he was there no longer. There was nothing to be done, nothing that could bring back Ewan Jackson McHugh.

28

Quentin never intended to fall asleep. He actually didn't think he would, not as he and Fatima were squished beside each other within one of the empty closets of the infirmary. He had decided that, of all the rooms on the upper floors, the infirmary was the safest and most conducive to their concealment, since Natalie had offhandedly mentioned last year that it was one of the few rooms that could lock from the inside. He didn't dare turn on any of the lights, didn't linger in the main wing of the medical quarter beyond their first few seconds after entering it; as soon as he secured the door, he had ushered himself and his smaller cohort into one of the closets. Fatima had been shaken when he first sealed the closet door behind them, but she knew to stay silent and not let out even the tiniest peep. He held her when she sobbed in silence, whispered that things would be better even though he mistrusted the utterances himself. Eventually, she fell fast asleep.

It was nearly pitch black in the closet, save for the wristwatch that glowed softly near Fatima's hip as Quentin held her. He couldn't take the risk of the light seeping out from the crack under the door, should someone have chosen to barge in, so he pulled his sleeve over the watch face. Eventually, his eyes adjusted to the dark and made out their breaths hovering before them, saw that Fatima was shaking from the cold even more than he was. They couldn't stay there, he knew that. *But where to go?* he wondered. Anywhere beyond the walls of the infirmary was too dangerous. He didn't want to imagine what Roxy would do if she had them within her grasp.

Quentin shook Fatima with one of his numbing hands, but she didn't wake. That came as no surprise to him. The last time any of them had slept more than three consecutive hours was the day of the 6th, and when he checked his watch in the infirmary, it read that it was three o'clock in the morning, on the 7th.

He did what he could to keep them warm, and he prioritized Fatima. He wrapped her significantly smaller form with his long arms. He blew hot air onto the back of her neck and hands, even rubbed his palms against hers to stimulate heat. He couldn't stand the pain of sitting on the frosty floor with unfeeling digits and a head that was becoming dizzy and confused, regressing in its clarity. He'd lived in New England once, had bore the chills of autumn and the blizzards of winter. This was nothing like that. This was a cold so ruthless that it numbed and stung him simultaneously. From the textbooks to one Colin H. Patterson, everyone was right. There was no cold like that of deep space's.

Unable to resist the temptation, Quentin checked the watch to find that only thirty minutes had passed. He placed his chin on top of Fatima's head as he ran shaking hands up and down her arms. *How long can we do this?* he thought. He blew breaths down to her forehead, covered her ears with her hair, and stared ahead to the wall in front of them while warming her. As he shifted his body to prevent a leg from falling asleep, the light of his watch hit the wall and he noticed something, something he thought he imagined just before he hid the gadget back under his sleeve. But driven by curiosity and desperation, he pulled his sleeve up and positioned the watch at a downward angle toward the wall, hoping to glimpse what he thought his imagination had conjured.

He wasn't delusional. A line was furrowed into the gray surface. He risked following it up with his watch's glow, and he saw that it came to form the shape of a square, which looked about three-feet tall, three-feet wide and ended just above the floor. He covered the watch again, relaxed his hold on Fatima, and uncoiled himself from around her. He prowled up to the surface and felt around. He made sure to especially touch the tips of his fingers along the line. At first touch, he thought it was carved in, but then he pressed against it more intently and highlighted it with the light. He found that tiny, painted-over screws had been driven inside each of the sharp corners of the square-shaped outline, presumably the cover of a vent or a small exit.

Mathias may have had the screwdriver, but Quentin was poised to believe that the scalpel fitted into his left boot could act as a decent substitute. He jammed the edge of the scalpel into the bottom-right screw and persistently twisted it counterclockwise. Removing the screw wasn't easy, but the effort kept him moving and, resultantly, warmer. At three-thirty-nine, his blistered fingers wrapped around the head of the screw as it started to pop out toward him. Paint and plaster particles chipped off and fell to the floor. At three-fifty-two, all four screws were strewn about the small expanse of floor between his knees and the unbolted pane. He peeled it back by its top corners and let it fall against his legs; the slight sound of the release woke Fatima. Quentin rotated the pane, leaned it against the wall to his right, and sat back. Fatima sidled up beside him and gazed ahead to what he had just unveiled. He bent his head down so that it was level with hers, and they looked into a narrow, metallic passage inside the wall. It was dark, darker than the closet, but he had his wristwatch to light the way, however faint it was.

Fatima turned to him. Her cheeks and the tip of her nose were pink from the cold. "Is that our escape?" she asked him timidly.

"Yes," Quentin said.

"Where will we go?"

The question jolted him. He hadn't actually considered where they would flee to, exactly. There were many rooms, but there were also many people who could have been inhabiting them.

"The basement?" Fatima suggested. "Our basement?"

Our, Quentin thought. "Our shuttle," he said to himself. That may have been an ideal option, were he not solely encumbered by the responsibility of keeping the child safe.

"It's our shuttle," Fatima said to him.

Quentin dwelled on the idea. "I guess, if we do go down there," he said, "we could just choose an empty room. Or stay in the vents."

"But in our shuttle, right?"

After having gone months without one, Quentin allowed himself a smile. "You want it back, don't you?"

"It's our shuttle," Fatima said once again, like there was nothing else to explain. To her, their goal was obvious.

"All right, all right," Quentin gave in. "But we're not taking over the ship tonight. We just need to get somewhere warmer and then…"

Fatima watched him with anticipation.

"And then we'll see," Quentin said.

It appeared to be a satisfying compromise. She stopped asking him questions—or, rather, the same one over and over again.

Quentin entered the small passage first. It wasn't so restricting that he had to wiggle his way through, but it was high enough that he could crawl comfortably. He placed his hands along its flooring and felt cool metal. It wasn't a robust material; this metal flexed and clanked every time he moved a bit too heavily or applied moderate pressure. Right on his heels, Fatima followed.

A while later, they came to a wider space that was about a foot taller, where a wall-mounted ladder awaited them. Quentin climbed first. The ladder went higher than he expected. He counted twenty-three rungs as they ascended it. At the top, his head and shoulders protruded into another vent passage. He studied the space, detected that there wasn't one passage in front of him, but, rather, one on each side of him. He peeked down and watched as Fatima started hugging one of the rungs by her face to remain securely propped up.

"What's wrong?" she asked.

Quentin let go of his hesitation. It wasn't like he could somehow endanger them by taking an incorrect turn. As far as he was concerned, they were already safely stowed away from the searching eyes of everyone downstairs. It was merely a matter of where he wanted to go, so he hoisted himself up and then reached down to take one of Fatima's chubby hands into his parched ones. He pulled her up with him.

For some reason, he thought back to the much simpler times back home, to the giant, inflatable obstacle courses through which he and Lucas used to wander during the summertime birthday parties of their friends. When they were little, such festivities felt like they had taken place every other week, from the first day of June to the concluding days of August each year. Quentin shook his head, ridding it of the memories of blow-up realms that had once seemed sprawlingly large, but were no bigger than one of the smaller rooms of the ship. He didn't appreciate the nostalgia rush, especially then of all times.

He and Fatima crawled for a long while, turned many corners, shuffled across countless crossings, and proceeded down even longer expanses of their hideout. They came upon their second ladder at five o'clock in the morning, which offered them both a way up and a way down. They selected the downward option, seeing as how their objective was to reach the basement, not the upper levels. At the base of the ladder, as they recommenced their crawling, Fatima asked him if he thought Frances and the others were all right. He told her he didn't know, but that the others would want the two of them to stay safe and remain out of sight.

Behind him, he heard Fatima say, "I thought they were our friends." For the split second Quentin was curling his body around a corner, he was finally able to look back and see her face. She was difficult to read, but most children were. "I never liked Derek," she said. "I don't think he liked me either." She turned the corner and followed Quentin down the straighter path. "But, actually, I don't think any of them did."

"Did what?" Quentin asked.

"Like us. Like…if I think about it, I guess not."

Quentin felt the same. The more he recalled his interactions with members of the first division, it became clear to him that most of them only ever conversed with him when they needed something or if they were assigned by Patterson to be in Quentin's general proximity. And when he thought back to their days back home, he couldn't remember ever speaking to any of them beyond the topics of schoolwork.

"I think—" Quentin said, but he cut himself short.

He swore he heard a muffled groan, or something like it. It sounded close, but he knew that it definitely hadn't come from the girl at his heels. He held up an index finger, and Fatima knew not to speak. They froze and cautiously waited to hear another sound like the one he thought he had heard. For a moment, he suspected that his mind was playing tricks on him. But then they heard a voice below them. It was muffled. *Two voices,* Quentin observed. One was an increment softer than the other, although both were pronounced enough to be audible from above, even if he couldn't make out any specifics of the words that were spoken. He knew that he and Fatima had to have reached the third floor a while back, after they climbed down the second ladder.

The voices died out.

Neither Quentin nor Fatima made a move or a sound. He brought the watch up to his face and waited for two minutes to pass, growing hypnotized by the thin arrow skittishly completing its clockwise journey twice. That was when they started moving again. They barely pressed their hands and knees into the surface as they went on, but they were also wary of making any dragging noises. It was a thin line they had to walk—in that case, crawl.

A corner was ahead. Eager as he was to round it, Quentin knew he had to continue the steady, gradual pace that had kept their travel clandestine. When he reached the junction of the two passages, he folded his body around the edge of the wall as flexibly as possible.

Mere seconds after promising to be stealth, his left boot bumped against the wall behind him. Fatima gasped. Quentin did too. They locked eyes and their faces morphed into tight grimaces as they tried to will away the horror of the brief ruckus he made, however small it was.

From below, a *"bang!"* disrupted the silence. It hadn't originated from where the muffled voices were, but, instead, in the vicinity of the surface they crawled upon. Quentin flinched. Fatima whimpered.

Quentin knew a gunshot when he heard one. Fatima squealed and she did it again when two more shots rang out. She crawled backwards. They focused their attention on the ground of their passage, to the couple of spots that started jutting up. The metal was waving up hard, and they heard the banging return for a fourth and a fifth time. Fatima covered her ears with her hands while Quentin beckoned her closer, trying to get her to leave that particular terrain and join him around the corner, where the problem wasn't occurring. The *"bangs!"* didn't stop, and the intervals between each one became shorter. The metal kept rising. In some spots it was struck repeatedly and started to break bit by bit, rising and becoming more brittle. Fatima wasn't coming any closer to Quentin. He kept reaching forward, trying to goad her off her spot, but she wouldn't move. He abandoned the junction between the two passages and went to her, aiming to yank her forward.

One of the protruding spots of metal burst, opening inward and twisting into a jagged-rimmed chink. A bright flash erupted from the tiny opening. In a fraction of a second, Quentin glimpsed a projectile sheathed by a flash of light. In the next fraction, the bullet found its place inside him, lodging itself into the right side of his torso, just above his hip.

Quentin screamed. He fell prone, could feel Fatima clawing at him and telling him to get up. His hand went to the side of his stomach and covered it, attempting to lock in what he knew would inevitably leave him, but all he felt was the escaping outpour of red, hot blood.

"The vents!" someone, a male, alerted everyone below. "They're going through the vents! Get Oscar in the basement now! Go!"

"Derek!" Fatima whispered. *"Quentin, that's Derek!"* She pushed Quentin's shoulders, urging him to keep moving.

Quentin didn't. He felt Fatima weakly wrestling with him to try and get him up, but all he did was writhe in place, sinking into the metal surface. His blood spilled heavily. It was on his hands, all over the vent, and dripping through the open gap of the passage. He all but stuck his fingers into the hole in his gut. The pain was intolerable, immeasurable. It was nothing he could have ever imagined. He blacked out to the sound of Fatima screeching.

29

From what Marina saw with the help of the few speckles of light provided from outside the window, Athol's head was on Frances's chest and his arms were wrapped around her midsection. He couldn't stop crying, was sobbing and sniveling as she likewise clung to him. Connor, Mathias, and Jaymes were huddled together.

Ewan was on the floor, his eyes closed and his blue lips still parted. No one knew what to do with the body.

Marina couldn't stop shaking, not because of what had happened to Ewan, but because she was agonizingly cold. She could no longer feel her hands as she rubbed her fingers together. The outsides of her ears burned. The bit of her clavicle that was exposed above her vest line began to redden. Her stitched spots crinkled every time she shook, the flesh on the brink of splitting after having grown taut in its frozen state. She said that they had to leave, brought attention to the fact that Athol's tears were solidifying on his face. But no one listened to her. They ignored her call to the cold.

"We *have* to leave," Marina said a second time, more forcefully.

"Marina," Frances said her name, her voice cracking. "Ewan just di—"

"We don't have time for this. Two subjects are somewhere out there and if they're on the second floor, like us, they will freeze to death." Marina's hands stung as she slid them farther down her shirtsleeves. "This…this is painful…"

"Wh-What do we do?" Jaymes asked.

"We have to go now," Marina said. "We're a day away from our Grains running out of their oxygen supply, and we will freeze to death." She blew a breath down her neck, to her chest. "We know Roxy's in the control room, the one in the cargo hold. It's the only way she could have shut off the oxygen."

"I…I don't get it," Connor said. "She can't do that without our permission."

Marina wiggled her toes inside her sneakers. Even that small act hurt her.

"I'm going to skin that bitch alive," Mathias said very slowly as he looked down to the motionless Ewan. Mathias said it so smoothly that Marina would have sworn he wasn't shivering like the rest of them, like he was his normal, unaffected self again.

"We need to get our shuttle back," Marina said, suppressing the natural urge to stutter as she shook. "We need to get back that shuttle and its control rooms."

"Both of them?" Connor asked.

"Yes, both of them. Roxy's probably in the one in the cargo hold. Oscar or Amber, or both of them, might be in the smaller one, the one that we used." Marina blew another breath down her shirt. "Athol, can we get to the shuttle control room through the vents?"

He didn't answer.

"Athol," Marina gritted out.

Aggravation replaced the sadness on Frances's countenance. "Give him a minute," she said to Marina.

"If we wait any longer, we'll die," Marina said. "That would leave Roxy with the chance to do whatever she wants downstairs. Athol, we need an answer."

"There's a way," came muffled from Athol's mouth. He unwound himself from Frances and put his hands on the gelid wood of the floor to balance himself. His hair was askew and his were eyes swollen; Marina could barely see his pupils. "We can get into both control rooms through the vents. But it's not…It's not simple."

"Why?"

Athol sniffed as he watched Frances reach forward and run a shaking hand over one of Ewan's. She held it, her warmer fingers stroking the cold digits beneath them.

Athol overcame the distraction. "There are two vent systems, one for each side of the ship," he said. "They don't connect. So… like…on the left side, where we are, we're in line to go to the first shuttle's control room. But if you're on the right, you can go down to the other control room, which is in the other half of the basement."

"We should split up," Mathias said. "I'll look for Fatima."

"That's too dangerous," Connor warned.

"I don't care. I'll find her. I'll crawl through every vent if I have to. I'll check every fucking room."

"I'm going with you, then," Frances said. She ran her thumb over Ewan's pulse point, where a beat was once steadily present. "I'm one of the people responsible for this, anyway."

"You're not going just the two of you," Marina said.

"We'll make it," Frances insisted. "We will. We'll stay hidden. I have a scalpel. It's not much, but it can do some damage."

"That's one knife," Jaymes said. "Why don't you take the Nox with you?"

"No way," Connor said. "Searching through the vents, they're way safer than the rest of us if we're going into the basement. Right?" He looked to Marina. "Right, Marina?"

Marina's mind roamed elsewhere. It had begun to drift as soon as Jaymes spoke of Frances and Mathias's modest arsenal. Jaymes's argument evoked a forgotten moment Marina had once mistakenly thought to be unimportant, but was glaringly crucial when she actually thought back to it. She was thinking of the morning of their flight, the 2nd of February, when she insisted to Quentin that the kitchen knives were not to be moved to the cargo hold, but were to stay in their cages, in the kitchen. In those few seconds of recalling the event, the bitter cold that swept through the library went unnoticed by her. "Oh my god," Marina said, her hand flying to her forehead. "*Oh my god.*"

"What?" Jaymes asked.

Marina looked to Connor. "I did give Roxy my biometrics," she said. "Ivy came to me and Quentin before the flight. She asked for our fingerprints so Patterson could make portable IDs. I never once considered that it was Roxy, not Patterson, who sent Ivy."

Her admittance stopped Athol from slipping into another grief-stricken trance. "You *what?*"

Connor dropped his head. His breathing was more labored. "I did the exact same thing," he said. "I fell for the exact same fucking thing. Fuck. Fucking fuck."

"Here's what we'll do," Marina said. "We'll split up in the vents. Frances and Mathias, do whatever it takes to get back Quentin and Fatima. The rest of us, we'll enter the basement through the control room of the first shuttle, not the one in the cargo hold. We'll have Athol lock the basement so that no one gets in and no one gets out. If we get that shuttle, we'll have the advantage over everything."

"And if there are people in there?" Athol asked. "If there are people in our control room, what do we do?"

Marina pat her breast pocket, where she felt the Nox Bomb poking out beneath the fabric. "We'll knock them out before we go in ourselves." She stood, but it was harder to do than she expected. Her already rigid legs further stiffened despite the movement, and she felt her toes sting under the pressure of her weight, despite how light she was. "We move now," she said. "Mathias, get the vent."

Before Mathias left, he bid Ewan farewell with a dispirited glance. It was cursory, a mere flicker of his formerly outward show of pain. Marina almost didn't notice Mathias doing it.

Other farewells were antithetically demonstrative. Athol gave one of Ewan's blue hands a light squeeze and Frances kissed the top of his head.

"One day," Frances said to Athol, "we'll be with him again."

Connor and Jaymes didn't say anything. They didn't move closer to express their sorrows and affections to what had once been a living, breathing friend. They did, however, jointly help Athol up to his feet.

Marina walked past everyone, tromped her way up the staircase, and followed Mathias to the loft.

Marina oftentimes forgot how monstrous their ship was, but a manifest reminder of its immensity occurred during the early hours of February 7th. They crawled for hours. No one knew the way, not even Athol. He relied on hunches and distant recollections of blueprints he had once reviewed with Patterson and Ewan, but neither were alive to be consulted. Mathias had been right: they really were alone.

Marina's body ached during the whole journey down. It was the pressure that the crawling applied on her hip that made her feel like a fixed twinge had settled into uncomfortable permanency throughout her. Everyone else bemoaned the ladders they happened upon, but she was always relieved. The temporary verticality alleviated the knots in her shoulders and the physical stress that crawling applied to her hip. Jaymes always offered to carry her while they moved up the ladders, but she consistently refused.

Frances and Mathias were no longer with them. They had left for their pursuit of Fatima and Quentin early on in the crawl, about five minutes in. The group had splintered at the first fork they came across, where the advisers, their last pilot, and Jaymes split left and the other two split to the right. Connor, Jaymes, and Athol gave their unneeded suits to Frances and Mathias, citing that the cold would only become more unbearable the higher they went into the upper levels. Mathias took one, Frances two, and then they were gone, determined to avoid being empty-handed when they reunited.

If, Marina thought. *If we reunite.* She previously believed that they would, but she knew not to lead herself down a path of overblown expectations. By the looks of everything else that had occurred over the previous two days, she knew to trust her pessimism.

Athol lost his way many times. His inklings were often wrong, and horribly so. He would lead them one way and hit a dead end, which would prod Marina, at the back of the pack, to scuttle in reverse, which pained her hip. He would apologize profusely, rubbing his swollen eyes and guiding everyone down another path, typically a wrong one. He tried to remember things, would mutter to himself of the blueprints he mentioned, but he was rarely accurate in his mental mapping of the ship. Marina never complained, though. Connor did, as he was unfairly impatient that way, but she, by comparison, knew to not grate on the tender nerves of the one person who could bring them back to their rightful territory.

It took three hours for Athol to lead them to the basement. They had crawled through nearly fifty interconnected passages and descended seven ladders. He said lowly, cautious of being heard by anyone beyond the vents, "We should be in the basement by now. The next opening we see, I'll open it to check where we are."

Mathias had given them the screwdriver, which Athol put to use when they worked themselves into another small, metal enclave a couple minutes later. Marina couldn't see anything besides Jaymes's backside. She heard the painstakingly slow unlatching of a vent cover, the crusts of dried paint and plaster breaking. Athol spent some time inspecting the area he opened and then loosely returned the cover to the wall. He didn't bother screwing it back into place.

"Where are we?" Jaymes asked, cautious to remain quiet but not really whispering.

"I was right, we're in the basement," Athol said. "It was the third room. I recognized the water heaters."

"What number's your shuttle entrance?" Connor asked Marina.

"Eighty-five?" Marina asked. She was unsure.

"Yeah, eighty-five," Athol confirmed.

"So does that mean we go by another forty-one-ish rooms?" Connor asked.

"If only, but it's not designed in a straight line, remember?" Athol reminded them. "I do know our shuttle is left of here. But we'd have to, like, go left, take a right, keep going right, take another right or something, and then we'll get there."

"Do you know where the vent exit will be in the shuttle?" Jaymes asked. "I'd hate to get out through the control room and come face to face with the other pilots or something."

"I really don't know," Athol said. "Let's just go."

They resumed their crawling. Marina hurt all over, and more intensely than before. To assuage the strains in her left hip, she shifted her weight onto her right side. After every ten vent covers, Athol would open one. The fleeting moments of him checking which rooms they were passing allowed her some time to lie on her right side and rest. She kneaded her bruises and listened to his reports on what the lighting and equipment in the spaces ahead looked like, from which he recalled exactly where they were. And then they would keep crawling. Just when she thought she might yield to the soreness and stinging, Athol stopped them in their tracks.

"Shh, we should be here," Athol announced, the dread in his voice evident. They were likely somewhere near their shuttle, if not actually inside it. Marina heard the newly familiar tick as he fit the head of the screwdriver into the screws that held the vent cover in place.

She took advantage of the lag in their crawling and laid herself down on the metal surface. She kept only the top of her torso up as she folded her arms on top of each other. Her stitched neck hurt from the strain.

"Wait, wait," Connor interrupted as Athol started to push the cover forward; light from the other side streamed into the passage. Connor pulled his scalpel out of his pocket. "I'll check this time," he said.

Athol shuffled aside. In spite of his height, he was thin enough to stick himself against one of the walls as Connor moved up beside him.

Marina and Jaymes stayed silent. She felt for her scalpel and pulled it from her pocket. He took out one of the syringes Frances had distributed.

Connor pushed the vent cover forward, gripping the top of it to prevent it from crashing to the floor. He held it out midair. He then stuck his head forward for a moment before drawing himself back in, and he returned the cover to its rightful place. It was thick enough to stand on its own, but flimsy enough to give way under the force of even the softest of touches.

"We're in the storage closet," Connor informed them.

Jaymes scooted aside so Marina could see past him again.

"Is the door closed?" Marina asked. She didn't have to keep her voice as quiet, since she was all the way in the back. "The one to the passengers' quarter?"

Connor shook his head. "It's open a little. I bet one of us could squeeze our head through and see the room from there."

"Except that there's also the bathroom," Athol said. "We can't tell if anyone's in there if we're in the closet." He turned to Marina. "But that's not my call. Have any plans up your sleeve?"

Marina slid her thumb up and down one side of her scalpel. "I do," she said a few seconds later. "We all have something on us. It's likely that only Amber and Oscar are in the control room. I doubt Roxy's here. If she's smart, which she is, she's probably hunkered down in the cargo hold. I say we leave the vent now, check the passengers' quarter, including the bathroom, and Nox the control room on the weakest setting."

"Do they have their Grains in?" Jaymes asked. "Because it won't work if they're in, correct?"

"Correct," Marina said.

"We took all ours out after the belt flight," Connor said.

"Everybody out," Marina ordered.

Scalpels, screwdriver, and syringe drawn, the four of them ejected themselves from the vent, one by one. Marina was the last to exit. She didn't bother with the vent cover behind her and left it on the floor. They tiptoed around the storage boxes, some of steel and others of cardboard, and maneuvered around the inflated mattress she had laid upon for the days that led up to that morning of the 7th.

Marina stood closest to the door of the closet. Connor was next to her, Athol beside him, and Jaymes at the rear. Marina thumbed the device in her pocket and pulled it out for the first time since she had showcased it to everyone. Her fingers tightened around it.

Her head rounded the corner of the closet doorway. She didn't extend herself far enough that her face was entirely visible; only the top of her head could be seen from the other side. She looked around and saw that the space was relatively unaltered. Her shabby suit, the medical kit, and Jaymes's unzipped backpack remained in a pile under the single table in the corner of the quarter; Mathias's and Ewan's Grains glimmered on the edge. The rows of seating were empty, but the aisle between them wasn't. She saw a womanly figure, rounded at the hips and thin at the waist, perched on the floor and facing the other way, toward the control room. The figure had long, fiery, red hair. There was a laptop on her knees; it dangled treacherously, daring to poke into her midsection every time she typed on it.

Marina slunk her head back into the closet. *"Amber,"* she mouthed to Connor.

Athol hit Jaymes's middle with the back of his hand, whispering the name into his ear.

Connor put his palms out, essentially asking what Marina had in mind. She gestured to him and then to his scalpel, and when his eyes were on hers again, she nodded her head toward the doorway. *"You first,"* she dared whisper. He nodded, squeezed past her, and he tiptoed through the doorway. She followed, waving a dismissive hand at Athol to indicate that he and Jaymes were to stay where they were, near but not on the threshold.

Prudent of Amber's laptop screen possibly providing a mirrored view, Marina and Connor hunched low as they moved through the passengers' quarter to avoid having their reflections shown on the device. She stayed behind him as he snuck up on the unsuspecting pilot. Once he was in the aisle between the seats, he squatted so low that his knees almost made contact with the floor. Marina hung back behind one of the seats—Quentin's—with her blade in one hand and the Nox Bomb in the other. Connor crept up behind Amber and then he lunged forward. He smothered her head from behind, his large arms swallowing up those red locks, which were all Marina could see of the young woman. The laptop fell to the floor, producing a clamor that made Marina cringe. One of Connor's hands was slapped over Amber's mouth while the other held the butt of his scalpel, which he kept in front of her neck so that it was close enough for her to feel it against her skin.

Marina showed herself from behind Quentin's seat and made her way up to Connor and his hostage. Amber attempted yelping, but he kept her muted. She didn't move. She didn't fight it. She simply cried, her tears moistening his hand.

"Is there anyone else here?" Marina whispered.

Amber eyed the control room.

Marina's grip tightened around the bomb just as Connor's did on the lower half of Amber's face. Marina cocked her head forward in one, quick motion, and Connor understood that she was urging him to advance to the control room doorway. He followed her to it, Amber in his grip, and he tracked Marina's every move as she hovered her thumb over the entry keypad.

"Ready?" Marina asked.

Connor nodded.

Amber caught sight of the object Marina held and let out a whimper.

Marina scanned her thumb on the keypad of the control room entrance, drew her hand back to the Nox Bomb, and flicked up the honeycomb cover. Her finger pushed down on the bomb's blue button just as the door beside her slid away from the wall. She threw the bomb inside. Connor shoved Amber in after it. The advisors stepped back, and the door, losing detection of their bodies, began to close automatically. They heard coughs come from inside, and from multiple mouths, but Marina couldn't tell how many. They watched the door, awaiting the unexpected, but feasible, possibility of someone escaping, teary-eyed and choking on the released fumes. When no one emerged, Connor took the opportunity to check the restroom. Marina, on the other hand, remained skeptical. She only stepped back once the coughing stopped, which was also when Athol and Jaymes emerged from the storage closet.

"Did you get them?" Jaymes asked.

Connor returned from the restroom. Marina almost didn't notice it when he loomed out from the darker area, but in his other hand, his right one, he held a gun. "Clear," he said. "Found this on the sink."

With the tip of her scalpel, Marina pointed to the closed-off control room. "It should be safe for us to go in. Let's get a move on. I don't know how long the effect of the gas will last."

Their earlier reluctance to make noise still applied during their venture into the control room. Despite the emitted gas, they were untrusting of the efficacy of its damage. After they snuck through the doorway and reached the tunnel, they processed the spectacle of three, unconscious people. Connor had pushed Amber in quite far, as she was facedown on the floor at the end of the tunnel. Derek was unconscious, sprawled outside of the electrical closet. Oscar snored in Ewan's seat. Marina and the others poked and prodded at the ostensibly insensible, and once they were certain that the intruders were not feigning sleep, they relocated the sleepers. A limping Marina dragged Amber away, careless of how often her face collided with the solid floor. *She'll bruise soon*, Marina thought self-satisfyingly. Connor and Jaymes hauled away the stocky Oscar. Athol had no trouble addressing Derek, who was still dangerously emaciated.

Athol sealed off the vent in the closet to prevent either of their intruders from escaping once they woke up. He screwed it shut and pushed a tall, heavy crate, in front of the escape route.

As soon as the intruders were limply flopped on top of each other in the closet, Marina headed into the passengers' quarter and rifled through the medical kit. She greedily smothered her stitches with cooling gel. She bandaged the sensitive wound on her left arm, the one Quentin had haphazardly tended to amid the frenzied evening of February 2nd. She dryly swallowed her overdue antibiotic pill, since Jaymes's canteen was empty and she was too tired to search under each seat and go backpack to backpack looking for another. After her throat recovered from the coarseness of the pill, she took in a single painkiller. She sat on one of the seats, Quentin's again, and yawned. The gel lessened some of the stinging, but it did next to nothing for her left hip. She tore off a significant length of the bandage roll and began wrapping it around her waist.

"Go lock this level," Marina told Athol, who dutifully made his way up to the front and vanished.

Connor and Jaymes began layering metal boxes against the front of the closed storage room door.

"How long do you think it'll keep them under for, the Nox Bomb?" Jaymes asked as he heaved his third box into the air.

"I don't know," Marina said. "Just assume the worst. Act like it's five minutes from now."

Connor slid his scalpel into his knee pocket and set the gun on the seat beside Marina, which was Frances's.

The doorway behind the seating whirred as Athol returned. "I locked the basement," he said. "That'll block off the elevator. Also, the door to here."

"And the vents?" Marina asked.

"Nothing I can do about those, unfortunately. But they'd have to figure that out on their own."

Satisfied with the barricade they had put into place at the last minute, Connor and Jaymes leaned against the nearest wall.

"What now?" Jaymes asked.

"We have to get back that main control room, the one in the cargo hold," Connor said.

"But how?"

"I haven't thought that far. Now, we told Frances and Mathias that they were to come back here, whether or not they found anything…"

Marina shook her head. "We can't wait for them. We have to do something now. Athol, is there any way you can block Roxy's actions from here?"

"No."

"Okay," Marina said snippily. She scratched her eyelids.

"Is the only way to stop them really through physical force?" Jaymes asked.

"I think so," Connor said. "I just don't know how we'll do that without weapons of our own."

"We have a gun now, don't we?" Athol asked. "The one you found in the bathroom?"

"It was left alone for a reason," Connor said. "I checked the magazine and the barrel, both were empty."

"That's the same one Derek used to hold us at gunpoint in the foyer, right?" Athol asked. "Do you think he already used all of its bullets?"

"You know what? Never mind," Marina said. "We wait."

Connor titled his head. "Wait for what?"

"For Frances and Mathias to return. I just realized that it's not really the four of us versus whoever else is down here. It's the two of you," she said to Connor and Jaymes. "I'm not in any shape to help you, and Athol's life can't be put at risk. He's our only pilot. Besides, I'm not comfortable with the idea of you two storming off on your own because, Jaymes, you are our only Listener left in my reach. We should wait until the others return. If they don't have Quentin and Fatima, at least we'll have Mathias to replace Jaymes, and Frances to treat you if something goes wrong. Best case scenario, they do return with our other Listeners. Quentin and Fatima would stay here."

"You wouldn't want Quentin fighting with us?" Jaymes asked.

"He's a subject, just as you are. And do you think he would even if he could?"

"True, true."

"Athol," Connor said.

"Hm?"

"Remove the other pilots' biometrics from our shuttle and undo whatever they programmed into it," Connor said. "And replace anything they might have removed. Make sure you've wiped all of their markings."

"I will."

"Go with him," Marina said to Connor. "I trust Athol but we're all overtired. Make sure he doesn't slip up accidentally."

"You should get some sleep, Marina," Athol said.

"I was planning on it." Marina listened as the others hurried out of the passengers' quarter and entered the control room. Their fading footsteps were the last sounds she remembered before her head bobbed down and her eyes fluttered shut.

Following nearly two consecutive days of sleep deprivation, she slept deeply. There was nothing that could have woken her, not a yell, a thud, or a rumble—not even the searing pain that lingered in her hip. Her rest, however, did eventually come to be interrupted. It was one of the worst sensations she felt in all her twenty years, and it was that her bladder, of all things, woke her. She supposed it wasn't an unforeseeable disruption. In retrospect, she realized her division hadn't had the opportunity to use a restroom since the last time they were in their shuttle. She groaned and rose from her seat. She stumbled forward, shirked the pounding headache that indicated how inadequately she had slept, and all but rammed herself against the restroom door before she tripped inside.

After she took care of her bodily burden, she stood before the mirror and washed her hands. She looked at herself. She never had the chance to before; for all her time in the belt, she spent it laid across the mattress in the storage closet, drifting in and out of an uneven sleep pattern. The cut on the left side of her face was graying. The bags under her eyes were so weighty that they met the tops of her cheeks. Her hair was billowed around her shoulders like a cloud, and the strands extended outward instead of shooting down straight, like her mother's. The wound on Marina's neck, the one that should have killed her, made a grisly, choppy line across her sickly, sallow skin. She looked like an embodiment of the death she had narrowly escaped. *An anomalous occurrence if there ever was one*, she thought. It was a mystery she was inclined to solve, but it would have to wait for another time.

Marina shut off the sink faucet and dried her hands against her pajama bottoms. She languidly walked back to the seating area. In her limping, she dizzily passed the table, the open lid of the shuttle entrance, and the medical kit she had left standing on its own with no other boxes in close proximity to it.

She stopped walking. Her head may have been reeling from the pounding ache that rattled it, but for all the sharpness of her vision that had substantially withered in the last few hours, she knew what she saw. It was blurry, but she saw it. She turned on her heels, ever so slowly, to enable her sunken eyes to view the open lid which she knew had been closed when she was last awake. It was possible that Athol might have asked someone in their group to climb through the passage and confirm that the door downstairs, the eighty-fifth one, was locked. It wouldn't hurt to confirm that with him.

She turned around with the intention of enquiring, if only to lay her mind to rest so she could return to sleep. Yet she never had the chance to ask Athol anything. She saw only the metal wrench as it battered the side of her head.

30

Sometime in the night, Athol had lost himself in a rant regarding his discomfort over the new interconnectivity between his control room and the one Roxy had presumably occupied. Normally, the concern would have won Connor's attention, if not render him disoriented from a surge of worry, but it didn't on that night. He was so tired that he hadn't listened to a single word Athol said as he rambled on for minutes on end. At first, Connor thought that the lone pilot was trying to mindfully include the others in his thoughts for their sake, but the continuously yawning Connor soon realized that it wasn't so much for anyone else than it was for Athol himself, who used it as a tactic to stay awake. Connor, for his part, drifted in and out of feigned listening.

"...On me for not expecting it," Athol was saying. "I'll just have to..."

Jaymes tapped Connor's shoulder. They were sitting beside each other on the floor, right on the edge of where the tunnel to the passengers' quarter began.

Connor stifled a yawn. "Hm?"

"I heard something," Jaymes said. His facial features, what Connor could see of them under the glasses, rumpled together in a way that expressed disconcertment.

"Athol, we'll be back," Connor said.

"Is something wrong?" Athol asked.

Connor didn't know, so he didn't answer. Neither did Jaymes, who was surprisingly quick in springing to his feet and had already started toward the door. Connor followed him, the two of them stalking down the tunnel until they came to the end and entered the passengers' quarter. Connor fully expected to see a dozing Marina on one of the seats, her head propped against a hand and her eyes pinched shut, the way they always were when she slept. He thought it would be physically impossible for her to still be awake; he was worn out, but his minor pains were nothing compared to the unsightly disarray that was her body. However, when Connor entered the room with Jaymes, Marina was in no such position on one of the seats. She was on the floor, awake, leaning back on one elbow with a hand clamped to her forehead. Her body was supported by an open tool box behind her. The closet door was ajar. The boxes that had once guarded the entrance were messily strewn in front of it; the makeshift, second wall was undone. Holding a wrench, Oscar stood over Marina. His heavy expulsions of breaths released like the growls of a recently uncaged animal, which, in some ways, he was. When he caught sight of Connor and Jaymes appearing at the other end of the room, the fury on Oscar's face waned for moment. Connor thought he saw a shadow of remorse flit across Oscar's face, but it vanished so quickly that Connor wondered if he had wishfully projected the perception rather than having actually seen it.

Without even realizing it, Connor was sprinting forward with Jaymes beside him. They sped across the room and lurched themselves toward Oscar, but he fled. Just in time, he squatted to the floor, threw his legs over the edge of the quarters' entry lid, and scrambled down.

Connor and Jaymes stopped to inspect Marina. Jaymes held her up and pressed her for answers, asking if she was hurt and if anyone else had been with Oscar. She gave only grunts and groans. Jaymes's left hand worked its way to the back of her head. He slotted his fingers under her hair, feeling for blood. There wasn't any.

With the knowledge that she wasn't severely harmed, Connor lowered himself down the entry lid.

"What're you doing?!" Jaymes asked.

Connor didn't feel the need to explain himself.

Athol rushed out of the control room. He gawked at Marina, but didn't approach her like Connor thought he would. Instead, Athol's eyes flicked to the ajar door of the storage closet. The last thing Connor saw before his head dipped away was Athol slamming the metal barrier on the three, middle fingers of someone's hand. A female shriek echoed throughout the quarter, and he knew the sound was Amber's.

"Connor, stay here!" Jaymes yelled.

But Connor climbed down, and he disappeared from the room. Faced with the reality of what he was doing, he didn't exactly know why he chased after Oscar. It wasn't the pragmatic choice, but Connor supposed that just because one tended to oftentimes act rationally didn't necessarily make them a rational person. He always was something of a selective pragmatist; throughout his childhood, he befriended the wrong people despite his awareness of their negative influences on him; not a week ago, he had endangered himself by openly expressing outrage at his peers' treason rather than deceptively pretending to agree with them to keep himself safe.

He burst open the eighty-fifth door of the basement, stood in a dark hallway that was similarly soot-stained to the upstairs foyer, and clenched his jaw as he turned his head one way and then the next.

Behind him, Jaymes squeezed through the heavy door before it closed on him. "Connor, let's go back inside. It's not worth it."

"He killed Ewan," Connor said, his chest rising and falling as he spoke. "At the very least, he was complicit."

"Connor."

But the advisor didn't stop. He turned a corner.

Jaymes ran in the same direction. "Look, let's just go back while we can."

Connor shook his head. "I'm tired of them terrorizing us."

Jaymes kept up, his hand scraping the back of Connor's shoulder, trying to get him to stop. "And do you think it's going to get better if we go looking for him? No, obviously. Let's go back. We're thin on resources and we have no energy."

Connor resigned. He stopped walking.

"Thank you," Jaymes said. He dropped his hand. "Besides, we can't leave Athol and Marina."

"No, I know. I know."

They retraced their steps around the same corner they had just rounded.

Huffing, Connor swiped a hand through the front of his hair as he looked to Jaymes. "I just wish that bastard had stayed uncon—"

Connor didn't finish his sentence because the audience for it froze in place. Jaymes looked nauseous as he held steady, so Connor looked away from him, to the rest of the long hallway that extended out in front of them. With the dimness of the orange light bulbs in the ceiling muted against the fume-stained surfaces, Connor had to squint. But he managed to spot what it was that frightened Jaymes, what made him stop in his tracks. Ahead of them, Chris and Terry blocked off the rest of the hallway. They weren't lecherously angry or taunting like Connor thought they would be, had he run into them again. They looked tired, spent of all their anger, as if wanting the tension to be over with. What vindictiveness they divulged earlier had surrendered to an air implying that they weren't enthusiastically at odds with the other pair, but saw it as an exhausting necessity. Behind Connor and Jaymes, there was a scratching sound. The faint disturbance strained the already uncomfortable silence. Oscar was approaching, his hands clenched into fists. There weren't any guns, Connor made note of that. He supposed, in the grand scheme of things, it was a kind decision by the other three. But not kind enough to keep him still.

He elbowed Jaymes and they ran away, down an adjoining corridor. As they fled, they were constantly reminded of how limited they were in their escape route options. Connor felt the fatigue rush out of his body. He shed it like a second skin. They swept through corridor after corridor, and always at their heels were the screeches of Terry's sneakers and the *"thunks!"* of Chris's boots on the cement. Every time the opposing pair came closer, their breaths were loud in the others' ears. They didn't know where Oscar was, but wherever he lingered, they knew they were bound to reunite with him in one of those hallways ahead, where he'd likely pop out around a corner and force them to a halt.

Connor had an idea for an escape. It was one which he assumed would be met with opposition by Jaymes, but Connor reasoned that their scramble through the basement provided them the rare opportunity to storm a certain place, one that they desperately needed to claim as their own. When he recognized where they were, he yanked Jaymes by the back of his shirt and sent them charging into a seemingly random corridor on their left. Jaymes didn't protest. He knew to follow the advisor, who was fluent in everything that pertained to the navigation of the basement. He probably expected Connor to lead them down a route that would bring them back to the door of Division One's shuttle, but that wasn't what Connor had in mind. He led them through several more corridors. All the while,

Chris and Terry advanced so much that they seemed nearly an arm's reach away. Connor barreled himself and Jaymes, and by extension their pursuers, through a closed door.

When they reached the middle of the basement, where the western and eastern wings narrowly melded together, Connor sent them east.

"No you don't!" Terry bellowed behind them, but whether or not they liked it, they were headed to the cargo hold.

Connor kept tugging Jaymes's shirt to steer him down the accurate path. They cut diagonally, then they ran forward. Despite the fact that his previous excursions to the hold were often as slow as a leisurely stroll, running to it, in that instance, felt much longer. He heard the sound of someone tripping. A bout of shouted profanities followed, but then the footfalls resumed. He dared a glance, saw that it was Terry who had faltered, and noted that Chris hadn't stopped.

Oscar finally closed in, but not enough to catch them. He emerged from an intersecting corridor and found himself a few feet behind Chris. He must have thought that pursuing an opposite route would work and throw the others off guard, but his plan fell short.

At the one-hundred-and-thirtieth door, which was down the twentieth corridor in the east wing, Connor ran them inside. There was just a single hallway and no crossing ones in sight. He had not time to close the door, so they kept on forward.

Jaymes gasped for air. "You're not bringing us to my shuttle, are you?" he asked, hurrying his pace.

Connor stared down a pair of doors ahead of them. "No," he said.

Connor thew himself against the slit where the two barriers of the cargo hold entrance were adjoined; they swung open, then closed behind them once the frantic duo made it inside. He took in the giant space, his feet screeching to a stop for the first time since they started running. The cargo hold was unchanged, pristinely organized, and, at first glance, seemingly unoccupied. He knew it wasn't, though. As Marina had said, there was a high likelihood that Roxy Thompson was up the escalator, down the ramp, and inside the room at the end of the platform.

They couldn't linger. Connor guessed it would be another five seconds before their pursuers threw themselves into the room with them. He led Jaymes behind a tall storage unit located on their right. They narrowly missed being spotted and concealed themselves a split second before Terry, Chris, and Oscar came barging in. Terry was enraged, his anger reawakened. He was shouting, demanding that Chris and Oscar spread out and find the others. The sound of metal hitting the floor echoed throughout the area, bouncing off the steel objects around them. Connor heard all kinds of things being tossed around, the clamor intensifying and the echoes dizzying. They must have been checking every possible nook and cranny he and Jaymes could have fit themselves into. Heavy footsteps became progressively louder on the other side of the storage unit that hid them. They tiptoed backwards, moved to their left and positioned themselves behind a pyramid of spare, water heater tanks, five of them stacked atop one another. There was a large gap between two of the piled appliances. As the footsteps became louder, Connor led Jaymes through the gap, to the other side of the temporary wall that the tanks formed for them. The tanks were neighbored by five storage units; three on their left and two on their right. The footsteps of their pursuers fell farther away and became significantly quieter.

"Why did you bring us here?" Jaymes hissed, whispering.

"Frances and Mathias never came back," Connor said. *"We're on our own."* He didn't need to elaborate, didn't need to explain that Frances and Mathias had probably been caught sneaking around or that Quentin and Fatima, if they were hidden upstairs, had

possibly already died from the upper floors' deprivation of heating and oxygen. All that was left of the first division were Jaymes, a single pilot, and an injured advisor who balanced precariously on the cusp of life and death. *"With my biometrics, I can take back the control room,"* Connor whispered. He looked over his shoulder, to the towering escalator that was still a lengthy distance away from where he and Jaymes were squatted on the floor. *"I need to get up there."*

"They'll see you," Jaymes warned.

"Maybe we can sneak our way to the escalator. Let's go."

Staying low and hunched over, they stood. Although both were tall, they were tiny beside the storage units, which they stayed behind as they moved. Their tiptoeing was noiseless, but their breathing wasn't as subdued. An enormous crate, in which three, brand-new ovens were cased in hard plastic, stood across from the last storage unit. Connor thought it would make a decent obstacle to keep them unseen. It appeared wide enough to shield them during their progression toward the escalator. Much to his worry, though, there was a gap between the last unit and the crate. In order to reach it, they would have to expose themselves.

When they were a step away from abandoning the safety provided by the last unit in the chain of storage compartments, Oscar rounded the corner in front of them. He wielded the familiar weapon they had faced the previous night, in the foyer. His hand raised so that the barrel of the object was barely two inches away from Connor's nose. Oscar's index finger pulled back, and then there came a deafening sound.

Jaymes had jumped forward, plunging right onto Oscar. They fell to the floor. Another gunshot sounded, but luckily Connor staggered away from the spot where Oscar thought Connor would still be standing. Briefly blinded by the muzzle flash, he held a hand over his eyes to block the searing light. His ears rang from the harsh sound.

He heard a crash against the metal of one of the storage units, followed by the bullet ricocheting off another one before it embedded itself into the plastic that surrounded an oven that had been locked into the crate beside him.

Somewhere on the other side of the hold, Terry yelled to Chris.

Jaymes banged Oscar's head against the cement floor twice. Oscar rolled over. He cocked the gun again, pointed it up, and pulled the trigger. A bullet shot out. Connor ducked, sent his hands over his head, and prayed that the tiny, lethal shred of a thing wouldn't hit him. Once again, it missed. Having realized that, he was tempted to reach down and take the gun into his own hands, but it was too dangerous to intervene. Jaymes and Oscar were a jumble of knees and elbows and teeth, every single one of their body parts clashing against the other's. Another shot followed. That time, it came deathly close to Connor.

"Go!" Jaymes urged. He took an elbow to the face. His nose bled. His glasses cracked on one side. He had a strong grip on one of Oscar's hands, the one that held the gun, and Jaymes pushed it as far away from their faces as he could. He wasn't a fighter. For him, actions of violence were unorthodox. Connor appreciated Jaymes's change in character.

Oscar's gun released another bullet.

Connor breathlessly ran away. The wrenching guilt he felt nearly made him stay behind, but what use would that be? Whose benefit would that decision really serve? He was too self-aware to neglect how hypocritical it would be, when only the previous night, he had argued that the lives of a few had to be put at risk for the safety of many others. He couldn't betray his decision. It was grueling and it made him sick to his stomach, but he continued running. He cleared his mind during his sprint, not allowing himself to let the idea of regret consume him and lure him back to Jaymes. As Connor passed multitudes of piled utilities, barrels, chairs, crates, and boxes overstuffed with pillows from the library and bedrooms, he tried to ignore the screams behind him.

He ducked behind two, stacked, gilded-edged servers. From there, he had to round a corner to reach the lower landing of the escalator. It was powered off due to the recency of their flight and Patterson's incorrect assumption that there wouldn't be a need for anyone to enter the cargo hold during that week. It was too much of a risk to go forward and expose himself. The area that led up to the escalator was entirely vacant, not a storage unit or errant appliance in sight. If he had been followed and stepped right out, he would be seen.

He took in a breath and felt the air slip through the cracks between his front teeth. He took in another, and then he was gone, scrambling to the escalator. He had to do it.

He was out in the open and he wasn't alone. Terry appeared across from him, having stormed out from behind the cover of three refrigerators that were tied together to form a wall. He headed toward Connor, who was already past the escalator platform and bounding up the steps, three at a time. Because he wasn't allowed, he hadn't ever been on the escalator, had only glimpsed its height several times from below. He never ventured to consider just how high it reached, but as he skipped steps in his racing ascent, his stomach flipped about halfway up. He tried not to look down. Terry trailed behind by just twenty steps, and Connor figured that he was at least forty-feet high. A fear of heights made him reach out to the rubber-topped handrails that flanked him. He used the nauseating height to his advantage and chanced a second glimpse behind himself, to locate Jaymes. From Connor's new stature, he spotted a further embittered Oscar scouring the depths of the hold, evidently frustrated that Jaymes wasn't anywhere in sight. Connor didn't see the gun on Oscar's person, so perhaps Jaymes had taken it for himself. Chris, however, was where

Terry had been seconds earlier; at the base of the escalator, ready to climb.

Twenty-five feet. That was how much of a distance was left between the precipice of the escalator and where Connor was climbing. In the meantime, Terry sped up. He wasn't far away, and he was gaining on Connor quickly. Excited at the prospect of grabbing Connor, Terry hopped four steps at a time.

Connor tripped. After that one misstep, strong hands looped around his left arm. With his limb seized, he was jerked backwards, which also meant downward. Connor shoved Terry off him. They both wavered, each conscious of the height of their current position. Terry recovered faster, though. While Connor swayed in balancing himself, one of Terry's hands smashed against his chin. Connor wobbled again, but he regained a steady stance and turned around, heading up the steps once more. He was certain that something had chipped in his jaw, that something had broken. It hurt enough to distract him. As soon as he reached the platform above, the one that led to the control room, a wave of dizziness flowed through him. Pain coursed through his mouth and made its way down to his neck. He pushed through it and turned to head down the ramp on his left, but Terry flew up behind him. He took hold of Connor's nearest shoulder and spun him around. Terry thrust open hands against Connor's chest, pushing him back against the steel wall. Connor mustered a punch. It wasn't a great one, but it caused some damage.

Terry gripped the side of his face that had been struck. "How could you?!" He sounded heartbroken and gutted, not angry like Connor expected. He'd never seen Terry like that—hurt. Terry Montgomery could bear collisions to the head, could rise to the challenge of pushing the limits of his physicality. It wasn't the physical element of being weakly punched that made him cry, it was that *Connor* was the one who did it to him.

Chris was halfway up the escalator.

Terry quickly swiped away his tears.

"You killed Ewan," Connor said.

Terry lunged forward. In doing it, he took a blow to his right eye, but he reciprocated with a ram of his fist along the column of Connor's neck. He wobbled back, gagging, before pushing Terry against the ramp's railing that overlooked the cargo hold. Connor took three rapid strikes to the face, all in spots above his aching jaw. After the second punch, nothing hurt anymore. He threw a flurry of punches, and they were all better than his last one. They made Terry bleed and groan. One of them even made him cower over and hold his forehead. After the sixth, the final, Terry fell to his knees. Chris reached the top of the escalator, and Connor ran down the ramp, toward the control room.

"Casey!" Terry yelled in the direction of the control room. He spat blood out of his mouth.

Chris passed Terry and reached Connor, forcing him to engage in their own skirmish. It was mainly Chris who did the attacking. Connor was exhausted. The pain flooded back into him, its return worse than when he first felt it. He took a beating, so much that his right eye went blurry. He felt dizzy. Everything hurt. He made a last-ditch effort to kick the space between Chris's legs, which worked. Connor still had his weighty, gravity boots strapped to his feet, and when his foot collided with Chris's groin, Chris stumbled away, wincing in pain and puffing breaths in and out in quick succession.

Connor sensed rather than saw a recovered Terry running toward him to rejoin the fight. "Casey!" Terry called out again, cowering over in his run as he did. He held his stomach. "Lock the door! Lock the control room!"

Connor tried to limp away, but the dizziness led him directly into the wall to his right. The approaching Terry stumbled and fell right behind him, but then rose immediately to become eye-level with his lower back. Connor attempted a backwards kick that missed its mark. Terry pulled Connor down by the collar of his jumpsuit, far enough that they were face to face. He was too dizzy, too late, to react when arms encircled his neck and started to squeeze him, closing off the airflow.

Connor gasped. "Terry!" He slapped at the arms around his neck.

"Home…" Terry grunted. He clasped his hands together. His arms squeezed tighter. "I *will* go…home…"

Two, wet things stuck to the back of Connor's neck before they slid down his clavicle. While suffocating, he realized that they were tears falling from Terry's eyes. Connor begged Terry to stop, but he didn't. He kept squeezing harder and harder, until Connor's entire vision blurred and his throat started closing, his skin shifting between red and pale and then red once more. He started pushing, just pushing. He gave power to his pushes by fixing his boots to the floor and slowly sliding back one foot at a time, until he had Terry pressed against the railing. Connor had such little strength left, but with the remnant of a near-dying breath and an overpowering will to live, he gave a backwards thrust.

He didn't know what he expected to happen, maybe hoped Terry would receive the thrust to his gut and finally stagger away or perhaps crumble to the floor of the ramp. But nothing could have prepared him for Terry holding him in a death grip one second and then disappearing in the next. There came a blood-curdling shriek, and in his concussed state, Connor thought it may have been his own. He didn't feel Terry behind him, nor was Terry on either side of his body. Connor blinked and turned around slowly, not knowing what he would see when he stepped closer to the railing of the ramp.

Terry was splattered. Spilled. His corpse laid mangled, devoid of the qualities that had made him look human not five seconds earlier. All that remained of him was a mound of his separated appendages and bursted insides smeared along the cement, unspooling and spreading in the molten blood that trickled down the floor, where the surface had a slight slope.

Chris backed himself to where the escalator and the platform met. He vomited, and profusely. The liquid he threw up wouldn't stop shooting from his mouth.

Oscar had been standing at the bottom of the escalator, where he was searching for Jaymes. He must have seen everything firsthand and up close, because he was collapsed on all fours near the stacked pair of gilded servers that recently hid Connor. Oscar was so distraught that he was ignorant to Jaymes hovering on the other side of the servers.

A whirring sound came from the end of the platform, and Casey strode out of the control room. Connor didn't look at her. He *couldn't* look at her. He wanted to, but he couldn't bring himself to move. "What is—?" he heard her begin to ask and Connor knew, and he hated that he knew, from the way she didn't finish her question, that she, too, saw what he had done.

In the seconds following Terry's death, Connor's first movement was the closing of his eyes. Memories of a life the two of them had once lived together came rushing to the forefront of his mind. He saw their afternoon bike rides through Shaw's forests when they were children, and later, the nightly drives when they were teenagers, free from the overbearing clutches of their parents. He remembered the smug, collected smirks Terry would divulge in public, but also the broad, goofy grins he permitted himself to show in private, when it was only himself and his friends within the walls of their homes or when it was just the two of them, alone. Connor remembered when Casey's parents died, the two who were also Terry's favorite aunt-uncle pair. He remembered the pain of that loss, the dramatic shift in the cousins' lives, how nothing beyond that point was ever the same for either of them. How they had thought, initially, that there was no one who would understand them, who would be there for them back in that cold, superficial world in which transactional relationships dominated the social circles of their town's youth. But they were not alone. They had each other, and they had Connor. Terry and Casey weren't Connor's siblings, but he held them when tears streaked their cheeks.

Casey's screech would haunt Connor forever. It tore him apart to hear it. He wasn't even looking at her face. He did eventually, when the screeching didn't stop and it rang in his head like the sounds that Quentin, Jaymes, and Fatima swore they had heard all their lives. Connor's eyelids hesitantly unpeeled and his head turned.

Casey was crumbled on the platform. Her hands gripped the railing's support beams and her face fit into the tiny space between the metal rods she clutched. Her skin paled as she looked at the bits and pieces of what had once been her cousin. Somehow, unlike Connor, in the thick of her grief, she found herself capable of speaking. *"You..."* she murmured, her head over her shoulder, staring right at him. *"You...You did..."*

Connor's head shook of its own accord. "I didn't mean to—" He didn't recognize his own sputtering voice. "Casey, I didn't mean to —You know I couldn't—*I wouldn't...*" But he did. He had. He was lying. He meant for it to happen, for Terry to die. Just not that way, and that didn't really make it any better.

Even as she spoke, Casey's eyes never strayed from the ground. *"I can't...I can't...believe you."* She rose up, but she kept holding the railing like it was a lifeline.

Connor didn't think as he approached her. He took her into his arms, wrapping himself around her. She sobbed into his chest, her tears wetting his shirt, pulling him closer, like he was going to slip from her grasp. *"Casey,"* he whispered, crying into her hair. She stilled in his arms. He backed his head up to see her.

She pushed him hard twice, and he stumbled back, to the peak of the escalator. She didn't say anything, was crying and hiccuping. He tried to clutch her wrist, but she kept pushing him away and he kept taking it, until he realized exactly where he was, with a sixty-foot drop and a squatted, puking Chris behind him. She pushed Connor again, and with extra force. He pleaded for her to listen, said empty statements of how he had never intended to hurt Terry. To her, Connor was transparent. He always was. It was Casey, after all. She pushed him one last time with both hands to his chest, and he slipped. He collided with Chris, and the two of them spiraled down the escalator stairs.

It didn't really register with Connor that he was airborne. He distantly felt his spine hitting the edges of several steps and his knuckles bouncing off the balustrades, but he didn't react. He simply allowed himself to go limp and land where he did, which ended up being several steps below Chris. They both raised to their knees and wrestled, banging heads, scratching at eyes, and twisting ears as they tumbled further down the steps. Their fall came to a full stop about halfway down, but Chris threw himself onto Connor and grabbed every bit of him. In fighting each other, they managed to regain momentum and started falling again.

Oscar had found Jaymes, had snuck up on him from behind and latched thick hands around his sinewy arms. He dragged Jaymes away from the protection of the servers and into the open space in front of the escalator's platform. "Connor!" Jaymes called out. "Help!"

The two on the stairs finally reached the bottom. Connor dizzily lifted his head. He and Chris were on the landing platform sixty feet down, each rolled onto their sides, pained from the tumbling fall. Connor's tongue swiped over one of his molars. It was cracked.

Derek arrived. His legs buckled at the sight of Terry's remains, but he quickly collected himself and set his sights on Jaymes.

Connor made to stand, but a tremendous weight landed on his back and pushed him to his knees on the landing platform. His face hit the jagged metal. His chin sliced open. Chris was heavy, and his hits were unforgiving. When he did allow Connor reprieve from being crammed against the ground, it was only to roll him onto his back, and Chris punched everything he could see.

Jaymes was propped up for the taking in Oscar's grasp, so, like Chris did to Connor, Derek started swinging. It wasn't long before Jaymes's head nodded to one side as he struggled for air between blows. He took one hit to the front of his face, a second to his right side, and yet another to his nose. There was a snapping sound, maybe a bone or his glasses. It could have been both.

Chris straddled Connor's stomach. The weight of him, combined with ribs which Connor thought might've been broken, was numbing more than it was painful. As he laid there, blood shot out from his face and rained back onto him. He was crying, and he saw that Chris was too. Tears slid down their pale faces, and the harder Chris cried, the harder he hit. If Connor continued to lay there, he would die. Suddenly, he thought, *I don't want to die like this,* before an even simpler thought came to mind: *I don't want to die.*

He heard the throaty groans from Jaymes close by, knew that he, too, was on the brink of departure, and that his survival depended wholly on Connor.

He couldn't feel his chest but he had sensation in his face. He recovered from one punch, which was followed by an unusually long pause of three seconds, so he shot himself up, expelling the blood that had filled his mouth. Chris was surprised. He had read Connor's pliant form as the prelude to the end of his life; it wasn't so faraway a feat. With his face to Chris's collarbone, Connor flipped him over, his head feeling heavy as he moved. Chris balanced himself on all fours, but before he could advance, Connor kicked him square in the face. He watched as the back of Chris's head hit the escalator newel behind him. He immediately put a hand to the back of his head, brought it forward to inspect it, and they both saw blood. By the time he went to reach his hand back for another inspection, the red liquid was streaming down to his shoulders.

Connor snapped up to his feet. The whiplash still had an effect on him, as he wobbled and couldn't discern where to go under a newfound spell of double vision; the limp Jaymes, restraining Oscar, and attacking Derek were hazy, each appearing alongside duplicate versions of themselves. Connor had to save Jaymes, who, even through blurred vision, showed a sagging, beaten face that would soon turn pale-white as he wilted away. He wasn't even letting out pained noises anymore. Connor had to reach him.

He took a step towards the other three, and in that moment, a sharp pain shot through the back of his shoulder. He let out a howl. Whatever it was that did that to him—whatever it was that was *inside* him—penetrated his upper back. He fell to the floor face-first and twisted an arm backwards to try and get a sense of what happened.

He felt the solid, cold metal of what he assumed was a knife. Hard and tapered inward, it had entered him too cleanly to have been anything else. He tried to pull it out, but it was lodged into something inside him, either tendon or bone. Laying on the floor, he twice rocked the protruding portion of the object to the right and to the left. He yanked it out. The heat of blood cascading down his back grounded him in the moment, made him stare ahead at nothing and swallow the shock that washed over him. He dropped the object to the floor, right in front of him, where he could see it. He was correct. It was a knife.

Connor turned around and balked at the sight of Chris, who was kneading the back of his head as blood spurted down his body; the whole escalator landing was wet with it. It couldn't have been him, Connor realized. Chris looked too disoriented to have stabbed so heartily and, had it been on his person before, he surely would have used it when they first fell. Connor looked up, to the peak of escalator, where Casey was collapsed and crying with her head in her hands, inconsolable and far too distracted to have targeted him with such expert precision from that distance. He looked farther down the platform, to the door of the control room, which was open for the second time during his short stint in the cargo hold.

Outside the open door, Roxy stood no more than an inch away from the railing. She was drawing her right hand back, in it a blade identical to the one he had just extracted from his shoulder. He was her focal point. With him fallen and disadvantaged by his injury, she hurled her arm forward and snapped her wrist in a sharp motion, and she let fly the second throwing knife. Not even the excruciating shoulder pain could have convinced Connor to surrender to his exhaustion. He twisted his torso to the side. The knife flew past him and scraped to a stop nearby.

He stared back up at Roxy. Disdain and dissatisfaction markedly governed her face. The knives hadn't sufficed. She had to do better, which she did: from one of the back pockets of her suit, she withdrew a revolver akin to the one Derek had brandished the prior evening. Connor crawled over to the knife that had misfired and seized it in one hand. He crawled more determinedly. He made his way to Derek, the first logical target to eliminate from the equation in Jaymes's ordeal.

A gunshot sounded from above. The bullet hit the area in front of Connor and chipped the floor. He watched Roxy as he kept low in his crawl, thankful that she was clearly more skilled at slinging knives than firing bullets. Yet the fear of better aim on her second shot prompted him to scramble as fast as possible and ignore the torment of his shoulder and the dizziness in his head. He heard her cock the weapon again, saw her eyes begin to narrow. Her thumb twitched. She brought her index finger closer to herself and pulled back slowly on the trigger.

She was bombarded, then, by a person whom Connor couldn't identify. He only discerned her body being jerked backward by a human form. His vision became a little clearer as he squinted to make out the disrupter of her attempted kill, his body pausing in its crawl due to the shocking turn of events. He saw blood-stained sleeves that coated long, lanky arms, which had wrapped around Roxy's neck from behind. Peeking past her silky hair was none other than Quentin Hanson's face.

The bullet shot forward, but not to the bottom of the cargo hold like Roxy intended. It shot straight down the platform, nearly hitting Casey, who saw that Quentin had emerged, seemingly from out of nowhere. Her shuddering legs straightened up and she ran toward him and Roxy.

Quentin choked Roxy harder. She directed the gun upward, to his face behind her, but as she pulled the trigger, he bumped his elbow into hers and it sent the gun focusing elsewhere, away from him. There was a clank against nearby metal and a shake of the railing beside them. The bullet must have ricocheted off the iron beam, because Casey collapsed to the floor. Connor sobbed her name. He begged that she would jump up in anger, anything other than what he dreaded. But she didn't move. She laid motionless.

Roxy squawked out a cry as Quentin loosened his grip on her neck, endeavoring to pry the gun from her hand. She never relented. Her grip on it was firm and she was determined to pull its trigger again, as soon as she could get the barrel pointed anywhere at Quentin in the distinct hope that one bullet would finally find its mark.

Connor didn't know what to do. Behind him, Chris's eyes had shut. Above, a visibly wounded Quentin battled an armed Roxy on his own. To his left, Jaymes was on the verge of fading as Oscar helped Derek hammer punch after punch into his body. One blade wouldn't be enough. There was one other option, a viable one which Connor warmed to fast. He put his hand in the front-right pocket of his jeans, slowly eased from it the Nox Bomb, and held it close to himself. He flipped open the cap and pressed the blue button—blue, for nitrous oxide.

No such gas released.

Connor pressed it again.

It still didn't work.

Jaymes's head sank to his chest, drool and blood and scraps of skin hanging by the edges of his mouth. Derek didn't stop punching and Oscar didn't stop supporting the one-sided foray.

Roxy pulled the trigger of her gun again. Just as it neared firing, Quentin tightened his grip on her wrist and rotated it back toward their heads, a murder-suicide move she likely never expected him to make. He ducked as the bullet struck her in the middle of her neck. Blood shot out of her. She dropped to the floor.

Connor pressed the red button. Red, for sarin. He sucked in a breath and held it, until realizing that he didn't have to. He had Grains in his nose; all he had to do was keep his eyes and mouth closed. He couldn't crawl, not with what was about to sweep across the space, and he stood despite how much it hurt. By the time three seconds passed, he was reaching Derek, who was pulling his arm back to punch Jaymes again, but stopped to scratch at his chest from the strange feeling that spread everywhere between his lungs and his nose. The gas didn't reach Oscar yet. He threw Jaymes aside, into a gap between two pyramids of cargo; he didn't realize how much that worked to Connor's advantage, how it made Jaymes accessible for the rescue. With the combativeness of a man who was unaware of what awaited him, Oscar bolted toward Connor, ready to finish him off. But as Oscar came closer, he began coughing and crying and scraping at his own neck.

Connor moved past them, not bothering to take time he could ill-afford to lose by watching what he had done. He limped to the passed-out Jaymes, slammed a hand over his open mouth to keep him safe, and dragged him away, back to the doors of the cargo hold. As they left, Connor saw Quentin tripping into the control room.

31

After locking the door to the main control room, Quentin beckoned Fatima out from the vent in which she had been instructed to hide. She crawled out from where he had exited earlier; a small, square-shaped slice in one of the walls inside the room's electrical closet. He knew she saw the tears that poured out of his eyes and the exacerbated state of his stomach, where the wound had been bad enough earlier in the day but even more irritated, then.

"The bleeding's stopped, though," Quentin told her, panting as he did. Despite how much he tried to assure her that everything was all right, that his tears would soon cease and his wound would eventually heal, he fell to the floor the moment she materialized from the opening in the wall. Outside the closet, he sat against the back of one of the pilot seats, his legs spread out in front of him and his head rolled to one shoulder. His hand flew back to his stomach and his teeth gritted repeatedly, almost snipping the edge of his tongue in the process. He didn't expect Fatima to come to him when he was like that, bloodstained and plagued by unmanageable sobs. But she did. He had forgotten how loyal and trusting children were to those who protected them. "We'll have to stay here awhile," he said once she approached, curled into one side of him and lightly hugged an unharmed area above his bullet wound, trying to not inflict any additional pain.

"Why?" Fatima asked.

"It's not safe out there," Quentin said. He recalled the little orb he had seen Connor reluctantly remove from one of his pockets, how with one press of a button it had rendered Derek and Oscar coughing, spluttering messes, how it had dragged each of them to the floor until their bodies were convulsing. But Quentin would never tell Fatima about that. There were some things which even the shrewdest of little ones didn't need to know about. She had likely heard it, anyway, which was more than enough.

Quentin barely held onto consciousness as they waited for more time to pass. He was acutely aware of how slowly the arrow ticked on his watch. When he put his mind to it, the act of him, of all people, begging for the hours to speed by was a great irony, considering how he had spent the last twelve months of his life praying for time to slow, if not freeze altogether.

Fatima didn't know what they were waiting for, why they weren't leaving the room, but she didn't question the decision. Her hair absorbed his tears, and her palm softly pet his heart every time he sobbed. His blood was all over her hands, yet the spillage never repelled her.

When Quentin assumed that the dangerous gases had finally dissipated, they left the room later in the morning, at nine o'clock. It not only hurt him to walk, but to carry Fatima as they departed. By all logical accounts, he shouldn't have juggled her, but he couldn't imagine living with himself if he had done it any other way. He wouldn't have been much of a protector if he allowed her to stroll out next to him. He couldn't do that to her. He couldn't let her see what he and Connor had done, however necessary all of it was. She didn't need to see the hole in Roxy's neck, the burst in Casey's chest, the puddled pile which Fatima would surely discern to have once been Terry, or the sallowed skins of the intact young men downstairs, whose faces were swollen and sickly. So, Quentin bore the pain. He held the back of Fatima's head firmly, wedging her into his collarbone. *"Don't look,"* he whispered the whole time he conducted the two of them outside with his uneven gait. *"Don't look, Fatima. Don't look."*

She did, though. He didn't realize it until they reached the bottom of the escalator, when he glanced down to ensure he was still properly shrouding her from the aftermath of the morning. But he saw that her eyes were wide open. Her lashes batted against her skin with each slow close of her lids. Her pupils flicked from one part of the cargo hold to the other; from one body to another. The pain of watching her do that was one which no bullet could have ever brought upon him.

He was numb the whole time they traveled through the basement corridors. When he was confident that there was nothing beyond that point which could further scar her, he let her go. He walked and clutched his stomach, guarded it from the warm air that felt burning-hot every time it touched him. Yet no matter how much it hurt, it was nothing compared to the resentment he had for himself as the recent scene replayed in his mind. Fatima seeing the bodies behind them pained him, but more so the fact that those would be the lasting images whenever she recalled any of those peers. She was silent too, and that didn't ease his suffering. It only made him feel worse. What she saw must have rightly disturbed her beyond comprehension. He wondered if she would ever speak again.

Their travel was long. He was limping and she was closely behind him, but not close enough. He sensed her footsteps slowing, her feet beginning to drag. The two occasions he looked back to her, he saw her head ducked, like she was hypnotized by the repetitive motions of her feet. Her arms hung by her sides, swaying as she moved, but she didn't lift her head to see him or talk to him.

"It's okay," Quentin heard Fatima say a bit later, when they reached the middle of the basement, at the terrain that bridged its four quarters. He turned around, one hand still on his stomach and the other open-palmed against a wall for stability. She was nodding at him. "It's okay," she repeated, her voice small.

"I'm sorry," Quentin said, dropping his hand from the wall.

Fatima was looking up at Quentin. It made him wonder what she saw. Did she think him weak, crippled, and pathetic? He couldn't blame her if she did. But whatever it was she thought of him, whether she admired him or was pitifully disgusted by him, or even a mesh of both, she padded forward and took his free hand into hers. He didn't know what it meant—if she was thankful for him, was seeking his comfort, or knew that he was the one who needed comforting—but he gave her small, squishy fingers a squeeze, and they were back on their way.

"Where are we going?" Fatima asked.

"You know the door number by now, don't you?"

"Eighty-five?"

"Eighty-five."

When they reached the passengers' quarter of their shuttle, Quentin hoisted himself up and dropped to the floor like his advisor once did. The first person that came rushing toward him, but not to him, was Frances. It was almost as if she didn't see him as she bypassed his bloody form and practically suffocated Fatima in a firm embrace. The only reason the young woman let the girl go, and only momentarily, was to pull back and check her for wounds. Noting that Fatima was unbroken by that one, awful night, Frances redoubled her embrace of the child.

There were others with them. On the floor, an almost excessively bandaged Connor and a stitched-up Jaymes were sitting side by side, their backs up against two storage containers. Marina was on her seat with an icepack held to her temple. Athol shot up from his spot on the floor and went to Quentin, calling attention to Frances when he saw the bullet wound that needed dressing, as it began bleeding again. Mathias made his way down the aisle between the seats, and Fatima, who caught sight of him, unwound from Frances. Fatima scuttled to him, bounded into his arms, and wrapped hers around his neck when he stuffed his head into her hair. After a minute, she squirmed to indicate her hankering to be released. They sat on the floor with everyone else.

Frances treated Quentin for over an hour. She had him laid upon the inflated mattress that was once reserved for Marina, where Frances punctured, inspected, and mended him with a new set of sterile instruments. He had to fight to stay awake. She would poke him with the butt of a needle or a tweezer every once in a while, which tended to help prevent his eyes from closing. One thing worked the most in keeping him awake. About forty minutes into the procedure, his head dipped off the edge of the mattress and his eyes had nowhere to look but behind him, to the wall next to the storage closet. Amber was there, consciously seated far apart from everyone else. She sat with her arms curled around her legs, catching glimpses of something on the other side of the quarter, which Quentin, with a turn of his head, saw was not something but, in fact, someone: Athol. He was directing enraged, twisted glares at her.

Suddenly, Quentin didn't feel Frances's hand probing his insides for the missing bullet. He had been delayed in realizing that there was one party of his division who wasn't in the room with them, a person who once had a single, deep dimple in his left cheek and large eyes that were blue like the sea. Quentin looked to Marina to appeal for an answer. She didn't know what he was referring to, vividly confused about why he was randomly enraptured by her and motioning to the closed control room. It took a minute, but when she deduced what he was asking about, she shook her head.

They found Natalie and Ivy in the cargo hold on the morning of the 9th. Natalie had placed herself on a cardboard box that was beside the pair of servers Connor and Jaymes had used to hide themselves during their run the night before. Her eyes welled, but she shed no tears. When the second division entered the room, she left as if on cue, silent and surrendered, wise to the fact that there would be no winning for her.

Ivy was knelt beside her twin on the cold cement floor. She held one of his hands in hers. Her thumbs skimmed over his left wrist, as if subconsciously feeling for a pulse she hoped to rise but never did. Quentin couldn't imagine how long she had been there, how many hours she must have spent with the cold hand of her brother stuck in hers as she waited to see him miraculously emanate some sign of life.

"How could you?" Ivy asked Connor specifically, and then she was up, storming out of the hold and following after Natalie.

Quentin should have felt guilty. He felt badly, felt a little sick and sad, but he didn't feel any guilt. He felt unburdened. He would never tell anyone how he felt. There was more than one way his feelings could be taken in the wrong context, but regardless, it was the truth. He had acted decisively, and he wasn't going to be ashamed of it. He had no intention of begging for mercy from the god in whom he scarcely believed.

32

March, 2048

Quentin couldn't sleep. It shouldn't have come as a surprise. It was hardly the first time insomnia had riddled a night of potentially deep rest with thoughts that spun his head out of control. Since February, his sleep had improved. For most others, it hadn't. Nearly everyone else battled nightmares and plaintive memories that kept them awake until their eyes became so heavy that staving off sleep any further was an impossibility. No such circumstances applied to Quentin anymore, though. After months of grappling with it himself, the unease had become a visitor that seldom came by, and, when it did, only stayed a few hours. He didn't know why that was. He wanted to tell someone about it, but with almost everyone struggling around him, he knew sharing such a fact would be inappropriate. For the time being, he had to pinpoint the reason himself to satisfy his curiosity. He wondered if it was a catharsis of some sort, if purging their ecosystem of those who were stuck in the past had in some way ripped him out of that same mindset. He definitely saw bits of himself in the likes of Casey, Terry, Derek, and Chris. Perhaps viewing them as antagonistic figures in his life finally made Quentin accept that he had been his own worst enemy all along. It wouldn't have surprised him, if many years in the future, he would be brave enough to view the situation in that light.

He recently decided that his life had been split into two chapters, that there was a Quentin who existed before they crossed the belt and that there was another Quentin who'd been born in the period directly after. He had many years to live before he would face the internal rebirth that came with accepting change, but it no longer seemed unattainable. He squirmed as he thought back to all those sleepless nights he used to idly waste, all the self-pity he had radiated at every single moment. He grew uncomfortable when he recalled his most frequent pastime on the ship; the hours he spent wallowing in a depression he had once thought underserved, only to discover, post-belt, that he thought differently. This wasn't to say that he was always so hard on himself. He recognized that, in order to alter his outlook and evolve for what he thought would be the better, a period of repulsed introspection was needed, however harsh it was.

"I won't pretend like some of this wasn't your fault," Connor had told him once in February, when they were taking a short break while refilling the upper levels of the ship with the adornments they'd been instructed to remove before their flight through the belt. "You had the chance to warn me about everything," he said, "yet you chose not to."

Quentin hadn't responded, just sat beside Connor on one of the boxes they were about to unload. They breathed in sync.

"But," Connor said, "I am grateful for you. Even though you knew we would stop you from going home, you saved my life. Why did you do that? Why did you kill Roxy?"

"Because I wanted something to return to," Quentin said. "If I want to go back to something, I have to make sure it still exists for me when I get there."

He meant it then, and he still meant it several weeks later, on the 3rd of March, when it technically wasn't night but the earliest hour of the morning. He was sprawled on one of the couches in the living room, as there were no longer residential third and fourth floors. He missed his bedroom often. The privacy was a privilege he wanted back, but when he thought about how much he pined for his old room, he also thought of what else had been lost in February.

Would Patterson have been happy with how it all ended? And if not happy, then satisfied? Quentin wasn't going to pretend that he missed the man and his flamboyancy, how he had tried to trick them into thinking their operation was a painless, measured work orchestrated from perfection and precision. Far from that, it was a haphazard attempt, an embodiment of just how desperate their home country and its allies had been to set in motion such a plan. But, in more than one way, like Connor had said about him, Quentin was grateful for Patterson despite all his faults and questionable fancies.

It seemed that few others were asleep on March 3rd. One of the conference rooms on the first floor wasn't necessarily packed, but Quentin considered it fairly astir for the late hour. Athol was sitting on the table with his feet rested where his body should have been, on the seat beside him. Everyone else sat normally at the same table; Marina; Jaymes; Connor; Mathias. Bowls of fruits and baked almonds were strewn in the middle of the table, occasionally being nibbled, but mostly by Mathias. In spite of the number gathered, as Quentin came to join them, he noticed that the mood of the room wasn't lively. It was somber more than anything else, and they were all staring at something Athol had in his hands.

Quentin sat down next to Jaymes. His nose was still in wraps, even though it was March. In spite of a slow recovery, his face was bettering with each day that passed. That part of his face would never be the same, though. It had taken a brutal beating.

"What's that?" Quentin asked.

There was a pink shell of an object split into four in Athol's hand. At first, Quentin didn't know what it was, but then he saw the rounded edges, the bits that protruded and then dipped where there were carefully architected fissures and bumps. It was one of the models for the Brain Development Pursuit, but cracked into pieces.

The realization dawned on Quentin. "Oh," he said.

"They must have broken it shortly after we all split up, after Derek made us go upstairs," Athol said, crestfallen. His bottom lip quivered for a few seconds.

"Is there no way you can fix it?" Connor asked.

"No, I...I can..." Athol circled one of the plastic gyri. "It's just that they burned all our notes and documents. I found them burned in a barrel in the cargo hold."

Quentin's stomach turned. "All of them?"

"All of them." Athol carefully placed the broken pieces of his project onto the glossy table. He slid himself off and landed on his seat.

"Do you think you can redo it before May?" Marina asked.

May was the target month for them to reenter a cryogenic sleep phase, the nap which Patterson had mentioned in 2047, during Quentin's first official meeting with him.

"Possibly," Athol said.

"You can do it," Jaymes said with conviction.

"Mm," Athol hummed. He wasn't soothed by the conjecture. He blinked quickly, like he wanted to change the subject, which he did. "So, hey," he said to Marina, "now that we've all bared ourselves, did you kick Roxy off that wall?"

Mathias threw an almond into his mouth and chewed very slowly, watching the young woman beside him.

"Yes," Marina said factually, unemotionally. "And purposely too."

"Why, though?" Athol asked.

"Honestly?"

Everyone nodded.

"I have absolutely no idea," Marina said.

"You don't know why you kicked someone off a rock wall in deep space?" Athol asked.

"I seriously don't know. Something about Roxy didn't sit right with me. From the beginning, it's always been like that, an inkling I never understood. I don't know where it came from, and then, for some reason, that day, I just saw the opportunity and decided to seize it. But if you want to ask me about the rationality behind it, there was none. It was pure instinct."

Athol shrugged. "Well, considering how I have to start from scratch for my BDP notes, what you just said is going on file."

"Really?" Connor asked.

"Really," Athol said. "There are so many things humans do that come off as irrational but end up being logically justifiable."

Mathias snorted. "You guys remember that history teacher we had in ninth grade…Douchefuck or something?"

"Mister *Dufois*, is that who you mean?" Jaymes asked. "Why are you dredging up that guy?"

Quentin recoiled. "Isn't he the pervert who got jailed for impregnating his teenage daughter?"

"Yeah, that one," Mathias said. "We were all freshmen when it happened."

"I knew he was a creep back before that shit went down," Athol said.

"*Exactly,*" Mathias said enthusiastically.

"What do you mean?" Athol asked.

"Well, why'd you think he was a creep?"

Connor reclined. "What are you talking about, man? Everyone knew that guy was a creep."

"Right, but why?"

"Ohh," Athol caught on to what Mathias was alluding to. "I see where you're going with this."

"It's true that he wasn't outright creepy," Quentin said. "He just kind of...Like, he never stared at anyone longer than he should have or touched anyone. It was just a vibe, I guess."

"But we knew, even as kids, that he would go on to do some strange stuff," Athol said. "We knew even before he was genuinely creepy, through the instincts in our bodies, or *minds*, that he would become a major league creeper. Now, what I do with this information, I don't know."

"You've got fifteen years to sleep on it," Connor said.

"Well, no, not fifteen years. It's cryo, remember? So my brain won't actually be functioni—"

"Killjoy," Mathias quipped.

Jaymes, who had been fairly subdued for most of the conversation, began to absentmindedly swivel in half-circles at the end of the bench as he spoke. "Since we're baring our souls here..."

"Confessional booth's open," Mathias said. "But Frances isn't here. She'd probably be better at this than any of us, what with her godliness and all."

"Actually, she already knows what I'm about to tell you," Jaymes said. He inhaled and shivered, like it was cold when it wasn't, since the heater was blasting overhead. "So does Natalie. They both do because, you know, they're the doctors up here. I guess I should have told you...Patterson should have, anyway. But he was right, it wasn't his place. It's just that I always wanted to be normal and for so long I feel like I've been able to be that way. But it's always been something of a lie, you know? Guys, I'm not...I'm not like you. I'm me, and I love myself, but there's always going to be a piece of me that's missing. That I will always miss, even though I never had it. And again, I feel like I owe you this because there might come a time when you need me for something and I can't help, and it kills me to think of that, especially after how close we've all gotten." He ran a finger over the edge of his glasses. "I'm not color blind. I'm blind, blind." He blew out a breath. "Okay," he said shakily, but relief was in his voice. "There. I said it."

"Yeah, we already knew that," Mathias said.

Connor laughed. It was the first time Quentin had heard that sound from anyone in months.

Athol scratched the side of his head. "I was like, who's gonna tell him?"

"Right?" came from Mathias.

Jaymes was frowning, his brows pinched together. "Wait, what do you mean you knew?"

"How could we not?" Quentin asked, poorly containing his amusement. "We'll literally be in pitch-black places and you'll always be the one to navigate your way through them, like you're crossing the street on a sunny day."

"Did you really think we're that slow?" Mathias asked.

"I just...I..." Jaymes was flustered, at a loss for words. "I thought—"

"See," Athol said, "we always thought that you knew that we knew. Like, c'mon."

"You sleep with those glasses on," Marina said, unsmiling and almost a little annoyed.

"Huh." Jaymes scratched the back of his head. "I guess I always was kind of obvious."

"Hold up, though," Mathias said. "What's always puzzled us is how you get stuff done. Like, for real."

"As in, navigation-wise?"

"Yeah."

"My parents had these weird sensory devices implanted in my head when I was a baby and I learned to grow up with them. They're super rare and I'm very fortunate to have them. They only came out in 2027 or something and were limited in supply. I always wondered how they managed to get me to the top of the waiting list, but now it all makes sense. I guess working for Colin Patterson had its perks back then too."

"Maybe," Athol said, "but it's also possible that he knew we'd need different perspectives for a mission like this one. You can't approach a problem like ours by looking through just one lens, with one mindset. You need a lot of different people up here. Different perspectives, as Quentin said."

Connor nodded. "It's worked, hasn't it? It's what got the BDP going in the first place, even if they did destroy it."

"It's nothing I can't fix," Athol said. "I'll spend the next two months rebuilding it."

"And we're here if you ever need anything," Connor offered.

"I know," Athol said. "I know." He thumbed one of the broken pieces on the table. "I kind of have to work on it, anyway. It's all I have left of Ewan, and I don't think he would want us to be held up by a few splinters in our project."

"No," Connor said sternly, "he wouldn't."

They dispersed a little later, when the clock struck three and yawns frequently disrupted the conversation. Since they had only makeshift beds at their disposal, some flocked back to the living rooms, others to the lounges, and a couple to the library, which was still a work in progress but had significantly improved from its deprived state following their flight through the belt.

Quentin couldn't sleep, though. Not yet. His body was tired but his mind remained active, an ongoing whirlpool of the invigorating thoughts that sometimes visited him.

He went to the observatory, of all places. It was still the most-hated spot on the ship by all, but it wasn't lost on him that it was also, antithetically, the one Patterson loved the strongest. Quentin didn't know how Patterson did it, how he could stand there for minutes at a time, sometimes hours, and soak up the darkness, unaffected by its proximity to him. Even after everything, Quentin still had to make a concerted effort to stay composed in there.

Fifteen years, that's what was scheduled for them. He often wondered where Lucas was, then, at fourteen; he had to be that age by March of 2048. Had he grown tall like their father or had his height stunted like their mother's, whom he surely missed? Sometimes Quentin's insides churned at the idea of his brother one day discovering how Quentin dishonored their mother's death with an attempted cover-up. Other times he swore he would do everything in his power to stop that from happening.

As much as Quentin would have liked to become liberated of the cumbersome questions that came to him, of anxieties like those, he was, if not happy, then satiated by the fact that he was no longer living in the past. He could complain about the grimness of the future, of the horrible possibilities that could very well come true, but so long as his head wasn't being softened by the dolor of a person who thought their self at an impasse when in fact there was an escape, he was more than willing to bear the brunt of a few sleepless nights rather than live through an endless cycle of total contempt for his existence. He started to understand Patterson a little more, how there were indeed things that had to be sacrificed for the sake of a greater cause; unlikely alliances, lost lives, and the suspension of personal morality were the prices that had to be paid for the outcome of more important things. In a perfect world, Quentin never would have met Patterson. Quentin would have graduated high school, attended college, married fairly young, and lived out his days normally, happily. But he didn't live in a perfect world. He wasn't even on one. He had to embrace the fact that individuality had no place in duty.

"Do bees buzz for butterflies?" Agata had asked him once. He only just realized what she was referring to, that it was the frailty of her mental clarity which had hindered her from actually voicing what she wanted to say, thus she had to resort to the simplest terms she could muster, an allegory. The translation was simple, he realized. The question was a hint she had tried to give to her grandson before he would disappear later that year, in 2045. She had been warning him that for one creature to thrive, another would have to labor in its shadows. And maybe it was a stretch. Maybe he would fall asleep and later wake, questioning how he ever pieced together the likelihood of those words being connected to the events of his life, but in that moment, he couldn't bring himself to care. What he took from it was that, yes, bees did buzz for butterflies. For him to return to home, to Lucas, Quentin would have to buzz for years for the sole purpose of providing his brother a chance to fly.

September, 2048

The Kilimanjaro sky was gray on the 15th of September. The clouds were usually sparse, mere dapples across a faultless, blinding, baby-blue pallet. That day, however, things were a bit different. Lucas couldn't see past the masses of dark puffs that lingered all around him, even though the camp was located on one of the lowest points of the mountain, where the sky, although never far away, felt significantly like a looming storm was trying to make itself known to forewarn him of its impending wrath.

Abul's head dipped down and he bitterly noticed the porch of their open tent flapping despite his and Lucas's weight being set upon it. "It will probably rain later today," Abul murmured glumly. He hated the rain, Lucas had learned.

Lucas hungrily stuffed his mouth with the half-peeled banana he was consuming for breakfast. When he finished, he dropped the fruit skin into the tiny can that stood inside the tent, in the corner closest to the entrance. "I don't mind the rain," he said. "I actually kind of like the new darkness. It adds an edge to the area."

They only started their ascent the day before, so they could easily turn back and make their way down to the safety of the base. But it wasn't concern that dampened Abul's mood. He just hated the rain. "It's early, though," he said. "Maybe the storm will pass quickly and die down in the afternoon. They typically do."

"Well, I want rain," Lucas said. "After Rome, I could do without the sunshine." He had spent his summer abroad, at a youth geology camp conducted by one of Naomi's former professors. She told Lucas it would be refreshing and mind-broadening for him to see other parts of the world, not just where she and Richard were stationed. The program took place from the beginning of June to the end of August, at which point Lucas had to return to Tanzania anyway, when some disheartening news had arrived, both for him and Naomi.

"It really surprises me that you like here more than southern Europe," Abul said.

"Does it?" Lucas asked. "If that's so, then why are you still here?"

Abul bumped his shoulder against Lucas's and smiled. "Mm," he hummed. "You have a goood point. It's not like here, is it? Other countries?"

"Not the ones I've seen or read about, no," Lucas concurred. "Everything's just so fresh and free here. Besides, you can't really find mountains like this in Europe, even though they have lots of them. In the US there are some good ones, but this is way better."

"Does that mean we get to keep you?"

Lucas nodded. "I hope so. I don't know where college will be, but I have a long way to go before I think about that. I'll make sure to come back, though."

The ground sheet of the tent rippled and crinkled as Richard ducked under the opening to step outside. He held a rubbery bottle in one hand and a slice of bread smothered in peanut butter in the other. Just as he bent to fit through the door, he spilled some of his cocoa on the front of his tee-shirt.

"Morning," Lucas greeted.

Richard shook his head at himself. "This is the most discombobulating time of day, isn't it, Mr. Hanson?"

"Quite."

Richard sat on the ground, on the other side of Lucas. "You know," he said, "Rome wasn't my favorite either."

Lucas reddened. "No, I didn't mean it like that. I'm thankful that I got to go. I was just saying that—"

"Geez, relax," Richard said in a laugh. "I'm not the one who sent you there, Naomi did."

"I don't want her to take it the wrong way. I'm really happy I got to go to the camp."

"I know you are, bud. Relax."

But Lucas couldn't. Words often failed him when it came to expressing his gratitude to Naomi and Richard, how they had taken him under their wing during his darkest days and then kept him.

Naomi and Jane came out of the tent. They shared a bowl of cereal, since neither were ever really hungry in the mornings.

Jack and Maryam were still inside the tent, packing up the last of their belongings. They were the deepest, and longest, sleepers.

Naomi, who was beside Richard, took the sign from his exaggerated coughs that her hair was stabbing into his mouth as the wind blew it around. She tied her strands back with an elastic, and Lucas noticed her knowingly smiling at him as she did. "For all your dissatisfaction with Rome," she said, "I hear Greece was a little more exhilarating."

Richard proffered his drink to Lucas, who took the canister into his hands and sipped some of the cocoa. "Greece was nice," Lucas said agreeably.

"I'm talking of Ming Zhao, of course."

Lucas choked on the cocoa that rushed into his mouth.

Naomi's grin widened.

"What's this?" Jane asked, an eyebrow quirked.

"Oh, nothing, as you can see," Naomi said.

Lucas wiped his hand against his mouth to clear it of the cocoa. "We're just friends. And how do you even know about that anyway?"

"Know about what, an innocent friendship?"

Lucas stifled a smile.

"What did I say when I signed you up?" Naomi asked. "That I've known Professor Welch since I was fifteen. Did you really think he wouldn't inform me of an *innocent friendship*, as you say?"

"So, growing up, in my household," Richard said, "it was kind of an unspoken rule that I wasn't allowed to date when I was home, but I was allowed when I was away at camp. Or, not allowed, per se. Just not lectured for it."

"Same here," Jane said. "If my dad had found a boy in my bedroom at home, he would have killed the kid. But if I were away at camp, that was a different story."

"In short, no one's judging you," Naomi assured Lucas, who felt his face grow hot. "But riddle me this, is that why you were asking to have your braces removed before next summer?"

"Very subtle," Abul chimed in.

Lucas groaned into the cocoa.

He wasn't annoyed, though. Despite the slight intrusion on his privacy and some embarrassment, he didn't actually mind the jesting pokes at his summertime romance. He didn't have it in him to complain, not with the way Naomi was smiling. He hadn't seen her cheeks indented with dimples since August, right before the news of the faraway deaths that had taken place in the sky above had finally reached them, six months later. If he thought she had been miserable following the discovery that she was incapable of having children of her own, it was nothing compared to the devastation that came as a result of learning about her father's death. She was inconsolable, had spent a full week in her bed. She never would move past it.

In some respects, the news rattled Lucas more than when his mother had been pronounced dead. The international conflicts that transpired around him had always been prominent and an intimate issue to him, given that they robbed him of a family member. But it felt like an even more dire matter when he heard about the deaths of Terry and Casey Montgomery, who had once been his next-door neighbors back in Shaw. Naturally, Lucas was grateful for the fact that Quentin was safe and only had to bear one, rectifiable injury. But the same couldn't be said for the others, for those other young people whom Lucas had known his entire life. Being informed of their deaths had struck a chord in him, one which he had long forgotten existed: fear. For the first time in years, Lucas was afraid. It made him fear for himself, for Quentin, and for the volcanology unit. Lucas still feared for the missing Hollis, who remained so impossibly faraway and unreachable.

"No one is safe," Topher had told Lucas when they had a moment alone during the night he had paid Naomi, Richard, and Lucas a visit to inform them of what had happened. The couple were sitting in the living room, where Naomi cried into her husband's chest. Lucas and Topher were in the kitchen. "This is the life we lead," Topher told him. "You have to understand that the loss of your mother is one of many that we face every day. There will always be liars among us. Is that clear?"

Lucas nodded. While he didn't need it to be explicitly told to him, he appreciated the reminder. Sometimes he forgot how complex the circumstances of his life were, how every move he made and intended to make would forever be dictated by the invisible tensions around him.

All throughout the night of Topher's visit to the house—the one that had once belonged to Lucas's mother—the wallpaper absorbed the adults' raised voices. Somehow the minutes of crying mutated into hours of shouting. Lucas kept quiet, having recognized that he shouldn't intervene. He heard the undertones of desperation in Topher's voice as he beseeched Naomi to stop working in the field, to finally make her long-contemplated transition to a career in higher education.

"You don't have to do this anymore," Topher said later in the night, when her tears had mostly dried and she was able to speak in coherent sentences. "You can go back home. Become a professor. You've always wanted to teach."

"I am not quitting," Naomi said defiantly. "Now more than ever we need people to stay where they are."

"Nani—"

"Dad never quit!"

"And look where that got him!"

Lucas felt like a tiny, unwise preteen all over again. He didn't think Topher was being unreasonable for suggesting that Naomi and Richard return home and make a life for themselves, one that didn't heavily rely on the ever-changing political climates of every country on the globe. But Lucas also understood their perspective, which was that if every operative or scientist were to quit due to a handful of deaths every year, there would be no one left on their side.

After many hours had passed, the high emotions and yelling died down. Naomi had fallen asleep on a couch in the living room, Topher at the kitchen island, and Lucas in his bedroom, where he had retreated to escape the conflict. Richard came into the room, sat down on the edge of Lucas's bed, and asked the awoken child, "Do you understand that we will never stop doing this, that we won't quit until our bodies can't handle this lifestyle any longer?"

"I know," Lucas said, sitting up and rubbing the sleep from his eyes.

"It's never too late to reach out to your father," Richard said. "If you don't want anything to do with this, if you think she and I are crazy—"

"I don't think that," Lucas said quickly. "Unless, of course, you're asking...asking me to go back to him."

Richard shook his head. "You know we'd love to keep you here forever if you wanted that."

"I do want that. Whatever happens, I want to stay here with you guys."

Richard ruffled Lucas's hair. It was longer, then. The uncut waves had started to make him look the way Quentin did in 2045.

"So be it," Richard said smiling, but Lucas saw beyond the calm visage the man attempted to display. There was worry in his eyes.

Life had already taken so much from Lucas. If there was anything he'd learned since being ripped away from Quentin, it was that people tended to leave when Lucas least expected it. If anything were to happen to Naomi and Richard, who were his remaining family, he wanted to be with them until their last breaths.

———

"You're getting better at this," Naomi said to Lucas as she watched his ECG reading on the screen of Abul's handheld monitor. Lucas passed the altitude sickness test with flying colors. His blood pressure still exceeded the normal level for someone of his height, weight, and age, but no one was perfect, not where they were, at an elevation of twelve-thousand feet. "You're acclimatizing so much faster than last time," she said.

Abul peeled off the sticky bottoms of the electrodes from Lucas's bare chest. "I definitely feel better," Lucas agreed. He layered his shirts and jacket back onto his body. "I'll probably throw up tomorrow, though."

"Me too," Naomi admitted. She had climbed enough mountains in her life to recognize the pattern of sickness that came with the third day of hiking. She didn't know why, but on all other days she was fine. For some reason, when it came to the third, her stomach twisted on itself and she would be retching by nightfall.

"I'll probably let him use the oxygen tank before he goes to sleep tonight," Abul said. "Just for a few minutes, to even things out before morning." He took a few glances at the rocky stretch that extended for miles around them. "Should we set up the tent here?"

Naomi looked over her shoulder to the rainforest behind them, where they had slept the night before. From where they stood on the flatlands miles above it, the green of the trees was faded and small, a spread across the brown base. Jane was a couple miles south of them and would probably near their location in a few hours. "Here's a good spot," Naomi agreed. "It'll be easier for Jane when she's done working."

"Okay," Abul said. "Come on, Lucas."

The boy zipped up his jacket.

"I'll be back before sundown," Naomi said, kissing Lucas on the cheek. It wasn't as easy to do as the previous year, when they were eye-level with each other and all it required on her part was a forward push of her neck. But he had grown so much taller than her by September of 2048 that she had to stand on her tiptoes just to reach his face. He looked so much like his older brother.

"Pipsqueak," Lucas said to her.

"You're no hotshot just because you've had your first kiss," Naomi cracked.

Lucas smirked. "Where are you heading?"

"Northwest, near the desert. You remember that, don't you?"

"Isn't that where the military base is?"

"I'll be right near it." Naomi pulled up the end of her left sleeve and checked her watch; it read five. "As soon as the tent's up, go to sleep. The colonel expects us there by afternoon tomorrow."

"I will. See you later."

Naomi hoisted her backpack over her shoulders, took the smallest of the tiltmeters and one of the seismic monitors into each hand, and started climbing her way up the bumpy trail ahead. She wouldn't cross paths with anyone for at least a mile; Richard and Jack were west, and Maryam was a short distance behind them.

Naomi estimated that her climb would take two hours. She had a favorite spot, a section where the moorland zone blended with the first few miles of the alpine desert. Her legs ached throughout the journey and her shoulders could have benefited from a much lighter load, but she bore it by reminding herself how much easier an undertaking it was compared to that of the previous day, when the humidity of the rainforest and the beating sun had drained all of her energy by midmorning. Being higher was easier, and the climb that day was too. It hadn't rained yesterday like everyone predicted, but the odds of it happening on the current day seemed higher.

She had once told Lucas that she rather liked the high elevation, that it made her feel closer to her father. She said those words over two years earlier, but she didn't know how she felt about them in 2048, with her father deceased. If anything, she felt lonely again. There were still people in the sky to keep her occupied, she supposed. But the concept of their presence didn't console her the way her father's used to. Perhaps Topher was right about her quitting, that she should leave and do something for her own interest. Climbing alone on that September day, with her head bent down, her hands full, and her high-altitude-induced headache pounding as she slogged even higher up the trail, she realized just how much of her life she had spent, not quite in the shadows of her father, but tagging along after him. Sometimes she, too, had felt like another expendable piece in his puzzle, but she didn't mind it because of the simple fact that he was her father, and if following after him meant being close to him, then she was more than fine with the trying conditions his life often imposed on her. But he was gone. He was gone, and she was left climbing alone. She wondered what would happen later in life, when she and Richard grew old. Would continuing down their current path lead Lucas to where she was after her father's death, confused and questioning how much of her individuality expanded beyond her work? Did she want that for Lucas?

The trail under her feet shifted from steep and stony to grassy and flat. The barren earth of the desert was easy on her legs and she was grateful for the clouds above; the sun tended to burn her when she stood on the flatlands.

She unstrapped her backpack from her shoulders and set it to the ground with care, unzipped it, and peered inside. She was on her knees, leaned forward, her head deep in the bag, but she could hear, even with her ears hidden, the steady beat of fast-paced footsteps behind her. She sat back on her heels and looked behind herself, her head over one shoulder.

Topher was running her way. He wore black, fleece pants and the old, blue windbreaker she had bought for him one Christmas many years before. His face was flushed. He looked like he had run his way up from the base of the mountain.

"What the...?" Naomi whispered. She shot up to her feet, standing so she could go and meet him halfway. "What are you doing here?!" she exclaimed, jogging forward.

When he was right in front of her, Topher stopped moving. He cowered over with his hands on his hips and his mouth agape as he inhaled. He swayed in place, so Naomi shot an arm out to steady him.

"Topher, that was dangerous! Do you have any idea how foolish that was?! You don't have an oxygen supply with you! If you had passed ou—"

"We have to leave," Topher said.

"What? Why?"

"We need to, Naomi. While we can."

Naomi pinched the bridge of her nose. "What? No. I don't understand. How did you even get here?"

"Helicop..." Topher huffed out. "Nearby...helicopter...Need to leave."

"I don't understand, why do we need to leave?"

Topher fought even harder to take in air. "Infil...Infiltration... Hacked the...They're here."

"What are you talking about? Who's here?"

Topher stood upright. "You know who I mean!"

"No, I don't!"

"They came...this morning!" Topher pointed up high to the mountain behind her. "This morning...storm...knew we wouldn't be able to see...explosives...Dropped them...They dropped massive... this morning..."

Naomi froze. "Does Colonel Brandt know about this?" she asked soberly.

Topher gripped her forearm. "Let's go. While we can."

"Wait, Topher—!"

"We don't have time, Naomi!"

"But what about the others?! The whole base up north?! My unit south!"

Topher wrapped his other arm around her back in his continuing effort to lead her away from the trail. "Come, Naomi. We have no time. Forget your things. We'll get your unit."

Naomi followed reluctantly, letting him guide her further west. When they reached a small slope, she glanced back to the tiltmeter that was left abandoned beside her bag. "I can run a quick test!" she insisted. "I can check if they actually did anything!"

"No...no time..."

"Topher," Naomi said very calmly, "the last time this mountain erupted was over two-hundred-thousand years ago. I'm sure I—"

Topher let her go, but he spun around to face her. His jaw was tautly set and his gaze bore into hers. She had never seen him so angry. But then he was turning around, resuming his way down the slope, just expecting her to follow after him, which she did. "Do you recall what you told me?" he asked her. "Do you remember, four years ago, when you were assigned here?"

"Do I what?!" Naomi shouted, raising her voice, aggravated. "You know, I would really appreciate it if you'd be less opaque with me!"

Topher was out of breath, but he fought against the weariness in his lungs so he could speak to her. "No, Nani, it was you...you who was vague with me. You said you were excited."

"Yes?"

"But that you were afraid."

"All right?"

"You said, 'Topher, I can't wait, but I am so terrified. The possible eruption...of an actual...a volcano...as old as that one...not quantifiable.'"

"Perhaps I was being dramatic."

Topher sped up his walking. "If you were being dramatic, why do we have military guarding it?"

Naomi's foot caught on a rock and she tripped, but he didn't stop moving. "Christ, wait!" She hurried after him. "That was millenniums ago, Topher, no one knows what'll happen if it erupts again!"

"That's my point!" Topher yelled, his breathing fairly normal. "If even Naomi Patterson, one of the best geologists in the world, cannot prognosticate anything, then what's there to be said for the rest of us?!" He turned around and stopped. "Look me in the eyes right now and tell me you know what will happen if this mountain erupts. You tell me right now that the whole thing won't collapse in on itself."

Naomi did as he said. She looked into his eyes, remembered the decades she had spent sleep-deprived, poring over books and papers for her school studies, and then she peered into her adulthood, when she toiled mostly in places such as there, on that alpine desert, with so many unanswered questions stuck to her tongue, and not only hers, but those of her colleagues as well. "I don't know," she admitted.

Topher took her hand. He was back to leading her away. "It is close by," he said. "The helicopter, it's near."

"How near?"

"About another half mile."

"Okay," Naomi said, abiding by his instructions and trailing after him.

In a joint effort to conserve their oxygen, neither spoke the rest of the way down. Naomi, heavy-stepped, stayed on Topher's heels as he led her even further south. The desert ground was receding, fading away as the orange-brown of the moorland began to take over the terrain. Throughout the entire time they fled, Naomi was entranced by her footsteps.

Another infiltration. *Topher was right,* she thought. She should have quit when she had the chance. He had always been right. He spent all those years warning her, but never once did she ever listen to him. He was right in 2045, just before Hollis Carlyle went missing. He was right in 2047, immediately before Sydney Hanson was pronounced dead. He was right even as recently as 2048, both before and after Naomi's father and a plethora of young innocents were killed. And once again in 2048, Topher was probably going to be right about the dormant volcano that was Mount Kilimanjaro. Memories played in front of her distracted eyes, memories of Mark and Lucy Carlyle, of Sydney Hanson, of Naomi's own father, and of the Montgomerys, Laneys, and Martinezes, whose children were all gone. She remembered how Topher's hair grew grayer at the absence of the Carlyles along with the tears that streamed from his eyes when he delivered the news of Sydney, and the adamance that Naomi leave the field after he told her of her father's death. He was alarmingly punctual with his injections of opinion before each and every one of those tragedies. It should have, at the very least, impressed her that he was so astute in his observations and, subsequently, his extrapolations. It hadn't, though.

She didn't know why the realization of his accuracies made her want to recoil instead of marvel at him.

Her gaze on her feet grew blurry. She slipped and fell facedown on a pile of stones. Topher tried to catch her, but he failed. The serrated surfaces cut her forehead, scraped her uncovered fingers, and painfully pressed her wedding band into the bone of her ring finger. Topher attempted to help her to her feet, but she stayed in place on the stones. He was asking her what was wrong and why she had fallen, but she didn't answer.

The ground beneath them shook. They heard something of a rumble, an enormous, deafening growl.

Topher covered his ears, then pulled at one of Naomi's shirtsleeves, but when he couldn't win her attention, he waved a hand in front of her eyes, screaming that she needed to get up, that they were out of time, that they needed to leave. Crouched beside her, Topher took her face into his hands. "Naomi, look at me!" he pleaded. "Look at me! Look at me!"

Naomi did look up.

The world around them was shaking.

"We need to leave, Naomi! We need to go! Please!"

Naomi blinked. She smelled smoke, felt it trickle into her nose. She saw the gray sky begin to darken behind Topher, so that it was almost the same color as the stones that had cut her.

"*You*," Naomi said very quietly.

Topher stopped pulling her. She knew he could barely hear her, that he had to lean in as the rumbles intensified. "What?!" Topher asked. "Come on, we have to leave!"

"You," Naomi repeated. "It was always you, wasn't it?"

Topher's hands softened on her shoulders. They slipped down to the ground of the moorland.

"Hollis," Naomi said. "Sydney. Dad. Thompson." *Roxy Thompson*, she thought. *How had I missed it?*

Topher didn't look as frantic anymore. "I did what I had to do to save us," he said plainly, like they were anywhere else in the world, in a place where a calm, collected conversation could be held. It seemed that both of them forgot the deformation around them, the chaos and destruction that was doomed to strike them. Neither the graying sky nor the blazing red, the blood of the Earth, that they saw out the corner of their eyes could have possibly disrupted what either of them had to say. "I always did love you," Topher said, nodding. "Everything I have ever done is to protect you. That was never a lie, Nani."

Naomi blinked the tears away. She pushed herself up on her knees, unfeeling to the blood that slipped out of her hands as she pressed them to the ground to steady herself. She didn't look at him when she stood, but, instead, ran away to her post in the middle of the trail she had long strayed from, where she was sure she could navigate her way back to her husband and Lucas.

Topher didn't run after her. What he did after she left him, she had no idea.

—

Lucas shot up inside his sleeping bag. He dripped sweat. Salty beads flowed down the sides of his face, the back of his neck, and down his chest, some finding their way to his navel. He could hardly see a thing. Smoke pervaded the tent. It traveled in oscillating swirls around him, dancing in circles and rapidly hazing up the closed space. He felt weak when he started crawling for the half-unzipped exit, had to practically drag himself by his fingernails just to push his body through the flap. He called for Abul, but Lucas could only say the man's name in the raspiest of tones, as though his lungs were locked away and inaccessible.

There were few things that he could make out in the tent, but outdoors, after he had crawled through the tent doorway, nothing was distinctive. He couldn't see the rainforest in the distance, the alpine desert ahead, and save for the flapping, fabric door beside him, he couldn't see most of the tent either. Everything was dark, and he was choking on that very darkness. Ash rained onto him. He rasped Abul's name once more, even tried to say something beyond that, but Lucas found himself incapable. All he could do was cough. He choked on the smoke, his tongue coiling back every time he tasted it plowing into his mouth and his nose, piercing his open eyes as well. The smoke was profound, unavoidable. It completely swallowed him, and it became thicker, hotter. Suffocating.

He squeezed his eyes shut and traced the perimeter of the tent with his hands clawing along the rocky surface. There were fifteen lag bolts pinched through the bottom of the tent, so he decided to feel along them to comprehend his position. He did look up when he reached what he thought was the back of the refuge, and when he squinted, he was finally able to see something. It just wasn't what he had hoped for. It was a gradually moving redness that shone brightly far away and was visible through the gaps of a few smoke swirls. The red oozed down the slopes ahead, slinking down the mountain. He felt his eyes flutter, came close to fainting at the sight of it, but he couldn't pass out. Not then.

No matter how hard he tried, he couldn't stand. He kept crawling. He couldn't feel much, if any, air entering his body. It shouldn't have taken him as long as it did to come upon the sixth lag bolt, but it did. It did, and he felt entirely hopeless that he could no longer see beyond the premises of the tent. He felt around in front of it, reached his hand out as far as he could, hoping that he would feel something or someone.

Lucas felt skin. He grabbed onto whomever it was he found. They were no less than a foot away from where he was, and he scrambled forward, blaring loud coughs as he reunited himself with Abul, who was on the rocky ground. He laid supine and his eyes were closed. He wasn't breathing. Lucas spoke Abul's name, his voice raspier and more desperate. Lucas spoke it once, twice, and eventually up to ten times. He tightened his hand around Abul's.

"Abul," Lucas struggled to say. He sounded out the faintest, hoarse whisper, *"Abul, wake up. Please wake up."*

Lucas didn't want to be alone. He couldn't be alone. He didn't know how to be anymore.

The smoke was heavier. It wafted into Lucas's open mouth and blurred the vision of his teary eyes. He tried speaking Abul's name just one more time, but Lucas's throat was clogged. His lungs closed off. The smoke was everywhere, and the snaking redness in the distance was coming closer with each second. The sky was imperceptible. He couldn't even see the ground in front of him. Ash caught on his lips and he felt smoke heating his insides. He fell forward and laid there coughing, aching, heaving in his breaths. The last thing he saw were his fingers inching away from the rest of his body, sweeping against the stones beneath him, until they were entwined with Abul's. Unable to control it, Lucas's eyes closed.

———

Often people questioned the reason behind the deaths of innocents, the utility behind the heartlessness of ending the lives of those who had done little to deserve being prematurely taken from their world. Speculations had been made, and what blossomed from them were varying faiths and beliefs, but little had anyone known that the real answer, the undiluted truth of the reason behind that unfair mystery, would be discovered not very long after September of 2048, and by none other than one Quentin Frank Hanson.

Vol. I

Acknowledgements

It would be foolish of me to say that I embarked on the journey of completing this novel on my own. I have wonderful friends and family members who have stood by me throughout my mad endeavor of starting a career in fiction writing at the tender age of twelve. From my grandparents to my childhood friends, I am incredibly grateful for all your boundless love and support. I've known to never take your affections for granted.

To my father, my gratitude to you is indescribable. Thank you for lending your astute eyes to the effort of grammatically editing every single one of my scribbles.

To Sue-Ellen Lamb, the graphic artist of my cover artwork, I am eternally grateful for your boundless patience. I was especially thankful for you throughout all those times I told you that the book would be publishing in two weeks…which I said every month…for twenty-four months…

Ingram Content Group UK Ltd.
Milton Keynes UK
UKHW020648130723
425033UK00005B/70